STEPHEN DONALDSON

The Runes of the Earth

GOLLANCZ

LONDON

Copyright © Stephen Donaldson 2004
Maps by Dave Senior
All rights reserved

The right of Stephen Donaldson to be identified as the author of this work
has been asserted by him in accordance with the
Copyright, Designs and Patents Act 1988.

First published in Great Britain in 2004 by

Gollancz
An imprint of the Orion Publishing Group
Orion House, 5 Upper St Martin's Lane, London WC2H 9EA

Second impression 2004

A CIP catalogue record for this book is available
from the British Library

ISBN 0 575 07598 8 (cased)
ISBN 0 575 07599 6 (export trade paperback)

Typeset, printed and bound in Great Britain
by Butler and Tanner Ltd, Frome and London

www.orionbooks.co.uk

to Jennifer Dunstan –
the princess of my heart

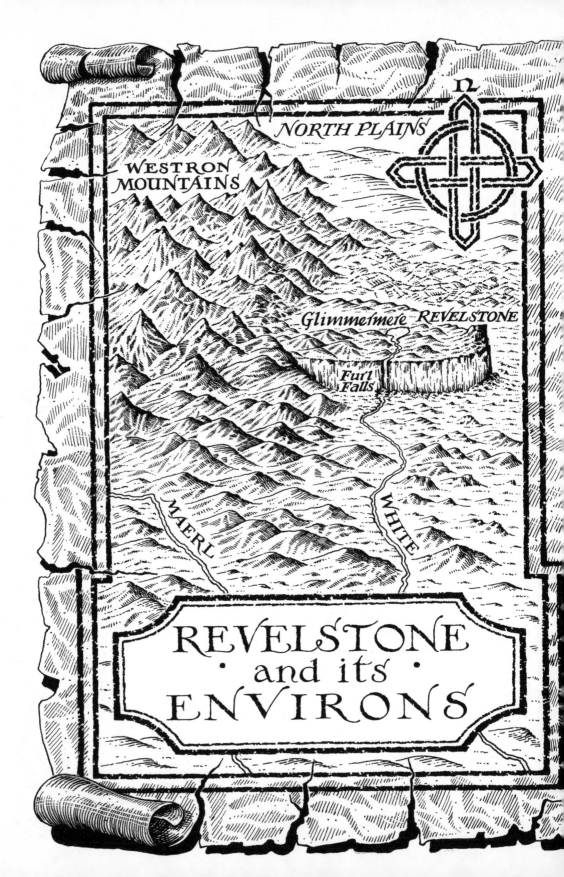

NORTH PLAINS

WESTRON
MOUNTAINS

Glimmermere REVELSTONE

*Furl
Falls*

MAERL

WHITE

REVELSTONE
· and its ·
ENVIRONS

Acknowledgements

My particular thanks to John Eccker,
who went 'above and beyond the call'
after the first draft and never looked back.

TABLE OF CONTENTS

PART II

WHAT HAS GONE BEFORE

THE CHRONICLES OF
THOMAS COVENANT THE UNBELIEVER

As a young man – a novelist, happily married, with an infant son, Roger – Thomas Covenant is stricken with leprosy. In a leprosarium, where the last two fingers of his right hand are amputated, he is taught that leprosy is incurable, and that his only chance of survival is to reject all hope of relief. Instead he must dedicate his life to avoiding anything which threatens his ability to protect himself. Horrified by his illness, he returns to his home on Haven Farm, where he finds that his wife, Joan, has abandoned and divorced him in order to protect Roger from exposure.

Other blows to his emotional stability follow. Fearing the inexplicable nature of his illness, the people around him cast him in the traditional role of the leper: a pariah, outcast and unclean. In addition, he discovers that he has become impotent – and unable to write. Grimly he struggles to go on living; but as the pressure of his loneliness mounts, he begins to experience prolonged episodes of unconsciousness, during which he appears to have adventures in a magical realm known only as the Land.

In the Land, physical and emotional health are tangible forces, made palpable by an eldritch energy called Earthpower. Because vitality and beauty are concrete qualities, as plain to the senses as size and colour, the well-being of the physical world has become the guiding ethical precept, the religion, of the people of the Land. When Covenant first encounters them, in *Lord Foul's Bane*, they immediately greet him as the reincarnation of an ancient hero, Berek Halfhand, in part because he has lost two fingers, and in part because he possesses a white gold ring – his wedding band – which they know to be a talisman of great power, able to wield 'the wild magic that destroys peace'.

However, Covenant chooses to interpret his translation to this magical place as a form of hallucination or dream. Shortly after he first appears in the Land, his leprosy and impotence disappear, cured by Earthpower; and this, he knows, is entirely impossible. Further, he knows that any acceptance of the idea that he holds some magical power will be a betrayal of the principles upon which his survival depends. Therefore he responds to his welcome and health in the Land with Unbelief: the harsh, dogged assertion that the Land is not real, and that attributing mystical or restorative powers to him serves only to undermine his ability to endure his actual life.

Because of his Unbelief, his initial reactions to the people and wonders of the Land are at best dismissive, at worst despicable (at one point, overwhelmed by his reborn sexuality, he rapes a young girl, Lena, who has befriended him). However, the people of the Land decline to punish or reject him for his actions. As Berek Halfhand reborn, he is beyond judgment. And there is an ancient prophecy concerning the white gold wielder: 'With the one word of truth or treachery,/he will save or damn the Earth.' The people of the Land know that they cannot make his choices for him. They can only hope that he will eventually follow Berek's example by saving the Land.

At first, such forbearance conveys little to Covenant, although he cannot deny that he is moved by the ineffable beauties of this world, as well as by the kindness of its people. During his travels, however, first with Lena's mother, Atiaran, then with the Giant Saltheart Foamfollower, and finally with the Lords of Revelstone, he learns enough of the history of the Land to understand what is at stake.

The Land has an ancient enemy, Lord Foul the Despiser, who dreams of destroying the Arch of Time – thereby destroying not only the Land but the entire Earth – in order to escape what he perceives to be a prison. Against this evil stands the Council of Lords, men and women who have dedicated their lives to nurturing the health of the Land, to studying the lost lore and wisdom of Berek and his long-dead descendants, and to opposing Despite.

However, these Lords possess only a small fraction of the power of their predecessors. The Staff of Law, Berek's primary instrument of Earthpower, has been hidden from them. And the lore of Law and Earthpower seems inherently inadequate to defeat Lord Foul. Wild magic rather than Law is the crux of Time. Without it, the Arch cannot be destroyed; but nor can it be defended.

Hence both the Lords and the Despiser seek Thomas Covenant's allegiance. The Lords attempt to win his aid with courage and compassion: the Despiser, through manipulation. And in this contest Covenant's Unbelief appears to place him on the side of the Despiser. He refuses to acknowledge the power of his wedding band. Like the Land's beauty and magic, it threatens his precarious grasp on life and sanity.

Nevertheless Covenant cannot deny his response to the Land's apparent transcendence. And as he is granted more and more forbearance and even friendship by the Lords and denizens of the Land, he finds that he is now dismayed by his earlier violence towards Lena. He faces an impossible conundrum: the Land cannot be real, yet it feels entirely real. His heart responds to its loveliness – and that response has the potential to kill him.

Trapped within this contradiction, he attempts to escape through a series of private bargains. In *Lord Foul's Bane*, he grants the Lords his passive support, hoping that this will enable him to avoid the demand that he learn how to use his ring. And at first his hopes are realised. The Lords find the lost Staff of Law; their immediate enemy, one of Lord Foul's servants, is defeated; and Covenant himself is released from the Land.

Back in his real world, however, he discovers that he has in fact gained nothing. Indeed, his plight has worsened: his experience of friendship and magic in the Land has undermined his ability to endure his outcast loneliness on Haven Farm. When he is translated to the Land a second time, in *The Illearth War*, he knows that he must devise a new bargain.

During his absence, the Land's plight has worsened as well. A number of years have passed in the Land; and in that time Lord Foul has gained and mastered the Illearth Stone, an ancient bane of tremendous power. With it, the Despiser has created an army which now marches to overwhelm the Lords of Revelstone. Although they hold the Staff of Law, they lack sufficient might to withstand the evil horde. They need the strength of wild magic.

Other developments also tighten the grip of Covenant's dilemma. The Council is now led by High Lord Elena, his daughter by his rape of Lena; and in her person, he begins to experience the consequences of his violence. It is clear to him – if to no one else – that she is not entirely sane. In addition, the army of the Lords is led by a man named Hile Troy, who appears to have come to the Land from Covenant's own world. His presence radically undermines Covenant's self-protective Unbelief.

Now more than ever Covenant feels that he must resolve his conundrum. Again privately, he offers a bargain. He will give the defenders of the Land his active support. Specifically, he will join Elena on a quest to discover the essence of Earthpower in its most concentrated form, the EarthBlood. But in return he will continue to deny that his ring holds any power. He will accept no responsibility for the ultimate fate of the Land.

This time, however, the results of his bargain are disastrous. Using the Illearth Stone, Lord Foul slaughters the Giants of Seareach. Hile Troy is only able to defeat the Despiser's army by giving his soul to Caerroil Wildwood, the Forestal of Garroting Deep. And Covenant's help enables Elena to find the EarthBlood, which she uses to sever one of the necessary boundaries between life and death. Her instability leads her to think that the dead will have more power against Lord Foul than the living. But she is terribly wrong; and in the resulting catastrophe both she and the Staff of Law are lost.

Covenant returns to his real world knowing that his attempts to resolve his dilemma ultimately serve the Despiser.

Nearly broken by his failures, he visits the Land once more in *The Power that Preserves*, where he discovers the full cost of his actions. Dead, his daughter now serves Lord Foul, using the Staff of Law to wreak havoc. Her mother, Lena, has become entirely insane. And the defenders of the Land are besieged by an army too vast and powerful to be defeated.

Covenant still has no solution to his conundrum: only wild magic can save the Land – and he cannot believe in it. However, sickened at heart by Lena's madness, and by the imminent ruin of the Land, he resolves to confront the Despiser himself. Powerless, he has no hope of defeating Lord Foul. Nevertheless he would rather sacrifice himself for the sake of a magical, but unreal, place than preserve his outcast life in his real world.

Before he can reach the Despiser, however, he must first face dead Elena and the Staff of Law. He cannot oppose her; yet she defeats herself when her attack on him draws an overwhelming response from his ring – a response which also destroys the Staff of Law.

Accompanied only by his old friend, the Giant Saltheart Foamfollower, Covenant finally gains his confrontation with Lord Foul and the Illearth Stone. Facing the full force of the Despiser's savagery and malice, he at last finds the solution to his conundrum, 'the eye of the paradox': the point of balance between believing that the Land is real and believing that it is not. On that basis, he is able to combat Lord Foul by using the dire might of the Illearth Stone to trigger the wild magic of his ring. With that power, he shatters both the Stone and Lord Foul's home, thereby ending the threat of the Despiser's evil.

When he returns to his own world for the last time, he learns that his new-found balance benefits him there as well. He knows now that the reality or unreality of the Land is less important than his love for it; and that knowledge gives him the strength to face his life as a pariah without fear or bitterness.

'The Second Chronicles of Thomas Covenant'

For ten years after the events of *The Power that Preserves*, Covenant lives alone on Haven Farm, writing novels. He is still an outcast, but he has one friend, Dr Julius Berenford. Then, however, two damaged women enter his life.

His ex-wife, Joan, returns to him, violently insane. Leaving Roger with her parents, she has spent some time in a deranged commune which has apparently been manipulated by Lord Foul to desire Covenant's destruction. Recognising the Despiser's handiwork, and hoping to spare anyone else the hazards of involvement, Covenant attempts to care for Joan alone.

When Covenant refuses his aid, Dr Berenford enlists Dr Linden Avery, a young physician whom he has recently hired to work with him. Like Joan, she has been badly hurt, although in entirely different ways. As a young girl, she was locked in a room with her father while he committed suicide. And as a teenager, she killed her mother, an act of euthanasia to which she felt compelled by her mother's illness and pain. Loathing death, Linden has become a doctor in a haunted attempt to put aside her past.

At Dr Berenford's urging, she intrudes on Covenant's treatment of his ex-wife. When Joan's commune attacks, seeking Covenant's death, Linden attempts to intervene, but she is struck down before she can save him. As a result, she accompanies him when he is returned to the Land.

During Covenant's absence, several thousand years have passed in the Land, and the Despiser has regained his power. As before, he seeks to access Covenant's wild magic in order to break the Arch of Time and escape his prison. In *The Wounded Land*, however, Covenant and Linden soon learn that Lord Foul has fundamentally altered his tactics. Instead of using armies and warfare to goad Covenant, the Despiser has devised an attack on the natural Law which gives the Land its beauty and health.

The overt form of this attack is the Sunbane, a malefic corona around the sun which produces extravagant surges of fertility, rain, drought and pestilence in mad succession. So great is the Sunbane's power and destructiveness that it has come to dominate all life in the Land. Yet the Sunbane is not what it appears to be. And its organic virulence serves primarily to mask Lord Foul's deeper manipulations.

He has spent centuries corrupting the Council of Lords. That group now rules over the Land as the Clave; and it is led by a Raver, one of the Despiser's most ancient and potent servants. Pretending to resist the Sunbane, the Clave extracts blood from the people of the Land to feed the Banefire, the true source of the Sunbane.

However, the hidden purpose of the Clave and the Banefire is to inspire from Covenant an excessive exertion of wild magic. And towards that end, another Raver afflicts Covenant with a venom intended to cripple his control over his power. When the venom has done its work, Covenant will be unable to defend the Land without unleashing so much force that he destroys the Arch.

As for Linden Avery, Lord Foul intends to use her loathing of death against her. She alone is gifted or cursed with the health-sense, the ability to directly perceive physical and emotional health, which once informed and guided all the people of the Land. For that reason, she is uniquely vulnerable to the malevolence of the Sunbane as well as to the insatiable malice of the Ravers. The manifest evil into which she has been plunged threatens the core of her identity.

Linden's health-sense accentuates her potential as a healer. In addition, however, it gives her the capacity to possess other people; to reach so deeply into them that she can control their actions and emotions. For this reason, Lord Foul has chosen her. He intends to cripple her morally: he wishes to transform her into a woman who will be willing to possess Covenant in order to misuse his power. Surely, the Despiser believes, either Covenant or Linden will give him what he wants.

And if those ploys fail, Lord Foul has other stratagems in place to achieve his ends.

Horrified in their separate ways by what has been done to the Land, Covenant and Linden wish to confront the Clave in Revelstone; but on their own, they cannot survive the complex perils of the Sunbane. Fortunately, they gain the help of two villagers, Sunder and Hollian. Sunder and Hollian have lived with the Sunbane all their lives, and their experience enables Covenant and Linden to avoid ruin as they travel.

However, Linden, Sunder and Hollian are separated from Covenant near a region known as Andelain. They are captured by the Clave while he enters Andelain alone. It was once the most beautiful and Earthpowerful place in the Land; and he now discovers that it alone remains intact, defended from the Sunbane by the last Forestal, Caer-Caveral, who was formerly Hile Troy. There he encounters his Dead, the spectres of his long-gone friends. They offer him advice and guidance for the struggle ahead. And they give him a gift: a strange, ebony creature named Vain, an artificial being created for a hidden purpose by ur-viles, former servants of the Despiser.

Aided by Waynhim, cousins of the ur-viles, Covenant hastens towards Revelstone to rescue his friends. When he encounters the Clave, he learns the cruellest secret of the Sunbane: it was made possible by his destruction of the Staff of Law thousands of years ago. Desperate to undo the harm which he has unwittingly caused, he risks wild magic in order to free Linden, Sunder, and Hollian, as well as a number of *Haruchai*, powerful warriors who at one time served the Council of Lords.

Unfortunately, a Raver has been at work torturing Linden, and she is now effectively comatose. When she has recovered somewhat, she and Covenant set out with Sunder, Hollian, Vain and a small group of *Haruchai* to seek for the One Tree, the wood from which Berek originally fashioned the Staff of Law. Covenant hopes to devise a new Staff with which to oppose the Clave and the Sunbane.

Faring eastwards, towards the Sunbirth Sea, Covenant and his companions encounter a party of Giants, seafaring beings from the homeland of the Giants of Seareach. One of them, mute Cable Seadreamer, has had a vision of a terrible threat to the Earth, and the Giants have sent out a Search to discover the danger.

Convinced that this threat is the Sunbane, Covenant persuades the Search to help him find the One Tree; and in *The One Tree* Covenant, Linden, Vain, and several *Haruchai* set sail aboard the Giantship Starfare's Gem, leaving Sunder and Hollian to rally the people of the Land against the Clave.

The quest for the One Tree takes Covenant and Linden first to the land of the *Elohim*, cryptic beings of pure Earthpower who appear to understand and perhaps control the destiny of the Earth. The *Elohim* agree to reveal the location of the One Tree, but they exact a price: they cripple Covenant's mind, enclosing his consciousness in a kind of stasis, purportedly to protect the Earth from his growing power, but in fact to prevent him from carrying out Vain's secret purpose. Guided now by Linden's determination rather than Covenant's, the Search sets sail for the Isle of the One Tree.

Unexpectedly, however, they are joined by one of the *Elohim*, Findail, who has been Appointed to ensure that Vain's purpose fails – and to bear the consequences if it does not.

Linden soon finds that she is unable to free Covenant's mind without possessing him, which she fears to do, knowing that she may unleash his power. When events force her to a decision, however, she succeeds at restoring his consciousness – much to Findail's dismay.

At last Starfare's Gem reaches the Isle of the One Tree. When one of the *Haruchai*, Brinn, defeats the Guardian of the One Tree, Covenant, Linden and their companions are able to approach their goal.

But their hope of obtaining the wood for a new Staff of Law is an illusion fostered by Lord Foul's manipulations – and by Findail's refusal to aid the Search in any way. Covenant's purpose is in fact the threat to the Earth which Cable Seadreamer has foreseen. Covenant's approach to the One Tree and his power begin to rouse the Worm of the World's End; and the Worm's awakening will accomplish Lord Foul's release from Time.

At the cost of his own life, Seadreamer succeeds at making Linden aware of the true danger. She in turn is able to forestall Covenant. Nevertheless the Worm has been disturbed, and its restlessness forces the Search to flee as the Isle sinks into the sea, taking the One Tree beyond reach.

Defeated, the Search sets course for the Land in *White Gold Wielder*. Covenant now believes that he has no alternative except to confront the Clave directly, to quench the Banefire and then to battle the Despiser; and Linden is determined to aid him, in part because she has come to love him, and in part because she fears his unchecked wild magic.

With great difficulty, they eventually reach Revelstone, where they are rejoined by Sunder, Hollian, and several *Haruchai*. Aided by a Sandgorgon of the Great Desert, they break down Revelstone's gates. Then Covenant, Linden and their friends give battle to the Clave.

After a fierce struggle, the companions corner the Raver which commands the Clave. There the Sandgorgon and Seadreamer's brother, Grimmand Honninscrave, succeed at 'rending' the Raver, although Honninscrave perishes in the attempt. Then Covenant flings himself into the Banefire, using its dark theurgy to transform the venom in his veins. With the danger that he will destroy the Arch thus diminished, he is able to quench the Banefire with wild magic.

When the Clave has been dispersed, and Revelstone has been cleansed, Covenant and Linden turn towards Mount Thunder, where they believe that they will find the Despiser. As they travel, still followed by Vain and Findail, Linden's fears grow. She realises that Covenant does not mean to fight Lord Foul. That contest, Covenant believes, will unleash enough force to destroy the Arch. Afraid that he will surrender to the Despiser, Linden prepares herself to possess him again, although she now understands that possession is a greater evil than death.

Yet when she and Covenant finally face Lord Foul, deep within the Wightwarrens of Mount Thunder, she is possessed herself by a Raver; and when she wins free of that dark spirit's control, she is no longer willing to interfere with Covenant's choices. And in fact he does surrender, giving Lord Foul his ring. But as the Despiser turns wild magic against Covenant, slaying his body, the altered venom is burned out of Covenant's spirit, and he becomes a being of pure wild magic, able to sustain the Arch despite the fury of Lord Foul's attacks. Eventually the Despiser expends so much of his own essence that he effectively defeats himself; and Covenant's ring falls to Linden.

Meanwhile, she has gleaned an understanding of Vain's purpose – and of Findail's Appointed role. Vain is pure structure: Findail, pure fluidity. Together they contain the necessary elements for a Staff of Law.

Using Covenant's ring, Linden melds Vain and Findail into a new Staff. Then, guided by her health-sense and her physician's instincts, she reaches out with the restored power of Law to erase the Sunbane and begin the healing of the Land.

When she is done, she fades from the Land and returns to her own world, where she finds that Covenant is indeed dead. Yet she now holds his wedding ring. And when Dr Berenford comes looking for her, she discovers that her time with Covenant and her own victories have transformed her. She is now truly Linden Avery the Chosen, as she was called in the Land: she can choose to live her old life in an entirely new way.

THE LAST CHRONICLES
OF THOMAS COVENANT

BOOK ONE

The Runes of the Earth

PROLOGUE

'My heart has rooms'

Chapter One:

Mother's Son

'No, Mr Covenant,' she repeated for the third time. 'I can't do that.'

Ever since he had entered her office, she had wished that he would go away.

He gazed at her as if he had not heard a word. 'I don't see the problem, Dr Avery.' His voice cast echoes of his father through her, flashes of memory like spangles off a surface of troubled water. 'I'm her son. I have the right. And it's my responsibility.' Despite the differences, even his features dragged a tangled net across her heart, dredging up aches and longing. 'She's nothing to you, just a problem you can't solve. A burden on the taxpayers. A waste of resources you could use to help someone else.' His eyes were too wide-set, his whole face too broad. The flesh of his cheeks and jaw hinted at self-indulgence.

And yet—

If he were clay, only a slice or two with the sculptor's tool, only a line of severity on either side of his mouth, and his cheeks would look as strict as commandments. A squint of old suffering at the corners of his eyes: a little grey dust to add years to his hair. His eyes themselves were exactly the right colour, a disturbed hue like the shade of madness or prophecy. Oh, he could have been his father, if he had not been so young and unmarked. If he had paid any price as extravagant as his father's—

He was certainly insistent enough to be Thomas Covenant.

He seemed to face her through a haze of recall, reminding her of the man she had loved. The man who had risen in fear and fury to meet his harsh fate.

Avoiding the young man's gaze, she looked around the walls of her office without seeing them. At another time, the strict professionalism of this space might have eased her. Her displayed diplomas, like her tidy desk and heavy filing cabinets, served to vouch for her. She had found comfort among them on other occasions. But today they had no effect.

How many times had she held Thomas Covenant in her arms? Too few: not enough to satisfy her hunger for them.

She still wore his white gold wedding ring on a silver chain around her neck. It was all that she had left of him.

'I can reach her, Dr Avery,' the son continued in a voice which was too bland to be his father's. 'You can't. You've been trying for years. I'm sure you've done your best. But if you could have reached her, she would be sane by now. It's time to let her go. Let me have her.'

'Mr Covenant,' she insisted, 'I'll say it again. I can't do that. The law in this state won't allow it. Professional ethics won't allow it.'

I won't allow it.

Joan Covenant was as unreachable as her son claimed. She might as well have been catatonic, in spite of every conceivable drug and therapy. In fact, she would have died long ago without constant care. But she was not 'nothing' to Linden Avery. If Roger Covenant believed that, he would never understand the woman who stood in his way.

His mother was Thomas Covenant's ex-wife. Ten years ago, Linden had watched Covenant trade his life for Joan's – and smile to reassure her. That smile had ripped Linden's heart from its hiding place, rent away its protective lies and commitments. Sometimes she believed that everything which she had now done and become had started then. Covenant's smile had triggered a detonation which had blown her free of her own parents' hunger for death. The new woman who had emerged from that explosion loved Thomas Covenant from the bottom of her soul.

For his sake, she would not abandon Joan.

Yet now Roger Covenant sat across her desk from her, demanding his mother's release. If she had been the kind of woman who found the folly of the misguided amusing, she would have laughed in his face. Where did he get the nerve?

Hell, where did he get the *idea*?

'I'm sorry.' Apparently he wanted to be polite. 'I still don't see the problem. She's my mother. I'm her son. I'm willing to take care of her. How can the law object? How can *you*, Dr Avery? I don't understand why she and I haven't already left.'

She turned away for a moment to look out the window. It gave her an unilluminating view of the parking lot, where her worn old car crouched over its rust, waiting for the day when its welds would fail and it could finally slump into scrap. She had kept it only because it had carried her to her first encounters with Thomas Covenant.

If Roger would not leave, surely she could simply drive away? Go out to her car, coax its engine to life and return to Jeremiah?

No. If she had wanted to be a woman who fled whenever her job became difficult, she should have bought herself a more reliable vehicle.

Old habit lifted her hand to press the hard circle of Covenant's ring through her blouse. Sighing, she faced his son again.

'Let me try to be plain. Whether or not you understand is beside the point. The point is this. Unless and until you bring me a court order signed by a judge instructing me to release Joan Covenant to your custody, she stays where she is. End of discussion.' She gazed at him expectantly. When he failed to take the hint, she added, 'That's your cue to leave, Mr Covenant.'

Don't you understand that you're not the only person here who cares about her?

However, she doubted that Roger Covenant cared at all for his mute mother. His oblivious manner, and the incipient madness or prophecy in his eyes, conveyed an entirely different impression.

He had explained that he had not come for Joan earlier because he had not been old enough. But he had passed his twenty-first birthday yesterday. Now he was ready. Yet Linden believed intuitively that he had some hidden purpose which outweighed love or concern.

In his unwavering insistence, he reminded her of some of the more plausible psychotics she had known in her tenure as Chief Medical Officer for the Berenford Memorial Psychiatric Hospital. But perhaps he suffered from nothing more treatable than terminal narcissism, in which case he was telling her the simple truth. He could not 'see the problem'.

This time, however, something in her tone – or in the conflicted fire mounting behind her eyes – must have penetrated his strange unction. Before she could offer to call Security, he rose to his feet as if he comprehended her at last.

Immediately she stood as well. She saw now that he was an inch or two shorter than his father, and broader in the torso. For that reason, among others, he would never evince the particular gauntness, the cut and flagrant sense of purpose – all compromise and capacity for surrender flensed away – which had made Thomas Covenant irrefusable to her.

He would never be the man his father was. He had too much of his mother in him. His carriage exposed him: the slight looseness in his shoulders; the tension which compensated for his poor balance. His arms seemed full of truncated gestures, expressions of honesty or appeal cut off prematurely. Behind his insistence, Linden heard hints of Joan's weakness, forlorn and fundamentally betrayed.

Perhaps his real desires had nothing to do with his mother. Perhaps he simply wanted to prove himself his father's equal. Or to supplant him—

When Roger had gained his feet, however, he did not admit defeat. Instead he asked, 'Can I see her? It's been years.' He offered Linden an affectless smile. 'And there's something I want to show you.'

In spite of her impatience, she nodded. 'Of course. You can visit her right now.' Strangely, his apparent emptiness saddened her: she grieved on his behalf. Thomas Covenant had taught her that ignorance – like innocence – had no power to ward itself against harm. Because Roger did not understand, he could not be saved from suffering.

When he saw Joan's unique plight, either his incomprehension would hold against her, or it would not. In either case, the experience might convince him to leave Linden alone.

For that reason, she gestured him towards the door. She had already done her rounds; and her paperwork could wait. Certainly her patients had no immediate need of her. At its heart, Berenford Memorial existed, not to heal its occupants, but to help them heal themselves.

Suddenly cooperative, as if he had gained an important concession, Roger preceded her out of her office. Now his smile struck her as reflexive; an unconscious expression of eagerness.

Closing the door behind her, Linden led him through the edifice where she did the work with which she attempted to fill Covenant's place in her heart. His place – and the Land's—

Inadvertently she remembered the sound of Pitchwife's voice as he sang,

> My heart has rooms that sigh with dust
> And ashes in the hearth.

At times the contrast between her experiences with Thomas Covenant and her years at Berenford Memorial discouraged her. Surely her contest with the madness of her patients could not compare with the sheer glory of Thomas Covenant's struggle to redeem the Land? Nevertheless she closed her throat and continued guiding Roger towards Joan's room. The ache which he elicited was familiar to her, and she knew how to bear it.

Her life here was not less than the one she had lived with Covenant. It was only different. Less grand, perhaps: more ambiguous, with smaller triumphs. But it sufficed.

A short corridor took her out of the Hospital's small administrative wing and across the lobby, past Maxine Dubroff's reception/information station. Maxine worked there nine hours a day, five days a week: an ageing woman who looked like a stork and smiled like an angel, responding to everyone who entered Berenford Memorial with unfailing solicitude. She was a volunteer who had simply attached herself to Linden one day after Linden, on call in ER as she was every third night, had saved the life of Maxine's husband, Ernie. He had been kicked in the chest by a horse: Linden had found and removed a sliver of bone from his left lung. He had recovered to teach the horse better manners; and Maxine had been at Linden's service ever since.

She smiled now as Linden and Roger Covenant crossed the tiled lobby. In spite of Roger's presence, Linden replied with a smile of her own – less seraphic than Maxine's, but no less sincere. Maxine reminded Linden that she was not alone in her dedication to her work. Like Linden herself, and most of Berenford Memorial's staff, Maxine had committed herself to a need which the county acknowledged but could not meet.

Ten years ago, Joan had been snatched from Thomas Covenant's care by a group of people who were – in the county's eyes – demonstrably insane. For weeks these individuals had nurtured their lunacy and destitution openly, begging for food and shelter and clothing, calling for repentance. Then, one night little more than twenty-four hours after Linden had arrived in town to accept a job at County Hospital, they had kidnapped Joan, leaving Covenant himself unconscious, his home splashed with blood.

They had taken her into the woods behind his home, where they had apparently planned to kill her in some bizarre ritual – a rite which included burning their own hands to stumps in a bonfire built for the purpose. Although no one except Linden knew the truth, that rite had achieved its intended aim. It had lured Covenant into the woods on Joan's trail. There he had exchanged himself for her, and been killed.

In the life which Linden had lived here, she had known him for scarcely thirty-six hours.

After his death, however, the people who had arranged his self-sacrifice had regained some measure of ordinary sanity. Their charred hands and starved bodies had been horrible enough. Those injuries had stretched County Hospital's limits. But the burden of their damaged minds, their aggrieved spirits, had proved harder for the citizens of the area to bear. Collectively the county felt responsible.

In public, most people admitted that they had failed to care for the most desolate and fragile members of their community. Surely unbalanced mothers and fathers would not have thrust, not just their own hands, but the hands of their children as well, into the flames if their destitution had not been neglected by the more stable souls around them? Surely those wounded men and women would have eschewed such violence if they had been offered any other recourse? No matter how many demented preachers urged them to fanaticism? Listening to children in cruel pain sob through the night taught the well-meaning people of the county to desire some form of prevention.

Yet this sense of communal guilt ran deeper than most people would acknowledge. On some level, the entire county understood that the terrible events which had led to Covenant's murder would never have happened if he had not been shunned and execrated, forced into the traditional role of the outcast, the pariah. He had been, inexplicably, a leper: he had what the doctors called a 'primary' case of Hansen's disease, one with no known etiology. Such cases were rare, even by the standards of an illness as rare as leprosy, but they occurred often enough to suggest the wrath of God; punishment for sins so vile that they sickened the sinner.

Viscerally frightened and full of loathing, people had spurned Thomas Covenant as if he were a carrier of corruption. For over a decade, he had occupied Haven Farm on sufferance: seeing no one, never coming to town, avoided by his neighbours; occasionally harassed by the county sheriff, Barton Lytton; uncomfortably tolerated by his own lawyer, Megan Roman; befriended only by Julius Berenford, then Chief of Staff at County Hospital. Indeed, the county's repugnance for Covenant's illness would have driven him into exile if he had not once saved the life of a snake-bitten girl. In addition, however, he made significant contributions to the care of the county's indigents – money which he earned by writing novels about guilt and power. In effect, he had supported the very people who brought about his death: the same people, presumably, who had driven his ex-wife mad. Therefore he was tolerated.

Then he was gone, irretrievable, leaving only Joan and Linden behind.

Dr Berenford believed that he had been too silent while Covenant lived. Afterward he raised his voice. Impelled by her own regrets, Megan Roman acted on his words. And the voters and politicians of the county felt more responsible than they cared to admit. They lobbied the state legislature: they passed mill levies: they applied for grants.

Eventually they built Berenford Memorial Psychiatric Hospital, named for Julius when he had slipped away in his sleep one night five years ago. And they appointed Linden as Berenford Memorial's CMO. She was the only one among them who had accompanied Covenant to his last crisis.

Now she presided over a small facility of twenty beds, all in private rooms. Her staff included five nurses, five orderlies, one janitor, one maintenance man and a coterie of part-time secretaries, in addition to volunteers like Maxine Dubroff. Berenford Memorial had two psychiatrists on call. And one physician – herself – with a background in emergency room medicine and family practice: trauma, triage, and pink eye.

From the lobby, she guided Covenant's son upstairs to the 'acute care' wing: ten beds devoted to patients who were inclined to injure themselves, assault the staff, or run away at random opportunities. Instead of proceeding to Joan's room, however, she paused at the top of the stairs and turned to face Roger.

'A moment, if you don't mind, Mr Covenant. May I ask you a question?' When he had seen his mother, he might not give her another chance. 'The more I think about it, the less I understand why you're here.'

Again his smile seemed merely reflexive. 'What is there to understand? She's my mother. Why wouldn't I want to see her?'

'Of course,' Linden countered. 'But what inspired your desire to take care of her? That's not as common as you might think. Frankly, it sounds a little' – the term she wished to use was *de trop*, existentially dislocated – 'daunting.'

In response, Roger's manner seemed to sharpen. 'The last time I saw her,' he replied precisely, 'she told me that if she failed I would need to take her place. Until yesterday I didn't have the resources to do that.'

Involuntarily Linden caught her breath as the bottom of her stomach seemed to fall away. 'Failed at what?'

Long ago, Joan had sought out Thomas Covenant – no, not sought out, she had been *sent* – in order to teach him despair. Despite her terrible plight, however, and her thirst for his blood, she had failed absolutely.

'Isn't that obvious?' Covenant's son returned. 'She's here, isn't she? Wouldn't you call that failure?'

No. For a moment, Linden's heart quailed. Memories beat about her head like wings: she felt harried by furies.

Her face must have betrayed her chagrin. Solicitously, Roger reached out to touch her arm. 'Dr Avery, are you all right?' Then he dropped his hand. 'I really think you should let me take her. It would be better for everyone.'

Even you, he seemed to say. Especially you.

Take her place.

Ten years ago, empowered by all of those hands thrust into the flames, all of that ceded pain, as well as by the fatal rush of Thomas Covenant's blood, a bitter malevolence had pierced the reality of Linden's life. It had drawn her in Covenant's wake to another place, another dimension of existence. The psychiatrists on call at Berenford Memorial would have called it a 'psychotic episode' – an *extended* psychotic episode. With Covenant, she had been summoned to a realm known as the Land, where she had been immersed in evil until she was altered almost beyond recognition. During the black hours of that one night, before Julius Berenford had found her with Covenant's body, she had somehow spent several months outside – or deep within – herself, striving to win free of her own weakness and the legacy of her parents in order to preserve the beauty of a world which had never been meant for corruption.

Now Roger's words seemed to suggest that she would have to face it all again.

No. Shuddering, she came back to herself. It was impossible. She was flinching at shadows, echoes. Roger's father was dead. There would be no second summons for her. The Land was Thomas Covenant's doom, not hers. He had given his life for it, as he had for Joan, and so its enemy, the dark being known variously as a-Jeroth, the Grey Slayer and Lord Foul the Despiser, had been defeated.

Trusting in that, Linden set aside her alarm and faced Covenant's son.

Roger's implied threat she ignored. Instead she asked, 'What do you mean, you have the "resources" to take her place?'

'It's simple,' Roger replied. He seemed to misunderstand her without being aware of it. 'I'm twenty-one now. I'm of age. Yesterday I inherited my father's legacy.

'Of course,' he explained as if Linden might have forgotten, 'he left everything to my mother. Haven Farm. His royalties. But she was declared incompetent when she was committed here. Ms Roman – you know her, my father's lawyer – has been trustee of the estate. But now it's all mine.' His smile hinted at self-satisfaction. 'Once I've persuaded you to release her, she and I will live on Haven Farm.

'She'll like that. She and my father were happy there.'

Linden swallowed a groan. Thomas and Joan Covenant had lived on Haven Farm until his leprosy had been diagnosed. Then she had left him, abandoned him; divorced him to protect their son from his illness. No doubt she had believed that she was doing the right thing. Nevertheless the knowledge of her own frailty – the awareness that she had broken her vows when her husband had needed her most – had given the Despiser a foothold in her soul. Her shame was fertile soil for the seeds of despair and madness.

And when she had been deprived of every conscious impulse except the desire to taste her ex-husband's blood, Covenant had cared for her on Haven

Farm until the end. The idea that Joan would 'like' living there again nearly brought tears to Linden's eyes.

And Roger had not answered her real question.

'That isn't what I meant,' she insisted thickly. 'You said she told you to take her place if she failed. Now you have the resources to do that.'

'Did I?' His smile remained expressionless. 'You must have misheard me. Now I can take *your* place, Dr Avery. I have enough money to care for her. We have a home. I can afford all the help I need.

'She isn't the only one who failed.'

Linden frowned to conceal a wince. She herself had failed Joan: she knew that. She failed all her patients. But she also knew that her failure was beside the point. It did nothing to diminish the value or the necessity of her chosen work.

And she was sure that she had not 'misheard' Roger.

Abruptly she decided not to waste any more time questioning him. For all practical purposes, he was impervious to enquiry. And he had nothing to say which might sway her.

Surely he would leave when he had seen his mother?

Without challenging his falseness, she drew him forward again, towards Joan's room.

Along the way, she explained, 'This is where we keep our more disturbed patients. They aren't necessarily more damaged or in more pain than the people downstairs. But they manifest violent symptoms of one form or another. We've had to keep your mother under restraint for the past year. Before that—'

Linden temporarily spared herself more detail by pushing open Joan's door with her shoulder and leading Roger into his mother's room.

Out in the hall, the characteristic smell of hospitals was less prominent, but here it was unmistakable: an ineradicable admixture of betadyne and blood, harsh cleansers and urine, human sweat, fear, floor wax and anaesthetics, accented by an inexplicable tang of formalin. For some reason, medical care always produced the same scents.

The room was spacious by the standard of private rooms in County Hospital next door. A large window let in the kind of sunlight that sometimes helped fragile psyches recover their balance. The bed occupied the centre of the floor. An unused TV set jutted from one wall near the ceiling. The only piece of advanced equipment present was a pulse monitor, its lead attached to a clip on the index finger of Joan's left hand. According to the monitor, her pulse was steady, untroubled.

On a stand by the head of the bed sat a box of cotton balls, a bottle of sterile saline, a jar of petroleum jelly and a vase of bright flowers. The flowers had been Maxine Dubroff's idea, but Linden had adopted it immediately. For years now she had arranged for the delivery of flowers to all her patients on a regular basis, the brighter the better. In every language which she could devise or imagine, she strove to convince her patients that they were in a place of care.

Joan sat upright in the bed, staring blankly at the door. Restraints secured her arms to the rails of the bed. Her bonds were loose enough to let her scratch her nose or adjust her posture, although she never did those things.

In fact, one of the nurses or orderlies must have placed her in that position. Fortunately for her caregivers, Joan had become a compliant patient: she remained where she was put. Pulled to her feet, she stood. Stretched out on the bed, she lay still. She swallowed food placed in her mouth. Sometimes she chewed. When she was taken into the bathroom, she voided. But she did not react to words or voices; gave no indication that she was aware of the people who tended her.

Her stare never wavered: she hardly seemed to blink. Standing or reclining, her disfocused gaze regarded neither care nor hope. If she ever slept, she did so with her eyes open.

Her years of catatonia had marked her poignantly. The skin of her face had hung slack on its bones for so long now that the underlying muscles had atrophied, giving her a look of mute horror. Despite the programme of exercises which Linden had prescribed for her, and which the orderlies carried out diligently, her limbs had wasted to a pitiful frailty. And nothing that Linden or the nurses could do – nothing that any of the experts whom Linden had consulted could suggest – spared her from losing her teeth over the years. No form of nourishment, oral or IV, no brushing or other imposed care, could replace her body's need for ordinary use. In effect, she had experienced more mortality than her chronological years could contain. Helpless to do otherwise, her flesh bore the burden of too much time.

'Hello, Joan,' Linden said as she always did when she entered the room. The detached confidence of her tone assumed that Joan could hear her in spite of all evidence to the contrary. 'How are you today?'

Nevertheless Joan's plight tugged at her heart. A sore the size of Linden's palm stigmatised Joan's right temple. A long series of blows had given her a deep bruise which had eventually begun to ooze blood as the skin stretched and cracked, too stiff to heal. Now a dripping red line veined with yellow and white ran down her cheek in spite of everything that could be done to treat it.

When the bruise had first begun to bleed, Linden had covered it with a bandage; but that had made Joan frantic, causing her to thrash against her restraints until she threatened to break her own bones. Now Linden concentrated on trying to reduce the frequency of the blows. On her orders, the wound was allowed to bleed: cleaned several times a day, slathered with antibiotics and salves to counteract an incessant infection, but left open to the air. Apparently it calmed Joan in some way.

Roger stopped just inside the door and stared at his mother. His face betrayed no reaction. Whatever he felt remained closed within him, locked into his heart. Linden had expected surprise, shock, dismay, indignation, perhaps even compassion; but she saw none. The undefined lines of his face gave her no hints.

Without shifting his gaze, he asked softly, 'Who hit her?'

He didn't sound angry. Hell, Linden thought, he hardly sounded interested—

She sighed. 'She did it to herself. That's why she's restrained.'

Moving to the side of the bed, she took a couple of cotton balls, moistened them with sterile saline and gently began to mop Joan's cheek. One soft stroke at a time, she wiped away the blood upward until she reached the seeping wound. Then she used more cotton balls to dab at the wound itself, trying to clean it without hurting Joan.

Linden would have cared for her carefully in any case; but her devotion to Thomas Covenant inspired an extra tenderness in her.

'It started a year ago. Until then we kept her downstairs. She'd been unreactive for so long, we never thought that she might be a danger to herself. But then she began punching at her temple. As hard as she can.'

Hard enough to wear calluses on her knuckles.

'At first it wasn't very often. Once every couple of days, no more. But that didn't last long. Soon she was doing it several times a day. Then several times an hour. We brought her up here, tied her wrists. That seemed to work for a while. But then she got out of the restraints—'

'Got out?' Roger put in abruptly. 'How?'

For the first time since he had entered the room, he looked at Linden instead of at Joan.

Avoiding his eyes, Linden gazed out the window. Past the institutional profile of County Hospital next door, she could see a stretch of blue sky, an almost luminous azure, free of fault. Spring offered the county days like this occasionally, days when the air reminded her of *diamondraught*, and the illimitable sky seemed deep enough to swallow away all the world's hurts.

Today it gave her little comfort.

'We don't know,' she admitted. 'We've never been able to figure it out.

Usually it happens late at night, when she's alone. We come in the next morning, find her free. Blood pumping from her temple. Blood on her fist. For a while we had her watched twenty-four hours a day. Then we set up video cameras, recorded everything. As far as we can tell, the restraints just fall off her. Then she hits herself until we make her stop.'

'And she still does?' Roger's manner had intensified.

Linden turned from the window to face him again. 'Not as much as before. I can get you a copy of the tapes if you want. You can watch for yourself. Now it only happens three or four times a night. Occasionally during the day, not often.'

'What changed?' he asked.

Gazing at him, she remembered that his father had done everything in his power to protect both Joan and her. Roger's stare conveyed the impression that he would not have done the same.

Her shoulders sagged, and she sighed again. 'Mr Covenant, you have to understand this. She was going to kill herself. One punch at a time, she was beating herself to death. We tried everything we could think of. Even electroshock – which I loathe. During the first six or seven months, we gave her an entire pharmacy of sedatives, tranquillisers, soporifics, stimulants, neural inhibitors, beta-blockers, SSRIs, anti-seizure drugs – enough medication to comatise a horse. Nothing worked. Nothing even slowed her down. She was killing herself.'

Apparently something within her required those blows. Linden considered it possible that the Land's old enemy had left a delayed compulsion like a post-hypnotic suggestion in Joan's shattered mind, commanding her to bring about her own death.

Not for the first time, Linden wondered what Sheriff Lytton had said or done to Joan during the brief time when she had been in his care. When Julius Berenford had driven to Haven Farm after Covenant's murder, he had found Joan there: confused and frightened, with no memory of what had transpired; but able to speak and respond. Wishing to search for Covenant and Linden without interference, Julius had sent Joan to County Hospital with Barton Lytton; and by the time they had reached the hospital Joan's mind was gone. Linden had asked Lytton what he had done, of course, pushed him for an answer; but he had told her nothing.

'And she was getting worse,' Linden went on. 'More frantic. Hysterical. She hit herself more often. Sometimes she refused to eat, went days without food. She fought us so hard that it took three orderlies and a nurse to fix an IV. She began to lose alarming amounts of blood.'

'What changed?' Roger repeated intently. 'What did you do?'

Linden hesitated on the edge of risks which she had not meant to take. Without warning the air of Joan's room seemed crowded with dangerous possibilities. How much of the truth could she afford to expose to this unformed and foolish young man?

But then she tightened her resolve and met his question squarely. 'Three months ago, I gave her back her wedding ring.'

Without glancing away from him, Linden reached to the collar of Joan's nightgown and lifted it aside to reveal the delicate silver chain hanging around her neck. From the end of the chain, still hidden by the nightgown, dangled a white gold wedding band. Joan had lost so much weight that she could not have kept a ring on any of her fingers.

Roger's smile hinted at sudden hungers. 'I'm impressed, Dr Avery. That was obviously the right thing to do. But I would not have expected—' He stopped short of saying that he would not have expected such insight from her. 'How did you figure it out? What made you think of it?'

Committed now, Linden shrugged. 'It just came to me one night.

'I don't know how much you know about the end of your father's life. For the last two weeks before he was killed, he took care of Joan.' On Haven Farm. 'She had already lost her mind, but she wasn't like this. In some ways, she was much worse. Practically rabid. The only thing that calmed her was the taste of your father's blood. When he needed to feed her, or clean her, he would let her scratch him until she drew blood. Sucking it off his skin would bring her back to herself – for a little while.'

Behind Linden's professional detachment, a secret anger made her hope that she might yet shock or frighten Roger Covenant.

'Now she hits herself, Mr Covenant. She wants the pain for some reason. She needs to hurt herself. I don't know why. As punishment?' For her role in her ex-husband's murder? 'It certainly looks like she's punishing herself.

'And she won't tolerate a bandage. Her own bleeding seems to comfort her. Like a kind of restitution. It helps her regain a little balance. I tried to think of some way to sustain that. If restitution calmed her, I wanted her to have more of it.

'Her ring,' the symbol of her marriage, 'was the only thing I had that I could restore.'

At the time, Linden had placed the chain around Joan's neck with acute trepidation. The language of that gesture could so easily have been mis-interpreted; taken as a reminder of guilt rather than as a symbol of love and attachment. However, Joan had lapsed into her comparatively pliant trance as soon as the ring had touched her skin.

Since then Linden had often feared that she had made a terrible mistake: that it was precisely the reminder of guilt which calmed Joan: that Joan's catatonia endured because she had been fundamentally defeated by the touch of white gold. Nevertheless Linden did not remove the ring.

Joan's present trance was all that kept her alive. She could not have survived her battering desperation much longer.

Roger nodded as if Linden's explanation made perfect sense to him. 'You did well. Again, I'm impressed.' For the first time since Linden had met him – hardly an hour ago – he seemed satisfied. 'I can see why you're reluctant to let anyone else take care of her.'

At once, however, he resumed his irrational insistence. 'But you've done all you can. She won't get any better than this unless I help her.'

He raised his hand to forestall Linden's protest. 'There are things you don't know about her. About this situation. And I can't explain them. Words won't—' He paused to rephrase his point. 'They can't be conveyed in words. The knowledge has to be earned. And you haven't earned it. Not the way I have.

'Let me show you.'

She should stop him, Linden thought stupidly. This had gone on too long. Yet she did nothing to intervene as he approached the bed. He had touched a forgotten vulnerability to paralysis deep within her.

Gracelessly he seated himself as close to his mother as the bed-rail permitted. A touch of excitement flushed his cheeks. His respiration quickened. His hands trembled slightly as he undid the restraint on her right wrist.

Flowers cast splotches of colour into Linden's eyes, deep red and blue, untroubled yellow. A few minutes ago, she had known exactly what kind of flowers they were: now she had no idea. The sky outside the window seemed unattainable, too far away to offer any hope. The sunlight shed no warmth.

Joan stared past or through Roger vacantly. Linden expected her to strike herself, but she did not. Perhaps the fact that her hand was free had not yet penetrated her subterranean awareness.

Roger lifted his palms to Joan's cheeks, cupped them against her slack flesh. His trembling had become unmistakable. He seemed to quiver with eagerness, avid as a deprived lover. Unsteadily he turned her head until he could gaze straight into the absence of her eyes.

'Mother.' His voice shook. 'It's me. Roger.'

Linden bit down on her lip. All the air in the room seemed to concentrate around the bed, too thick to breathe. In the bonfire where Joan's captors had destroyed their right hands, she had seen eyes like fangs look out hungrily at Covenant's impending murder. At the time, she had believed that they held malice. But now she thought that emotion in them might have been despair; an emptiness which could not be filled.

'Mother.'

Joan blinked several times. Her pupils contracted.

With an effort that seemed to stretch the skin of her forehead, her eyes came into focus on her son.

'Roger?' Her disused voice crawled like a wounded thing between her lips. 'Is it you?'

Suddenly stern, he told her, 'Of course it's me. You can see that.'

Involuntarily Linden recoiled a step. She tasted blood, felt a pain in her lip. Roger sounded disdainful, vexed, as though Joan were a servant who had disappointed him.

'Oh, Roger.' Tears spilled from Joan's eyes. Her free hand fumbled to his shoulder, clutched at his neck. 'It's been so long.' Her face held no expression: its muscles lacked the strength to convey what she felt. 'I've waited so long. It's been so hard. Make it stop.'

'Stop complaining.' He scolded her as if she were a child. 'It isn't as bad as all that. I had to wait until I was twenty-one. You know that.'

How—? Linden panted as if she had been struck in the stomach. How—?

How had Roger reached Joan?

How could Joan have known anything?

'I've been good,' Joan responded, pleading. 'I have.' Her damaged voice seemed to flinch and cower at his feet. 'See?'

Dropping her arm from his neck, she flung her fist at her bruised temple. Fresh blood smeared her knuckles as she lowered her arm.

'I've been good,' she begged. 'Make it stop. I can't bear it.'

'Nonsense, Mother,' Roger snorted. 'Of course you can bear it. That's what you do.'

But then, apparently, he took pity on her, and his manner softened. 'It won't be much longer. I have some things to do. Then I'll make it stop. We'll make it stop together.'

Releasing her cheeks, he rose to his feet, turned towards Linden.

As soon as he left the bed, Joan began to scream – a frail, rending sound that seemed to rip from her throat like fabric tearing across jagged glass. As if in sympathy, the pulse monitor emitted a shrill call.

'You see, Dr Avery?' he remarked through his mother's cries. 'You really have no choice. You have to let her go with me.

'The sooner you release her, the sooner I can free her from all this.'

Over my dead body, Linden told his ambiguous smile and his bland eyes. Over my dead body.

Chapter Two:

Gathering Defences

'Outside,' Linden ordered him aloud. 'Now.'

She was fortunate that he complied at once. If he had resisted, she might have hit him, trying to strike the certainty from his face.

As soon as she had closed Joan's door behind her, she wheeled on him. 'You knew that would happen.'

Joan's screaming echoed in the corridor, reflected by the white tile floor, the unadorned walls. Her monitor carried its alarm to the nurses' station.

He shrugged, untouched by Linden's anger. 'I'm her son. She raised me.'

'That's no answer,' she retorted.

Before she could go on, a woman's voice called out, 'Dr Avery? What's wrong?'

A nurse came hurrying along the hall: Amy Clint. Her young, diligent face was wide with surprise and concern.

Roger Covenant smiled blandly at Amy. 'Give her a taste of that blood,' he suggested as though he had the right to say such things. 'It'll quiet her down.'

Amy stopped. She stared in dismay at Linden.

'Ms Clint'– Linden summoned her authority to counteract Amy's shock – 'this is Roger Covenant. He's Joan's son. Seeing him has upset her.'

'She's never—' For a moment, the nurse fumbled to control her reaction. Then she said more steadily, 'I've never heard her scream like that.' Joan's wailing ached in the air. 'What should I do?'

Linden took a deep breath, mustered her outrage. 'Do what he says. Let her taste her blood.' To ease Amy's consternation, she added, 'I'll explain later.'

'Now,' she insisted when the nurse hesitated.

'Right away, Doctor.' With distress in her eyes, Amy entered Joan's room, shut the door.

At once, Linden confronted Roger again. 'You didn't answer my question.'

Still smiling as though his mother's screams had no effect on him, he held up his hand, asking Linden to wait.

Moments after Amy had entered the room, Joan suddenly fell silent. The abrupt end of her cries throbbed in the hallway like an aftershock.

'You see, Dr Avery?' replied Roger. 'I'm really the only one who can take care of her. No one else is qualified.' Before Linden could protest, he added, 'I knew what would happen because I'm her son. I know exactly what's wrong with her. I know how to treat it.

'You can't justify keeping her now.'

'You're wrong.' Linden kept her voice down. 'I can't justify releasing her. What you just did is unconscionable.'

'I reached her,' he objected. 'That's more than you can do.'

'Oh, you reached her, all right,' Linden returned. 'That's pretty damn obvious. It's the results I object to.'

Roger frowned uncertainly. 'You think she's better off the way she is.' He appeared genuinely confused by Linden's reaction.

'I think—' Linden began, then stopped herself. He was beyond argument. More quietly, she stated, 'I think that until you bring me a court order to the contrary, she stays here. End of discussion.

'The front door' – she pointed along the hall – 'is that way.'

For an instant, anger seemed to flicker in his dissociated eyes. But then he shrugged and the glimpse vanished.

'We'll resolve this later, Dr Avery,' he said as if he were sure. 'There's just one more thing.

'Can you tell me what happened to my father's wedding ring?'

Without transition, Linden went cold. In the Land, Covenant's white gold ring was the symbol and instrument of his power. With it, he had wielded wild magic against the Despiser.

Roger wanted more than a chance to take his mother's place. He wanted his father's theurgy as well.

'I understand he always wore it,' he went on, 'but it wasn't found on his body. I've asked Megan Roman and Sheriff Lytton, but they don't know where it is. It's mine now. I want it.'

Old habit caused her to raise her hand to the irrefusable circle of the ring under her blouse. Roger meant to bear white gold to the Land so that he could tear down the Arch of Time, set Lord Foul free. The Despiser had already renewed his assault on the beauty of the Earth, and an ordeal which had nearly destroyed Linden once before was about to begin again—

No. *No.* It was impossible. Such things had exhausted their reality for her ten years ago.

Nevertheless she believed it. Or she believed that Roger Covenant believed it.

And if he believed it—

He smiled his vacant smile at her.

—then she could not afford to let him know that she had guessed his intent. If he realised that his plans were endangered, he might do something which she would be unable to prevent.

Already she might have given away too much. He could have seen the ingrained movement of her hand.

People were doing to die—

A heartbeat later, however, she recovered her courage. 'I have it,' she answered. She did not mean to diminish herself with lies. And she would not disavow her loyalty to his father. 'I've had it ever since he died.'

Roger nodded. 'That's why Sheriff Lytton didn't find it.'

'Your father left it to me,' Linden stated flatly. 'I intend to keep it.'

'It belongs to me,' he countered. 'His will left everything to my mother. I inherited it yesterday.'

She shook her head. 'No, you didn't. It came to me before he died. It isn't part of his estate.'

In fact, Covenant had not handed her the ring directly: she had retrieved it when the Despiser had slain him with its argent fire. Nevertheless she considered it hers as much as if he had wedded her with it.

'I see.' Roger frowned again. 'That's a problem, Dr Avery. I need it. I can't take her place without it. Not entirely. And if I don't take her place, she'll never be completely free.'

He seemed unconcerned that he revealed so much. Perhaps he did not consider Linden discerning enough to understand him.

'But it's not *my* problem,' she said precisely. 'We're done here. Goodbye, Mr Covenant. The door is—'

'I know,' he interrupted. 'The door is that way.'

'*Doctor* Avery' – now he sneered her title – 'you have no idea what you're interfering with.' Then he turned and strode away.

Oh, she had *some* idea. Despite his power to disturb his mother, he clearly understood nothing about the woman who opposed him. But she could not imagine that she had any advantage over him.

She could only guess what he might do next.

Urgently she wanted to know how he had earned his knowledge.

Her stomach clenched as she reentered Joan's room to explain the situation as best she could to Amy Clint.

By the time she returned to her office, her resolve had hardened, taken shape. She could not allow herself to be drawn into Roger Covenant's mad designs, whatever they might be. She had made her life and her commitments *here*: people whom she had chosen to serve and love were dependent on her. And Joan deserved better than whatever her son might do to her.

Linden had to stop Roger *now*, before he carried his intentions any farther.

To do that, she needed to know more about him.

She also needed help. Joan was not her only responsibility. She had other duties, other loves, which she did not mean to set aside.

Clearing space on her desk, she pulled the phone towards her and began to make calls.

First she contacted Bill Coty, the amiable old man who ran what passed for Security at County Hospital. He was generally considered a harmless, ineffectual duffer; but Linden thought otherwise. She had often suspected that he might rise to a larger challenge if he ever encountered one. Certainly he had made himself useful during the crisis which had followed Covenant's death, when the hospital's resources had been stretched by burn victims, concerned citizens and hysterical relatives. His characteristic smile twisted with nausea, he had soothed some people and shepherded others while shielding the medical staff from interference. And he could call on half a dozen volunteer security 'officers', burly individuals who would rush to the hospital if they were needed.

'I know this is going to sound odd,' she told him when he came on the line, 'but I think there's a man in the area who might try to kidnap one of my patients. His name is Roger Covenant.

'You remember his mother, Joan. He thinks he can take care of her better than we can. And he doesn't seem to care about legal niceties like custody.'

'That poor woman.' For a moment, Coty sounded inattentive, distracted by memories. Then, however, he surprised Linden by asking, 'How violent do you think this Roger is?'

Violent—? She had not considered Joan's son in those terms.

'I ask, Dr Avery,' the old man went on, 'because I want my guys ready for him. If he's just going to break a window and try to carry her off, any one of us can stop him. But if he comes armed—' He chuckled humourlessly. 'I might ask a couple of my guys to bring guns. I'm sure you know we aren't bonded for firearms. But I don't want a repeat of what happened ten years ago.'

Linden scrambled to adjust her assessment of Roger Covenant. 'I'm not sure what to tell you, Mr Coty. I just met him this morning. I don't think he's in his right mind. But nothing about him seemed violent,' apart from his emotional brutality towards his mother. 'Guns might be an overreaction.'

Could she be wrong about Roger's intentions? Was she inventing the danger? That was possible. If so, he hardly deserved to be shot for his dysfunction.

'Whatever you say, Doctor.' Bill's tone suggested no disappointment. Apparently he did not fancy himself – or his volunteers – as gunslingers. 'We'll start to keep an eye on her room tonight. Unless he's stupid, he won't try anything during the day. I'll make sure one of my guys is on duty all night.'

Grateful as much for his lack of scepticism as for his willingness to help, Linden thanked him and hung up.

Could she leave the matter in his hands? she asked herself. Did she need to do more?

Yes, she did. Joan was not Roger's only potential victim. If something happened to Linden herself, Jeremiah would be lost. He was entirely dependent on her.

The simple thought of him made her glance out the window at her car. She felt a sudden yearning to forget Joan and go to him; make sure that he was all right—

Sandy would have called if he were not.

Roger did not know he existed.

Her hands trembled slightly as she dialled Megan Roman's number.

Megan had been Thomas Covenant's lawyer, and then his estate's, for more than twenty years. During much of that time, her diligence – as she freely admitted – had been inspired by shame. His leprosy had disturbed her deeply. She had felt towards him a plain, primitive, almost cellular terror; an innominate conviction that his disease was a contagion which would spread through the county as it would through her own flesh, like wildfire.

But she was a lawyer, a thinking woman, dismayed by her own irrationality. While he had lived, she had waged a running battle with her alarm, continuing to work for him because she was ashamed of herself. And after his death she had become a staunch and vocal advocate for the kind of tolerance and social responsibility which had eluded her during his life. The bloody events which had brought about his murder should not have been allowed to happen. Like Julius Berenford, she had made a personal crusade out of trying to ensure that they never happened again.

Linden considered Megan Roman one of her few friends. Certainly Megan had always given Linden her assistance unstintingly. After Jeremiah's maiming by his stricken mother, and his troubled history in the county's various foster facilities, his adoption had posed a legal tangle which Linden could not have unsnarled for herself.

While she waited for Megan's receptionist to put her call through, Linden had time to wonder why Megan had not already contacted her about Roger Covenant. As his father's executor, she must have been dealing with him for years.

'Linden.' Megan had a professionally hearty phone manner which Linden disliked. It sounded false to her. 'This is an unexpected pleasure. What can I do you out of?'

Vexed in spite of herself, Linden responded bluntly, 'Why didn't you warn me about Roger Covenant?'

At once, Megan changed her tone. 'Oh, God. What has he done?'

'You first,' Linden insisted. She needed a moment to absorb Megan's immediate assumption that Roger had done something. 'Why didn't you warn me?'

'Well, shit, Linden,' Megan muttered uncomfortably. 'Will you believe that it wasn't any of your business? He's a client. I'm not *supposed* to talk about him.'

'Sure,' Linden conceded. 'But that's not the only reason you didn't tell me.' Clearly Megan distrusted him—

The lawyer hesitated, then asked, 'Will you believe that I just didn't think of it?'

'No. That I won't believe. I've known you too long.'

'Well, shit,' Megan repeated. 'What good is having friends if they know you too well to believe you?

'All right, all right,' she went on as if Linden had objected. 'I didn't tell you because' – she faltered momentarily – 'well, because I was trying to spare you. I know, you're a big girl, you can take care of yourself. But he's Thomas Covenant's *son*, for God's sake. That means something to you, something I don't understand.'

Deliberately Linden bit at her sore lip. That smaller pain steadied her.

'You don't talk about it,' Megan said more harshly. 'You hardly knew him. You've always said you just wanted to help him with Joan. But whenever I ask you about it, you don't really answer my questions. Instead I get the distinct impression that you had more at stake than you let on. He *looms* for you somehow. Your whole face changes when his name comes up.

'I don't know what his son means to you, but I thought it might be something painful.' Her tone conveyed a brusque shrug. 'So I wanted to spare you.

'Now it's your turn,' she added before Linden could respond. ' "Warn" you? Why should I need to warn you about anything? What has he done?'

But Linden was reluctant to describe Roger's encounter with his mother. She feared hearing the experience put into words.

'He came to see me an hour ago,' she said slowly. 'He thinks I should give him custody of his mother.' Words would make it more real. 'And he's *very* insistent—' Linden trailed into uncertainty.

'Yes?' her friend prompted.

'Megan, you're going to think I've lost my mind.' She touched Covenant's ring for courage. 'He made me believe that he intends to take her if I don't let her go.'

When Lord Foul put forth his power, people died. The beauty of the world was torn apart. He had to be stopped here.

'Oh, God,' Megan groaned. 'Made you believe it how?'

'I don't know how to explain it,' Linden admitted. After all these years, she could not now suddenly tell Megan what had happened to her during Covenant's death. If she did so, she would lose all of her credibility. 'Will you believe that he just gave me a bad feeling?

'I've been working with unbalanced people for a long time, and I think I have an instinct for it. He's off-kilter somehow. And I know for a fact that he didn't listen to a thing I said.

'He seems obsessed with the idea of taking care of Joan. Nothing else affects him. As far as he's concerned, she belongs with him. End of story. I'm afraid there aren't any ordinary social or legal or even practical considerations that will hold him back.'

Megan did not reply for a long moment. During the silence, Linden heard a ticking sound like a heartbeat along the phone line. Then it stopped. At last Megan said slowly, 'In fact, I do believe you. I have a bad feeling about him myself. And I can't explain it either.

'Do you know—?' She paused, apparently gathering her thoughts. 'We started corresponding three years ago. He wrote to me when he turned eighteen. At that point he was still technically a ward of the state – his grandparents never actually adopted him – but the welfare people found it easier to let him start managing his own affairs.

'He wanted to know everything about his father's estate. How much money there was, where it came from exactly, how it was invested, what kind of real property was involved. He wanted to make all the arrangements to take possession of the estate the minute he turned twenty-one. He understood that much about the law, at any rate. And he wanted to know everything I could tell him about his father personally. Hell, he even wanted to know about *you*, even though you hardly knew Thomas Covenant.'

Linden stifled an impulse to ask Megan what she had told Roger. Instead she looked out the window again. Her car seemed to call to her, insisting that she drive home; that Jeremiah needed her protection.

'But he never said a word about his mother,' added Megan. 'Based on our correspondence and conversations, I would have thought he didn't know where she was. Or care.'

He had not discussed Joan with Megan because he had not wanted to forewarn anyone.

Linden forced herself to turn away from the window. 'So what do you know about him? Has he talked about himself at all?'

'He doesn't volunteer much,' Megan responded. 'But he answers direct questions. You may know some of his background.'

In fact, Covenant had told Linden a little about Joan's past; but she did not interrupt Megan to say so. When Joan had divorced Covenant, she had moved back to her home town to live with her parents. For several years, apparently, she had striven to relieve her shame with conventional forms of exoneration: counselling, psychotherapy. When that approach had left her pain untouched, however, she had turned to religion: religion in more and more extreme forms.

'According to him,' Megan began, 'he doesn't remember much of his early life. But I got him to tell me a bit about that commune she joined. I guess that was about a year before she came back here.

'He says the commune called itself the Community of Retribution. Reading between the lines, they sure sound like a bloody-minded group. They didn't believe in salvation for people who acknowledged their sins and accepted God's grace. They thought the world was too far gone for that, too corrupt—' Megan muttered a curse under her breath. 'It needed violence, bloodshed, sacrifices. Ritual murder to destroy sin.

'Anyway, that's how I interpret what he told me. According to him, they spent most of their time praying for revelation. They wanted God to tell them who had to be sacrificed. And how.'

In protest, Megan demanded, 'Where do people like that *come* from, Linden?'

Thinking about Lord Foul, Linden replied, 'From despair. They're broken by their own hollowness. It makes them implode.'

Roger and Joan had studied fanaticism in the same places, from the same sources. But his was of another kind altogether.

'I suppose you're right,' Megan conceded. 'I don't really understand it.

'The way he tells it,' she went on, 'he didn't understand it either. It didn't touch him. He was just along for the ride. What was he? Shit, nine years old?'

She swore again, softly.

'Then—?' Linden prompted.

Her voice heavy, Megan said, 'After the better part of a year watching hysterics work themselves into a lather, Joan took Roger back to her parents and left him there. I guess she'd had her revelation. He never saw her again. And I got the impression that his grandparents never talked about her. He knew she was still alive. That's all.

'I asked him if he had trouble adjusting to a normal life after all that. You know – middle school, ordinary teachers and classmates, clothes, homework, girls. Hell, he'd just spent a year helping the Community of Retribution pick its victims. But he said it was easy.' Sourly Megan concluded, 'He said – this is a direct quote – "I was just passing the time."'

'Until what?' asked Linden.

'That's what I wanted to know. If you believe what he says about himself, the only thing he's actually done since Joan abandoned him is wait for his twenty-first birthday. So he could inherit his father's estate. That's it.

'Why it matters to him, I have no idea.' Megan's tone conveyed her bafflement. 'Or what he wants to do with it. He has nothing to say on the subject. He doesn't seem to understand the question.'

Linden probed at her sore lip with the tip of one finger. It was no accident that she had become Joan's keeper, caretaker. With every nerve of her body and beat of her heart, she knew how Joan felt. She, too, had been paralysed by evil; left effectively comatose by the knowledge of her own frailty. Like Joan, she knew what it meant to have her mind erased—

But somehow Roger had made his mother look at him.

Still groping for comprehension, Linden said, 'I assume he graduated high school. What's he been doing since then?'

'Shit, Linden,' Megan growled. 'It's easier to get him to talk about the commune. But I pushed him pretty hard. He says he took some classes at the local community college. Pre-med, apparently. Biology, anatomy, chemistry, things like that.

'And,' she added in disgust, 'he worked in a butcher shop. Thomas Covenant was one of the most remarkable men I've ever known, not to mention a hell of a writer, and his son worked in a butcher shop. "Just passing the time" until he could live off his father's accomplishments.

'*You* make sense out of it,' she finished. '*I* can't.'

He wanted to take his mother's place. And his father's.

'That isn't much help,' Linden said distantly.

'I know,' Megan sighed. 'But it's all I've got.'

As steadily as she could, Linden replied, 'If you can believe it, he says he's been waiting all this time for Covenant's estate so that he'll have money and a place to live while he takes care of Joan. He's obsessed with the idea. It may be the only thing he thinks about. He believes he can reach her.'

Abruptly she leaned forward against the edge of her desk. 'Megan, he has to be stopped.' An urgency which she could not control crept into her voice. 'I'm absolutely sure about that. There's something about him that scares me. I think he's dangerous. With his background—' She shuddered. 'We all know perfectly decent people who've been through worse. But this place,' Berenford Memorial, 'has plenty of patients who haven't been through as much. What only bends one person breaks another. And I think he's broken.'

Unwilling to say more, she repeated inadequately, 'He has to be stopped.'

At once, Megan's manner became crisper, more business-like. 'You say dangerous. Can you give me anything more concrete than that? Anything I can take to a judge? I can't get a restraining order unless I have something solid to go on.'

In response Linden wanted to shout, Tell the judge people are going to die! But she controlled herself. 'I don't suppose you could just ask him to trust my instincts?'

'Actually, I could,' Megan answered. 'In this county, anyway. You have a fair amount of credibility.' Then she reconsidered. 'But even a judge who thinks you hung the moon will want some kind of evidence. He might give us a restraining order for a few days on your say-so, but that's all. If we don't offer him real evidence before it expires, we'll never get another one.'

Linden sighed to herself. 'I understand.'

Again she considered dropping the problem, washing her hands of it. She could leave work right this minute, if she chose. No one would question her. God knew she was entitled to a little time off every once in a while. And Joan's claim on her did not run as deep as Jeremiah's.

He was her adopted son: he filled her heart. Nothing could replace him. Indeed, his irreducible need for her only made him more essential to her. Simply remembering the way his hair smelled after she washed it for him could bring tears to her eyes.

Anything that threatened her endangered him profoundly. Any attack on her would find him in the line of fire: at risk because she loved him, and he was dependent on her.

He had already been damaged enough.

But she also belonged here. All of her patients had already been damaged enough. And Joan did *not* deserve what Roger intended for her.

Quietly Linden asked Megan, 'Can you think of anything else?'

Megan hesitated. 'Well,' she said uncertainly, 'you could call Lytton—'

Linden had already thought of that. 'He's next on my list.' Barton Lytton had been County Sheriff for nearly three decades. If anyone had the knowledge and experience to stop Roger Covenant, surely he did?

'Be careful with him, Linden,' Megan cautioned. 'He isn't what we might call a fan of yours. As far as he's concerned, Berenford Memorial is just a liberal ruse to keep crooks out of jail. From his point of view, that practically makes you an accessory.'

'I know.' Linden was familiar with Lytton's attitude. However, she hoped that he might feel otherwise about Joan. How could he not? Beyond question he had played a part in her condition. For the sake of his self-regard, if for no other reason, he might be willing to protect her now.

'Call me after you talk to him.' Megan's voice held an undercurrent of anxiety. 'I want to know what he says.'

'I will.' Now Linden was in a hurry to get off the phone. Her urgency had shifted its focus. She needed to get in touch with Sandy.

She was about to thank Megan and hang up when a new concern occurred to her; a possibility like a touch of foresight. Quickly she added, 'Call my pager if you need to reach me.'

Roger might call Megan, trying to enlist her aid—

'I will,' replied Megan. 'I always do.'

Finally they hung up.

Staring blindly around her office, Linden looked for some way to contain her primitive alarm. She had made it clear to Roger that he could obtain his father's ring only by theft or violence. He did not know that Jeremiah existed. Nevertheless she understood obsession well enough to be sure that her own claim on the ring meant nothing to Roger. Inadvertently she had placed her son in peril.

A *butcher* shop—?

Instead of calling Sheriff Lytton, she dialled her home number. Helpless to do otherwise, she counted the rings while she waited for Sandy Eastwall to pick up the phone.

Sandy answered after the third. 'This is Sandy.'

Brusque with concern, Linden asked, 'Is Jeremiah all right?'

'Sure, he is.' Sandy sounded worried, troubled by Linden's manner. 'Why wouldn't he be?'

Linden could not explain. 'Has anything happened this morning? Anything out of the ordinary? Phone calls? Someone at the door?'

'Nothing important,' Sandy replied defensively. 'Sam called. He wants to know if Jeremiah can come Tuesday instead of Monday next week. I was going to give you the message when you got home.'

Linden wished to soothe Sandy, but other considerations impelled her. 'And Jeremiah?' she insisted.

'Sure,' said Sandy again. 'He's fine. Why wouldn't he be? I've done everything—'

'I'm sorry,' Linden put in hastily. 'I didn't mean that. Of course you haven't done anything.' In fact, Sandy's unquestioning regard for Jeremiah, like her cheerful attendance to his needs, was precious to Linden. 'I trust you. I've just been worried about him this morning for some reason.' Trying to account for herself in terms that would make sense to Sandy, she said, 'You know those feelings you get sometimes? Out of the blue, you suddenly think that something bad has happened to someone you care about?'

'And they're almost always wrong.' Sandy's tone conveyed a mollified smile. 'But that doesn't make you feel any better. I know what you mean.'

'I'll be especially careful today,' she assured Linden. 'Just in case.'

For a moment, Linden hesitated, on the verge of telling Sandy about Roger. She wanted Sandy to understand her fears. But Sandy was easily frightened; and Jeremiah would not be better off if she panicked.

'Thanks, Sandy,' Linden said instead. 'I appreciate it.'

Abruptly she stopped, caught by the same anxiety which had urged her to insist that Megan page her. Without transition, she asked, 'Is there any chance you could be on call tonight? We have a situation here that might need me.'

If Bill Coty's men caught Roger lurking around the hospital—

'Sure.' The request was routine between them. Sandy often stayed with Jeremiah when Linden was needed at night. 'I don't have any other plans.'

Occasionally Sandy went out with Sam Diadem's son; but she always gave Linden plenty of warning when she would not be available.

Mustering gratitude to counteract her apprehension, Linden thanked Sandy again and put down the phone.

Thomas Covenant had watched over his ex-wife with all of his considerable strength and intransigence, but he had not been able to prevent her abduction. If Roger had designs on Covenant's ring, Linden hardly trusted herself to stop him. Sandy would pose no obstacle at all. And Jeremiah might be hurt in the struggle.

Grimly determined now to organise every possible resource, she put in a call to Sheriff Lytton.

*

Unfortunately Barton Lytton was 'unavailable'. Linden was promised that he would call her back. With that she had to be content.

For the rest of the morning, she struggled to concentrate. She wrote up her rounds; returned phone calls; read or re-read a sheaf of advisory faxes on how to treat some of her patients; signed requisitions for medications and supplies. Studiously she did not look out at her car.

When the pressure to do something, anything, about her gravid fears became too severe to be pushed aside, she went to check on Joan. But she found no relief there.

Over lunch, she pumped Maxine shamelessly for gossip, hoping that some rumour of Roger's actions or intentions had plucked a thread in Maxine's vast web of friends. Uncharacteristically, however, Maxine knew less than she did herself. In a town as small as this one, it was difficult for anyone to visit a lawyer – or wander onto a long-abandoned property – without being noticed; remarked upon. Yet somehow Roger Covenant had escaped comment.

Afterwards Linden tackled more of her procedural duties. But she cancelled her sessions with her patients, as well as her remaining appointments. The thought that Sheriff Lytton might ignore her vexed her too much for such responsibilities.

To her surprise and relief, however, he did call her back. As soon as she picked up the handset, he said, 'Dr Avery?' He spoke in a good-ol'-boy drawl, perhaps for her benefit. 'You wanted to talk to me?'

'Thanks for returning my call, Sheriff.' Now that she had her chance, Linden felt flustered, unsure of herself. He was decidedly not a 'fan' of hers. Somehow she would have to persuade him to take her seriously.

'We have a situation here that worries me,' she began unsteadily. 'I hope you'll be willing to help me with it.' Taking a deep breath, she said, 'I believe you've spoken to Roger Covenant?'

'Sure have,' he replied without hesitation. 'He came to see me yesterday. Pleasant young man. Son of that writer, the leper who lived on Haven Farm.' He stressed the word *leper* trenchantly.

'He came to see you?' Her voice broke. She had assumed that Roger had phoned Lytton. Had he known that she would call the sheriff? That he would need to forestall her?

'Sure. He's new in town,' Lytton explained, 'but he's going to be here from now on. He says he'll be living on Haven Farm. Seems he inherited the place. It's been abandoned so long, he didn't want me to think he's some vagrant squatting where he doesn't belong.

'Like I say, he's a pleasant guy.'

Pleasant, Linden thought. And plausible when it suited him, that was obvious. No doubt to Lytton his explanation sounded perfectly reasonable.

Her sense of peril mounted, carried by the hard labour of her heart.

But she did not quail. Medicine had trained her for emergencies. And she was Linden Avery the Chosen, who had stood with Thomas Covenant against the Land's doom. Men like Sheriff Lytton – and Roger Covenant – could not intimidate her.

As if she were merely making conversation, she asked, 'What did you tell him?'

Lytton laughed harshly. 'I told him to burn it to the ground, Doctor. That leprosy shit isn't something he should mess around with. His mother did him a favour when she moved out of that house.'

A flash of anger pushed away Linden's fear; but she kept her ire to herself. Calm now, settled and cold in her determination, she continued, 'Did he happen to say why he wants to live there? Did he explain why he came back?'

'No, he didn't. And I didn't ask. If he wants to live in the house where he was born, it's none of my business. I told him what I think of the idea. We didn't have anything else to talk about.'

'I see.' For a heartbeat or two, Linden hesitated, unsure of her ground. But then she informed Lytton, 'I ask because he came to see me this morning. He told me why he's here.'

'Do tell,' Barton Lytton drawled.

'He wants custody of his mother,' she said, praying for credibility. 'He wants to take care of her.'

'Well, good for him,' retorted Lytton. 'He's a dutiful son, I'll give him that. Too bad you can't just release her, wouldn't you say, Doctor?'

'Not without a court order,' she agreed. 'That's why I called, Sheriff.' Summoning all the force of her conviction, she said plainly, 'He made it clear that he doesn't intend to wait for legal custody. If I don't release her, he's going to take her.'

'*Take* her?' Lytton sounded incredulous.

'Kidnap her, Sheriff. Remove her by force.'

'Don't make me laugh.' Lytton snorted his scorn. 'Take her *where*? He's going to live on Haven Farm. He's probably putting clean sheets on the beds right now.

'Suppose you're right. Suppose he sneaks her out of your precious "Psychiatric Hospital" while Bill Coty is taking one of his permanent naps. Half an hour later, you call me. I send out a deputy, who finds Roger Covenant at home on Haven Farm, spooning cream of wheat into his mother's mouth and wiping her chin when she slobbers. That's not kidnapping, Doctor. That's an *embar-rassment.*' The sheriff seemed to enjoy his own sarcasm. 'For you more than for him, maybe.

'Tell me the truth now. Is that really why you called? You're afraid Roger Covenant might kidnap his own mother? You've been working in that place too long. You're starting to think like your patients.'

Before Linden could tell him why he was wrong, he hung up.

Chapter Three:

In Spite of Her

Damn the man.

For a while, she stormed mutely at the unresisting walls of her office. Lytton was wrong: Roger Covenant was not a 'pleasant young man'. He was dangerous. And Joan was not his only potential victim.

But her outrage accomplished nothing, protected no one; and after a few minutes she set it aside. The sheriff could not know what his disdain might cost. He had never been summoned to take his chances against despair in a world which baffled his comprehension. He lacked the experience, the background, to react effectively.

Although she chose to excuse him, however, her anger did not recede. It had settled to a thetic hardness in the centre of her chest. *Damn* him, she repeated, thinking now of Roger rather than the sheriff. His year with the Community of Retribution must have done him such harm – and of course he had been raised for weakness by his grandparents as well as by his mother.

Why in God's name did he want Covenant's ring? If he took Joan somehow, he would also gain possession of her wedding band. It, too, was white gold, no doubt essentially indistinguishable from her ex-husband's. Surely it was white gold itself that mattered, an alloy apt for wild magic, not any specific piece of the metal?

What difference could it make whose ring Roger wielded when he took Joan's place?

Thomas Covenant probably would have known the answer. Linden did not.

Was it possible that Lytton was right? Had she misread Roger? By any ordinary measure, this explanation made more sense. Anyone except Linden, anyone at all, would have accepted it without question.

And she had at least one other reason to believe that she was wrong: a reason which she had not yet had time to consider.

Leaving her anger in her office, she went to the staff lavatory to splash cold water on her face and think.

With the door locked and her cheeks stinging, Linden Avery contemplated her wet features in the mirror over the sink. She was not a woman who studied her appearance often. When she did so, she was occasionally surprised or bemused by what she saw. This time she was taken aback by the alarm which darkened her gaze. She seemed to have aged in the last few hours.

In some ways, the past decade had marked her noticeably. Oh, her hair retained most of its wheaten lustre, trammelled by grey only at the temples. The structural harmony underlying her features made her look handsome, striking, in spite of the years. She had what men called a good figure, with full breasts, slim hips and no unnecessary weight – a womanliness which had seemed gratuitous to her until she had met and loved Thomas Covenant. The right light gave the ready dampness in her eyes radiance.

But her once-delicate nose had become prominent, emphasised by curved lines of erosion at the corners of her mouth. That erosion seemed to drag at her features, so that her smiles often looked effortful. And the knot between her brows never lifted: apparently she frowned even in her sleep, troubled by her dreams.

Nevertheless if she had examined her face yesterday she might have concluded that she wore her age lightly. Her days with Thomas Covenant, and her years with Jeremiah, had taught her things that she had never known about love and joy.

Now, however, she saw hints of Joan's mortality in her troubled scrutiny. Roger's intrusion had brought back more than her memories of struggle and pain in the Land. He made her think as well of her own parents: of her father, who had killed himself in front of her; and of her mother, whose pleading for release had driven Linden to end the suffering woman's life. Like Joan, if in her own way, Linden had known too much death, paid too high a price for living.

If she had been asked to explain why she worked for Berenford Memorial Psychiatric Hospital, instead of practising some other form of medicine, she would have replied that she was here because she understood her patients. Their damaged spirits were eloquent to her.

At the moment, however, she had more immediate concerns. Her dilemma, she thought as she watched water drip from her cheeks and jaw, was that she might be wrong about Roger Covenant. Her time with his father gave her at least one reason to doubt herself.

She had seen no harbinger.

Before her first encounter with Thomas Covenant, she had found herself unexpectedly striving to save the life of an ochre-clad old man with thin hair and foetid breath. When at last he had responded to her frantic CPR, he had pronounced like a prophet, *You will not fail, however he may assail you. There is also love in the world.* Then he had disappeared into the strange sunlight on the fringes of Haven Farm.

Do not fear, he had commanded her. *Be true.*

Less than thirty-six hours later, she had fallen to the summons of the Land. At Covenant's side, she had been assailed and appalled past bearing. But in the end she had not failed.

And ten years earlier, Thomas Covenant had met the same prophet himself. Walking into town in a desperate and doomed attempt to affirm his common humanity, he had been accosted by an old man with compulsory eyes and an ochre robe who had asked him, *Why not destroy yourself?* When Covenant had responded to the man's manifest need by offering up his ring, he was refused.

Be true, the old man had instructed him. *You need not fail.*

Shortly thereafter, Covenant had been drawn to the Land for the first time. His devotion to Lord Foul's defeat had finally cost him his life. Nevertheless he, too, had not failed.

So where, Linden had to ask herself, was the old man now?

If Roger's intentions threatened the Land in some way, surely that ragged figure must be somewhere nearby? And if he did not appear to forewarn her, surely Roger could not be as dangerous as she feared?

Deliberately she chose to believe that. Roger might well attempt to take his mother. But as long as the old man did not accost Linden, the Land was safe – and neither she nor Jeremiah were truly at risk.

Pulling a couple of paper towels from their dispenser by the sink, she dried her face and hands. Then she returned to her office to call Megan again, as she had promised.

When she had done that, she warned her staff to call Security as well as her if Roger put in another appearance. But she could think of no other precautions to take.

If the old man appeared, she would have to choose between the Land and Jeremiah. She could not challenge Lord Foul in the Land's defence without abandoning her son; and *that* she would not do. No matter how many people died, or how much beauty was destroyed.

Driving home after work, she involuntarily scrutinised every face she saw, every figure she passed. Anxiety daubed her peripheral vision with ochre, added years and desuetude to every man whom she failed to recognise. Yet she saw no sign of peril.

And soon she reached her home: a small two-storey wooden-frame house which she had bought when she had decided to adopt Jeremiah. Parked in her short driveway, she remained in her car for a few minutes, granting herself that brief opportunity to set aside her concerns in order to concentrate on her son.

The gratitude that she so often felt when she came home helped settle her attention. She did not have to care for her house herself. A neighbour whose son she had treated after a crumpling car wreck tended the lawn for her. The family of a woman who had been one of her early successes at Berenford Memorial supplied her with maintenance, patching her roof when it leaked, conditioning her heat-pump for the changing seasons, repainting her walls every few years. And twice a week an appreciative wife came in to clean, cook and do laundry: simple thanks for Linden's attention to her disturbed husband.

Linden valued the help. It simplified her life enormously. And she was grateful that she lived in a community which honoured what she did.

In addition, her gratitude for Jeremiah was too great to be contained in words. He was the centre of her life. He gave her a use for the capacity for love which she had learned from Covenant; from Sunder and Hollian, the First and Pitchwife; and from the Land. His mere presence seemed to validate her. He was like a flower which had bloomed within her, fragile and inestimable. She could not have removed it, or turned away, without tearing herself open. The fact that its petals had been crushed in the Despiser's fist, and had never regained their natural shape and scent, only caused her to cherish him more. As long as he remained to her, she would never entirely lose heart.

Thomas Covenant had told her that some decisions could not serve evil, no matter how severely they appeared to harm the Land. When he had been summoned to Revelstone's last defence, he had refused to comply: not because he had no love for the Land, but rather because a little girl in his present world had been bitten by a rattlesnake and needed his help. That refusal had delayed his arrival in the Land by many days. And during those terrible days many of the Land's most valiant champions had fallen. Yet the conditions of the delay had enabled him to challenge Lord Foul in ways which might never have been possible otherwise. In the end Covenant's rejection of the Land for the sake of a little girl had provided for the Despiser's defeat.

Fervently Linden prayed that Covenant's promise would hold true for her as well.

With that, she left her car, climbed the steps to the front porch, and let herself into her home.

The door admitted her to Jeremiah's domain; and at once she had to duck her head. During her absence, the short hallway which joined the living room on one side, the dining room on the other, and the stairway to the second floor, had been transformed into the site of a high, ramified castle of Tinker Toys.

Turrets of wooden rods and circular connectors rose above her on both sides. If she had not ducked, she would have struck her head on the flying rampart stretched between them. Other ramparts linked the turrets to a central keep: more turrets proliferated beyond it. The whole edifice was at once enormously elaborate, thick with details like balconies and bartizans, and perfectly symmetrical, balanced in all its parts. Its strangeness in her entryway, a pedestrian place intended for the most ordinary use, gave it an eldritch quality, almost an evanescence, as though some faery castle had been half translated from its own magical realm, and could be discerned by its outlines in slim rods and wheels like a glimpse into another dimension of being. Seen by moonlight, blurred and indistinct, it would have seemed the stuff of dreams.

As perhaps it was. Jeremiah's dreams – like his mind itself – lay beyond her reach. Only such castles and his other constructs gave her any hint of the visions which filled his head, defined his secret life.

'Sandy?' she called. 'Jeremiah? I'm home.'

'Hi,' Sandy answered. 'We're in the living room.'

'Jeremiah,' she added, 'your mother's home.'

One of the things that Linden appreciated most about Sandy was that she consistently treated Jeremiah as if he were paying attention.

Smiling, Linden worked her away between the turrets to the living room.

Sandy put down her knitting as Linden entered. 'Hi,' she said again. 'We were going to put the Lego away, but I wanted you to see what he made.' She gestured around the room, pleased by what her charge had accomplished.

Linden was accustomed to Jeremiah's projects. Nevertheless this time she stopped and stared, stricken with shock. At first she could not grasp the import of what she saw.

Sandy sat in an armchair in one corner of the room. Opposite her, Jeremiah knelt on the floor as he usually did when he was not busy, feet splayed out on either side of him, arms across his stomach with both hands folded under them, gently rocking.

And between them—

From the floor up onto an ottoman in the middle of the rug, he had built a mountain of interlocking Lego. Despite the stubbornly rectangular shape of the Lego, and their uncompromising primary colours, his construct was unmistakably a mountain, ragged ravines cut into its sides and foothills, bluffs bulging. Yet it also resembled a titan kneeling at the edge of the ottoman with its elbows braced on the ottoman's surface and its crown raised defiantly to the sky. A canyon widened between its legs as its calves receded into the floor. The whole structure stood almost to the level of Linden's shoulders.

The mountain or titan faced the sofa; and there Jeremiah had been at work as well. He had adjusted one of the seat cushions so that its corner jutted outward; and out onto the floor from that corner as from a promontory he had devised another castle. However, this one was entirely unlike his towering, airy construct in the entryway. Instead it resembled a wedge like an extension of the cushion's corner – a wedge which had been hollowed out rather than built up for habitation. Its high walls were marked with tiny windows, clever ramparts and delicate battlements, so life-like in spite of the materials from which they had been formed that they might have been limned from memory. And at the tip of the wedge stood a sturdy watchtower, nearly half the height of the wedge itself, connected to the main castle by a walled, open courtyard. In the base of the tower, and again in the base of the high keep, he had built entrances like tunnels, guarded by gates that closed like teeth.

'Jeremiah,' Linden gasped involuntarily, 'oh, Jeremiah,' while all her fears rebounded through her, and her heart laboured in her throat as if she might choke.

She had seen such shapes before. She recognised them, even though they had been constructed of bright plastic, all flat sides and right angles. The resemblance was too exact for confusion. The mountain was Mount Thunder, ancient Gravin Threndor, its bowels full of Wightwarrens and buried evil. And the castle was Revelstone beyond question, Lord's Keep, delved from the gutrock of its mountain promontory by Giants millennia before she had known it during her time with Thomas Covenant.

She had seen them, but Jeremiah had not: never in his life. He had not accompanied her to the Land after Covenant's murder.

Yet somehow he seemed to know such places—

His knowledge alarmed her. During the years that she had been his mother, he had produced hundreds or thousands of constructs; but until now none of them had hinted at the Land in any way.

'Linden?' Sandy asked anxiously. 'What's the matter? Is something wrong? I thought you would want to see—'

Although Linden had gasped his name, Jeremiah did not look up at her or react to the sound of her voice. Instead he rocked himself gently, blankly, as he always did when he was not assembling one of his constructs – or tearing it down. He must be finished with this one. Otherwise he would have been difficult to deflect from working on it.

Dear God! she thought in dismay and outrage. He's threatening my son. Lord Foul meant harm to Jeremiah.

Ignoring Sandy for the moment, she moved to kneel in front of Jeremiah. There she put her arms around him as if her mere embrace might ward him from the Despiser's malice.

Passively he accepted her hug without touching her, or turning his head, or focusing his eyes. She only knew that he noticed her on some level – that his nerves felt her presence if his mind did not – because he stopped rocking until she let him go.

Although she had known him for ten years, and had been his adopted mother for eight, he still gave her only the subtlest of indications that he was aware of her existence.

However, she had long ago accepted him as he was. Subtle indications were enough for her. She loved him intensely enough for both of them.

'Linden?' Sandy repeated. 'Have I done something wrong?'

Linden closed her eyes, took a deep breath to steady herself. 'I'm sorry,' she told Sandy. 'I didn't mean to scare you. There's nothing wrong. You haven't done anything. It's just another of those feelings. When I saw all this' – she swallowed convulsively – 'I panicked. I can't explain it.'

'I understand.' Sandy's relief was evident. She loved Jeremiah: Linden did not doubt that. 'Don't worry about it.' Then she asked, 'Is there anything I can do—?'

Linden tried to put aside the shock of seeing Jeremiah's construct, but it clung to her. Seeking reassurance, she opened her eyes and looked into his face.

He gazed past or through her exactly as Joan did, blankly, without any shadow or flicker of cognisance. Yet the effect on Linden was entirely different. He was so much more active than Joan, demonstrated so much more capability, and was at times so much less compliant, that Linden often forgot this one resemblance between them.

She had witnessed his growth since he was five, and had cared for him in every possible way since he was nearly seven, studying each increment of change over the years. She had brushed his teeth and washed his body, wiped his nose, bought him clothes, dressed and undressed him. She had seen him take on size and bulk until he was nearly as tall as she was, and weighed slightly more. She had watched his features shift from the starved and haunted shapelessness of the unregarded five-year-old who had placed his right hand in the bonfire at Lord Foul's command to the lean definition of a teenager. His eyes had the muddy colour of erosion run-off. His first few whiskers marked his passive cheeks. Saliva moistened his open mouth. In spite of his blankness, he had the face of a boy on the verge of manhood, waiting for sentience to give it meaning.

When Linden had satisfied herself that the eerie impulse which had inspired him to construct images of Mount Thunder and Revelstone had not caused him any discernible distress, she rose to her feet and turned to Sandy.

Sandy Eastwall was a young woman, perhaps twenty-eight, still living with her parents, and apparently content to do so. After high school she had trained as a practical nurse; but she had taken care of Jeremiah for seven years now, and exhibited no ambition to do anything else. Responsibility for one charge instead of many, and always the same charge, seemed to suit her emotional instincts and warm heart, as well as her natural complacence. Although she dated Sam Diadem's son, she showed no particular impulse to get married. As far as Linden could tell, Sandy was comfortably prepared to tend Jeremiah for the rest of her life.

That unlikely attitude was high on Linden's list of reasons for gratitude.

'If you don't mind,' she asked, answering Sandy's offer to help, 'can you stay long enough to get his Lego put away? I have something I need to do.' Then she added, 'You can leave the Tinker Toys. I like that castle. And it's not in the way.'

'Sure.' Sandy responded with an uncomplicated smile. 'I'll be glad to.'

'Come, Jeremiah,' she said to the kneeling boy. 'It's time to put your Lego away. Let's get started.'

Crouching to the floor, she took one of the many cartons clustered at the side of the room and set it near Mount Thunder's ankles. Then she detached a piece from the construct and placed it in the carton.

That was all she had to do to trigger Jeremiah's hidden awareness. At once, he left his knees and moved to squat beside the carton. With the same unhesitating meticulousness with which he built his constructs, he began to disassemble Mount Thunder, arranging the Lego in compact rows in their carton as he removed them.

Linden had spent many hours watching him do such things. He never moved quickly, never appeared to feel any hurry or tension – and never paused for thought or doubt. She herself might have needed two or three hours to put away so much Lego – or to put them away with such precision – but he moved so efficiently, using his maimed hand as deftly as the whole one, that his Mount Thunder appeared to melt away before her eyes. He would probably be done in forty-five minutes.

Because she needed to speak to him, hear his name in her mouth, she said, 'Thank you, Jeremiah. You're very good with Lego. I like everything you make with it. And I like the way you put it away when it's time.'

Then abruptly she turned and left the room so that Sandy would not see the sudden tears in her eyes, or notice the lump of love and fear in her throat.

While Jeremiah took Mount Thunder apart, and Sandy resumed her knitting, Linden went upstairs to master her alarm.

He's threatening my son.

She had tried to believe that there would be no danger unless the old man in the ochre robe appeared to warn her. But she no longer trusted his absence to mean that anyone was safe.

Alone in her bedroom, she asked herself for the first time whether she should flee.

She could do that, in spite of her responsibilities. The necessary arrangements would require nothing more than a few phone calls. She could pack and drive away in an hour or two; take Jeremiah out of harm's reach. In fact, she could make her calls when she had driven far enough to avoid any conceivable peril.

Lord Foul was threatening her son.

Roger Covenant had no idea that Jeremiah existed. Nevertheless it could *not* be an accident that Jeremiah had created images of Mount Thunder and Revelstone on the same day that Roger had demanded his mother's release.

And if Linden were wrong? If Roger proved to be as harmless as Barton Lytton claimed? Why, then she could simply bring Jeremiah home again, with no damage done.

Aching to protect her son, she gave serious consideration to the possibilities of flight.

But the prospect shamed her. And she had learned the necessity of courage from the most stringent teachers. Love and beauty could not be preserved by panic or flight.

The ruin of Jeremiah's hand was in some sense her fault; and she did not believe that she could bear to see him hurt again. But he was not the only one who had been maimed that night. And Thomas Covenant himself had died for the same reason: because she had failed to intervene. When she had seen what was happening, she had been appalled by horror, stunned motionless. In dread she had simply watched while Covenant had smiled for Joan; while men and women and children had sacrificed their hands to the Despiser's malice; while the barriers between realities had been torn asunder by blood and pain.

Now she knew that that night's evil could have been prevented. When she had finally broken free of her dismay and charged forward, towards the bonfire, Lord Foul's hold on his victims had been disrupted. If she had acted sooner, that whole night's carnage might have been averted. Even the Land might have been spared—

If she fled now, no one would remain to stand between the Despiser and more victims.

She did not mean to be ruled by her fears again. Not ever. No matter how severely Roger Covenant provoked her.

Here, however, she faced a conundrum which she did not know how to untangle. To flee for Jeremiah's sake? Or to remain for her own, and for Joan's, and for the Land's? Trapped by indecision, she found herself sitting on her bed with her hands over her face and Thomas Covenant's name on her lips, listening as if she were helpless for sounds of danger from downstairs.

There were none. Occasionally the distant murmur of Sandy's voice reached her. At intervals a car drove down the street. Erratic gusts of wind tugging past the eaves of the house suggested a storm brewing. She heard nothing to justify her gathering apprehension.

Sighing, she told herself that in the morning she would make another attempt to enlist Lytton's aid. Or perhaps Megan could sway him. For tonight she would watch over Jeremiah with all her vigilance, and let no harm near him.

By now, he had probably finished with Mount Thunder and begun to separate the pieces of Revelstone. Nothing in his manner had suggested that Gravin Threndor and Lord's Keep held any significance for him. As far as she could tell, his life remained exactly as it had always been, despite the Land's strange intrusion into his lost mind.

This was how he had spent his time for years: he put things together and took them apart. Indeed, he seemed incapable of any relationship except with physical objects which could be connected to each other. No human being impinged on his attention. He did not react to his name. If he were not involved in making one of his constructs, he simply knelt with his feet angled outward beneath him and rocked himself soothingly with his arms across his stomach. He walked only if he were raised to his feet and led by the hand. Even animals found no focus in his muddy gaze.

Presented with Tinker Toys, however, with Lego, Lincoln Logs, or an Erector set, or any other form of non-mechanical object designed to be attached to or inserted into other non-mechanical objects, he became a wizard. The castle in the entryway, and the models of Revelstone and Mount Thunder in the living room, were only today's examples of his talent. By the hundreds, by the thousands, obsessively, he devised structures of such elegance and imagination that they often made Linden hold her breath in wonder – and of such size that they sometimes filled the available space. Perhaps they would have expanded indefinitely if he had not run out of materials. And yet they always appeared complete when he did run out, as if somehow he had calculated exactly what could be done with the Lego or Tinker Toys at hand.

Often Linden sat with him while he built his edifices. She had conceived a method of playing with him; of producing a personal reaction from his inattention towards her. She would take a piece – a block or connector – and place it somewhere in his construct. He would not look at her when she did so – but he would pause. If by his inarticulate standards she had placed the piece incorrectly, he would frown. Then he would rectify her mistake. But if by chance she had set the piece where it belonged, he would nod slightly before he continued.

Such indications assured her that he was aware of her.

Two years ago, guided by a flash of intuition, Linden had spoken to Sam Diadem about Jeremiah. Sam ran a small assembly-line business which produced wooden playthings for children, primarily rocking horses, marionettes and various wooden puzzles in strange shapes which interlocked to form balls, pyramids and the like. At her urging, Sam had discovered that if he left Jeremiah alone with a supply of ready parts, Jeremiah would quietly and steadily produce finished toys. He would not paint or package them, and never played with them. But they were always perfectly assembled.

Now Jeremiah 'worked' in Sam's shop two mornings a week. His 'pay' Linden spent faithfully on K'nex, or 3-D jigsaw puzzles of palaces, or more Lego and Tinker Toys.

Some of the psychologists whom Linden had consulted called Jeremiah's condition a 'dissociative disorder'. Others spoke of 'hysterical conversion reactions' and 'somatoform disorders'. His symptoms resembled autism – specifically, he appeared to be an autistic savant – yet he could not be autistic. Autism was congenital, and beyond question Jeremiah's condition had been induced by trauma. His natural mother had described him as 'a normal boy' before the bonfire – whatever those words might mean in her deranged lexicon. Certainly none of the known therapies for autism had produced any change in him.

Memories of that trauma still woke Linden at night, sweating, with cries which she had failed to utter locked in her throat.

His natural mother was a woman named Marsha Jason. She had had three children, all adopted now by other parents – Hosea, Rebecca and her youngest,

Jeremiah, prophet of woe. She had chosen that name, apparently, because her husband had abandoned her during her last pregnancy.

For the first few years of Jeremiah's life, Marsha Jason had subsisted at the mercy of various welfare agencies. In one form or another, she had kept herself and her children alive through the charity of strangers. And then, when her self-pity and ineffectiveness had reached unendurable proportions, she had discovered the Community of Retribution.

From that point onwards, as she proclaimed afterwards, she had had no control over anything that happened. She must have been brainwashed or drugged. She was a good mother: without brainwashing or drugs, she would never have sacrificed her dear children to the Community's mad crusade against Thomas Covenant. Had she not been victimised of her own right hand at the same time? Surely she did not deserve to have her sons and daughter taken from her; placed in foster care?

Yet she had not been able to deny that in the last weeks before Covenant's murder – soon after Joan Covenant's departure – she and her children, along with perhaps thirty other members of the Community of Retribution, had left the commune and made their way towards Haven Farm, supporting themselves by beggary when they could not gain donations by preaching. Entranced, perhaps, by some form of mass hysteria, they had snatched Joan from her ex-husband; had slaughtered a cow so that they could splash his home with blood. Then they had taken her into the woods behind Haven Farm and built a bonfire. When Covenant had at last appeared to redeem Joan, Mrs Jason and her children had been the first to hold their right hands in the blaze, Hosea after his mother, then Rebecca, and then five-year-old Jeremiah.

With years to study the question, Linden still could not explain how ordinary adults, much less their uncomprehending children, had been impelled to endure the pain long enough to burn the flesh from their bones. But the fact remained that Marsha Jason, Hosea and Rebecca had done so. Jeremiah had been damaged almost as badly. And after them, more worshippers had followed.

And in the bonfire, Lord Foul had emerged to claim Covenant's life.

Linden still too easily remembered the Despiser's eyes as they had appeared in the bonfire, carious as fangs. She would never forget his figure forming in the deep heat of the blaze. Alive with fire and offered pain, he had stopped her life in her veins. And she had remained paralysed while the leader of his worshippers had set a knife to Joan's throat, intending to sacrifice her if Covenant did not surrender himself.

Then Covenant had retrieved Joan from her doom; and Linden had at last broken free of her immobility. She had rushed towards the bonfire, striving frantically to block the knife from his chest. But the worshipper with the knife had struck her senseless; and as she lost consciousness she had seen the blade pound into Covenant's heart.

A few hours or a lifetime later, in the dawn of a new day, Dr Berenford found her where she lay beside Covenant's corpse. Mrs Jason had rousted him from his home, seeking treatment for herself and her children. He and Sheriff Lytton had discovered Joan asleep in her bed in Covenant's house, all memory of the night's events apparently gone. While Lytton had taken Joan to County Hospital, Julius had searched the woods behind Haven Farm until he located Linden and Covenant.

Thus he had spared her any accusation that she had played some role in Covenant's death. Legally, of course, she had not. Morally, she knew better.

She had suffered acutely during the long months of that one night. Nevertheless she had gone into surgery as soon as Julius had driven her back into town. Together, they had spent interminable hours fighting to save as many flame-savaged hands as they could.

For Hosea and Rebecca, Linden had been able to do little except amputate. With Jeremiah, however, she had met somewhat more success. Through simple stubbornness as much as by skill, she had found a way to save half of his thumb and two of his fingers: the last two.

They remained shorter than they should have been. Yet they were strong now: he could use them. To that extent, at least, she could forgive herself for what had happened to him.

At the time, she had given no thought to other forms of restitution. The particular sense of responsibility which she had learned from Covenant and the Land had asserted itself slowly. After the initial crisis, she had occupied herself for months adjusting to her new life: to the county itself; and to her work at County Hospital. And then Julius had involved her in the complex efforts which had eventually led to the construction of Berenford Memorial Psychiatric Hospital, and to her appointment as its Chief Medical Officer.

Nearly two years passed before she recognised the residual ache in her heart for what it was: not grief over Covenant's death, although that pang never lost its poignancy, but rather a hollow place left by the Land. Her parents had dedicated her to death, but she had transcended their legacy. Now she realised that her new convictions and passions required more of her. Her work with her patients suited her abilities; but it did not satisfy the woman who had sojourned with Giants, contended with Ravers, and opposed the Sunbane at Thomas Covenant's side.

She wanted to heal as well some of the harm which Lord Foul had done in her present world. And she needed someone to love.

She had heard Pitchwife sing:

> My heart has rooms that sigh with dust
> And ashes in the hearth.
> They must be cleaned and blown away
> By daylight's breath.

She could not allow the hollow place within her to remain unfilled.

Her own damaged childhood had taught her an intense empathy for children forced to pay the price of their parents' folly; and before long she remembered Jeremiah Jason. She had already done him a little good. Perhaps she could do more.

When at last she tracked him down and arranged to meet him, she recognised immediately the missing piece of her heart, the part which might make her whole. His little face spoke to her as clearly as a wail. She knew what it was like to be a conscious prisoner inside her own skull, defeated by power and malice. The Clave and Ravers had victimised her in that way. Indirectly the *Elohim* had done the same. The thought that Jeremiah might be in a comparable state, knowing and alone within his mental cell, wrung her utterly.

In the Land, she had been called 'the Chosen'. Now she did the choosing. Doggedly, with Megan Roman's help, she pursued Jeremiah through the legal and bureaucratic snarls of the county's floundering foster care until he was made her son.

At first, the task which she had assigned to herself was arduous and costly, in spite of Sandy Eastwall's assistance. The closure of Jeremiah's mind rebuffed any penetration. He was lost, and her love could not find him. If he had so much as wept, she would have celebrated for him, rejoiced in that victory over an intimate ruin. But he did not weep. Nothing breached the hard stone wall of his plight. His only response to every situation was an unresisting absence of cooperation. He did not stand, could not walk. Voiceless and alone, he could not engage in a child's necessary play; and so she had no lever with which to spring him from his prison.

And then one day— The memory still brought tears of joy to her eyes. One day in his paediatrician's office, surrounded by toys enjoyed by other children, he had suddenly reached out uninvited to place one bright wooden block upon another. When he was satisfied with what he had done, he had positioned another block; and then another.

Within an hour, hardly able to contain her excitement, Linden had bought him a mountain of blocks. And when she had seen him use them to build an impromptu Greek temple, she had rushed back to the store to purchase Lincoln Logs and Tinker Toys.

There his life had changed; and hers with it. In a few short weeks, he had learned – or re-learned – to stand so that he could reach higher, build higher. And mere months later he had regained his ability to walk, seeking to move around his constructs and position pieces more readily.

His newly discovered gift transformed him in Linden's sight. With every construct, he built hope for the future. A child who could play might someday be set free. And his strange talent seemed to have limitless possibilities. Connecting one Lincoln Log or Tinker Toy to the next, he might at last devise a door to his prison and step out into her arms.

She would not, she swore to herself now, *would not* sacrifice that hope, or him, for any purpose. Roger Covenant had to be stopped. But if she were forced to a choice between Jeremiah and Lord Foul's other victims, she would stand by her son.

Thomas Covenant had believed that the Land could not be damned by such decisions.

Linden was still afraid, but her indecision had passed. Deliberately she readied herself to go back downstairs.

On the way, she heard Sandy call, 'Linden? We're done with the Lego. Is there anything else you need before I leave?'

In the living room, Linden greeted Sandy with a smile; tousled Jeremiah's hair where he knelt, rocking, beside a tall stack of Lego boxes. 'No, thanks. You've done enough already.' To Jeremiah, she added, 'Thanks for putting your Lego away. You've done a good job. I'm proud of you.'

If her reaction gave him any pleasure, he did not reveal it.

When Sandy had gathered up her knitting, Linden walked her to the door. 'I can't thank you enough,' she told the other woman sincerely. 'I can't explain what came over me today, but it shook me up. I really appreciate everything you've done.'

Sandy dismissed the subject with a comfortable shrug. 'He's my sweetie.' Over her shoulder, she asked, 'Aren't you, Jeremiah?' Then she finished to Linden, 'I'll see both of you tomorrow, if you don't need me tonight.'

Refraining from more unnecessary thanks, Linden ushered her outside and said good night.

For a moment after Sandy left, however, Linden did not return to Jeremiah. Instead she leaned against the door and considered the castle which had transformed her entryway. It seemed to contradict her fears, as though it had the power to guard the sanctuary that she had made for her son.

Relieved for the first time since she had met Roger Covenant, she heated a casserole and fed Jeremiah while she ate. At intervals she paused to talk about anything she could think of – horses, Sam Diadem's toys, places of wonder in the Land – hoping that the sound of her voice would also feed him, in its own way. When he stopped opening his mouth for the spoon, she took him upstairs to bathe him. Afterward she dressed him for bed in his – actually her – favourite pyjamas, the sky-blue flannel shirt and pants with mustangs ramping across the chest.

In his bedroom, she took a moment, as she often did, to marvel at how he had decorated it.

One day two or three years ago, she had purchased a set of flywheel-driven model racing cars that featured tracks which could be snapped together into structures as elaborate as roller coasters, complete with loop-the-loops and barrel-rolls. She had been drawn to the set because it included materials like plastic Tinker Toys for building towers and pylons to support the tracks. And because Jeremiah appeared to prefer large projects, she had bought every set in the store, four or five of them.

He had shown no interest in the cars. In fact, he had disappointed her by showing no interest in the tracks either. He had not so much as touched the boxes, or turned his eyes towards them.

Maybe he needed time, she had told herself. Maybe his occult, hidden decisions required contemplation. Reluctant to surrender her hopes, she had carried one of the boxes up to his bedroom and left it there for him to consider.

That night he had gone to bed still oblivious to the box. The next morning, however, she discovered that during the night he had opened it and used every available piece to build towers on either side of the head of his bed. Through the towers he had twined tracks twisted into implausible shapes. And – uncharacteristic of him – the construct was plainly unfinished. He had run out of parts before he could connect the towers and tracks to each other above the head of his bed.

At once, she brought the remaining boxes up to his room. Like the first, they were ignored all day. And like the first, they were opened during the night; put to use. Now supports like drawbridges and catwalks extended along the walls, under the window, over the bureau and past the closet towards the door. Sections of track linked themselves and their pylons like the ligaments of some self-proliferating rococo robot.

The racing cars themselves lay in a clutter on the floor, unregarded. And still he obviously had not completed his design.

After a fervid search, Linden finally found a few more sets. Fortunately they sufficed. When Jeremiah had used every last plastic beam and connector, every section of track, he was done.

Now towers festooned with curlicues of track reached up on either side of his bedroom door to meet in an arch at the height of the lintel. Raceways in airy spans linked those structures to the ones which he had already finished. Yet the design would have been useless to its cars. The track through all of its loops and turns and dives formed an elaborate Möbius strip, reversing itself as it travelled so that in time a finger drawn along its route would touch every inch of its surface on both sides.

She had never asked him to take it down. Surely it was special to him? Why else had he only worked on it late at night, when he was alone? In some sense, it was more uniquely his than anything else he had built.

Respecting what he had accomplished, she left it as it was. Cheerfully she ducked under its spans whenever she needed to reach his closet.

The racing cars remained where she had placed them, arrayed like a display on top of his bureau. She hoped that one day he would take an interest in them; but they were still meaningless to him.

Shaking her head now in familiar astonishment at his arcane gifts, she settled him into bed and asked him which of his books he would like her to read. As ever, he did not respond; but on the theory that the adventures of a lone boy triumphing over impossible odds might convey something to his snared mind, she took out one of his 'Bomba the Jungle Boy' books and read a couple of chapters aloud. Then she kissed him, adjusted his blankets, turned out the light, and left him to sleep.

In one respect, at least, he was a normal boy, even a normal teenager: he slept deeply, unselfconsciously, his limbs sprawling in all directions as though they belonged to some other body. Only on very rare occasions did she find him awake when she checked on him before she went to bed herself. And she never knew what had roused or troubled him.

If this had been some other night, she might have used her time to catch up on some paperwork, or perhaps read. But tonight she was not alone. A throng of memories accompanied her through the house: they seemed as restless and compelling as ghosts. In particular, she recalled Thomas Covenant's gaunt face and stricken eyes, as dear in their own way as Jeremiah's undefended slackness, and as precise as etch-work.

Others also she could not forget: Sunder and Hollian; the Giants of the

Search; all her friends in the Land. Thinking that she would spend an hour alone with them, sharing at least in memory her gratitude and grief, she went downstairs to the kitchen to heat water for tea. Steaming mint might console her while she ached.

As she boiled water and prepared a teabag, filled a cup, she chose to concentrate on the Giants. She found consolation in remembering their open hearts, their long tales and their ready laughter. She had not seen the First of the Search and her husband, Pitchwife, for ten years. No doubt in their own world they had passed away centuries or millennia ago. Nevertheless they had a healing power in her thoughts. Like Jeremiah's faery castle, they seemed to defend her from her fears.

They alone had willingly accompanied Linden and Covenant to their confrontation with the Despiser. They alone had stood with Linden after Covenant's death while she had formed her new Staff of Law and unmade the Sunbane; begun the restoration of the Land. And when she had faded away, returned to her old life, they had carried with them the hope which she and Covenant had made for all the Earth.

Thinking of the First and Pitchwife reminded her that her worries were like the difficulties of caring for Jeremiah, or of working at Berenford Memorial: transient things which could not disturb the choices she had made.

She would have gone on, drawing solace from her memories; but an unexpected idea stopped her. Perhaps it would be possible to hide Joan from Roger. If the nurse on duty, Amy Clint's sister Sara, moved Joan to another room – no, to a spare bed in County Hospital – Roger might not be able to find her. Certainly he would not be able to search for her without attracting attention. Bill Coty or one of his men – or even Sheriff Lytton – would have time to intervene.

Then what would Roger do? What *could* he?

He would have no difficulty discovering Linden's address.

The phone's shrill ring startled her so badly that she dropped her cup. It hit the floor as if in slow motion and bounced once, apparently held together by hot peppermint tea splashing past its rim: then it seemed to burst in mid-air. Shards and steaming tea spattered around her feet.

None of her friends called her at home. Neither did her colleagues and staff. They all knew better. When they wanted or needed to get in touch with her, they dialled her pager—

The phone rang again like an echo of the shattered cup.

Roger, she thought dumbly, it was Roger, someone must have given him her number, it was unpublished, unlisted, he could not have found it out unaided.

He meant to impose his insistence on the private places of her heart.

And then: no, it was not Roger. It was about him. He had done something. Something terrible—

The phone rested on an end-table in the living room. She pounced for it as it rang a third time. Snatched up the handset; pressed it to her ear.

She could not make a sound. Fright filled her throat.

'Dr Avery?' a voice panted in her ear. 'Linden? Dr Avery?'

Maxine Dubroff, who volunteered at the hospital.

'I'm here.' Linden's efforts to speak cost her a spasm of coughing. 'What's wrong?'

'Dr Avery, it's Bill—' Maxine's distress seemed to block the phone line. What she needed to say could not get through. 'He's— Oh, dear God.'

Linden's brain refused to work. Instead it clung to the sound of Maxine's voice as if it needed words in order to function. Still coughing, she managed to croak out, 'Slow down, Maxine. Tell me what happened.'

Maxine sucked in a harsh breath. 'Bill Coty,' she said in pieces. 'He's dead.'

The room around Linden seemed to veer sideways. Of course Maxine knew Bill: she knew everyone. But if the old man had collapsed at home—

Linden had asked him to protect Joan.

'Shot.' Maxine's voice came through the handset, jagged as chunks of glass. 'In the head. By that – that—' She paused to swallow convulsively, as if her throat were bleeding.

'Maxine.' Linden fought down more coughing. 'Tell me what happened.'

'I'm sorry, Doctor.' Now Linden heard tears in Maxine's voice. 'I'm just so upset— I should have called you sooner. I came as soon as I heard the sirens' – she and Ernie lived only a block and a half from Berenford Memorial – 'but it didn't occur to me that somebody hadn't already called you. I wanted to help. Ernie told me you were worried about trouble. Bill called him about it. But I never expected—

'That young man. The one who was here this morning. He shot Bill Coty.'

Ice poured along Linden's veins. Her hands started to shake. 'What about Joan?'

Again she heard wind thrashing under the eaves of the house. One of the kitchen windows rattled plaintively in its frame.

'Oh, Linden.' Maxine's weeping mounted. 'She's gone. He took her.'

Automatically Linden answered, 'I'll be right there,' and put down the handset.

She could not think: she was too full of rage. The old prophet had betrayed her. He had given her no warning at all.

Apparently he no longer cared what happened to the Land.

Chapter Four:

Malice

The sirens were police cars, then: Sheriff Lytton responding too late to Berenford Memorial's call for help.

Bill Coty must have failed to rally enough of his volunteers to Joan's protection. Or he had simply cared too much to forget about her when he went off-duty—

Hands shaking wildly, Linden picked up the handset again and dialled Sandy Eastwall's number.

For the first time in years, she wished that she had bought a cordless phone. She wanted to rush upstairs and check on Jeremiah while she waited, shivering, for Sandy's voice.

Buffeted by wind, the front door thudded dully against its latch. Surely nothing had happened to Jeremiah since she had left his room? But Bill Coty had been shot – by Roger. Who obviously had a gun.

Linden had told Bill that Roger was not dangerous enough for guns. Now she knew better.

Providentially Sandy answered the phone almost at once. 'Hello?'

'Sandy, it's Linden. I'm sorry, I'm needed at the hospital. It's an emergency.'

Bill Coty was dead because Linden had underestimated Roger's madness.

Sandy did not hesitate. 'I'll be right there.'

'Thanks.' Linden hung up and headed for the stairs.

Joan's son would be in a hurry now. He meant to precipitate the crisis for which his heart hungered immediately.

With her hand on the knob of Jeremiah's door, Linden paused to gather herself. How could anything have happened to him? Scarcely twenty minutes had passed since she had put him to bed. Yet she feared for him. Her whole body trembled at the possibility that Roger wished him harm.

Easing open the door, she peered into his room.

Light from the hall behind her reached across his floor to the raceway towers guarding the head of his bed. Between them he lay outstretched, his blankets already rumpled and twisted around him, one arm extended like an appeal. He made faint snoring sounds as he slept.

Roger had shot Bill Coty in the head.

Linden's trembling grew more acute. She shut the door and hurried downstairs to wait for Sandy.

At the bottom of the stairs, standing amid Tinker Toy spires and buttresses, she heard the front door rattle again as if someone outside struggled to open it. Sandy could not have arrived yet – and in any case, she always rang the doorbell. Nevertheless Linden ducked under a rampart to unlock the door, pull it aside.

Wind slapped into her face, snatched tears from her eyes. The gust felt unnaturally cold; and abrasive, full of grit. A storm was on its way, a serious storm—

In the porch light, Linden saw Sandy lean towards the house as if she were tacking through the wind. Gusts plucked at her coat so that it fluttered like a loose sail.

Swept forward, Sandy mounted the steps to the porch. Linden let her into the house and pushed the door shut, then said, 'That was fast.'

Light chased the shadows from Sandy's face. Strain pinched her mouth, and her eyes were dark with doubt.

'Are you all right?' Linden asked quickly.

'I had a feeling—' Sandy began, then stopped herself to attempt an unconvincing smile. 'Whatever bothered you today must be catching. It came on me while I was driving home. I couldn't relax—' She smiled again, more successfully this time. 'I knew you were going to call. I already had my coat on when the phone rang.' Then her expression resumed its indefinite distress. 'I hope nothing bad has happened.'

'I'll let you know,' Linden replied to avoid explanations. 'I'll call as soon as I can.'

Sandy nodded. She appeared to be listening to the wind rather than to Linden.

Still shivering, Linden took her own coat from the entryway closet, belted it around her and impelled herself out into the night.

When she had pulled the door closed after her, however, she paused where she was until she heard the lock click home. She could not imagine what had unsettled Sandy's usual phlegmatic calm, but she was fiercely glad of it. Scared, Sandy would be particularly cautious; and Linden desired every scrap of care which Sandy could provide for Jeremiah.

She needed that reassurance to help her bear the inchoate conviction that she was abandoning her son. She yearned to flee with him now, take him and run—

Surely Roger was unaware that she had a son?

She had to close her mouth and squint her eyes against the grit in the wind. Clutching her resolve around her like another coat, she forced herself to hasten down off the porch and across the lawn to her car.

A hard gust nearly tore the car door from her hand as she pulled it open. She stumbled into the driver's seat as if she had been shoved. The door resisted her tug for an instant, then slammed shut after her. At the impact, the car staggered on its springs.

The starter ground briefly before the engine came to life. With as much caution as she could muster, she backed out into the street and turned towards the hospital.

For a block or two, the wind left her alone. Then it staggered the car again, whining in the wheel-wells, striking the hood and trunk until they vibrated. The street lamps lit dark streaks in the air like handfuls of dust thrown along the leading edge of a gale. They swirled when they hit the car, curled momentarily on the windscreen, danced away.

Fortunately Berenford Memorial was not far. And street lamps were more common in the centre of town: they seemed brighter. Nevertheless dust tainted the air in swift plumes and streamers, scattering into turbulence at the edges of the buildings. Scraps of paper twisted like tortured things in the eddies.

Past the bulk of County Hospital, she wheeled into the parking lot between it and Berenford Memorial. From the lot she could not see the front door. But three patrol cars had reached her domain ahead of her. Their lights flashed empty warnings into the night.

Blinking hard at the dust, and at the wind's raw chill, she hugged her coat around her and hastened along the walk towards the front door. She could have used the staff entrance and saved herself thirty yards, but she wanted to enter the building as Roger must have entered it, see the sequence of what he had done.

Around the corner of the building and along its front she hurried. The front steps she took two at a time, nearly running.

Lit by the lights from the small reception lobby, as well as by its own lamps, the outer door seemed to appear in front of her as if it had been swept into existence from some other reality. She was reaching for its handle when she saw the ugly hole which had been torn in the metal where the lock had been. From the hole, cracks spread crookedly through the glass.

Berenford Memorial's entrance had two sets of heavy glass doors, one inside the other. At night the outer door was kept locked. The people who worked here used the staff entrance and their own keys. Visitors after dark had to ring a doorbell which summoned the duty nurse or an orderly; and they were not admitted until they had introduced themselves over the intercom by the door.

Apparently someone had refused to let Roger in.

Sara Clint was the duty nurse: who were the orderlies? For a moment, distracted by Roger's violence, Linden could not remember. Then she did: Avis Cardaman and Harry Gund. Harry would have been useless against an intruder. He was a freckle-faced young man with an ingratiating demeanour and a positive genius for paperwork; but he tended to flinch whenever he heard a loud voice. Avis, however, was a huge and compulsively responsible man whose gentle manner concealed his prodigious strength. Linden had often suspected that he could have intimidated the paint off the walls, if he had considered it a threat to his patients.

If Roger had taken Joan in spite of Avis—

How many other casualties had he left in his wake?

Snatching a quick breath for courage, she heaved open the outer door, then the inner, and strode into the lobby.

The space was crowded with police officers: Sheriff Lytton and at least six of his deputies. They all looked towards her as she entered.

Behind them, Harry Gund attended the reception desk. His manner seemed at once frightened and defiant, as if he had shamed himself in some way and now sought to make amends with a display of attention to duty. Near him stood Maxine Dubroff and her husband, Ernie, their arms around each other.

In a rush, Linden scanned the lobby past the shoulders of the officers, but she saw no sign of Sara Clint.

Helplessly she wondered how her patients were reacting to gunshots and turmoil.

Just inside the door, nearly at her feet, Bill Coty sprawled in his life's blood. He still wore his navy-blue Security uniform, with his walkie-talkie and his nightstick attached to his belt. A splash of blood obscured the useless silver of his badge. But a small holster at his belt was empty.

In one slack hand, he held a can of Mace: the only real weapon sanctioned by County Hospital's insurance. Apparently Roger had not given him time to use it.

Strands of his white hair showed through the wreckage of his head. Roger's bullet had smashed in his left temple. The exit wound in the back of his skull was an atrocity of brains and bone. A dark trickle across his cheek underscored the dismay in his sightless eyes.

Instinctively Linden dropped to her knees beside him; reached out as if she believed that the touch of her hands would somehow bring him back to life. But the sheriff stopped her.

'Don't touch him!' Lytton barked. 'Forensics hasn't been here yet.'

As if there could be any doubt about the cause of death.

Briefly Linden covered her face as if she could not bear the sight of Bill's lifeless form. Almost at once, however, she dropped her hands; and as she did so her trembling fell away as if one aspect of her ordinary mortality had sloughed from her. The crisis was upon her now: it smelled of copper and ashes. Grimly she rose to her feet to meet it.

Bill had been shot so long ago that most of his blood had already dried. How much time had passed? Half an hour? An hour?

How much of a head-start did Roger have?

'Dr Avery,' growled Barton Lytton when she faced him. 'It's about time.'

He was a blunt, fleshy man with a gift for seeming bigger than he actually was. In fact, he stood no taller than Linden herself; yet he appeared to loom over her. No doubt that contributed to his incessant re-election: people thought of him as dominant, effective, despite his real stature. Typically he wore mirrored aviator sunglasses, but now they were shoved into the breast pocket of his khaki shirt opposite his badge. Various heavy objects dragged at his belt – a radio, a cell phone, handcuffs, Mace, a handgun the size of a tinker's anvil, spare clips – making his paunch appear larger than it was.

'I—' Linden began. She wanted to say, I tried to warn you. But the look in his eyes, haunted and raging, closed her throat. They were the eyes of a man in trouble, out of his depth, with no one to blame but himself. Roughly she swallowed some of her anger. 'I came as soon as I could.'

'Dr Avery!' When she spoke, Harry Gund left the reception desk to push his way through the clustered officers. 'Thank God you're here. I've done everything I can, but we need you.

'This is real bad, Dr Avery,' he told her earnestly.

'Harry,' Lytton muttered: a warning.

Harry ignored the sheriff. Ordinarily he was deferential in the face of authority; but now his need to exonerate himself overshadowed his timidity.

'We couldn't stop him.' His voice trembled with the aftereffects of dismay and shock. 'We tried – Avis and me – but we couldn't. I didn't let him in. He rang the doorbell, used the intercom. He was smiling, and he sounded just as reasonable as could be. But I remembered your orders' – which he must have heard from Sara – 'and didn't let him in.'

'Harry,' Sheriff Lytton rasped again. He reached out a thick hand to silence the orderly.

Linden interrupted the sheriff. 'He was here. You weren't. Let him tell it.'

Lytton dropped his hand. His shoulders appeared to slump as if she had made him smaller.

A moment of gratitude flashed in Harry's eyes.

'I tried to stop him,' he repeated. 'But he had this gun, this huge gun. He shot the lock.

'I yelled for help. Then I tried to get behind the desk so I could use the phone. But he pointed his gun at me. If I did anything, he was going to shoot me.

'He kept smiling like we're friends or something.'

Linden listened carefully, setting her own thoughts and her secret knowledge aside. Roger had to be stopped. *He's in my mind,* Joan had once told Thomas Covenant, *and I can't get him out. He hates you.*

'Then Bill Coty came in.' Harry's tension mounted as he continued. 'He wasn't supposed to be here. He's off-duty, isn't he? But he had his Mace, and he held it up like it could stop bullets. He told him to put the gun down.'

The harm that Roger could do was incalculable.

'Avis was there,' Harry said, trembling now. 'And Mrs Clint. They must've heard me yelling.' Or the sound of Roger's handgun. 'Avis wanted to do something, you know what he's like, but she made him stay where he was.

'Bill was scared, you could see that, but he kept telling him to put the gun down, put the gun down. *He* just smiled and smiled, and I thought he wasn't going to do anything, but all at once he pointed the gun at Bill and fired, and Bill went down like someone kicked him in the head.'

Linden closed her eyes slowly, held them shut for a moment to contain her regret. She had told Bill that Roger was not dangerous.

Harry was saying, 'That's when Avis ran at him, even though Mrs Clint was yelling at him to stop. Avis tried to tackle him, but he just turned and hit him with the gun, hit him so hard his head bounced.'

Deliberately she opened her eyes again.

Behind Harry, Sheriff Lytton waited with badly concealed impatience. His officers listened as if they were stunned, although they must have heard Harry's story earlier.

Where had Roger acquired such murderous skills?

'Avis fell down,' Harry said, shaking. 'He had blood all over him.

'Then he wasn't here anymore. I didn't even see where he went, but he took Mrs Clint with him. He made her go.

'I called the sheriff right away, right away. I was going to call you, too, but I had to take care of Avis.'

Belatedly Linden noticed another pool of blood off to the side of Bill's body. Drying smears marked the front and sleeves of Harry's pale green orderly's uniform. He must have taken Avis' head in his arms, cradled the big man like a brother.

'He kept bleeding—' Harry's voice shivered on the verge of hysteria. 'I couldn't make it stop. I called Emergency, I told them stat, Avis was dying, I couldn't look at Bill but I thought he was already dead.

'I did everything I could, Doctor.' His eyes implored Linden to tell him that he was not to blame. 'Honest, I did.'

His appeal touched her, but she had no room for it.

At the back of the lobby, Maxine released herself from Ernie's arms. Moving between the silent officers, she came forward to stand beside Harry, place a reassuring hand on his shoulder. Her kind face regarded him sadly.

The officers began to shift their feet and look around as if they were rousing themselves from a trance.

'Dr Panger has Avis in surgery,' Maxine told Linden. 'He may have bone splinters in his brain.'

Linden nodded an acknowledgement – Curt Panger was more than competent – but she was not done with Harry. 'Did you see him leave?' she asked quietly.

'Oh, yes,' Harry answered. 'Right after I called Emergency. He had Joan, and Mrs Clint. Joan went with him like she wanted to go, but he had to keep his gun pointed at Mrs Clint. I hid behind the desk so he didn't see me.'

Lytton cleared his throat fiercely. 'He has a hostage, Dr Avery.' His voice seemed to grate against his teeth. 'We're wasting time here. I need to talk to you.'

Linden turned her attention to him at last. 'And I need to talk to you.' The fact that Roger had taken a hostage meant that he was not finished yet. If he had simply wanted his mother, a hostage would only slow him down.

He intended more harm.

Sara Clint was a good nurse, level-headed and compassionate. She had a husband and two daughters. She did not deserve this.

Joan herself did not deserve it.

'Fine,' Lytton growled. 'So tell me just how the hell you knew this was going to happen.'

'Not here,' Linden countered. 'In my office.' He was more likely to tell her the truth if they were alone.

Stifling an impulse to hurry, she took a moment to ask Maxine to call for a nurse to replace Sara. She did not want to leave Harry on duty alone in his condition. Then she beckoned for the sheriff to follow her and headed towards her office.

His heavy boots stamped behind her on the tile as if he were cursing.

In her office, she sat down behind her desk, anchoring herself on her medical authority. She wanted Barton Lytton to know that she was not a woman whom he could intimidate.

He began at once. Towering at the edge of her desk, he announced in a rough voice, 'I need to know what you know. We have to find that little shit.' He glowered down at her as if she could free him to act on his outrage and frustration. 'He sure as hell won't take her to Haven Farm. Not unless he's begging to get caught. The Clints are decent people. I'm not going to let him get away with this.

'Tell me now, Doctor. How the fuck did you know what he would do?'

The sheriff was wrong. Roger expected to be caught; wanted that for some reason. Why else did he need a hostage?

'I knew,' she retorted firmly, 'because I pay attention.' The haunted ire and need in his eyes had not changed, but now it did not sway her. 'I could see as soon as I met him that he was unstable. He kept repeating that he wanted to take care of Joan, but his manner was all wrong. He didn't act like a loving son. The way he talked convinced me that the only thing he really cared about was getting her away from here.

'I tried to tell you. He wants to do something to her.'

Lytton propped his fists on her desk, leaned his bulk onto his arms. In spite of his posture, however, his eyes flinched. 'You're not helping, Doctor,' he said softly. 'Telling me I fucked up doesn't do shit for Sara Clint. We've got to get her back.

'I need to know where he's going. Hell, he could be halfway out of the county by now. I can call in help. We can set up roadblocks, try to stop him. But there are too many small roads. We can't block them all. Hell, we don't even know what kind of car he drives. That fool Gund was too scared to look.

'And while we're sitting at roadblocks, he can hole up anywhere he wants. We'll never find him. Until he's already done' – Lytton swallowed hard – 'whatever the fuck he has in mind.

'It's too late to tell me I should have listened to you. Tell me how to find him.'

Linden recognised the justice of his response. In some sense, she respected it. But she was not moved. The look in his eyes disturbed her. Their mix of fear and fury seemed to promise butchery.

Terrible things might happen to Joan and Sara if Lytton tried to kill Roger—

Linden held the sheriff's gaze until he looked away. Then, distinctly, she said, 'There's something I need to know first.'

'Are you shitting me?' he protested. 'Roger Covenant has a fucking *hostage*, he has *Sara Clint*! We need to *move*! What can you possibly need to know *first*?'

Linden did not relent. Instead she said precisely, 'When Julius Berenford found Joan on Haven Farm ten years ago, she was sane. She couldn't remember what had happened to her, but she could talk. She could *function*, at least to some extent. But by the time you delivered her to County Hospital, Sheriff Lytton, she was a vegetable. Entirely out of reach. If we didn't take such good care of her, she would have died years ago.

'What happened while you were driving her back into town? What changed her?'

With a jerk, Lytton pulled himself upright. A sudden flush darkened his cheeks. Glaring at the centre of Linden's forehead, he said, 'We've had this conversation, Doctor.'

'Yes, we have,' she insisted. 'But I need a better answer. It's time to talk about it. Tell me what happened.'

Her pager chirped at her, but she ignored it. She had come too far and waited too long to let Barton Lytton evade her now.

Darkness spread down Lytton's neck, staining his skin with threats. Yet he could not conceal his fear. His eyes seemed to cower in their sockets. Linden thought that he might refuse to answer; but she had underestimated his rage – or his shame. Abruptly he bared his teeth as if he were grinning. His eyes found hers in defiance.

'Oh, it's nothing much,' he answered between his teeth. 'I didn't *hurt* her or anything, if that's what you think.

'Of course, I cuffed her. She was a fucking *accessory*, for God's sake. For all I knew, she'd killed her damn ex.' He faltered for an instant, wincing. Then he rasped, 'After that, I made her ride in back.'

The back of a police car: the cage. Bars between her and the front seat. No handles inside the doors. Like a dangerous criminal.

After what she had suffered—

'She asked me why,' he went on. 'She was fucking hysterical about it. So I told her.'

Linden stared at him. His gaze held a throng of conflicts. Her pager signalled again; but now she could not force herself to glance away from him.

'Told her—?' she asked weakly.

'The truth, Dr Avery.' His tone was thick with disgust. 'Her ex was a fucking *leper*. And she was married to him before she knew he had it. She probably had it herself. Hell, she probably still does. If nothing else, she's a damn carrier.

'I made her ride in back because I didn't want to be *infected*.'

Linden heard him clearly. He was trying to sound justified. But he failed. The plain cruelty of his actions defeated him.

Before she could react, he leaned over her desk again. 'That upsets you, doesn't it, Doctor. You don't think I should have been so *mean* to her.

'Well, fuck you. We should have talked about your complicity in that murder *ten years ago*. You're an accessory too, but the sainted Julius Berenford protected you. The two of you hid the truth. I'm the *sheriff* of this county, and you didn't let me do my *job*.

'Now you're at it again. But this time you won't get away with it. I'll find them without you. And when I do, I'm going to make *damn* sure you get your share of the blame.'

Then he stood up and wheeled out of her office. Before he reached the lobby, he started shouting orders at his deputies.

Linden swore to herself. She could have told him where to look for Roger. She should have. But she did not trust him. He was too eager for violence. His solution to Joan's dilemma might leave no one alive.

Her pager beeped again, insisting on her attention. Reluctantly she looked down at its display.

For a moment, she did not recognise the number. She stared at it, frowning, while she pushed the button to make the pager stop chirping.

Who—?

Then she had it: Megan Roman. That was Megan's home phone number.

She groaned under her breath. She did not feel equal to the challenge of telling Megan about Bill and Joan and Sara.

But what else did she propose to do, now that she had driven Barton Lytton away? Go after Roger on her own? No. She would not risk her life – risk abandoning Jeremiah – in that way. And it was possible that Megan would be able to help—

She might know someone in the State Highway Patrol. Or, better yet, the FBI. Kidnapping was a Federal crime, was it not? Megan might be able to have Joan's plight, and Sara's, taken out of Lytton's hands.

Swallowing her reluctance, Linden reached for her phone and dialled Megan's number.

The lawyer picked up almost instantly. 'Yes?'

'Megan, it's Linden.'

'*Linden,*' Megan cried at once, '*where are you?*'

Her urgency seemed to knock Linden back in her seat. She heard crises in Megan's voice; dangers she had not imagined. Quickly she asked, 'Megan, what's wrong?'

'*Damn* it, Linden!' Megan yelled back. '*Listen* to me. Where *are* you? At the hospital?'

'Yes, I—' Linden began, floundering.

'Then go home!' Megan demanded. 'Right now! No matter what you're doing. *Listen!* I heard what happened. Roger and Joan. Sara Clint. Bill Coty.

'I've—' Abruptly she faltered; fell silent. Dead air filled the phone like keening.

'Megan?' Linden urged her friend. 'Megan?'

'Oh, Linden.' Without transition, Megan's voice changed. Now she sounded like she was in tears. 'I've made a horrible mistake.

'I mentioned Jeremiah to Roger. A few days ago. He was asking questions about you. I told him you have a son.'

Somewhere in the background of herself, Linden started screaming.

Chapter Five:

The Cost of Love and Despair

She saw everything with a terrible clarity. The edge of her desk looked sharp enough to draw blood. Across its surface, sheets of paper in confusion whetted each other to the incisiveness of anguish. The clock hanging on the wall above her seemed to jut outward, its hands as stark as cries. In her grasp, the black plastic of the phone's receiver looked desperate and fatal. Its cord coiled about itself, binding her to Megan's voice.

She had lost her chance to flee with Jeremiah. It would never come again.

Her friend was saying, 'Linden, I am so sorry.'

She was saying, 'Go home *now*. Maybe I'm wrong. Don't take the chance. Don't let this become any worse than I've already made it. No one else needs you the way he does.'

Linden did not reply. If she had, Megan would not have heard her: she had already dropped the handset. Borne along by screams, she left her office at a run. The skirts of her coat flapped behind her like Furies.

Stop, she tried to tell herself, go back. Assume he has Jeremiah. Get Lytton's help. Tell him where to look, make him take you with him, with your help he might find Roger in time.

But she did not stop running, or turn. The voice of her own sanity could not reach her. She flung aside the staff door, and the wind caught it: she might have cracked the safety glass. But she did not pause to close it. Instead she raced headlong for her car. The wind battered at her; struck tears from her eyes. The heels of her shoes slapped the sidewalk awkwardly, making her stumble. One of them flipped from her foot. She kicked the other away and ran on.

He is threatening my son!

How far ahead of her was Roger? Half an hour? An *hour*?

Even half an hour was too much.

As she neared her car, she tugged the keys from her coat pocket. The wind seemed to snatch them out of her fingers: they dropped to the pavement in a buffeted arc through the false illumination from the light poles. Without pausing, she stooped to retrieve them.

She did not need to unlock her car: she seldom locked it. Gusts and turbulence resisted her momentarily, then tumbled away to let her pull open the door, slide into the driver's seat.

As soon as she closed the door and shut out the wind, she began to quake. Her hands faltered and shook like scraps of paper enclosed with gusts. She could not fix her fingers to the right key. It fumbled from her grasp as she strove to push it into the ignition. Her heart beat interminably while she struggled with it.

Raging through her teeth, she clutched the keys in her fist and punched the dashboard hard enough to gouge metal into her palm.

If she failed I would need to take her place.

Jeremiah needed her. No one else needs you the way he does.

She thumbed the key into the ignition; cranked the starter. The old engine roared to life like an act of will. Violent as gunfire, she aimed her car out of the parking lot and jammed her foot down on the accelerator.

Roger did not know this town. He did not know where she lived. Even given directions, he would have to drive slowly, peer through the darkness for street signs and house numbers. And Sara Clint—Joan would not resist him, she was already lost. But Sara would do whatever she could to escape him, frustrate him. He could not make an attempt on Jeremiah unless he controlled her somehow.

He could not move quickly. If Linden did not reach her house ahead of him, she might catch him while he was there.

If Sandy had been forewarned—

The wind or her tyres shrieked through a corner. The car lurched on its springs. Again she punched the dashboard. *Damn* it, she should have called Sandy from her office; or asked Megan to do it for her. She had been too long away from the Land. She had got out of the habit of fighting against Despite.

Three more houses. Two. Then she reached her home.

Tyres squalling, her car slammed to the curb. She made no effort to pull into her driveway, or park sanely; did not turn off the engine. Lightning shrieked overhead, a static discharge rubbed to life by the pressure of the wind. It left a glare across her vision as she shoved out of the car and saw the door of her house gaping open to the night.

Jeremiah—!

She seemed to rush forward in sheets and tatters, lifted by wind and slapped at the front of her house. The lawn and the steps were nothing to her. She noticed only the door banging on its hinges and the bullet-torn lock; only the ruined castle which littered the entryway.

Roger had left all of the lights on as if to welcome her home. Of course. How could he have known where to look for Jeremiah? He must have held Sandy at gun-point while he searched from room to room. Or else he had killed—

Fearing more blood, Linden scanned the Tinker Toys quickly, the living room carpet, the hallway to the kitchen. But she saw nothing to suggest that he had harmed Sandy.

He had another use for her life.

She took the stairs three at a time, surged upwards in her fluttering coat and her exposed feet to confirm her worst fears.

Every light blazed. Roger had been into every room, left no part of her home unviolated. The whole upstairs shone as if she were being welcomed to a wake.

He had searched—

Jeremiah's bed lay empty. Roger Covenant had not touched the race track and towers. He had disturbed nothing. He had taken only her son.

There Linden stopped running.

Her terror and fury did not let her go. Instead they seemed to drive her into another mode of being, onto a new plane of existence. Between one heartbeat and the next, she ceased to be the Linden Avery who could panic or be paralysed. In that woman's place, she became Linden Avery the Chosen, who had transcended Ravers and despair in the name of those she loved.

She knew what Roger would do. And she had already made all of the choices that would be required of her.

Deliberately, sure of herself now, she went to her bedroom to change her clothes. She could not go to meet the Despiser barefoot, clad only in her loose coat and the impersonal blouse and skirt which she had worn to work.

That room also Roger had violated. He had swept everything off the top of her bureau and dressing-table; emptied her drawers onto the floor; rummaged out the contents of her closet. Cosmetics, earrings, and shampoos complicated the floor of her bathroom.

He wanted something more than Jeremiah from her.

He could no longer surprise her: she had already guessed the truth. He had hoped to find his father's wedding band.

Now she knew why Roger had taken Jeremiah. It was not simple malice; a desire to hurt her for refusing him – or for opposing the Despiser. Jeremiah had no worth in himself: no power, no ring. And Roger did not need another hostage to protect him from Sheriff Lytton's outrage. Jeremiah's only value was to Linden herself.

Roger wanted him as leverage against her. Either here or in the Land, Roger intended to use her son to extort what he needed from her.

Would he have claimed Jeremiah if he had found her ring? Perhaps. It was possible that white gold lost its power if it were stolen, or reft by violence. She did not know – or care.

Steadily, without haste, she stripped off her clothes. As she did so, she found a dull pain throbbing in the palm of her right hand; and her touch left slight smears of blood on her skirt and blouse. When she looked at her hand, she saw crusted blood around a crescent cut into her palm, a small rent of vulnerability. She had cut herself when she had punched the dashboard with her keys in her fist.

If she failed I would need to take her place.

From the litter on her floor she selected comfortable jeans, a warm red flannel shirt which Jeremiah had seen her wear many times and might recognise, and a pair of sturdy boots. Soon she was dressed very much as she had been when she had followed Covenant into the night behind Haven Farm in order to rescue Joan.

Her coat she rejected. It could not protect her from the mounting storm. Without it, she went back downstairs to call 911.

Speaking precisely, she told the operator to give Sheriff Lytton a message. *Roger has taken my son. He has another hostage, Sandy Eastwall. Look for him on Haven Farm.*

Now that she had stopped running, she no longer feared what Lytton might do. He had harmed Joan out of spite, not malice, because Julius Berenford – and Linden herself – had made him feel emasculated after Covenant's murder. With so many lives at stake, he would act with more restraint. And she needed his help. She was no match for Roger's gun, or his madness.

There were other people whom she could have called, Sam Diadem and Ernie Dubroff among them. Megan Roman would have begged for a chance to make restitution. But Linden was unwilling to risk any more innocents.

Leaving her house as she had found it, she strode down the steps and across the lawn back to her car.

The wind seemed to grow stronger by the moment. She had to lean against it in order to walk forward. Stark in the cloudless dark, friction lightning streaked among the treetops. She had never seen a storm like this before: it appeared to rip at the laws of nature, altering realities with every strike. When she gained her car, she was vaguely surprised to find that it still ran; that the street itself had not been torn apart. She half expected the trees to crash and fall under the force of the wind and the lightning.

Her car shuddered at every blast, as if at any moment it might shiver itself to scrap; yet it brunted stubbornly ahead. A few blocks took her to the main street through the centre of town. From end to end, the whole town looked deserted. There were no other cars at the intersections, no vehicles moving anywhere. Every inhabitant of the area had gone to ground like a threatened animal. If Sheriff Lytton or his deputies were abroad, Linden saw no sign of them.

Alone, she passed the phone company offices, the town's only department store, the county courthouse. The sheer intensity of the wind seemed to dim the street lamps, truncate their illumination; but for a moment lightning etched the courthouse out of the crowded night, casting a bright wail across the old columns which upheld the roof. In the harsh white glare, the giant heads atop the columns gaped like ghouls.

Thomas Covenant had lost his marriage there. He had nearly lost his home.

And Linden had adopted Jeremiah—

How far ahead of her was Roger now? How much harm could he inflict before she caught up with him?

She clung to the steering wheel, forcing the car forward. Sweat stung her gouged palm.

Abruptly every lamp along the street let out an incandescent blare and went dark. Midnight seemed to tumble out of the sky, filling the town as all the lights failed. Lightning must have hit a transformer somewhere; or a tree had fallen across the power-lines. The beams of her headlights appeared to sag to the ground directly in front of her, unable to penetrate the sudden blackness. Reacting on instinct, she stamped at the brakes and her car slewed to a stop.

At once, however, she punched the accelerator again, battling the wind for speed. She knew this road: it had few intersections and hardly curved between town and Haven Farm. And Haven Farm itself was only two miles away. Clearly she did not need to worry about traffic. If the mounting gale did not blow her off the road – and if lightning did not strike her—

Roger was already there: her fears discerned him too vividly for her to believe otherwise. She seemed to see him through her windshield, his bland unction whetted to eagerness, his teeth bared. He had reached the farmhouse. He was inside. With one hand, he dragged Jeremiah along: the other brandished his gun. In her imagination, terror flashed from Jeremiah's eyes, and his slack mouth quivered on the verge of wailing.

She could not see Sara or Sandy; could not guess what Roger would do without electricity. Perhaps his madness had grown so lucid that he did not need light—

Gusts kicked the car hard, and its front wheels seemed to lift from the road. Lightning brought the pavement to life, then snatched it away into darkness. Fighting for control, Linden shoved down on the gas and went faster. She was afraid that Lytton might reach Haven Farm ahead of her – and afraid that he would not. Roger's actions would become more extreme as time passed.

There, on her right: the dirt road that served as Haven Farm's driveway. A quarter of a mile away beyond open fields, invisible against the wood which clustered around Righters Creek, stood the small farmhouse where Thomas Covenant had lived. Linden knew it well, although she had not been there for years. In memory she had preserved its rooms. Even now, with Jeremiah in danger, and her nerves primed for battle, she could see Covenant's flagrant eyes as he had striven to prevent her from sharing his peril.

And *there*, not twenty yards from the main road, lay the spot on which she had swallowed nausea and fear in order to save the life of the old man in the ochre robe—

—who had told her to *Be true*—

—and who should have by God *warned* her that Jeremiah's life was at risk.

Wheels skidding in the dirt, she drove towards the house through winds that gathered a tornado's force.

Then the scant reach of her headlights found one wall of the farmhouse. It had once been white, but over the years neglect had peeled the paint away to grey wood, and a few of the boards had sprung from their frame. No light showed in the windows: apparently the power-failure covered this whole section of the county. Otherwise, she felt sure, Roger would have left every lamp lit here as he had in her home, welcoming her to his handiwork.

In a spray of dirt that disappeared instantly along the wind, Linden stopped.

Beside the house stood a dark sedan: Roger's car. He had closed the doors, but left the trunk open. Its interior light gave off a faint glow that seemed to efface the rest of the vehicle, so that only the trunk retained any reality in this world.

Only the trunk and whatever Roger had transported in it—

For a moment, she thought that he must have carried Jeremiah there; and she nearly burst raging from her car. But, no, Roger would not have done that for the simple reason that there was no need. Like Joan, Jeremiah would have caused him no trouble, put up no resistance. Regardless of what happened, her son would have remained rocking wherever he was put, passive and doomed.

Roger must have used the trunk to contain Sara or Sandy. Or both—

Linden saw no other cars. Either the sheriff had not received her message in time, or he had elected to ignore it.

Still she did not hesitate or hurry.

Leaving her headlights on, she turned off her car, grabbed the keys and surged out into the wind.

Behind his blankness, Jeremiah would be terrified. She could not know what he remembered of his terrible past; but on some level, he might recognise what was being done to him now. Or he might believe that he had been returned to that cruel time when his mother had given him into the Despiser's power.

Cries which he would not be able to utter for himself filled Linden's heart as she pushed through the blast to the back of her car. Again she had trouble handling the keys: they dug at her gouged palm as she fumbled to open the trunk. Then she jammed the right key into place.

From the trunk she took her medical bag and a heavy flashlight, and turned towards the house.

A sizzling flash snatched the house into light, rendered it stark and bleached against the black night. Without warning, gusts caught in the trunk of Roger's sedan. The lid slammed shut like the jaws of a trap.

She wanted to clutch for courage at Covenant's ring hanging against her sternum; but she needed both hands. Grimly she thumbed the switch of the flashlight. Like her car's headlights, its beam seemed to fall ineffective to the ground. It barely reached the house; cast no illumination at the front door.

Wind snapped her sleeves against her arms. Holding the flashlight before her like a weapon, she advanced on the dark farmhouse.

He is threatening my son.

Her light traced the outlines of the door. It had no windows, offered her no way to see past it. Its panels had held their paint better than the wall, and that white made the door look somehow newer than the rest of the house, fresher: a portal pulled forward in time by recent use.

Shifting the flashlight in her grasp, she used two fingers and the tip of her thumb to test the doorknob.

It turned easily; and at once the wind ripped it away, kicked the door open inwards. It hit the limit of its hinges hard enough to shake the frame.

Her flashlight could not penetrate the darkness. Wind and dust lashed more tears from her eyes. She had to rub the moisture away with her wrist before she could step over the threshold, force the beam of her light into the house.

The open door let her into the living room.

If she had not remembered the room so clearly, she might not have recognised it. Seen in the brief gleams and streaks cast by her flashlight, it seemed ruined, uninhabitable: the scene of an earthquake or some other catastrophe. Amidst funnels of wind-driven dust lay chunks of plaster from the ceiling and broken boards from the walls. The couch against one wall had been gutted, eaten alive by rats and roaches. Its stuffing blew like snow among the dust-devils. Shards from shattered windows lay on the armchairs, the coffee table, the rank carpet. Sections of the walls looked like they had been blown apart by shotguns.

Roger Covenant had made no attempt to pretend that he and his mother would actually live here. If anyone – Megan Roman, Sheriff Lytton, Linden herself – had had the foresight to visit his intended 'home', they would have seen the truth beyond any possible contradiction.

At first, Linden could find no sign that Roger and his victims had been here. Any marks which they might have left in the dust had been blown to confusion. But then she noticed darker patches among the room's debris. She had taken them for clotted dust and dirt. Now, however, she saw that they clung to the floor as if the wind had no power over them. Some of them caught a moist gleam from her flashlight.

Crouching to examine them, she found without surprise that they were blood: viscid and thickening, but still wet; recently shed.

'God *damn* you,' she muttered at Roger through her teeth because she already knew what he had done; knew what he was doing. 'You will not get away with this.'

Linden had sworn that he would claim Joan over her dead body; but she had not kept that oath. She had talked herself out of taking her fears seriously enough. Now she knew better. She would not make that mistake again.

In God's name, that bland bastard had not even had the decency to slaughter an animal instead—

Knowing the truth, and dreading it deep in her guts, she tightened her grip on her bag and went forward, into the short hallway which connected the living room and the kitchen.

The kitchen was as bad as the living room. Half the windows had been blown out. Splintered fluorescent bulbs intensified the litter of glass, plaster, and broken cabinets on the floor. And knives and utensils: whoever had cleaned out the house after Covenant's death – Megan Roman? – must have neglected the kitchen. Open drawers had spilled their contents like scree.

Here, too, Linden found smears and puddles of blood.

She should have been terrified for Jeremiah, but she was not. Her fears were certain: Roger's intentions for her son would not end so soon.

He had not yet had time to offer Jeremiah to the Despiser.

From the kitchen another short passage led to three doors, a bedroom, the bathroom and another bedroom. Her flashlight showed the way in splashes of illumination. Dark drips and smears marked the floor as if Roger had blazed a trail for Linden to follow to the end of the hall.

She did not have far to go to reach the last room, where Covenant had cared for Joan. Six forthright strides: ten hesitating steps. The door stood open ahead of her, inviting her deeper into the night. Even though she knew what she expected to find, her dread mounted.

She clung to the handle of her bag. Its weight comforted her. She had neglected it ten years ago, when she had followed Covenant into the woods after Joan. It might have helped her then, counteracting her terror. Perhaps it would aid her now.

Stabbing her light ahead of her, Linden approached the open door; stepped past the edge of the frame.

With a splintering crash like rent heartwood, lightning struck somewhere nearby: so near that she seemed to feel the impact in her stomach. For an instant, fierce white filled the hall as though it shone straight through the walls into her eyes; as though in that moment the hallway and Linden herself had been ripped into another reality by the accumulated ferocity of the blast. Every hair on her body seemed to stand on end as darkness recoiled over her, stifling her flashlight, leaving her blind. The ripe reek of ozone shouted in her nostrils.

She had time to think, God, that was close—

Then her struggling flashlight brought the room beyond the door back into being.

She gazed inwards at more ruin, the wreckage of a dwelling which had been left without love or care for ten years: fallen plaster and sprung floorboards, broken window glass, drifted refuse and dust. Abandoned so, the bedroom looked toxic, fatal, as if during his years here Thomas Covenant's illness had seeped into the walls.

Like the cushions of the living room couch, the mattress on the single bed had been torn apart by time and vermin. Briefly Linden seemed to see the bed as it had lain since Joan's abduction and Covenant's death; forlorn and unused. But then her flashlight asserted its tangible vision; and lightning glared from the windows; and she saw the truth.

On the bed lay Sara Clint, desolate in her own blood.

Beside her head, a large kitchen knife had been driven into the remains of the pillow. Perhaps Roger had found it here, and had used it because it had belonged to his father. It stood like a marker at Sara's head. A warning—

Involuntarily Linden dropped her bag. It could not help her now. No medical power would undo Roger's cruelty.

Blood dried on the edges of the cuts which had been made in Sara's uniform, soaked from the wounds in her flesh. As Linden stepped into the room, she saw more and more places where the white fabric had been sliced through; and at first she feared that Sara had been cut and cut and *cut* until she had simply bled to death: slowly, helplessly; in terror. Sara's wrists and ankles had been secured to the bed frame with what appeared to be duct tape. She could not have avoided Roger's knife to save her soul. Then, however, Linden saw the raw wound which grinned under Sara's chin across her carotid arteries. Roger had pulled his blade through her life there, ending it quickly.

Apparently he had wanted more blood than he could gather from less fatal cuts.

Or he had known that he was running out of time—

Had he seen Linden's headlights approach from the road? How far ahead of her was he?

She should go after him: *now*, before he increased his lead. She could move more swiftly than he did. She did not have to drag Sandy Eastwall along, shepherd both Jeremiah and Joan. She might be able to catch him before he carried out the next phase of his madness. Before he butchered Sandy as he had Sara, to open the way for the Land's destruction, and Jeremiah's.

She would go. She would. As soon as she had given a moment of shock and grief to Sara's corpse. The nurse deserved that much. She had been among the best people at Berenford Memorial. And her husband—

Linden should have been able to smell blood. Not at first, her nose full of ozone. But that heavy scent was gone now, torn away by conflicting winds which seemed to tumble through the walls. Surely standing so near the bed she should have been able to smell Sara's blood?

She could not. She smelled smoke.

As soon as she became aware of it, it seemed to gather strength: the fug of burning wood; smoke like the malice of the Despiser's bonfire. Tension mounted in her chest. She must have been holding her breath; or smoke had already begun to ache in her lungs. Now her flashlight caught wisps of it amidst the gloom. Tendrils curled towards the bed until the winds clawed them apart.

Dear God! That blast of lightning: the one which had blinded her outside this room. It must have struck the house—

All this dry, untended wood would burn like tinder.

For an instant, her peril trapped her as it had ten years ago, when she had failed to save Covenant's life. The thought that Roger had recreated Lord Foul's blazing portal *here*, with her snared in its centre, stunned her like a fist to the heart. Roger might be outside at this moment, waiting for her agony to open the way—

Then she remembered that he still lacked his father's ring; and she surged into motion. Snatching up her bag, she retreated from the room to hasten towards the kitchen.

Already worms of fire gnawed at the edges of the boards between the bathroom and the other bedroom, Covenant's room, glowing in the benighted space. Before she could take a step, a blast like the slap of a hurricane struck the house, and the whole building staggered.

The door to Covenant's room jumped from its latch and blew open. At once flame like a breaking wave tumbled along the sudden release of air into the hall: a roar of torment from the throat of the house. Heat struck at her face, a palpable blow. Staggering herself, she fell backward against the end of the hall. Rotten boards flexed at the impact.

The hungry howl mounted. A tumult of flame cascaded from Covenant's room, barricading the hall. She could not escape that way. The fury of the heat warned her: if she strove to pass, she would catch and burn like an auto-da-fe.

Smoke piled towards her, too thick already for her light to dispel. Ducking under it, she sprang back into the room where Sara Clint lay. Instinctively she swung shut the door, although she knew that it would not protect her. For a moment, she gaped at air which had already lost its capacity to sustain her. Then she rushed to the nearest window.

Half of its glass had cracked and fallen long ago. She used her bag to break the rest from the frame. Then she tossed the bag and her flashlight to the ground outside. Bracing her hands on the sill, she climbed out through the window. Scraps of glass tore fresh blood from her right palm.

Sitting on the sill, she dragged her legs out of the room, dropped to the ground. She landed with a jolt that jarred her spine, as if she had fallen much farther; but she kept her balance. Gasping for good air, she retrieved her bag and her flashlight, and stumbled away to put distance between herself and the blazing house.

Helpless to do otherwise, she left Sara for cremation.

When the heat no longer hurt her skin, no longer threatened to set her hair on fire, she turned to watch Thomas Covenant's home die.

Now gouts and streamers of flame poured from all of the windows. Fire licked between the roof's remaining shingles, showed in the gaps which marred the walls. Every lash of wind spread the flames, intensified the conflagration. Sparks gyred into the sky and were torn away. In minutes the structure would collapse in on itself, reduced to ash and embers by the eerie storm.

From Linden's perspective, Roger's sedan seemed too close to the house. Surely it would catch fire as well? Her own car might be safe—

In the flagellated light of the blaze, she saw no sign of Roger Covenant or his other victims.

He had not gagged Sara. Jeremiah must have heard her cries. Sandy and Joan must have heard them. Perhaps Joan was beyond caring: Sandy was not. And for Jeremiah—

Running now, frantically, Linden turned her back on the roaring house and headed into the woods behind Haven Farm.

Wind kicked at her legs, tried to trip her among the first trees: it caught at her clothes. She knew where Roger would go, now that he had destroyed his father's home, his father's example of concern and devotion. She had not returned to these woods since the night of Covenant's murder, but she was sure of them. Where else *could* Roger go, if he wished to undo his father's self-sacrifice?

The woods twisted like a thrown ribbon among the fields of the county, following the crooked course of Righters Creek. Scrub oak, sycamore and ivy crowded against each other along the gully of the stream. As soon as she had outrun the light of the burning house, she had to slow down. The wind or a fallen branch or a gap in the ground might trip her.

Gusts of wind flung limbs and leaves at her face, confused her senses with the wet odor of rotting wood and loam. Repeatedly her bag banged into her leg. Her flashlight was ineffective against the scourged dark. It had a will-o'-the-wisp frailty; cast only enough light to lead her astray. No trod ground opened in any direction: the woods were cut off from the world she knew. If she had not been sure, she might have wandered there for hours.

But she had forgotten nothing of the night of Thomas Covenant's death: she followed her memories. The wind whipped branches to bar her way, sent tangles of ivy reaching for her neck. But she could not be turned aside.

Roger's pace would be slower than hers. He could not be far ahead of her.

Standing somewhere else in these woods, on a hillside above Righters Creek, Thomas Covenant had once seen a young girl threatened by a timber rattler. On his way down the slope to help her, he had fallen – and found himself summoned to Revelstone. Yet he had refused the Land's need. Instead he had chosen to do what he could for the child in his own world.

Roger would avoid such a place. The ground itself might retain too much of his father's courage. But Linden clung to it in her mind as she forged among the trees, following her faint light through the rending wind.

She had every intention of refusing the Land, if she had to; if Roger left her no other choice.

Lightning flared and snapped overhead, flooding the woods and then sweeping them into darkness. Repeatedly she pressed the heel of her right hand against the uncompromising circle of Covenant's ring. She needed to assure herself that she still possessed one thing which Roger wanted; one talisman with which she could bargain for Jeremiah's life.

Her cut palm stung whenever she shifted her grip on the flashlight. Its plastic case had become sticky with her blood. How far ahead of her was Roger? A hundred yards? A quarter of mile? No, it could not be so far. She remembered the way. He was already near his destination.

Over my dead body.

Then the ground began to rise, and she recognised the last hill, the final boundary. The cluttered terrain climbed to a crest. Beyond it, the ground dropped down into a hollow, deep as a stirrup cup, its sides steep and treacherous. Within the hollow nothing grew, as if decades or centuries ago the soil had been anointed with a malign chrism which had left it barren.

As Linden reached the crest, she half expected to find fire burning below her. Roger could have readied a conflagration here. Not tonight: he had not had time. But he could have begun to prepare for this night from the moment when he had first known what he meant to do.

However, there was no fire; no light of any kind. In the bottom of the hollow, she knew, lay a rough plane of exposed stone like a rude altar. Covenant had been sacrificed on it: she had fallen there herself. But she could not see it now. Her flashlight's beam did not reach so far. Before her, the ground seemed to sink away into deeper blackness like a plunge into an abyss.

Then lightning split the heavens; and in its shrill silver glare she saw the hollow as if it had been etched onto her retinas. When night closed back over the flash, she saw the scene still, limned in argent and terror.

Flecks of mica in the native stone glittered so that Roger Covenant appeared to stand amid a swath of sparks. He faced up the hillside towards Linden as if he had been expecting her – and had known exactly where she would appear. His smile had the empty pleasantry of an undertaker's.

In his right hand, he held a gun as heavy as a bludgeon, pointing it at Sandy Eastwall's head. She knelt on the stone beside him, her hands clasped over her heart in prayer. Her features were swollen, aggrieved with tears.

She knew her peril. Roger must have forced her to watch while he had shed Sara Clint's blood, preparing the way—

At his back stood Joan, her head bowed in submission. Around the betrayed sticks of her arms and legs, her nightgown fluttered like a pennon.

With his left hand, Roger gripped Jeremiah's wrist. The boy's maimed hand dangled in his captor's grasp. He held his free arm over his stomach, rocking himself as best he could on his feet. His lost eyes stared at nothing.

In the image burned onto Linden's retinas, sparks surrounded them all like a nimbus: the first touch of power which would translate them to ruin.

She could see nothing except dismay. Her flashlight hardly revealed the ground at her feet. Wind rushed wailing among the trees, lashed their limbs to frenzy. Its gusts seemed to cry out her son's name.

'*Jeremiah!*' she called like an echo of the storm. 'I'm here! I won't let him hurt you!'

At once she plunged down the hillside, heedless of the dark.

Again lightning hit the night. Stone and sparks seemed to reel towards her as she rushed downwards. In the flash, she saw fresh blood stream from Joan's right temple. Joan had smeared the blood into her mouth. Without that lunatic strength, she would surely have collapsed.

'My dear Doctor,' Roger answered, 'I have a gun. I don't see how you can stop me.'

Linden heard no strain in his voice, no effort to out-shout the wind. Nevertheless his words reached her as though he had spoken them directly into her heart.

She jerked to a stop half a dozen paces from him. Her flashlight reached the plane of rock now, found four dim shapes poised in the dark. Its beam seemed to concentrate of its own volition on the black weight of Roger's gun.

'Linden!' Sandy gasped, 'oh, my God, he killed Mrs Clint, back in the house, he cut her apart—'

With a negligent flick of his wrist, Roger swung the gun against Sandy's head. She sagged to the side; nearly fell.

'You don't talk now,' he informed her, smiling through another wrench of lightning that seemed to endure for a heartbeat too long. 'This is between me and the good doctor. You don't have anything more to say.'

Wind shoved at Linden's back, urged her forward. She held her ground. She wanted to spring at Roger and tear the smile from his face; but she understood the danger too well. He needed nothing from Sandy now except her blood. He could pull the trigger at any moment, any provocation, to supply his desires.

With an effort, Linden turned her flashlight away from the gun and Sandy's stricken face towards her son.

More lightning rent the night. The blasts were growing more frequent, fiercer; accumulating towards a convulsion which would crack the boundary between realities. In silver fire, she saw Jeremiah gaze blindly through her, his sight and his mind imprisoned. Horses reared uselessly across the blue flannel of his pajamas. If Roger's grip on his wrist caused him any pain, he did not show it.

He still held his free arm across his stomach, the hand closed into a fist. Lightning and the wan touch of Linden's torch caught a brief flare of red from his fist: the artificial red of bright paint, as raw as a cry.

The next furious flash showed her clearly that he gripped one of his racing cars in his tight fingers. He must have picked it up from his bureau as Roger dragged him away.

Forgotten screaming rose in her. When he had been captured, her mute, blank, helpless son had reached out—

On some level, he must have understood his danger.

At any other time, she would have wept at the sight; but now she had no tears. The moisture which the wind and her whipped hair drew from her eyes was only water, not weeping.

'You bastard!' she yelled at Roger through the gale. 'What do you want?'

She knew what he wanted.

He gazed at her. 'Don't embarrass yourself, Doctor.' His voice reached her effortlessly. 'You already know.'

At his back, Joan made sounds that might have been pleading; but Linden could not identify words through the wind's roar and the sizzling ire of the lightning.

'Linden,' Sandy panted, 'get help. He has a gun. He'll kill you, he's going to kill all of us. You can't—'

'Yes!' Linden shouted at Roger to forestall another blow. 'I know! I have it.' It hung on its chain against her chest. 'But I don't understand.'

'That's right. You don't.'

He struck again, despite Linden's attempt to distract him. This time, Sandy slumped to the stone and lay still. Respiration stirred her chest slightly. Blood oozed through the hair on the side of her head.

Nothing touched Roger's bland smile.

A bolt of lightning struck the ground scarcely twenty feet from the plane of rock. It burned in the air, impossibly prolonged, for two heartbeats; three. Static flashed along Linden's skin as if she were about to burst into flame.

In the hot core of the blast, she saw two curved yellow marks that might have been fangs. Or eyes.

Then darkness slapped the light away. Her flashlight revealed nothing. Until her eyes adjusted, she could not see.

The wind might have been the voice of her own cries.

When the lightning came again, it had receded from the stone as if to make room for Roger's madness. It struck now with horrific frequency; pounded into the hollow at quick, erratic intervals, first on one side, then on the other, behind her, off to her left. Each blast clung to the ground for two or three seconds, sealing off the bottom of the hollow from the rest of the woods; interdicting help. The trapped space between the bolts swarmed with static. Linden's hair seemed to crackle about her head. Roger, Jeremiah and Joan were wrapped in a penumbra of potential fire.

If a bolt hit the trees, these woods might burn like Covenant's home—

'You said,' Linden shouted at Roger, 'you know things I don't.' Each word wore an aura of electricity. 'You said I haven't earned the knowledge. But you don't know anything about me.

'How did *you* earn it?'

She did not care how he answered. She wanted only to make him talk. Distract him. Encourage him to drop his guard.

He may have believed that her right hand shook with fear; but it did not. Rather it trembled at the severity of her restraint. Every nerve in her arm burned to swing the flashlight into his face, hit him and *hit* him until she had destroyed his false image of his father. But his gun still threatened Sandy. Linden could not risk attacking him until he gave her an opening.

Had she seen *eyes* in that one long discharge? When he had split open Sandy's scalp, spilled her blood?

'By being her son,' he replied without a glance at Joan. 'And Thomas Covenant's. My parents were a leper and a victim. Really, Doctor. You could at least try to imagine who I am.'

Linden did not need to imagine it. She saw him clearly, revealed by the harsh silver stutter of lightning.

'So what?' she shouted back. 'My father killed himself in front of me. My mother begged me to put her out of her misery. I know what having damaged parents is like. As far as I can tell, the only thing you've earned is the right to *not do this!*'

Roger shook his head. Joan's thin fingers plucked weakly at his shoulders, beseeching him. Her touch left faint streaks of blood on his shirt.

'It's too late,' he told Linden. 'You're already lost. You should be able to see that.

'Your hand is bleeding, Doctor.' His tone betrayed a hint of eagerness. 'Why do you suppose that is?'

She gaped at him, momentarily silenced. How had he—?

But he gripped her son by the wrist; pointed his gun at Sandy's head. For their sake, Linden retorted, 'Because I cut myself.'

'No.' Again he shook his head. 'It's because you're already doomed. You can't get out of it now.'

Her blood also was necessary to him.

Another prolonged shaft of lightning hit and held the ground. For a moment, its brilliance dazzled Linden, cast Roger's face into shadow. This time from within the heart of the blaze Linden felt rather than saw the hungry yellow reach of fangs. They seemed to strain towards her while the bolt endured.

Calmly Roger added, 'But I like you, Doctor. I like what your parents did to you. I'll give you a choice.

'I see you brought your bag.' He nodded at the weight which anchored her against the compulsion of the wind. 'I'm sure you have a scalpel in there somewhere.

'Get it out. Cut off your right hand.'

He smiled avidly. 'Do that, and I'll let this woman live.' His gun indicated Sandy's crumpled form.

Joan lifted a tremulous hand to her wounded forehead.

Another long shaft of lightning: another impression of fangs like eyes, carious and malevolent.

In that instant, Linden was transformed. The fierce strobe of the lightning no longer staggered her. Shock and horror had no power over her.

'What about Jeremiah?' she cried into the storm.

Roger's inhuman gaze held her. 'First your hand.' No light reflected from his eyes. They remained as dark as catacombs. 'Then we'll discuss it.'

She let the wind and her bag's bulk buffet her forward a step as if she were stumbling. Just one step, to the edge of the stone. Sparks in shards of silver mica swirled before her feet.

Jeremiah's mouth hung open, slack. His gaze was closed to her. He was her chosen child, the son whom she had loved and tended in spite of his shuttered blankness. But nothing in him hinted at comprehension except the red metal racing car clutched in his left hand.

Deliberately she aimed her voice and her fury and her trembling flashlight at Roger.

'You've got it all wrong, asshole! I'll give *you* a choice. You give me Jeremiah. And Joan. And Sandy. *Alive!* And I give you your father's ring.'

He blinked as if she had surprised him. Joan made small mewling noises at his back, apparently begging him to hasten.

Lightning struck near the plane of rock again; so near that its force sent a stinging wave across Linden's skin. This time she was sure that she could see eyes and hunger in the depths of the blast.

'Now why would I do that?' Roger asked her. 'That ring is already mine. When I'm ready, I'll just shoot you and take it.'

'No, you won't.' Another step. Now she stood among the sparks. 'That craziness in your head. Lord Foul. He won't let you. He can't get what he wants that way. If he could, you would have killed me already.'

'Roger,' Joan gasped audibly. 'Roger!'

Prone at Roger's side, Sandy shifted inconsolably, trying to twist away from the pain in her head.

Roger ignored his mother to concentrate on Linden. Briefly he seemed to consider her proposal. Then he announced, 'It's an interesting suggestion. There's just one problem. Why would I ever trust you? If I let them go, you'll just run away.

'No, let's keep it simple. I have the gun. I have your son. If you don't feel like cutting yourself, I'll shoot this nice lady.' Sandy. 'Then I'll start on – what did you call him? – Jeremiah.

'He's just meat. Don't you know that? An empty carcass. There's nothing you could do to save him. There hasn't been anyone in there for ten years.'

The lightning had become almost constant, firing the sky and the earth in violent blasts only a small handful of heartbeats apart. And in the core of each bolt hung Lord Foul's eyes, rapacious and unmistakable, flickering in and out of this world as each flash clung and faded.

Instead of answering, Linden took another step. Blood from her cut palm crusted her hand to her flashlight. With every flash of lightning, pain pulsed in her grasp as though her heart kept time to the music of the storm.

'You're wrong!' she shouted over the wind. 'You don't understand. You haven't earned anything. You're no better than your mother. The only thing you've ever done with your whole life is let a crazy woman' – and Lord Foul – 'tell you what to do!'

Still smiling, always smiling, Roger lifted his right arm in a slow arc to point his gun at Linden's head. Its muzzle seemed to gape at her like a mouth, open and hungry.

'Hold it right there!' Sheriff Lytton yelled through the tumult. 'Put the gun down! Let's talk about this!'

'Roger!' Joan moaned distinctly, 'I can't stand it. I can't stand it anymore.'

Roger's weapon did not waver as he slowly turned his head in the direction of Lytton's voice.

Deliberately Linden turned as well, letting her knotted arm lower the flashlight to her side, tightening her grip on her bag.

Sandy groaned painfully. Her hands made small scratching movements on the stone.

Lit by the strobing frenzy of the lightning, and watched by fangs, Barton Lytton picked his way down the slope into the hollow. He walked with a rigid, stiff-kneed gait as if he fought panic at every step. Silver snatched reflections of fear from his staring eyes. Nevertheless he advanced until he neared the boundary of the storm-blasted ground around the plane of rock. There he halted, swaying on his feet as if he were about to fall.

His holster was empty. He had come down into the hollow unarmed.

'Sheriff Lytton,' Roger remarked. 'You're a brave man.' The ease with which he made himself heard through the wind's outcry mocked Lytton. 'I didn't think you had it in you.'

Lightning flared and yowled, accelerating towards a crisis. Fangs hung poised for violence in every flash. Static mounted in the air. The wind gusted like a wail torn from the throat of the night.

'You're in trouble here, boy.' Lytton's voice shook. Somehow he forced himself to stand his ground. 'You need to understand that. I've got half a dozen men up there.' He jerked his head at the rim of the bowl. 'They're all around you. And some of them shoot pretty good. If we can't talk our way out of this, you and me, they are going to cut you down.'

Linden glanced towards him, then shifted her gaze back to Roger. Her concentration left no room for surprise at Lytton's presence – or his actions.

Roger gave Jeremiah's wrist a warning wrench that nearly snapped her restraint. 'You've been listening to the things Dr Avery says about me,' he commented to Lytton. 'That's a mistake. A law enforcement officer like yourself can't afford mistakes.'

Facing the steady muzzle of his gun, Linden eased forward cautiously.

Lytton swayed on his locked knees. 'You can't either, boy. Do you understand that you've already killed two people? Bill Coty is dead. Avis Cardaman is probably going to die. And God knows what you've done with Sara Clint.' In the lightning, he looked pallid and frail, as if he were about to faint. 'That's life in prison. *Life*, boy. But if you stop now, that's all it is. You fire that gun one more time, in cold blood, and my men will *execute* your ass.

'Even if you live through being shot a couple dozen times, you're still dead. You'll get the death sentence for this. They'll stick one of those big needles in your arm, and you'll sleep until you *rot*.'

Apparently he thought that he might be able to frighten Roger into submission. Plainly, however, he did not comprehend Thomas Covenant's son at all.

Yet he did not give up.

'But you drop that gun now,' he went on, 'and maybe they'll just declare you incompetent. If that happens, you'll end up in a psychiatric hospital with women like Dr Avery taking care of you.

'What's it going to be, boy? You want a soft bed in a hospital? Or are you so *pitiful* you would rather be dead?'

Sandy moved one arm, braced her hand on the stone and tried to push herself upright.

In that instant, Joan slumped backwards as if she were about to fall. For one heartbeat, she seemed to sag down into herself, breaking inwards like a woman with crumbling bones. Then she raised her face to the dark heavens and cried out with her last strength, '*Make it stop!*'

As if in response, a long harsh shaft of lighting rife with eyes caught her where she stood, impaling her to the stone. It burned her life away; must have seared the marrow of her bones. While it endured, she hung in the bolt as though her death upheld her. When the blast ended, however, she dropped like shed spilth.

Linden tottered. The rock on which she stood had become a plunge into darkness. Jeremiah gazed vacantly past her. On the hillside, Lytton staggered backwards; barely caught himself.

Placidly Roger made his reply as loud as the wind, as large as the hollow. 'You're wasting your time, Sheriff,' he said as if Joan's death could not touch him. 'What makes you think I would believe a word you say?'

Without warning, he swept his gun from Linden to Lytton and fired.

The gun made a hard, flat, coughing sound, immediately torn away by the wind. The heavy slug caught Lytton high on his right shoulder, kicked him off his feet with the force of a thunderclap. He landed on his back without a sound. His arms and legs recoiled, bouncing. Then he lay still.

No time had passed. Linden's heart had not yet beat again. But already Roger had shifted his aim. His right arm dropped as he pointed his gun at Sandy's struggling form.

His left hand gripped Jeremiah's wrist as though he meant to hold her son forever.

In that sudden absence of time, Linden made her choice. Releasing her pent arm, she flung her flashlight at Roger's head.

Her cut hand betrayed her. Drying blood stuck the flashlight to her skin just long enough to reduce its momentum. It appeared to tumble across the short gap towards Roger in slow motion. When it struck the side of his neck, it had no impact.

He ignored her failure.

She did the same. With all the strength of her legs, heaving upwards from the soles of her feet, she swung her physician's bag into motion and let it fly.

It collided with Roger's ribs just as he fired at Sandy.

This time the shot seemed to make no noise. Instead Linden heard only the slug as it spanged off the stone beside Sandy's head and whined away into the ravenous lightning.

At last Linden's heart beat again. She drew breath; gathered herself to spring for Jeremiah—

—and the rim of the hollow on all sides exploded in a barrage of gunfire.

The sheriff's men.

Helpless to stop them, she watched muzzle flashes and streaking death, fire as destructive as any conflagration of wood and flesh. She would have cried out for the men to stop, to spare her son, but she had no air and no voice. She could only strain with all her heart towards Jeremiah.

As she moved, Roger's chest erupted in a spray of blood.

Still he did not release his grip on her son.

Then his life splashed into her eyes, and she could no longer see. Instead she felt the heavy punch of lead slap her down as if she, too, had been struck by lightning.

In that brief falling interval, she tried to find her voice and cry out Jeremiah's name; but she made no sound that he could hear.

An instant later, gunfire and Lord Foul's blasts burned all light away, and she fell into the bottomless night.

PART I

'chosen for this desecration'

Chapter One:

'I am content'

Gunfire seemed to track her down into blackness like a cannonade: each harsh blast drove her deeper. Concussions shocked breath and pulse and pain out of her until only silent cries remained. She had abandoned her son to bloodshed. She tried and tried to shout his name, strove to twist her body so that she might shield him from the rush of death; but she only plunged further into the dark.

She had sworn that she would protect Joan with her life. And she had promised that she would allow no harm to touch Jeremiah. This was how she kept her vows.

She was dying; was already close to death. Lytton's deputies had granted Roger the outcome he most desired.

Nevertheless she felt no pain. She knew only the force which had struck her to the stone, and which struck her still, ceaselessly, impelling her always deeper into the abyss of the Despiser's despair.

And Jeremiah—

Blinded by blood, she had not seen him fall. He may not have been hit: the fusillade might conceivably have spared him, when he could not have warded himself. But Lord Foul did not require his death in order to snare him. Linden herself had once been taken alive in Thomas Covenant's wake. If Roger had not relaxed his grasp on Jeremiah's wrist—

God, let it be true that Lord Foul did not require his death!

Yet the outcome would be the same, whatever the Despiser demanded. She had failed to protect her son, failed utterly. She had not so much as witnessed his fate.

Barton Lytton had probably survived. And Sandy Eastwall might live still. Prostrate, they had sprawled below the wild gunfire. They had no part in this.

Nevertheless everything which Linden had ached to cherish and preserve had been lost. She had failed her son, the frail boy with one red racing car clutched in his good hand. *No one else needs you the way he does.* Dead or alive, he must believe that she had forsaken him.

Falling, she could only pray that they would not be separated; that by some miracle he would be swept after her as she had once followed Thomas Covenant, rather than being borne away by Roger's madness. If the Despiser took Jeremiah, claimed him; *possessed* him—

The thought went through her like flame through the abandoned tinder of Covenant's home; and her own fire answered it, as extravagant as lightning. Without transition she became a blaze of passion and argence. She had fallen so far from herself that Covenant's ring responded. Its heat seemed to demand life from her when her heart had already burst; laboured its last. Hot silver knitted desperation into her tissues, her bones, and made them whole. It burned the stigma of Roger's blood from her face.

Jeremiah.

If there had been any justice – any justice in all the world – her anguish would have undone the darkness. Such power should have been stronger than loss and time; should have allowed her to fling herself back to the desolate hollow in the woods, and to gunfire, so that she might shield her son with her own flesh.

Did not the Land believe that white gold was the keystone of the Arch of Time? How else had Thomas Covenant defeated the Despiser, if not by sealing time against him?

But Covenant was dead. Alone, she contained nothing which would enable her to withstand the loss of her son.

Still the sound and impact of shots receded, smothered by her measureless fall. Their violence blurred and deepened until it became a low tectonic rumble, the ancient grinding of the world's bones. She could feel realities shift as she plunged through them, translating her away from the people and commitments to which she had dedicated herself.

And as she fell, she felt a blow strike her right temple.

Its force snatched a phosphene flare across the blackness in her eyes. The abyss into which she fell became vivid with consumed comets, bursting suns, scattered stars. She shook her head, trying to dispel them, but they did not fade. Rather they took on coherence, definition: like a cleaned lens, they resolved suddenly into vision.

She saw him sitting on the edge of the bed in which she lay: Thomas Covenant as she had known him on Haven Farm, gaunt with pain and empathy, his stricken gaze fixed on her. She saw fingers which must have been hers rise to rake their nails along the back of his right hand. Appalled, she watched herself smear her fingers in his blood and lift them to her mouth.

Her fall had carried her into the abysm of Joan's memories. With her white gold ring, Joan now wielded her power to rip open the barrier between worlds; summoning—

Another blow reached Linden. Again she rocked to the impact, and found herself stretched out in a bed in Berenford Memorial, her arms tied to the rails. At the same time, she sat beside herself, wearing a doctor's white coat and a plain skirt. In scorn, her external self snorted, *Of course you can bear it. That's what you do.*

Compulsory as hallucinations, times and places and identities reeled through her.

She had a son, a ten-year-old boy. He gazed at her earnestly, absorbing every word, while she held his face between her hands. He goes somewhere, she told him. I know he does. She loved and loathed Roger's features as though they were his father's. It's a powerful place. He matters there. He makes a difference. Everyone makes a difference. Now the face she held was Thomas Covenant's, the man she had known and loved and betrayed. I have to go there. I have to find that place.

He met her tormented stare as if he understood her; as if he acquiesced.

If I fail, she adjured him, you'll have to take my place.

His acceptance was another blow.

Time blurred and ran; and Linden folded to her knees. Even in death, Joan's pain consumed her. Kneeling, she heard fanatics preach over her like Roger or Thomas Covenant hurling imprecations. You failed him. You broke your vows. You abandoned him when he needed you most.

The preachers might have been Jeremiah.

Her knees hurt as if she had dropped to the hard floor from a great height. The figure before her had become Roger again, impossibly tall and cruel. Behind him rose a gleaming brass cross. Within each of its arms hung a bitter eye like a fang suspended in fire. Gothic letters on a banner beyond the cross announced like a shout:

The COMMUNITY of RETRIBUTION.

You are worthless. Broken. Empty of faith. Without value to God or man or Satan. Unworthy even of damnation.

Joan! she cried into the grinding silence. Dear God. Is that what they told you?

You must expiate, her son retorted. Sacrifice. But you are worthless. You have nothing to sacrifice that God or man or Satan would want. The sacrifice must have some value. Otherwise it counts for nothing.

Is that what they told you?

Only the man you betrayed can expiate for you.

Righteous and enraged, Thomas Covenant turned his back on her.

She was Joan, trapped in Joan's torment. As Roger and Lord Foul must have intended, she reached out with power and pain to draw others after her. But she was also herself, Linden Avery, and she had felt the touch of Covenant's ring. Reborn resources strove for definition within her: the health-sense, the spiritual discernment, which she had known in the Land. Tentative and fragile, her former ability to *see* opened itself to the abyss and denunciation, to the excoriation of soul which tortured Joan—

—and felt a Raver.

She knew it instantly, recognised its evil. Its craving for destruction was familiar to her. It called itself *turiya*: it was known as Herem.

The bare memory of its hunger *hurt*.

It had no face, no hands, no flesh: it was a black soul, the ancient foe and ravager of the great forest which had once thrived in the Land. Its presence was suppuration and horror, the old screaming of trees.

In Revelstone, one of *turiya*'s brothers, *samadhi* Sheol, had touched her. *You have been especially chosen for this desecration*, it had told her, glad of her terror. *You are being forged as iron is forged to achieve the ruin of the Earth. Through eyes and ears and touch, you are made to be what the Despiser requires.*

Then *samadhi* Raver had withdrawn. But that had been enough. Appalled, she had fallen so far into the knowledge of evil that she knew only despair; desired only death. To herself she had appeared as ruined as the wasteland which the Ravers coveted; lost in her own crimes.

Now a Raver had taken hold of Joan. Perhaps it had lived in her for years. Certainly it filled her now, feeding on her madness, consuming her with its voracious malevolence.

And it possessed Joan's ring. *Turiya* Herem could wield wild magic in the service of the Despiser. Coerced by the Raver, Joan had summoned others after her. Roger. Linden herself.

And Jeremiah—?

The woman she had once been would have quailed and fled.

But that Linden Avery was gone, unmade by Covenant's love and the Land's need. So many of the people who had opened their hearts to her had surpassed her: Sunder and Hollian, Pitchwife and the First, Honninscrave and Seadreamer. Covenant himself had gone to glory in the Land's name; had defeated

Lord Foul and passed beyond her. Nevertheless they had all helped her to become who she was now: not the frangible woman who had fled within herself from her own darkness, but rather the healer who had raised wild magic and the Staff of Law against the Sunbane.

In the abyss between worlds, Thomas Covenant or his son had just told her, Only the man you betrayed can expiate for you. Now he turned from her in contempt.

She stared after him with conflagration in her eyes.

She would not accept his denunciation. Joan had betrayed only her own heart. Fear had undermined her until she became too frail to stand: fear for herself, and for her infant son. A stronger woman might have made a different choice. But no one could condemn her for what she had done. No one had the right.

Joan herself did not have the right.

Inspired by passion and flame, Linden refused to endure it.

With fire she dismissed Joan's self-loathing. With white power she swept her own pain aside. The ring burned between her breasts as she shocked the dark with argence. As if wild magic were words, she shouted a blaze of defiance into the void of Lord Foul's malice.

Thomas Covenant – the real Covenant, not the tormentor in Joan's mind – had taught Linden that no contempt or cruelty or hurt could defeat her, if she did not choose to be defeated. The Despiser might assail and savage her as a predator attacked prey, but he could not deprive her of herself. Only her own weaknesses could wreak so much harm.

That she believed utterly.

Jolted by her sudden strength, reality veered again: a nauseating reel like the plunge of heavy seas. She seemed to tumble as if she had been snared by breakers until she came down hard on a flash of vision like a shingled beach.

For the second time in her life, she stood with Covenant and the rest of their companions in the depths of the Isle where the One Tree spread its limbs. There Seadreamer suffered and perished; and Vain met salvific harm; and her other companions came near to death. But this time—

Oh, this time it was not Covenant who raved with white fire, disturbing the Worm of the World's End in its slumbers, threatening to rouse the destruction of the Earth. Now it was Linden herself. In her hands she held more power than she could comprehend or control; and with it she lashed out in a frenzy of desperation, seeking to reclaim her son, and achieving only cataclysm.

Unchecked, her needs goaded the Worm to wakefulness. It lifted its vast head, seeking havoc. For a moment as terrible as eternity, it looked into her eyes with recognition.

No! she cried in protest. No! This was more of Joan's madness; more of Lord Foul's malice. But it was not: it was prophecy. She had regained her health-sense, and knew the truth.

If she did not quail and flee, this augury could come to pass. With Covenant's ring, she might indeed be capable of rousing the Worm.

Nevertheless she did not falter. Her fury held. She had lost her son, and would dare any devastation to win him back. In her scales, he outweighed the life of worlds. If Lord Foul believed that she could be daunted—

Abruptly reality veered again, flinging her from vision to vision. For a moment, she tumbled through a chaos of outcomes: moments of outrage and stark evil; instances of slaughter and betrayal, the cruel scything of death. Then she staggered to a halt.

Now she stood on a bluff overlooking a plain of rich life and ineffable loveliness. The ground below her undulated among hills and woodlands; luxuriant greenswards; streams delicate as crystal, cleansing as sunlight. Here and there, majestic Gilden trees lifted their boughs to the flawless sky, and vast oaks shed beneficent shade. Birds like reified song soared overhead while small animals and deer gambolled alertly among the woods. With her enhanced discernment, Linden beheld the vibrant health of the plain, its apt fecundity and kindliness. She might have been gazing down at Andelain, the essential treasure of the Land, bourne of its most necessary beauty; the incarnation of everything which she had striven to attain when she had fashioned the new Staff of Law.

This, too, felt like a form of prophecy.

As she drank in the gentle grandeur below her, however, a spot of *wrongness* like a chancre appeared amidst the grasses. It was not large – not at first – but its intensity multiplied moment by moment as she studied it in dismay. Soon it seemed as bright as a glimpse into a furnace, incandescent, malefic, and brutally hot. And from it writhed forth a fiery beast like a serpent of magma; an avatar of lava with the insidious, squirming length of a snake and the massive jaws of a kraken. While she watched, appalled, the monster began to devour its surroundings as if earth and grass and trees were the flesh on which it fed.

And around it other chancres appeared. They, too, gathered intensity until they gave birth to more monsters which also feasted on the plain, consuming its loveliness in horrifying chunks. A handful of the creatures would destroy the entire vista in a matter of hours. But more of them clawed ravening from the earth, and still more, as calamitous as the Sunbane. Soon every blade and leaf of life would be gone. If the beasts were not stopped, they might eat through the world.

Then her vision fell to darkness like the closing of an eye. And she fell with it, blind and dismayed; full of woe. If this were death, then she could only believe that she was being translated, not to the Land, but to Hell.

But instead of the shrieks of the damned she heard a voice she knew.

It was fathomless and resonant, as vast as the abyss: her fall itself might have been speaking. And it brought with it a sweet and cloying reek, a stench like attar, as vile as putrefaction.

'It is enough,' Lord Foul said softly. 'I am content.' His tone wrapped around her caressingly, like the oil of cerements and death. 'She will work my will, and I will be freed at last.'

He may have been speaking to Joan. Or to *turiya* Herem.

Then the shock of Linden's power rebounded against her, and she was flung away as if in rejection; as if the abyss itself sought to vomit her out.

For a moment longer, she could hear the Despiser. As his voice receded, he said, 'Tell her that I have her son.'

She would have wailed then: the pain would have sundered her. Now, however, she tumbled headlong through the tectonic groan of shifting realities; and she could draw no breath with which to cry out. Percipience came to her in scraps and tatters, granting her glimpses of emptiness: the unspeakable beauty of the spaces between the stars. The passion of Covenant's ring faded from her, quenched by the sheer scale of what might suffer and die.

Only the loss of her son remained.

Jeremiah—

It might be better for him if he had been slain.

Later she no longer tumbled, although she was unaware that anything had changed. She did not notice the smooth cool stone under her face and chest, or the high, thin touch of open air. Tell her that I have her son. At their fringes, her senses tasted the immense expanse of the sky; but the Despiser had taken Jeremiah, and nothing else conveyed any meaning.

No one else needs you the way he does.

Yet the old stone insisted against her face. Her hands at her sides felt its ancient, flawed strength. The danger of another fatal plunge tugged at her nerves. Along her back the breeze whispered of distant horizons and striding crests of upraised, illimitable rock.

Where was Thomas Covenant, now that her need for him had grown so vast? She was no match for the Despiser. Without Covenant, she would never win back her son.

She remembered Sheol's touch. At its behest, she had fled from consciousness and responsibility. But she was no longer that woman: she could not flee now. Jeremiah needed her. He required her absolutely.

Covenant was gone. She lacked the strength to stand in his place.

Nevertheless.

Finally she noticed that Roger's blood was gone from her face. It had clogged her nostrils, blinded her eyes: she could still taste its coppery sickness in her mouth. Yet it no longer stained her skin.

Despite the bullet wound in her chest – the death which she could not feel – she lifted her head and drew up her hands to confirm that she had been burned clean.

When she opened her eyes, she found herself on stone in deep sunlight. Finished granite formed a circle around her, enclosed by a low parapet.

She was alone.

Tell her that I have her son.

Once more she cried Jeremiah's name. For a moment, the sound echoed back to her, vacant and forlorn under the wide sky. Then it vanished into the sunlight and left no trace.

Chapter Two:

Caesure

At first Linden could not move. Her cry had taken the last of her strength. Haunted by echoes, she folded her arms on the stone and lowered her head to rest.

She knew where she was. Oh, she *knew*. Her brief look around had confirmed it. She had been here once before, ten years and a lifetime ago. This stone circle with its parapet was Kevin's Watch, a platform carved into the pinnacle of a leaning stone spire high above the line of hills which divided the South Plains from the Plains of Ra.

How much time had passed since her first appearance here? She knew from experience that months in the Land were mere hours in her natural world: centuries were months. And Thomas Covenant had told her that between his imposed translations the Land had undergone three and a half millennia of transformation.

If a comparable interval had passed again, the healing which she had begun should have worked its way into every stretch of rock and blade of grass, every vein of leaf and trunk of tree, from the Westron Mountains to Landsdrop and beyond.

But thirty centuries and more were also time enough for Lord Foul to restore himself, and to devise a new corruption of this precious, vulnerable place.

She would have to search for her son in a country which had almost certainly changed beyond recognition.

According to Covenant, the Land had once been a region of health and beauty, rich in vitality. In those days, the natural puissance of the world had flowed close to the surface here; and the Land's inward loveliness had been tangible to everyone who gazed upon it. But the Sunbane had tainted that elemental grace; had twisted it to desert and rain, pestilence and fertility. As a result, Linden had only grasped the true worth of the Land when she had at last visited Andelain.

There, in the final bastion of Law against the Sunbane, she had seen and felt and tasted the real wealth of Earthpower, the anodyne and solace of the Land's essential largesse. Her preternatural discernment had made its health and abundance palpable to her senses.

Inspired by Andelain and Covenant, she had striven with all her love and compassion to remake the Land as it had been before Lord Foul had launched his attack on its nature.

Three and a half *millennia*? Time enough, and more than enough, for everything which she and Covenant had accomplished to change, or be forgotten.

And the prophetic figure who should have warned her of her peril had given her nothing. He had denied her any chance to protect her son.

Dear God, how bad was it this time? What had Lord Foul *done*?

What was he doing to Jeremiah right now?

That thought stung her; galvanised her.

In her own world, she was dead, or dying. Her life there was gone, stamped out by a leaden slug. She had failed all of her promises.

Here, however, she remained somehow among the living, just as Covenant had remained after his murder in the woods behind Haven Farm. And while she retained any vestige of herself, only Jeremiah mattered to her.

Tell her that I have her son.

He, too, had survived: here at least, if not in his former existence.

As long as she could still breathe and think and strive, she would not, *would not* allow the Despiser to keep him.

Yet she did not leap to her feet. Already she knew that any attempt to rescue Jeremiah might well require months. She could not simply descend from Kevin's Watch and step to his side. The place where Lord Foul had secreted her son could be hundreds of leagues distant. Hell, she might need days simply to gain an understanding of her own circumstances – and the Land's.

She had seen herself rouse the Worm of the World's End. She had witnessed monstrous creatures devouring the ground as though they fed on life and Earthpower.

And this time she was alone. Entirely alone. She did not even know whether the village of Mithil Stonedown, where she and Covenant had found Sunder to aid them, still existed. She had no supplies or maps; no means of travel except her untrained legs.

All she had was power: Covenant's white gold ring, *wild magic that destroys peace.* Enough power to crumble Time and set the Despiser free, if she could learn how to use it.

Lord Foul had prepared her well to understand despair.

Nevertheless her alarm for Jeremiah had restored her to herself; and she recognised that she had one other resource as well. During her fall from her own life, she had tasted her former health-sense. Now she felt it fully: it sang in her nerves, as discerning and keen as augury. It told her of the cleanliness of the sunshine; of its untrammelled, life-giving warmth. It described to her senses the high purity of the air and the breeze, the sky, the heavens. It made her aware of the bold reach of the mountains behind her, ancient and enduring, although she had not glanced towards them.

And it warned her—

Involuntarily she flinched; jerked herself onto the support of her hands and knees. Had she misunderstood the sensation? No, it was there, in the stone: a suggestion of weakness, of frailty; a visceral tremor among the old bones of the spire. The platform did not literally move or quiver. Still the message was unmistakable.

Something threatened Kevin's Watch. It had been strained to the breaking point. Any new stress might cause it to collapse—

—dropping her a thousand feet and more to the hard hills.

Panic flared briefly through her, and she nearly sprang erect. But then her percipience gained clarity, and she saw that the danger was not imminent. She could not imagine what manner of force had done the Watch so much harm, when it had withstood every assault of weather, earthquake and magic since at least the time of High Lord Kevin Landwaster, a thousand years before Covenant's first appearance here. However, no such power impinged upon it now.

Kevin's Watch would stand a while longer.

Breathing deeply, Linden Avery closed her eyes and at last turned her discernment on herself.

She had been shot. She had felt the shock in her chest, the irreversible rupture which had severed her link to the life that she had chosen for herself.

Yet she was not in pain now. Probing gingerly inwards, her reborn senses descried no damage. Her heart beat too rapidly, spurred by Jeremiah's plight and her own fear; but it remained whole. Her lungs sucked in the clean air without difficulty, and her ribs flexed with each breath, as if they had not been touched by frantic lead.

Anxiously she opened her eyes and looked down at her shirt.

A neat round hole had been punched through the red flannel directly below her sternum. Yet the fabric at the rim of the hole showed no blood. Even that sign that she had been slain had been burned away.

When she unbuttoned her shirt, however, to study the skin between her breasts, she found a round white scar in the V where her ribs came together. Covenant's ring hung on its thin chain only an inch or two above the newly healed flesh.

Undoubtedly there was another scar in the centre of her back, a larger and more ragged wound, impossibly repaired. And her palm had been made whole as well.

Moments or hours ago, in the darkness of Joan's mind, she had felt power flare through her; the argence of white gold. Had she healed herself? Covenant had once done something similar. He had borne the scar of a knife throughout his remaining time in the Land.

Such healing violated every precept of her medical training. Nevertheless it was natural here. Wild magic and Earthpower worked such wonders. She had experienced them at Covenant's side too often to doubt them.

Still her former life was gone; irretrievable. She would never see Berenford Memorial again, or her patients, or her friends. She would never know whether Sandy and Sheriff Lytton had survived—

But she could not afford such griefs. Lord Foul had taken Jeremiah. She had lost something more precious to her than her own life.

Her healed scars gave her courage. When she had rebuttoned her shirt, she climbed slowly upright.

She knew what she would see; and at first the scene which greeted her was just as she remembered it. The circle of stone and its parapet had been smoothed from the native granite of the mountains; and its spire leaned northwards, towards Andelain. The sun, nearly overhead and slightly to her left in the southern expanse of the sky, suggested that she had arrived in late morning, despite the violent darkness which she had left behind. Confirming her other senses, the light showed her immediately that there was no flaw upon the sun; that no vestige or reminder of the Sunbane remained.

In this one way, if in no other, she resembled Thomas Covenant. She had not failed the Land.

Turning slowly with the sun's health on her face, she saw the familiar mountains rearing up over the spire to the south. Here, she recalled, the Southron Range jutted some distance northwards, forming a wedge of peaks which ended at Kevin's Watch and the north-lying hills. From among those peaks to the west arose the Mithil River, which then flowed along a widening valley out into the South Plains. But on the other side, the mountains were more strongly fortified. They stretched east and then north-east like a curtain-wall from Kevin's Watch to Landsdrop, separating the Plains of Ra from the distant south.

Linden had never seen or heard what lay beyond the Southron Range. East of Landsdrop, however, past Lord Foul's former demesne in Ridjeck Thome, was the Sunbirth Sea. And as the littoral ran northwards, the Spoiled Plains lapsed into Lifeswallower, the Great Swamp, which in turn eventually rose from its fens to form the verdant land of Seareach, where the Unhomed Giants had once lived.

Her head swirling with memories, she sat down in the centre of the Watch so that she would not fall again. She had already plunged too far: further than she could measure; perhaps further than she could endure. While her eyes scanned the crests and valleys of the mountains, and her memories gyred across the Land, she steadied herself on the stone's stubborn endurance.

She faced there because she did not want to remember Revelstone, Lord's Keep, three hundred leagues to the west and north: the huge granite habitation which Jeremiah had re-created in Lego in her living room; in the life she had lost.

But beyond the Keep, high in the cold-clad fastness of the Westron Mountains – so she had been told – lived the *Haruchai*. She thought of them more willingly, recalling their distrust of her and their fidelity to Thomas Covenant; their extravagant strength; their costly rejection of compromise.

Had they survived the uncounted centuries of her absence? Were they still a presence in the Land?

If so, she could hope for help.

And if the tale of what she and Covenant had accomplished for the Land had withstood so much time, she might find other allies as well. Covenant's first victory against Lord Foul had survived the telling and retelling of it over a comparable stretch of centuries. In Mithil Stonedown, Sunder had cast in his lot with Covenant and Linden because his father had taught him to preserve the memory of the Unbeliever.

She needed aid of *some* kind. She had to trust that she would find it somehow. Otherwise she might not have the courage to creep down the long, precarious stair which descended from Kevin's Watch. She would certainly not be brave enough to search the entire Land for her son.

Joan was out there somewhere, the summoner with her madness and her white ring. And Roger was there as well, serving his bitter master. He had to be. How else could Lord Foul have claimed Jeremiah?

At that moment, she felt Thomas Covenant's loss so acutely that it wrung her heart. She could have borne anything, faced any peril, endured any hardship, if only he were alive to stand beside her.

Yet when she had rested a while, she climbed to her feet again. Yearning for her dead lover was a weakness she could not afford. The Despiser had captured her son. While she lived, she would do everything in her power to win him back.

Wrapping her fingers around Covenant's ring for comfort, she shifted towards the western side of the Watch. She wanted to look down at the valley of the Mithil River.

She had hardly taken a step, however, when she froze in surprise and dismay. Her first glance past the parapet showed her that the entire vista from horizon to horizon was shrouded in a thick layer of yellow cloud.

No, not cloud, she corrected herself almost immediately: smog. It looked like *smog*. The air thickened to obscurity no more than a hundred feet below her; as dense as thunderheads. But it had the hue of pollution, the stifling and damaged shade of industrial exhaust. From the mountains behind her, it stretched as far as she could see in every direction, hiding even the base of the spire. Beneath it, where her senses could not penetrate, the Land might have become a wasteland.

And it was *wrong*. Her eyes and nose, the nerves of her face, even her tongue, were certain of that: the shrilling of her health-sense permitted no doubt. It was as vile as the Sunbane, and as pervasive, lying like cerements over slain flesh as though the vital beauty, the very Law, which she had once given her utmost to preserve had been arrayed for burial.

I am content. God in Heaven! What had the Despiser *done*?

Her percipience told her only that this acrid yellow shroud was an act of violence against the fundamental Law of the Land's nature. It could not reveal the smog's cause, effects, or purpose.

Instinctively she retreated into the centre of the Watch; hugged her arms around her stomach to contain her distress. Now she feared the descent from Kevin's Watch in a new way. The stair was exposed, dangerous. And it would take her into that yellow shroud. Remembering the Sunbane, she believed that the eerie smog would savage her open nerves. It might hurt her so severely that she would lose her balance—

While she squirmed in alarm, however, she heard a new sound through the gentle breeze. Its susurration was punctuated by the noise of scrambling, the frantic movement of skin on stone.

Where—? She looked around quickly; saw only the clean sky and the bluff mountains and the acrid shroud.

The sound appeared to come from the stair – from someone climbing towards her.

Because she was frightened, she dropped to the stone. Then she eased forward on her belly to peer furtively through the gap in the parapet at the top of the stair.

There she heard scrambling more clearly. Hands and feet against rock: hoarse, ragged breathing.

A few heartbeats later, a head emerged from the yellow cloud.

A tangle of rank grey hair straggled to the shoulders of a torn and filthy tunic which may once have been brown. A man: she knew that at once. An old man. His hands clutching at the treads looked gnarled and bent, almost crippled. She sensed their arthritic straining as if they ached aloud. His laboured breathing threatened to choke him.

He was mortally afraid. His ascent was an attempt at escape.

Linden's percipience was too sharp: she felt his difficulties too acutely. She had forgotten how to manage the sensations which inundated her. Carefully she retreated to the far edge of the Watch and sat with her back against the parapet, bracing herself for the moment when he would emerge from the gap.

What could he flee by coming here? There was no escape for either of them now.

Lifting Covenant's ring out of her shirt, she folded it in both hands as if she were praying.

With a gasp of desperation, he heaved himself over the rim of the last stair and collapsed, panting. His legs still dangled off the Watch.

The nature of his prostration told her at once that he had lost his mental balance a long time ago; had toppled into a kind of madness. And he had not eaten for days. Hunger and sorrow had taken his mind.

He reminded her of Nassic—

When she and Covenant had arrived together in the Land, they had been greeted by Sunder's father, Nassic, who had inherited a vague knowledge of the Unbeliever from a long line of half-mad hermits called Unfettered Ones. In spite of his confused grasp on events, he had done everything in his power to aid them.

A Raver had killed him for his trouble.

This old man might be in similar danger.

At once she set her own fears aside. Kneeling forward, she gripped him by his arms and pulled him fully onto the Watch. Then she crept to the gap and looked downwards again, searching the shroud for anything that resembled *turiya* Herem's malice.

Still the cloud baffled her percipience; concealed its secrets.

Come on! she urged the long fall. *Try* me. I am in no mood for this!

Until now, she had been helpless to save any of Roger's victims. But

Covenant's ring had power here. She was done with helplessness.

Nothing appeared out of the shroud.

Slowly she withdrew from the gap; returned her attention to the collapsed old man.

For a moment, she studied him with her health-sense, trying to determine how close he had come to death. Now that she could observe him more precisely, however, she saw that he had not exhausted his life. In fact, he possessed an astonishing resilience, in spite of his inanition. He was sustained by—

New surprise rocked her back onto her heels.

—by Earthpower.

Automatically she rubbed at her eyes, trying to sharpen her senses.

The old man was a being of some puissance. Human, undoubtedly: old, arthritic, and frail. Nevertheless an active pulse of Earthpower throbbed in his worn veins. It made her think of Hollian, who had been brought back from death by Caer-Caveral's sacrifice and the *krill* of Loric. Linden remembered her vividly as she had stood at Sunder's side, lambent with Earthpower made tangible and lovely – and mortal. Sunder himself had shared her numinous glow. Even the child in her womb had shared it.

But neither Sunder nor Hollian had been mad.

And there was something else in the old man, another ill in addition to his arthritis and his instability. When Linden first became aware of it, she could not define it. But then he groaned, stirred and raised his head; and she saw that he was blind.

He had a face like a broken rock, all ragged edges and rough planes, softened by an old tangle of neglected beard and a patina of ingrained grime. His mouth resembled a crack in dried mud.

And above it, his eyes were the milky colour of moonstone, devoid of iris or pupil. She thought at first that he suffered from cataracts; but when she looked more closely, she realised that his sightlessness ran deeper. His mind itself appeared to have rejected vision. In some way – perhaps by Earthpower – he had blinded himself.

With the Staff of Law she might have been able to heal him. She could certainly have eased his arthritis. But with Covenant's ring? She had used its power on herself successfully. Yet she hardly knew how she had done so. And she had been guided by her instinctive awareness of her condition. For this tattered old man—

She had little experience with wild magic; was not even sure that she could call it up at will. And it was called *wild* magic for a reason: it tended always towards increase; rampant flame; chaos. After his confrontation with the Banefire, Covenant had turned his back on the use of such power. He had feared that it would tower beyond the reach of his restraint: that it would rage and grow until it shattered Time, and the Despiser was set free.

Linden's control would not be delicate enough to help the abused figure in front of her.

If he had rejected sight, he might not want to be helped.

Nevertheless she was a physician: she wished to succour him in some way, despite the desperation of her circumstances – and, apparently, of his. Putting aside the surprise of his presence, she cleared her throat, then said cautiously, 'Don't try to move. You're too weak – and this place isn't exactly safe. I'm here. I'll try to help you.'

In response, he faced her with his blind eyes and broken mien. 'Protect Anele.' His voice was a cracked whisper, hoarse with exhaustion, uncertain with disuse. 'Protect—'

'I will,' she answered without hesitation. 'I want to. I'll do what I can. But—'

Who or what was Anele?

As if she had not spoken, he moaned, '*They* search for him. *It* pursues him. Always he is pursued. If *they* take him, he will not be able to escape *it*. His last hope. Poor Anele, who has lost his birthright and harms no one. His sacred trust—' He reached one trembling hand towards her. '*Protect.*'

A sound like a dusty sob escaped from his chest.

'I will,' she said again, more strongly. 'You aren't alone.' She had too many questions – and he was plainly in no state to answer them. 'We're in danger here. I don't trust this stone. And the only way down is the same way you came up. But I'm sure there's something I can do.'

Covenant's ring would serve her somehow.

'Power,' the old man croaked, 'yes. Anele feels it. He climbed to find it.'

On his knees, he shuffled towards her, groping with his gnarled hand until he touched her arm. Then, however, his hand flinched away as if he feared to presume – or feared the sensation of contact.

'*They* search for him,' he offered abjectly, 'but Anele tricks *them*. *They* can be tricked, a little.' Again he touched her arm, appealing to her – and flinched back. 'But *it* is not tricked. *It* knows where Anele is. *It* pursues him. If *it* takes him—

'Ah!' he cried out weakly, 'lost! All lost.' Another sob broke his voice. 'Anele climbed high. His last trick. If *it* comes close, he will jump and die.'

His distress twisted Linden's heart. 'Anele,' she responded, sure now of his name, 'listen to me. I'm here. I'll do everything I can. Don't jump.'

She had already felt too much falling.

His hand fumbled towards her and away as though he feared to believe her. 'Lost,' he said again. 'All lost.'

'I understand,' she told him, although she did not; could not. 'I'm here. Whatever happens, you aren't alone.'

He gaped at her blindly as if she were the one deranged, not he.

'But I need—' she began. Then, however, she hesitated. She hardly knew where to start. Even if he had been sane, she would not have known which question to ask first. She had to guess at the things he might be able to answer.

But she had spent years dealing with damaged minds. She had learned how to probe them gently. 'You're Anele?' she inquired quietly. 'That's your name?'

Begin with something concrete. Unthreatening.

He nodded as if in confirmation.

'And you have enemies?' A frail old man in his condition? 'What do they want?'

What was *it*?

His white eyes stared at her. '*They* seek to catch Anele. Imprison him. *They* are terrible, terrible everywhere. *It* will take him. *They* can be tricked. *It* is not tricked.'

His reply explained nothing. She tried a different approach.

'Why does it pursue you? Why do they?'

'Ah!' Anele broke into a low wail. 'His birthright. Sacred trust. Lost, failed. Anele failed. Everything, all lost.'

Apparently he was too badly hurt to answer in terms that she could comprehend. Perhaps her questions were too abstract; too far removed from his immediate plight.

'I understand,' she repeated, striving to calm him. 'I'm here. I have power.' He had said as much himself. 'Whoever they are – whatever it is – they have no idea what I can do.'

Then she remarked as though she felt no threat herself, 'It pursues you. Is it close?'

'Yes!' he returned instantly. 'Yes!' His head nodded vehemently. '*Protect* him. He must be protected!'

'Anele!' Linden spoke more sternly. 'I'm *here*.' Perhaps severity would pierce his confusion. 'I know you need protection. I want to help you. But I need to know. How *close* is it? *Where* is it?'

Without warning, Anele sprang to his feet. His blind eyes remained fixed on her, but his left arm gestured wildly behind him, indicating some portion of the shrouded cliff-face.

'There!'

'Now?' she asked in disbelief. Her senses had detected nothing. 'It's there now?'

'Yes!' Lifting his head, he shouted into the clear sky, '*It pursues him!*' Frantically he brandished his arms at the clean sunlight. Under their dirt, they looked as brittle as dry twigs. 'Poor Anele. His last trick. He will jump. He *must!*'

Then he began to weep as if he had come to the end of himself and even the vibrant Earthpower in his veins could no longer sustain him.

At once Linden stood as well. 'Anele!' she called softly, taking hold of his shoulders so that he would not fling himself from the Watch. 'Anele! Listen to me. I'm here. I'll protect you.'

A heartbeat later, however, a swirl of distortion against the mountains snagged in her peripheral vision: caught and tugged so hard that she almost staggered.

Still gripping one of Anele's shoulders, she turned her head.

God in Heaven! What's *that*?

Standing had lifted her high enough to see the thing Anele dreaded.

The sight of it seemed to crawl over her skin like a rush of formication. The eerie kinesthesia of her health-sense was so intense that she could hardly restrain her impulse to slap at the squirming sensation.

Hundreds of feet tall, it stood against the western edge of the blunt cliff-face: a spinning chiaroscuro of multicoloured dots like the phosphene aura of a migraine. Towering in the shape of a whirlwind, it seethed and danced hotly, each spot of colour incandescent with force, each indistinguishable from the others. Its initial impact struck Linden so hard that she could not focus on it clearly: it appeared to be superimposed on the impenetrable shroud below her, as if it swirled in a different dimension. But then her senses sharpened, and she realised that she was seeing the manifestation *through* the cloud. It was definitely below her, beneath the obscuring blanket.

In all the region under Kevin's Watch, that aura was the only thing powerful enough to pierce the shroud.

And like the shroud, it was *wrong*. It violated her percipience in similar ways, but more acutely, as if it were the distilled essence of violation. In that swirl, fundamental Laws which enabled this world's existence were suspended or distorted: reality seemed to flow and melt into itself like the confusion in Joan's mind. Any living thing swallowed by it might be torn apart.

And it was moving; advancing along the cliff-face towards the Watch. Soon it would be near enough to touch the spire.

Moaning in distress, Anele wrenched at Linden's grasp. Now she understood his reaction. She might leap from Kevin's Watch herself, if that aura came near her.

'Release Anele!' he panted urgently. 'It pursues him! He must escape!'

His alarm helped her to step back from her own. Pursues him? she thought fiercely. Not damn likely. His madness misled him. That fatal aura had no interest in him. It had no interests at all; no consciousness and no volition. Her senses were certain. It resembled a force of nature hideously perverted: blind, insentient, and entirely destructive.

Yet it continued to advance on the Watch, drawing closer with every beat of her heart.

'Anele, no!' she called with as much authority as she could summon. 'Don't!' Deliberately she turned her back on the aura so that she could hold him more tightly. 'I said I'll protect you. I can't do that if you jump.'

His white, staring eyes glistened as if they were sweating in terror.

Why did he think that the mad distortion *wanted* him?

But she could not phrase her questions in words that he would be able to answer. With the whirlwind approaching at her back, she could hardly think. And it moved nearer at every moment. Clutching Anele, she abandoned her confusion and reached instead for the memory of her fall to this place. The memory of wild magic.

Under her boots, the stone seemed to shiver in anticipation or dread.

Linden had healed her wounds somehow. Yet wild magic was not inherently apt for healing. Its impulse towards rampage limited its ordinary, mortal uses. She did not know whether she could oppose the aura with white gold. She was not even sure that she could muster its fire consciously.

But she did not doubt that both she and Anele would die if the seething swirl touched them.

Moment by moment, the aura advanced. At the same time, the shivering of the stone mounted; became insistent. Earlier she had felt a flaw in the spire, a suggestion of frangibility. Her health-sense had told her that the Watch had been damaged—

Its instability undermined her balance. Only her grim grip on Anele kept her from stumbling.

—but she had not been able to guess what form of power had done the spire such harm.

Now she knew.

The aura was not the only manifestation of its kind. Or it had existed for a long time – a very long time – roving the Land as its energies dictated. In some form, it had been here before.

Then it had left Kevin's Watch barely standing. Even through her boots, the tremors in the stone assured her that the next touch would be the last.

The swirl would reach the base of the spire in moments.

'Anele!' she yelled frantically, 'get behind me! Hold on! Don't let go, whatever happens. *We're going down!*'

With all her strength, she wrenched him aside so that she stood between him and the danger.

Obedient to her desperate command, he flung his arms around her neck, caught her in a hug of panic. When he shoved the side of his head against hers, his gasping sounded like a death-rattle in her ear.

Seething viciously, the aura approached the base of the spire.

Enveloped it.

For an instant nothing happened. The stone quivered and quailed – and held.

Then a rending shriek shivered the Watch, and the ancient granite twisted to splinters like torn kindling.

Chapter Three:

In the Rubble

Through a din like the destruction of the heavens, the massive spire of Kevin's Watch shuddered and snapped. Between one heartbeat and the next, it became rubble hopelessly poised a thousand feet above the hills.

Dust and flung detritus obscured the sun. Ponderously at first, and as poignant as augury, it sagged away from the cliff. Stone screams stunned the air as the platform on which Linden and Anele stood tilted outwards.

She had time for one last cry; barely heard Anele's lorn wail. Then the weight of so much granite took hold, and the ruined Watch collapsed like a cataract.

With Anele clutching her neck, Linden fell down the sky, accompanied by shattered menhirs – hundreds, thousands of them – heavy enough to crush villages. As she and her burden dropped, they seemed to rebound from one tremendous shard to the next, striking one to be deflected towards another. At any instant, they might have been smashed to pulp between stones; slain long before their flesh was flung against the hard hills.

Anele's grasp threatened to crush her larynx: she could not breathe. Already she might have broken bones. Her last outcry was the rending of Kevin's Watch, an eternity of terror and protest compressed into one small splinter of time.

And again she was struck, as she had been struck before: her temple collided with a boulder the size of a dwelling, and the whole inside of her head – her mind and her scream and her frantic heart – turned white with pain.

White and silver.

In the plunge of her translation here, she had given no thought to wild magic; had made no attempt to call it forth. Instead, beneath or beyond consciousness, she had reached out instinctively for her own strength. But this time she had already begun groping towards Covenant's ring when the stark *wrong* of the aura had overwhelmed the spire's ancient intransigence.

While the cruel bulk of stones swept her downwards, and helpless collisions battered her bones, Linden Avery became a detonation of argent fire.

In the imponderable gap between instants, she felt that she had dropped into the core of a sun. Its glare appeared to catch and seethe in the earth's yellow shroud, lighting the obscurity to its horizons like a lightning-strike.

Then rampant flame bore her away, and she vanished into a whiteness like the pure grief of stars.

Stars, she had heard, were the bright children of the world's birth, the glad offspring of the Creator, trapped inadvertently in the heavens by the same binding which had imprisoned the Despiser. They could only be set free, restored to their infinite home, by the severing of Time. Hence their crystalline keening: they mourned for the lost grandeur of eternity.

And wild magic was the keystone of Time, the pivot, the crux. Bound by Law, and yet illimitable, it both sustained and threatened the processes which made existence possible, for without causality and sequence there could be no life; no creation; no beauty.

No evil.

Joan held a white gold ring.

Lord Foul had taken Jeremiah.

Although she had failed at everything else, Linden took hold of Covenant's power and with it transcended the necessary strictures of gravity and mass, of falling and mortal frailty. Bearing Anele clasped at her neck, she became the centre of a fire which emblazoned the sky. Not knowing what she did, guided only by instinct and passion, she briefly set aside the bonds of life.

For a time which she could not have measured or understood, she passed among the sorrows of the stars, and wept with them, and felt no other hurt.

Eventually, however, the stars drew nearer until they became the pressure of the sun against her eyelids. Warmth soothed her battered face while constellations danced into dazzles across her vision. A vast silence seemed to cover her where she lay – a silence given depth and definition by the delicate soughing of the breeze, and by the distant call of birds. Under her, cool edges of rock punctuated the encompassing warmth.

A deep lassitude held her, as if she had expended all her strength, and could have slept where she lay.

Every breath hurt her chest. She felt battered from head to foot: a woman caught in a profound wreck, and surrounded by devastation. Yet she *could* breathe. As far as she knew, she had been merely bruised, not broken. The air tasted of dust and torn earth, and soon it would make her cough; but for now she responded only to its sweetness.

The stone beneath her seemed recently damaged. Faintly she tasted its granite pain, the raw hurt of new wounds. If she could have slowed her perceptions to the pace of its ineffable pulse, she might have been able to hear it groaning.

Somehow she had landed atop the fragments of the Watch rather than under them. And she had survived the impact. Falling so far, she had come down gently enough to live.

Wild magic again.

But where was Anele? She had lost him while she fell. His arms were no longer around her neck.

At the thought, she inhaled sharply, and immediately began coughing. Tears welled in her eyes to wash away grit and dirt. When the pressure in her chest eased, she found that she could blink her sight clear and look around for the old man.

Damn it, she had to be able to save *somebody*.

She lay amidst a chaos of shattered stone. Apparently the collapse of Kevin's Watch had struck a hillside and spread itself down into a low valley, burying grass, shrubs and trees under mounds and monoliths of granite. Hillcrests softened by verdure constricted her horizons on all sides. In the direction of her feet, the vale wandered away towards more hills.

Above her, a new scar marked the cliff-face where Kevin's Watch had clung for all its millennia. The sun hung almost directly over the mountains, suggesting that she had not been unconscious long. Yet the dire swirling which had caused the fall of the spire was gone. It had dissipated or moved on.

Still enough time had passed for the heavy debris of the Watch to settle, and for most of the dust to drift away. And the birds had apparently forgotten the event. Already they had resumed their piping soars and flits among the hills.

After a moment, she realised that the tumbling stone must have been seen or heard by everyone who lived in the vicinity. Simple curiosity might bring them out to look at the wreckage. The help she needed might be on its way to her.

Or Anele's enemies might come—

In spite of the intervening shock, she remembered his fears. He had been right to fear that aura of *wrongness*. He might be right to fear *them* as well.

Were there truly people in the Land now who meant harm to crazy old men?

She needed to find him.

If she could move—

Groaning and wincing, she shifted her arms in an attempt to prop herself up. But her limbs were as weak as an infant's: she could hardly move them. And when after a while she succeeded, the effort left her gasping. Although her bones were apparently intact, she felt as broken as the stone.

Sitting, she rested. Unaware at first of what she did, she gazed dully at her hands as though she wondered what had become of them. They seemed strange to her; pallid with powdered stone. Dumbly she stared at them, trying to determine how they had changed.

How had they grown so frail?

They were caked in dust, but the blood which had marred her right palm was gone. Like her other wounds, the cut which she had inflicted on herself had been healed. Even the blood had been scoured away. Still the sight of her hands disturbed her. Something was wrong with them.

She was too tired to think.

She had lost Anele.

Surely he was around here somewhere? She had saved herself. Surely she had done the same for him?

Vaguely she lifted her eyes to the cerulean expanse of the sky. Northwards only the crests of the hills defined the horizon, their slopes blurred by trees and brush. Behind her, however, mountains lambent with sunlight piled into the heavens. The more distant peaks held snow.

When she glanced back down at her cut palm, she realised that she could not discern whether it had healed cleanly. She could not tell whether the nerves were whole, or the tendons. If blood flowed in the veins, it lay beneath the reach of her perceptions.

From the Watch, she had not been able to see the ground. The whole region had been covered by a smog of *wrongness*. Now nothing obscured her view in any direction. Yet the sun shining down on her had lost its impression of beatitude. It might have been any sun in any world.

Suddenly frightened, she dropped her hands to the stone edges under her, probed their rough planes with her fingers – and felt only cool stone, superficial and crude; mute; lifeless.

The Land's yellow cerements had vanished—

—taking her health-sense with them. She had lost her sensitivity to the Land's rich vitality and substance. A remnant of her percipience had endured after she had regained consciousness: now it was gone.

Goaded by new fears, she forced herself to her feet, standing awkwardly on the broken stones so that she could search for Anele.

The rubble covered the hillside where it had fallen. Above her, massive fragments of granite balanced precariously on other stones of all sizes. She had not felt Anele slip away. For all she knew, wild magic had burned out his life. Or he might have been crushed under the jagged menhirs around her.

He was all she had.

But then, ten or fifteen paces above her on the slope, she spotted a hand clutching at the stone as if it groped for help.

Without her health-sense, she could only see its surface; could discern nothing about the body to which it belonged. Yet it moved. The fingers searched feebly at the rocks.

In a rush, Linden scrambled towards it.

She was weak, and haste made her careless. She slipped repeatedly on the treacherous rubble, fell; caught herself and climbed again, panting with urgency. Without her boots and jeans, she would have scraped her legs raw; but she took no notice.

When she reached the stone where the hand clutched, she found Anele among the wreckage behind it.

He lay on his back, blind eyes staring whitely upwards. With both hands he clawed vaguely at the granite as if he sought to dig his way out of a grave. His breath laboured painfully through his filthy beard.

'Anele,' she gasped thinly. Bending over him, she tried to force her senses into him; tried to see beyond the surface of his seamed, unwashed skin. But of the madness and Earthpower which had defined him earlier she caught no glimpse. He was closed to her now.

Oh, God. She did not *understand*.

A moment of sharp grief overtook her, and her vision blurred as she mourned the loss of her health-sense. For her, the beauty had gone out of the world. And she had tasted it so briefly—

During her previous time in the Land, percipience had exposed her to evils against which she had no armour and no weapons. The Sunbane and *samadhi* Raver had nearly shattered her spirit. Nevertheless she had learned to treasure such discernment. It had shed light into beauty as well as evil. It had enabled her to understand why Covenant loved the Land. It had taught her to view healing in a new way, less as a repudiation of death and more as an affirmation of life. And it had given her purpose, a reason to continue striving when her burdens, and Covenant's, and the Land's, seemed more than she could bear.

A Raver had told her, *You are being forged as iron is forged to achieve the ruin of the Earth. You have been chosen, Linden Avery, because you can* see. But Lord Foul had misjudged her. Because she *could* see, she had learned to loathe and oppose him. In the end, her health-sense had made her effective against the Sunbane.

She had lived without it for ten years now, but she treasured it still. For a while, the loss of it rent her heart.

However, she had no time for grief. The hole in her shirt and the scar on her chest changed nothing. She needed answers; understanding. And she hungered for companionship. Therefore she needed Anele.

She repeated his name more strongly. 'Can you hear me? Are you all right?'

He jerked as though she had slapped him. 'You!' For a moment he rubbed at his eyes as if he wanted to force his blindness aside. Then he rolled over and lurched upright. 'You are here.' Coughing at the dust in his throat, he leaned against the boulder behind which he had lain, braced his feet on a canted shelf of stone. 'I did not delude myself. You have saved me.'

Before she could respond, he fumbled towards her. Instinctively she reached out to help him. One of his hands found her arm, gripped it hard. With the other, he reached up to explore her face as if he thought that he might recognise her by touch.

In spite of herself, Linden flinched. But the old man held her.

'The Law of Death was broken,' he murmured, apparently speaking to himself while his fingertips traced her expression, 'long ago.' He held his head cocked to one side, considering her eyelessly. 'The Law of Life was sundered in And-elain. Such things are possible.'

She stared at him, baffled at first by the change in his manner. The angle of his head suggested a derangement of some kind. Yet his madness had apparently passed with the smog. He sounded sane now, in possession of himself.

Capable of answers.

'I'm Linden,' she told him at once. 'Linden Avery. I just got here. I don't know if you've ever heard of me. I don't know what's going on. But I—'

Abruptly he dropped his hand. With one trembling finger, he pointed at Covenant's ring hanging outside her shirt.

'And you have power. That is well. You will have need of it.'

His words disturbed her as if they had been pronounced by an oracle. He had become strangely knowledgeable since the collapse of the Watch. She did not know how to approach him.

'I was worried,' she responded awkwardly as she slipped the ring back under her shirt. 'You disappeared while we were falling. I was afraid you were dead.'

He cocked his head further. 'I feared you. You might have been—' He shuddered; and with his free hand he rubbed the top of his head roughly. 'The folk of this region are kindly towards me. Kevin's Dirt blinds them, and they cannot see me. Upon occasion they grant me food and shelter. But *they* are not blinded. If any Master came upon me, I would be taken and doomed. Therefore I did not seek you out.'

Cautious with him, Linden did not ask him to explain who *they* were. That question could wait. First she needed to know more about his mental state; his apparent recovery. Gently she enquired, '"Kevin's Dirt"? What's that?'

In spite of her care, he winced. Suddenly impatient, he demanded, 'You have beheld it, have you not? From the Watch? An evil which concealed all the Land? *That* is Kevin's Dirt.'

'Yes, of course,' she replied, confused. 'A dirty yellow cloud, like smog. But it's gone now.'

Anele snorted. 'It is not. You are merely blind.'

Floundering, she said, 'I don't understand.'

With a jerk, he cocked his head over to the other side. 'Do you behold me now? Do you discern what I am?'

'Of course—' she began, then stopped herself. 'Not the way I did,' she admitted. There the distortion of his mind, and the Earthpower in his veins, had been plain to her. Now she could not detect them.

'You are blind,' he repeated scornfully. 'Kevin's Dirt blinds you. On the Watch you stood above it. It could not affect you. Now—' He smacked his lips as if in disdain or regret. 'You are unaware of it because it blinds you. You do not see *me*. Only the Masters—'

Abruptly he tightened his grip on her forearm. Without transition, his manner became fearful. 'Do they come?' he whispered. 'I have no sight, and their stealth exceeds my hearing.'

Although he could not watch her, Linden made a show of looking around the hillsides, studying the slope of rubble. 'I don't see anyone. We're alone, at least for now.'

Anele clutched at her with both hands. 'They will come.' His voice shook. 'You must protect me.'

That was the opening she needed. Taking him by the shoulders, she held him firmly. 'I will. I've already promised that. And I've kept you alive so far. No one will hurt you, or trap you, while I can do anything about it.'

Slowly his features relaxed. 'From the breaking of the Watch,' he responded softly, 'yes. With power. Such things are possible.' He released a low sigh. 'I have failed my power. It was given into my hands, but I have betrayed that trust.'

His Earthpower? Linden wondered obliquely. Had 'Kevin's Dirt' deprived him of his nature, as it had blinded her health-sense? Or did he refer to something else?

But she did not pursue such questions. Instead she broached her own needs. 'That's right,' she began. 'I saved you. Now you can help me.

'Anele, I'm a stranger. I was here once before, but that was a very long time ago. Now everything has changed.' She appealed to him as she had so often appealed to her patients, asking them for hints to guide their treatment. 'You have to understand that I don't know what's going on. I don't know anything about Kevin's Dirt, or Masters, or that sick aura—'

'The *caesure*,' he offered helpfully. If his eyes had been whole, they might have been as bright as a bird's.

Linden nodded. 'All right, that *caesure*. I don't know what it is. I don't know what it does,' except cause harm and dread. 'I can't even imagine what Lord Foul is trying to accomplish—'

At the Despiser's name, Anele winced again. Shrugging her hands away, he crouched against the stone. His head turned fearfully from side to side: he might have been trying to locate a threat.

'The Grey Slayer,' he breathed. 'Maker of Desecration. He seeks to destroy me. He sends his *caesures* to achieve ruin. Kevin's Dirt blinds the Land. The Masters name him their foe, yet they serve him and know it not.'

'Anele.' Linden stooped to his side, sure now that he was still mad. 'I said I would protect you.' She did not believe for a moment that the Despiser's *caesures* were aimed at him. 'You know how powerful I am.'

Carefully she touched him again, stroked his shoulder, hoping to convince his nerves, if not his faulty mind, that he was safe with her.

'But Lord Foul has taken my son. My *son*, Anele.' This old man had once been someone's son, cherished as she cherished Jeremiah. If he could remember— 'I have to get him back.'

For Jeremiah's sake, she risked saying, 'That means I have to find the Despiser.'

Anele did not respond. She could not be sure that he had understood her. Nevertheless some of the tension in his shoulder eased.

'I don't know how to do that.' She took a deep breath and held it for a moment to steady herself. 'I have a white gold ring. I have power. But I can't help my son if I don't know where Lord Foul *is*. I can't even imagine where to look.

'Anele, I need answers. I need you to answer my questions.'

Still the old man did not speak. However, he appeared to be considering her words. She fell silent herself, trusting her hand on his shoulder to communicate what she could not.

After a while, he shifted so that he could sit with his back to the stone. His scrawny legs sprawled pitifully in front of him. His feet were twisted and scarred, gnarled with old injuries and calluses. He must have lived without the benefit of sandals for many long years.

At last he said, 'You have a son.' His voice was a forlorn sigh, filled with decades of bereavement and suffering. 'His birthright has been torn from him. Mine I have lost. I am not worthy of protection. I live only because I am the Land's last hope.

'Ask your questions. I will attempt to answer.'

Oh, Anele. His reply caught at Linden's heart. The last hope? Was that possible?

What had happened to him? How had he been so badly damaged?

Still striving for caution, she asked in a musing tone, '"Kevin's Dirt". Why is it called that?'

He leaned his head to the other side and looked around, apparently searching for an explanation. 'These stones do not know,' he replied gruffly. 'Kevin Landwaster they know, the last of the Old Lords. The Ritual of Desecration is written within them. But Kevin's Dirt is a human name. It is too recent to be discerned here.'

Linden did not understand. She was too tired; and the mounting ache of her many bruises confused her. She, too, had known the High Lord. Kevin's shade had accosted her in Andelain, trying to persuade her to turn against Thomas Covenant. The dead Lord had believed that Covenant's intentions would damn the Land.

His tormented spirit had been difficult to refuse. He was familiar with despair; as familiar as Linden herself. Yet in the end she had set her doubts aside to join Covenant against the Despiser.

Kevin's Dirt. It was not a good omen that Lord Foul's blinding shroud had been named for the man who had helped perform the Ritual of Desecration.

While Linden tried to comprehend Anele's response, the old man continued to study the shattered rocks blindly. After a while, he asked, 'Are you content? I must not remain here. They will discover me.'

She made an attempt to go on. 'How long—?' But her throat closed, choked by auguries and dust. She had to swallow several times before she could ask, 'How long has the Dirt been up there?'

Her companion shrugged. 'Twenty-five score years? Fifty score? The bones of the Earth do not regard such details.'

'And these *caesures*?' she pursued. 'Have they been around that long?'

He shook his head. 'I read nothing certainly. It appears that they have hunted the Land for perhaps five score years. No more than that, I judge.'

'And you?' Linden asked. 'How old are you?'

Anele sagged as though her question diminished him. 'The stones do not know.' An undercurrent of bitterness ran beneath the surface of his tone. 'I also am too recent. And I cannot answer you. My recall is disturbed. Have my parents perished? Did I receive my birthright from their failing hands?' He sighed again. 'I am uncertain.'

The more he spoke, the more confused he seemed.

'But you said the *caesures* hunt for you,' she objected. 'If they've been around for a hundred years, they must have appeared before you were born. You aren't that old.'

'Did I? It may be that I did.' By degrees, his bitterness lapsed into mourning. 'My mind wanders betimes.

'Certainly they did not threaten the Land when I was born.' His head fell further to the side as if he lacked the strength to hold it up. 'Yet I cannot be so aged. I have been harried beyond endurance, lost and alone, footsore and battered and hungry to the marrow of my bones. It is not possible that I have lived so long. My flesh could not have borne it.'

Softly he finished, 'The *caesures* do not desire me. I am scant threat to the Grey Slayer. Yet I fear them utterly. If they take me, I am doomed and damned.'

As Anele spoke, Linden's frustration grew. He had been born before the *caesures* began, yet they were older? Impossible. Clearly she could not trust his apparent sanity. His mind existed in fragments dissociated from each other, and he had lost the ability to combine them into a coherent whole.

Pausing to gather her resolve, she gazed around at the rocks and hillsides. If or when someone came to investigate the collapse of Kevin's Watch, she did not want to be taken by surprise. Then she returned her attention to Anele.

'What do they do,' she asked, 'these *caesures?*'

'They sever,' he answered. 'Dislocate. I cannot name it. Five score years is too short a time. These stones do not speak of it plainly.'

Sever? Dislocate? Vexation tugged at her restraint. With an effort, she fought it down. 'The stones speak to you? You can read them?'

In spite of Kevin's Dirt? Did his inherent Earthpower give him that discernment?

He turned to face her squarely. His white eyes regarded her like closed shutters, concealing the strange rooms of his mind. 'Look about you,' he said with a touch of his former impatience. 'The truth is visible here.'

Ah, visible, she groaned to herself. To him, perhaps: not to her. In crucial ways, she was as blind as her companion. And she felt so weak— She had eaten nothing for several hours; drunk nothing. And since then she had been stretched to her limits.

She only continued questioning Anele because she could not imagine where she might find food or water.

'All right,' she murmured. 'You already know I can't see whatever is in the rocks.' She had never been a woman who could read stone. 'Never mind that. Earlier you said the Law of Death was broken. And the Law of Life. What did you mean?'

'Only what all folk know.' His air of impatience grew as he answered: he may have felt as frustrated as she did. As if he were reciting part of a liturgy, he intoned, 'High Lord Elena wrested Kevin Landwaster from beyond death. She drank the Blood of the Earth and coerced him with the Power of Command. Thus was the boundary which distinguishes the end of life made fragile. In her folly, she violated the Law of Death.'

Linden had heard such things from Thomas Covenant.

But then Anele faltered. 'The Law of Life—' For a moment, he fell silent, angrily slapping the top of his head with both hands. Next he rubbed his face roughly. 'Do I read or remember? Nothing is certain, nothing sure. Have I heard a tale? Do the stones remember?' His impatience vanished, engulfed in sorrow. 'The fault is mine. All this' – he gestured wildly around him – 'Kevin's Dirt and *caesures*, the Masters and the dread fire of the *skurj*. All the Land's pain. The fault is mine.'

Shaken by his distress, Linden reached out to comfort him; but he struck her hand aside.

God help me, she thought. Protect me from people who punish themselves. She had spent far too much of her own life doing the same.

Sadly she said again, 'All right. Never mind. I can live without knowing that. Just tell me what the Law of Life *is*.'

She already knew the answer. She only wanted to keep him talking while she groped for courage.

'It is hope and cruelty,' he replied like a tocsin, 'redemption and ruin. It is the boundary which distinguishes the end of death.'

She had been in Andelain when Sunder and the last Forestal had brought Hollian back to life – and with Hollian her unborn child.

Surely thousands of years had passed since that fraught night? It had nothing to do with Anele. It could not. Nor could Linden imagine that it pertained to her dilemma now.

By its very nature, the new Staff of Law which she had fashioned should have stabilised the disturbed boundaries between life and death. And its wielders – Sunder, Hollian, and their descendants – would have wished to restore the Land's essential health. Surely their use of the Staff would have healed the strictures which separated the living from the dead long ago?

Such evils as Kevin's Dirt and *caesures* should not have been able to exist in the presence of the Staff of Law. Had her efforts for the Land accomplished *nothing*?

Everything Anele said carried her further and further from sanity.

Roughly she demanded, 'And you had something to do with it? It's your "fault"?'

In response, he clutched for the sides of her face. His hands shook feverishly. 'Gaze about you!' he cried. 'Consider the stones!' His eyes burned as if he had gone blind with terror and abhorrence. 'Do not torment me so.'

Trying to ease him, Linden softened her tone. 'Does the Law of Life have anything to do with your birthright? You keep saying that you failed somehow. You lost your birthright. Do you want to recover it? Is that what you mean when you talk about hope?'

None of this made any *sense*.

Anele answered with an abject wail.

Then he whirled away from her to scramble over the shattered rocks, heedless of his old flesh and brittle bones. She shouted after him urgently, but he did not stop. Groping for holds and footing, he fled as swiftly as his frail strength could take him.

Again she looked around. Had he sensed some peril? But she saw nothing to alarm her. The sky and the sun hung over the quiet hills as if they could not be touched.

The old man did not flee from her. He fled because of the question she had asked.

'Anele!' she called again, 'wait!' Then, groaning to herself, she started after him.

Her bruises had begun to throb, draining her endurance. Unable to move quickly, she concentrated instead on placing her feet and bracing her hands so that she did not slip or tumble. If Anele desired her protection, he would wait for her when his distress receded. And if he did not—

He was her only link to the Land's present.

When she had traversed half the rock fall, she glanced up and saw Anele standing on the rough grass of the hillside a few steps beyond the rubble. He had turned to watch her progress.

He appeared to be grinning.

Beyond doubt, he was a lunatic.

He had stopped just below a bulge in the hillside. There the ground swelled into an outcropping, as if under the soil a massive fist of gutrock had been trapped in the act of straining for release. His position provided him with cover from the east while allowing him a clear view over the rock fall to the western hills, towards Mithil Stonedown.

Had he thought of such things? Did his sanity – or his cunning – stretch so far?

Linden sorely wished that she knew.

At last, she left the broken stones behind, crossed a band of gouged dirt, and reached hardy grass. Pausing for a moment's rest, she looked up at Anele.

The blind old man held his head oddly askew, grinning at her open-mouthed. His smile exposed the gaps between his remaining teeth.

Despite his expression, the white glare of his eyes resembled anguish.

Linden felt a pang of concern. Without hesitation, she ascended the slope until she stood no more than a pace below him.

He was not tall: his head was nearly on a level with hers as she tried to gauge his condition; discern what lay behind his mad grin and tormented stare.

'Anele,' she asked softly, 'what's wrong? Help me understand.'

His grin suggested that he wanted to laugh at her. When he replied, his voice had changed; gained depth and resonance so that it seemed to reach past her towards the far hillsides, warning them to beware.

Distinctly he pronounced, 'I see that you are the Chosen, called Linden Avery. At one time, you were named "Sun-Sage" for your power against the Sunbane. I have your son.'

Then he began to laugh as if his heart would break.

Chapter Four:
Old Friends

Linden staggered backwards, downhill: she nearly fell. *I have your son*, her son, at Lord Foul's mercy. The eerie change in Anele's tone echoed the Despiser's resonant malice.

It was as though—

Oh, God!

—as though Lord Foul spoke through the blind old man.

She wanted to shout back at him, repudiate him somehow; but stark silence smothered her voice. Even the birds had ceased calling, and the breeze had fallen quiet, shocked still by the hurtful sound of Anele's voice. In an instant, the air seemed to lose its warmth: a chill crept through her clothes. The sun mocked her from its unattainable height.

Anele continued laughing in mad agony.

'That dismays you, does it not? You have cause. He lies beyond you. At my whim, I am able to command or destroy him.'

Stop! she tried to cry out, stop! but her voice choked in her throat.

'Which shall I perform?' he mused cruelly. 'Would it harm you more to observe him in my service, or to witness his death in torment?' He laughed harder. 'Wretched woman! I do not reveal my aims to such as you.'

For a moment, Linden could not breathe. Then she gasped, 'Anele, stop this. *Stop it.*'

Anele did not comply. Insanity or Despite held him like a *geas*: tears streamed from his white eyes. Barking harsh laughter, he took a step towards her.

'Yet this I vow. In time you will behold the fruit of my endeavours. If your son serves me, he will do so in your presence. If I slaughter him, I will do so before you. Think on that when you seek to retrieve him from me. If you discover him, you will only hasten his doom. While you are apart from him, you cannot know his sufferings. You may be certain only that he lives.'

His voice knelled in her ears. It was no wonder that the old man had lost his mind.

The woman she had once been might have covered her ears and cowered; but she was different now. In response, an abrupt torrent of rage flashed through her, and she did not doubt herself. Inspired by memories of argent, she surged back up the hillside like a rush of fire. As she caught her fists in the front of his tattered raiment, she seemed on the verge of wild magic, almost capable of erupting in flame at will.

'Foul, you sick bastard,' she hissed into Anele's weeping face, 'hear me. If you can talk through this miserable old man, I'm sure you can hear me. You're finished. You just don't know it yet. Whatever you do to my son, I'm going to tear your heart out.

'Your only hope' – her fury rose into a shout – 'is to *let him go unharmed!*'

Anele struggled weakly against her grasp, but Lord Foul did not release him. His lips trembled as he jeered at her, 'Fool! I have no heart. I have only darkness. For that reason, I strive to free myself.' His blindness sneered at her. 'For that reason, I do not relent, though my torments are endless. For that reason, you may no longer oppose me.

'No mortal may stand in my path. I have gained white gold, and my triumph is certain.'

'Just watch me,' Linden muttered. Deliberately she stepped back, letting Anele go as her anger took another form. She was too furious to bandy threats with the Despiser. 'Talk all you want.' And she did not mean to take her ire out on the old man. He was not responsible for the words in his mouth. 'I'll have more to say when I find you.'

Turning her back, she sat down on the grass and closed her eyes. Briefly her exhaustion became a blessing: she could sink into its depths and shut her ears to anything Anele might say.

I have your son. Oh, Jeremiah. Hang on. Please. I'll get you back somehow. I swear on my soul.

I have gained white gold—

He had access to Joan's ring. That poor aggrieved woman had been brought here. And she must have drawn Roger after her, as she had drawn Linden. Linden could not imagine that he had been left behind to die of his wounds.

—and my triumph is certain.

How many enemies did she have? she thought, aching. How many people would she have to fight in order to reach her son?

But she had more immediate concerns. She was near exhaustion and needed to concentrate on water and food. Shelter. Rest. If she turned her mind to them, such necessities would defend her against feeling overwhelmed.

The Staff of Law should have made Kevin's Dirt impossible.

Opening her eyes, she scanned the hills. There might be a stream somewhere among them. If there were not, she should be able to reach the Mithil River. As for food—

Surely treasure-berries still thrived in the Land, in spite of *caesures* and Kevin's Dirt? Long ago the Sunbane had been unable to quench them: they had endured its depredations even without the beneficent influence of the original Staff. At times she and Covenant, Sunder and Hollian, had lived on *aliantha* alone, and had grown stronger. If the gnarled shrubs had not been destroyed somehow, they should be easy to locate now.

Groaning at her bruises, Linden forced herself to her feet.

Anele remained rooted to the grass with his head on one side and moist distress in his moonstone eyes. He still wept, although he no longer spoke. Tears spread streaks through the grime on his cheeks into his ragged beard. His mouth worked in silence, forming imprecations or appeals which made no sound.

'Come on,' she breathed to him wearily. 'If you're done threatening me, let's go find water. And food.' Touched by his mute distress, she added, 'I'll start crying myself if I don't at least get something to drink soon.'

Perhaps he would comprehend that she did not intend to abandon him, and would take heart.

In a cracked whisper, he replied, 'You have delayed too long. The Masters are here.'

The Masters—?

Quickly she glanced around at the wide tumble of rock and the hills beyond; the rolling slopes on either side of her. But she saw no one, no movement of any kind—

Facing Anele again, she asked, 'Where? I don't see anyone.'

'Then you are blind,' Lord Foul retorted while Anele's features twisted in fear, 'as you should be.' The old man's chest heaved for air as if he were choking.

Linden raised a hand towards him, made her tone as soothing as she could. 'Try to stay calm. I said I would protect you. Just tell me where they are, if you can. Or point them out.'

Anele chuckled between painful breaths, but did not respond.

She started to turn away, then froze as a figure dropped out of the sky and landed on the grass half a dozen paces from her.

He must have leaped from the edge of the bulge behind Anele, nearly a stone's throw above her. Nevertheless the newcomer landed with feline grace and an easy flex of his legs and stood facing her like a man who had spent long moments waiting patiently to be noticed.

After her first fright, Linden felt a jolt of recognition. He was one of the *Haruchai*.

Panting, Anele plunged to his knees as if the tendons in his knees had been cut.

Relief nearly undid her as well.

The *Haruchai*— Thank God!

She had not known them when they were the Bloodguard, the guardians of the old Lords: faithful beyond sorrow or sleep. She had first met them as the victims of the Clave, sacrificed to feed the Banefire with their potent blood. After that, however, they had served Thomas Covenant – and Linden herself – with a severe and absolute fidelity.

For a long time, they had not trusted her. Committed to their own certainty, they had not endured her internal conflicts graciously. Nevertheless she had learned to consider them friends. They were men who kept their promises. And they had the strength to give their promises substance.

They demanded of themselves commitments more strict than anything that they required from others.

Friends, she told herself again. Answers. Anele feared the *Haruchai*, that was plain; but she did not doubt that they would aid her against Lord Foul.

Their name for the Despiser was Corruption. He was their antithesis, their sovereign foe.

The man before her had the characteristic features of his kind: a stocky and muscular frame; a flat, undecipherable countenance that seemed impervious to time; brown skin; dark curly hair cropped short. Above his bare feet and legs, he wore a short tunic made of a material that resembled vellum dyed ochre. A sash of the same hue cinched the tunic to his waist.

A ragged scar, long healed, marred the skin under his left eye.

If the *Haruchai* had not changed since she had known them, this man was a fearsome warrior, full of great force, prodigious skill and uncompromising judgment. Even to her truncated senses, he seemed impenetrably solid, weighty enough to have gouged holes in the hillside when he landed.

'Protect!' Anele gasped in his own voice. 'Oh, protect. You swore. You *swore!*'

The *Haruchai* glanced towards Anele. 'She cannot protect you,' he stated with an awkward inflection. 'We have sought you long and arduously. Now you are done. You will no longer threaten the Land.'

For her companion's sake, Linden moved to stand between him and the

Haruchai. 'Wait a minute,' she said unsteadily. 'Wait. Let's not rush into anything. I don't understand any of this.

'I know you. I mean I *knew* you. A long time ago. Back then, the *Haruchai* were another name for faithfulness. Don't you know me? I was hoping that your people would remember—'

She sagged into silence, momentarily defeated by the man's lack of expression.

'How can we know you?' countered the *Haruchai*. 'You have not spoken your name.'

Of course, Linden thought. She should have realised— Too much time had passed.

As clearly as she could, she announced, 'I'm Linden Avery the Chosen. I was with Thomas Covenant when he fought the Clave and the Sunbane. I don't know how long ago that was. Time' – she rubbed a blur of memory from her eyes — 'moves differently here.' Then she added, 'Some of your people helped us search for the One Tree. Don't you remember?'

The *Haruchai* stared at her inflexibly.

She stood her ground. 'This poor old man is terrified of people he calls "Masters". I promised I would protect him. I won't let you hurt him.'

The newcomer continued to stare at her. After a moment, however, he replied, 'We remember, though many centuries have passed. We remember the Lords before the Ritual of Desecration. We remember the destruction of the Staff of Law, and the slaughter of the Unhomed. We do not forget the malevolence of the Clave. The name you have given is known to us.'

The edge of discomfort in his tone reminded Linden that among themselves the *Haruchai* communicated mind to mind. They did not naturally express themselves aloud.

'It is spoken with respect,' he went on. 'And your raiment is strange. The same is said of the white gold wielder, ur-Lord Thomas Covenant, and of his companion, Linden Avery the Chosen. It may be that you speak the truth. Later we will grant you opportunity to persuade us that we must honour you.'

Then the *Haruchai* glanced at Anele. 'But the old man is ours. He has eluded us for many years. We are indeed the Masters of the Land, and we do not permit freedom to such as he.'

She regarded the *Haruchai* in dismay. The Masters—?

Damn you, Foul, what have you done?

The people whom she had known here had never sought to rule any aspect of the Land. Only the Despiser and his servants nurtured such ambitions.

Certainly the *Haruchai* had displayed no interest in sovereignty. They had defined themselves by their devotion to people whom they deemed greater than themselves; to causes which they considered worthy of service. Linden remembered vividly those who had accompanied the Search for the One Tree, Brinn and Cail among them. In her experience, no one had ever matched their fierce rectitude.

She would have been proud to call them friends.

Now they were the Masters of the Land—?

But the *Haruchai* before her had not finished speaking. 'Do not fear for him. He will come to no harm. We do not desire his distress. We will only deliver him to Revelstone so that he may work no ill.'

The Master apparently thought that this would reassure her.

It did not. She had been through too much, and could not bear to fail another commitment. 'You aren't listening,' she told the *Haruchai*. 'I said I promised to protect him. He's old and confused, he's no threat. And he's terrified of being trapped. He won't be able to avoid those *caesures*.'

'We name them "Falls",' said the *Haruchai*.

Linden ignored that. 'I don't know why he's so afraid of them. But I think they're what broke his mind in the first place. Being helpless is the worst thing that could happen to him. He's so scared – any kind of restraint might destroy him. Even if you're gentle about it, you could ruin what's left of him.

'I made him a promise,' she finished. 'You of all people should understand what that means.'

The *Haruchai* showed no reaction. He did not so much as blink.

A moment later, however, she heard an impact on the grass behind her: the sound of a body landing lightly. In alarm she wheeled towards Anele and saw another *Haruchai* already standing behind him.

This one bore no scars. He may have been younger than his companion.

'Where is your power now?' Anele cackled at her in Lord Foul's voice, 'the wild magic that destroys peace?'

'He belongs to us,' the new arrival said flatly. 'We will permit him no more freedom.'

Bitter with anger and fatigue, Linden turned back to the first *Haruchai*.

He had moved one or two steps closer to her.

'I *told* you—!' she began.

He interrupted her. 'I have said,' he repeated without expression, 'that we will grant you opportunity to persuade us that we must honour you. Until that time you must accompany us. We will treat the old man gently.'

'No!' Linden shook her head, infuriated by his impenetrability. 'You will not *touch* him!'

The *Haruchai* shrugged as if in dismissal.

Anele went on chortling. 'They are *Haruchai*. Did you believe that they would heed you?'

Roger Covenant also had refused to hear her.

Before she could defend herself, the *Haruchai* swept forward. Swiftly his fist lashed out; struck her in the centre of her forehead. Her head snapped back. The hills reeled drunkenly around her.

As she lapsed into darkness, she heard Anele's cry of woe.

Haunted by lamentation, Linden Avery rode a dark tide of pain and futility, as helpless as a dried leaf on a wave. She chose nothing, determined nothing: she merely reacted to events. The Despiser had laid a snare for the people of the Land, and they walked towards it blindly. She could not even warn them. They refused to listen.

Why should they heed her? She had no name for their peril. She had no idea what the Falls and Kevin's Dirt were *for*.

Jeremiah's plight was only more immediate, not worse. Lord Foul threatened the life of the Land, and of all the Earth, and she had no means to save any of them, except by wild magic. Yet any use of white gold endangered the Arch of Time. For that very reason, Thomas Covenant had forsworn his power.

Now the man she loved lay forever beyond her reach. No matter how acutely she had yearned for him over the years, she would never see him again, or feel his touch, or hold him in her arms.

She had learned to yearn instead for her son. Whatever happened, she intended to save Jeremiah.

Borne along by the current of her unconsciousness, she endeavoured to slough away all other considerations; to concentrate her whole heart on her vulnerable son. But the dark scend did not float her to Jeremiah. Instead it brought Covenant's voice to her ears.

He sounded as he had sounded in life: harsh and compassionate; driven to extremes, deeply wounded, and dear; full of comprehension and rue.

Linden, he said distinctly, *you aren't listening*.

Oh, Covenant! she cried out within herself. Where are you? Why can't I see you? Are you all right?

I'm trying to tell you. He seemed as strict as the *Haruchai*. *You need the Staff of Law*.

For a moment, he surprised her questions to silence. *I don't know where it is*. She might have wept. *It doesn't seem to work anymore*.

Violations of Law like Kevin's Dirt and *caesures* could not have flourished in the presence of the Staff.

You aren't listening, he repeated more gently. I said, I understand how you feel. It's too much to ask of anyone. Don't worry about that. Do something they don't expect.

Like what? she countered in tears. All I have is your ring. It isn't mine. It isn't me. It doesn't belong to me the way it did to you. I don't understand any of this.

Foul has my *son!*

Don't worry about that, he said again. Already his voice had begun to recede from her. Trust yourself. She could barely hear him. Do something they don't expect.

Then he was gone. She sobbed his name, but only breakers and seething answered.

Eventually a swell lifted her up to deposit her upon a plane of stone above the tide. When she returned to herself there, her cheeks were wet with weeping.

For a time, she lay still, resting her bruised body on the cool smooth stone. Her former life had not prepared her for physical ordeals. All of her muscles throbbed with over-exertion. In addition, her tongue felt thick with thirst, and her stomach ached for food.

Nevertheless those pangs hurt her less than the knowledge that she had failed to keep her promise to Anele. Covenant had told her to trust herself. He might as well have advised her to fly to the moon. Too many people had already died.

Groaning softly, she opened her eyes on darkness like the inside of her mind.

She lay face-down on stone worn or polished smooth. The air felt cool and clean in her sore lungs. When she tried to shift her limbs, they moved as easily as her injuries allowed. To that extent, at least, she was intact. She simply could not see.

But when she raised her head, pain lanced into her neck: whiplash from the blow she had received. At once, a sharp throbbing began in her forehead and the stone under her seemed to tilt. Cursing to herself, she lowered her head again.

Damn them anyway. The *Haruchai* she had known – Brinn, Cail, and the others – had not made a practice of striking down strangers.

And where had she been taken? Underground? No. The air was too fresh, and the stone not cold enough, for a cave or cavern.

Night must have fallen while she was unconscious. Or the *Haruchai* had left her in a windowless cell somewhere. Mithil Stonedown? To the best of her knowledge, that was the nearest village.

The *Haruchai* did not need cells to control their prisoners.

For a while, she postponed the challenge of rising to her feet. Instead she reached under her chest to confirm that Covenant's ring still hung on its chain around her neck; to reassure herself on its hard circle. Then she turned her attention to the scents of this space.

At first, she detected only grime and old sweat, the sour odour of an untended body: probably hers. Stone dust still caked her hair, clogging her senses. When she reached past those smells, however, she caught a faint whiff of water and the unmistakable aroma of cooked food.

Suddenly eager, she braced her arms on the stone, wedged her legs under her. Then, carefully, she pushed herself up onto her hands and knees.

The pain in her neck brought tears to her eyes; and for a moment the stone seemed to cant under her. Briefly she rested where she was. Then she began to grope forward, hoping for water.

Her right hand found an emaciated ankle.

It jerked away from her touch as she snatched back her hand. Hoarsely an old voice croaked, 'Leave Anele alone. Cruel Masters. Let him perish.'

Anele. Her throat was too dry for sound: she could not say his name. Nevertheless she felt a rush of relief. At least the *Haruchai* had not separated them. Presumably they were prisoners together.

She might yet be given a chance to keep her promise.

Shifting her knees to the left, she continued searching.

After a moment, the edge of her left hand encountered a hard shape. Quickly she reached for it.

It was round and curved: a large bowl. Its surface felt like polished stone, cooler than the floor. When she dipped her fingers into it, she found water.

At once, she lowered her pounding head and drank.

Every swallow was bliss on her swollen tongue and parched throat. She could easily have emptied the bowl. As the level of the water dropped, however, she pulled back her head.

'Anele,' she panted softly into the dark, 'it's me. Linden. I found water.'

The *Haruchai* had told her that they treated their prisoners gently.

A prompt scuffling answered her. 'Where?' her companion asked. 'Anele is thirsty. So thirsty. *They* are cruel. *They* give him nothing.'

One of his hands grasped at her side.

'Here.' She reached for his wrist and guided him to the bowl. As he clutched its sides, she added, 'Take all you want. I'm sure they'll bring us more.'

Anele's only response was to lift the bowl so that he could drink more deeply.

While the old man satisfied himself, Linden resumed her search. She was confident that she had scented food.

Their captors would have left it near the water.

Less than an arm's length away, she discovered a second bowl. It had been fashioned of stone like the first, but its sides were warm. When she poised her face over it, she felt a waft of steam stroke her cheeks.

Stew, definitely: meat and broth; vegetables of some kind. And— Was it possible? Had she caught a hint of *aliantha*?

Dear God.

Saliva filled her mouth. Sweeping the floor with one hand, she found a pair of wooden spoons. Without hesitation, she dipped a spoon into the bowl and tested its contents.

They retained some warmth, but were no longer hot. Mutton and gravy thick with flour. Small round shapes that tasted like spring peas. And yes, beyond question: *aliantha*. As her first mouthful comforted her tongue, it left behind a distinctive savour of peach tinged with salt and lime.

For the first time since she had arrived on Kevin's Watch, Linden remembered hope. The *Haruchai* had told her the truth. If they stirred healing treasure-berries into their viands, they did not intend their prisoners to suffer.

To that extent, at least, Anele had misapprehended the Masters. They had not fallen entirely under Lord Foul's sway.

Linden ate several spoonfuls of the stew while her companion drained the bowl of water. Then she whispered to him, 'Over here, Anele. It's food.'

'It is fatal,' he answered anxiously. 'They seek to poison Anele.'

'No, they don't,' she replied as calmly as she could. 'I've already tasted it. It's good.' Unsure how to persuade him, she added, 'They put treasure-berries in it.'

Immediately he shuffled to her side. '*Aliantha* sustains Anele,' he muttered as she pressed a spoon into his hands. 'Often naught else preserves his life.'

Together they crouched over the bowl.

She stopped before she was satisfied, leaving the rest for her companion. But Anele continued ladling stew into his mouth until he had scraped the bowl empty.

Half to herself, she murmured, 'Poor man, how long have you been lost?'

He did not answer. No doubt in his present condition he could not. His manner of speaking told her that his madness had reasserted its hold over him.

'In a minute or two,' she breathed absently, 'I'm going to look for a way out of this place – whatever it is. But first I'm going to rest a bit.'

Her torn muscles and bruises demanded that.

Turning away from Anele, she crawled until the tips of her fingers brushed a wall. Like the floor, it was formed of smooth, cool stone. She sat with her back against it and leaned her head on it to reduce the strain on her neck.

Water and food. *Aliantha*. And captors who were prepared to treat her kindly. The *Haruchai* had only struck her because she had opposed his desire to take Anele. Perhaps she did indeed have reason to hope.

If she could convince the Masters that she was the Linden Avery who had accompanied Covenant to the Land so many centuries ago, she might win back their amity. Then she would get answers. Guidance. Aid.

If.

You need the Staff of Law.

Otherwise she would have to find a way to escape. She would have to tackle the whole Land with only Anele's insanity to direct her.

Do something they don't expect.

What in hell was *that* supposed to mean?

She ought to move; start exploring. But she was entirely out of her depth. She hardly knew how to tread water in this situation: she could not imagine how she might extricate herself. And she was so tired— Her last night in her own bed, her last experience of comparative innocence, seemed to have occurred weeks or months ago.

Somewhere in the darkness, her companion sighed. 'Anele is weak,' he muttered to himself. 'Too old. Too hungry. He should refuse food, water. Better to perish. *They* only prolong Anele's life to hurt him. Hold him for *it*.'

He meant a *caesure*.

Quietly Linden asked, 'What will it do to you, Anele?' In spite of her fatigue, she could still be moved. 'What're you so afraid of?'

His voice shuddered as he replied, 'It severs.'

She swore to herself. 'So you said. What does it sever?'

'Life.' Anele moaned as though she had dismayed him. 'Anele's life. It is the maw of the Seven Hells. Betrayed trust. Failure. Sorrow.'

Linden did not press him. His distress restrained her.

And she remembered the Seven Hells.

During their generations of dominion over the Land, the Clave had preached that the Earth had been created as a prison for a being called a-Jeroth of the Seven Hells, whose domain was pestilence, desert, fertility, war, savagery, rain and darkness. Thus Sunder had explained the Sunbane to Covenant and Linden. It was the manifestation of a-Jeroth's evil; and it was also retribution against those who had failed to oppose the lord of the Seven Hells.

After so many centuries, Linden was appalled to think that any vestige of those teachings still persisted. Surely she and Covenant and their friends had discredited the Clave utterly when they had driven it out of existence?

The Masters name him their foe, yet they serve him and know it not.

Ah, God. She was out of her depth in all truth: floundering in quicksand. *Caesures* were the gullet of the Seven Hells, swallowing people away from life? The *Haruchai* served Lord Foul?

Catching her lower lip between her teeth, Linden braced her hands on the floor and pushed herself to her feet. Forget whiplash and bruises. Never mind exhaustion or murder. More than sleep or healing, she needed answers. She had to find out what was going on.

The pain in her neck undermined her balance; but she leaned against the wall and followed it with her hands. If nothing else, she might be able to determine the dimensions of her prison.

She had hardly taken two steps, however, when a flicker of light caught at the corner of her vision.

She flinched, clinging to the wall as if for protection.

She saw nothing. Blackness seemed to swim about her head, tugging her towards a fall.

Staring into the dark, she held on.

There. A small flame reappeared in front of her. She saw it through a thin vertical slit like a cut in the wall of her gaol. An instant later, it shifted out of reach. But she had *seen* it.

The slit had appeared tall enough to be the edge of a door. Or the gap between a doorframe and a hanging curtain—

Before she could move forward to investigate the opening, she saw the flame again. This time it did not disappear. Instead it came towards her.

A heartbeat later, a figure swept aside a heavy leather curtain and stepped through the doorway.

He held what appeared to be a cruse cupped in one hand; and from within it a burning wick flamed upwards: an oil lamp. The thin yellow light nevertheless seemed bright to her darkened sight. She could see his garments and features clearly, his short vellum tunic, the jagged scar under his left eye.

He was the *Haruchai* who had struck her down.

'Protect!' gasped her companion. 'Protect Anele!' Hissing through his teeth, he scrambled backwards to crouch against the far wall of the chamber.

The *Haruchai* gazed at Anele for a moment, then shifted his attention to Linden. 'You understand that we will not harm him. We seek only to ward him, and the Land.' He faced her like a man who could not be impugned.

However, he may have been able to sense her distrust. Stooping, he set his lamp down at his feet. Then he asked awkwardly, 'Are you well?'

Making him wait while she tried to calm herself, Linden glanced around the space.

The lamp showed her a square room that she could have crossed in five or six strides. The wall at her back – she stood to the right of the doorway – held a wide window sealed with rocks. Another curtain hung opposite her, filling a second doorframe; and a third marked the wall near Anele. Presumably they both opened on other rooms.

This place had not been built as a gaol. It may once have been a small dwelling, abandoned now to the Masters' use.

Perhaps they did not routinely take prisoners.

Holding that scant comfort, Linden faced the *Haruchai* again.

'How could I be well?' she countered sourly. 'You damn near broke my neck.'

The man returned an impenetrable stare. The unsteady flame of his lamp cast shadows like streaks of repudiation across his countenance. 'You will heal.'

Instead of answering, she held his gaze as she had held Sheriff Lytton's, daring him to believe that she could be intimidated.

He was *Haruchai*: his manner did not waver. 'Do you desire more water? More food? We will provide for your comfort.'

'Thank you.' His offer softened Linden's attitude. His people had already demonstrated that they meant to treat their prisoners kindly. 'We do need more food and water. As for our comfort—' She paused, wondering how much he would be willing to tell her.

If he had not struck her, she might already have blurted out Jeremiah's name.

Her captor waited stolidly. After a moment, she suggested, 'You might start by telling me your name.'

'I am Stave,' he replied without hesitation. 'With Jass and Bornin, I ward this Stonedown.'

Ward it from what? she wanted to ask. But that could wait until she had convinced him of her identity. And until she had discovered whether or not she could trust him.

If Anele were right about the Masters, they would strive to prevent her from reaching her son.

Rather than dive into those murkier waters, she enquired, 'This is Mithil Stonedown?'

He nodded. 'Yes.'

'Good.' That small confirmation of her assumptions made her feel stronger. 'I'm glad to find something that hasn't changed.

'Now, about our comfort—'

Stave faced her with no discernible impatience.

Linden took a deep breath. 'What Anele needs is to be set free, but I already know you won't take my word for that. At least not yet. So let's start with me.

'I'm Linden Avery. People called me "the Chosen". I came here a long time ago with Thomas Covenant.' Ur-Lord and Unbeliever. 'For a while, I was a prisoner of the Clave. So were a lot of the *Haruchai*. Brinn, Cail and several others joined us on a quest for the One Tree. We wanted to make a new Staff of Law. Eventually we succeeded.'

Several of the *Haruchai* had given their lives to make that possible.

'You said,' she continued, 'you would let me prove I'm telling the truth. When are you going to do that?'

Stave continued to study her. 'How will you persuade us?'

Linden stifled an impulse to reach for Covenant's ring. Instead she offered, 'You said you remember. Ask me questions.'

Behind her as she faced her captor, Anele made frightened noises deep in his throat.

'Very well.' Stave's manner stiffened slightly. He might have been listening to other voices than hers. 'Name the *Haruchai* who failed to refuse the Dancers of the Sea.'

His people set inhumane standards for themselves. They had no mercy for those who demonstrated mortal desires and flaws.

'Brinn and Cail.' She had forgotten nothing of her time with Covenant. 'Ceer and Hergrom were already dead. Hergrom was killed by a Sandgorgon. Ceer died saving my life.' Grimly she refused to relive the events she described. Her memories would only weaken her here: she needed to keep her concentration fixed on Stave. 'Brinn and Cail were the only ones left to hear the *merewives*.'

On his hands and knees, Anele crept forward a little way, leaving the protection of the wall as if he wanted to be near Linden.

The Master studied her with apparent disinterest. 'What became of Brinn and Cail?'

She sighed. Such things should have been common knowledge; the stuff of legends. Sunder and Hollian had heard the story. The Giants of the Search had participated in the events. Surely they had told the tale?

What had happened during the millennia of her absence? What had gone wrong?

Stung by loss, she replied stiffly, 'Brinn decided to challenge *ak-Haru Kenau-*

stin Ardenol. Otherwise we wouldn't have been able to approach the One Tree.' She and her companions had been lost in mist until Brinn had released them. 'The Guardian was invisible. Brinn didn't stand a chance.' Gaps in the gravid mist had allowed glimpses of his struggle. 'But he found a way. When the guardian drove him off a precipice, he dragged *Kenaustin Ardenol* with him. He bought us access to the One Tree by surrendering his life.

'We thought he was dead.' No living flesh could have survived the punishment Brinn had taken, or the fall from that height. 'But his surrender defeated the Guardian. Instead of dying, he took *Kenaustin Ardenol's* place. He became the *ak-Haru*.'

The Guardian of the One Tree.

'As for Cail—'

Linden paused to swallow memories and grief. Stave waited for her like a man who could not be swayed.

Again Anele advanced slightly. Apparently her tales meant something to him.

'Your people judged him pretty harshly,' she told the *Haruchai* when she was ready to continue. 'He was faithful to Covenant and the Search,' and finally to Linden herself, 'for months, and they practically beat him to death. They considered him a failure.'

And Cail had accepted their denunciation.

'But in spite of that,' she went on, 'he helped us against the Clave and the Banefire.' Against Gibbon Raver and the na-Mhoram's *Grim*. 'He didn't leave us until Covenant put out the Banefire, and we were all safe.'

All but Grimmand Honninscrave, who had given his life to rend *samadhi* Sheol.

There she stopped. Stave gave no sign that he had understood her answer; that the heritage of his people meant anything to him. Yet he was not done. In the same awkward, ungiving tone, he asked, 'When Cail departed from you, where did he go?'

Again Linden restrained an impulse to reach for Covenant's ring. 'Your people called him a failure,' she repeated. 'Where else could he go? He went to look for the *merewives*.'

Their song had planted a glamour in his soul which he had not wished to refuse. Bereft of home and kinship and purpose, he had embarked on a quest for the depths of the sea.

If Stave challenged her further, she feared that she would rage at him. Like all of those who had been lost in the Land's service, Brinn and Cail deserved more respect than he appeared to give them.

However, he did not demand more answers. Instead he studied her flatly. His mien conveyed an impression of absence, as if he were no longer entirely present in the room. Then without transition he seemed to return. Holding both fists together at the level of his heart with his arms extended, he gave her a formal bow.

'You are Linden Avery the Chosen,' he said uncomfortably, 'as you have declared. We do not doubt you.

'Be free among us.' Reaching behind him, he held the curtain aside for her. 'Tell us how we may honour your fidelity to ur-Lord Thomas Covenant and your triumph over Corruption.'

Sudden relief nearly dropped Linden to her knees. Thank God! She had hardly dared to acknowledge how badly she needed his aid: his, and that of all the *Haruchai*.

She let her head drop mutely, a bow of her own to repay his acceptance. *You need the Staff of Law.* Perhaps now she would be able to begin her search.

Scrambling forward, Anele startled her by throwing his arms around her calves. 'Free Anele!' he panted. 'Oh, free him. *They* will slay him and name it kindness.'

Linden looked down at his face. Shadows shed by the shifting flame of the lamp seemed to chase a stream of expressions across his visage: terror and hope, disgust, profound bafflement. Light in flickers turned his moonstone eyes to milk.

He must have meant that as a prisoner he would be exposed to a *caesure*. The *Haruchai* had never been killers. They fought with transcendent skill: they slew when the exigencies which they served required it. But to harm a forlorn creature like Anele was surely beneath them.

Yet she had promised the old man her care. She could not set aside her word merely because she was weak and in need.

Groaning to herself, she dragged up her head to meet Stave's gaze.

'You heard him.' The words sighed between her lips. 'Honour me by letting him go. He's just a crazy old man.' A madman rife with secrets and inbred Earthpower. 'I'll make sure he doesn't hurt anyone.'

Stave regarded her implacably. 'Linden Avery,' he replied at last, 'we regret that you have asked this of us. We wish to honour you, but in this we will not comply. We have taken upon ourselves the guardianship of the Land. We are its Masters because we cannot preserve the Land from Corruption in any other way. We do not permit such beings as this Anele to work their will. They serve Corruption, whatever they may believe of themselves.'

Anele clung harder to Linden's legs, breathing in sharp gasps like mouthfuls of dread. If he leaned on her, he would topple her to the floor. Her sense of balance already had too many flaws.

'Anele.' She stooped to him, urged him to ease his grasp. 'I won't leave you. You can trust me.' The thought of freedom blew to dust in her chest. 'If the Masters won't let you go, I won't go either. I'll stay with you until they come to their senses.'

She knew the *Haruchai* too well to believe that they would change their minds.

Anele groaned as if she had betrayed him. Dropping his head, he pressed his face against her shins. However, he loosened his hold slightly; enough to let her keep her feet.

Like a shrug, Stave released the curtain. The leather fell back into place, swaying heavily.

'All right,' Linden told him faintly. 'I'm staying here. But I need answers. I've been away for a long time. I need to know what's going on.'

The *Haruchai* acquiesced with a slight nod.

She still did not know whether she could trust him.

She ached to learn who held the Staff of Law – and why it had apparently lost its effectiveness. But she withheld those questions. First she needed to test Stave as he had tested her; needed to hear him prove himself.

She wobbled for a moment, barely caught herself. 'Forgive me,' she breathed as though he might disdain her weakness. 'I'm very tired. It's hard to think.'

'What is it about Anele that worries you? Why is it so important to keep him prisoner?'

What harm could the poor old man possibly do?

Stolidly Stave responded, 'He is a man of Earthpower.'

'You can *see* that?' Anele had told her that the Masters were not hampered by Kevin's Dirt, but she had been suspicious of his sanity.

'You have stood upon Kevin's Watch, have you not?' the *Haruchai* replied like a shrug. 'We felt the force of wild magic there. From that height, you surely beheld a yellow cloud like a shroud upon the Land. Did it not appear to cloak the Land in evil?' When she nodded, he said, 'It is named Kevin's Dirt. It has blinded the folk of the Land. It deprives them of their' – he seemed to search for a word – 'penetration. The life of the Land has been closed to them.

'But we are *Haruchai*. We retain our discernment. Thus we are able to guard the Land.'

In spite of his mental confusion, Anele had told her the truth – about a number of things.

But Stave's explanation raised another question. Guard the Land from *what*? He and his people were strong and fearless; but they had no power to oppose evils like Kevin's Dirt and the Falls. She was not sure that they could *be* opposed.

What *else* threatened the Land?

She kept that fear to herself, however. She did not mean to be distracted from Anele's plight.

'All right,' she repeated. 'He's full of Earthpower. So what? How does that make him dangerous?'

'We do not know,' Stave admitted. 'Yet the Earthpower is his. It cannot be taken from him. Therefore we will not release him.'

'Because you think he might use it someday? What's wrong with that?'

It was *Earthpower*, the vital substance of the Land, and infinitely precious.

'You do not comprehend,' the *Haruchai* informed her dispassionately. 'Any use of Earthpower serves Corruption.'

Now Linden stared at him in dismay. 'What, *Earthpower*? You think *Earthpower* is wrong?'

How could any sentient being consider the spirit and essence of the Land evil?

Straining at her knees, Anele gasped, 'Do not permit *them*! *They* are fierce and terrible. Can you not see? *They* will destroy Anele.' Then he cried out, 'He is the hope of the Land!'

Convulsively he began to cough, as if he were suffocating on sorrow.

Stave ignored the old man. 'You are indeed weary, Linden Avery,' he stated. 'You have not heard me. Earthpower is not "wrong". That is impossible. My words were that any *use* of Earthpower serves Corruption.'

Linden reeled inwardly, staggered by too many assaults on her perceptions. *He is the hope of the Land*— Who, *Anele*? How? And how could using Earthpower serve Lord Foul? The two were fundamentally antithetical. *Any use*—? How in sanity's name had Stave's people reached such a grotesque conclusion?

She could not—

Suddenly urgent, she stooped again, clasping her hands to the sides of Anele's face to demand his attention. 'Anele, listen to me. I heard you. I won't forget. But I can't deal with this many questions at the same time. I need you to let go of me. I need you to be patient. Before I do anything else, I have to concentrate on what Stave is saying.

'I'll stay with you. I'll get to the bottom of all this.' Somehow. 'But first you have to let go.'

Anele's eyes stared into hers blindly. Bits and streaks of lamplight cast desperation across his features. Between bursts of coughing, he groaned deep in his chest.

By slow increments, he released her.

When his arms had finally dropped free, he crawled back to the rear wall and curled himself against it as though he found more comfort in blank stone than in her avowals.

Cursing to herself, Linden faced the *Haruchai* again.

'You'd better explain yourself,' she said darkly. 'Earthpower is good, but using it isn't?' All life in the Land throve on Earthpower. 'How is that even possible?'

And who in hell gave you the right to judge the natural essence of any living thing?

Stave may have shrugged: shadows made her uncertain. The scar on his cheek gleamed like a small grin in the wavering light. 'We do not account for it,' he replied. 'That is not our place. We lack the lore for such explanations. We only remember, and learn.

'But the Staff of Law which you formed was soon lost. Doubtless if it had remained in wise hands, the peril of Earthpower would be diminished.

'You are Linden—'

'Just a minute.' Without knowing what she did, she covered her ears to close out his words; as if she might cause them to be unsaid. 'Give me a minute.'

The Staff was *lost*? That explained—

It explained too much.

But it should have been impossible. Soon lost— People like Sunder and Hollian would not have been careless with something so precious. And after his defeat Lord Foul would have needed centuries, millennia, to recover his strength.

The touch of hope which she had felt earlier fell to ashes as she lowered her hands. Without the Staff of Law, the Land was effectively defenceless. Cryptic evils like the *caesures* and Kevin's Dirt might prove as ruinous as the Sunbane had ever been.

'This is terrible,' she began weakly. 'I had no idea.' She could barely force herself to meet Stave's flat gaze. 'I don't know what to say.'

Unconscious, she had heard Covenant tell her, *You need the Staff of Law.* But if the Staff were lost— Lord Foul may have sent Covenant's voice to taunt her, as he had caused her to be tormented during her translation to the Land.

'Who lost it? How could this happen?'

Anele squirmed against the wall, apparently trying to find a comfortable position.

'We do not know what transpired,' the *Haruchai* replied. 'We were not present. We know only that the new Staff of Law was delivered into the hands of the Graveler Sunder and the eh-Brand Hollian when the Sunbane had been quenched. Among their kind, they were long-lived, and for perhaps five score years they served the Land with great care, healing what they could and easing what they could not. Without them, many villages would not have survived the abrupt cessation of the Sunbane, for the folk of the Land knew no other way to live.

'Yet at last Sunder and Hollian grew weary and wished to set aside their labours. To their son they gave the Staff so that he might continue their service. Of a sudden, however, he disappeared, and the Staff with him.' A liquid rattle disturbed Anele's respiration. 'We have discovered no account of his doom. The Staff has not been found, though the *Haruchai* and the folk of the Land sought for it long and arduously.'

Stricken, Linden sighed, 'All right. Go on. I just' – weakly she retreated to the nearest wall and slid down it to the floor – 'just need to sit down.'

She lacked the courage to hear the rest of Stave's explanation on her feet.

Apparently considerate, he allowed her a moment to compose herself. Then he began again.

'You are Linden Avery the Chosen. The *Haruchai* are known to you. You must grasp that to speak as you do is' – again he hunted for the right word – 'graceless for us. Our thoughts are not easily contained in uttered speech. I can only assure you that we remember, and learn.

'And we remember much.

'The *Haruchai* recall High Lord Kevin son of Loric in his grandeur, with Revelstone his glorious habitation, and all the Council at his side in strength and peace.'

As he continued, Stave's voice took on a slight sing-song cadence. Occasionally he touched on details which had been mentioned to Linden by Covenant and others, but most of what he said was new to her.

'Many times many centuries ago,' he related, 'the *Haruchai* marched from their icy fastness in the Westron Mountains seeking opposition against which they might measure themselves. They had no wish to diminish or command those who dwelt elsewhere. Rather they sought to discover their own true strength in contest. Therefore they entered the Land. And therefore, when they had seen the might of High Lord Kevin and felt the astonishment of his works, our distant ancestors challenged him.

'However, he declined contention. He desired only peace and beauty, he treasured the richness of the Earth's life, and he welcomed the *Haruchai* in friendship and honour.

'Your words will not convey his effect upon our people. Above all else, they desired to show themselves equal to those admirable Lords. Because they could not test themselves in combat, they elected rather to demonstrate their worth in service.

'Together they swore an undying Vow, enabled and preserved by Earthpower. They became the Bloodguard, five hundred *Haruchai* who set aside the fierce love of their women and the stark beauty of their homes and who neither slept nor rested nor wavered in the Lords' defence. If one were slain in that service, the Vow brought another to take his place.

'For centuries the Bloodguard kept faith. They knew the marvels of Andelain and the eldritch Forests, extravagant with Earthpower. They knew the love and fealty of the Unhomed, the Giants of Seareach. They knew the broad backs and strong thews and boundless fidelity of the Ranyhyn, the great horses of Ra, in whom the Earthpower shone abundantly. In their Vow, the Bloodguard themselves became men of wonder.'

An undercurrent in Stave's tone suggested that he would have gladly lived in that ancient time; shared that Vow.

'Yet High Lord Kevin's greatness was misled by Corruption. In his love of peace and health, he countenanced Corruption's place among the Council of Lords, not recognising the truth of the Despiser. And from that honourable blindness arose the enduring ills which have befallen the Land. For when Corruption unveiled his face, he had grown too puissant to be defeated in any contest of arms and powers, though the attempt was made at great cost.

'The Bloodguard burned to challenge the Despiser themselves, to exceed his might with their own valour. They believed that they were indomitable. Corruption had not yet taught them otherwise.

'But the High Lord forbade them. He could not bear to chance that they might fail and fall. Concealing the darkness in his heart, he ordered the Bloodguard from the Land. And because they honoured him – because they trusted him – they obeyed his will, dispersing themselves among the mountains.'

A note of sadness entered the faint music of Stave's tone. 'They did not grasp that darkness had mastered the High Lord's heart. In despair he had conceived a stratagem of desperation. By his command, both the Bloodguard and the Unhomed were barred from the Upper Land. Likewise he sent the folk of the Land from their homes and instructed the Ramen to guide the Ranyhyn away. Then he met with Corruption in Kiril Threndor, and there challenged the Despiser to the Ritual of Desecration.'

Bits of lamplight reflected from Stave's gaze as if his eyes were full of embers and kindling, primed for fire.

'It is said that Corruption acceded gleefully. Desecration is his demesne, and he knew as High Lord Kevin did not that from such an expression of pain no life or being or power could emerge unscathed.'

Linden lowered her head to her knees to rest her throbbing neck. She remembered Kevin's tormented shade as keenly as the cut of a blade.

Anele lay hugging himself with his knees against his chest. He had turned to face the wall, away from Linden and Stave. He may have fallen asleep.

'Together,' Stave continued, 'Corruption and the Landwaster wrought devastation. In that Ritual, the old Lords and many of their most precious works were swept from the Land. Much of beauty was crippled, and much destroyed utterly. When those who had been dispersed returned to the Land, they found a wilderland where they had left vitality and health. A thousand years passed before the many healings of the new Lords bore fruit, and the beauty which belonged to the Land could grow anew.'

There the *Haruchai* paused briefly.

Linden did not raise her head. She did not want to see sparks gather into conflagration in his eyes.

When Stave resumed, however, his voice had regained its familiar dispassion.

'From Kevin Landwaster, the Bloodguard learned the peril of trust. Linden Avery, you have felt the doubt of the *Haruchai*. You know that these words are truth.'

She did indeed. The persistent suspicions of Brinn, Cail and their companions had caused her more pain than she could recall without trembling. But she said nothing that might deflect Stave's narrative.

'The Bloodguard served the new Council as they had served the old. Once again, they honoured the Giants and the Ranyhyn. Where they could, they gave battle to Corruption's minions. But they had learned to doubt, and now they did not relax their vigilance, or grant unquestioning compliance to any act or choice of the Lords.'

Once more the cadences of distant singing claimed Stave's tone. 'Yet their strength was proven weakness. In the battles of the new Lords against Corruption's armies, the Unhomed, whom the Bloodguard loved, were utterly destroyed. Confronting a Raver in the flesh of a Giant – a Raver that held a fragment of the Illearth Stone and was thereby made extravagant in power and malice – the Giants could not rouse themselves to oppose their own doom. Therefore they were slaughtered.

'There the Bloodguard glimpsed the onset of a new Desecration. For that reason, they determined to take the Despiser's defeat into their own hands. When the Illearth Stone had been wrested from the Raver's hand, three of the

Bloodguard, Korik, Sill and Doar, claimed that fragment of great evil. Seeking to prevent a greater ruin, they fulfilled the desire of all the Bloodguard to challenge Corruption.'

Now Stave's tone hinted at bitterness. 'They were mastered easily and entirely. Their skill and fidelity had no force against Despite. They were enslaved. They were maimed to resemble the Unbeliever. And they were dispatched to Revelstone to declare the Lords' last defeat.

'There the Vow was broken.' Vistas of sorrow filled the background of his voice. 'The Bloodguard were *Haruchai*. They could not suffer it that they had been so turned against themselves. The beauty and grandeur which had inspired the Vow required flawless service, and they had shown themselves flawed. Earthpower had enabled their service, but it had not preserved them from dishonour.

'In the name of the purity which they had failed to equal, the *Haruchai* returned to their cold homes, turning their backs in shame on the Council and the Ranyhyn, on Andelain and all the Land. Aided by the last of the Unhomed, ur-Lord Thomas Covenant defeated Corruption, and so the Land was spared another Desecration, but the *Haruchai* had no hand in that triumph.'

Still Stave's inbred dispassion sustained him. 'From their shame, they learned that they could not endure it. And from their Vow, they learned that they had been misled by Earthpower. Such puissance both transcended and falsified their mortality. Without Earthpower, they would have remained what they were, *Haruchai*, inviolate. They would have known themselves unequal to such banes as the Illearth Stone and Ravers.'

That Linden understood. She, too, was certain of her own inadequacy. And she had learned from Thomas Covenant that such knowledge could be a source of strength.

'Yet evil continued to flow from the use of Earthpower,' Stave explained. 'For thirty centuries and more, the *Haruchai* remained among their mountains and their women, and at last their memories gave birth to a wish to see what had become of the Land. Again some among them sojourned eastwards. Thus they discovered the Clave and the Sunbane.

'So much of their tale you know. The *Haruchai* were imprisoned by the Clave. Their fierce blood was shed to feed the Banefire. When they, and you, were freed by the Unbeliever, they again set themselves against Corruption in anger and repudiation.

'But they did not renew the shame of their past arrogance. Instead they contented themselves in Thomas Covenant's troubled service, and in yours, and in defence of the folk of the Land. Therefore they were not again turned against themselves.

'And again the ur-Lord triumphed over his foe. That tale the *Haruchai* heard from the Giants of the Search. And they heard as well that Linden Avery the Chosen gave form to a new Staff of Law. Thus you triumphed over the Sunbane, so that the Land might once again be allowed to heal.'

She found herself nodding, although the movement hurt her neck. Hardly aware of what she did, she had raised her head to gaze into Stave's indecipherable face.

'Desiring a service in which they might also triumph,' he said, 'the *Haruchai* remained when you had returned to your world. The new Staff was given to the folk of the Land, but it was soon lost, and there were no Lords who might have defended Earthpower from darkness. The Land required our care.'

Anele whimpered as if in nightmare; but he did not turn from the wall.

'Do you understand me, Linden Avery? We had learned that the Ritual of Desecration and the Sunbane were expressions of Earthpower. We had learned that Earthpower could not preserve any service from shame, neither ours nor the Lords. We had learned that mortal hearts are weak, and that Corruption is cunning to exploit that weakness. And we had learned to love the Land, as the Lords did before us.

'In the end, we learned that the Land and all its life would not have suffered such renewed and again renewed cruelty if Earthpower were not' – again he paused to search for a word – 'accessible for use. Certainly it is not Corruption. But in the absence of the Staff of Law, only Corruption is served when mortal hearts exercise Earthpower. Even in the presence of the Staff, great evil may be wrought. Therefore we have taken upon ourselves the guardianship of the Land.

'We do not rule here. We command nothing. We demand nothing. All life is free to live as it wills. But we do not permit any exertion of Earthpower.'

Linden stared at him, but she could no longer see him. Tears blurred her vision. *Only Corruption is served*— How was it possible to have learned so much, and to understand so little?

Earthpower was life: no mere decision or belief on the part of the *Haruchai* could gainsay it. Everything that had form and substance here was in some sense an 'exertion of Earthpower'. The true peril lay not in its use, but in the hearts of those who did not understand their own vulnerability to despair.

Against that danger, Linden Avery, like Thomas Covenant before her, was defended by the knowledge of her inadequacy. She could not be misled by despair because she did not expect herself to be greater than she was.

Kevin's Dirt held sway, and *caesures* stalked the Land, because the Staff of

Law had been lost – and because the *Haruchai* did not 'permit' any other use of Earthpower to oppose those evils.

But Stave was not done. 'Nor are we content,' he stated more stiffly. 'We do more. Though we remember much, we do not share our memories. We seek to end all recollection of Earthpower, so that no new use may arise to thwart us.

'We command nothing,' he insisted. 'We rule nothing. But we discourage tales of the past. We relate none ourselves. We confirm none that others relate. Human memories are brief, and we nurture that brevity.

'For many centuries now, the folk of the Land have known little which might harm them. You are forgotten, Linden Avery. The ur-Lord himself, whom we greatly honour, is no longer remembered. If it is your wish to oppose us, you will find no aid in all the Land.'

Now Linden dashed the blur from her sight to gape aghast at the *Haruchai*, silently begging him to stop. But he did not.

'In this the Giants have been our gravest hazard. The folk of the Land are short of life as of memory, but the span of the Giants is measured in centuries. They remember. They return to the Land at intervals, when their wide sojourning tends hither. And they speak of what they remember.

'They love long tales, which they recount at all opportunities. Therefore we are wary of them. As it lies within our power, we dissuade their travels to the Upper Land. And we do what we may to prevent the folk of the Land from hearing their tales.'

Linden flinched as if Stave had struck her – and still he was not done. 'The Giants have not forgotten you, Linden Avery,' he assured her, 'yet you will find no aid among them. Their last sojourn to the Land ended scant decades ago. They will not return in your lifetime, or the next.'

Good *God*, she groaned in protest. And you think you've given up arrogance? Stave's people had gone beyond folly. Anele was right about them. They might call Lord Foul their enemy, but they served him and did not know it.

She should have risen to her feet; faced him with her anger and dismay. But she did not. He had shaken her profoundly. The flame of the lamp guttered in her face, and all of her courage had fallen to ash.

However, her face must have betrayed her reaction. After a moment, Stave observed, 'Still you do not understand.' He addressed her from an unattainable height. 'This manner of speech misrepresents us. It misrepresents truth. And I have deflected myself from the pith of that which I must convey.'

He appeared to reconsider his approach. 'All other matters are secondary,' he said then. 'Only the question of Earthpower signifies. Grasping that, you will grasp all else.'

He began again as though he could read the floundering incomprehension written in the play of lamplight on her features, and knew now how to answer it.

'Consider, Linden Avery. The *Elohim* are beings of Earthpower, and they serve only their own freedom rather than the needs of the Earth. And the Worm of the World's End is Earthpower incarnate.

'The peril is manifest. It cannot be denied.

'When he had concealed the old Staff of Law so that it would not constrain him, Kevin Landwaster enacted the Ritual of Desecration. That was Earthpower.

'Though she held the old Staff in her hands, and Thomas Covenant urged restraint, High Lord Elena exercised the essential ichor of the Earth to lift dead Kevin from his grave. Disdaining his agony, she compelled his shade against Corruption. Thus was the Law of Death broken, and the Staff lost, to no avail.

'That was Earthpower.'

And still Stave was not done.

'The ancient Forestals were beings of wonder. Long they laboured to preserve the remnants of the One Forest. Yet when they had dwindled to the last, and Caer-Caveral stood alone in Andelain, he surrendered all use and purpose to break the Law of Life so that Hollian eh-Brand might live again. Now no guardian remains to the trees, and their long sentience has faded away.

'That was Earthpower.

'The Vow which misled the honour of the Bloodguard was made possible by Earthpower. Like the Sunbane before it, Kevin's Dirt is an expression of Earthpower. Beasts of Earthpower rage upon Mount Thunder, and the lurker of the Sarangrave grows restive. Of the evils which now threaten the Land, only the Falls appear to spring from another fount. In all other forms, it is by Earthpower that the Land is imperilled, as it has been from the beginning.'

There the Master finished. 'Give answer, Linden Avery. As you have said, Brinn of the *Haruchai* has become the Guardian of the One Tree. In this he surpasses our knowledge of ourselves. He both exalts and humbles us. We must show that we are worthy of him, in guardianship and devotion.

'We have determined that we will serve the Land. How then may we countenance any exercise of Earthpower?'

Still Linden could not muster the strength to stand. She needed help from *someone*. She had no idea how to free her son. She did not even know where to look for him. Nor could she imagine where the lost Staff might be found. For that search also she would need help. And she was certain now that the

Haruchai would not 'countenance' such a quest. How could they? The Staff was an instrument of Earthpower.

She did not answer Stave as he might have desired. Instead she countered his query with one of her own.

Bowing her head, she asked past the swaying veil of her hair, 'If you're so determined to suppress the past, why are you willing to let me go?' She was a portion of the Land's history incarnate. 'Aren't you afraid of what I might do?'

Another man might have sighed. Stave only lifted his shoulders slightly. 'You are Linden Avery the Chosen. You have stood at the Unbeliever's side, and have kept faith. To our knowledge, no harm has arisen from you, or from the wild magic which you now wield. With white gold, ur-Lord Thomas Covenant has twice defeated Corruption. And when we have doubted you, your choices and actions have shown their worth.

'We will' – once more he searched for the right word – 'accept the hazard that you may seek to oppose us.'

Oh, I'll oppose you, she wanted to say. I haven't forgotten a thing. I'll tell it all, and to hell with you.

Don't you understand that Earthpower is *life*?

Nevertheless she kept her anger to herself. Her plight was too grave; and she was too weak: she feared to declare herself. And Stave would not be swayed by Jeremiah's peril.

Instead of responding to the Master's assertion, she said obliquely, 'That smog – that yellow shroud. Why is it called Kevin's Dirt?'

His answer had the finality of a knell. 'We name it so because we deem it to be a foretaste of Desecration. Its pall covers the Land in preparation.'

Have mercy, Linden groaned to herself. A foretaste— Was Lord Foul *that* sure of himself?

Hiding behind her hair, she told the *Haruchai* softly, 'If that's true, I need time to think. I want to be alone for a while.'

She had come to the end of what she could bear to hear.

Until she heard the soft rustle of the curtain and knew that Stave was gone, she did not raise her head.

Incongruously considerate, he had left his lamp behind.

His people did not allow any use of Earthpower. Deliberately they had caused its very existence – the Land's true heritage – to be forgotten.

If Covenant could have heard her – if he had been anything more than a figment of her dreams – she might have groaned aloud, I need you. I don't think I can do this.

Abruptly her companion rolled away from the wall. His arms trembled as he braced himself into a sitting position. Tears glistened in the grime on his cheeks, formed lamp lit beads in his tattered beard. His lower lip quivered.

Miserably he breathed, 'Anele is doomed.'

She could not contradict him. She did not know how.

Chapter Five:

Distraction

After a time, Anele wore out his inchoate sorrow and lapsed from weeping.

A low breeze seemed to blow through Linden, scattering the ashes in her heart until nothing remained to indicate that she had ever known fire. But she could not remain where she was. The stone of the floor and walls offered her no accommodation. Instead its hard surfaces pressed on her bruises when she already felt too much distress.

Eventually she rose to her feet, picked up the lamp, and limped across the room to investigate the other chambers of their gaol.

The curtained doorway near Anele admitted her to Mithil Stonedown's version of a lavatory. A stone basin and a large ewer full of water sat on a low wooden table. Beside them was a pot of fine sand, presumably for scrubbing away dirt. A clay pipe angled down into the floor answered other needs.

She wanted to wash. A lifetime of ablution might not suffice to make her clean again. However, her hurts were too deep and tender to be rubbed. And she was nearly prostrate on her feet, hardly able to hold up her head.

Unsteadily she left the lavatory.

In the next chamber, she found what she sought: beds; two of them standing against the side walls. They had trestle frames well-padded with bracken and grass covered by blankets woven of rough wool. A window interrupted the far wall above the level of her eyes: it, too, had been wedged full of rocks.

Turning her head, she informed Anele wanly, 'Two beds.' When he did not respond, she added, 'You probably haven't slept in a bed for years.'

Still he showed no reaction. He had slumped until his body appeared to mould itself against the stone.

Sighing, she entered the bedchamber and let the curtain drop behind her.

For no particular reason, she chose the bed on the left. Stumbling to it, she sat on its edge and unlaced her boots, pulled off her socks. Then she stretched out between two of the blankets and fell instantly asleep.

Pain disturbed her at intervals, but it could not rouse her. Exhaustion held her hurts at bay. Jeremiah appeared to her in spikes like coronary crises. She saw the supplication in his muddy gaze. Tousled by neglect and rough treatment, his hair hung in poignant clumps. Horses reared, unregarded, across the blue flannel of his pyjamas.

She wept for him without waking.

Covenant spoke to her distantly, too far away to be heard. Honninscrave screamed as he contained *samadhi* Sheol so that Nom the Sandgorgon could rend Lord Foul's servant. Covenant insisted, but his desire to console or guide her could not cross the boundaries between them. Warped ur-viles fell in butchered clusters, crushed by the unexpected vehemence of Vain's midnight hands.

In life, Covenant had drawn her into the light when her darkness had threatened to overwhelm her. He had done so repeatedly. He had taught her that her fears and failures, her inadequacies, were what made her human and precious; worthy of love. But he could not reach her now.

Because the ur-viles had turned against the Despiser, he had destroyed them all.

To free Covenant from the fatal stasis imposed by the *Elohim*, Linden had possessed him with her health-sense. There she had found herself in a field of flowers under a healing sun, full of light and capable of joy. Covenant had appeared as a youth, as dear to her as Jeremiah. He had opened his hands to her open heart, and had been made whole.

Linden, he called to her faintly, find me.

If her son could have spoken, he might have begged her for the same thing.

In dreams she cried out his name, and still slept.

Followed by an echo of her lost loves, she drifted finally out of slumber. Tears cooled her cheeks when she opened her eyes.

A weight of lassitude clung to her limbs, holding her down. Yet she was awake. Dimly lit by small motes and streaks of sunshine from the blocked window, the stone walls of her gaol rose around her.

When she glanced at the other bed, she saw that it lay vacant, untouched. Anele had slept in the outer room.

Or the *Haruchai* had taken him during the night; delivered him to Revelstone—

He is the hope of the Land.

Her only companion.

Stupefied with rest and dreams, Linden rolled her stiff body out of bed.

Her joints protested sharply as she forced herself to her feet. Standing motionless, she rested for a moment or two; tried to summon her resources. Then she shambled forward like a poorly articulated manikin.

Beyond the curtain, gloom filled the outer chamber. The lamp had burned out. The only illumination angled in strips past the edges of the leather which hung in the gaol's entrance.

She could hear no sound from the village around this small dwelling: no calls or conversation, no passing feet, no children at play. Mithil Stonedown seemed entirely still; lifeless as a graveyard. Only Anele's hoarse breathing humanised the silence.

He lay where Linden had left him, curled tightly against the wall as if for comfort. In sleep and gloom, he looked inexpressibly forlorn. Nevertheless she felt a muffled relief to find that he had not been taken from her.

While she slept, fresh bowls of food and water had been placed on the floor. But they were half empty: Anele must have eaten again during the night.

For herself, she was not conscious of hunger or thirst. Somnolence and dreams filled her head, crowding out other sensations. But she knew that she needed food; and so she crossed the floor to sit beside the bowls. In Jeremiah's name, she spooned cold stew into her mouth and drank cool water until she had emptied both bowls.

Covenant had told her to find him. *Trust yourself. Do something they don't expect.*

Her dreams were going to drive her crazy.

In an effort to undo their effects, she struggled to her feet and went into the lavatory. There she splashed herself with cold water and rubbed her skin with sand until her bare feet began to cramp against the unwarmed floor. Then she returned to the bedchamber to don her socks and boots.

Simple things: trivial actions. Meaningless in themselves. Nevertheless they helped her shrug aside her sense of helplessness.

She had made promises to Anele. She did not regret that. Because of them, however, she was trapped here as much as he. But she was a physician, trained to patience and imprecise solutions; the circadian rhythms of devotion. If she were a woman who gave way to frustration – or to despair – she would have lost courage and will long ago.

Thomas Covenant had taught her that even the most damaged and frail spirits could not be defeated if they did not elect to abandon themselves.

When she had secured her resolve, she left the bedchamber again, intending to open the outer curtain, locate the nearest *Haruchai* and insist on talking to

Stave once more. She wanted to hear everything that he might be able to tell her about how the Staff of Law had been lost.

She needed to understand what had become of the Land.

In the larger room, however, she found Anele awake, sitting with his back to the wall.

Clearly sleep and food had done him good. His skin tone and colour had improved, and some of the wreckage was gone from his features. He did not rise to greet her; but his small movements as he turned his head and shifted his shoulders seemed more elastic now, less fragile.

'Anele,' she enquired quietly, 'how are you? Why didn't you use the bed? You would have slept better.'

He dropped his chin to his chest, avoiding her gaze. His fingertips moved aimlessly over the stone on either side of him. 'Anele does not sleep in beds. Dreams are snares. He will be lost in them. They cannot find him here.'

Without her health-sense, Linden felt profoundly truncated, almost crippled. But she needed to understand him. As gently as she could, she pursued him.

'Here?' she prompted, her voice soft. 'On the floor?'

'On stone,' he acknowledged. 'You do not protect Anele. He has no friend but stone.'

In another phase of his madness, he had claimed that the rocks around him spoke.

'Anele—' Muttering to herself at the pain in her muscles, Linden squatted to sit beside him. Deliberately she set her shoulder against his, hoping to reassure him. 'I said I would protect you. I meant it. I just haven't figured out how yet.'

Then she asked, 'What does stone do for you? Why do you need it?'

How could walls and floors guard him from dreaming?

The old man struggled for an answer. 'Anele tries— He strives— So hard. It pains him. Yet he tries and tries.'

She waited.

After a long moment, he finished, 'Always. Trapped and lost. Anele tries. He must remember.'

Remember what? she wanted to ask. What kind of knowledge did his fractured mind conceal from him? Why had he chosen madness?

But if he could have answered that question, he would not have been in such straits. Seeking a way to slip past his barricades, she asked instead, 'Do you remember me?'

He flashed her a blind glance, then turned his head away. 'Anele found you. High up. The Watch. It pursued him. He fled. You were there.'

So much he retained, if no more.

'Do you remember what happened to us?' Linden kept her tone calm, almost incurious. She wanted him to believe that he was safe with her. 'Do you remember what happened to the Watch?'

In spite of her caution, however, she had disturbed him. He seemed to shrink into himself. '*It* came. Anele fell. Fire and darkness. White. Terrible.'

Perhaps she had not phrased her question simply enough. Gently, softly, she tried again.

'Anele, are you still alive?'

If he could have caused the wall to swallow him, he might have done so. '*It* came,' he repeated. '*They* came. Worse than death.'

Linden sighed to herself. Her brief percipience on Kevin's Watch had given her the impression that he was fundamentally responsible for his own condition. He had chosen insanity as a form of self-defence. Having chosen it, however, he could not simply set it aside. He would have to find his own way through it, for good or ill.

The same necessity ruled her, as it ruled Jeremiah.

Hoping to comfort him, she reached out to squeeze the old man's shoulder. 'Don't worry about it.' Covenant had said the same to her. 'It's easier to remember when you don't try too hard.

'Once I figure out what to do, we'll get out of here. In the meantime, I'm sure the Masters will bring us more food and water. And I need someone to talk to' – a new idea occurred to her in mid-sentence – 'preferably someone who isn't one of them.'

She wanted to talk to a Stonedownor. If the *Haruchai* would allow her.

Deliberately she climbed to her feet. Limping to the outer doorway, she pushed the leather curtain aside and leaned her head into the sunlight.

The door opened on a narrow passage of packed dirt between flat-roofed stone dwellings. A mid-morning sky arched overhead, deep blue and apparently untrammelled in spite of Kevin's Dirt. A few birds called to each other in the distance, but she heard nothing else; saw no one. The whole village might have been deserted.

She wanted to bask in the sun's warmth for a moment, let its touch sink into her hurts; but almost immediately one of the *Haruchai* appeared around the corner of her gaol.

She recognised the unscarred Master who had helped Stave capture Anele and her.

'Linden Avery.' He bowed as Stave had done, with both fists extended from the level of his heart. 'I am Bornin. You are welcome among us. What is your desire?'

She nodded a bow. His characteristic stolidity brought back her sense of betrayal and outrage. However, she kept her reaction to herself. 'Thank you, Bornin,' she replied evenly. 'There are a couple of things you could do for me, if you don't mind.'

Expressionlessly he waited for her to continue.

'We could use more water and something to eat,' she explained. 'And I want to talk to one of the Stonedownors. Is there anyone around who can spare me a little time?'

If she could not seek out comprehension, she would make it come to her.

Bornin appeared momentarily uncertain. 'What will a Stonedownor reveal to you that we cannot?'

'I'm not sure,' she answered noncommittally. 'I might ask what it's like to live without Earthpower. Or I might just want some company. Anele isn't much of a conversationalist.'

The *Haruchai* seemed to consult the open air. Then he nodded. 'Very well, Linden Avery. Do you wish to accompany me, or will you await my return?'

Thinking of Anele, she swallowed her desire for freedom and sunshine, and let the curtain drop between herself and Bornin.

The old man lifted his head briefly, then returned to his fractured thoughts.

'Anele,' she said on an impulse, 'you've scrambled to survive for a long time. Decades. Does anyone ever help you? Do you have any friends?'

How was it possible for a demented old man to keep himself alive? Hunger and injuries, if not sheer loneliness, should have killed him long ago.

Again he raised his white eyes. For a moment, he appeared to consider her question seriously. 'Anele is lost,' he said almost calmly. 'Always alone. And always harried. *They* seek him.

'But—' Concentration and gloom filled his sightless gaze. 'Folk are kind. When *they* are far away. Even here— Anele is fed. Given raiment. When *they* are far away.

'And—'

His voice trailed off as if he had lost the thread of a memory.

'And?' Linden prompted.

Come on, Anele. Give me *something*. I can't do it all alone.

'And—' he began again. He seemed to cower against a wall deep inside himself. 'Creatures. Dark. Fearsome. Lost things, long dead. Anele fears them. He fears—

'They feed him. Force blackness into him. Make him strong. Heal him, whispering madness.

'Madness.'

Without warning, he shouted in protest, 'Creatures make Anele *remember*!'

Then he collapsed to his side, clutching his knees to his chest, hiding his face.

'Anele!' At once, Linden dropped to the floor beside him, tugged him into the cradle of her arms. 'Oh, Anele, I'm so sorry. I know you suffer. I didn't mean to remind you. I just—'

She had no way of knowing what might cause him pain. Helpless to do otherwise, she held him and rocked him until his tension eased and he grew still.

At the same time, she tried to comfort herself. She had been in worse straits than this. The Clave had imprisoned her for days: a Raver had demeaned her utterly. In Kiril Threndor, *moksha* Jehannum had tortured her while Covenant confronted the Despiser. Oh, she had been in worse straits. Much worse.

But Jeremiah had not. Even when he had held his right hand in the bonfire: even then. That agony had been relatively brief; and he had found a way to escape from it. It could not be compared to the torments Lord Foul might devise for him. His dissociation would not defend him from the malice of a being who could *possess* him—

While you are apart from him, you cannot know his sufferings.

And he could hope for nothing from her. She did not know where to look for him – and might not have been able to reach him if she had known.

Anele's state frustrated and pained her; but it also protected her. If she had not felt compelled to care for him, she might not have been able to contain her own anguish.

Later the old man left her to use the lavatory. When he returned, he sat beside her again, his shoulder touching hers like a recognition of companionship. For that she was grateful.

Eventually a hesitant scratching came to the outer curtain; and the stocky frame of a Stonedownor ducked inwards with a large stone bowl cupped in each hand. 'Anele?' he asked uncertainly. 'Linden Avery? You wished to speak with me? I was told—'

His voice faded into doubt. Unsure of himself, he stooped to set his bowls on the floor.

Without hesitation, Anele rose to cross the room and drink from one of the bowls.

Linden struggled to rouse herself. She had asked to speak to a Stonedownor, but she no longer remembered why. Nothing that he might say would enable her to help her son.

The man waited for a long moment, indecisive. Then he made an attempt to pull up his dignity.

'I see now that I was mistaken. Pardon my intrusion.'

With the constrained light behind him, his face lay in shadows. Yet his eyes found a way to appeal to her. Somehow he conveyed the impression that he had come, not because a Master had requested it, but because he wanted to.

'Wait,' Linden murmured hoarsely. 'I'm sorry. Wait.'

Somewhere she found the strength to gain her feet.

'I don't mean to be rude.' Her own voice seemed to reach her from a great distance. 'I'm just' – her throat closed convulsively – 'just scared.'

She took a step or two forward. While the Stonedownor waited for her, she rubbed her hands across her face; pulled her hair back over her shoulders.

'There's something I didn't tell the Masters.' She sounded too far away from herself to speak coherently. 'The *Haruchai*.

'It's my son—'

Unable to go on, she stopped, hoping that her visitor would reach out to her in some way.

He seemed to swallow conflicting responses. After a last hesitation, he said, 'I am Liand son of Fostil. The Master did not say that you wished to speak to me. He said only that you wished to speak to a Stonedownor. I presumed to offer myself.'

As if he understood that she needed an explanation – a chance to gather herself – he continued, 'My duties are among the horses rather than in the fields, and horses are easily tended. They are few in any event, and not needed today. Having no other demands upon me, I often accompany the Masters, or do their bidding.

'I was—' Sudden embarrassment made him falter. 'I had concealed myself nearby when they took you and your companion. I helped them to bear you here.

'Since that moment, I have wished to speak with you. You are strange in the South Plains, and to me, and I am hungry to learn of new things.'

While he spoke, Linden rallied her resources. She felt the delicacy of his manner, the instinctive consideration: his unprompted account of his presence gave her time to prepare. He may have felt awkward, but he did not appear so to her. Instead he seemed spontaneously kind.

That contrast with Stave and the *Haruchai* encouraged her to gather her courage.

'Thank you, Liand,' she said when she could breathe more easily. 'I'm glad you're willing to talk to me.'

Anele turned his back, dismissing the Stonedownor, and moved to sit once again against the far wall.

'Oh, I am willing in all truth.' Liand's voice was an intent baritone, full of concentration and interest. 'Your speech is foreign to my ears, and your raiment is unlike any I have beheld.' Frankly he admitted, 'I am eager to offer whatever I may.'

'Thank you,' she said again. Inadvertently she had provided herself with an opening, an approach to her immediate concerns. As she considered how she might proceed, she tried to see his face more clearly. However, the gloom shrouded his features, blurring their definitions. Tentatively she asked, 'Can you let in more light? The Masters won't release Anele, and I promised not to leave him. But I want to be able to look at you.'

'Surely.' Liand reached at once to the side of the doorframe, located a hook which must have been formed or attached for the purpose, and hung the curtain there. 'Will this suffice?'

The sunlight did not stretch far into the chamber; but enough reflected illumination washed inwards to brighten the room considerably.

'It will' – Linden smiled wanly –'as soon as we sit down.' Easing herself to the floor, she indicated a spot for him inside the doorway. 'Anele and I had a rough time yesterday,' she explained as neutrally as she could. 'I haven't got my strength back yet.'

When Liand complied, the light revealed him plainly. He was a young man, perhaps half her age, with broad shoulders and sturdy, workman's hands, wearing a jerkin and leggings of rough wool dyed the hue of sand. Thick leather sandals protected his feet. His features reminded her distantly of Sunder, the only Stonedownor whom she had known well: he had Sunder's blunt openness without the bereavements and guilt which had complicated her friend's native simplicity. And he was characteristically brown-skinned, brown-eyed. Above his square jaw, imprecise nose and eager gaze, his loose hair and eyebrows were a startling black, as dark as crow's wings.

His mouth seemed made for smiles; but he was not smiling now.

'I witnessed your capture,' he told Linden gravely. 'The Masters were not gentle with you. And I cannot conceive what you must have endured in the fall of the Watch. Indeed, I cannot conceive how it is that you yet live.'

Dropping his eyes, he observed noncommittally, 'The Masters may comprehend that wonder, but they answer enquiries rarely – and never when what has transpired surpasses our experience. To justify your captivity, they say only that Anele requires their care, and that you opposed them.'

He did not need to add that he was eager to hear a better explanation. His excitement was plain in the feigned relaxation of his posture, the quick clench and release of his hands. However, she was not ready to put him in peril. Anything that she revealed might turn the *Haruchai* against him. Hell, they might decide to treat him like they did Anele. She could not take that kind of chance with him: not yet.

And she did not know if he were truly as guileless as he appeared. The health-sense which she had regained and lost again would have discerned his essential nature. Without it, she had to be more careful.

'Maybe we can talk about that later,' she answered. 'There's a lot at stake, and right now I don't know who I can trust and who I can't.' To forestall an interruption, she went on more quickly, 'I was here once before, but that was a very long time ago. I gather my name doesn't mean anything to you?'

The Stonedownor shook his head.

'Thomas Covenant?' she continued. 'Sunder son of Nassic, the Graveler of Mithil Stonedown? Hollian eh-Brand?'

The First of the Search? Pitchwife?

Liand shook his head again. 'This is Mithil Stonedown. These other names I have never heard.' He hesitated, then asked, 'What is a "Graveler"?'

Linden swallowed indignation. Those damn Masters had suppressed *every-thing*. If the people of the South Plains had forgotten the lore on which their lives had once depended—

Controlling herself with difficulty, she told Liand, 'You see my problem. Too much time has passed. If you don't even know what a Graveler is—' She sighed. 'I can't tell you who I am, or what I'm doing here. You wouldn't understand unless I explained the whole history of the Land first.'

Liand leaned forward, undaunted by her response. 'But you are able to explain that history. The Masters do not speak of such things. If they are asked, they do not answer.

'Linden Avery, I would do anything that might serve you, if in return you would share with me the Land's past. I know naught beyond the small tale of my family and Mithil Stonedown for a few generations only, a few score years. Yet I have—'

Abruptly he stopped; pulled himself back from his enthusiasm. 'My heart speaks to me of greater matters,' he said more warily. 'Simple fragments of the Land's lost tale would content me. There is little that I would not do for you in exchange.'

His words nearly broke down her defences. An offer like that— She could have taken advantage of him shamelessly.

Betray the Masters for me. Help us escape. Guide us. I'll tell you stories that will turn your head inside out.

She might be able to find her son.

Surely the *Haruchai* deserved no restraint from her? God, no. In the name of their own self-esteem, they had deprived the Land of its history and power; its access to glory. They deserved anything that she could do to subvert them.

But she knew better. Stave's convictions may have offended hers; but that did not detract from his essential worth: his rigorous honesty and candour; his readiness to judge himself more stringently than he judged anyone else.

And—

Unhappily she told herself the truth.

And Liand was no match for them. They were the *Haruchai*, preternaturally potent and defiantly uncompromising. If she set him against them, they might kill him. They would certainly damage his spirit. She would have his pain on her conscience, and would gain nothing.

In spite of Jeremiah's plight, she could not turn her back on her own scruples.

Restraining herself, Linden gazed into the Stonedownor's face. 'Convince me,' she countered quietly. 'Tell me what you were about to say. "Yet I have—"'

Liand hesitated. Apparently she had asked him to take a significant risk. Her nerves stretched as he debated within himself. In a moment, however, his excitement – or his trusting nature – won out.

He glanced around quickly; leaned forward. Lowering his voice to a whisper, he said, 'I have ascended the Watch, though the Masters forbid it. I have seen a vast pall of harm upon the Land, a dire cloud which I cannot now discern. And I have beheld the peaks of the south rise mighty and glorious above that pall, fraught with majesty. I have ached to sojourn among them, to taste their rare substance with my own flesh, though such savors may destroy me.

'Surely at one time the Land itself was home to similar marvels.'

He brought tears to Linden's eyes: she could not quench the burning he inspired. He had stolen a brief glimpse of something that should have been readily apparent to everyone in the Land at all times. Ignorant of what his people had lost, he did not grieve over it as she did. Nevertheless the loss was real, and abominable.

She wanted to match his honesty with her own, in spite of the danger to him.

'Liand—' Roughly she rubbed back her tears. 'I can't explain things to you right now. Not here,' where any *Haruchai* might overhear her. 'But I'm in trouble, and I need help.

'I knew the Masters a long time ago. They remember me. They were my friends then, but I don't think I can trust them now. They've changed. I want to hear anything you can tell me about them.'

Anele snorted as if in disgust, but did not speak.

Liand's stare showed his concern. 'I do not understand,' he admitted. 'Your knowledge of them is surely deeper than mine. They seldom answer our enquiries. Indeed, they seldom speak. I know only what all in Mithil Stonedown know, and that is little. There is a place which they name Revelstone, though what it may be, or where, they do not say. Upon occasion, they sojourn there, and return.' After a pause, he finished, 'I have observed no alteration in them.'

She sighed. 'All right. I'll ask it a different way. What do you know about Lord Foul the Despiser?' She searched his face. 'The Grey Slayer? The Masters call him Corruption.'

At the back wall, Anele flinched, then covered his head with his arms.

The Stonedownor gave her a perplexed frown. 'I fear that I know nothing. I have never heard these names.'

'There,' Linden responded bitterly. 'That's my problem.

'The Land has an ancient enemy. If he isn't immortal, he might as well be. Over the centuries,' the millennia, 'he's done more harm than I could possibly describe. And you've never heard of him.

'The Masters know more about him than I do, and I know him too damn well.' The Despiser had found an echo of himself in her, and had nearly destroyed her with it. 'He's here. He's still here. But they don't talk about him.

'Liand,' she told the young man as openly as she could, 'that terrifies me.'

Stave had explained his position only too well, yet still she could not comprehend it.

'This Lord Foul,' Liand asked uncertainly, 'this Despiser? He remains among us? What has he done?'

Unable to contain her fear and anger, Linden rasped, 'He has taken my son.'

Her words seemed to shock the Stonedownor. He straightened his back; clasped his arms over his stomach. Alarm darkened his frank gaze.

Anele whimpered softly to himself as though he feared to be overheard.

'That's my problem,' she repeated. 'Lord Foul has my son, and you've never heard of him. The Masters want you ignorant. They think they can defend the Land by themselves, even though they're no match for him.

'I've got to find my son. To do that, I need help. But I didn't tell Stave about him. I don't want to turn the Masters against me. If they knew the truth – what I have to do—' She was already sure that she would not be able to search for Jeremiah without Earthpower and the Staff of Law. 'I'm afraid they'll try to stop me.'

More quietly, she concluded, 'I need to make some decisions. I can't just sit here.' And Anele required freedom. 'Anything you can tell me might help me make up my mind.'

Plainly out of his depth, Liand unfolded his arms and spread his hands. 'Linden Avery, I know not how to reply.' Uncertainty confused his gaze. 'To me as to all my people, the Masters have ever been what they are. Upon occasion, as I have said, they are absent from Mithil Stonedown. More commonly they are not. They do not aid us in tilling the soil, or in harvesting crops, or in gathering fruits. They neither tend the weak nor succour the infirm. Yet they countenance all that we do. In no way do they intervene in our pursuits, or alter our lives.'

Linden studied him sharply. 'But you said they forbade you to climb Kevin's Watch.'

'Yes,' he admitted. 'That they have done.' His expression suggested that until this moment he had not considered the prohibition unusual. It was merely one more item on a long list of things which the Masters did not explain. 'I did not dare to defy their command until a sojourn of some days took them from among us.'

As Liand spoke, a cloud seemed to pass over the sun. The light reflecting through the doorway grew dim, bleeding illumination from the room. Shadows obscured his face as he added, 'And they discourage wandering. They say that our lives are better lived in proximity to Mithil Stonedown.'

Then his tone quickened. 'Yet we have horses because the Masters provide them.' Apparently he considered it important to describe the *Haruchai* fairly. 'Our herd is too scant to be replenished by breeding, and they say that we must have means to bear tidings swiftly at need.'

After a brief pause, he said, 'Also they aid us against the *kresh*. And—'

'*Kresh?*' interrupted Linden. That name was new to her.

'The yellow wolves,' Liand explained, 'more terrible in size than the grey wolves we know, and savage beyond description. Our old songs and tales speak of a time when no such beasts harried the Plains. For three generations, however, or perhaps four, *kresh* have fallen upon us at intervals, hunting blood in fearsome packs. Lacking the aid of the Masters, we could not withstand them.

'In this our mounts are precious. At any warning – often it is the Masters themselves who warn us – we ride abroad to gather our people so that we may make defence in Mithil Stonedown.'

Linden had expected the light to improve as the cloud drifted past; but it did not. Instead twilight gathered in the room, and a faint chill breathed past the open curtain. The weather was changing. When she glanced away from Liand to check on Anele, she saw that the old man had begun to shiver.

For a moment, she yearned for percipience so keenly that she could not continue. In the Land as she had once known it, the simple touch of the air on her cheek would have told her what the deepening gloom presaged.

But aching for her lost health-sense weakened her as much as the loss itself. With an effort, she set the pang aside.

'You said sometimes the Masters go away. For days?'

'Upon occasion,' the Stonedownor affirmed. 'Other absences are less prolonged.'

Revelstone was three hundred leagues away. Even on horseback, the journey would take more than a few days.

'Do you know where they go?' she asked. 'I mean, when they aren't going to Revelstone. Why do they need to go anywhere?'

Liand shrugged. 'They are the Masters. They reveal little and explain less.

'However,' he added more slowly, 'at times they accept my company, when my duties permit it. Thus I have learned that in certain absences they searched for your companion.'

Linden caught her breath. In this also, Anele had told the truth.

'I know not,' Liand went on, 'why they have attended so to the capture of one frail old man. Nor am I able to describe how he has eluded them. I could not have done so in his place. Yet it is certain that their desire against him is no recent wish.'

She nodded in the gloom. The sun's light had faded further, and as it did so the air grew noticeably cooler. Soon she might start to shiver. Liand's account was consistent with what both Stave and Anele had told her.

How had the old man been able to evade capture? She could not imagine. Like Liand, she would have been helpless to foil the *Haruchai*.

If she wanted to escape, she needed to learn Anele's secret.

He had mentioned dark, fearsome creatures. Lost things, long dead. Creatures that forced him to remember—

That question would have to wait. Something that Liand had been about to reveal nagged at her. Instead of pursuing his sporadic travels with the Masters, she said, 'A minute ago, you started to say something else. You mentioned *kresh* and—?'

He frowned, momentarily confused. '*Kresh* and—?' But then his expression lifted. 'Ah, yes. I meant to add that the Masters aid us also against the Falls.'

As if to himself, Anele muttered, '*Caesures.*'

'Go on,' Linden urged the young man.

Liand sighed. 'By some means which we do not comprehend, and which the Masters do not explain, they discern the Falls at great distance. We are scarcely able to behold the Falls when they are nigh, yet the Masters perceive their presence and their movements from afar. Destructive as they are, and unpredictable to us, they might well have torn us from life if the Masters did not forewarn and guide us.'

The Stonedownors could not detect the *caesures* because they had been blinded; yet the *Haruchai* had not so much as mentioned Kevin's Dirt to Liand's people.

Cursing to herself, Linden asked, 'Could you see the Fall that broke Kevin's Watch?'

Liand shook his head. 'We could not. The distance was too great for our eyes. We only guessed at its presence when the spire fell.'

She understood none of this. What did Lord Foul gain by it? Nevertheless the yellow smog baffled her less than did the *caesures*. If she could not imagine its ultimate purpose, she could grasp the nature of its evil. But the migraine aura which had shattered Kevin's Watch was another matter. She had seen that it was potent and harmful; but what was it *for*?

Groping, she probed further.

'You said you've had trouble with *kresh* for three or four generations. How long have you had to worry about Falls?'

'Four score years, perhaps, or five. Falls are more' – he grimaced – 'more remarkable than *kresh*, fearsome though the wolves may be. They disturb our lives more profoundly.' Liand thought for a moment, then offered, 'If I question my people, I may be able to determine the time of their first appearance among us.'

Eighty or a hundred years. Three or four generations. *Caesures* and *kresh* had begun to afflict the South Plains at about the same time.

'What do the Falls do?' Linden asked intently.

The young man's mouth twisted again. 'They are destructive, as I have said.' He did not enjoy the taste of his memories. 'Trees and shrubs are often blasted, and crops are ruined as though ploughs by the score had torn through them. At times we have been brought near to starvation by the loss of our fields, and winter has been cruel to us because we could find little wood to feed our fires.' He sighed. 'Beyond question the aid of the Masters has enabled us to endure.'

His voice held a note of fatality as he concluded, 'Stone may withstand a

Fall, though it does not do so repeatedly. But any beast or bird or human that nears a Fall is swallowed away and does not return.'

Linden stared at him. Swallowed away? Actually devoured? God! No wonder Anele was terrified –

Fearing Liand's answer, she asked, 'How often do you see Falls?'

He shrugged uncomfortably. 'We cannot foretell them. They are not constant. However, the interval between them is commonly measured in years. Some pass, harmless, across the Plains. Others disappear among the mountains, or emerge from them. It is rare that a Fall enters this valley.'

As he spoke, Linden winced at an abrupt flash of intuition. *Caesures* had begun to afflict the Land, say, ninety years ago. Covenant had told her that roughly a year passed in the Land for every day in her ordinary world. And three months had passed since she had restored a white gold ring—

Was it possible? Behind Liand's shrouded form and the blank stone walls and the gloom, Linden seemed to see Roger's mother in her hospital bed raising her fist against herself. Had Lord Foul taken hold of Joan's mind so completely that she had been able to reach across the barrier between realities with wild magic? Had Joan *caused* the Falls by beating out her pain on the bones of her temple?

If so, the danger was about to get a lot worse. She was *here* now; able to strike directly at the Land.

And Linden was inadvertently responsible. Nothing in her experience had prepared her for the possibility that Joan's madness might have power across such distances.

Even the Staff of Law – if Linden could somehow contrive to find it – might prove useless against such wrong.

Her voice shook as she asked, 'Do the *kresh* ever attack while you're threatened by a Fall?'

How far did Joan's insanity – and Lord Foul's machinations – extend? Kevin's Dirt effectively masked the *caesures*. Did the Falls similarly disguise the peril of the wolves?

'I have beheld one such attack,' Liand admitted, 'no more. Yet when they neared the Fall, the *kresh* attempted flight. Those that failed were consumed.'

His answer gave her a small relief. It suggested that Joan – or the Despiser – was somehow constrained; limited. Or that separate intentions were at work; hungers driven by differing impulses.

Nevertheless she did not understand it. It did not sound like Lord Foul. Surely his appetite for ruin would be better fed by a coordinated assault? The Masters alone could not repeatedly withstand such an attack.

Stave's people had spent centuries ensuring that the Land had no other defenders.

Linden needed more information. She lacked some crucial fact or insight which would have allowed her to grasp the Despiser's purpose.

'So *kresh* and Falls are new,' she mused. 'Comparatively. Have there been any other changes? Maybe not in your lifetime, but in the past few generations? Do your people talk about anything unusual? Has anything strange happened?'

'Do you mean apart from the fall of the Watch, and your own presence?' Liand's tone suggested a grin, but the accumulating gloom concealed his features. 'Do you enquire of stillbirths, or twins, or unwonted blights?' Then he shook his shadowed head. 'Surely you do not.

'One event,' he said more seriously, 'which we would deem "strange" without hesitation has transpired. Indeed, I was present at its occurrence. Though I was little more than a child, I recall it well – as do we all.'

'Tell me,' Linden urged.

He rubbed his arms roughly for a moment, as if the thought of what he would say left him vulnerable to the growing cold. Outside the day had turned crepuscular and somehow ominous: she could hardly make out the wall of the home beyond her gaol. An erratic breeze began to scrub up dust from the packed dirt between the dwellings.

'The occasion itself,' he said quietly, remembering dismay, 'was in no way remarkable. Our folk had gathered at day's end in the centre of the Stonedown to speak of that which had been accomplished, and to prepare for the morrow's labours. Also such gatherings provide opportunity for songs and tales and ease. Thus do the folk of Mithil Stonedown combine their hearts for the aid and comfort of all.'

Wind plucked at the curtain. An accumulating tension in the air hinted at thunder. For reasons of his own, Anele left the rear wall and crept forward on his hands and knees. He may have wished to hear better.

Liand continued.

'The occasion commenced in the ordinary fashion, occupied with matters which held little interest for a child of my few years. Labours were discussed, plans made. I attended to them scantly, awaiting tales.

'Yet of a sudden it became apparent that a stranger stood among us. His visage was merely unfamiliar, for we had never seen him before. And his raiment resembled ours. We found it surpassingly strange, however, that none of us had observed his approach. Indeed, the Masters themselves had given no sign that they were aware of him ere he appeared.

'He did not ask for our notice. He merely awaited it. Yet soon every eye and ear was concentrated towards him. Then he began to speak.'

An abrupt gust pulled the curtain from its hook. The leather slapped down, sealing out the last of the light. Startled, Linden clutched at Covenant's ring. Now she could see nothing of Liand except his outlines. Anele was an undefined blur in the centre of the chamber, breathing feverishly through his teeth.

Almost whispering, the Stonedownor said, 'The stranger spoke of matters which conveyed no meaning to us. Sandgorgons. *Croyel.* A shadow upon the heart of his kind. *Merewives* and other bafflements. To none of them could we make response. We did not comprehend them.

'Then, however' – Liand faltered as though the memory still discomfited him – 'he informed us that a bane of great puissance and ferocity in the far north had slipped its bonds, and had found release in Mount Thunder.

'"Mount Thunder"? we enquired of him courteously. "We know nothing of that place. Is it near? Does it concern us? We are imperilled betimes by Falls. But packs of *kresh* are the only harm which has visited us from the north."'

Linden groaned like the mounting wind. In the gaps between gusts, she heard a faint sizzling noise like rain on hot stone. Liand's people had never even heard of Mount Thunder— The thoroughness with which the *Haruchai* had expunged the Land's past shocked her.

But Liand could not see her reaction; knew nothing of her concerns. He had not stopped.

'At first the stranger answered us with anger. Were we blind? Had we grown foolish across the centuries? Did we disdain the harsh evils of the world?

'There, however, Stave of the Masters intervened. I have not forgotten his words.

'"*Elohim,*" he said, "you are not welcome here."'

Oh, hell. Linden gaped at the dark. An *Elohim*? What were those arrogant, Earthpowerful beings doing in the Land?

In the distance, thunder opened a cannonade. Crushing volleys echoed from the mountains which sheltered Mithil Stonedown. Anele quailed at the sound as though each barrage were aimed at him.

'"These folk are ignorant, *Haruchai*," replied the stranger. "You have maimed them of knowledge. Their doom is upon your heads." But he did not tell us what he meant.

'Instead he gave warning. "Beware the halfhand," he pronounced in a voice which shook our hearts. Then he appeared to dissolve into the air as salt does in water, and was gone, leaving only the taste of disturbance on our tongues.'

If she could have cleared her throat, Linden might have protested, Beware the *halfhand*? Distress crowded her chest. That title had been given to Thomas Covenant during his first visit to the Land.

But Jeremiah was also a halfhand, in his own way.

She hardly heard Liand ask, 'Do you deem that strange, Linden Avery? Do you know of this "halfhand"?'

The *Elohim* had never trusted Covenant. They had feared his white ring; feared its power to compel even them, despite their fluid transcendence. But he was dead—

What did they know of her son?

They were *Elohim*. They knew everything that transpired throughout the Earth. It was their nature to know. Of course they were aware of Jeremiah's plight.

Surely they understood Lord Foul's intentions precisely?

'It troubles us still,' Liand admitted when she did not respond, 'though the stranger has not returned. For that reason, my heart speaks to me of matters greater than the Masters permit us to know.'

Beware the halfhand.

Find me, Covenant had pleaded in her dreams.

She had assumed that her son had been taken as a hostage against her, so that she might be coerced into surrendering Covenant's ring. But the warning of the *Elohim* seemed to imply a larger danger.

Larger than the destruction of the Arch of Time and the extinction of the Earth—?

Seconded by thunder, Liand finished, 'And therefore I ascended the Watch, defying the prohibition of the Masters, though to do so may have been foolish and perilous. I wish to know the name of our doom.'

Linden stared at him, seeing nothing. Worse than Lord Foul's complete victory—?

'Protect Anele,' the old man whimpered through the thrashing of the wind. 'Power comes. It will shred his heart.'

'Linden Avery.' Liand's voice held a note of supplication. 'Speak to me. You grasp much which is denied to us. Do you comprehend this doom? Who is this *Elohim*? What is the "halfhand", that we must be wary of him?'

Magnified by the wind, thunder thudded against the ground so heavily that the floor under her shook. The air flurrying past the curtain had turned as cold as frost.

She had encountered the *croyel*. They were parasites which gave power in exchange for mastery. She had seen them unify the primitive savagery of the *arghuleh*; exalt Kasreyn of the Gyre's dangerous theurgies.

What might such a creature do to Jeremiah?

The *croyel* posed no threat to the *Elohim*. The danger must be to the Land, and to the Earth. Or to her son—

'What's happening?'

She did not hear herself speak aloud. She only knew that the thunder had grown as violent as the rending of Kevin's Watch.

'Protect,' Anele repeated. His voice quavered in fright.

Abruptly a ragged wail carried along the wind. 'We are assailed!'

At once, Liand sprang to his feet. '*Kresh?*' he gasped. 'Now?'

In a rush, he flung himself past the curtain; disappeared between the dwellings.

Instinctively Linden surged upright, echoing Liand's question. Wolves? In a storm like this?

No. Not unless the Despiser had compelled them to attack.

Mithil Stonedown would need all of its defenders. Even the *Haruchai* might find themselves overwhelmed.

'Come on,' she told Anele urgently. With her right hand, she gripped Covenant's ring. 'They need help, and I can't leave you. You're coming with me.'

Her companion did not react. He could not have heard her. Wind and thunder like detonations smothered her voice.

'Come *on!*' she yelled, beckoning furiously at the thick gloom. Then she slapped the curtain aside and hurried into the storm.

There, however, she staggered to a halt.

She stood in the narrow passage between her gaol and the nearest home. It was deserted: every passage in sight was deserted. The Masters had abandoned their watch on Anele. The force of the wind had swept them away.

Clouds frothed like spume overhead, black and grey tangled together, and racing for the horizons. The dwellings around her appeared in shades of dark-ness, as comfortless as sepulchres. Dust stung at her eyes and flared away.

She expected rain, but there was none.

Out of the gloom, Anele stumbled against her back. He caught himself, staggered to her side. His lips worked feverishly, but she could not hear him.

If Liand's people and the *Haruchai* fought *kresh*, they did so without a sound: no snarling; no cries of effort or pain.

Not wolves, then; or any other form of attack that Linden knew. A running battle could not be waged in silence between shocks of thunder.

The whole Stonedown had lost its voice. She and Anele might have been the only ones left alive—

The next slam of thunder brought no lightning. She had seen none since the storm began. Instead the shrouded air ahead of her seemed to congeal into a knot of perfect and impenetrable blackness: distilled ebony or obsidian. Even her blunted senses felt its concentration and power like a shout of wreckage.

As she stared at it in dismay, it shattered downwards.

Dirt and broken stone spouted from the ground where the power struck; too much stone. Stunned moments passed before she understood that a home had been blasted to scree and flinders.

No natural force drove this storm. It was the Despiser's handiwork. Nothing in Mithil Stonedown could hope to stand against it.

Except wild magic—

She started forward again.

A heartbeat later, she stopped once more.

If Lord Foul had caused this storm, what did he hope to gain? Gratuitous destruction? Homelessness and pain? He delighted in such things. But she remembered him vividly. Always he hid one purpose within another. He would not be content with tearing Mithil Stonedown apart. He wanted more—

What would happen if she allowed herself to be lured into a contest of powers, white fire against black havoc? She did not know how to use Covenant's ring. If she found the way, she might break the storm, save some of Liand's people. Or the seething clouds might prove too potent for her. She might be impelled to flee for her life. Or worse, might lose control completely—

Or she might find that she could not raise wild magic by any act of will. Unable to defend herself, she might be struck down by the storm. Jeremiah's last faint hope would be gone.

In either case, the Masters would imprison Anele again when the danger passed. Her chance to escape – perhaps the only chance she would get – would be gone. *That* would serve the Despiser beyond question.

No, she panted to herself. No. She would not. Not while she could still breathe and think—

Do something they don't expect.

—and run.

If this storm was aimed at her, it might follow. Some of the Stonedownors, at least, would be spared. And Stave's people might not be able to pursue her.

Wheeling, she reached out for Anele, grabbed him by the shoulder of his tattered tunic. Instead of trying to shout through the wind, she shoved him ahead of her, away from the boiling centre of darkness.

He complied as though she had set a goad to his ribs; as though he were not hindered by blindness.

Together they ran with all their strength between the dwellings and out of the Stonedown: away from thunder and Masters and the Land she knew.

Chapter Six

The Despiser's Guidance

South: Linden prayed that she and Anele ran south; deeper into the valley. Surely that black storm arose from the north? – from the peril which had found its release in Mount Thunder? If so, she needed to flee southward, towards the place where the mountains rose like barricades.

Away from Masters and dark thunder and Jeremiah.

Something they don't expect.

Away from any hope that she would find people to help her.

Dreams are snares.

Running, hardly able to see, she and the old man made their way between the homes and out of Mithil Stonedown. Anele stayed near her without urging or explanation. In every phase of his madness, apparently, he understood flight and did not need vision. Indeed, when they gained open ground he began to pull ahead. Guided by some instinct which she could hardly imagine, his feet seemed to find and follow a path of their own accord, despite the dense cloud and trailing thunder.

She did not want that. The *Haruchai* would come in pursuit. They were too doughty, and too familiar with power, to die in the darkness which assailed the village. And they had access to horses. Any path would guide the Masters swiftly after her.

Hoping that she had chosen the right direction and knew where she was, Linden panted at Anele's back, 'Not that way! Head for the river!'

Liand's village lay on the eastern bank of the Mithil. If she and Anele were going south, they could reach the watercourse by veering to their right. Perhaps they would be able to confuse the *Haruchai* by crossing the river – or by travelling along it.

Or by floating down it, as she and Covenant had done with Sunder under a sun of rain.

Would Stave make that assumption? He might. Certainly he would have to consider it seriously. If she could slip past Mithil Stonedown on the river, aiming towards the open expanse of the South Plains, she would be difficult to track.

And if she rode the current of the Mithil long enough, it would carry her to the southern edge of Andelain. There she might discover the counsel and guidance of the Dead—

It was possible that those shades no longer occupied the Hills. The Masters would know. But they would also know that she did not. Surely they might believe that she would head in that direction?

Fearing that she might lose him in the heavy gloom, Linden ran hard after Anele as he angled away from the path. He must have understood her, in spite of his derangement. And must have believed, as she did, that they fled for the south.

She could hardly see her feet, but her boots found easy footing on the tough cushion of the grass. And in moments the turf seemed to lean gently downwards, perhaps declining towards the watercourse. For a few strides, she ran more easily.

Nevertheless she soon knew that her attempt to escape would fail.

She did not have the strength to run far. Already she could scarcely breathe. The heavy cloud filled her sight like dusk, swirled like phosphenes before her: darkness seeped into her eyes as if her life and blood were oozing away. Again and again, she missed her balance and nearly fell; or the harsh wind knocked her off her stride.

She had been battered too severely; had found too little rest. Her flesh demanded days of healing, not hours. And she had not prepared herself – for ten years, she had done little to sustain the physical toughness which she had developed on her travels with Thomas Covenant.

If the Despiser had appeared before her here and now— And if she could have drawn one full breath – she would have flung everything she had against him without hesitation. But she could not, simply could not, evade the *Haruchai* by running.

Yet Anele sped ahead of her over the dim grass as though all fatigue, every vestige of his mortality, had been left behind in the gaol of the Masters. Galvanised by Earthpower or dread, and hardened by years of privation, he outdistanced her easily. Already he had begun to fade from sight, evanescent as a spectre in the fog. In another moment, she would lose him altogether.

She thought she heard him cackle as he ran, overflowing with mad glee. She would have begged him to slow down if she could have made any sound except gasping.

Then without transition she saw him clearly for an instant, and a glimpse of sunlight flared ahead of her. The outer edge of the storm—? Goading herself forward, she struggled after him.

Another flash of sunlight: a sweep of hillside, sloping mildly downwards. Abruptly the cerements of the strange storm unwound from her limbs and she broke free into dazzling light and clean day.

Momentarily exhausted, she dropped to her hands and knees, panting while the grass seemed to sway under her and the low breeze tugged her sideways.

For a while, she heard nothing except her hoarse breathing and the unsteady labour of her heart. The hills around her seemed silent as a grave, deprived of birds and life by the passage of the storm. She meant to lift her head, look for Anele, but the muscles in her neck and shoulders refused to obey her. For all she knew, he had continued running; would continue until he had left her behind forever.

After a few moments, however, the sound of movement upon the grass reached her, and a pair of old feet, abused and bare, appeared at the edge of her vision. Anele had returned for her.

He chortled in tight bursts like a man who could not catch his breath for mirth.

Linden tried to say his name, but she had no breath. How far had she stretched her frail attempt at escape? A hundred yards? Two hundred? The Masters would recapture her swiftly when the attack on Mithil Stonedown ended.

'Pathetic,' Anele cackled in Lord Foul's voice. 'Entirely abject. You disappoint me, Linden Avery. I would delight to see you grovel thus, but I have not yet earned your prostration.

'If you had not released this failing cripple, my servants the *Haruchai* would have aided you. They would have fostered your false hopes. Now they will hunt you down and imprison you.

'This displeases me.'

She had no stamina; but she could still feel outrage. At once, she surged to her feet, clutching for Covenant's ring with fury in her gaze.

Anele flinched involuntarily. His blind eyes wept dread and misery as his mouth articulated the Despiser's bitter laughter.

'Damn it, Foul!' she panted through her teeth. 'Leave him alone. If you need a victim, try me. Take your chances.'

'And if I do not?' Lord Foul retorted. 'If I elect rather to mock you with this cripple's torment? What then? Insipid woman! Will you scour the life from these displaced bones for my amusement?'

Linden yearned for strength; for the validation of white fire. Wild magic would have given force to her repudiation. If Covenant's ring had not lain inert in her grasp, she might have been able to daunt even the Despiser. But she was not Covenant. His power did not belong to her.

Nevertheless her anger was enough for her. With ire and determination, if not with fire, she confronted Anele's anguish.

'Are you having fun, asshole?' she lashed out. 'Enjoy it while you can. Sooner or later, I'm going to recover my health-sense.' Somehow. 'And when I do, you will *leave Anele alone. That* I guarantee.

'If you don't, I'll be able to get at you.' More than once, percipience had enabled her to take possession of Covenant. 'I'll tear you out of him with my bare hands.'

For what he did to Jeremiah as much as for his cruelty to Anele.

The old man recoiled in fright. The spirit within him chortled harshly.

'Do you believe so?' he retorted. 'That would please me. I would find satisfaction in such a contest. And this mad vessel, that clings so stubbornly to continuance when he should have perished ages ago' – Lord Foul laughed outright –'ah, he would be quite destroyed.'

Not necessarily, Linden assured him in silence. You have no idea what I can do.

As matters stood, however, she posed no true threat. She knew that. Though Anele's plight wrung her heart, she gained nothing by exhausting herself with anger.

Sagging, she released the ring. 'Then what is all this for?' she countered bitterly. 'Does mocking us please you so much that you just can't resist? Hell, you can't escape unless you destroy the whole Earth. Don't you have anything better to do?'

Come on, Foul. Reveal something I can use. Tell me what you've done.

'At this moment?' the Despiser asked merrily. 'Indeed I do. You must be restored, lest you prove unable to serve me. I mean to assist you.'

Abruptly her companion turned away, beckoning her to follow. 'Come, woman. Accept our guidance. We will show you hurtloam.'

For the first time since she had regained her feet, Linden looked past him and saw the Mithil River at the bottom of the slope, bright with sunshine hardly a stone's throw away. Beyond it, mountains reared upwards, jagged as teeth, forbidding the sky. Off to her right, they declined towards the plains; but in the south they gathered into a rugged wall at the head of the valley.

Behind her, partially hidden by the shape of the terrain, the storm still boiled and frothed over Mithil Stonedown. Apart from the occasional thunderclap of violence, the only sounds she could hear were the damp rush of the river between its banks, murmuring of high cold and distant seas, and her own laboured respiration.

Somewhere she had heard of 'hurtloam', but she could not remember what it was, or who had mentioned it.

In spite of the storm, the air held a crisp tang that hinted at snow and ice among the distant peaks. The breeze on her flushed cheeks felt like spring; and the Mithil's current was turbulent, heavy with melted winter.

The *Haruchai* would come in pursuit as soon as the attack on Mithil Stone-down ended.

Seeing that she had not moved, Anele beckoned more urgently. 'You require healing,' Lord Foul assured her. 'Without it, these self-maimed Masters will ensnare you blithely, and this time you will not win free. They will hold you helpless until I am forced to foil them on your behalf.

'Without hurtloam, also,' he added as though he were explaining himself to a dotard, and weary of it, 'you will not regain the discernment which renders you able to serve me.

'Come, I say. I find little sport in your wretchedness. Be assured that this abject old man does not wish harm upon you.'

The sweat had begun to dry on Linden's forehead. Hurtloam? She could not run further: escape was no longer possible. But she could think, and probe, and stand her ground.

I mean to assist you.

She did not believe him for an instant; could hardly credit that Lord Foul had spoken such words. Nevertheless his bizarre offer gave her an opportunity which she did not intend to miss.

Feigning boldness, she retorted, 'And you think I'll do what you tell me *why*? Because I've lost my mind? I'm suddenly stupid? Shit, Foul, you've had things your own way too long. You're getting complacent.'

'Blind fool!' the Despiser jeered. Anele's moonstone eyes rolled in desperation. 'Do you doubt that the *Haruchai* will give chase? Do you conceive that they will now offer you friendship and aid?'

Linden replied with a laugh full of warning. 'Of course not. But I *know* you, Foul. I know better than to believe anything you say.'

'Paugh!' he spat. 'You have never known wisdom or discernment sufficient to comprehend my designs. Your defiance serves no purpose. It merely feeds my contempt. You disdain me at your peril.'

'So convince me,' she countered promptly. 'Give me a reason to listen to you.'

Anele squirmed as though she had threatened him with fire. Tears formed a sheen on his seamed cheeks. His head flinched from side to side as if he feared to speak. But the Despiser ruled him, and he could not remain silent.

'I have said,' Lord Foul answered, 'that the *Haruchai* serve me, albeit unwittingly. That is sooth. Also it is sooth that they will imprison you.

'Whether you partake in them or no, my designs will be fulfilled. Forces have been set in motion which will shatter the Arch of Time, putting an end to the Earth, and to all that I abhor. If you are imprisoned, however, certain aspects of what will ensue remain clouded to my sight. On that path, I cannot determine that my Enemy will not again find means to snare me.

'But if you remain free, apt and able to satisfy me, my release is assured. Your attempts to oppose me will secure it. The Arch will be torn asunder, and I will reclaim my rightful place among the eternal Heavens. My Enemy will be unable to thwart me.'

Cunningly the rank voice added, 'There is more, but of my deeper purpose I will not speak.'

Then the Despiser stated brusquely, 'It must therefore be plain that I do not desire your capture. And it must surely be plain as well that you will fail to evade the *Haruchai* if you are not restored to your fullest strength. You require hurtloam. The *Haruchai* have ensured that no lore remains which might aid you. Only Earthpower will suffice.'

Linden stared at him, momentarily horrified and transfixed. Forces have been set in motion— But then she fought down her dismay. Gritting her teeth, she demanded, 'Stop it. Don't be so damn cryptic. It's petty. And you're wasting time.

'Just tell me what you've done.'

Anele's mouth twisted, although his trapped soul made no sound. *'Done?'* the Despiser chortled. 'I?' His delight wrung Anele's scrawny frame. 'Naught. Apart from the claiming of your vacant son, I have merely whispered a word of counsel here and there, and awaited events.

'The *caesures* are none of mine. Also I had no hand in your blindness, for I did not utter the fine riposte of Kevin's Dirt. If you fear what has been *done*, think on the *Elohim* and feel despair. They serve me as do the *Haruchai*, unwittingly, and in arrogance.'

Linden muttered a curse. 'And you expect me to *believe* you? You didn't send that storm?'

Anele's hands jerked to his head, pulled at his scraps of hair. 'Shame upon you, woman. Shame and excruciation! You undervalue my enmity. That pitiable assault serves me well enough, but it is too crude, far too crude. I would not deign to raise my hand for such an unsubtle ploy.'

Not? Shaken by uncertainty, Linden fell silent. In this, at least, she did believe her foe. Lord Foul was not one to refuse credit for his actions. He enjoyed his own malice too much.

Yet if he did not send the storm—

She was weak; too weak. She could not summon strength which she did not possess.

—who did?

How many enemies did Mithil Stonedown have?

For a moment longer, Anele squirmed as though his guts were being torn. Then he whirled away, sprinting for the Mithil.

As he ran, Lord Foul called back at her, 'Refuse me and be damned! That you will be captured is certain! Then you will be helpless while your son remains in my hands!'

She had been holding her fears at bay: now they broke past her restraint. She had so little power, and had lost so much time. The river might be her only chance to avoid the Masters.

Stiffly she let the slope carry her downwards after Anele.

Ahead of her, the old man sprawled on his belly at the edge of the water-course. His head stretched past the rim of the grass: he might have been searching for his lost mind among the ripples and eddies of the river. From her angle, the current appeared to twist past within reach of his face.

One step at a time, she closed the gap; jerked to a stop at his side. 'What now, Foul?' she panted heavily. 'Do you tell fortunes by staring into riverbeds?'

'More than you know, fool,' retorted the Despiser. 'Men commonly find their fates graven within the rock, but yours is written in water.'

Then his arm flapped, pointing downwards. 'There,' he announced, 'as I promised.' An undercurrent of distress or loathing marred his glee. 'Hurtloam.'

Ah, shit. The last of Linden's resistance leaked away and she folded to her knees. Hurtloam, is it? She felt herself falling into a defeated weariness. *Now* what was she supposed to do? Trust the *Despiser*?

Yet Anele's distress was terrible to behold. He needed to be healed of his vulnerability, freed from madness, more than he needed anything else in life; perhaps more than he needed to live.

That would never happen while the *Haruchai* kept him and she remained blind.

She had promised to protect him. And he was her only link to her son. The old man was possessed by Lord Foul, who also held Jeremiah. Whenever the Despiser taunted her through Anele, he connected her, however tenuously, to her son. If she could *see*, she might be able to reach Jeremiah—

In fact, Anele might be the only link she would ever have.

Below her, the Mithil complicated the air with whispers of escape. Her panting silence seemed to make her companion frantic. Grimaces and revulsion clenched his features as he pointed downwards again. 'There!' His eyes glistened with white terror. 'Are *you* mad as well? It is *hurtloam*, I tell you.'

You require healing.

Half hypnotised by his intensity, Linden looked over the riverbank; but she saw nothing to account for his insistence. Absorbed by its own concerns, the river moiled past little more than an arm's length below the grassy rim of its bank. Where Anele pointed, in a notch between slick stones at the lapping edge of the water, lay a roughly triangular patch of fine sand. She could not distinguish it from other patches of sand nearby, among similar stones.

The murmuring of the water filled her head.

'*There!*' Lord Foul repeated; but it might have been Anele who pleaded with her. 'This doddering cripple is rife with Earthpower, which I loathe. In this he can not be mistaken.'

He had told her that hurtloam would renew her health-sense. Without it, she might never learn how to use Covenant's ring. Only percipience offered her any hope—

The Despiser sought harm and freedom. If hurtloam could truly restore her, then her foe had something to gain by offering it to her: something virulent and dangerous.

But she also might gain something. She might be able to turn his designs against him.

Do something they don't expect.

Holding her breath to contain the clamour of her heart, Linden stretched her arm over the rim of the bank as if she had at last become sure of herself.

With her palm, she touched the damp triangle of sand – and felt nothing.

Anele had squeezed his eyes shut. His head bobbed furiously, signalling lunatic assent.

Carefully she pushed her fingers into the sand; scooped up a handful.

For a moment, she felt only cool moisture against her skin.

Her companion rolled over onto his back; covered his face with his gnarled hands. He made whimpering sounds that she could not hear.

Then Linden saw a faint gleam like a spark in the sand. She nearly winced in surprise as spangles of light began to tingle over her palm. Glints of gold seemed to catch the sunlight, swirling like cast embers or the tiny reflections of Wraiths.

As they swirled, they spread a sparkling sensation into her hand. Bits and motes of vitality soaked her fingers and palm, then swept along her forearm to her elbow and shoulder. Involuntarily, hardly aware of what she did, she raised the sand closer to her face so that she could peer into it; and gleaming like a taste of renewal expanded into her chest, wiping away weariness and exertion as though they had never touched her.

Soon the exuberant tang of Earthpower, numinous and ineffable, thronged throughout her senses, lifting her into a realm of perception as keen as crystal, as vibrant as the language of the sun.

From her hand to her arm, from her shoulder to her ribs and thighs, one by one her bruises evaporated as though they had been blessed away. Her abrasions faded. Palpably caressed, her torn muscles and strained ligaments regained their elasticity and vigour; their eagerness. The harsh effort of flight slipped from her as though she had forgotten it. In a wave of transformation, she felt herself exalted to health.

That was hurtloam, there in her palm. That tincture of pure health had been stirred like wealth by the washing of the river into the plainer substance of the sand: a subtle and transcendent instance of the Land's essential mystery. It was not common, oh, no, not common at all: most of the sand and soil on either side of the Mithil gave no hint of it. But now she could discern it without difficulty here and there, in small whorls and traces between the stones, as though it called out gladly to her nerves.

The river itself called out to her as it curled and chuckled in its course. Its waters sang to her of nourished growth and protracted journeys; of life renewed after sleep. In its bright running, she heard the music of winter storms among the peaks, the yearning chords of the current's long hunger for the sea.

Wherever it found her, the grass on which she lay pressed its green and burgeoning richness to her skin. It spoke of health won by fine, cunning roots from the thin fertility of the sand and loam which cloaked the underlying stone: soil too recently worn from granite, obsidian, and schist to provide the abundant sustenance that enriched the Center Plains and the Andelainian Hills.

And beneath the grass and the soil and the first rocks, she felt the living skeleton of the slopes and crests: obdurate stone that hugged to its heart secrets at once enduring and elusive, tangible enough to be tasted, yet too vast and slow to hear.

Gradually the hurtloam in her hand lost its gleaming as it expended its potency. Nevertheless it had lifted her to her feet: it had lifted up her heart. Tears of gladness blurred her sight as she faced the crisp morning, the burnished sunshine. All around her, the savour of the new season filled the air with possibilities. From its place near the height of noon, the sun warmed away the last of her bruises and fatigue.

In that way, one small handful of sand and hurtloam and Earthpower restored to her the glory of the Land. She felt positively reborn. For reasons which she could not begin to comprehend, Lord Foul had guided her here so that she might set aside her blindness and futility.

At last, she turned her renewed percipience towards her companion.

He still lay on his back with his hands covering his face. Now, however, she did not need to see his features or hear his voice in order to discern his insanity. His posture and his skin, his breathing and the angle of his bones, proclaimed it to her. She knew beyond question that his mind had been broken by more loss than it could endure.

And she knew as well, though the knowledge surprised her, that the Despiser had played no part in Anele's derangement. The incoherence of Anele's mind allowed Lord Foul entrance; permitted the Despiser to speak. Yet the Land's foe had not caused that madness.

Anele's straits brought an ache to her heart. He required healing; absolutely required it. He had already suffered far too long.

Now, suddenly, she had the means to help him.

'Anele,' she asked softly, 'can you hear me?'

He did not respond. His hands covered his eyes urgently. Lord Foul still held him: she could see that. However, the Despiser had withdrawn from the surface, from mastery, leaving the old man at the mercy of his fears.

Linden did not hesitate. Her health-sense seemed to set her free. Two quick steps along the riverbank carried her towards another swirl of fine gleams in the sand. Crouching, she reached down to wash the expended hurtloam from her hand and scoop up more.

Glad fire sang in her fingers as she moved to Anele's side, knelt near his head. 'Anele,' she said again, 'if you can hear me,' if Lord Foul permitted him hearing, 'I have more hurtloam. I'm going to put it on your forehead. It should heal you.'

She was not sure that even this power could knit his mind together. But she had no doubt that it would do him good. If nothing else, it would reduce the damage which years of flight and dread had done to his old flesh.

Immediately Anele jerked down his hands. Terror shone in his sightless eyes. His mouth fumbled to form a cry which might have been *No!*

Still Linden did not hesitate. She expected the prospect of healing to dismay him. He had created his madness for reasons which had seemed compulsory to him. Until he recovered his mind, how could he know whether his need for insanity had passed?

Ignoring his distress, she overturned her hand and wiped hurtloam across his forehead.

Instantly the Despiser's presence vanished from him, fled as if from the touch of dissolution – and Anele went into convulsions.

Before Linden could react, his whole frame snapped rigid. Blood spurted from his bitten tongue. His eyes rolled up into his head, protruding as if they were about to burst. From his skin sprang an acrid sweat that smelled like gall.

Anele! Too late, she saw what she had done. The hurtloam was too potent for him. He was already rife with Earthpower: his body could not contain more. It would scorch the marrow of his bones.

Desperately she slapped at his forehead, trying to remove the sand; but his preterite anguish had already carried him beyond her reach. One fatal scream ripped his throat: he seemed to explode to his feet. In a flurry of thrashing limbs, he flung himself from the riverbank out into the depths of the Mithil.

And the current bore him away.

He made no attempt to swim. Instead he pounded water at his forehead while he sank.

Christ!

Linden surged upright; dashed after him along the bank. Ahead of her, he broke to the surface, still floundering; foundering. Three more strides, four. Then she gathered herself to dive after him.

But she had no chance to save him. As she prepared to spring, a length of rope uncoiled through the air from somewhere above her on the slope.

It splashed the water within Anele's grasp. Instinctively he threw his arms over it; closed his hands on it; clung to it fervidly as it dragged him across the current towards the bank.

Linden staggered to a halt.

Now she saw Liand. Her concentration on Anele had left her blind and deaf to his approach. Unnoticed, he had ridden down the hillside towards her on a hardy mustang, responding to Anele's peril more swiftly than she could.

For a moment, he anchored his rope from horseback while Anele struggled towards the riverbank. Then, when the old man began to gain footing, Liand dismounted. Keeping the line taut, he hurried down the slope to help Anele scramble out of the Mithil.

Soon Anele stood on the grass, streaming and unhealed. Blood spilled from his mouth: the hurtloam was gone from his forehead. While Linden stared at him, Lord Foul let out a snarling laugh.

Then the old man crumpled to the ground, coughing as if he had filled his lungs with water.

Chapter Seven

Companions in Flight

Linden stood on the riverbank, so shocked for the moment that she had ceased to move. Anele grovelled in the grass in front of her. She saw him as distinctly as if he had been etched in sunfire. Water poured like tears off the broken landscape of his face: he coughed as though he had swallowed too much blood.

Hurtloam had given back to her the beauty of the Land.

Beyond question he was full of Earthpower: she could not be mistaken now. Its vitality shimmered in every line of his emaciated limbs, every twist of his abused features. And hurtloam was Earthpower as well, an indisputable instance of healing and glory. It should have lifted him into light like an annunciation. The hurt which he had taken from it contradicted its essential nature.

Now she saw that the loam had not been too potent for him. It had exerted its natural effect. But his inherent energies had become part of his madness, and had opposed his restoration.

Fortunately she had done him no lasting harm.

Retrieving his rope swiftly, Liand demanded, 'Linden Avery, hear me.'

But she did not. She saw only Anele.

He stank of the Despiser.

However, Lord Foul remained beneath the surface, leaving the old man free to gasp and cough. Linden found that she could still distinguish between the Despiser's presence and Anele's madness. But now she discerned other things as well. She saw clearly that the Despiser did not control the phases of Anele's condition; could not grasp possession of Anele at will. Instead he merely took advantage of a flaw in the defences which the old man had erected to protect his deepest pain. And that flaw shifted and changed with the unexplained modulations of Anele's mental state.

She had no idea how this could be so. Her health-sense did not reach so deeply: not like this, separate from him. If she truly wished to understand his sufferings, she would have to immerse herself in him utterly; intrude upon his fundamental relationship with himself.

She had done such things before, long ago, and knew what they cost.

'Linden Avery,' Liand insisted, 'do you not hear me? Is this madness?'

She might have been deaf to him. His voice could not pierce her awareness of Anele's plight. Yet when she turned towards the Stonedownor, she saw him distinctly as well.

He was a sturdy young man, full of toughness and health: the more ordinary and friable health of the Land, nourished and sustained by Earthpower, but not transformed by it. He would not survive to an improbable age, or endure decades of bitter privation, as Anele had.

And he contained no hint of Despite. Instead he emitted sincerity and yearning. The lines of his form expressed an excitement which was turning rapidly into alarm. He was just who he had appeared to be when she had spoken to him earlier: an honest young man, capable of courage and devotion, and largely untried.

Nothing in his aura or his manner suggested that he could sense Lord Foul's presence.

'Do you intend flight?' he asked urgently. 'Then why do you tarry here?'

His mount shared his natural, Land-born vigour, his capacity for toughness – and his apparent blindness to the proximity of evil. It was not entirely whole, however. At one time, it had fallen awkwardly, scraping faint scars into the coat of its chest and fraying the deep muscles around its lungs. That old injury had damaged its stamina. The pinto might be as willing as Liand, but it lacked his endurance.

And over them all the sky arched like a vault of crystal: it seemed to chime to the pitch of its essential cleanliness. At first, Linden descried no hint of Kevin's Dirt. But when she had refined her senses to the memory of that stifling yellow shroud, she tasted it faintly above her, distant and imprecise, like a thin smear of *wrong* across the crisp purity of the air. It was still there.

Eventually it would blind her again.

'Linden Avery!' Liand cried at her. 'What ails you? Soon the Masters will hasten in pursuit. If they have not yet discovered your flight, they will do so at any moment. If you desire to avoid them, we must *go*. We must go *now*!'

We?

At last she heard him.

Of course she had to go. She had lost too much time; far too much. Indeed, she could hardly imagine why the *Haruchai* had not retaken her already. How had Liand found her when they had not?

But such questions could wait. Escape might still be possible. And Anele might not be able to bear it if he were captured again.

They had to *go*.

We?

Damn it, she could not afford the time to argue.

'I'm sorry, Liand.' With an effort, she wrenched herself out of her distraction. 'You're right.' *Do something they don't expect.* 'Anele can ride with you. I'll try to keep up.'

The young man stared, frankly unsure of her. He did not – could not – understand what had happened to her. Or what she had done to Anele.

At every moment, Linden expected to see *Haruchai* rush past the rim of the hills; descend on her like raptors. Cursing, she hurried to Anele's side, tugged on one of his arms.

Even that small approach to the Despiser filled her nerves with revulsion. But she did not let go.

'*Now*, Liand!'

If Liand could pull Anele after him onto the pinto's back, she intended to run and run as long as her new strength lasted, as far and as fast as she was able.

The old man tensed against her grasp; propped his free arm under him. Unsteadily he climbed to his feet. Behind the blood on his lips, his skin had a pallor of weakness, as if his stubborn fortitude were failing.

Liand was tangibly unsure of Linden, but he did not hesitate. Springing to his mount's back, he secured his coil of rope to the rudimentary saddle, then extended his hand to Anele.

We?

Linden gave Anele's arm to Liand, and with her help the Stonedownor heaved Anele up behind him. Inarticulate frights clenched Anele's face as he clung to Liand for support.

Yet every hint of Lord Foul's presence was suddenly gone from him. Between one heartbeat and the next, he had become himself again.

At once, Liand wheeled his mount. With Linden running beside him, he cantered south along the riverbank, towards the head of the valley; away from Mithil Stonedown and the Masters.

Marvelling at herself, Linden matched Liand's pace while the terrain allowed the pinto to canter. If she had been less familiar with the wonders of Earthpower, she might have believed that she was dreaming. She was not the same woman who had fallen to her knees only a short time ago. One small handful of hurtloam had apparently erased her mortality. While she ran, exaltation filled her heart. Buoyed by springy grass and soft soil, by the mountain tang of the air and the luxuriant quest of the river, and by hurtloam, she felt that she could run, and go on running, until she arrived at hope.

The riverbank changed as the valley rose, however, forcing Liand to slow his mount. The hillsides grew steeper, constricting the Mithil in their climb towards the mountains, and rocks and hazards littered the ground along the watercourse. The mustang could have broken an ankle there, or stumbled into the Mithil.

Above Linden and her companions, the mountains had become sheer and forbidding without apparent transition: a high, jagged wall glowering against intrusion. As she slackened her pace, she felt her lungs strain for breath as if the air had turned abruptly thin, inhospitable.

Panting, she asked Liand to halt. 'Just for a minute. I need to think.'

Liand reined in the pinto, but did not dismount. The lines of his arms and shoulders told her as plainly as words that he wanted to press on. And Anele needed his support. Worn out by the effects of Lord Foul's presence, the old man had fallen asleep against Liand's back.

The Despiser had not returned. For some reason, he could not.

That was a relief, for Linden as well as for her battered companion. Now she could talk to Liand without being overheard.

She needed to understand him. Why was he here? Why was he helping her? And how far was he willing to go—?

As her pulse slowed, she found that she could feel Kevin's Dirt more clearly. It seemed to clog her lungs, depriving her not of oxygen but of some more subtle sustenance. Already it had begun to erode her health-sense, fraying her nerves towards blindness. This time the process was slow: the lingering power of hurtloam hindered it. She might not lose true percipience before nightfall. Yet it would eventually fail her.

By degrees, her exhilaration leaked away, leaving her to the realities of her situation.

There appeared to be no hurtloam anywhere around her. The hillsides were bare of its eldritch glitter. And the banks of the Mithil had grown steeper as the ground rose to the foothills, putting the river itself effectively out of reach. She would not be able to refresh her health-sense a second time.

Nor could she share the wonder of such vision with Liand. While her discernment lasted, she would have to *see* for both of them.

Muttering curses to herself, she scanned her surroundings.

The hills which shouldered the watercourse blocked her view of Mithil

Stonedown. Past their crests, however, she could still make out the highest seething fringes of the storm which had enabled her escape. They boiled with violence and darkness; but their *wrongness* was of a different kind than Kevin's Dirt and *caesures*. The stormtops violated Law and nature in less harmful ways. Nor did they gust in pursuit of her – or of Covenant's ring. Instead they remained to harass the village.

I would not deign to raise my hand—

Lord Foul had told her the truth about more than hurtloam.

And as long as the Masters remained to ward the Stonedown, they could not search for her. Hell, they might not yet know that she was gone. It was possible—

'So far, so good,' she said to Liand's impatience. 'Now what? If we want to escape' – she indicated the mountains – 'we need to get up there somehow.'

To the east lay her easiest road. There the valley diverged more and more from the course of the Mithil; and as it curved into the southeast it rose steadily until it became a vale between mountainheads. From this distance, its slopes appeared to remain grassy and gradual two thousand feet and more above Mithil Stonedown. If she and her companions angled in that direction, they would be able to travel as fast as her stamina could carry her.

And they would be in plain sight of the valley bottom for at least a league, until they rounded the curve up into the vale. The *Haruchai* would spot them as soon as the storm over Mithil Stonedown dissipated. Linden's red shirt assured that.

She needed another route.

Even if Liand knew of one, however, she would not be able to stay ahead of the Masters for long. They would travel faster than she could. Ultimately her only realistic hope was that Stave and his people would believe she had fled north, into the open Land.

Responding to her question, Liand pointed towards the rising cliffs south and slightly west of him. When Linden looked there, she saw a rift between crags ending in a fan of scree above the foothills. The shape of the rift and scree suggested that the slope of loose stone piled higher as it reached out of sight. If it piled high enough, it might provide a route into the Range above the rift.

But it stood on the far side of the Mithil. And as the watercourse neared the head of the valley, it gathered into a crooked ravine tending somewhat east of south: too ragged and sheer to climb; too wide to cross. Then, at the base of the nearest cliff, it sprang up into a waterfall which thundered from a damp cut high and unattainable in the rock face.

The rift might as well have been on the dark side of the moon.

'Great,' Linden muttered in disappointment. 'How can we get there? The last I checked, none of us can actually fly.'

'It will not be difficult.' Lifting his head, Liand indicated the waterfall. 'That fall we name the Mithil's Plunge. For a portion of its way, it pours beyond the cliff, and there we may pass behind it. We must take care that Somo does not slip, but we will be able to do so.

'Certainly the Masters know of this, as I do. But mayhap they will not readily notice my absence from Mithil Stonedown. I am only a young man whom they tolerate, not a valued companion. And if they do not guess that I accompany you, they may not pursue you there, believing that you have no knowledge of it.'

Linden nodded. 'Good.' So it was possible: she still had a chance.

But the young man's answer brought her back to another question. What in hell was he *doing* here? He was risking more than the disapproval of the Masters; far more than he knew. She could not accept his help simply because he chose to offer it.

Frowning, she waited until he turned to face her. Then, more harshly than she intended, she said, 'But before we go any further, you have some explaining to do.'

His eyes widened in surprise.

'Where do you get this "we" stuff, Liand?' Because she was afraid and unsure, and could not afford to be, she sounded angry. 'What are you doing here? Why aren't you defending Mithil Stonedown, where you belong?'

The young man swallowed uncomfortably, but did not drop her gaze. 'Would you have been able to save your companion without my aid?'

'That's not the point. Of course I would have saved him. I can swim, for God's sake.'

'And will you save him now?' countered Liand. 'You are able to gain the mountains, but how will you feed him among the rocks? How will you feed yourself? Can you bear the cold of the peaks?'

Linden scowled at him. 'Oh, hell. You know I can't. I didn't exactly plan any of this. I just—' She knotted her fists to contain her frustration. 'I just can't do anything for my son while I'm a prisoner.'

Liand indicated bundles tied to his saddle. 'Then it is well that I have given the matter forethought which you could not. Here I have food and waterskins. Robes and blankets. Rope.

'Somo alone enhances your flight.' Apparently Somo was the mustang. 'I have done much to provide for your escape. All that I can.'

His eyes begged her to accept him.

'But—' With an effort, Linden restrained her impulse to swear at him. His manifest sincerity did not deserve it. 'But,' she said more quietly, 'that's still beside the point. Obviously I need any help I can get. But your people need you, too. They were fighting for their lives when I ran. How could you leave them?'

Her demand increased his discomfort. For a moment, he looked away towards the mountains as if he were measuring himself against them. When he met her gaze again, the sunlight on his face exposed the difficulties within him.

Nevertheless he faced her squarely.

'At first I did not,' he admitted. He had set his impatience aside. 'You know this. I ran to the defence of the Stonedown, thinking that we were assailed by *kresh* in the storm. But the Masters halted us, saying that there were no *kresh*, that only the storm itself threatened us.

'Against that power we could do nothing. And it struck no one. For reasons which I do not grasp, the storm's violence harmed only our homes. Indeed, it fell only upon those homes which had been left empty. Their families were at work in the fields, or attending other concerns. And the Masters assured us that no lives had been lost – that none would be lost if we did not approach the storm.

'How they had gained their knowledge, I do not know. But I believed them. And I thought of you, Linden Avery.'

Homes which had been left empty? She frowned to herself. It made no sense. Why would any foe wish to damage empty dwellings?

'I considered your need for escape,' Liand continued, 'and my desire to aid you. Then I stole away. Leaving the Masters and my people to regard the storm, I hastened to the stables for a mount. Gathering all that I could to assist your flight, I rode in search of you.'

Linden studied him, trying to understand. 'All right. I get that.' She could read the nature of his emotions readily enough, but not their content, their causes. 'But why did you head south?'

He had found her too easily.

The Stonedownor shrugged. 'You had no mount. If you sought escape north-wards, the Masters would shortly ride you down, and no aid of mine would free you.

'Also,' he added a bit sheepishly, 'the storm lay there, and I feared to hazard it.'

Perhaps his reply should have eased her anxiety. The *Haruchai* might not reason as he did. Surely they did not remember her as a woman who fled from eldritch storms?

Yet her trepidation increased as she considered the young man. The Masters had deprived him of a kind of birthright: he lived in the Land, but knew nothing of its power or peril. His desire to join her would have consequences beyond his comprehension.

Gritting her courage, she placed one hand like an appeal, a hint of exigency, on his thigh.

'That's not enough, Liand. You still haven't answered my question. Not really. Mithil Stonedown is your home.' It was all he had ever known. 'Everyone and everything you've ever cared about is there. Why do you want to risk all that for me?'

He did not hesitate. To this extent, at least, he was prepared for her questions.

'Linden Avery,' he replied gravely, 'I might answer that I find no satisfaction in the life of my home. I sense the greatness of the Land, but I know nothing of it, and I crave such knowledge.

'Or I might answer that I mistrust the Masters, for it is plain that their knowledge is great, yet they reveal nothing.

'Or I might answer that I have no family or attachments to hold me.' His tone hinted at loneliness. 'My father and mother had no other children, and both have fallen to time and mischance in recent years. Nor have I found other loves to fill their place in my heart.'

Again he looked away. When he faced Linden once more, his yearning had found its way to the surface. Stiffly he told her, 'I might well answer so, for it is sooth.' Then he appeared to lose resolve. Ducking his head, he murmured awkwardly, 'Yet there is another truth, of which I do not presume to speak.'

She nearly turned away from his discomfort. It was too obvious: his open nature held no concealment. And she could so easily have let the matter drop—

Yet she did not release him, in spite of his vulnerability. She had her own qualms, her own conscience: she could not set them aside merely to gain aid from a man who could not imagine what his assistance might cost him.

Roughly she knotted her fingers in the rough wool of his leggings. 'I'm sorry. That's still not enough. You have friends and neighbours who feel the same way, you must have, but they aren't here. I need to hear the rest.

'I can see it in you. I just don't know what it means.'

Liand appeared to groan inwardly. However, it was not in his nature to refuse her probing, regardless of his own unease. And he had a palpable courage which enabled him to tell the truth.

'In my life,' he said, 'I have beheld wonders.' The words seemed to come slowly from deep within him. 'Linden Avery, you are one. The storm which provided for your escape is another. The Falls are both wondrous and dire. And the sight from Kevin's Watch of the shroud which blinds the Land fills my dreams with fear.

'But it is the memory of the strange being whom the Masters named *Elohim* which impels me to your side. His words are a knell within me, though I was but a child when I heard them.

'All that he said lies beyond my ken. Yet I comprehend clearly that he has prophesied our doom. And I grasp also that he did not speak only of Mithil Stonedown. His words pronounced the destruction of the Land.'

The angle of the sunlight filled Liand's eyes with shadows as he gazed down at Linden. 'I am as I appear to be, merely a young man among my people. But I have seen that the Land is lovely. I wish to defend it. And if I am too small for so great a task, still I will not be content until I have learned the name of our doom.'

Now he did not look away. She wished that he would. His undefended innocence wrung her heart, and she did not want to witness his reaction when she answered him.

Quietly, almost whispering, she said, 'Liand, listen to me.' Her fingers tugged at his leggings of their own accord, urging him to understand her. 'I can't let you help me unless you hear what I have to say.

'You called me a wonder, but there's nothing wonderful about me. I love the Land. I love my son.' In spite of her bereavement, she loved Thomas Covenant. 'I try to keep my promises. And I'm carrying a power I don't know how to use. That's all there is.'

Grimly she spared herself nothing. 'But it's worse than that. In my own life, I'm already dead.

'Do you see this?' Releasing his leg, she used both hands to show him her shirt. 'It's a bullet-hole. I was shot through the chest. I'm only alive because this is the Land.'

Because she had healed herself. And because Joan had summoned her.

Liand stared at her, plainly unable to grasp what her assertions entailed.

'On top of that, it looks like the whole Land is against me. The Masters don't mean me any harm, but they're deaf to everything I care about.' The weight of her concerns grew as she listed them. 'You've seen Kevin's Dirt. You know the *caesures*, the Falls. There are *kresh* and *Elohim* and Sandgorgons and Ravers.' Anele had mentioned *skurj*, whatever they might be. 'There are at least two lunatics with too much power,' Roger and Joan. 'And there's Lord Foul, who has my son.

'Do you want to know the name of your doom? Do you really? It's the Despiser. He's trying to destroy the entire Earth.'

The mere act of speaking such words seemed to bring the peril nearer. Yet she could not stop. Liand needed to know what he risked in her company.

'And as if all of that weren't enough, the Staff of Law has been lost. It's the only weapon I know of against Kevin's Dirt and the Falls, and it disappeared after only a couple of generations. I need it back, but I have no earthly idea where to look.'

Raising her hands, she clenched them into fists between her and the Stonedownor as if to fight off his growing chagrin.

'Do you think the Land is bigger than the Masters have ever told you? Do you think the danger is more terrible than anything you've ever imagined? You have no idea. Men with the power of gods could scarcely stand against what Lord Foul is doing, and I can't begin to compare myself with them.

'I need your help, Liand. That's painfully obvious. I'll be glad for your company. But if you've got some confused notion that all we have to do is escape the Masters, you should go home now. They are the least of our problems.' Absolutely the least. 'If you come with me, I can't promise you anything except anguish and death.'

There she stopped, shaken by the danger of what she had said. If Liand chose to turn away now – as he should – she would have nothing except Covenant's ring and her failing health-sense and Anele's fractured guidance to aid her.

But she had struck a spark of anger in the young man. He glared at her, squaring his shoulders and straightening his back until he appeared to tower over her, bright with sunshine.

'Linden Avery,' he retorted sternly, 'have you not said that you sojourned to Mithil Stonedown once before, in years long past? At that time, did it appear to you that the folk of my home were careless of their word, or lightly swayed from the path of their convictions and desires?'

She shook her head helplessly, remembering Sunder with rue and admiration. The Graveler she had known had held fast to all his choices, regardless of their consequences. Without him, she and Covenant would not have survived—

'If they did,' Liand went on, 'then we have come far from that time, and do not regret what we have become.' Every upright line of his frame seemed to reproach her. 'I am not so flighty of heart that I would recant my wish to aid you merely because the peril is great. I do not merit your doubt. And I will not abandon you.'

Linden bowed her head to hide her sudden tears. His unexpected dignity made him impossible to contradict. And she saw now, without warning, that he was taking the same stand that she had taken ten years ago, when she had involved herself in Covenant's ordeal with Joan. Covenant had warned her in the simplest and most honest terms, *You don't know what's going on here. You couldn't possibly understand it. And you didn't choose it.* But she, too, had refused to be dissuaded.

She had paid a high price for her intransigence. Yet she had learned to regret none of it. Even her time in Revelstone, when *samadhi* Raver had touched her soul with evil, had proven to be worth the cost.

She had neither the foresight nor the wisdom to assure Liand that he was wrong now.

Blinking her eyes clear, she looked up at him again. 'I'm sorry. I didn't mean it that way. I don't doubt your honesty – or your word. I can see the kind of man you are. I'm just trying to be honest myself.

'I've been where you are. I met a man who needed help. I wanted to help him,' needed to help him. 'And I could never have imagined what I was getting into. If I'd known how bad it was going to be, I don't think I could have done it.

'But I wouldn't be who I am now if I hadn't refused to abandon him.'

As she spoke, the young man's indignation eased. The way his shoulders relaxed told her that he accepted her apology. 'I hear you, Linden Avery,' he replied firmly. 'I am content to aid you.'

'Good,' she repeated with more conviction. 'In that case, we should go. I've already wasted too much time.'

They might make better progress while Anele slept. She could not predict how he might react when he awakened.

Liand nodded his agreement. With his heels, he nudged Somo into motion.

Now they will hunt you down—

Summoning her reserves, Linden trotted at his side as he began to angle across the hillside towards higher ground.

Chapter Eight:

Into the Mountains

At first the climb was not arduous. The slopes had not yet swelled to true foothills and Liand ascended them at a slant, aiming for the head of the valley. Nevertheless the joy of the Land's health and vitality continued to fade from Linden's muscles and she began labouring to match his pace. Hurtloam had healed her, but it could not give her stamina. Inevitably her new strength diminished.

Before long, however, as she and her companions rounded a hilltop on their way to the next rise, something ahead of her tugged at her senses; and when she looked towards it, she saw a clump of *aliantha*.

No wonder she loved the Land. Its providence delighted her.

Without urging, Liand guided his mount towards the low shrubs.

They had twisted limbs and dark green leaves shaped like a holly's; and beneath the leaves grew clusters of viridian fruit the size of blueberries. Under the Sunbane she had never found more than a single bush in any one place, but here they had proliferated into a group of six or eight. Perennial and hardy, and resistant to all Lord Foul's depredations, they produced treasure-berries in every season, even during the winter – or so Covenant had once told her.

When she and her companions reached the clump, Liand might have dismounted; but Linden asked him to remain where he was so that he would not disturb Anele. The old man's need for rest was as palpable as an ache. Gathering berries eagerly, she handed some to Liand, then placed several in her mouth.

They tasted like a gift, the distilled essence of the Land's natural beneficence: light and sweet, with a flavour of peach followed by a refreshing suggestion of salt and lime. Her whole body seemed to sing with appreciation as their savour and juice washed the strain from her throat.

One by one, she dropped the seeds into her hand and cast them around the grassy slope as she had been taught, so that more *aliantha* would grow to nourish the Land. And from the pinto's back, Liand did the same. Seeing him do so comforted her. Apparently his people had retained that aspect of their birth-right, whatever else they may have lost.

At another time, she might have wished to linger here, relishing the taste of the berries. But the certainty that the *Haruchai* would come after her rode her pulse as if her heartbeats were the rhythm of feet and hooves. And when she looked back down the valley, she saw the thunderheads over Liand's home dissipating at last, their violence expended. The search for her, and for Anele, would begin soon – if it had not already commenced.

Leaving some of the treasure-berries behind for others who might need them, Linden and Liand resumed their flight.

Now the terrain piled upwards more strenuously, accumulating towards the heights. Liand's path had temporarily diverged from the watercourse; but Linden measured their progress by watching how the mountains towered ever more grandly over them, single peaks and massifs jutting urgently into the heavens. Ahead of her, the Mithil's Plunge loomed until it seemed to pour from the heart of the range, bearing the private thunder of mountains in its writhen turmoil.

She could see no sign of any path behind the Plunge. Already the roar of the water seemed to barricade the way against her.

And when she reached it, what then? Behind the fall: across the more obdurate foothills beyond it to the steep fan of scree: up that precarious slope to the concealment of the rift. And what *then*? She had no clear plans. In a general sense, she proposed to work her way eastwards among the mountains until she could regain the Land somewhere beyond the remains of Kevin's Watch. Then, if she had baffled the pursuit of the Masters, she might head towards Andelain, hoping to find an unspecified form of insight or support.

The vagueness of her intentions frustrated her. But what else could she do? Liand knew only Mithil Stonedown and its environs; nothing about the larger issues of the Land. And anything that Anele might comprehend was masked by madness.

She wanted to find the Staff of Law; but she had no idea how to look for it. It had already eluded the meticulous searching of the *Haruchai*.

Prompted as far as she knew by nothing but prescience, Jeremiah had constructed images of Mount Thunder and Revelstone in her living room. Perhaps he had meant them as hints; guidance. But she did not know how to interpret them.

Then a tug of the breeze brought spray to her cheeks; and when she looked up into the water's buffeting roar, she saw that she and her companions were approaching the base of the Mithil's Plunge.

The cataract pounded down from its heights as though it were driven by anger as well as eagerness; as though the cold force of the peaks filled the torrents with a fury for spring and renewal. Liand shouted something to her, pointing, but she could not hear him through the tumult. Spray chilled her skin in spite of her exertions: her shirt had begun to stick to her skin. Looking where Liand pointed, however, she saw that the waterfall tumbled free of the cliff-face for several hundred feet before it smashed into the head of its ravine. Still she would not have imagined that a passage existed behind the Plunge, if her companion had not urged her forward.

Behind him on the mustang, Anele had awakened. As if he could see, the old man studied the waterfall intently, but he showed no alarm. Beads of moisture clung in his hair and whiskers, and sunlit sparks of reflection transformed his face as if he were being made new.

As they ascended, the spray became as thick as rain, and the water's tumult seemed to blare away every other sound.

A stone's throw later, Liand dismounted; helped Anele to the ground. Panting against mist that threatened to fill her lungs, Linden climbed to join them as the Stonedownor unpacked a blanket from his supplies and wrapped it over Somo's eyes, protecting the pinto from panic. Then he looped the reins around his hand and pointed again. His yell barely reached her.

'There!'

She made no effort to see what he indicated. She felt that she had begun to suffocate, smothered as much by the water's weight as by its roar and spray. Liand meant to lead her behind that cataract. If they allowed its force to touch any part of them, it would snatch them down, crush them to pulp.

Unable to answer, she simply nodded and waved Liand ahead. As the young man pulled Somo into motion, she joined Anele; took his arm as if to remind him of her promise. Then she began to move towards the Plunge, forcing her way down a throat of sound.

Anele accepted her grasp. Perhaps in his blindness he trusted her as he did Liand. Or perhaps he was already familiar with this passage. In his long years of hiding and fear, he might have discovered it for himself.

Gradually Liand guided them nearer and nearer to the waterfall; but Linden did not so much as glance at it. It frightened her profoundly. Her clothes clung to her now, entirely soaked. Sodden hair straggled across her face. She had difficulty keeping her eyes clear. The complex thunder of the fall seemed to pull at her, urging her towards its touch.

Clutching Anele as much for her own protection as for his, she followed Somo's hooves behind the massive curtain of the Mithil's Plunge.

At first, she could not see: the water's roar seemed to efface light. But then reflected illumination from the ends of the passage leaked through the spray, lifting her way out of the darkness.

Liand led her onto a ledge in the cliff-face, wide enough to be traversed safely, but complicated with piled stones and small boulders, as well as with moisture and moss as slick as ice. She had to test her footing carefully as she moved, holding back her weight until she had confirmed that the sole of her boot would grip the next step. Constantly the water howled at her to fall, and fall, and fall again. She had entered the demesne of irrefusable forces. Reality seemed to deliquesce along her nerves, soaking into her clothes and running from her skin in rivulets, chilling her heart.

Ahead of her, Liand let the mustang pick its way over the rocks at its own pace. Somehow the sodden blanket and Liand's grasp on the reins kept Somo's alarm within bounds.

With her hand on Anele's arm, Linden felt his fear. Preoccupied with her footing, she initially tasted only a featureless apprehension in him; nothing more. By degrees, however, the character of his distress seeped into her like the waterfall's power.

One timorous step at a time, he had passed into a realm of threats altogether his own; a crisis beyond her grasp. When she noticed the change in him at last, it shocked her out of her own frights.

He may have been becoming sane. If her senses discerned him accurately in this tumult—

On an uncluttered and comparatively level section of the ledge, he halted suddenly, drawing her to a stop beside him. His teeth gnashed the laden air as if he sought to tear loose bitten chunks of meaning. He may have been crying her name, calling out for help or attention in a voice too mortal to be heard.

Linden flung her arms about him, holding him still; restraining herself from the howl of the water. She could hardly identify his features. Pressing her forehead against the side of his skull, trying to reach him bone to bone, she shouted, 'Anele! Are you all right? I can't hear you!'

His voice reached her like a distant vibration in her brain. '*Skurj!*' he shrieked. '*Skurj* and *Elohim*. He has broken the Durance. *Skurj* mar the very air. Oh, the Earth!

'Its bones—' Freeing one arm from Linden's embrace, he pressed his palm to the cliffside as if he meant to thrust himself away from it; out into the water and death. 'Its bones cry out! Even here, they *wail!*'

'Anele!' she yelled again. She had nothing to offer him except his name. 'Anele!' He had gone beyond her comprehension. Every clench and tremor of his emaciated frame told her that he was sane at last.

For him, sanity held more horror than any madness.

'My fault!' he cried as if he were being shattered. '*Mine!* The *Elohim* did naught to preserve the Durance. They are tainted. Arrogant. *I* lost the Staff! The treasure and bulwark of Law. My birthright. I *lost* it!'

Sane? Linden gripped him with all her strength. Chills shook her. This was sanity? According to Stave, the Staff of Law had been lost more than three thousand years ago.

'Anele! What's wrong? What's happening to you?'

Liand could not have heard them. He continued to lead Somo cautiously towards daylight and the westward foothills, abandoning Linden and Anele to the exigency between them.

Abruptly Anele released the stone of the cliff and wrenched himself around in her grasp. When they were face to face, he pressed his forehead against hers. Earthpower latent in his veins throbbed for conflagration. Furiously he drove his anguish into her mouth; down her throat.

'Are you blind?' he howled; and the greater howl of the Plunge swept his words instantly away. 'Do you see nothing? *I held it in my hands!* It was given into my care. *Trusted to me!* For years, I studied the Earth, striving for courage. *And I lost it!*'

She could not understand him; could hardly think: spray and thunder smothered her mind. Shivers ran through her bones. Lost? The Staff of Law? *Millennia* ago? Sweet Christ! What manner of sanity had overtaken him? His deprived flesh had suffered the erosion of too much time, but nothing on that order of magnitude. Even her diminished perceptions could not have misread him to such an extent.

Water streamed down their faces, ran from their chins. His revulsion towards his own failings had become a whirlwind of rage and grief.

'I could have preserved the Durance!' he cried. 'Stopped the *skurj*. With the Staff! If I had been worthy. *But I did not!* Instead I betrayed my trust! My word. My birthright.' He might have been weeping. 'All the Earth.'

'Anele!' Desperation surged in Linden. She had to get him out of this place. 'Anele, come on!' She could not think. If the storm within him mounted any higher, he might hurl himself from the ledge, and her with him.

But his passion demanded release. Forcing his forehead against hers, he begged her fervently, 'Oh, break me! Slay me! Tear away this pain and let me die! Did you sojourn under the Sunbane with Sunder and Hollian and learn nothing of *ruin*?'

Did you sojourn—?

Had he recognised her at last?

In a tumult of confusion and thunder, she jerked her head away. '*Damn* it, Anele! Of *course* I understand ruin. It doesn't give you the right to do this to yourself! For God's sake, don't make me drag you out of here!'

Perhaps in sunlight under an open sky he would become comprehensible to her.

For an instant, a flare of Earthpower burned in his white eyes, set light to the water beading in his beard. When it passed, it appeared to leave him chastened; covered in gloom. He nodded as if she had doomed him.

Suddenly frantic to escape the Plunge, Linden took his arm once more and urged him forward, after Liand and the pinto.

A moment later, Liand's form restricted the passage. He had come back for them. 'Why do you tarry?' he called anxiously. 'What is amiss?'

She did not try to answer him. Instead she waved her arm to send him back the way he had come. As he complied, she continued to scramble grimly over the treacherous stones.

With all the will that she could muster, she concentrated on her footing. Anele's sanity confounded her. She yearned for the safety of the sun and understanding.

Tear away this pain and let me die!

Elohim she knew; but what in hell were *skurj*?

Her boot skidded off a patch of wet moss. She caught herself on Anele's arm. She was supposed to protect him. She knew him better when he was mad.

Liand receded ahead of her, drawing her on. He did not appear to fear falling. Perhaps on some atavistic level his people retained their ancient relationship with stone.

Oh, the Earth! Its bones cry out!

When at last she and Anele emerged into the bright solace of day, everything between them had changed.

'Linden Avery.' Liand demanded her attention. 'Why did you tarry? Are you harmed?'

The day's spring warmth shone through the spray. She kept her grip on Anele. Blinking against the sun's dazzle, she peered at him with all of her senses.

He had been *sane*: her nerves were certain of it. Now, however, a roil of confusion distorted his emanations. His mind had relapsed to madness.

And his plight was changing. The character of his derangement shifted –
and shifted again. Before her eyes, he modulated between the various phases
of his insanity; and the landscape of his face appeared to shimmer and blur,
smeared out of clarity by the heat of his rapid alternations. She could read
nothing in him surely except that he was no longer the man who had cried
out to her behind the Mithil's Plunge.

He said nothing. For the moment, at least, even language was lost to him.

Finally Linden allowed herself to turn towards the Stonedownor. 'I'm sorry,
Liand.' She wiped tears of brightness from her eyes. 'Something happened to
Anele in there.' She had to shout to make herself heard. 'He changed. All of
a sudden, he seemed sane,' although everything he had said sounded crazy. 'But
it's gone now. I don't know what came over him.'

'But you are not harmed?' Liand persisted.

She shook her head. 'Just scared. Everything here' – she gestured at the sky,
the mountains, the foothills – 'looks so normal.' Undisturbed. 'The way the
Land is supposed to look. But the things Anele said—'

She shuddered. 'He was terrified. He sees dangers I've never even heard of.'

They were gone now, locked behind his madness.

In response, Liand's expression darkened. 'The Masters.' His disgust was
barely audible through the waterfall's roar. 'The most dire perils stalk the Land,
and they tell us nothing.'

Then he straightened his shoulders. 'It would please me greatly to elude
them. We must continue our ascent. Exposed on these hillsides, we may yet be
discovered.' Frowning, he added, 'The hue of your raiment will be easily seen.'

Linden needed no urging to move away from the mind-numbing thunder of
the Plunge.

He had left his mount a short distance away, its reins loosely secured under
a hunk of rock. While he wrung out the blanket he had used to cover Somo's
eyes, she said suddenly, 'Don't put that away. I can use it to cover my shirt.'

The blanket was damp, but it might warm her.

With a nod of approval, Liand handed it to her. As soon as she had draped
the rough brown wool over her shoulders, she returned to Anele.

The old man did not react to her presence, or her voice. However, he allowed
her to reclaim his arm. Pulling him with her, she started up the hillside.

With Liand and Somo a pace or two below her, she headed in the general
direction of the rift.

Their path angled to the west as it challenged the tumbled foothills. Further
in that direction, along the northward reach of the mountains, the foothills

were like fingers knotted in the valley-floor, pulling the valley wider; and between the fingers lay steep vales and clefts. Here, however, in the head of the valley, the slopes were more even, draped down from the cliffs like a mussed skirt. Linden and her companions were spared the abrupt rises and drops of the northwestward hills.

Nevertheless their ascent was arduous. The stubborn grasses and wind-twisted brush which marked the hillside could not always hold the soil in place under the pressure of their feet, and they often had to scramble in order to gain ground. At the same time, the slope grew steadily steeper, with less vegetation to anchor the dirt. The distance from the passage behind the Mithil's Plunge to the fan of scree below the rift may have been no more than a stone's throw for a Giant; but after an hour's labour Linden and her companions still had not reached their immediate aim.

They must have been visible from the vicinity of Mithil Stonedown. Until they reached the shelter of the rift, they had to hope that they were too small to be noticed from so far away.

Clinging to the blanket, she paused for a moment's rest. Her respiration had become a deep heaving, and her legs trembled with each step. Sunlight and exertion had dried the blanket as well as her clothes; but that had proved to be a curse as much as a blessing. For a while, she had been grateful for anything which eased her various chills. Gradually, however, her dampness had become sweat and hard breathing, and even the crisp breeze of this elevation could not cool her. As the strength which she had gained from hurtloam and treasure-berries faded, she began to believe that she would prove too weak for her task.

More and more, she relied on Anele's support. In spite of his emaciation, he remained hardy: he seemed to forge upwards as if he had never done anything else. His eldritch toughness helped her continue the climb.

His skin against hers described the irregular fluctuations of his mental estate. At odd intervals, he veered close to sanity: less frequently, she felt the Despiser's dark scorn moil in his depths. Masques of rage and grief and appalled endurance drifted through him like shadows. But he did not speak; and she had no energy to spare for his complex lunacy. As she forced her trembling steps upwards, her awareness of him withdrew. She only clung to him, and laboured onwards.

Ahead of her, Liand and his horse ascended more easily; had to wait for her more often. Although Somo's hooves dragged the untrustworthy hillside downwards, the mustang had stamina to spare in spite of its old wound. And Liand possessed the characteristic toughness of Stonedownors. He and his mount would be able to keep going long after Linden dropped.

They were here on her account; and yet their chances of escape would have been much higher without her.

Then Liand called softly, 'Soon, Linden Avery!' and she looked up from her benumbed concentration to see him standing at the edge of the scree.

Lowering her head, she forced her quivering muscles to bear her to his side.

He had already taken a waterskin from one of his packs. Now he handed it to her. She held it shaking to her lips and drank until she had soothed her dry mouth and raw throat. Then she passed the waterskin to Anele.

While the old man sucked at the skin, Liand unpacked a little bread and sun-dried fruit. 'We should not tarry here,' he remarked, 'exposed to the sight of the Masters. I fear, however, that you near the end of your endurance. And Somo cannot bear you on this terrain. Our flight will fail if our haste exceeds your strength.'

He handed food to her first, then to Anele.

Linden thanked him with a nod. She was breathing too hard to speak.

Slowly she chewed bread and fruit, and tried to imagine sustenance flooding through her veins, filling the courses of her heart. Jeremiah *needed* her. She did not mean to fail him. While she ate, she surveyed the climb ahead and endeavoured to believe that she could master it.

That she could master herself.

For a while, Liand gave her silence; a chance to gather her resolve. But his tension increased as he waited, and eventually he asked, 'Are you able to continue, Linden Avery? Until we gain shelter, every delay is perilous.'

'I'll do it,' she muttered. 'Able or not.' Then she gave him a wry frown. 'But you have *got* to stop calling me "Linden Avery". I feel like I'm in church.'

She had spent too many hours there as a child, wearing her one nice dress and fidgeting while a preacher levied strictures against her; a preacher who knew nothing about her pain – or her mother's.

But she could not expect Liand to understand such things. 'I'm "Linden",' she added. 'That's enough. I don't need so much formality.'

He studied her as if she had asked him to commit an act of irreverence. 'Very well,' he said cautiously. 'You will be "Linden" to me.'

Then he turned away and began to repack Somo's burdens.

Anele also seemed eager for movement. He had grown restive, shuffling his feet on the scree. He started upwards without any urging.

Setting her teeth, Linden stumbled into motion and followed her companions.

There the ascent became harder for her. The slope of shale and loose stones increased the likelihood that she might fall; perhaps break an ankle. At the same time, however, she found that she could use her hands to help her climb. If she simply let the blanket hang across her shoulders, her arms could ease some of the strain on her legs. In that way, in spite of her weakness, she was able to keep pace with Anele, Liand, and Somo for a time.

She scraped her palms; bruised her newly healed elbows and shins. The thinning air stung her lungs until phosphenes plucked erratically at her vision, dissolving boulders and wedged stones to bright swirls and then resolving them to granite again, schist and obsidian, feldspar and quartz. But she fixed Jeremiah's face before her and went on climbing.

Halfway to the rough edges of the rift, however, she began to fall behind her companions. The blanket slipped from her shoulders, but she was unaware that she had lost it. The tremors in her legs expanded to her arms and chest. Eventually she found herself approaching each step as a discrete event, isolated in time from the one before it and the one which would come next. During that instant, nothing existed for her except the effort of heaving herself upwards.

Then finally she discovered that her legs no longer shook and her cheek lay along a sheared plane of stone. Flakes of mica sent small gleams of sunlight into her eyes, but she could hardly distinguish them from the dissociated dance of anoxia. Had the air become so thin already? And why had the sun not warmed the chill from these rocks? She seemed to enjoy their cool touch, but could not understand it.

There was something missing, she knew that, but it eluded her until Liand grasped her arms and urged her upright. 'Linden, come,' he panted softly, 'the rift is nigh, you will be able to rest soon,' and she realised that she had stopped moving. Her legs must have failed without her knowledge or consent.

Stunned by exertion, she let Liand help her to her feet.

Anele had apparently disappeared, perhaps translated upwards and out of reach by a rush of Earthpower; but Somo stood nearby. The pinto had flecks of froth on its nostrils: its chest heaved for breath. Still it had more strength than she did.

She had lost her son. She would have wept, but she had no tears.

Feigning a confidence which he palpably did not feel, Liand told her, 'Here,' and placed her hand on one of the bindings which secured his mount's packs. 'Hold here. Somo will support you. The way is not far. In the shade of the cliffs, we will rest.'

Obediently she closed her fingers on the leather. She may have nodded: she could not be sure. Like her legs, her neck seemed to twitch for reasons of its own; but she had gone numb, and its motions lay beyond her awareness.

After that, the instances of effort which had defined her became a blur and she climbed without recognising what she did, drawn upwards by Somo's strength and Liand's courage; and by the knowledge – the only thing she knew – that she needed to grow stronger.

When she returned to herself, she lay among boulders in the shadow of high cliffs, one near her head, the other a stone's cast from her feet. Far above her, the sky still held the sun, and would for some time yet. But where she lay, a deep gloaming covered her, and all her courage had fallen away.

Liand stood nearby, watching her; making no attempt to hide his anxiety. When she met his gaze at last, he knelt beside her. Gently he put her hand on the throat of a waterskin. Then he reached under her arms to help her sit up.

'First water,' he said as if he knew what she needed. 'Then bread. Later I will give you meat and fruit.'

Sitting, she felt cold air tug through the bullet-hole in her shirt, noticed its dry touch on her forehead. Her skin was no longer damp. She did not particularly need water. Or she had stopped sweating some time ago—

Perhaps that explained her weakness.

With Liand's help, she guided the waterskin to her mouth, drank a few swallows. Almost instantly, sweat seemed to spring from all her pores at once.

Dehydration, she told herself weakly. Stupid, stupid. She was a doctor, for God's sake; familiar with the effects of exertion. She ought to know better.

'My fault,' she murmured when Liand had helped her drink again. 'I forgot about water.' Until she dropped it, the blanket must have heated her; increased her fluid-loss. 'I'll be all right.'

The Stonedownor looked sceptical. 'I am unsure. Our sojourn has only begun. If we are not taken by the Masters, we will face many days more harsh than this one. I fear that you will be unable to endure.'

She wanted to say, You and me both, but refrained for his sake. Instead she indicated the waterskin and asked, 'Can we refill this?'

He frowned. 'Linden Av – Linden. I have never ascended so far above Mithil Stonedown. I know nothing of what lies before us.' Then, as if he were taking pity on her, he said, 'Yet I believe that we will discover streams and springs among the mountains. And snow remains upon the heights. Drink all that you require. Doubtless we will need to ration aliment, but it will be false caution to stint on water.'

'In that case,' she replied, 'don't worry about me. I'll get tougher.' She would have to. 'And I'll take better care of myself.'

Liand nodded, clearly unconvinced, and turned away to unpack the food he had promised her.

While he did so, Linden looked around for Anele.

To her right, in the direction of the Mithil valley and the South Plains, she found her view blocked by a hill of rocks like a fold in the detritus spilling down the rift. Somehow Liand had urged her high enough up the scree to reach the shelter of a hollow in the scree. Past the rise, she could see only mountains and sky: she and her companions were hidden from the valley. If they had not been spotted before they reached the rift, the Masters would catch no sight of them now.

Of course, she also could not see if they were pursued—

To her left, the broken slope climbed southwards into the narrowing cleft; and there she located the old man. He sat on shards of granite and obsidian several paces above her, his head cocked to one side, blindly studying the cliff opposite her and mumbling to himself.

Linden drank more water and tried to focus her fading health-sense on him.

Physically he looked no worse than when she had first met him: tired, certainly, and ill-fed; but sustained by old stubbornness and Earthpower. He conveyed the conflicting impressions that he had already suffered more privation than ordinary flesh could bear, and that he had reached none of his limits. As for his mental state, she could discern little through the shaded dusk. However, the phases of his madness had apparently stabilised, leaving him in a condition which resembled his partial sanity when she had talked to him among the rubble of Kevin's Watch.

There he had spoken of reading the wreckage of the Watch. In his fractured way, he had tried to tell her what he saw.

He has no friend but stone.

She had no one else who could so much as hint at what had happened to the Land.

Unsteadily she rose to her feet. When she had reached a fragile poise, unsure of her centre as she was of her muscles, she picked up the waterskin and carried it to Anele's side, wallowing like a derelict in the troughs of the rocks as she moved.

He did not turn his head at her approach: he might have been unaware of her. As soon as she placed the waterskin in his lap, however, he raised it to his mouth and drank, automatically, without shifting his sightless scrutiny of the cliff.

Stifling a groan, she eased herself to the rocks beside him. A low wind tumbled down the slope, cooling the sweat from her skin. Its faint susurrus covered his voice: she only knew that he spoke because his lips moved. For a moment, she rested, gathering herself. Then she asked softly, 'Anele, what do you see?'

At first, he did not respond. She thought that perhaps he could not. His concentration resembled a trance: he might have been bespelled, caught by granite incantations audible only to him. His head hung to one side as if that might improve his hearing. But then he seemed to shudder, and a sad anger reached out to her senses.

'These stones are old.' A flick of his hand indicated the detritus in the rift as well as the cliffs themselves. 'Old even by the ancient measure of mountains. They know nothing of *caesures*. Or Masters.' Gradually his voice took on a cadence which she had not heard from him before, a rhythm hinting at music and gall. 'Rather they speak of great forests filling all the Land. In their hearts they lament the rapine of trees.'

He is the hope of the Land.

Linden leaned close to him; breathed, 'Tell me.'

'Their sorrow is no fault of mine,' he replied as if he were answering an accusation so old that its meaning had perished long ago. 'That at least I am spared. It is aged beyond antiquity, and they neither forget nor cease to keen.

'Here is written the glory and slaughter of the One Forest.'

The One—? She had heard the name before; but she could not imagine why the stones of the world would remember the transient lives of wood. Nevertheless she yearned for anything he could reveal which might place the Land's plight into some kind of context.

'Tell me,' she repeated softly.

Liand approached over the rocks to offer his companions a little bread, but Anele ignored him. When Linden had accepted it, however, the old man answered her, impelled to words by a threnody in granite.

'It is a tale of humankind and destruction, of defenceless beauty unheeded, ripped from life. A tale of Ravers and *Elohim* and Forestals and sleep, the fatal sleep of long time and unmitigated loss.'

Facing the cliff, Anele let his anger flow. His head leaned, first to one side, then the other, as though he followed a tune that passed from stone to stone around him.

'Then was not the age of men and women in the Land, and neither wood nor stone had any knowledge of them. Rather it was an era of trees, sentient and grand, beloved by mountains, and the One Forest filled all the Land.

'Its vast life spread from the ancient thighs of *Melenkurion* Skyweir in the west to the restless song of the Sunbirth Sea in the east, from the ice-gnawed wilderness of the Northron Climbs to the high defiance of the Southron Range. Only at the marges of Lifeswallower did the One Forest stand aside, for even in that lovely age evils and darkness seeped from the depths of Gravin Threndor, leaking harm and malevolence into the Great Swamp.

'And in that age, the spanning woodland was cherished in every peak and fundament of the Land, held precious and treasured by slow granite beneath and around it, for the One Forest knew itself. It had no knowledge of malevolence, or of humankind, but of itself its awareness was immense beyond all estimation. It knew itself in every trunk and limb, every root and leaf, and it sang its ramified song to all the Earth. The music of its knowledge arose from a myriad myriad throats, and was heard by a myriad myriad myriad ears.'

Linden listened as if she were ensnared. She moved only to eat the viands which Liand handed to her. In the rhythm of Anele's voice as much as in his words, she recognised the Land she loved.

She knew little of the Land's deepest past: even this much of its history was new to her. But she had sojourned in Andelain, her every nerve alight with percipience and Earthpower, and she felt the fitness of Anele's story. It was condign: it *belonged*. She could believe that the Earth's gutrock would remember such things.

At her side, Liand crouched down to listen, caught by wonder; but she hardly noticed him. For a time she forgot pursuit and black storms. The tale of the One Forest had no bearing on her immediate plight, but she drank it in as if it were hurtloam and *aliantha*; another form of nourishment.

'Yet in those distant years,' Anele related, 'neither men nor women had true ears.' His anger sharpened as he continued, as if he had absorbed the passion of the stones. Linden heard his heart in every word. 'When they came to the Land, they came heedless, providing only for themselves. And the malevolence within Lifeswallower had burgeoned, as all darkness must, or be quenched. It had grown great and avid, and its hunger surpassed satiation.

'No tongue can tell of the shock and rue among the trees when human fires and human blades cleared ground for habitation. The mountains know it, and in their hearts they yet protest and grieve, but mortal voice and utterance cannot contain it. A myriad myriad trunks, and a myriad myriad myriad leaves, which had known only themselves in natural growth and decay, and which had therefore never considered wanton pain, then cried out in illimitable dismay – a cry so poignant and prolonged that the deepest core of the peaks might have answered it, were stone itself not also defenceless and unwarded.'

Anele clasped his arms around his knees to contain his distress. 'Yet men and women had no ears to hear such woe. And even if they had heard it, their single minds, enclosed and alone, could not have encompassed the Forest's betrayal, the wood's lamentation. Only the malice within Lifeswallower heeded it – and gave answer.

'For a time, those who had come to the Land felled trees and charred trunks only because they knew not how else they might achieve space for homes and fields. Thus was their cruelty at first restrained. But their restraint was brutal and brief by the measure of the One Forest's slow sentience. And after those generations, humankind discovered malevolence, or was discovered by it. Then the murder of the trees was transformed from disregard to savagery.

'Hence came Ravers to the Land,' the old man rasped bitterly, 'for they were the admixture of men and malevolence, an enduring hunger for evil coalesced and concentrated in transient flesh generation after swift generation until they became beings unto themselves – spirits capable of flesh, yet spared the necessities of death and birth. Thus they gained names and definition, three dark souls who knew themselves as they knew the One Forest, and who aspired above all things to trample underfoot its vast and vulnerable sentience.

'And humankind had no ears to hear what had occurred. Men and women were only ignorant, not malefic, for their lives were too brief to sustain such darkness, and when they perished their descendants were again only ignorant.

'Yet even that renewed and ever renewed ignorance could not spare the One Forest. Humankind was deaf to malevolence as to lamentation, and so it was easily led, easily mastered, easily given purpose, by the three who had learned to name themselves *moksha*, *turiya* and *samadhi*. Therefore the butchery of the trees swelled and quickened from generation to generation.'

There Anele paused; released his knees in order to scrub unbidden tears from the grime on his cheeks. His blind eyes stared at the broken rocks as if he could see the ancient moment of their shattering. Around him, the breeze flowed slowly, and the chill of high ice seeped into the rift as the westward peaks began to bar the sun.

Linden waited for him in a kind of suspense, as though she needed the old man's tale.

When he had gripped his knees again, he said, 'Still the One Forest could only wail and weep, unable to act in self-defence.' Voiceless tears spread anger and sorrow into his torn beard. 'Despite its vastness, it, too, lived in ignorance. It knew only itself and pain, and so could not comprehend its own possible strength. Born of Earthpower, sustained by Earthpower, knowing Earthpower, the One Forest could not grasp that Earthpower might have other uses.

'Thus the destruction of the trees grew as the ambitions of humankind and Ravers mounted. And with that bereavement came another loss, inseparable from the first, but more bitter and deadly. In the slaughter of each tree, one small gleam of the Forest's Land-spanning sentience failed, never to be renewed or replaced. Thus the wishes of the Ravers were fulfilled. As the butchery of the trees increased, so the One Forest's knowledge of itself diminished, lapsing towards slumber and extinction.

'That grief was too great to be borne.' Anele himself seemed hardly able to contain it. His voice rose to a low cry. 'Even mountains could not endure it. Peaks shattered themselves in sorrow and protest. This very cliff split as a heart is torn asunder by rage and loss, and by helplessness.'

For a moment, he gaped at the riven walls. Their yearning had come upon him like a *geas*. They needed his mortal tongue to articulate their interminable rue. Cold exhaled down the rift like a sigh of protest and loss.

But then his head jerked to the other side, and he seemed to find a new vein of song. His voice dropped to a murmur which Linden would not have been able to hear if he had not chipped each word off his stone lament like a flake of obsidian, jagged and distinct.

'The Earth itself heard that cry. Every knowing ear throughout the Earth heard it. And at last, when much of the Lower Land had been slain of trees, and the devastation of the Upper had truly begun, the cry was answered.'

Abruptly Anele leaned forward, shifted the angle of his head. 'There.' With one trembling, gnarled finger, he pointed into the centre of the sloping rubble. 'It is written there – the coming of the *Elohim*.'

Gloaming filled his moonstone eyes. 'Many centuries after the rising of the Ravers, at a time when much of the One Forest's sentience had dwindled to embers, a being such as the trees had never known came among them, singing of life and knowledge, of eldritch power beyond the puissance of any Raver. And singing as well of retribution.

'Why the *Elohim* came then and not earlier, before so much had been lost, these stones cannot grasp. Yet come she did – or he, for the *Elohim* are strange, and such distinctions describe them poorly. And with her song, the remaining leagues of the One Forest awoke to power.'

This part of the story Linden had heard before. Findail the Appointed had told it to the assembled Search for the One Tree aboard Starfare's Gem. Still she listened with all her attention. Anele conveyed an impression of urgency, of necessity, which she could neither name nor ignore.

'The trees,' he told the gathering shadows, 'could neither strike nor flee. Their limbs were not formed to wield fire and iron.' Findail had said, *A tree may know love and feel pain and cry out, but has few means of defence.* 'Yet even that remnant of wakefulness which remained was vast by mortal measure, and its power was likewise vast. Capable then as well as aware, the One Forest turned its loathing and ire, not against the deaf ignorance of humankind, but rather against the Ravers.

'Nor did the trees count the cost of their new might. The *Elohim* had sung to them of retribution, and she was more puissant than any Raver. Her nature granted them the power to deny. Therefore they took her and bound her, and with Earthpower set her in bonds of stone at the edge of Landsdrop as a barricade, a forbidding, against the Ravers. And such was the strength of their ramified will that while she lived, while she retained any vestige of herself, *moksha*, *turiya* and *samadhi* were entirely barred from the Upper Land. No Raver in any form could pass that interdiction to threaten the remnants of the One Forest.'

There Anele stopped, although his tale was not done. He had lost the thread of memory in the granite, or his ability to discern it had faltered. Nevertheless its compulsion held Linden. When he did not continue, she finished his tale for him as if she, too, had been bound in place by the exigency of the trees.

'But that's not all,' she added. 'People didn't stop cutting down forests just because the Ravers couldn't goad them to it.' Covenant had told her this. 'The trees had spared them, but they were still too ignorant to know it. Ordinary people kept on hacking and burning whenever they thought they needed more open ground. They didn't know,' could not know, 'that they were murdering the mind of the One Forest.

'So the trees went further. After they formed that forbidding,' the Colossus of the Fall, 'they used what they learned from the *Elohim* to create the Forestals. Guardians to protect the last forests.' Morinmoss between Mount Thunder and the Plains of Ra. Dark Grimmerdhore east of Revelstone. Fatal Garroting Deep around the flanks of *Melenkurion* Skyweir. Giant Woods at the borders of Seareach. 'Because most of the time we humans don't seem to care what we're doing to the world.'

Then she had to stop as well. She needed time to pray that the ending of the Sunbane and the creation of a new Staff of Law had undone some of humankind's harm; that the Land had regained enough vitality to enable the growth of new forests.

'It may be so,' Anele sighed into the gathering chill. 'That knowledge is not written here.'

After a long moment, Liand stirred. He rose to his feet; gathered up the food and waterskins. 'No one remembers it.' His bitterness echoed Anele's tale. 'The Masters do not speak of it. This treasure of the Land's past, these memories of glory, they keep to themselves.'

Linden groaned inwardly. He was right. The *Haruchai* had left the people of the Land as ignorant and blind – and as potentially destructive – as their first ancestors had been.

In their own way, the Masters might prove as fatal as Ravers.

'Thank God,' she murmured obliquely, hardly aware that she spoke aloud, 'there are only two of them left.'

No ordinary death could claim a Raver. But *samadhi* Sheol had been rent, torn to shreds, by the sacrifice of Grimmand Honninscrave and the power of the Sandgorgon Nom.

'Two?' Liand asked in confusion.

And, 'Masters?' croaked Anele, rousing himself. 'Masters?'

Linden brushed them aside with a flick of her hand. Anele's tale filled her head. 'I'm just thinking—'

She felt now that she had never before grasped the full atrocity of the Sunbane. Oh, she had experienced its horror in every nerve. Her knowledge was both personal and intimate. But she had not guessed what such devastation meant to the fading sentience of the trees. Or to Caer-Caveral, the last Forestal, who had lost more than he could bear.

It was no wonder, she thought, that he had given up his defence of Andelain for the sake of Hollian and her unborn child. He had known too much death and needed to affirm life.

Suddenly Anele flung himself to his feet. Wailing, 'Masters!' he began to scramble frantically up the raw sharp rocks.

Masters—?

Remembering forests and slaughter, Linden struggled upright in time to see Stave top the rise which blocked her view of the South Plains.

He approached swiftly. Deepening shadows obscured his face. Even with her full health-sense, she had never been able to read the emotions of the *Haruchai*. Nevertheless her thin percipience was enough to let her feel the urgency of his stride.

Behind her, Anele rushed upwards like a shout of fear.

'Linden Avery,' Stave barked as he drew near, 'this is folly.' The timbre of his voice suggested anger, although its inflection did not. 'Do you seek to flee? Then why are you not far from this place? While you linger, they have caught your scent.'

Instinctively, uselessly, Liand moved to interpose himself between Stave and Linden. 'It is *you* we flee, Master.' Once again his innocence and resolve conveyed a dignity that she could not match. 'If we have erred, it is because we were granted opportunity to hear a tale which you have denied us.'

Stave ignored him; seemed to slip past him without effort. 'Abandon your supplies, Stonedownor,' he ordered as he advanced on Linden. 'You must flee at once. The Chosen will require your aid.'

Then he stood before her.

'They have caught your scent,' he repeated. 'Already they have severed any retreat. You must make haste.'

Liand started after Stave as if he meant to leap on the Master's back. But then he seemed to hear something in Stave's tone that halted his attack. '"They"?' he panted. '"They"?'

An instant later, he wheeled; rushed towards his packs and Somo.

Linden stared at Stave in blank shock. The mourning of the cliffs still gripped her: slain trees thronged in her mind. She could not grasp—

Your scent—?

'Have you forgotten your peril?' he demanded. 'Alone, I cannot withstand them. Yet I will slay as many as I may. They will be hindered somewhat. Perhaps they will be daunted. Or perhaps you may gain some covert before they assail you.'

'Linden!' Liand cried out to her. 'Run! Do not delay for me!' Feverishly he threw bundles onto the pinto's back. 'I will follow!'

'Stave?' she breathed dumbly. 'What—?'

'Linden Avery, you are hunted by *kresh*.'

In his flat tone, the words sounded as deadly as Ravers.

Chapter Nine:

Scion of Stone

Had she heard of *kresh* in huge packs possessed by Ravers? Did she imagine the memory? Aboard Starfare's Gem she had seen a black swarm of rats driven by a Raver's malice. In a terrible storm burning eels had come near to crippling the Search for the One Tree. But *kresh*—?

Had she ever heard of those great yellow wolves before Liand had mentioned them?

The Stonedownor yelled, 'Linden!'

Stave insisted inflexibly, 'Linden Avery.'

Her son needed her, and she had come to this.

The twilight of deep shade filled the cleft. Overhead the sun had passed into mid-afternoon, but the ragged cliffs rose too high to admit direct sunshine. Beyond them, the sky held an illimitable blue tinged to the verge of gloaming with purple and majesty. Its lambency was all that lit the rift.

Liand fumbled to secure Somo's burdens. 'Stave!' he shouted. 'How far?'

'Half a league,' Stave answered as if Linden had asked the question, 'no more.' His hands touched her shoulders. 'If you do not flee, you will perish here. They will tear you asunder.'

'Flee?' she countered. 'What for?' Disoriented by images of ruin, she could hardly concentrate on the Master. 'I mean, seriously. I can't outrun them. I can hardly walk. It's been too long—'

She lifted Covenant's ring out of her shirt and closed it in her fist. 'You can't protect us. You said so. Maybe I can.' She had no idea how. 'If I can't—' She shrugged. 'We weren't going to survive anyway.'

But Stave immediately wrapped one hand over her fist. 'Do not,' he urged her. His hard eyes and the scar high on his left cheek seemed to call out to her through the gloom. 'Linden Avery, I forbid you. Old evils inhabit these mountains. You will rouse them, or draw them down upon us. Better the threat of fangs and claws than some darker peril.'

Finally Liand finished with Somo's packs. At once, he hauled the pinto into motion, half-dragging the beast up the slope.

Linden stared back at Stave, floundering within herself. Old evils—? She could not imagine what he meant; but he was *Haruchai* and commanded belief.

And she did not know how to summon wild magic. It arose according to laws or logic which she had not yet learned to understand. Without percipience to guide her—

'Linden, come!' Liand cried as he laboured upwards. 'You do not know the ferocity of these *kresh*! They will devour us flesh and bone. We must find some shelter which we are able to defend.'

'Then it's up to you.' She faced Stave as squarely as she could. 'I'm too weak.'

For a brief moment, no more than a heartbeat, Stave appeared to hesitate. He may have realised that there was more at stake between them than simple frailty and flight. His people remembered her as the Chosen, the Sun-Sage; worthy of service. But he could not simultaneously aid her and recapture Anele. Every step upwards would carry him further away from the driving convictions of his people.

An instant later, however, he surged at Linden, swept her into his arms and began to spring easily up the rocks.

His feet were bare, yet he crossed the sharp edges and splinters of the rubble as though mere stone had no power to hurt him. In a dozen strides he caught up with Liand and Somo; passed them. When Linden glanced up the rift, she saw that he was gaining on Anele, in spite of the old man's frenetic haste.

An inestimable distance above Anele, the glow of the sky lit the place where the fallen rock met the rims of the cliffs. Those slopes might or might not provide a route onto the higher mountainsides: Linden was too far away to see them clearly.

Too far away to reach them at all.

Below her, the wolves had not yet appeared. If they had gained the scree, or even the rift, they were still hidden by the rise behind which she had rested. How far was half a league? A stone's throw? For a Giant? More? She should have known: she had travelled leagues by the hundreds during her earlier time in the Land. But she could not remember.

Anele's pace appeared too headlong and frantic to be sustained; but she did not fear for him. *He has no friend but stone.* He had endured for decades in and around these mountains. Even now, he might well outlast her.

When she glanced down at Stave's feet, their swift certainty frightened her. If he tripped, he would fall to the jagged stones atop her. To ease the strain of his task, she hooked her arm over his neck. Then she watched behind her for the first glimpse of the *kresh*.

In his arms, she mounted the slope as if she were moving backwards through time. With every step, Stave's feet touched memories which only Anele could perceive. The *Haruchai* carried her up over broken pieces of song, fragments of lamentation.

No wonder Anele was mad. Such music might have fractured anyone's mind.

Covenant's ring bounced on its chain outside her shirt. It seemed to reproach her with its mystery and power. Its true owner would have known how to use it; save his comrades. She had seen him in the apotheosis of the Banefire, mastering the source and fuel of the Sunbane even though his veins were full of Lord Foul's venom. In spite of his self-doubt, he had found within himself the passion and control to quench long generations of bloodshed.

But afterwards he had foresworn power. He had refused to defend himself against Lord Foul.

In her dreams, he had told Linden to trust herself – and yet she did not believe that she could raise enough flame to hold back a pack of wolves. When minutes had passed and the *kresh* did not appear, she caught Covenant's ring in her free hand and put it back under her shirt. He had left it to her, but she could not claim it as her own.

Liand tried to match Stave's pace, but could not. Somo slowed him. The beast was a mustang, bred to mountains; but the scree demanded great care.

Jostled in the cradle of the *Haruchai*'s arms, Linden panted, 'Wait for Liand. We have to stick together.' With *kresh* on her scent, she would not have left even a Master behind.

She did not expect Stave to heed her. So far he had shown little regard for her wishes. Yet he slowed his strides for Liand's sake. Apparently he and his people took their guardianship of the Land seriously.

When Liand and Somo had drawn level with him, Stave suited his pace to theirs. Ahead of them, Anele was able to maintain his lead. In that formation, they climbed as if they were ascending into recollections of the One Forest. To Linden, it seemed that the old man's tale drew them upwards.

She peered back at the horizon of the rubble below her. Stave had carried her perhaps a quarter of the way up the rift; possibly less. Still she saw no sign of any wolves. However, she did not doubt that the *kresh* would soon surge past the rise.

Liand may have felt otherwise. Breathing easily in spite of his exertions, he guided Somo closer to Stave and Linden. 'I am disturbed, Master,' he said tensely. 'You name yourselves the guardians of the Land. And you have recognised Linden Avery from the forgotten past.' His distrust reached through the dim light to Linden's nerves. He had left his diffidence towards the *Haruchai* behind. 'Yet you have come alone to her aid.

'You conceal many truths. Will you reveal one here, in the Chosen's presence? Why have you come alone to ward her?'

Stave made a sound like a snort. Linden felt his strength flow; and for a moment, he surged ahead of Liand. Irredeemable crimes passed beneath his feet. But then he seemed to reconsider. 'Do not presume to challenge us, Stonedownor,' he retorted flatly. 'You do not suffice. Enquire of the Chosen whether the word and the honour of the *Haruchai* have worth.'

Together humankind and Ravers had decimated a vast and marvellous intelligence. With the Sunbane Lord Foul had completed their cruel work.

Stave paused, apparently waiting for Linden to speak. When she did not, however, he added, 'Yet I will acknowledge that we were unprepared for her flight.' His tone conveyed a two-edged disdain: for Liand's disapproval as for Linden's escape. 'The Linden Avery who is remembered among us would not have done so. Rather she would have borne the white ring to the Stonedown's defence. Therefore we were taken unaware.'

His words stung her. In his dry tone, she heard a criticism with which she was intimately familiar. Often in the past, the *Haruchai* had made no attempt to conceal their scorn for her doubts and hesitations.

He may have been right. Perhaps she should have remained to fight for the Stonedown. But Covenant had told her, *Do something they don't expect.* And Stave knew nothing of Jeremiah.

If she had stayed behind, she would not have heard Anele's tale.

The Master continued to answer Liand. 'Nor could we estimate the direction of her flight. The Chosen has repudiated our knowledge of her. For that reason, we separated when the storm had passed, so that we might search more widely.

'We could conceive of no purpose which would impel her here, but we feared that she might attempt these mountains in ignorance, thinking them a sanctuary. Thus it fell to me to ride southwards, while Jass and Bornin hastened to consider more likely paths.

'I found no sign to guide me. Almost I turned aside. But then I saw *kresh* gather among the hills beyond the Mithil. I saw the direction of their hunt, and was concerned that the Chosen had become their prey. Therefore I made haste to place myself ahead of the pack. At the Mithil's Plunge I left my mount so that it might not fall to the *kresh*, and continued on foot.'

Stave looked into Linden's face as if she rather than Liand had questioned him. 'Linden Avery, are you answered?'

He might have asked, Will you trust me now?

Because he distrusted her, she replied, 'I thought Lord Foul sent that storm. I wanted to draw it off.'

In his arms, she was entirely vulnerable to him. No doubt he could have broken her neck with one hand. Nevertheless she had enough faith in him to add, 'And no, I don't trust you. What you Masters are doing appalls me. The *Haruchai* I knew weren't that arrogant.'

She could not bring herself to tell him about Jeremiah.

By rough increments, the rift narrowed, its walls leaning towards each other as though they yearned to seal away the ancient pain of the stones. As the gloom grew deeper, it brought with it a cold that seemed to congeal against Linden's skin. Above her on the slope, Anele had begun to falter. Apparently he had exhausted his desperation. In spite of Somo's difficulties with the ascent, Stave and even Liand diminished the old man's lead.

'The *Haruchai* whom you knew,' Stave told Linden stiffly, 'had not yet experienced the meaning of Brinn's victory over *ak-Haru Kenaustin Ardenol*. We had seen the Staff of Law lost and regained. We had seen it un-made and then made anew. When it was lost yet again, we could not continue as we were.

'Brinn has proven himself equal to the guardianship of the One Tree. Will you tell us that we may not prove equal to other guardianships as well?'

'Of course not,' Linden murmured through the soft whisper of Stave's breathing and the harder rhythm of Liand's. 'But I've seen your people die. It's your *definition* of guardianship that frightens me. You're asking too much of yourselves.'

He responded with a slight shrug. 'What would you have us do?'

Still grieving for the trees, she turned her gaze downwards, and her heart lurched as she saw a moiling line seethe past the rim of the rise. A darkness heavier than shade poured up the scree like a viscid spill flowing in reverse, running backwards in time into the storehouse of the mountains' memories. If she had not lost most of her health-sense, she might have felt ferocity and fangs pelting over the rocks after her scent.

In moments the upwards-cresting tide of *kresh* had filled the cleft from wall to wall. And still it crashed higher and gathered to crest again: God, *hundreds* of them, more wolves than she could have imagined in one pack.

'Hurry,' she panted to Stave as if that were her only reply. Alarm clogged her throat. 'They're coming.'

One Master and an untried Stonedownor would never hold back that tide.

Liand flung a look over his shoulder, cursed under his breath and began to haul on Somo's reins, trying to hasten the pinto with his own strength.

But Stave did not quicken his pace, or glance behind him. 'They will outrun us,' he said stolidly. 'That cannot be altered. Over these rocks the mount travels poorly.' He had told Liand to abandon the supplies – and Somo. 'Haste will only exhaust your companions to no purpose.'

Then how—? she wanted to ask; demand. How do you expect us to survive? An instant later, however, she realised that Stave had no such expectation. Her flight into the rift had created this plight. He had merely pursued her so that he could fight on her behalf.

While she could, she rested in his arms and tried to focus her remaining percipience inwards, searching for the link or passage which might connect her to the limitless power of Covenant's ring.

The howling of the pack echoed up the rift; and the sound seemed to sharpen the chill on Linden's skin. In it she heard more than ordinary animal ferocity. As they raced upwards, the *kresh* gave tongue to a more personal and fervid hunger; a desire not merely for food and blood, but for destruction. Redoubled by the cliffs, their howls suggested Lord Foul's eager malice.

The Despiser had guided her to hurtloam. He had taunted her with Jeremiah's suffering, the Land's pain. And now he sent wolves to feast on her flesh?

No. She did not believe it. Lord Foul did not desire her death. Not yet.

He had sent the wolves to *prevent* her.

Prevent her from what? She could not imagine. Nevertheless she was abruptly certain that the true threat of the *kresh* surpassed mere fangs and rending.

When Lord Foul had aided her earlier, he may have expected her to flee in the opposite direction, towards the Land she knew. And he had not touched Anele again, however briefly, until after she and her companions had passed the Mithil's Plunge.

If she gained the mountains, she might thereby foil some aspect of the Despiser's machinations.

Even here, her foe had something to fear from her.

Ahead of her, Anele had stopped climbing. He had mounted no more than halfway up the cleft. A harsh ascent remained between him and the possibilities of the mountains. Yet he knelt among the rocks as if he had come to the end of his stamina – or his heart.

Peering through the shadows in alarm, Linden saw that he had halted at the lower edge of a rising plane of unbroken stone. There the fall of rubble had exposed a stretch of native granite which reached from cliff to cliff and perhaps a dozen strides upwards.

The rough surface offered a few moments of easier flight. Yet the old man had faltered below it—

'Anele!' she called up to him. 'Keep going! We have to keep going!'

With a twist of his shoulders, he looked back at her in Stave's embrace; at Liand and Somo and the rising wave of wolves. A faint cry reached her among the howls and echoes as he floundered to his feet and staggered onto the exposed gutrock.

He managed three steps, or four. Then he fell on his face and lay still.

'Hurry!' Linden panted to Stave. 'God, *Anele*.'

This time the *Haruchai* heeded her. Springing into a run, he sped forward.

Behind them, Liand laboured over the rocks as swiftly as his mount could climb.

Scant heartbeats later, Stave reached the plane of stone; strode to Anele's prone form. There he set her on her feet.

At once, she dropped to her knees and found the old man gasping as if in terror.

'Anele? What's wrong?'

Her health-sense had declined too far: she could not discern the source of his distress. She only knew that he had not exhausted his strange strength. But when she touched his arm, she realised that he was indeed terrified; that he was wracked, nearly undone, by remorse and sanity.

Behind the Plunge, he had radiated similar emanations. Yet the character of his aura here had substantial differences. There he had writhed in self-recrimination, scourged by the consequences of his supposed crimes. I *lost the Staff*! He had blamed himself for impossible faults; mistakes which he could not have made. Here his dismay was more intimate. His fears seemed to come from the foundation of his being, the bedrock upon which his commitments and beliefs had once stood.

Although he did not move, he seemed to rise to meet her as if her touch had evoked him in some way; called him up from an abyss to speak to her.

'How was it possible?' he panted as if he were answering her. 'I was not blind. Not deaf.' Echoes of hunger chased his words away. 'I felt the *wrongness* of it. A thing which severed Law from Law. Yet I—

'Why am I not slain? I do not merit life. How is it that I am permitted to continue, when I have imperilled all the Land?'

Abruptly Somo's hooves clattered on the plain stone. Tugged forward by Liand, the pinto came to Stave's side and halted, blowing froth and trepidation from its nostrils. Its eyes rolled wildly. If Liand had not gripped the mustang's reins, held them hard, Somo might have wheeled and fled into the jaws of the wolves.

'Anele.' Urgently Linden grasped the old man's shoulders, rolled him over so that he lay on his back. If he had truly become sane at last— 'Go on. Keep talking. I can't help you if you don't talk to me.'

Distant howls beat about her head, resounding from the cliffs to harry her. The wolves had already swarmed halfway to her position. Any hope, however irrational, that she and her companions might out-race the pack was gone.

Even Stave's transcendent skill and force could not meet so many slavering predators. Liand had a Stonedownor's bulk of muscle: he would give a good account of himself before he went down. Somo's hooves might stop a few wolves. Nevertheless the end would be swift and savage. And soon.

Stave's warning no longer mattered. If Linden could not summon wild magic against the *kresh*, she would never help anyone again, or anything: not Anele; not Jeremiah; not the Land.

Still she knelt beside the old man. His moonstone eyes stared at her sightlessly. He needed to talk. She knew of no other way to lance the psychic suppuration of his pain.

Tears smeared grime into his beard, down the sides of his neck. 'It seemed a small thing,' he said brokenly. 'Such a small thing. Yet I have wrought such evil—'

'Anele!' she breathed like a cry, 'make sense! You're sane now. I can feel it. For God's sake, tell me something I can understand!'

He must have heard her. Abruptly his attention turned to her. Although he could not see her, he gulped in surprise, 'I know you. You are Linden Avery the Chosen. The *Haruchai* has said so. You accompanied Sunder my father as he bore the corse of Hollian my mother into Andelain and life.'

Linden gaped at him as though he had shocked the air from her lungs. He might have spoken in an alien tongue: she recognised each word individually, but together they conveyed no meaning.

'That's impossible,' she protested.

Impossible.

God in Heaven—

How much time had passed since she had travelled with Sunder and Covenant into Andelain and seen Hollian reborn? Stave could tell her, if she asked him. Millennia, certainly.

This was Anele's sanity?

Now Stave stood beside her. He gazed down at the old man like a denunciation. 'It cannot be,' he announced flatly. 'He remains mad, though he appears sane. Do not heed him.'

'What—?' She surged erect to confront the *Haruchai*. 'You want me to *ignore* this?'

Stave faced her steadily. He hardly seemed to blink.

'Linden Avery, you must not harken to him. He is mad. And the *kresh* will soon be upon us. You must flee. If you do not, the hope of white gold will be lost to the Land. The Stonedownor and I will strive to provide for your escape.'

When she did not move, he said in a tone like a shove, 'You must flee now.'

Compelled by his appeal, she turned to look down the slope.

As the *kresh* boiled over the rubble, they moved from deep shade towards the borrowed light of the sky; and for the first time Linden saw them clearly.

The sight staggered her.

They were yellow, as Liand had told her, the hue of pestilence. And they were huge. God, they were *huge*: taller than ponies at the shoulders. A fulvous fire shone from their hot eyes, and their gaping fangs seemed to slather acid across the rocks. To her senses, their fury for death was a scream pouring ahead of them up the rift.

They horrified her. Lord Foul drove them somehow: their ferocity was the febrile hunger of scourged animals. When they had ripped away her flesh, they might turn on each other to quench their coerced savagery.

Yet through her dismay she heard Anele murmur, 'Linden Avery the Chosen. You alone—' Tears spilled ceaselessly from his eyes, although he did not sob. 'You have known those who trusted me. You alone may comprehend what I have done.'

So saying, he altered everything.

Instantly Linden shrugged off her shock and horror. Before all else, she was a physician; and Anele had suffered too much. She could not abandon him now: this window into his shame and pain might never open again. Somehow she had to help him unlock the bars which had closed his mind.

When the *kresh* attacked, she would trust herself to repulse them with white fire. Surely the same instincts which had preserved her during the collapse of Kevin's Watch would come to her rescue again?

In a rush, she stooped to the old man and helped him to his feet. Then she positioned herself so that she could watch his face as well as the rising tide of *kresh*.

'Tell me,' she urged him softly. 'I'm listening. I won't leave you. Tell me what happened.'

A frown intensified Stave's scar. For a moment, he appeared to consider the merits of simply snatching her into his arms again and running upwards with her; leaving Liand and Anele to die. But then he shrugged slightly.

Without haste or fear, he called Liand to him; readied the Stonedownor and Somo to fight for their lives.

Liand cast Linden a look fraught with apprehension. But he showed no hesitation as he plucked a pair of stone knives from Somo's packs and braced himself against the multiplied howling of the *kresh*. Events had not granted him time enough to learn regret.

Anele clung to her with supplication on his face. Tears still ran like blood from his eyes, although he spoke more steadily.

'This stone remembers,' he told her. 'Therefore I remember. I am Anele son of Sunder and Hollian.' The child Hollian had carried in her resurrected womb. 'In Mithil Stonedown I was born to them. I came to life in their care and their love.'

It was impossible: all of it. For him, sanity was only a more profound form of madness. Nevertheless he invoked names which Linden could not ignore. In spite of the danger, she listened to him as if they stood leagues rather than moments away from the charging pack and had no cause for fear.

'Though they made their home in Mithil Stonedown, their concern was for all the Land.' Again Anele's voice took on the cadences, the implied threnody, of the stone. The advance of the *kresh* might have ceased to exist for him. 'The Staff of Law had been entrusted to them, and they knew what was required of them. Indeed, they felt no wish to shun it, for their task was one of healing, and its necessity lifted their hearts.'

Facing him, Linden tried to estimate the speed of the wolves. How much longer could she delay before she reached for fire? She had already sacrificed any margin for failure. If Covenant's ring did not answer immediately to her hand, she and her companions would be lost.

Still Anele spoke as if he were oblivious to everything beyond his incomprehensible sanity.

'I was born after the passing of the Sunbane, yet I recall its ravages, for the harm was vast, and my parents journeyed throughout the Land for many years, bearing me with them. From earliest childhood, I watched them wield the Staff for the Land's healing. From them, I learned of love and hope and courage, and of commitment to beauty.

'And I learned also to be astonished at them, though they did not desire to astonish me.'

'Linden Avery,' Stave instructed distinctly, 'you must not heed him. The old man is entirely mad.'

The *kresh* had come so near that their fangs seemed to reflect the sick fire in their eyes. Their massive shoulders heaved as they bounded closer: in another moment their claws might strike sparks from the rocks.

Yet Anele was saying, 'Their past you know. Ere I was born, Sunder and Hollian had already accomplished the most wonderful deeds. Knowing nothing of wild magic and true Law, they had nonetheless given themselves utterly to the Land's redemption. So great was their love and devotion that even death did not stand against them. I would not otherwise have found life.'

Now, Linden thought, *now*, and as she came to readiness her last doubts slipped away. Anele might be a demented old man, but he had known Sunder and Hollian, whom she had loved. If this were madness, she preferred it to sanity.

In some sense, the last remnant of the One Forest had restored to Sunder his wife and unborn son.

Holding Anele's blind gaze as the stone held his mind, she reached into herself for argence—

—and could not find it.

Covenant's ring hung inert against her sternum; uninvoked. Though her entire being cried out in mute and sudden anguish, she felt no power anywhere within her. Three times before, Covenant's vast fire had answered her needs. Yet now, with Anele's life, and Stave's, and Liand's, in her hands, her desperation called up no response from the hard metal.

The exertion of wild magic had never been a conscious choice for her. Without the guidance of her health-sense, she did not know how to transcend the constraints of her thinking mind.

Before her dismay could find its voice, however, a concussion like the shattering of tremendous bones shook the rift and a blackness more fathomless than ebony and midnight blossomed between the cliffs. It had the force of a great conflagration: in spite of its blackness, it shed illumination like flame, silent and blazing, and as ruddy as magma.

At the first touch of the blast, she feared that the storm which had threatened Mithil Stonedown had found her; that ruin had begun to thunder down. For an instant, all of the cleft around her shone, etched out of shadows until every bulge and edge and cranny seemed to blaze with fire. Stave and Liand and even Somo stood erect in the blare of heat and flame as if they had been transformed.

At once, the advance of the *kresh* collapsed onto itself in bestial panic. Taken unprepared, momentarily blinded, they flinched and shied away, stumbled under each other's paws, wedged themselves between rocks. Terrified, they lashed out with fangs and claws, trying to drive back the strange violence which had fallen upon them.

Then the red light was quenched and darkness swept back down the rift, redoubled by the sudden cessation of fire. The wolves might have vanished: only a tumult of snarls, yelping and fear remained to define their presence.

Holding her breath, Linden braced herself on Anele's voice and waited to regain her sight.

'They loved me dearly,' he insisted as if he were deaf to the *kresh*, blind to fear, 'Sunder and Hollian. They shared with me the glory and loveliness of the Land, which they made new from the devastations of the Sunbane.'

Gradually the sky's afternoon glow macerated the darkness.

'When I came to manhood, they taught me all that they had learned of the Law and the Staff.'

First one and then another, the *kresh* took form from the shadows.

'It was always their purpose that I should inherit their task when they had grown old and weary, and they taught me with all their hearts.'

Then a shudder seemed to run through the pack. Between one heartbeat and the next, the wolves reclaimed the scent of their prey.

'Also they had learned much from the *Haruchai*, and from the far-sojourning Giants, and this as well they granted to me as my birthright.'

Hurtling up from the rocks, the leading *kresh* launched themselves in pursuit again.

Now Linden knew that she was powerless. Her hope of wild magic had failed her: she had no time to learn its use. But she also knew that she and her companions were no longer alone. She had recognised the force of that concussion. Earlier a similar force had enabled her to escape from the Masters, and had damaged only empty homes.

Some lore-wise being or beings had fired this blackness to delay the hunt. So that help could reach her—?

Without warning, men and women appeared among the stones as if they had reshaped themselves like *Elohim* from within the granite itself.

'Alas for the Land!' groaned Anele softly. His past gripped him and he regarded nothing else. 'Loving me as they did, my parents did not understand that I had learned to be astonished.'

Ten of them, or more: as many as twenty? Men and women, short, slim, with swift lines to their limbs and dark hair sweeping like wings about their heads. Some of them stood between Linden's companions and the pack: others rose up among the wolves.

Knotted in their hands they held lengths of thin rope like garrotes.

Tears streamed from Anele's eyes. 'Returned to life in Andelain, I was born of flesh and Earthpower.'

They were too small. None of them stood more than three hand spans taller than the *kresh*; and the wolves carried more weight. Bits of rope could not master fangs and claws: fewer than twenty men and women could not oppose so many of the great beasts. Yet the newcomers attacked without hesitation.

'I knew my nature, for my own strength answered to the strength of the Staff, and all the Land sang to me of its vitality and grandeur.'

Liquid with swiftness and precision, each man and woman flipped rope around the neck of a wolf, then leaped past it. Linden expected to see the *kresh* shrug off their assailants. But the newcomers used the wolves' bulk and momentum to augment their own. Some of the beasts went down, writhing against strangulation. Others heard their own necks snap as they died.

'Nevertheless I had been astonished beyond bearing, amazed to the core of my spirit.'

Again the rush of the pack collapsed in turmoil. Wolves collided with each other in their frenzy to rend their assailants. They sprang to attack and their jaws closed on fur rather than human flesh. All of the men and women disappeared under a thrashing chaos of wolves—

'I knew beyond doubt or appeal that I could not equal the example of my parents.'

—and reemerged riding the backs of *kresh*, their garrotes cutting into the necks of their ravening mounts.

'Though I laboured at emulation eternally, I would never rise to the greatness of their deeds.'

Linden wanted to shout Stave's name. Neither he nor Liand had moved. Liand's inexperience might have done more harm than good; but Stave, at least, should have joined the newcomers. He was *Haruchai*: surely he could have slain wolves with his bare hands?

'And in time I grew to understand that I required a different path.'

Instead, however, the Master turned away. Striding up the exposed gutrock, he approached Linden. 'Beware, Chosen!' he called through the struggle of fangs and ropes. 'The evil has been roused. We are assailed!'

With one hand, he pointed up the rift behind her.

Behind her?

'The wolves—!' she protested. In moments her unexpected defenders would all be dead. *Kresh* would surge past the fallen to leap on Liand and Somo.

Nevertheless Stave's manner compelled her. Releasing Anele, she looked back over her shoulder.

At once, the old man fell silent. Perhaps he had recognised this new threat, in spite of his blindness. Or perhaps he could not speak without Linden's attention to anchor him.

Down the broken slope like a wave of dark chrism flowed a compact wedge of black forms, barking to each other in guttural voices.

They resembled creatures she had once known, the Waynhim that had defended Covenant's quest amid the ice and cold of the Northron Climbs. Like the Waynhim, these beings had long, hairless torsos and short limbs, better formed for running on all fours than for walking upright. Pointed ears perched atop their bald heads. And they had no eyes. Instead moist gaping nostrils filled their faces above the cruel slits of their mouths.

But these creatures were much larger than the Waynhim. Their skin was an unilluminable black, the colour of obsidian and murder. And they carried knives of bitter iron: knives like fangs, with blood-red blades which seethed like vitriol.

Their wedge seemed to concentrate their power. The creature at its tip held a short iron staff, almost a sceptre, pointed like a spike at one end. With this instrument the leading creature could wield the force of the whole formation.

The sceptre seemed to splash acid over the rocks as the wedge swept downwards. Its power hit hard against Linden's last percipience; struck sparks into the sudden tinder of her fear.

'Ur-viles!' Stave told her firmly. 'The old evil. Against their might we cannot stand. Only wild magic may ward us.

'You must strike down the loremaster. There' – he pointed again – 'at the focus of the wedge. Otherwise we perish, and the Ramen with us.'

Ramen—? she wondered dumbly. Had she heard that name before?

She had seen ur-viles: she recognised them now. Long ago, they had turned against Lord Foul, and been punished by the Sunbane. With Sunder and Hollian, she and Covenant had been attacked by a horde of them made monstrous and insane. They had caused Hollian's death. Indirectly, they were responsible for her resurrection – and Anele's.

Yet these creatures were not monstrous. Dire though they seemed, they remained themselves: nothing had twisted their given nature.

'I thought they were dead,' she panted. Surely Lord Foul had destroyed them all? They had betrayed him by creating Vain.

'As we did,' Stave replied. 'We cannot account for them. We know only that they are Demondim-spawn, servants of Corruption.

'Chosen, you must strike at them while you may.'

Like Anele – if the old man spoke the truth – they did not belong here. Somehow they had appeared out of time.

'I can't!' she countered urgently. 'I don't know how.'

Who else could have produced the black concussion which had cast the *kresh* into confusion?

Before Stave could protest, a woman came swiftly towards them over the rock. Like the human fighters – the Ramen? – she seemed to emerge from within the stones. She too was slim and lithe, ready for quickness, with long black hair and dark skin, and clad in leggings of leather and a snug leather jerkin. But she wore her hair tied back with a length of rope: her garrote. About her neck hung a small band of yellow flowers.

'The Ringthane's power is not needed, sleepless one.' Her voice sounded like nickering. 'The ur-viles will not harm you.'

Stave stared at her for an instant, then bowed as if she had appeared out of legends to greet him. 'Manethrall.' He sounded stiff, like a man deliberately withholding wonder. 'This cannot be. Ur-viles are evil, and the Ramen do not serve Corruption.'

The woman did not return his bow. 'Nevertheless,' she retorted. 'They will harm none of you.'

'Stave!' Liand shouted frantically. 'They come!'

Below the Stonedownor, the Ramen fought fiercely, fluidly. And they seemed improbably successful. Some of them must have fallen by now, bitten and torn. Yet they continued to disrupt the pack's course, ten or more of them: rearing up from the struggle, leaping past teeth and claws; wielding their ropes to dislocate limbs, break necks, crush windpipes.

But they could only hamper the *kresh*, not halt them. Already wolves had broken from the mêlée to pelt upwards.

Towards Liand and Somo.

The first of them sprang for Liand's chest. At the last instant, he stepped aside. As the wolf passed him, he ripped both of his knives underhand through its belly. It crashed to the stone, screaming at its wounds.

Before he could recover, another beast charged. Two more went for the mustang's throat.

Liand fell, overborne by the wolf's impact. Together they rolled and thrashed on the stone.

Bounding downwards, the woman whom Stave had called Manethrall flipped the rope from her hair and in the same motion looped it around the neck of Liand's attacker. Her momentum carried her over the *kresh*; wrenched the beast aside.

At the same time, another Raman sped to Somo's aid. Jumping onto one wolf's back, the man bunched himself and leaped to plunge down onto the spine of another. Bones broke with a sickening crunch. The man rolled free while the *kresh* collapsed, grovelling helplessly.

Wheeling, Somo lashed out with its hooves to crush the other wolf's skull.

Still the wedge of ur-viles poured downwards, barking in cadence like an incantation. Power flared and spat from their glowing blades. In another heartbeat, they would reach the plane of native stone which had snared Anele in his memories.

Linden stared at them. They will harm none of you. She believed the Manethrall. Yet the force which she felt from the ur-viles was harm incarnate: it had been devised for death.

Covenant had told her of such creatures – and of butchery in Andelain—

Grimly she held herself back, though her knuckles were white with fear, and the raw din of fighting *kresh* filled her head. She could see now that the wedge was not aimed at her.

The woman who had spoken to her trusted ur-viles.

And Stave must have trusted the Ramen. Instead of urging Linden to power, he followed the Manethrall into battle; met the brunt of the attack with his imponderable strength and skill.

Anele's hands plucked at Linden's shoulders. When she turned to him, he gripped her weakly, needing her support. 'Linden Avery,' he pleaded. 'Chosen.' He had ceased weeping: his pain had grown too great for tears. 'You must heed me.' His head flinched from side to side, straining his thin neck. 'I cannot bear it else.'

The ur-viles went past her at a run. Shouting in their harsh, incomprehensible tongue, they swept across the open rock and drove their wedge deep into the heart of the pack.

Crimson blades flashed. The staff of the loremaster lashed black acid to both sides. Ramen vaulted out the path of the wedge; began to withdraw from the struggle.

Wherever the fluid force of the ur-viles touched fur, black flames burst. Acid knives parted flesh and bone as easily as rotten fabric. The frantic snarling of the *kresh* became torn yelps and shrieks.

Trembling, Linden met Anele's supplication. The muscles of her legs quivered so that she could scarcely stand. Nevertheless she gazed into his ravaged face.

'I'm here.' Speaking required so much effort that her words came out in gasps. 'I'm listening. Go on.' There was nothing that she could do to aid her defenders. And the old man needed her. 'Tell me what you remember.'

He replied with a fragile nod. For a moment, he mumbled to himself, apparently searching to find his place in the tale. Then he resumed the granitic dirge of his life.

'After many and many years of service,' he said, half-singing his grief and remorse, 'Sunder and Hollian my parents elected at last to rest, and so they placed the Staff of Law in my hand.'

Below them, the fight intensified as the *kresh* raved for some point of weakness which would allow them to break open the wedge; but Linden no longer attended to the battle. Events had exceeded her frayed capacity to understand them. Instead she concentrated on Anele. His tale had become the only thing that made sense to her.

'Yet I could not continue their work.' His distress ached to her senses. 'Daunted by astonishment and inadequate to their example, I needed to discover my own use for my birthright. All other courses led to despair.

'So it transpired that when my parents had lapsed gently into death, and I had shared in the inexpressible mourning of Mithil Stonedown, and of all the Land, I did not take up the task left to me. Instead I took the Staff of Law and departed from my home so that I might seek out some more personal form of service.'

At the edges of the wedge, a few ur-viles fell to claws and fangs. Instantly, however, ur-viles within the wedge shifted to replace the fallen. And the loremaster's distilled puissance dealt out fury as though it could not be quenched. Already more than a score of *kresh* writhed in flames; and still more caught fire with each acrid splash of power. Stave guarded the bare gutrock, delivering death whenever a wolf dared challenge him. Liand and Somo remained safely behind him, watching the fight. And at the walls of the rift, using the cliffs to guard their backs, the surviving Ramen crippled or slew every beast that came within reach.

Anele ignored them all. He might have forgotten their existence.

'High among these crests and vales,' he explained, nodding to the mountains, 'I made a place for myself – not so distant from Mithil Stonedown that I could not hasten to the Land's aid at need, but far enough to attain the silence and loneliness, the freedom from astonishment, which my spirit craved.

'There I became Unfettered. The *Haruchai* had spoken of such men and women. From them I had learned the words, though I did not know the song.'

In a frail voice, he recited:

'Free
Unfettered
Shriven

Free—
Dream that what is dreamed will be:
Hold eyes clasped shut until they see,
And sing the silent prophecy—
And be
Unfettered
Shriven
Free.'

Then he continued his story.

'Sunder and Hollian my parents had set themselves to heal the life of the Land. For myself I chose another task.'

Abruptly the character of the battle changed. Too many of the *kresh* had been slain: too many howled at the fire in their fur, or at the torment of their crippled and dangling limbs. First one at a time, then by twos and threes, then all together, the pack turned to flee.

'I wished to comprehend the Land's spirit. I did not purpose healing. In my astonishment, I did not conceive that I might attempt so great a task. But I dreamed that if I could teach myself to hearken to the essential language of the Land, I might hear of truths or needs which would enable those who came after me to provide deeper balms, more fundamental restorations.

'And betimes,' the old man admitted, 'I imagined that if I could but tune my ears and Earthpower to an adequate acuity, I might learn from the gutrock itself how the Land might be rid of its most ancient and implacable evil.'

The ur-viles followed, killing every beast within reach of their power. The cries of the *kresh* filled the rift, a forlorn ululation. But the Ramen did not give chase. Instead they began to move among the fallen, searching for any of their comrades who were dead or injured, and ending the pain of the maimed wolves.

'For many years – a generation and more among the folk of the Land – I came here, to this place, this rock.' More and more, Anele leaned on Linden's support. He had no strength left for anything but words. 'Here with the Staff of Law and Earthpower, I studied stone in every flake of mica and complication of granite, every cunning mineral vein, every trace of recollected heat. Each ripple of texture and flake of loss I memorised until it became the substance of my heart. And when at last I had brought my mortal flesh into consonance with the Earth's bones, I found that I could hear the speech of mountains.'

Bearing three dead comrades, and five sorely wounded, the Ramen ascended the rubble, led by the Manethrall.

He has no friend but stone.

'Have I spoken of years and generations? Sunder and Hollian my parents far surpassed the span of ordinary men and women. By the measure of other folk, I was an old man when I inherited the Staff of Law – and more than old before I discovered true hearing – for I had inherited also the longevity of Earthpower and Law.'

When the Ramen reached the gutrock, Stave joined them. And Liand did the same, drawing Somo behind him. Blood streaked his left arm, but Linden could not gauge the extent of his injury.

'Much I learned here,' Anele breathed hoarsely, 'more than I am able to contain. I heard hints of the Durance, and of the *skurj*. In such matters the *Elohim* played a part entwined with Earthpower and the Worm of the World's End. Yet always I remained myself, incapable of the burden of astonishment. With the Staff and my own nature, I had opened a storeroom crowded immeasurably with memories and lore. Yet I was who I was, and could not attain the stature of such knowledge.'

On the open stone, the Ramen set down their hurt and fallen comrades. The dead they placed respectfully aside, then turned to tend the wounded. Some of the hurts looked grievous, but none of the Ramen cried out or made any sound.

'A better man might have felt the *geas* of the Earth's need and found an answer. I did not. I could not imagine that the peril pertained to me, for the Staff exceeded me always. Therefore I only listened, and heard, and did naught.'

The Manethrall did not stay with her people, but instead approached Linden and Anele, with Stave beside her. The other Ramen gestured for Liand to join them, but he ignored them to accompany the Manethrall and Stave.

'Thus my doom came upon me at last, and I fell from the Land's service through no cause but my own littleness and folly.'

As soon as the Master reached her, he said impassively, 'Linden Avery, we must not tarry here. If these ur-viles will permit us, we must return to Mithil Stonedown while daylight holds. You have seen that I do not suffice to ward you. We require the greater safety of habitation and other *Haruchai*.'

But the Manethrall woman forestalled him with a severe movement of her hand. 'Depart if you will, Bloodguard,' she told him sternly. 'We will permit the old man to speak. Long have we wished to hear his tale.'

Obliquely Linden heard in the woman's voice that she did not trust Stave. For some reason, she considered ur-viles less threatening than Masters.

Anele had not paused. He seemed to hear no voice except the lament of the stone's memories.

'In one clean dawn, pristine and cherishable, while I rested from hearing in the kindly cave which had become my home, I felt the thing of *wrong* – the thing which destroyed me – and was fearful of it, for I had never known its like.'

At last, the ur-viles ceased harrying the *kresh*. Still in formation, they turned to climb back up the jumbled slope.

'In some fashion it resembled the Sunbane's touch upon the Land. And in some fashion it echoed the seeping vileness which mars the waters flowing from Mount Thunder's depths into the embrace of the Great Swamp. Yet it was neither of those. Rather it was *fresh* – new-born to harm, and virulent beyond my comprehension. This stone could not have described such abomination to me. It would have rent itself asunder in the telling.'

The wedge ascended steadily; but the Manethrall gave it no heed, although Stave regarded it askance.

'For a time,' Anele moaned, 'my fear held me, and I faltered. Yet gradually I remembered courage, and determined that I would go forth to gaze upon this thing of evil.

'A simple choice, I assured myself, to go forth and gaze only. I would decide upon a better response when I had perceived its nature. Or perhaps when I had learned to understand it—'

Abruptly Stave insisted on the Raman woman's attention. 'Do not miscomprehend, Manethrall.' He may have wished to interrupt Anele's tale. 'Your presence among these mountains is a great boon to the Land, unexpected among the perils of these times. If you will consent to accompany us, or to return to your ancient homes upon the Plains of Ra, all the *Haruchai* will rejoice in your presence.'

He did not sound joyful, however. Instead his tone conveyed an adamantine resolve as he added, 'I intend no disrespect when I say that we must depart now.

'I do not speak for the Chosen. As you have discerned, she is the Ringwielder, and will do as she must. But the old man is in our care, and we do not permit his freedom. He must return at once to Mithil Stonedown.'

Gasping, Anele stumbled to a halt as if in dread; as if the Master had laid cruel hands on him. His thin form sagged against Linden's support.

The thought that he might not be able to continue – or that Stave might prevent him from saying more – sent a flush of anger through her. Before she could react, however, the Manethrall interposed herself between Stave and Anele; and Liand stepped closer to offer his aid.

Quietly, harshly, the woman said to Stave, 'Then it is you he fears. You who have become Masters.'

Stave nodded, untouched by her accusation.

'Have a care, sleepless one.' The Manethrall lifted her garrote, stiff with the drying blood of wolves. 'The Ramen do not forget. We remember that you have ridden Ranyhyn to their deaths.' Bitterness gave her voice a flaying edge. 'In those years, we withheld our enmity only because the Bloodguard had sworn fealty to the Lords. But we remember also that you turned from fealty to the service of Fangthane the Render.'

The Manethrall's assertion startled Linden. She had heard the tale from Stave: the defeat and maiming of Korik, Sill and Doar had led the Bloodguard to turn their backs on their Vow. But that had been, what, *seven thousand years* ago? And the Ramen *remembered* it?

'We suffer your presence,' the Raman woman continued, 'because we loathe the *kresh*, which you oppose, and because you do not bear the scent of evil. Also we seek to comprehend that which impels these ur-viles. But this old man has found a place in our hearts, and we will not withdraw our aid.'

'Your hearts mislead you.' Stave neither raised his voice nor spoke sharply; but his judgment was absolute. 'This Anele has claimed kinship with a man and a woman who perished three millennia and more ago. He is mad, and speaks only madness.'

'Be quiet, both of you, please,' Linden pleaded. 'I need to hear Anele.'

Stave did not relent. 'Chosen, you profess concern for the Land.' He studied Linden past the Manethrall's shoulder. 'If you truly wish to serve it, you must not hearken to him.'

'Then tell me something,' she retorted. 'You people remember *everything*. Your ancestors must have known Sunder and Hollian's son. What was his name?'

Stave's eyes widened slightly, but he did not hesitate. 'The inheritor of the Staff of Law was named Anele.' At once, he added, 'It signifies nothing that this old man claims that name for himself.'

'Nothing?' countered Linden. 'What else do you call "nothing"? Do you think it's an *accident* that he can read stone?'

Before Stave could reply, the Manethrall put in, 'If *you* truly wish to serve the Land, sleepless one, you will have patience. The Ramen do not desire to thwart you. We will do so only if we must.

'Grant us this tale. Grant us two days in which to take counsel, and to seek comprehension. Then if you have persuaded us to trust you, we will accompany you to Mithil Stonedown, to ensure your safe passage. And if you have not persuaded us, we will attempt to persuade you.'

'Finally,' Linden muttered between her teeth. 'A suggestion we can use.'

She had no idea what two days among the Ramen might entail – and did not care.

Stave gazed inflexibly at the Manethrall. After a moment, still stiffly, he repeated his earlier bow. 'Your distant ancestors held our respect. At the last, their devotion exceeded ours. In their name, and in that of the great Ranyhyn, which we adored, I will abide by your word.'

Thank God—!

Below Linden, the ur-viles had regained bare gutrock. They were so near that even her faint percipience felt the leashed savagery of their lore and their blades. But they could not frighten her now. Everything that remained to her, she focused on Anele.

He had not stirred in her grasp. Gently she shook him, tried to bring up his head. 'Anele, please. I'm ready now. Can you go on?'

No one would ever be able to help him if he could not speak of his distress; complete his tale.

Guided by instinctive empathy, she gently kissed the top of his head.

With an effort, one bone and joint at a time, he roused himself. By small increments, he dragged his eyes up to the level of Covenant's ring hanging inside her shirt. There he fixed his gaze, staring blindly. When he finally found his voice, he spoke as if he were addressing that small metal band—

—appealing to it as though it represented the life of the Land, and might forgive him.

His own recollections had broken him once before. Now they threatened to tread the shards of his mind underfoot.

'A simple choice I made. Ah, simple. Such simplicity gives birth to woe, and its outcome is lamentation. In my place, a wiser man might have deemed so much harm sufficient. Yet I was not content, for with one choice I made another, again a simple one. I left the Staff of Law in the covert of my cave.

'I wished to preserve it from harm until I had gazed upon this thing of *wrong*, and determined my best course. So I assured myself. Was I not in my own flesh a being of Earthpower, capable of much? Surely I would be safe enough until I had learned to name the evil.

'Yet the truth—'

There remorse seemed to close his throat, and he could not continue. Linden murmured soothingly to his bowed head; tried to project her support into him so that he would be able to go on. And gradually he felt her encouragement; or his need to finish his story grew stronger. When he had mastered himself, his quavering voice resumed.

'Ah, the truth was that I left behind the Staff because with power comes duty. I feared that if I bore with me the implement of Law, I would be compelled to measure my littleness against the thing of *wrong*. And I knew that I would fail.

'Thus I went out to my doom, leaving behind the Staff.'

Liand and the Manethrall moved closer to hear him: the plaintive ache of his tale had become almost inaudible. Even the ur-viles drew near. Only Stave listened with his arms folded as though his heart were a fortress.

'Alas, the evil which I there beheld was one which you also have witnessed.' Briefly the old man found a bit of strength, and his voice rose. 'Among the Masters they are known as Falls. Others name them *caesures*. They are a spinning of vile power, an illimitable bane, and when I had beheld it I was appalled.' Then his energy faded and he lapsed to whispering. 'No, more than appalled. I was stricken immobile. My littleness unmade me.'

Weak and sorrowing, he gave his pain into Linden's embrace; let her hold him so that he could reach an end.

'There the *caesure* took me. Its evil swept over me, and when it had passed my life and all that I had known had been swept away. Only the shape of the Land remained to me. These mountains. The valley of the Mithil. The reach of the South Plains. All else had ceased to exist.

'Oh, Mithil Stonedown endured, but it was no longer my home. Its folk knew nothing of the Land that I had known. All of my loves and lore had been effaced. The very stone on which I stood was not as I remembered it.

'And the Staff of Law—

'Ah, the Staff also had ceased to exist. It had vanished, lost by my folly. This Land knew nothing of it, and Law itself had given way to Falls and Kevin's Dirt.'

Oh, Anele. Hugging him, Linden found that she could still weep, although he did not. Her tears dropped to his old head and dripped away, unregarded.

'That is the harm from which I flee, though I bear it with me always. I have lost the Staff of Law. It was my given birthright, entrusted to my care, and I failed it. I was too fearful for my task. The blame for the Land's plight is mine.

'I am marked for damnation, and yet I cannot so much as die. If Sunder my father had known what the outcome of his love would be, he would have buried Hollian my mother beside the Soulsease, and the Land would have been spared the ill which I have wrought.'

When he was done, Linden simply stood and held him for a long time. She did not know how to comfort him. She could only bear witness to his bereavement.

Yet she had heard him: she knew that he needed more. For that reason, she told him softly, 'I understand. I believe you, Anele.' The stone on which he stood would not have permitted falsehood. 'Now I know the truth. You said it yourself. You're the Land's last hope.'

There was no one else who could even attempt to locate the Staff again.

Chapter Ten:

Aided by Ur-viles

When Linden said it, she knew it to be true, although she could not have explained how she knew – or how it could be true. She was in no condition to question herself. Anele's need for forgiveness had nearly exhausted her.

He knew where the Staff had been lost.

She could not continue to support him. Fortunately something in her voice roused him a little. He lifted his head from her chest, made an attempt to straighten his legs.

'Did I? It may be so. Why otherwise am I precluded from death?'

He was the son of Sunder and Hollian – which made him three and a half thousand years old.

Unless—

Intuitive perceptions hunted for clarity within her, but she was too tired to concentrate on them.

'Old man,' Stave put in without warning, 'hear me. Linden Avery has granted you credence. The *Haruchai* do not.'

In response, all of the ur-viles began to bark at once, apparently reacting to what they had heard. Their voices meant nothing to Linden, however: their speech resembled no language she knew. She turned a questioning look towards the Manethrall; but the woman shook her head.

'They comprehend us, but cannot form words in our tongue, and we know not how to grasp theirs.'

Stave ignored the exchange. 'Have you made search?' he asked Anele. 'Have you returned to your cave?'

Linden wanted to sigh, Oh, leave him alone. Don't you think he's been through enough? But the old man rallied before she could reply.

'What else have I ever done,' he answered like a spatter of gall, 'since the accursed day of my failure?' He had grown sane enough to feel affronted. 'The cave remains. I have searched it over upon occasions without number. I wander from it in despair, and in despair I return. Every span of its stone and dirt I have probed with my eyes and touched with my hands, even tasted with my tongue. The Staff is not there. No hint or memory of it is there. It passed out of knowledge when the Land I knew was erased by the evil of the Fall.'

Then he turned to face up the rift. 'You will betray me,' he muttered. 'I must not abide your presence.' A moment later, he shuddered. 'And these creatures' – he indicated the ur-viles – 'are harsh to my distress.'

In Mithil Stonedown, he had spoken of *Lost things, long dead*, creatures that had forced him to remember—

Gathering strength by the moment, as though he had left his frailty in Linden's hands and was no longer hampered by it, he strode up the bare rock and began once again to climb the rubble.

Stave started upwards as well, clearly intending to reclaim the old man. But the Manethrall stopped him with a frown. 'Two days you have granted us, Bloodguard. We will ensure that your prey is not lost to you.'

At her word, the *Haruchai* nodded and let Anele go.

Linden's health-sense was gone: she could no longer read her companions. Even the power of the ur-viles had faded from her nerves. Their blades had become mere lambent iron, eldritch and undefined. The Ramen might have been honest or treacherous, and she would not have known the difference.

Gazing after the old man, she asked the Manethrall, 'You've met him before. How much do you know about him?'

'Little or naught,' replied the woman. Her tone remained stern, but her severity seemed to be directed at Stave rather than Linden. 'We only pity him. Therefore when by chance our paths have crossed, we have given him what succour we may. However, he accepts little, and trusts less. He flees when he has been fed or healed. For that reason, we have not comforted him as we wish.'

'Will he be all right?' Linden continued, 'climbing by himself? I don't want to lose him. He's too important—'

She had only just begun to grasp how important.

'Do not fear for him,' the Manethrall responded. 'He is accustomed to this place. And we will watch over him. Since you wish it, and because I have given my word to the sleepless one, he will be returned to you at need.'

Her kindness brought another moment of tears and blurring to Linden's eyes. If these Ramen had treated Anele so, she would trust them for a while. Apparently their convictions and purposes were more humane than Stave's.

'I'm sorry,' she told the Manethrall. 'You and your people saved our lives, and I haven't even thanked you. I'm Linden Avery. Stave calls me "the Chosen" because that's what I was called the last time I came to the Land.'

The woman used her rope to tie back her hair, then bowed as she had not bowed to Stave, with her hands before her head and her palms turned outwards, empty of danger. 'Linden Avery,' she said in the nickering voice she had used earlier, 'Ringthane, be welcome among us. I am Manethrall Hami of the Ramen, and they' – she indicated her companions where they tended their injured – 'are my Cords.

'Your words suggest a tale which we will hear eagerly. However, we will not burden you with the telling of it until we have gathered at the Verge of Wandering, according to the word that I have given the Bloodguard. For the present, you are weary and in need. Before we ascend, we would offer you what aid or comfort we may.'

Linden hardly knew how to ask for what she needed. Help me find Jeremiah. Lead me to the Staff. Tell me why you distrust Stave. None of that would enable her to do more climbing. Instead she answered indirectly, 'You know Anele and Stave.' Well enough, anyway. 'This is Liand son of Fostil, from Mithil Stonedown.' She nodded towards the young man. 'Anele was a prisoner there. He helped us escape.'

As if for the first time, she noticed the streaks of blood on his left arm. They leaked from under his slashed sleeve: she could not see how badly he was hurt. But the tearing of his sleeve suggested claws.

Infection, she thought dully. Sepsis. If his wounds were not treated— Without percipience, she could not guess how grave the harm might be.

The Manethrall granted Liand a gracious bow, which he returned, emulating her movements awkwardly. He had already shared dangers and seen wonders far outside his experience, and his eyes sparkled with excitement.

'You honour me, Manethrall Hami. The Ramen are unknown in Mithil Stonedown, but you are doughty and generous, and would be made welcome' – he glanced pointedly at Stave – 'if the Masters permitted it.'

She frowned at this reference to *Masters*. 'Thank you, Liand of Mithil Stonedown. We will trust your welcome, if not that of the Bloodguard.'

Fearing that Stave might take offence, Linden put in, 'With your permission, Manethrall, I want to look at your injured. Where I come from, I'm a physician. I don't have any drugs or supplies with me, but I might be able to do something for them.' Uncertainly she added, 'You lost lives for us. I want to help, if I can.'

Hami shrugged. 'As you will, Ringthane. But your aid is not necessary. The Ramen are hardy, and I have taught my Cords the care of such wounds. Also' – a fierce grin twisted her lips – 'our grievance against all *kresh* is ancient and enduring, ill-measured in mere centuries. Had you not been threatened, we would have assailed them still.'

Linden wanted to ask, And the ur-viles? Would they have joined you? But she was too weary for such questions. Murmuring, 'Thanks,' she gestured for Liand to join her as she crossed the gutrock to join the Cords who were treating their hurt comrades.

They nodded to her courteously when she squatted among them, but did not pause in what they were doing.

They were nine, and none unmarked by the battle. However, they had suffered only scrapes and scratches, bruises. The wounds of the other five were more serious. Torn flesh hung in strips from the arms and legs of two of them, a man and a woman. Fangs had ripped grisly chunks out of one man's shoulder and another's thigh. As severe as those hurts appeared, however, they were small compared to the injuries of the fifth Raman.

The woman had been nearly eviscerated.

Three Cords laboured to keep her alive. The rest tended the other four.

'Damn it,' Linden muttered to herself. Peritonitis for sure. Even if the woman's intestines were not too badly rent, and could be sewn intact back into her abdomen, she would develop a killing infection almost at once. Indeed, all of the wounds would turn septic: the claws and teeth of the *kresh* assured that.

Fire, she thought. We need a fire.

And then: hurtloam.

With an effort, she swallowed the fatigue clogging her throat. 'Do you know hurtloam?' she asked the Cords.

'We do,' one of the men answered, abrupt with concentration. He appeared younger than Liand: too young for such work. Strain and pride stretched a pallor across his cheeks. All of the Cords were little more than adolescents. 'It is not found here.' Not among these broken stones. 'Nor do we often bear it with us. Its virtue slowly fades when it is lifted from the earth, and we lack the lore to sustain it. But we are Ramen. That which we have must suffice.'

From a pouch at his waist, he sifted into his palm a few sprigs of what appeared to be dried ferns or grass. Petals lay among them: the same flowers that Manethrall Hami wore around her neck. The Cord separated one sprig from the others, returned the rest to his pouch. Then he spat onto the herb in his palm; and at once a sharp tang pricked Linden's nose.

'This is *amanibhavam*,' he told her, 'the flower of health and madness. Fresh, it is too potent for human flesh, bringing ecstasy and death. Dried, however, it may be borne.'

Rubbing the damp herb between his hands, he wiped it into the gutted woman's wound.

She gasped in pain; and Linden nearly gasped as well, shocked by the crudeness of such care. *Damn* it. She needed her health-sense; needed to know what *amanibhavam* was and did.

The suffering of the Ramen hung about her head; agony stifled by pride and fortitude. The other Cords had similar pouches. They dabbed bits of saliva and fern under strips of ripped tissue and bound the skin back into place with cloth bandages; rubbed the same mixture as though it were a sovereign poultice into bitten shoulders and thighs. She had witnessed miracles of healing in the Land. With percipience and power, she had wrought a few herself. But this—

The last blood of the dead oozed from their wounds to stain the gutrock. Its lost scent tightened the back of her throat. They had died brutally, mangled almost beyond recognition. One had had her face ripped away. Another's spine had been crushed in the massive jaws of a wolf.

These dead and injured young people had saved Linden's life. She remembered evil; but on a purely visceral level, she had forgotten the real cost of Lord Foul's malice.

Staggering, she heaved herself upright. 'Manethrall,' she breathed urgently. 'Hami. They're going to die.'

The Manethrall came smoothly down the stone to consider the plight of her Cords. Then she met Linden's troubled stare. 'It may be so,' she admitted sadly. '*Kresh* are in all ways dire and filthy beasts. Yet *amanibhavam* has rare virtue. It may yet redeem these wounds. We can do naught else in this place. We must depart.'

'No.' Linden shook her head unsteadily. 'It's too dangerous. We can't move them.' Especially the gut-torn woman. In a rush, she added, 'Liand and I know where to find *aliantha*.'

Hurtloam was out of the question. Without percipience, she would not be able to identify it. And Liand had never seen it.

Manethrall Hami raised her eyebrows. 'That would be a benison. Is it near?'

Linden gestured down towards the Mithil valley. 'Send one of your Cords with me,' she urged. 'Or with Liand, if I'm too weak. They can bring some back.'

'Will they return before nightfall?'

Linden swallowed roughly. 'No.'

'Then I will send no one. You have knowledge of the Land, but mayhap you do not know these mountains. With the setting of the sun, a wind as harsh as ice will blow here. Lacking shelter, they' – she meant her injured Cords – 'will perish. Also you may succumb, for you are not hardy.

'We must ascend. Beyond the rims of this cleft, we will be capable of shelter and fire.'

Fire to boil water, cauterise wounds, burn away as much infection as possible. There was no wood for fuel in the rift.

Linden felt a pang of despair, and she faltered.

'Or we could go down,' she offered hesitantly. 'Get out of the wind. Find *aliantha*.' Do what Stave wanted. 'Mithil Stonedown will help us.'

Severity sharpened the Manethrall's face. 'Ringthane, we love the Land. It is the long dream of the Ramen that we will one day return there – to the Plains of Ra and Manhome, where we belong.' Her voice implied a suppressed outrage. 'But we will not enter any place where these Masters hold sway.'

Turning away, she added, 'My Cords will endure, if they are able. They are Ramen.'

Stave regarded her impassively, as though he did not deign to take umbrage.

Linden could not imagine what grudge the Ramen held against the *Haruchai*. However, she herself feared to return to Mithil Stonedown. Stave had surprised her by promising the Manethrall two days. In her experience, his people neither compromised nor negotiated.

When she had absorbed the hard fact that she could do nothing for the Cords – that all her years of training were useless here – she sat down to save her strength. The shadows in the rift approached true twilight, and the tops of the walls seemed too far away to reach. She did not believe that she would be able to climb so high.

Dumbly she watched one of the Cords treat Liand's arm. She had become certain that the Ramen meant him no harm.

The Cord applied a touch of *amanibhavam* and saliva to the gash, then bound it with a bandage of clean cloth. As he felt the effects of the poultice, Liand frowned at first, then gradually relaxed into a smile. 'I know not what other benefits this grass may have,' he told Linden when he had thanked the Cord, 'but it assuredly softens pain. For that I am grateful.'

Linden nodded vacantly. Her uselessness galled her. For the time being, at least, she had come to the end of herself.

Scant moments later, however, Manethrall Hami called her Cords into motion. Around Linden, the comparatively whole young men and women prepared themselves to carry their dead and fallen comrades, some in slings across their backs, others cradled in their arms. Liand readied Somo for an ascent they could scarcely see. And Linden realised that she was staring at a darkness deeper than shadows: the ur-viles.

Without thinking about it, she had expected them to depart. Surely they had already done what they came to do? Yet they remained, obviously waiting for something. Did they mean to accompany the Ramen? Did they anticipate another attack? Or were they wary of the moment when their interests might diverge from those of the Ramen?

Then Stave came to her side. 'Chosen,' he announced, 'I must bear you again.' Gloom obscured his features. If he had bared his teeth at her, she would not have known it. 'If I do not, your weariness will hold you here, and you will be exposed to cold beyond your endurance.'

Too worn out to do otherwise, she surrendered herself and the immediate future to his ambiguous care.

As the Cords settled their burdens, the ur-viles also prepared to move. Apparently the disturbing creatures intended to accompany them.

Then the Ramen began to climb. Linden had assumed that they would move slowly and rest often, laden as they were. But she soon saw that she had underestimated their toughness. They managed the jagged slope more swiftly than she could have imagined.

And the ur-viles ascended with ease. The proportions of their limbs aided them here: although they looked awkward upright, they could use their hands for climbing as readily as their feet. Somehow they had put their weapons away, so that their hands were empty; unencumbered.

Soon it became obvious that only Liand and Somo could not match the pace of the Ramen. Alone, he might have kept up well enough; but in the deepening twilight the mustang had to pick its footing carefully. Otherwise it might snap a foreleg among the stones.

At a word from Manethrall Hami, the lone unburdened Cord dropped back to Liand. 'Join your companions,' the young woman told him brusquely. 'I will guide your mount.'

'No.' Liand may have shaken his head. 'I brought Somo to this. The responsibility is mine.'

The Cord might have argued; but Stave put in, 'You have wrought sufficient folly for one day, Stonedownor. Do not be foolish in this. The horselore of the Ramen surpasses you. Your mount will fare better in her care than in yours.'

'Linden?' Liand asked out of the darkness. He may have meant, What should I do?

He may have meant, Tell this damn Master to leave me alone.

Sighing to herself, Linden answered, 'I think the Ramen know what they're doing. Somo should be safe with her.'

'Very well,' Liand muttered to the Cord. 'I have tended the mounts of Mithil

Stonedown since I grew tall enough to curry them. If you do not return Somo to me, you will answer for it.'

The young woman snorted under her breath, but made no other retort.

Liand scrambled up the rocks to Stave's side. 'I know nothing of these Ramen, Master,' he said softly. 'You have concealed them from us. If I am foolish, how could it be otherwise? You have kept secret all that might have made us wise.'

Stave ignored the justice of Liand's accusation.

Overhead the sky had turned purple with evening. Slowly it dimmed towards black. For some time now, the breeze had gathered force as cold poured like a stream into the narrows of the rift. Linden felt chills seep into her skin in spite of Stave's intransigent warmth. Soon she would start to shiver under the mounting weight of the wind.

A day and a half in the Land, hardly more than that, and she had already become as helpless as an infant. Jeremiah needed her. More than that: he needed her to be a figure of power, the stuff of legends; rapt with wild magic and efficacy. Yet here she lay, cradled weakly in the arms of a man who had turned his back on such things.

Ahead of her, the Ramen and ur-viles moved in their distinct groups, as obscure as clouds against the vague background of the rocks. Yearning to find some use for herself, she asked abruptly, 'Stave, will you talk to me?'

He replied without turning his head. 'What do you wish me to say?'

'Tell me what you know about ur-viles.' She desired a concession from him; something more personal than the forbearance he had shown the Ramen. 'You called them a great evil, but they don't act like it.'

Out of the gloaming, Stave said, 'They are as strange to us as to you. We cannot account for them. We have never understood them.'

Linden persisted. 'You still know more about them than I do. Their history. Where they come from. All I've ever heard is that they were made, not born. Created by the Demondim – whoever *they* were. I need more.

'Isn't there anything else you can tell me?'

For a long moment, Stave appeared to consider the deeper ramifications of her question. Deliberately over the centuries, the *Haruchai* had suppressed the history of the Land. Now she asked him to speak of it – and in Liand's presence.

Finally he countered, 'Chosen, do you comprehend what you request? This foolish young man has elected to dare his fate with you. If I give you answer, and he seeks later to relate what he has heard, we must prevent him.'

'You appear to value kindness. Will you treat him so roughly?'

Before Linden could object, Liand put in stiffly, 'Your words sow confusion, Master. You threaten me rather than the Chosen. Therefore the choice is mine to make. To pretend otherwise is not honest. It ill becomes you.'

A subliminal tension seemed to run through Stave's chest. 'Have a care, Stonedownor,' he replied. 'You are not equal to such determinations.'

'Because,' Linden protested, 'you don't allow him to be.' Stave's inflexibility exasperated her. 'He's right. If you think he's too ignorant to understand the risks, that's *your* doing. No one else's.'

The *Haruchai* had made themselves responsible for all the Land. Under the circumstances, the unexpected aid of the ur-viles must have undermined Stave's convictions. And he may have felt disturbed by the way in which the presence of the Demondim-spawn lent credibility to Anele's impossible tale. Perhaps his need to understand the creatures was as acute as Linden's.

'Very well,' he said at last. His voice held no hint of concession. 'I will answer. This Stonedownor must be wary of us as he sees fit.'

The indistinct group of the Ramen appeared nearer than it had earlier. Stave was gaining on them – or they had slowed their pace to listen.

'You have been told, Linden Avery, that the *Haruchai* first came to the Land in the time of High Lord Kevin Landwaster.' Having accepted this task, Stave spoke steadily, in spite of his taciturn nature. Nevertheless his tone conveyed an impression of awkwardness, as though he were translating a richer and more numinous tongue into blunt human language. 'I say this again to explain that they did not know the High Lord's father, Loric son of Damelon, who earned the name of Vilesilencer. They heard only tales of those years, and of the black Viles which had haunted the Land. We cannot now declare which of those tales were true.'

Linden settled herself in the Master's arms. His decision to speak gave her an obscure comfort. It suggested that he could still compromise, in spite of his native severity.

'It was said by some,' he told her as well as Liand and the listening Ramen, 'that the Viles were creatures of miasma, evanescent and dire, arising from ancient banes buried within Mount Thunder as mist arises from tainted waters. Others claimed that they were spectres and ghouls, the tormented spirits of those who had fallen victim to Corruption's evil. And yet others proclaimed that they were fragments of the One Forest's lost soul, remnants of spirit rent by the slaughter of the trees, and ravenous for harm.

'On three things, however, the tales agreed. First, the Viles appeared where they willed, elusive as swamp lights, wreaking mortification and horror. Next, their lore, which they had gained from the buried banes of the Earth, was black and ruinous, delving into matters which the Old Lords could not penetrate. And last, the evil of the Viles was inspired by their loathing of themselves.

'Doubt-ridden, perhaps, by the cleaner spirits from which they had arisen, or by the havoc which Corruption required of them, they desired above all things to become other than they were. And towards that desire they bent all their terrible lore.

'Therefore they created the Demondim, labouring long in the Lost Deep. And for a time it appeared that they had succeeded in their self-loathing, for the Demondim were unlike their makers. Among the Lords, they were described as "powerful and austere". It was said of them that they were "once friendly" to the trees.

'Still the Viles were a bane upon the Land. For that reason, High Lord Loric took up the challenge of silencing their evil. And in this he prevailed, though at great cost. Because their lore was a mystery to him, beyond his conception, he enlisted the aid of the Demondim against their makers. There he learned dismay, and could never again be truly whole, for he did not know that Corruption had been at work among the Demondim, sending his Ravers to teach them self-Despite, the same abhorrence of themselves which had long tormented the Viles.

'Because they had been swayed, the Demondim became the foes of the forests. For the same reason, they returned to the breeding dens of the Viles in order to begin the making of the ur-viles. And for that same reason, the aid which the Demondim granted to Loric Vilesilencer was Despite in another form, for it arose from their self-loathing. They turned against their makers because Corruption is cunning, and because they saw no value in their own creation.

'Thus was High Lord Loric's victory over evil made possible by Corruption. So were planted the seeds of doubt and chagrin which later blossomed in Kevin Landwaster and the Ritual of Desecration.'

Shades of evening still held the sky, but night now filled the rift, welling up from the memories of the rubble; flowing downwards from the dark past of the ur-viles. And with it came the ice-sharp wind which Manethrall Hami had promised. Cold soughed and hissed in the background of Stave's words.

Yet he was not chilled. His people made their home among the ice and snows of the Westron Mountains. The passion in his veins gave him all the warmth he required.

Bearing Linden upwards appeared to cost him no effort at all.

'The Bloodguard,' he stated flatly, 'heard only tales of the Viles, but of the Demondim their experience was certain. Among other causes, High Lord

Kevin was driven to Desecration by his failure to answer the darkness of the Vile-spawn.

'The Viles were in some form wraiths, as enduring and insidious as mist. The ur-viles were' – he hesitated momentarily, corrected himself – 'are as you see them, tangible flesh which may be slain, despite their deep lore. But the Demondim possessed a middle nature, at once both and neither, partaking of miasma and flesh together. As did the Viles, they persisted outside or beyond life and death. As do the ur-viles, they had forms which could be touched and harmed.'

'I do not understand,' Liand put in. 'How is it possible?'

'The Demondim were animate dead,' Stave answered, 'creatures such as those which came near to causing the fall of Revelstone in the time of High Lord Mhoram. Those creatures, however, were mere lifeless forms serving the power of the Illearth Stone. The Demondim were the lore and bitterness of the Viles made manifest in slain flesh, corpses with the puissance of Lords. The vitriol which the ur-viles wield for destruction pulsed in their hearts. Clad in cerements and rot, the Demondim arose from the graves of the fallen, and their touch was fire.

'They might be halted by blade or flame, but they could not be extinguished. From them, High Lord Kevin learned lessons of despair which doomed his spirit. Given time, an army of such creatures might overrun the Earth.'

Out of the night, Manethrall Hami said, 'The Ramen remember. We named them Fangs, the Teeth of the Render, and all their deeds were dire.'

'Indeed,' Stave responded. 'The Ramen fought valiantly and often along the Roamsedge to bar the Demondim from the Plains of Ra, and were not defeated.

'Yet the Demondim did not comprise an army. Their numbers were too few. Neither scruple nor opposition restricted them, but they had turned against their makers, and therefore the Viles were gone. Nor did the Demondim turn their lore to the spawning of yet more Demondim. They had learned to abhor themselves, and had no desire to seek their own increase. Rather they studied and laboured to re-fashion themselves in living flesh.'

Covenant had told Linden similar things. She had met both ur-viles and Waynhim. However, she had no wish to interrupt what Stave was saying.

'While Corruption wrought covertly to mar the Council of Lords,' he told the dark climb, 'the Demondim also laboured in secret, wielding their lore over breeding vats and fens in the Lost Deep, the lightless pits and caverns beneath the Wightwarrens of Mount Thunder. There among forgotten banes and ancient cruelties, they strove with lore and power to make of themselves new creatures.

'And from their labours emerged living flesh at last. Some were ur-viles, while others came forth as Waynhim, smaller than ur-viles, more grey than black, and less inclined to bloodshed. Why this should be so, the *Haruchai* do not know. Perhaps among the Demondim lingered the memory that they had once stood apart from the lust and loathing of the Viles. Perhaps some aspect or faction of the Demondim had not been entirely seduced by Despite. Whatever the cause, the truth remains that both ur-viles and Waynhim were created in the same fashion. Yet the Waynhim sought to heal their abhorrence in service rather than to quench it in slaughter, as the ur-viles did.

'So the downfall of the Demondim came upon them. They were undone by the Ritual of Desecration. Corruption had not forewarned his servants, or they had declined to heed their peril. It may be that they desired their own destruction. Thus the Landwaster's despair achieved this one victory. Though ur-viles and Waynhim endured, the Demondim were swept aside.'

'That also,' announced Manethrall Hami softly, 'the Ramen do not forget. We have known both Waynhim and ur-viles. In that time, an extravagant cruelty ruled the ur-viles, and all the Land feared them. They had indeed become mortal, however, and could be slain.' Her voice held relish. 'Many were the creatures which perished at the hands of the Ramen.'

Stave nodded. 'Yet they had become less than they were, for in the Ritual of Desecration even such beings as ur-viles and Waynhim were diminished. Much of the black lore of the Viles and the Demondim endured to them – and much did not.

'This the new Lords knew because in numbers both Waynhim and ur-viles continued to dwindle. Indeed, both had become the last of their kind. They created no descendants, and when they were slain nothing returned of them.'

Linden squirmed, suddenly uncomfortable in the *Haruchai*'s arms. He seemed to imply that the success of the Ramen against the ur-viles would not have been possible if the lore of the Demondim-spawn had retained its original force.

The Manethrall responded sharply, 'And do you therefore discount us, Bloodguard? Do you deem that our battles were less fiercely fought, or our blood less freely spilled, because our foes had become less than they were?

'Much has been altered since the Bloodguard were turned to Fangthane's service. You are Masters now, and a threat to harmless old men. Yet I see that the arrogance of your kind persists.'

Linden groaned to herself. She could not imagine what had caused the almost subcutaneous animosity between Stave and the Ramen. They had just met; could not know each other. Any grievance between them was several thousand years old.

However, Stave's reply sounded courteous enough, if not conciliatory. 'You mistake me, Manethrall. I speak only of ur-viles and Waynhim, not of Ramen. The courage of the Ramen was beyond question, and their devotion to the Ranyhyn proved greater than the fidelity of the Bloodguard.'

But then his tone grew harder. 'Yet we "persist" in the Land's service. What has become of the Ramen and their devotion?

'In the time of the Sunbane they withdrew the Ranyhyn from the Land. That was wisely done, for the Ranyhyn required preservation. Yet many centuries have now passed, and where are the great horses?

'The Ramen remain. That we see. They live secretly among these mountains, for purposes which are likewise secret. But what of the Ranyhyn? Do they also remain, Manethrall? Have they expired in some inhospitable region? Were they led from ruin to ruin by their Ramen? Or have you returned without them, thinking to deny them the birthright of their true home?'

Linden expected an angry rejoinder from the Manethrall; but instead she heard the rush of bare feet, the whisper of skin running over stone. The dark felt suddenly ominous around her, fretted with cold.

In the last glow of the sky, she saw ur-viles crowding between her and the Ramen. They barked to each other harshly, or to her, but she could not understand them.

Oh, shit.

Trying to forestall a conflict, she snapped, 'Stave, stop. Put me down. We don't need this. The Ramen are helping us. What more do you want?'

For a moment, the *Haruchai* strode up the rocks in silence. Then he stopped against an abrupt wall of ur-viles. The creatures had barred his way completely.

Facing them, he dropped Linden's legs to set her on her feet. Liand scrambled to her side as she groped for balance on the uneven surface. She feared that she would see red blades gleaming among the black creatures, but no weapons marked the night.

The ur-viles smelled of decaying leaves and carrion; things which had become rotten.

What in hell was going on?

And what were 'Ranyhyn'? Both Hami and Stave had mentioned them earlier, but she did not know what the name implied.

She wished urgently that she could understand the ur-viles.

'Manethrall,' she called out softly, 'I'm sorry. He doesn't speak for me. I don't even know what he's talking about. But you don't have to be enemies. The

Haruchai I've known have always been faithful. No matter what happened, they stood by us.'

'Chosen,' Stave put in impassively. 'The Ramen do not hear you.'

What—?

'Indeed,' Liand confirmed acidly. 'They have gone ahead. The Master's words have driven them away.'

Linden gaped into the black mass of ur-viles, trying to see past them. 'Why?' She was blind in the shrouded rift. 'What are they doing?'

She could not believe that the Ramen had forsaken her.

'I do not know,' Stave answered. 'Their purposes are hidden.'

'Yet if they do not guide us,' Liand muttered, 'we cannot escape this place. We do not know the way.'

Linden turned from the innominate threat of the ur-viles.

'Stave, I don't understand you.' He was no more than a vague shape in the night: indistinct; beyond persuasion. 'They saved our lives. You acted like you respect them. You even *compromised* with them, which is more than you've been willing to do for me. And now you want to pick a fight?'

Darkness and cold made the aid of the Ramen essential.

If Stave felt endangered by the ur-viles, his tone did not show it. 'Linden Avery, you do not accept us. For that reason, perhaps, you are quick to place faith in these Ramen, though you know nothing of them. Yet I mistrust them. You should understand that I have cause.'

He may have been asking her to take sides.

'What cause?' she countered.

'You have not known the Ranyhyn,' he replied. 'And spoken words cannot contain their worth. They are' – he hesitated briefly –'or perhaps were among the most precious of the Land's glories.

'The great horses of Ra were Earthpower made flesh. Their beauty and power played no small part in the wonder which bound our ancestors to the Vow, and the Bloodguard rode them in pride and service. Their absence diminishes us. Without them, the Land is incomplete, and our care can never suffice to make it whole.'

He paused, then continued more severely, 'The Ramen were the tenders of the Ranyhyn. Perhaps they continue in that devotion. Yet where are the Ranyhyn? Why have the great horses not returned to the Plains of Ra? And why do the Ramen conceal themselves among these mountains, consorting with ur-viles and succouring madmen, when the Land is their home, and the Ranyhyn are needed?'

Strictly he finished, 'I fear Corruption's hand upon them.'

He had called the ur-viles *a great evil*. For that, also, he had cause.

'Are you sure?' Linden demanded. 'Do you *see* it?' The *Haruchai* were proof against Kevin's Dirt, and mere night could not blind the other dimensions of health-sense.

'I do not,' he admitted. 'Yet we are the Masters of the Land and must consider such perils.'

'Linden.' Liand's voice shook in the cold. 'We cannot remain here. This wind will undo us. And our cloaks and blankets are with Somo, behind us. We must continue to climb, and attempt to discover the way.'

Damn it. He was right. The Ramen had left her and her companions in an untenable position.

For his sake, however, she said, 'We'll be all right. They haven't abandoned us. They'll help us when we need it.'

Grimly she determined to try the broken slope with her own hands and feet. She had had enough of Stave. If the ur-viles did not stand in her way—

But they continued to block her path. As she started forward, several of them began to bark more loudly. From the clotted darkness of their formation, one of them confronted her, holding an object in its hands.

'Chosen,' Stave said: a warning.

If she were in danger, surely he would be able to sense it?

The ur-vile extended a blurred shape towards her. It may have been a small cup.

Liand grabbed her arm. 'Linden. No. They are ur-viles. Demondim-spawn.'

Until this evening, he had never heard of such creatures. Like Ramen and Ranyhyn, the One Forest and Ravers, they had not existed for him even as legends.

Linden shook off his hand. 'They saved us,' she breathed.

She had already accepted aid from Lord Foul himself.

'And they are descendants of evil,' Liand objected. 'The Master has said so.'

Haruchai did not lie.

Yet the ur-viles barked at her insistently. The nearest creature prodded its cup at her hands.

Their rank, decayed odour repulsed her. It seemed to blow against her skin like the steam of a corrosive—

—bringing another scent with it, musty and potent: an aroma compounded of dust and age and vitality.

She knew that smell. For a moment, the memory troubled her; elusive, fraught with bloodshed and loss. Then it returned in a rush of clarity.

The Northron Climbs and bitter cold, accompanied by Cail and Giants. A preternatural winter brought down from the north by *arghuleh*. And a Waynhim *rhyshyshim*, a gathering.

To Linden and her companions, the Waynhim had given succour and safety; warmth and rest and food. And a dark, musty drink which had nourished them like distilled *aliantha*.

'Stave,' she murmured in wonder and surprise, 'that's *vitrim*. They're offering us *vitrim*.'

'"*Vitrim*"?' asked Liand. 'What is *vitrim*?'

Stave stood beside her opposite the Stonedownor. 'Are you certain? The *Haruchai* have not forgotten Cail's tales of the Search for the One Tree. He spoke of *vitrim*. But ur-viles are not Waynhim.'

She could have asked him to take the cup for her; sample its contents. She did not doubt that he would do so, trusting his senses and strength to protect him from any subtle poison. But she was fed up with suspicion, and already had too many enemies.

Abruptly she opened her hands for the proffered cup.

The ur-vile placed cold iron in her palms and stepped back, still barking. Perhaps it meant to encourage her.

So that she would not falter, she raised the cup at once and sipped from it.

The liquid tasted like dust and neglect: she had difficulty swallowing it. Nonetheless it seemed to fill her flesh with excitement, eagerness transformed almost instantly to sustenance as soon as it touched her stomach. With every beat of her heart, the cold lost its grip on her. The edges of the wind still drew tears from her eyes; but now they were tears of relief and possibility.

A kind of giddiness came over her and she nearly laughed aloud. 'Here,' she said, handing the cup to Liand. 'Try it. You'll like it. If you can ignore the taste.'

He hesitated, hampered by confusion.

'Go on,' she told him. 'Just a sip.' Rejuvenation in waves washed her weariness aside, riding the scend of her pulse. Light seemed to shine from her nerves, mapping its own life within her. Liand should have been able to discern the glow she emitted.

Stave certainly could.

The young man would not refuse: she knew that. He had already wandered too far beyond the boundaries of his experience, and had no one else to guide him. Cautiously he eased the iron cup to his lips and tasted its contents.

The Master did not move or speak. Instead he faced the ur-viles as though he were carved of darkness.

For a long moment, Liand remained motionless over the cup. Then, softly, he began to laugh: a quiet, clean sound like the sweep of a broom brushing away cobwebs and anxiety.

'I am astonished. The savour is indeed unpleasant. I have tasted brackish water and dying mosses which were kinder to my tongue. Yet it outshines *aliantha* in my veins.

'Linden Avery, I would not have believed it possible.'

She nodded gladly; but before she could reply, the nearest ur-vile retrieved its cup, then retreated among its fellows. At once, a larger creature bearing a pointed iron rod like a jerrid stepped forward: the loremaster. Instinctively she braced herself, uncertain of the creature's intentions.

But the loremaster only barked at its weapon; and gradually a crimson flame flowered from its tip, blooming until it resembled the blaze of a torch. Soon the fire shed a pool of incarnadine over the broken tumble of the slope; and Linden realised that the loremaster meant to light the way.

The ur-viles were still trying to help her. Spilling red illumination on all sides, the loremaster and its followers began to retreat up the rubble as if to draw her and her companions forward.

According to Stave, they were a great evil. And they should all have died millennia ago. Lord Foul had certainly tried to destroy them. Yet, impossibly, they were here. Like Anele, they seemed to have been displaced in time. If Anele's account of himself could be trusted—

Linden glanced at Stave; at Liand. The Master regarded her flatly, conceding nothing. But Liand nodded. 'Let us go. This *vitrim* warms me strangely. While its virtue endures, we would do well to escape the wind.'

Linden faced the loremaster. 'Lead the way. We'll follow you.'

Manethrall Hami had told her that the creatures understood human speech.

In response, they retreated further; and she began to climb after them, lifted over the rocks by their weird encouragement.

Even with their help, the climb was painful and prolonged. *Vitrim* was not hurtloam: it gave her energy, but could not heal sore muscles or aching joints. Before long, her legs began to tremble, and her balance wavered in the sullen light. Nevertheless she was glad that she no longer needed Stave to carry her. She could not afford to be dependent on him.

The ur-viles had given her more than sustenance. The illumination in her veins had enabled her to reclaim some necessary sense of herself.

Still the ascent was arduous. Gradually she grew numb, worn down by the effort of forcing her boots upwards, scraping her shins and palms over the jagged memories of the rocks, expending her given warmth and strength.

Anele's past, and the One Forest's, ceased to pain her. The strange aid of the ur-viles lost its disturbing eloquence. As she climbed and climbed, the rift and the wind and the darkness shrank down to a splash of crimson light, a precarious tumble of stones. If anyone spoke to her, she no longer heard them.

At some point, one of the Ramen appeared. Perhaps Hami had sent the young man back as a guide. Then the way became steeper; more perilous. Linden might have been scaling a precipice from which she could have slipped at any moment to fall for the rest of her life. But she did not slip – or her companions upheld her – and after a time the wind lost its flensing edge. Then she found herself kneeling on soil and grass instead of stone, under a fathomless expanse of stars.

There she could walk more easily; and Liand or one of the Cords supported her when she sagged. Several Ramen accompanied her now, although the ur-viles had vanished somewhere, leaving her to darkness and starlight. Eventually she rounded a hill into the shelter of an escarpment lambent with fires.

Ordinary campfires of brush and wood, three of them, shed warmth and flames against a jut of stone which protected a hollow at the base of the scarp; and around them were gathered several Ramen, more than Linden remembered. Some of them tended their injured comrades, boiling water and preparing salves. Others readied food, while still others devised lean-tos to soften the last of the wind, or gathered bracken for bedding. Linden smelled *amanibhavam* and stew.

While she could, she went to help the Ramen clean and bandage the wounds of Cords who had nearly died saving her life, and Liand's, and Anele's.

The old man had reached the camp ahead of her, guided here by Ramen if he had not found the way on his own. Already he lay in one of the lean-tos, apparently sleeping, felled by exhaustion.

Linden aided the injured until she reached the young woman who had been nearly disembowelled.

The woman lay on her back near one of the campfires; unconscious; pallid as wax. Several Cords squatted around her. Someone had placed a strip of leather between her jaws. She must have needed it earlier, to help her endure the jostling climb from the rift. Now her lips hung slack around it, baring her teeth.

Without her health-sense, Linden felt fundamentally truncated. She did not need percipience, however, to know that the woman's condition had worsened. The Cords had lifted flaps of torn skin and muscle aside so that they could attempt to cleanse the wound; and through the pulsing ooze of blood, Linden saw that the claws of the *kresh* had ripped into the woman's intestines and liver. In addition, a number of the fine ducts which connected the liver and the bowel had been severed: they leaked bile into the blood. That alone could cause the wound to mortify.

Linden needed a scalpel and sutures, clamps and sponges, IVs – and some very powerful antibiotics.

She had nothing.

With boiling water the Cords had made a salve of their *amanibhavam*. Surely they were right about its healing properties? But even so— She knew of nothing in the Land except hurtloam which might be potent enough to save this woman's life.

Or wild magic, if she had known how to raise it – and if she could have wielded its fire with exactly the right delicacy and precision – and if she could have *seen* what she was doing—

Sighing to herself, she asked the nearest Cord, 'Is there any hurtloam around here? Can you find it? Or do you have some other way to treat her? She'll die if we don't do something soon.'

At once, the Cord jumped to his feet and hastened away, apparently intending to consult with Manethrall Hami. The other Ramen stared at Linden, mutely asking for her help.

Grimly she set aside her exhaustion. 'All right,' she murmured. 'I need soft cloth. Something to soak up the blood and bile. And more boiling water. We'll use your salve when we've cleaned her as much as we can.'

Two of the Cords withdrew promptly. One returned with several pale brown blankets which he tore into strips. The other brought an earthenware bowl full of steaming water.

Trusting her instincts, Linden took the first strip of cloth, showed it to the Cords. 'Here's what we're going to do.' When she had dipped the cloth into the bowl just enough to moisten it, she lowered it softly into the puddled bile along the woman's descending colon. By increments, the fabric absorbed splotches of red and yellow; stains of mortality. When it was sodden, she lifted it away; wrung it out over the grass; dipped it again into the bowl.

'Do it *gently*,' she instructed the Cords. 'We want to clean out as much of this mess as we can. Especially the bile' – she pointed – 'that yellow ooze.'

They nodded. Three of them joined her, setting moist cloths in the wound to sponge up small amounts of fluid, then squeezing out as much as they could and repeating the process.

The woman's bleeding slowed as they worked: she had already lost too much blood. She needed a transfusion as badly as antibiotics. But Linden had no means to provide it.

She did not notice that an audience had gathered until Liand said her name in a way that made her lift her head. As far as she could tell, they were all there, Liand and Stave, Manethrall Hami, perhaps as many as thirty other Ramen: everyone except Anele. They studied what she did with uncertainty in their eyes; but none of them sought to interfere.

The intensity of their attention reminded Linden that she did not know the injured Cord's name. She knew none of their names, except Hami's.

Liand cleared his throat. 'Linden,' he repeated. 'The Ramen know a place where "hurtloam" may be found. The Manethrall has sent Cords. But it is five leagues distant, and the way is difficult. They cannot reach it and return before midday.'

He hesitated, then asked, 'Will Sahah live so long?'

Hami may have nodded: Linden was not sure. She returned her blunted gaze to the young Cord. Sahah, she thought. A young woman named Sahah with her guts ripped open: younger than Liand, hardly more than sixteen. If she had not been in such pain, she would have looked like a girl.

Abruptly Linden's hands began to shake, and a blur of weariness filled her gaze. 'I don't know. Probably not.' If she did, she would spend her last hours in agony. 'Unless *amanibhavam* is some kind of wonder drug.'

Sahah.

But there was nothing more she could do: not without power. 'That's enough,' she told the Cords helping her. 'Now your salve.' The Ramen had said that it was too potent for human flesh. 'Give her as much as you think she can tolerate.'

Somehow she struggled to her feet. If Liand had not put his arm around her, she might not have been able to stand. 'Close the wound,' she added. 'Keep her warm. And give her water, if she can swallow it.'

Falling blood pressure might kill the Cord before sepsis and trauma took her.

'Linden Avery,' said the Manethrall firmly. 'You are in sooth a healer. Yet you feel distress. Do you fear that you have failed Sahah? That she will perish because your care does not suffice?'

Linden nodded dumbly.

'It may be so,' Hami admitted. 'I think not, however. Ringthane—' She faltered momentarily. 'How may this be said? You have strange lore. I cannot know its extent.'

Linden might have murmured something; but the Manethrall was not done.

'There is a shroud of evil upon the Land. Mayhap you know this. It is one reason among several that we do not return to our ancient homes.

'It hampers discernment.'

Again Linden nodded. 'Kevin's Dirt.'

'You have felt its bale,' Hami explained. 'We do not. For you, sight and touch and scent are constrained. You cannot see what is plain to us.'

Unsteadily Linden reached out to Hami; gripped the Manethrall's shoulders for support. Blinking to clear her sight, she tried to understand Hami's kindness. 'See—?'

The Ramen were like the *Haruchai*? Still able to *see*?

'Indeed,' the Manethrall answered. 'You do not perceive that the pall of Sahah's death has been diminished by your care. Nor do you discern the surpassing balm of *amanibhavam*. You cannot see that her end is no longer certain.'

Fatigue and relief clogged Linden's throat. She could hardly find enough breath to ask, 'How—?'

'Ringthane?'

Linden had spent barely a day and a half in the Land; and already too many people had died for her. But Sahah might live?

She tried again. 'How can you *see*?'

Now Hami understood her. 'It is no great wonder. Among these mountains, we stand above the ill which you name Kevin's Dirt. It does not hinder us because it does not touch us.'

Linden's legs folded under her, but she hardly noticed it; hardly recognised that she would have fallen if Liand had not upheld her. Relief had taken the last of her resolve. She might yet recover from the effects of Kevin's Dirt.

Somewhere she found the strength to say, 'Thank you,' for more gifts than she could name.

Then she let herself sleep.

This time she did not dream. Perhaps she had moved beyond the reach of dreams.

Hungers woke her, several of them, the need for food among others. Her arms ached as though she had spent the dark longing to embrace her son. She craved the necessary sustenance of comprehension. And an inchoate anticipation ran in her veins. She opened her eyes with the suddenness of surprise, like a woman who had been told that the world around her had been made new.

She found herself lying on bracken under the shelter of a lean-to in the first grey promise of dawn. The air was cold enough to sting her skin; but blankets and warmth enclosed her. Someone – Liand, probably – had put her to bed.

When she raised her head to look around, everything that she saw and felt had been transformed.

The dimness of dawn shrouded details; and yet she knew beyond question that the season was spring. The air itself told her: it whispered of thawing snows and new growth; of readiness inspired to germination. The bracken assured her that it had dried and fallen long ago, and would sprout again; and dew wet the hardy grass in profusion, already restoring the soil's life.

The Ramen were up before her, moving about the camp in preparation for food and departure. The wide sky did not yet shed enough light to let her study their faces; but she needed no illumination to discern their essential fortitude, or to feel the clarity of their devotion. She could see beyond question that they were a people who kept faith: as unwavering in their service as *Haruchai*, and as unwilling to compromise.

Yet they were more human than Stave's kind. They lacked the surpassing strength of *Haruchai*; did not live as long. And their fidelity took another form. They were not men and women who aspired to measure themselves against the perils of the wide Earth. They nurtured no ambitions which might seduce them. Instead they strove only to remain who they were, generation after generation, without doubt or hesitation.

Gazing at them from her warm bed, Linden felt both humbled and exultant. *Do something they don't expect.* Somehow she had found her way to people who would give her every conceivable aid – as long as what she asked did not interfere with their deeper commitments. What those commitments might be, she could not guess, and did not try. At this moment, she was content to know that she could trust the Ramen.

While she slept, she had regained her health-sense. Now life and Earthpower throbbed palpably beneath the surface of all she beheld. Even in the crepuscular air, her surroundings and her companions were lambent with implications. The sensations of percipience sang in her nerves like joy.

Pushing back her blankets, she arose into the chill to see how Sahah fared; and as she did so the mountains seemed to spring up around her as if they had been called into being by the dawn.

Beyond the escarpment which sheltered the camp, peaks reached into the heavens on all sides. These were the lower and more modest crests which buttressed the Land, rather than the higher bastions, hoary with age and rime, deeper in the Southron Range. Few of them still held ice and snow, and those only in patches which seldom felt the sun. Nonetheless they reared around the camp like guardians, massive and vertiginous: the true titans of the Earth. The air drifting down their rugged sides tasted like an elixir, sharp and pristine. With their bluff granite and their enduring hearts, they formed a place of safety in their midst.

Splashing her boots with dew, she strode towards the campfire where she had left Sahah; and even the heavy aching of her muscles could not blunt her anticipation. Torn fibres and strained ligaments merely hurt. They did not dim the restoration of her senses.

At once, Liand called her name, waved and hastened to join her. Seeing him, she knew instantly that he had been awake for some time, too eager and young to sleep long in the company of Ramen. And she recognised that he, too, had felt the renewed touch of health-sense. He revelled in discernment as if he were exalted; drunk on the new depth and significance of everything around him. Excitement seemed to crow and preen in every line of his form.

'Linden,' he called joyously, 'is it not wondrous?' Clearly he felt too many wonders to name them all.

Smiling at his pleasure, she continued towards the campfire.

She was still ten paces away when she began to feel Sahah's wracked distress.

Manethrall Hami and two of her Cords squatted beside the woman; and Linden saw at a glance that they had been there all night: their vigil haunted their eyes. Hami's matter-of-fact manner the previous day had conveyed the impression that she did not greatly value the lives of her Cords; that other considerations outweighed individual life and death. Now, however, Linden discerned the truth. The Ramen lived precarious lives, threatened at all times by privation, predators and self-sacrifice: they could not afford to bewail the cost of their convictions. Nevertheless the bonds which sustained them were strong and enduring.

One look told her that Sahah's grasp on life had become tenuous, stretched as thin as a whisper. Fever glazed her eyes, and pain had cut lines like galls into her cheeks. Internal bleeding left her skin the colour of spilth, as if her flesh might slump from her bones at any moment.

The state of her abdomen cried out to Linden's senses.

It could have been worse; far worse. Care and *amanibhavam* had accomplished this: Sahah still lived.

Antibiotics and transfusions might yet save her.

But the left side of her belly was swollen and seeping, crimson with sepsis. The internal ooze of bile had undone the effects of hot water and *amanibhavam*. Infection ate like acid at her fading endurance.

The Cords whom Hami had sent for hurtloam might return by midday; but Sahah would not last so long.

'Ringthane.' The Manethrall's voice was a rasp of weariness. 'We have considered opening her wound to apply more *amanibhavam*.' She showed Linden a small bowl of the Ramen's sovereign poultice. In water the pulped leaves emitted such potency that the scent stung Linden's nostrils. 'But I determined to await your counsel. Hampered in discernment, you have shown that you are capable of much. If you are now able to *see*, perhaps you are also able to tell us what we must do.'

Pride made what she wanted to say difficult for her. The previous day she had discounted Linden's offer of help.

'Three Cords have fallen at my word. They are honoured among us, for they were valiant against the *kresh*. Yet they were Ramen, flesh and bone, and we are too few for the promises we have made. If you possess any lore or power which may retrieve Sahah from death—' For a moment, her eyes misted as though she might weep.

Linden turned away to spare Hami the sight of her own uncertainty. The Ramen knew that she had power. They had felt the presence of Covenant's ring under her shirt.

She could read Sahah's condition in frightening detail. Every rent tissue, every oozing duct, every mangled vessel was plain to her percipience; as vivid as a dissection. And everywhere within the Cord's abdomen thronged the killing secretions of bile and pus. Sahah's belly might have been the Great Swamp in miniature, its waters and growths and life made toxic by the leakage of Mount Thunder's terrible banes.

Studying Sahah's plight, Linden groaned to herself. She was a *doctor*, for God's sake. She was supposed to *know* how to heal people.

She had done so in the past—

Long ago aboard Starfare's Gem, she had once saved the life of a crushed Giant using only her health-sense. She had reached into him with her percipience, had *possessed* him, and caused his own nerves and muscles to pull closed some of his wounds, staunch some of his bleeding. In that way, she had kept him alive long enough for other aid to reach him.

But he had been a Giant, inconceivably strong by human standards. And she had rushed to his side immediately, before his condition could worsen. And his life had been sustained by the healing vitality of *diamondraught*. And there had been no danger of infection: no polluted fangs and claws; no spilled bile; no punishing climb up the rift.

Her health-sense alone would not suffice. Sahah could not be saved without power: without hurtloam or the Staff of Law.

Or wild magic.

Linden had already demonstrated to herself that she did not understand how to access white gold.

But even if she had been a master of argence, she might still have failed.

Covenant's ring was too puissant: its forces could more readily gouge out mountainsides than cleanse infections or seal internal wounds. And he had taught her that wild magic grew more rampant with use, not more delicate or subtle.

Yet the Manethrall and the Cords watched her as Liand did, as if she had led them to expect miracles.

Finally, because she did not know what else to do, Linden looked around the camp for Stave.

He stood apart from the Ramen as though he had been there all night, alone, and had no need for rest or friendship. He may have been waiting for her, however: as soon as she met his gaze, he came to join her.

The *Haruchai* had never been known as healers. They lived by their skills, or they died, and did not count the cost.

'Stave,' she said when he had acknowledged her with a nod. 'Manethrall.' She could not have explained what she had in mind. For all she knew, she would be unable to make it work. For Sahah's sake, however, she did not hesitate. 'I want to try something.'

Mutely Hami proffered her bowl.

Linden shook her head. 'Not that. She's too weak. It'll kill her. First we need to make her stronger.

'Do either of you know where the ur-viles went?'

The Manethrall shook her head; and Stave said, 'They were ever secret creatures, more accustomed to caverns and warrens than to open sky. I cannot guess where they have hidden themselves, but I deem that you' – his tone implied, *even you* – 'would be loathe to follow.'

Linden dismissed his point with a jerk of her head. 'Can you summon them?' she asked Hami.

Again the woman shook her head.

'Then how were they brought to our aid?' Liand asked impulsively.

The Manethrall shrugged. 'They come and go as they wish. I know not how your plight came to their notice. We do not speak their tongue.'

Linden stared at Hami. For a moment, she heard a vibration that sounded like dishonesty in the Manethrall's tone. Something in her response was meant to mislead—

Yet Linden saw immediately that Hami had told the literal truth: she did not know how to call the ur-viles. The Manethrall wished to conceal or avoid something; but it had no relevance to Sahah's straits. Hami might well have sacrificed all her Cords in battle, but she would risk none of them for the sake of an untruth.

'Then I'll have to do it.' Abruptly Linden started to walk away from her companions. 'Keep everyone back. I've never done this before. I don't know what's going to happen.' Before anyone could question her, she headed out of the camp away from the escarpment.

She had no particular direction in mind: she only wanted a little distance. At her back, she heard Liand object to being left behind. The Manethrall's command restrained him from following, however, if Stave's did not.

Anxious and uncertain, Linden paced the wiry grass until she felt in the sensitive skin between her shoulder-blades that she had reached a safe remove. There she stopped, facing away from the camp. Because she had no lore to guide her, and no experience, she sank to her knees. Perhaps that suppliant stance would convey what words could not.

'I don't know how to do this,' she told the dawn and the mountain breeze. 'I don't know if you can hear me. Or if you care. But you've already helped us once.

'And once you saved the world.'

As she spoke, she slowly closed her eyes; turned her concentration inwards. Without watching what she did, she pulled Covenant's ring from under her shirt and folded it in her cupped palms as if she were praying. Somewhere hidden within her lay a door which could be opened on silver and conflagration. She knew that: otherwise she would already be dead. But it seemed to occupy a place in her heart and mind which she could only approach as if by misdirection. She had not yet learned how to find that door at will.

'You know who I am.' She spoke softly. If the ur-viles could or would not hear her, no shout would reach them. 'With this white gold ring and my own hand, I used Vain to make a new Staff of Law, as you intended.' Vain had been given to Covenant, but he had acknowledged and served her. 'With your help, I went as far as I could go against the Despiser.'

Far enough to heal the ravages of the Sunbane. But only Covenant's self-sacrifice had sufficed to contain Lord Foul's malice.

'Now I'm back. This time I intend to do more.'

She thought of Jeremiah, alone and tormented. Of Anele's terrors and bereavements. Of Lord Foul's words in the old man's mouth. Of a yellow shroud tainting the Land.

She had heard Covenant say while she dreamed, *Trust yourself.*

And within her a door which she could not find shifted on its hinges.

'I want your help again,' she continued, 'if you'll give it. Not against the Despiser this time,' although she sought that as well. 'One of the Ramen is dying. She needs *vitrim*. You can save her.

'In Vain's name I ask it, and my own. Hear me, please. Otherwise a young woman,' hardly more than a girl, 'who fought with you against the *kresh* is going to die.'

Reaching out as if blindly with the fingers of her volition, the hand of choice, she grasped for the handle and unfurled white flame into the new day.

It could have been a high sheet of fire or a small tendril: she neither knew nor cared. Only a moment of wild magic; scarcely more than a heartbeat. Then she opened her hands and let Covenant's ring fall; left it dangling against her chest. Still with her eyes closed, she bowed her forehead to the grass.

If the ur-viles helped her now, they might do so again.

They might help her save Jeremiah.

She heard nothing except the mild curiosity of the breeze; felt nothing except the gravid silence of the mountains. Yet when she raised her head and opened her eyes, she saw an ur-vile standing before her on the grass with an iron cup in its hands.

In the burgeoning dawn, the aroma of *vitrim* – dusky, thick as silt – could not be mistaken.

Chapter Eleven:

Hints

The Ramen broke camp when Linden and Liand had eaten a brief meal. Then they set off along the escarpment, travelling generally eastwards towards a narrow gorge between two of the surrounding mountains.

Somo had arrived during the night, guided by Ramen. The mustang appeared hale and ready, undamaged by the difficulties of the rift. That visibly erased Liand's last doubts about the Ramen. Now he shared their company, and Linden's, with a young man's eagerness.

Sahah they left behind with a few of her companions to care for her. Under the sustaining influence of *vitrim*, the injured Cord had rallied. She could not be moved: her life still hung precariously from the strings of her native toughness. Nevertheless the infection in her belly and the fever in her eyes had receded. She sipped water as well as *vitrim* willingly. At intervals, her mind cleared enough to let her speak. Linden believed – and Manethrall Hami agreed – that Sahah would live until the Cords who had been sent for hurtloam returned.

As the company moved, one of the Cords retrieved Anele from the mountainside above the scarp. Linden had noticed the old man's absence only after her concern for Sahah had eased. She had felt little alarm, however, although she needed Anele in ways which she could hardly name: the Manethrall had promised that the Ramen would not lose him. When Linden asked after him, Hami answered that he had roused early and wandered away, she could not say why: to avoid the Master's presence, perhaps, or to commune with his demons alone. In any case, he rejoined Linden and the Ramen without any obvious reluctance. As he accompanied them towards the gorge, he mumbled to himself incomprehensibly, as if he were engaged in a debate which no one else could hear or understand.

He had been reclaimed by madness, and his blindness had the distracted cast of a man who wandered among ghosts and saw only death.

With her renewed senses, Linden might have tried to pierce his confusion.

But she feared the prices they both might pay for such an intrusion. Any possession was a form of psychic violence which might damage the last shards of his sanity. And she herself would be in danger from his madness. When she had entered Covenant years ago to free him from the imposed stasis of the *Elohim*, his blankness had overcome her, and for a time she had been as lost as Jeremiah. Ceer had died protecting her because she had been so completely absent from herself.

For the present, at least, she was unwilling to take the risk. Her own emotional state was too frangible.

Her success with Covenant's ring had given her a grim, febrile exhilaration. She had found the door to power within herself, and would be able to do so again. In addition, the restoration of her senses seemed to fill her with possibilities. To that extent, at least, she had regained her ability to make effective choices. To influence her own fate – and Jeremiah's. She was no longer entirely dependent on the willingness of others to guide and aid her.

Unfortunately her more profound dilemmas remained unchanged. Beneath her transient joy lurked frustration and despair like a buried lake of magma, a potential volcano. Every step that she took in the company of the Ramen, like every tale that she heard – like wild magic itself – was necessary to her. Yet none of them brought her nearer to Jeremiah.

If her muscles had not stiffened to an acute soreness during the night, so that merely walking demanded most of her concentration, she might have been defenceless against the larger difficulties of her situation.

Off to one side of the vale where the Ramen had camped, snow-melt gathered to form a stream which ran along the floor of the gorge. There the company paused briefly to refill their waterskins. Then they entered the gorge itself.

The narrow defile squirmed between its crude walls, following an ancient seam in the substance of the peaks. At intervals, fallen boulders littered the way, constricting the stream to pools and small rapids. Stave, Anele, and the Ramen seemed oblivious to such obstacles, too sure-footed to be hindered. But Linden, Liand, and Somo had to pick their footing carefully.

By the time they reached the far end of the gorge, the sun had risen past the shoulders of the lowest mountains. In the new light, she saw crests piling southward until they grew dark with distance. In shadow their cloaks of ice looked grimy and tattered, eroded by time. Direct sunlight, however, gave the ice a purity that seemed almost blue. As if exalted by the sun, the peaks lifted their grandeur proudly into the sky.

There the route of the Ramen traversed an open mountain slope southeastwards. This easier surface allowed Linden's muscles to grow accustomed to movement. In addition, the sun warmed some of the tension from her joints. Gradually the aching in her thighs and calves faded and her knees began to feel less brittle.

Liand walked at her side, leading Somo after him; and his buoyant company also helped her along. He was new to percipience, delighted by it, and every unfamiliar vista among the peaks, every type of grass or shrub or tree which he had never seen before, every soaring bird, enhanced his excitement. For him, the world was being made fresh as he moved through it.

Linden still believed that he should have remained in Mithil Stonedown; that he should return home as soon as he could. Nevertheless she found that she relied upon him more with every passing hour. He helped her believe that a world which gave birth to such people could never be entirely ruined by Despite.

Then the Ramen began to descend to the south, avoiding a gnarled bluff that jutted from the mountainside, and Linden was forced to concentrate on her steps again. Walking downwards strained her knees and thighs until they threatened to fold under her. She had to grit her teeth as well as her determination in order to stay on her feet.

Whenever she glanced at Anele, she saw that his madness was modulating between its various phases, responding to necessities or catalysts which she could not begin to grasp.

Ahead of her, the slope dropped towards a place of torn and jagged boulders, great blocks and monoliths, where two of the lower mountains appeared to have collided with each other. Studying the granite chaos, she feared that the Ramen would ask her to clamber there. However, they reassured her by turning so that their path angled more towards the east. As they rounded the mountainside beyond the tumbled monoliths, she saw that they were headed towards an arête between massive cliffs, a ridge like a saddle. It had been formed by tremendous rockfalls which had echoed each other off the higher cliffs and crashed together in the intervening valley, filling all of the space between the mountainsides with rubble.

Linden groaned to herself. *More* rubble— She could not conceal her chagrin as she asked Manethrall Hami, 'Is that where we're going?'

The woman nodded. 'The Verge of Wandering lies beyond. There we will attempt to answer the Bloodguard's doubts – and our own.'

Temporising, Linden inquired, 'Can Somo make it?' She was not sure that she could. 'It looks rough from here.'

Hami concealed a smile. 'We have learned a path among the stones. The mustang will not find it difficult.' Then she looked at Linden and said more gravely, 'Your weariness is plain, Ringthane. Your mount will be able to bear you, if you wish it.'

Linden stiffened. 'No, thanks,' she muttered. Her weakness the previous day had injured her self-confidence. 'If Somo can manage it, I probably can too.'

The Ramen leader nodded. 'I do not question it.'

'But tell me something,' Linden went on, 'before I start breathing too hard to talk.' She had not forgotten the apparent disingenuousness of Hami's earlier claim that her people had no communication with or comprehension of the ur-viles.

'If it will ease your way,' the Manethrall replied, 'I will answer as I can.'

Her tone conveyed sincerity, although Linden also heard hints of hesitation. The Ramen had their own secrets, which they did not mean to reveal.

Troubled by her sense of unspoken intentions, Linden asked, 'How did you know about the *kresh*?'

Hami gave her a perplexed frown. 'Ringthane?'

'It all seems too tidy to me,' Linden explained awkwardly. 'I don't see how you could have known that I was in danger. But you came to my rescue anyway, right when I needed you.

'How did you do that?'

'Ah.' Hami nodded. 'Now I comprehend. Our presence was indeed timely. It need not surprise you, however.

'It is our custom betimes to scout the borders of the Land, seeking some glimpse of what transpires there. Yesterday with my Cords I had elected to keep watch on the Mithil valley, for only there are these mountains readily entered – there, and from the Plains of Ra. Elsewhere the cliffs forbid passage.

'From the heights above the valley, we saw the *kresh* gather to hunt. We did not know what they hunted. We sought only to assail them when they dared the mountains. That you were their prey we did not discover until we had prepared our ambush.'

Her explanation sounded plausible. Linden would not have questioned it if she had not heard hints of avoidance in the Manethrall's tone.

She stopped walking so that she would be able to stand her ground. When Hami halted as well, Linden said, 'Yet somehow you picked yesterday to be right where I needed you. And so did the ur-viles.

'Don't misunderstand me,' she added quickly. 'I'm grateful. I trust you already. But I'm' – she shrugged uncomfortably – 'suspicious of coincidences.'

Lord Foul had taught her that.

She could believe that the ur-viles had known of her presence in the Land,

and of her need. Millennia ago, they had recognised that Covenant would return. But nothing about the Ramen suggested that they had such lore.

Cords gathered around her as she waited, but she ignored them; concentrated on Hami.

'You keep saying,' she went on when the Manethrall did not answer, 'you don't speak the ur-viles' language. But that's not the whole story, is it? You communicate with them somehow. You have some way of working together.'

'And the Demondim-spawn,' Stave put in harshly, 'have ever served Corruption.' He had placed himself at Linden's shoulder. 'They opposed their ancient master in the time of the Sunbane. Yet plainly he did not destroy them, as he appeared to do. Perhaps he preserved them covertly across the centuries, in preparation, it may be, for the return of white gold to the Land.'

Now Linden took notice of the Cords, drawn by the tension emanating from them. When she studied them, she realised that they shared Hami's secrets; that all of the Ramen knew the things which the Manethrall would not say.

Hami bristled at Stave's words. Her fingers twitched to take hold of her garrote. Stave faced her impassively, however, unswayed by her indignation.

'Does it offend you, Manethrall, that the *Haruchai* are not gladdened by your return to the borders of the Land? That we question your actions and your troth? Then reply to the Chosen's query. Permit us to judge the nature of your purposes.'

No doubt he could discern the presence of secrets as clearly as Linden did.

Hami gauged him darkly: she seemed eager for combat. But then, distinctly, she closed the door on her ready pride.

'You speak of that which lies beyond you, sleepless one,' she answered like a sigh. 'Two days I asked in which to take counsel and seek comprehension. This you accepted. Therefore there can be no contest between us. You are safe among the Ramen. We will permit no harm to you, or to your companions.

'Nor will we take offence. To provoke us is unseemly. Such impatience ill becomes you.'

Stave regarded Hami for a moment, apparently appraising her. Then he surprised Linden by bowing as he had in the rift.

'I hear you, Manethrall. I will be patient, as I have agreed. I have named the causes of my doubt. But know also that I am grieved to encounter the Ramen after so many generations, and to be denied knowledge of the Ranyhyn.

'You misjudge the Bloodguard. They did not ride Ranyhyn to their deaths, as you avow. Rather they accepted service which the Ranyhyn offered freely. No life or power in all the Land was honoured or loved more highly than that of the great horses.'

Again Hami did not return his bow. Instead she retorted, 'The Bloodguard might have refused that service. The Ringthane did so. Yet he prevailed.'

Then she returned her attention to Linden's question.

'As for the timeliness of our aid,' she answered like a shrug, 'it is no great wonder. We were drawn to the region of the Mithil Valley by the fall of Kevin's Watch. I have said that we scout the borders of the Land. Such destruction could not escape our notice.'

Without another word, she turned away, leading her Cords on towards the base of the arête.

Linden wanted to stay where she was. The animosity between Stave and the Ramen disturbed her. Their every exchange was fraught with history; with memories and passions which she had not shared and could not evaluate. She did not know what to expect from them.

But the Ramen were moving, and so she followed them. She could not afford the severity which seemed to rule Stave and Hami.

At once, Liand came to her side, radiating confusion like heat. However, he waited until she acknowledged him with a glance before he murmured privately, 'I do not understand. What troubles the Master? Can he not descry the worth of the Ramen?'

'Sure, he can,' Linden replied softly. 'It isn't their honesty he's worried about. It's their secrets.'

The Stonedownor looked surprised; but he did not contradict her. Perhaps he, too, had felt the undercurrents in Hami and her Cords. Instead he mused as if to himself, 'I had not known that the Masters are capable of grief.'

Linden sighed. 'Of course they are.' If they had not felt love or known loss, they would not have sworn the Vow which had bound them to the service of the Lords. 'They're just too strict to admit it most of the time.'

Liand frowned. 'Does that account for their denial of the Land's history and wonder? Do they fear to grieve?'

Linden looked at him sharply. 'Maybe.' She had not thought of Stave's people in those terms. 'I don't know anything about Ranyhyn, but it's obvious they were precious to the *Haruchai*. Stave is afraid something terrible has happened to them.'

The young man kept her company in silence for a while. Then he said slowly, 'I do not believe so. I know nothing of these Ramen. Nor am I accustomed to the new life which fills my senses. Perhaps it misleads me. Yet—' He paused again, then said more strongly, 'Yet I do not believe that any great harm has befallen the Ranyhyn. The Ramen would not countenance it. They would have died, all of them, to prevent it.'

Linden nodded. The Ramen had given her the same impression.

But surely Stave could see the Manethrall and her Cords as clearly as Liand did? As clearly as Linden herself? If so—

If so, his suspicions sprang from a deeper source.

Like him, she wanted to know why the Ramen would not speak of the great horses.

In silence, the company finished their descent to the foot of the rubble piled between the cliffs, the base of the arête.

By the time they reached it, the sun had risen near noon, and Linden could feel its force beginning to scorch her face and neck. She could not gauge how much elevation she had gained since leaving Mithil Stonedown; but the air was noticeably thinner, sharper, and the sun's fire, masked by the cool atmosphere, had a deceptive intensity. Before long, every exposed inch of her skin would be burned.

She felt vaguely faint as she joined the Ramen below the arête, light-headed with too much exertion and sun. Fortunately Manethrall Hami called a halt so that the travellers could rest and refresh themselves before tackling the knurled litter of the ridge. No doubt she had done so primarily for Linden's benefit. Nonetheless Linden was grateful.

Seen from its base, the arête looked unattainably high: an enormous wrack of boulders piled precariously towards the sky. Its sides appeared to lean outwards, impending ominously over anyone foolish enough to attempt them. And some trick of perspective foreshortened the brusque cliffs on either side so that they seemed to emphasise rather than dwarf the ridge. Staring upwards, Linden lost her balance and stumbled as though she had felt a tremor in the rubble, a hint of shattering like the unsteadiness which had presaged the fall of Kevin's Watch.

The rock remembered its own breaking. If she could have heard granite speak, as Anele did, it might have shared with her the convulsion which had ripped it down from the cliffs.

She looked around for the old man. He would heed stone wherever he found it, she was sure of that. If he were in one of the more lucid phases of his madness, he might tell her what he gleaned.

However, she found him seated on a swath of grass sprinkled with wildflowers, gnawing on a strip of jerky which one of the Cords had given him, and muttering imprecations at anyone who went near. His aura reeked of Despite.

Even here, beyond the familiar borders of the Land, Lord Foul could still reach him.

Could still know where he was – and Linden with him.

She had become convinced that the Despiser had sent *kresh* after her because he had learned of her movements through Anele and sought to stop her. Therefore she assumed – prayed? – that her present course thwarted Lord Foul in some way. Yet as long as he retained his ability to inhabit Anele, however erratically, he could ambush her anywhere.

She told herself that she should approach the old man now; but the fears which had stopped her earlier restrained her still. She lacked the courage to take his madness into herself.

For a time, at least, she also might become accessible to the Despiser. And if Lord Foul could reach her, he would reach Covenant's ring as well.

Trust yourself, Covenant had urged her in dreams. *Linden, find me.* But he was dead: she had seen him slain ten years and several millennia ago. She was no nearer to him now than she had been two days ago.

When the Manethrall called the company forward again, Linden complied with a groan.

Hami had told her the truth, however: the Ramen knew a way among the boulders that did not surpass her strength. Although the path wove and twisted upwards, contorting itself back and forth across the slope, it offered stable footing and a gentle ascent. And it was wider than she had expected, in spite of the towering bulk and knuckled shapes of the stones. Somo navigated the path with little urging: she was able to climb it almost easily.

Still the ascent took some time. Linden had to stop more and more frequently to rest her quivering muscles. Under other circumstances, she might have accepted a ride on Somo's back. But she was no horsewoman; and the pinto already looked heavily burdened by Liand's supplies. And being carried would not make her stronger.

Lord Foul had Jeremiah. The Land needed her. And the fact that she was entirely unequal to such demands changed nothing. If she did not free her son, no one would. The time had come for her to exceed herself.

This ridge was as good a place as any to start.

Somehow she made it. By the time she reached the saddle between the mountains, the sun had moved into the mid-afternoon sky and her legs had gone numb with strain. Sweat dripped from her cheeks, stained her shirt under her arms and down her back. At intervals, the pangs of cramps or blisters jabbed her feet. Yet she made it. And when she stood, cooling in the breeze, at the crest of the piled stones, she could see what lay ahead of her.

Beyond the arête, a cluster of mountains leaned away from each other to unfurl a wide valley in their midst: a rich grassland, verdant as a meadow in springtime, fed by a network of delicate streams and small pools. In the afternoon light, the whole floor of the valley had a lush hue, an aspect of luxuriance, far deeper than the green sprouting of buds and grass around Mithil Stonedown; and the streams and pools seemed to catch the sun like liquid diamonds. It might have been a place out of time, sheltered from winter by the surrounding peaks: an instance of late spring or summer made possible by an abundance of water and sunshine amid the lingering cold of the mountains.

The eagerness of the Ramen assured Linden that there lay the Verge of Wandering. From this distance, however, she saw no signs of habitation. If the Ramen lived here, they concealed the evidence well. They may not have been a people who valued structures or permanence. Perhaps they preferred to roam, touching the Earth lightly wherever they paused.

They were waiting for a chance to return home. To the Plains of Ra, where they belonged.

Reflexively Linden looked around for Anele. At first, she was unable to locate him: he was not among the Ramen. Then she spotted him a short way off the path. He had clambered away from his companions in order to sprawl on a sheet of stone and wedge his face into the gap between two weathered chunks of granite.

Anele? Frowning in concern, she limped towards him.

He had not collapsed there; was not unconscious. Rather her health-sense detected a sharpened awareness, as if his nerves had been tuned to a higher pitch. His aura had taken on a hue of concentration, lucid and helpless. Automatically she assumed that he was listening to the stone; that he had jammed his face against it in order to hear its whispering.

When she reached his side, however, she saw that she was wrong. He was not listening: he was cowering. Fear boiled off him like steam. He had forced his head between those two stones as though they might stop his ears.

Earthpower throbbed in him like the labour of a stricken heart.

'Anele, what's wrong?' She had asked him that too often. He needed more than her concerned incomprehension. 'What do you hear?'

The stones he had chosen were comparatively smooth. Wind and water and time had worn away their roughness until they resembled the floor of his gaol in Mithil Stonedown; the surface of Kevin's Watch.

'Be gone.' Rock muffled his voice. 'Anele does not speak. He is commanded. He obeys. Anele obeys.'

Commanded? By the *stones*? Linden resisted an impulse to grab at the threadbare fabric of his tunic; tug him out of his protective covert. Confusion and sunburn pulsed in her temples.

'Anele,' she repeated as calmly as she could, 'what's wrong? Talk to me.'

'Be *gone*,' he croaked again. 'Anele demands. He begs. He is commanded. He must not speak.'

'Christ on a crutch,' Linden muttered at him. 'You're making me crazy.' She could not restrain herself: the ascent of the ridge had stretched more than her physical limitations. 'I'm the best friend you've ever had. The Ramen want to help you. Liand wants to help you. Even Stave,' God *damn* it, 'doesn't want to see you in pain.

'Come out of there and *talk* to me.'

While she lacked the courage to challenge his plight, she had no one to blame but herself for her frustration.

'Do you not feel it?' protested the old man. 'Are you not commanded? Anele *must not* speak.'

Liand, Stave and the Ramen gathered behind Linden, drawn by Anele's strangeness and her intensity. She paid them no heed.

'No,' she countered, 'I *don't* feel it. The only power here is yours.' In her spent state, she might have surrendered to any coercive force. 'Make sense. Why in God's name would the *stones* command you not to speak?'

So suddenly that she fell back in surprise, Anele jerked his head up, flung himself around to face her. The rush of returning blood stained his cheeks crimson, stark as stigmata. His white eyes glistened with fury.

'The *stones* do not command it, fool! This is the true rock of the Earth, too honest to be impugned. It only remembers, and holds fast.'

Then he sagged. He may have felt Linden's shock, although he could not see it. With every word, his anger seemed to fray and drop away, leaving him defenceless.

'Do you not understand?' His voice shook. 'It *holds*.'

'Then who?' she returned quickly, trying to catch him while he could still answer. 'Who commands you?'

What secrets had the stones told him?

Urgently she searched him for hints of the Despiser's presence – and found none.

'*He* does not wish it.' Now each word cost Anele more effort, greater distress. Compulsion seemed to accumulate against him. '*He* commands. If Anele did not obey, he would whisper what this rock' – he flapped his arms, apparently indicating the cliffs as well as the ridge – 'cries out. He would tell of the Appointed Durance, the *skurj*, the *Elohim*.

'He would name Kastenessen—'

There Anele's resistance crumbled. Whimpering, he leaped to his feet and fled over the rocks as though he were being whipped away from utterance.

Linden hung her head. Oh, Anele. Was there no end to his sufferings? He could not tell her the things she needed to know without being tormented in some way. Only his inherited Earthpower kept him alive: a cruel gift which enabled or coerced him to survive more anguish than any mortal heart should have been able to bear.

He commands—

Not Lord Foul: not this time. Some other being or power—

She was being stalked. A potent enemy hunted her steps; someone who wanted her to fail— Someone other than the Despiser.

After a moment, Manethrall Hami told one of her Cords, 'Go. See that no harm comes to him.' At once, the Cord hastened away.

Liand cleared his throat. 'Linden? Do you comprehend him? What are *skurj*? Who is Kastenessen?'

Cursing mutely, Linden forced herself to stand. Anele had spoken a name that she recognised.

Stave must have recognised it as well—

Instead of answering Liand's questions, she sighed, 'Give me time. I need to think.'

Anele had referred to *skurj* several times now, and to a Durance. Under the Mithil's Plunge, he had wailed those names against the water's thunder. They meant nothing to her.

Kastenessen, on the other hand—

'There is darkness nigh,' Stave announced abruptly, 'potent and fatal. We have been warned of such perils. Perhaps it lives among the Ramen, concealing itself from their discernment.'

Dumb with bafflement, Linden stared at the Master. Liand's eyebrows rose. Quick indignation flashed from Manethrall Hami to her Cords.

Stave ignored the Ramen. 'We cannot oppose a being who remains hidden from our senses,' he told Linden, 'and who is yet able to command the old man's madness.' Holding her gaze, he added, 'Who but the *Elohim* wield such power?'

Still she stared at him. She understood him too well. The *Elohim* were certainly capable of masking their presence from any form of percipience.

And beyond question the Masters had been forewarned. Years ago, according to Liand, an *Elohim* had visited Mithil Stonedown. That strange, Earthpowerful being had spoken of terrible banes, which he had not explained.

Beware the halfhand.

But Hami was not swayed. She held herself on the balls of her feet, poised for combat. 'You conceive that we harbour darkness,' she said through her teeth. 'You credit that of us.'

Despite her stiff pride, an undercurrent in her tone hinted to Linden that Stave might be right.

With an effort, Linden shook off her confusion. 'We have to know,' she sighed to the Master. 'You can see Anele as well as I can.' Better. 'Lord Foul isn't the only power that uses him. There's so much he could tell us. We need to know who commanded him not to talk.'

Whoever it had been, that being lacked the Despiser's ability to take full possession of the old man. An *Elohim* could certainly have done so. But this *he* had not entirely succeeded at coercing Anele. In some sense, he was a weaker foe.

Damn it, Anele was using too many indefinite pronouns. Behind the Plunge, he had cried, *He has broken the Durance*. Was that the same *he* who had just tried to silence the old man? Apparently not.

How many enemies did she have?

She needed to know what the stone had told Anele. Somehow she had to confront his insanity. She had to find the courage somewhere—

Stave paid no heed to the Manethrall's anger. Briefly he appeared to consider Linden's statement. Then he nodded in agreement.

'The answer lies with the Ramen. We must discover it among them.' He paused again before saying, 'There is no other way for us. The Masters must know of this new threat.'

The scar on his cheek underlined his hard gaze as he turned away, leaving Linden to Liand and the Ramen.

At the same time, Hami also turned away, concealing her secrets.

Leaning on Liand for support, Linden followed them to begin the long descent from the ridge. Her frustration had become a swollen blackness within her, a thunderhead fraught with lightning. She did not know how to contain the storm.

If she did not discover some clear answer to her questions soon, the cistern of her soul would crack open.

At the foot of the arête, with her boots on the marge of the sheltered vale's rich grass, she released Liand in order to raise her eyes from the long path and look around.

The mountains seemed to have grown while she stumbled downwards. From the perspective of the ridge, they had not appeared so tall; and the grassland cupped among them might have stretched for leagues. Now, however, they reared ponderously into the heavens, stern visages of granite gazing down with the august hauteur of titans. And the lower terrain of the valley looked smaller, reduced in scale by its place among the high massifs. The far mountainsides seemed almost attainable.

In contrast, the grass was even more lush and prodigal than it had appeared from the ridge. Over the millennia, time and weather had filled the vale with fertility. Grass the colour of distilled emeralds grew to the height of Linden's thighs, so thick that she wondered whether she would be able to forge through it.

Reassured by the sight of so much untrammelled vitality, Linden cast her health-sense wider; and when she did so, she spotted *aliantha* only a few dozen paces away.

With treasure-berries to sustain her, she might be able to walk as far as the Ramen wished, and need no help.

Hami had already sent several of her Cords ahead of the company to announce their coming; and the young Ramen seemed to flow away through the tall grass without disturbing it or forcing passage. They were attuned to it beyond hindrance. The rest of the group had gathered around Linden, apparently waiting for her to recover her strength.

But Stave remained apart, isolated by the strict intentions of the Masters. And Anele had moved out into the grass, presumably to put a little distance between himself and the *Haruchai*. One of the Cords had led Somo down the arête in Liand's place so that the Stonedownor could concentrate on Linden.

Weakly she headed through the grass towards the *aliantha*.

She could not pass as the Ramen did, like a breeze among the blades and tassels. Grass caught at her boots and shins, tearing when she pushed her legs through it. Streaks of green sap stained her jeans below the knees. She might have felt mired in the grass, hampered, opposed, if its simple abundance had not soothed her senses.

Like the grass, the *aliantha* flourished in the valley's soil. The shrubs spread their twisted branches widely, and they were heavy with fruit. Plucking clusters of viridian berries hungrily, she fed as if she were feasting until their juice had washed the ache of defeat from her throat, and her exhausted muscles began to relax in relief.

When she was done, she felt lightened, fundamentally restored, as though she had partaken of a Eucharist. The gifts of the Land touched her to the marrow of her bones.

Liand and the Ramen had followed Linden to the *aliantha*. They each ate two or three berries, casting the seeds aside by ancient custom; but their need was not as great as hers, and they did not consume more.

Thoughtfully, as if to herself, the Manethrall observed, 'No servant of Fangthane craves or will consume *aliantha*. The virtue of the berries is too potent.'

As though he had been challenged, Stave stepped forward, claimed one of the berries and chewed it stolidly.

Around her, Linden felt a subtle shift in the emanations of the Ramen. Perhaps she and her companions had passed a test of some sort.

She wanted to pass another. Atop the ridge, she had asked Liand and the Ramen to be patient while she considered Anele's outburst. Now she felt that she owed them an explanation.

It would be easier to talk while she rested.

'Kastenessen,' she said when she felt able to speak at last. 'That name I've heard before. He was one of the Appointed.' Findail had described them, seeking to explain himself to the Search for the One Tree. 'An *Elohim*.'

The memory filled her with foreboding. And her tension was reflected in Liand's eyes. He moved closer as though he feared to miss a word.

'I don't know what to tell you about the *Elohim*. They aren't mortal. I guess you could call them incarnate Earthpower. They give the impression that they can do anything, and they do what they do for reasons of their own, no matter what anyone else thinks or wants.' Findail himself had often behaved like an enemy, encouraging Linden and Covenant to fail. 'They live far away, on the other side of the Sunbirth Sea. Most of the time, it seems, they ignore the Land.

'But sometimes they see a danger and decide to do something about it, I don't know why.'

Liand had heard Anele speak of the One Forest and the *Elohim*.

'When they do, they pick one of their people, they Appoint him or her, to answer the danger. To be the answer.'

Findail had said that the Appointed passed *out of name and choice and time for the sake of the frangible Earth*. He had sung:

> *Let those who sail the Sea bow down:*
> *Let those who walk bow low:*
> *For there is neither peace nor dream*
> *Where the Appointed go.*

Manethrall Hami and her Cords regarded Linden gravely, waiting for her to go on. The quality of their attention seemed to hint that they were not ignorant of the *Elohim*. Liand listened avidly, hungry for understanding. But Stave gazed away as if he disapproved of the *Elohim* and all their deeds.

For the time being, at least, Anele had disappeared into the grass, perhaps seeking to avoid reminders of coercion.

'Kastenessen was Appointed a long time ago,' Linden explained as the implications of her memories crowded around her. 'Dozens of millennia, for all I know,' if the years had any meaning to the *Elohim*. 'Apparently something deadly happened in the north,' *the furthest north of the world, where winter has its roots of ice and cold.* 'Some kind of catastrophe. A fire that might have split open the Earth.

'Kastenessen was Appointed to stop it.' *Set as a keystone for the threatened foundation of the north.*

Thus was the fire capped, and the Earth preserved, and Kastenessen lost.

'But he didn't go willingly. He'd broken one of the commandments of the *Elohim*,' violated their Würd or Weird, 'by falling in love with a mortal woman. His people chose him, Appointed him, to punish the wrong he did her.'

He had brought harm to a woman who could not have harmed him, and he had called it love.

'He refused to go. He didn't want to give her up. For her sake, he rejected his people and their Würd.' Their destiny – or the Earth's. 'When the *Elohim* demanded submission, he fought back. Finally they had to force him into place. So that the world wouldn't end in fire.'

Was that what 'Durance' meant? Did it refer to the power that had contained Kastenessen? And had he found some way to free himself? If so, a fire would be set loose fatal enough *to rive the shell of the world.*

During her translation to the Land, Linden had seen fiery beasts suppurate from the ground in order to devour all that lived.

She sighed, then spread her hands. 'That's as much as I know about Kastenessen.'

The Ramen plainly wanted to question her further; but it was Liand who admitted, 'I still do not understand. Did this Kastenessen not pass away?' Certainly that was the fate of the *Elohim* who had become the Colossus of the Fall. 'How then does he command Anele not to speak of him?'

Linden shrugged, trying to do so without bitterness. 'I don't think that was Kastenessen. The *Elohim* wouldn't command him to be quiet. They would just shut him up.'

Behind the Mithil's Plunge, no force had demanded silence from the old man. Yet here, so close to the Verge of Wandering—

'I can't explain it,' she added after a moment's hesitation. 'All I know is that we have enemies we haven't even met yet.'

'Yet your knowledge surpasses ours,' the Manethrall announced quietly. 'The Ramen remember much, but we have no tales of these matters.' Once again, her tone implied that she could have said more. 'It becomes ever more imperative that we take counsel together. We must banish misapprehension between us.

'Ringthane' – she faced Linden squarely – 'our encampment is but two leagues distant. Are you able now to walk so far? Does your heart hold other troubles to delay you?'

Two leagues, Linden thought. Six miles? On even ground, with *aliantha* in her veins— She attempted a smile; failed. 'I think I can make it. I need all the counsel I can get.'

She had enough other troubles in her heart to delay her until the end of time; but she did not mean to let them hold her back.

Fortunately several of the Cords travelled ahead of her, and she found that if she followed in their steps the grass did not hinder her. Somo could have borne her easily now – Liand offered her that – but she preferred to keep her burdens to herself.

She needed time to think; to prepare for what lay ahead.

At first, the distance passed easily. *Aliantha* sustained her, and the vernal grassland itself seemed to lift her from stride to stride. Every instance of health and Earthpower nourished her in some way. For a time, she watched the mood of the mountains modulate as the westering sun shifted shadows across them. When she encountered the occasional bursts of *amanibhavam*, she studied their dancing yellow flowers and their sharp scent, trying to understand their potency.

By degrees, however, she lapsed to numbness again. Step after step, her walking became a kind of ambulant doze. Guided by the Ramen, she made her slow way towards the centre of the Verge of Wandering, and did not notice how far she had come.

Yet around her more and more Ramen appeared out of the grass, answering the summons of Hami's Cords. From the crest of the arête, Linden might have believed the vale empty, but it was not. When she finally shook herself out of her somnolence, she found that perhaps three score Ramen had joined her companions. Most of them were Cords, garrotes at their waists, hair flying loose; but three or four wore their hair as Hami did, tied back by their garrotes, and around their necks were garlands of *amanibhavam*.

And still more of them merged with the company as Linden took note of them. Soon they became a throng among the grass. Yet somehow they sifted through it rather than trampling it down. In spite of their numbers, she could hardly tell where they had been.

She had not expected to find so many of them thriving here: five or six score now, with more continuing to arrive. Before long, however, she noticed that they had no children among them – and no old men or women. Two or three of the Manethralls had grey in their hair, and their scars had acquired the pallor of years. A certain number of the Cords appeared older than those who followed Hami. But no children? No grandmothers or grandfathers?

Either the Ramen were dying as a people, or they had left all those who could not fight elsewhere.

Or both.

What had happened to them during their centuries of exile from the Land?

Linden might have questioned Hami then, although the Manethrall had made it plain that she did not wish to speak prematurely. But as Linden's concern grew, she caught her first glimpse of their destination.

It appeared to be a dwelling of some kind, a tall, open-sided construct planted in the grass. Bare poles at the corners, and at intervals along the sides, supported a latticed ceiling of smaller wooden shafts like latias; and sod had been placed over the lattice to form a roof of deep grass. Within this shelter lay mounds of grass and bracken and a scattering of bundles like bedrolls; and at its centre a space had been cleared for a ring of hearthstones and a cooking fire.

Two Cords tended the fire, apparently preparing a meal, while others came forward with their Manethrall to join the Ramen around Linden.

And beyond this dwelling stood others, she could not see how many, all with open sides and sod roofs. Now she knew why she had not been able to spot any structures from the vantage of the ridge: their design camouflaged them.

Yet the vale was treeless. The Ramen must have dragged their poles and latias from somewhere beyond the surrounding mountains. Presumably, then, the camp was not a temporary one, but rather a habitation either permanently or regularly occupied.

Still Linden saw no children; no aged Ramen.

Moving between the shelters, Hami and the Ramen escorted Linden, Liand, Stave and Anele into a broad open circle where the grass had been worn to stubble and dirt by the passage of many feet. This clearing might have been visible from the ridge: it was certainly wide enough to stand out from the surrounding grass. The height of the shelters around it must have concealed it.

At the edge of the circle, Cords led Somo aside, promising to tend the pinto well; and Linden and her companions were invited into the centre of the clearing.

'This, Ringthane,' Hami announced quietly, 'is the Ramen place of gathering. Here we will share food so that you may rest and regain your strength. In this way, we hope to encourage ease between us. Then we will take counsel after the fashion of the Ramen. We will speak of ourselves, and you will tell us your tales, that there may be friendship between us.'

Linden began to acquiesce automatically; but the Manethrall forestalled her. The crowd around her had shifted. All of the Cords had withdrawn to the rim of the clearing, taking Anele with them. Only Manethralls surrounded Linden and her companions.

'But above all there must be understanding,' Hami said more sternly, as if she spoke for all her people. 'You will also be challenged. Thus we will distinguish honour from treachery.'

Oh, God. An involuntary wince twisted Linden's mouth.

Liand turned to her in alarm: obviously he had not expected this of the Ramen.

Stave opened his mouth to protest; but Hami stopped him with a harsh gesture. Still addressing Linden, she said, 'We desire friendship with you, Ringthane. You have been hunted by *kresh*, and have eaten *aliantha*. Of your own spirit and lore, you have brought Cord Sahah back from death when we could not. Also you bear that which commands respect, a ring of white fire such as Thomas Covenant wielded against the Render. If friendship is ours to give, we will offer it gladly.'

Linden did not react. Challenged? Treachery? Had she been stalked to this? Exposed to it by Anele's compelled silence?

Who here had tried to prevent Anele from speaking?

'To Liand of Mithil Stonedown as well,' the Manethrall continued, 'we mean no harm. We see that he is honest, though he has little skill. It would please us to welcome him without mistrust.'

Liand watched Hami anxiously, his eyes full of conflicted reactions.

The Manethralls glanced at him as Hami said his name, then returned their attention to Linden. They studied her in silence, sombrely, as if they were prepared to pass judgment.

Finally Hami indicated the *Haruchai* with a nod.

'In your name, Ringthane, we would welcome Stave of the Bloodguard also. Our grievance against his kind is ancient and enduring. Yet the Bloodguard were long Fangthane's foes, until they were twisted from fealty. For that reason, we do not wish to spurn him, though the sleepless ones have become Masters now, diminishing the people of the Land.'

Stave faced the Manethralls without expression. Linden could not read his emotions, but his aura felt as blunt and uncompromising as knuckles.

Still she did not speak. For no clear reason, she found herself wondering if any ur-viles occupied the valley. Had those dark creatures played some role in the attitude of the Ramen? What was the connection between them? – the connection which Hami sought to conceal.

The woman met Linden's apprehension steadily.

'Yet I must say plainly that if you do not answer our challenges, all of the Ramen will stand against you.' Her voice carried the sound of implied nickering. 'If you attempt no harm, you will be offered none. We will care for you as kindly as we may. But you will not be permitted to depart from us. Whether you wish it or no, we will retain you with us, that there may be no hazard of betrayal to the Land.'

There the Manethrall paused, apparently awaiting a response.

Stave allowed himself a disdainful snort. 'You are false with us, Manethrall. When you persuaded us to this place, you said nothing of challenges.'

'Master,' retorted Hami, 'the past of the Bloodguard flows in your veins. How did you imagine that we would take counsel together, except by challenge?'

Unexpectedly the *Haruchai* nodded. He seemed to accept her answer. He may have understood it.

'Linden?' Liand asked, nearly whispering. 'Do you know of this? They cannot mean to measure us in combat? I may strike a blow as well as any Stonedownor, but I have no skill to match theirs. In this they have described me truly.'

Linden shook her head, trying to face too many questions at once. But Manethrall Hami did not give her a chance to reply.

'Ringthane,' she pronounced formally, 'Linden Avery the Chosen, do you consent to all that I have said?'

Linden felt that she had no choice; that she had done nothing to determine her own course, or to help Jeremiah, since she had appeared on Kevin's Watch. But the concern of all the Manethralls, and their essential goodwill, were clear to her; plain and palpable. She had no idea why they chose to behave as they did. Nevertheless she had nothing to fear from them, no matter how much they might seem to threaten her.

'Manethrall,' she answered with a formality of her own, 'I do. I don't know what you're worried about. I hope you'll explain it. But I respect your caution. I'll consent to whatever you want.'

Then she added, 'You've already accepted Anele. And I think Liand will agree with me.' She did not wait for his nod: she trusted him to follow her example. 'As for Stave—' She shrugged. 'I get the impression that he knows more about what's going on here than I do. He'll probably welcome a challenge.'

In fact, however, the *Haruchai* appeared to have lost interest in the situation. He stood with his arms relaxed at his sides and his gaze fixed on the mountains as if he had decided to await the arrival of someone or something more worthy of his attention.

Then Hami bowed in the Ramen fashion. When Linden did the same, the gathered Manethralls relaxed somewhat.

At a word from Hami, the Manethralls turned towards the crowded ring of Cords; and at once the ring broke apart as the Cords hurried purposefully away. In moments, some of them returned carrying wooden blocks, apparently intended as seats, which they arranged in smaller circles within the clearing. Linden soon realised that they were preparing for a communal meal.

In the frugal lives of the Ramen, the occasion may have been considered a feast.

She did not need a feast: she needed rest. Liand wanted to talk to her, she could see that. No doubt he hoped that she might relieve some of his confusion. And Stave might have been willing to explain his unexpected air of indifference. But she had had enough of them for the moment.

Ignoring her companions as well as the activity of the Cords, she sat down on one of the wooden blocks, propped her elbows on her knees, and dropped her face into her hands.

She needed to think. God, she needed—

Lord Foul had guided her to hurtloam – and then had sent *kresh* to hunt her down. He disavowed responsibility for both Kevin's Dirt and the Falls.

An *Elohim* had passed through Mithil Stonedown, warning Liand's people against *the halfhand* even though Thomas Covenant was long dead and Jeremiah threatened no one.

Anele spoke repeatedly of *skurj* and the Durance. Some being who might or might not have been Kastenessen had commanded him not to reveal what he had learned from the stones of the arête. Kastenessen himself should have passed *out of name and choice and time* tens of thousands of years ago.

The Ramen planned challenges for Linden and her companions. They had apparently lost or abandoned the Ranyhyn somewhere, although they had once been the inseparable servants of the great horses. Occasionally Hami had hinted at other secrets.

Somehow the ur-viles had avoided Lord Foul's attempts to destroy them.

Linden believed that they had enabled her escape from Mithil Stonedown.

The Despiser held Jeremiah. The Staff of Law had been lost.

Anele claimed to be the son of Sunder and Hollian, who had died three and a half millennia ago.

And somewhere Roger Covenant and his mind-crippled mother walked the Land, seeking ruin as avidly as Lord Foul himself.

It was too much; *too much*. Linden could not absorb it all, or find her way through it. Because she understood nothing, she could do nothing. Covenant was dead: her dreams, illusions. Anele spoke only when his madness permitted it; and then his revelations gave her no guidance. And Stave, she suspected, knew little more than she did. Denying the Land's past, the Masters also denied themselves.

Liand may have been right about them. Perhaps they feared to grieve.

She did not need a feast, or more stories. She had no use for unspecified challenges. Hell, she hardly needed life. She already had a bullet-hole in her shirt.

She needed *help*.

When at last she lifted her head from her hands, she saw Anele standing on the grass beyond the edge of the clearing. A kind of fever shone from his blind face, and his whole body seemed to concentrate towards her.

He was beckoning as though he had heard her prayers and wished to answer them.

Briefly Linden considered ignoring him. Surely he would only confuse her further? Even from this distance, however, she could see that his madness had entered a new phase, one unfamiliar to her. He was in the grip of an intention so acute that it made him frantic.

Dusk had entered the vale while she counted her dilemmas. Behind the mountains, the sun declined from the Land and their shadows filled the air with omens. Cold drifted furtively down from the heights. Soon the Ramen would be ready to share their meal, and the challenges would begin.

Sighing, Linden forced her stiff body upright and walked across the open ground to meet Anele among the grass.

As soon as she drew near, he reached for her with both hands; took hold of her shoulders and pulled her closer as if he meant to fling his arms around her. 'Linden,' he breathed in a voice suffused with weeping. 'Oh, Linden. I'm so glad to see you.'

A voice she knew.

Tears streamed from his moonstone eyes, shocking her as sharply as the sound of that voice in his mouth. She had seen him weep often; but this was different. Until this moment, she had never seen him shed tears of sympathy.

Sympathy and pleasure.

'I didn't think I would ever see you again.' He spoke quickly, almost babbling, as if he had too much to say, and too little time. 'I wouldn't have believed it. But it fits. It's right. You're the only one who can do this.'

Thomas Covenant's voice.

She knew it as well as she knew her own, and loved it more. Through his madness, Anele spoke Covenant's words to her in Covenant's voice.

Her lungs heaved for air and found none. Covenant, she panted, nearly fainting. Oh, my love. The sound of him struck the whole vale to stillness. In an instant, the Ramen and all their doings had ceased to exist; lapsed to dreaming. Stave and Liand occupied the clearing in some other world, a dimension of reality which no longer impinged on hers. Her beloved did not speak to them.

Anele embraced her, a hard clasp with all the strength of Covenant's heart. Then he held her at arm's length so that he could gaze at her blindly. His eyes were awash in yearning.

'Linden,' he said, 'listen to me,' still hurrying. 'I don't have time. There's so little I can tell you.'

Covenant was dead, here and in the world they had once shared. She had spent ten years grieving for him. But this was the Land, and the Laws governing Life and Death had been broken.

She faced him mutely through her own tears, helpless to find words for her sorrow and rue. If she had opened her mouth, she would have sobbed like a child.

'The Law binds me in so many ways.' Anele was Covenant's surrogate, his only voice. 'If it didn't, it wouldn't be worth fighting for.

'And he opposes me. Here, like this, he's stronger than I am. Poor Anele can't hold me. I'm already fading.'

As he said so, she saw that it was true. The old man remained palpable before her. His fingers gripped her shoulders urgently: in some other life, they might have hurt her. But within him another form of lunacy struggled against Covenant's presence. In spite of Covenant's desire, and Anele's rapt submission, a rabid force gathered loathing to expel her love.

He opposes me. The same *he* who had commanded Anele not to speak earlier? Or some other foe?

Anele's madness now did not resemble his near-sanity on the ridge.

'You're in trouble here.' Already her beloved's voice sounded like tatters, scraps of presence. 'Serious trouble.' She was losing him again. 'You need the ring. But be careful with it.' His death had nearly undone her. 'It feeds the *caesures*.'

Covenant!

She could not bear to lose him a second time.

'Linden,' he urged at the limit of himself, '*find* me. I can't help you unless you find me.'

The next instant, Anele shoved her aside with such vehemence that she nearly fell. Before she could grasp at him, cry Covenant's name, try to pierce Anele's turmoil with her health-sense, the old man rushed past her onto the bare dirt and stubble of the clearing.

She pursued him at a run. She was too late: she saw that clearly, although his face was turned away. The transformation of his aura could not be mistaken. Nevertheless she raced to catch up with him; hold him.

He opposes me. The being who now possessed Anele had made a mistake. He had manifested himself within her reach.

She had forgotten fear, caution, peril. She intended to know her enemy, this one if no other. If she could, she meant to wrest his presence from Anele's tortured soul.

Anele halted a few strides into the clearing. She caught up with him almost at once. Without hesitation, she grabbed at his shoulder so that he would turn to face her; so that she could see his possessor in his blinded eyes.

Even through his filthy raiment, that touch scorched her fingers.

Cries of surprise and warning went up from the Cords. Manethralls snatched for their garrotes. Instinctively Linden flinched back. Anele's old flesh had become fire; reified flame. Without transition, he roared with heat like scoria. His skin should have been charred from his bones by the burning ferocity of the being within him.

Earthpower wrapped the old man like a cocoon, however, and his fiery possessor could not harm him.

Wildly Linden clutched at Covenant's ring as Anele's head swung in her direction. But then she froze, shocked helpless by his appearance.

Anele took a single, predatory step towards her. His jaws stretched open, impossibly wide: his few teeth strained at the air: his throat glowed like a glimpse into a furnace.

From the pit of his power, he exhaled straight into Linden's face.

His breath struck her like a blast off a lake of magma; like the fume of a volcano. Instantly her eyebrows and lashes were burned away. The hair around her face crisped and stank, and her sunburn became agony. Around the clearing, the air itself ignited in flames and dazzles.

She had already begun to fall when Stave leaped to the old man's side and struck him down.

Anele's heat vanished so suddenly that she feared Stave had broken his neck.

Chapter Twelve:

The Verge of Wandering

For a while, Linden went a little insane herself, demented by an excess of confusion and pain. There were no words in all the world to contain her dismay. At a command from Manethrall Hami, several Cords shouldered Stave away from Anele's outstretched form. The Manethrall examined Anele swiftly, confirmed that he was no longer filled with fire, then assured Linden that he was merely unconscious, not slain. Cords lifted him from the dirt and bore him away. But Linden regarded none of it. She hardly understood it.

From beyond death, Covenant had tried to reach her. His spirit still endured somewhere within the spanning possibilities of the Arch of Time. Under other circumstances, her heart might have been lifted by the knowledge that he sought to communicate with her; that he strove to answer her prayers—

But he had been so viciously thrust aside. Some flagrant power had dismissed him as though he had no significance. He seemed to be at the mercy of some malignant being. Like her son in Lord Foul's hands—

Her gaze streamed with grief. She could not shut it out. Even when she closed her eyes, her heart blurred and ran. She could not bear it that her lost love had tried to help her, and had been silenced.

Find me.

Liand knelt at her side: he spoke to her softly, trying to ease her in some way. Stave stood nearby, unrepentant. No doubt he believed that he had saved her and the Ramen from a futile grave. Perhaps he had. Linden neither knew nor cared.

It fits. It's right. You're the only one who can do this.

Covenant's assurance could not comfort her now: not after what had happened to Anele.

But then one of the Cords handed Liand a small clay bowl. When he began to stroke the poultice of the Ramen lightly onto her scorched features, the whetted aroma of *amanibhavam* stung her nostrils. In Covenant's name, she allowed herself one harsh sob as if she were gasping for air; for life. Then she struggled to sit up.

Her beloved had told her in dreams, *You need the Staff of Law.* That she understood.

She was sick to death of helplessness.

Liand supported her; propped her so that she could lean against him while she gathered herself. 'Do not be in haste,' he advised, whispering. 'You are burned and utterly weary. I see no deep hurt in you, but I am no healer and may be mistaken.'

Softly he murmured, 'Surely now the Ramen will forego their challenges. They must grasp that you can bear no more.'

The Stonedownor had first met Linden less than two days ago. Clearly he did not yet know her very well.

She swallowed to clear her throat; pushed away the poultice in his hand. Once again, she was struck by the blackness of his eyebrows. Frowning, they shrouded his eyes with foreboding; omens of loss.

Through her teeth, she breathed, 'Help me up. I can't do this without you.' *You're in trouble here.*

The young man braced her to her feet easily: he felt as sturdy and reliable as stone. When she tried to stand on her own, she wavered for a moment, undermined by the heat like guilt on her burned face. But Liand upheld her; and she did not hesitate. As soon as she found her balance, she said, 'Take me to Anele.'

Manethrall Hami had come towards her as she rose: the woman tried to intervene. But Linden insisted, '*Now*, Liand. Before it's too late.'

Before all trace of the being who had possessed Anele vanished.

Before she remembered to be afraid.

At once, Hami stepped back. She gave instructions to one of the nearby Cords, a young woman with flowing hair the same hue as Liand's eyebrows. The Cord moved like her hair as she led him and Linden out of the clearing.

Linden clung to him. She was not done with him; not at all.

The Cord walked quickly past two or three shelters, then entered one near the edge of the encampment. Following her, Linden and Liand found Anele sprawled on a bed of piled grass and bracken.

Linden saw at once that Hami had described the old man accurately: he was unconscious, stunned, not broken. Yet his breathing had an obstructed sound, fraught with pain. His eyes were closed; mercifully, so that their blindness did not accuse her of failing him. His neck and the side of his head ached in response to Stave's blow. But the *Haruchai* had measured out his strength precisely. He had cracked no bones, done no lasting harm. Anele would heal cleanly.

Because of the Earthpower in him, his hurts would probably heal more swiftly than Linden's sore muscles and burned skin.

But she was not concerned with his bodily recovery. Other exigencies drove her. And still she did not hesitate. If she paused for thought or doubt, she would remember that what she meant to do was perilous. It might destroy her.

'Here.' Hurrying now, she released Liand and lifted the chain from around her neck; thrust the chain and Covenant's ring into Liand's hands. 'Take this. Hold it for me.' Without its weight, her neck felt instantly naked, exposed to attack. 'Guard it.'

He stared at her in shock. His hands cupped the chain and the ring as though he feared to close his fingers.

'If anything happens to me,' she ordered, 'anything at all – anything that scares you – get the hell out of here. *Do not* try to help me. Take that,' the ring, 'and *run*. Don't come back until one of the Ramen tells you I'm all right.'

Otherwise—

He could not have known the reason for her command. Nevertheless he nodded dumbly, unable to speak.

Trusting the Stonedownor, she spared no consideration for what might happen if any of the powers that wracked Anele succeeded at entering her. Instead she dropped immediately to her knees beside the old man's bed, pressed her palms to the sides of his head and plunged her percipience into him as if she were falling.

At that moment, her attempt to possess him seemed a lesser evil than abandoning him to more torment.

Later she climbed unsteadily to her feet and reclaimed Covenant's ring from Liand's anxious hands.

She understood her failure well enough. And God knew that she should have expected it. She simply did not know how many more defeats she could bear.

'Linden?' Liand murmured, still fearful that she had been harmed, although he must have been able to see that she had not. 'Linden—' His voice trailed away.

Weak with regret, she answered, 'He's protecting himself.' Of course. 'I can't reach him.' How else had he survived his vulnerability for so long? 'There's a wall of Earthpower in his mind.' It was wrapped like cerements around the core of his identity. 'I can see how badly he's been hurt. But I can't get in to where the damage is.'

The flaw in his defences which permitted him to be possessed was sealed away; beyond her reach. She knew now that she would never be able to help him without power. She needed some force potent enough to cut through the barriers which he had erected.

Covenant's ring would do it. Anele's inborn Earthpower preserved him, but it could not withstand wild magic. Even at its most delicate, however, that fire was too blunt and fierce to be used on anyone's mind. She might blast every particle of his psyche long before she discovered how to make him whole.

Her beloved was right. Even if she had imagined him in dreams. She needed the Staff of Law. Without it, there was nothing she could do for Anele.

'I grieve for him,' Liand offered helplessly. 'He has been made a plaything for powers which surpass him. It is wrong, Linden.' Then the young man's tone sharpened. 'It is evil. More so than *kresh*. As evil as Falls and Kevin's Dirt.'

Linden nodded. If she spoke, she would not be able to contain her bitterness.

She had forgotten the presence of the woman who had guided her to Anele until the Cord touched Liand's arm, asking for his attention. When he glanced at her, the young woman – like Sahah, she was hardly more than a girl – said bashfully, 'If the Ringthane is willing, and Anele requires no other care, the gathering of the Ramen awaits her. Her need for sustenance is plain.'

Liand snorted. Taking a step forward as if to defend Linden, he demanded, 'And do the Ramen intend still to affront the Ringthane with challenges which they do not name?'

In response, the Cord lifted her chin, and her Ramen pride flared in her eyes. 'You are discourteous, Stonedownor. *I* do not doubt that the Ringthane is equal to any challenge.'

Tiredly Linden interposed herself between them. 'Please tell Manethrall Hami that we'll be there in a few minutes.'

To her own ears, her voice sounded too thin to be heeded; too badly beaten. However, the Cord quickly ducked her head, gave a deep Ramen bow and hastened away, as graceful as water.

Sighing, Linden turned to meet Liand's protests.

'Linden—' he began. 'I fear you are unwise. You cannot behold yourself as I do. The weariness in you—'

She lifted her hands. Instead of contradicting him, she said as clearly as she could, 'Thank you.'

He shook his head. 'I have done naught deserving of thanks. And I would be an ill companion if I did not—'

Again she interrupted him. 'For being here. For being my friend. I'd almost forgotten what that feels like.

'Don't worry about me. The Ramen won't hurt me. Even if they decide they don't trust me, they won't hurt any of us. They aren't like that.'

Frowning, he studied her for a moment. Then he acceded. 'Your sight is more discerning than mine. And the Cord spoke truly. Your need for aliment is great.'

She smiled wanly. 'Then let me hold onto you. I don't want to fall on my face in front of all those Manethralls.'

Liand replied with a sympathetic grimace; offered her his arm. Together they walked back to the clearing in the centre of the encampment.

As soon as they stepped from the grass onto the beaten dirt, Manethrall Hami approached them with concern in her eyes.

'Ringthane,' she said sternly, 'it shames me that you were harmed in our care. Such fire is an aspect of the old man's plight which we have not witnessed before. Believing you to be safe among so many Ramen, we relaxed our vigilance. Plainly we should not have done so.'

Linden shook her head. 'It's not your fault. You couldn't have known. And I'm not badly hurt.' No doubt Hami could see as much. 'But I'm very tired. Can we get this over with?' She meant the challenges. 'I want us to start trusting each other.'

Hami bowed an acknowledgment. 'As do we.'

'Come.' Respectfully the Manethrall touched Linden's arm. 'The Cords have completed their preparations. Let us eat together, that we may be sustained for the telling of tales.'

When Linden nodded, Hami guided her to a circle of seats in the centre of the clearing. There the Manethrall gathered eight or ten of her older Cords, and they all sat down with Linden. At the same time, Liand was taken to another circle nearby, and Stave to a third. As with Linden, one Manethrall and several Cords joined them. Soon each ring was occupied by a Manethrall and his or her Cords.

Within each circle, a fire had been set to illumine the meal. The younger Ramen stood around the rim of the clearing, holding small trenchers of food and bulging waterskins, waiting for some signal to serve the food.

Once everyone in the circles had seated themselves, the Manethralls stood together. In unison, they turned to the northeast, holding their heads high. From a circle near Linden, an older man with grey-streaked hair and a fretwork of scars on his arms raised a voice like an old whinny.

'We are the Ramen,' he called softly to the deepening twilight, 'long-exiled from our ancient home in the Land. For a hundred generations and more have we sojourned without place or welcome, carrying our dispossession upon our backs as nomads, wanderers, and telling to no one but ourselves the long tale of who we are.

'Yet have we kept faith with the past. Still we tell the tale of ourselves, and tell it again, precisely as it was told to us generation after generation, so that we will forget nothing, fail nothing, and our great purpose will never waver.'

The Cords bowed their heads as the older man spoke. But his fellow Manethralls stood tall in the clearing, and reflections of firelight glistened in their eyes.

'We are the Ramen, bereft and redeemed by service, and we will see our home again. This time we have not been promised an end to exile, as we were when High Lord Kevin Landwaster warned us from the Land. Yet we keep faith. Though the Earth may crack, and the Heavens fall, and all the peoples of the world be betrayed, we will hold fast to the tale of who we are. In the end, when our exile has run its course, we will return to the Plains of Ra.

'So our tale was told to our sires and dams, and to theirs, and to theirs again, for a hundred generations and more to the Ramen who first began our wandering. So it will be told to our children, and to theirs, and to theirs again, until the Ramen have been restored to the Land which is theirs.'

Then the gathered Manethralls sang together, raising their voices as one against the dark.

> 'We roam the world, lost, and learn
> We have no place but home.
> While time wears out its ceaseless grind
> We wander still, the rind
> And pulp and juice of our return
> Forever unconsumed.
>
> 'For hope we have not rock but loam
> Eroded by our sons
> And daughters. Generations pass
> And leave us as the grass,
> Or as the froth on waves, the foam,
> The rede of years unlearned.
>
> 'To eastward we have sought the sun's
> Acceptance. But the seas

We find too restive to give rest.
To southward lie the best
Of lands and hills. Yet endless runs
Still leave us unfulfilled.

'And in the west lie bitter leas
And forage that will burn
The throat of each last roaming heart.
Their folk despise our part
In wandering. Nor can we seize
A dwelling undenied.

'Thus we return, and still return
While years and ages end.
We cannot let our yearning sleep,
And so we roam, and keep
Our hearts alive, for we must earn
Our dream of home fulfilled.'

In response, the Cords raised their palms before their faces, still holding their heads bowed.

When they looked up again, the Manethralls had seated themselves once more. Then some of the younger Cords hurried forward with their trenchers, carrying food and drink to the circles, while others brought waterskins so that the sitting Ramen and their guests could wash their hands.

Linden rubbed the grime of hard travelling from her hands gratefully, and splashed a bit of water on her face to cool her burned skin; but she did not drop her guard. *You're in trouble*— Here food and even stories were a prelude to threats.

If you do not answer our challenges, all of the Ramen will stand against you.

She did not doubt that she was in serious trouble, in spite of the sincerity of her hosts.

A boy younger than Jeremiah knelt beside her to place a trencher on the ground in front of her. 'I am Sahah's brother,' he murmured softly so that only she would hear. 'My name is Char.' Then he was gone before Linden could look at his face.

Frowning uncertainly, disturbed without knowing why, she considered her platter.

It held stew, steaming and savory, cupped in a bowl of glutinous white mush which might have been cereal or potatoes, but which smelled like neither. Instead it had a loamy scent that suggested it had been made by boiling and pounding some form of tuber. Glancing at the nearby Cords, she saw that they ate by taking a bit of the mush, shaping it with their fingers and then using it to scoop stew into their mouths.

She may have been hungrier than she realised.

When she leaned towards one of her neighbours, thinking to ask him what the mush was called, what the stew was made of, she found another Ramen kneeling beside her: the young woman who had guided her to Anele.

The woman's black hair hung past the edges of her face, hiding her features. Apparently she still felt shy in Linden's presence. As Linden looked at her, she whispered, 'My sire is brother to Sahah's dam. My name is Pahni.'

Surprised, Linden glared at her involuntarily.

Hurrying in apparent embarrassment, Pahni breathed, 'The stew is hare and wild eland and shallots spiced with rosemary and the leaves of *aliantha* dried and ground fine. The *rhee*' – she indicated the mush – 'is boiled from the roots of the grass of this valley. It has little virtue alone, but eaten with meat and shallots it is a sustaining food.'

As soon as she finished speaking, she withdrew.

First Sahah's brother: then her cousin. What was going on?

Linden turned her head and found three Cords standing directly behind her: Pahni, Char and a man who looked old enough to be a Manethrall. When Linden met his gaze, he also knelt to introduce himself.

'Like Char,' he said, smiling awkwardly, 'I am Sahah's brother. We are children of the same dam, though we do not share sires. My name is Bhapa.'

Linden stared at them dumbly. She could not think of any polite way to ask, What the hell is going on? What are the three of you doing?

Did they consider themselves responsible for her because she had tried to help Sahah? Or was it the other way around? Had she somehow become responsible for them?

However, they seemed to expect nothing from her. When he had given her his name, Bhapa rose to his feet. With Char and Pahni, he simply stood behind Linden as though the three of them had been asked to guard her back and had no other interest in her.

Troubled for reasons which she could not name, Linden turned back to her food.

As an experiment, she tasted a bit of the *rhee* by itself. In spite of its smell, it had virtually no flavour. But when she combined it with the stew, she found that it added a taste like spelt bread to the spiced meat and shallots.

She was definitely hungrier than she had realised.

At intervals while she ate, Char or Bhapa or Pahni offered her a drink from a waterskin. She thanked them impersonally, trying not to think about the possible implications of their service. Whatever else may have been true about them, the Ramen clearly valued kinship.

Finally the meal was over. When the younger Cords had passed around more water for the washing of hands, they cleared away the trenchers and waterskins. The other Ramen remained seated, however, now obviously waiting.

Hami gave Linden a long, probing look. Then the Manethrall rose lightly to her feet and moved into the centre of the circle so that she stood near the small fire.

As she did so, the Ramen in the clearing turned their seats so that the whole gathering faced her together.

To Linden, Hami announced, 'It is not the way of the Ramen to give trust where trust has not first been offered. At another time, we would not speak of ourselves until you had described to us your past and purposes.'

Then she raised her voice and her eyes so that she addressed her assembled people. 'But she is Linden Avery, called the Chosen by the sleepless ones. And she is the Ringthane. The presence of her white ring is plain to all who behold her. And with my Cords, I have witnessed her argent flame.

'The name of the Ringthane we remember with reverence. Seeing that the Ranyhyn both honoured and feared him, Covenant Ringthane refused their service. He rode no Ranyhyn into peril and death. Instead he hazarded only himself against the Render. Therefore he is honoured among us. Though our lives are as brief as grass upon the Earth, our memories are long, for we have told the tale until it cannot be forgotten.'

Manethrall Hami held her head up to the valley and the dark mountains. 'And there is more. With her companions, Linden Avery Ringthane came among us hunted by *kresh*. She has befriended the mad old man whose plight has long touched our hearts. She consumes *aliantha* with respect and gladness. And she retrieved Sahah of my Cords from death when Sahah's wounds had surpassed our skills.

'For these reasons, I will speak first, in gratitude and acknowledgement.'

Around the clearing, Manethralls and Cords nodded their acquiescence. And Linden nodded as well, although she had not been asked for her assent. She was simply glad that she would not be required to account for herself before she knew what was at stake.

'I will speak briefly, however,' Hami promised, 'as our lives are brief, for the matters which must be resolved here are urgent and compelling.

'This place we name the Verge of Wandering.' Her words may have been meant for Linden, but she gave them to the whole assembly. 'It is here that the Ramen first gathered when the Sunbane had driven us from the Plains of Ra. Here we considered how we might fulfil the meaning of our lives in exile.'

Hami paused to drop a faggot or two onto the campfire so that its flames rose higher. As she continued, her voice became bleak, almost desolate, devoid of the nickering inflections which occasionally enlivened it.

'Twice before, we had fled the Land, but now there were no Lords to promise us an ending. As we withdrew to this place, we prayed that one day the Sunbane would be quenched – that the Ringthane or another like him would arise to again cast down the Render – but our hopes did not console us. We could see no outcome to the Sunbane except extinction.'

Now her desolation was unmistakable. Recalled loss ached in her words.

'Our memories were long then, as they are now. Here we told the tale of ourselves, and found that the toll of bloodshed had become greater than we could countenance. The Render had exacted too much death. His slaying of the Ranyhyn must cease.

'Therefore we determined that we would never again subject the meaning of our lives to Fangthane's ravage.'

The Manethrall sighed. 'Yet we had no power against him, no means by which we might end his malice. We could not impose the relief we craved.' The muscles at the corners of her jaw bunched with remembered resolve. 'For that reason, we swore then, as each generation has sworn anew, that we would not return to the Plains of Ra until the Land's foe had met his last doom, and would nevermore arise to shed the blood of Ranyhyn.'

Linden listened with growing discomfort. The Ramen were as draconian as the *Haruchai*, as absolute in their judgments. Both people rejected the reality of Lord Foul's malevolence and the Land's vulnerability. Where the Masters sought to alter that reality, however, the Ramen had simply turned their backs on it.

Compared to the stance which the *Haruchai* had chosen, that of the Ramen was more human; certainly less ambitious. Nevertheless it disturbed Linden profoundly. The Land would never be saved by people who believed and judged as the Ramen did.

She feared suddenly that her need for help had misled her; that the Ramen were not the allies she required. Even the intransigence of the Masters might be of more use to her.

Still Hami continued her tale. However, her tone had eased. The memories she described now did not hold as much hurt.

'Thus this place became the Verge of Wandering, the northernmost limit of our exile. From this valley, we found our way southwards among the mountains, sojourning by decades and centuries among strange and distant lands, living as nomads among peoples who knew nothing of the Land and Fangthane. Perhaps at another time we will speak of such things. For the present, I will say merely that we found no home there. But neither have we returned to the Land.

'Once in each generation, however, we visit the Verge of Wandering. Here we remain for a season, or a year, or for several years, scouting the Land until we have discovered that Fangthane yet lives – that the Land has not yet been healed of evil. Then we depart to wander again.

'For a hundred generations and more, no Ramen has set foot beyond these mountains, except to observe the life of the Land and to carry word.'

And do you like what you see? Linden might have asked. Has the life of the Land become better since you abandoned it? Have you made it better? But she said nothing. She was out of her depth, and knew it.

The things which Hami had not said were as loud in the darkened gathering as those she had. Where were the children of the Ramen? The old people?

Where were the Ranyhyn?

Then the Manethrall's voice took on a new edge, a sound of keen wrath. For the first time, her tale implied challenges.

'Once in each generation, therefore, we have witnessed the rise of the Masters in the Land, the men who were formerly the sleepless ones, the Bloodguard. We have discerned no sign of Lords, or of other powers, that might bring about Fangthane's end. Instead we have watched with growing anger, generation after generation, as those who once served the Lords now name themselves Masters and do nothing.

'The Land is in their care, and in their care it has been made helpless. Now the Render flourishes once again, and there are only Masters to oppose him.

'We have known the Bloodguard. We have seen them turned to Fangthane's service. We know that they do not suffice.'

Threats seemed to mount around the clearing as Hami spoke. The ancient animosity of the Ramen towards the Bloodguard had been vindicated by the attitude of the Masters.

'At last, however, a new Ringthane stands among us. Because she is here, we might feel hope. But because the Masters are also here, we fear that she will be thwarted.'

In that, at least, Linden understood Hami perfectly.

'The Ramen have kept faith,' the Manethrall concluded severely. 'What have the Masters done? How will Linden Avery bear the burden of wild magic against the Render, when the Masters have quelled any strength which might have aided her?

'These questions, and more, we will have answered.'

For a moment, silence greeted her demand. Ramen nodded to themselves, and to her, grimly. They seemed to feel their exile as if they had experienced the loss themselves, although they had known no other life but wandering. Their tales had the force of commandments, compulsory beyond the limits of flesh and time.

Concentrating on Hami, Linden sensed rather than saw Stave surge erect in the circle where he had been sitting.

'Do you claim the right to challenge us?' he replied flatly. He may have been full of ire and repudiation, but he did not show it. His hard form revealed only that he could not be swayed. 'I also claim that right. My questions also require answers.'

His tone was calm. Nonetheless it drew tension from the Ramen like the touch of a flail.

'Manethrall,' he continued, 'you speak harshly of the Masters, but you say little of the Ranyhyn. Did you not guide them into exile? And are they not the meaning of your lives? Why then are they absent from this place?

'What has become of them? How are you able to avow that you have kept faith with the past, if you have not been true to the great horses of Ra?'

No. Linden reached her feet without realising that she had moved. She was fed up with people who never forgave, the Ramen as much as the *Haruchai*. They shared a combustible pride, as sensitive as tinder, primed for conflagration. If she did not intervene, they might strike blows which they would never be able to take back.

And she was suddenly furious. Lord Foul held Jeremiah. Like the Land, he would never be saved by people who gave ancient grievances precedence over their immediate peril and responsibility.

'Sleepless one,' Hami countered, 'I am done speaking.' She held her garrote taut between her fists: it seemed to have appeared there without transition. 'It is you who will answer here.'

'No. *Wait* a minute.' Fighting to quiet her heart, Linden confronted Stave across the circles. 'Don't say a word. Please. Whether your people are right or wrong – it doesn't matter. It makes no difference. Not here. The Ramen don't know why you became Masters. They can't evaluate your reasons. And you're only here because of me.' Because she had fled from Mithil Stonedown. 'If they have questions, I'll answer them.'

Facing her without expression, Stave opened and closed his fingers deliberately, cocked one eyebrow – and said nothing. Instead he shrugged as though he recognised that she had told him the simple truth.

Gratitude for his restraint helped Linden manage her anger as she turned to Manethrall Hami. 'If you want to challenge someone,' she told Hami, 'challenge *me*. My companions are under my protection. *All* of them.'

Leaving her place in the circle, she approached the campfire until she stood near enough to see every spark and shadow in the Manethrall's face; near enough to let Hami gauge her honesty as accurately as the woman's senses allowed.

'When Covenant came back to the Land to fight the Sunbane, I was with him. We would have failed if the *Haruchai* hadn't helped us. I owe them a debt I'll never be able to repay.

'I know you have grievances. Old ones. I understand that. And I understand your distrust. I'll answer your questions, anything you want to ask me. But tell me one thing first. Please.'

Hami frowned sternly across the flames. She seemed reluctant to set aside her belligerence towards Stave. Yet her desire to trust Linden was plain: Linden could see it in her. After a moment, she conceded stiffly, 'If I may.'

If Linden's question did not exceed the limits of what the Ramen were willing to reveal.

Still wrestling with her own outrage, and trembling with effort, Linden said harshly, 'Lord Foul has come back, that's obvious. You've seen Kevin's Dirt. You've seen *caesures*. It's *your* return I don't understand.

'You say you scout the Land "once in each generation". But how did you happen to pick *this* year? *This* season?' Had the Ramen been told that she would appear? Had the ur-viles forewarned them? 'A generation is a long time. You could have come last year – or next year.' If they had, she and her companions would probably have died. 'But you didn't. Instead you're here now.

'How did that happen?'

Linden closed her eyes briefly, praying for an explanation that she would be able to accept. She needed to gain as much comprehension as she could before the Ramen put her to the test. Then she looked at Hami again.

There is darkness nigh. Perhaps it lives among the Ramen, concealing itself from their discernment.

Hami appeared to consider the question. Linden half expected her to consult with her fellow Manethralls, but she did not. Apparently she could be sure that her people would support her, whatever decision she made.

Finally she nodded. 'In sooth, Ringthane,' she replied, 'we have not come by happenstance. We are a decade and more ahead of our appointed time. However, two events persuaded us from our wonted round. The first I may relate.'

The Manethrall paused as if to compose herself, then began.

'Perhaps half a generation ago, in an unpeopled woodland many leagues to the south and west, a strange being came among us. His power must have been great, for we descried nothing of his approach or presence until he stood before us.' This point seemed important to Hami: her pride insisted on it. 'Skills and senses which would have acknowledged an unfamiliar butterfly within a league of our camp caught no sign of the stranger until he deigned to make himself known to us.

'He offered us no harm, and therefore we acted similarly, though we misliked him at once, for his mien was haughty, and he appeared to hold us in scant regard.' Hami's voice was tight with disapproval. 'His raiment was of sandaline, without shade or tint, and his eyes held the coldness of gemstones. When we had granted him welcome, he said that he intended to forewarn us.'

A chill ran down Linden's spine. She knew what was coming.

'He named himself one of the *Elohim*, dispatched by his people in their distant land to speak of perils which stalked the Land from the ends of the Earth.'

Behind her in the clearing, Linden heard Liand catch his breath; whisper her name. Silence held the rest of the gathering, however, and Hami did not heed the Stonedownor.

'He said nothing of Fangthane, nor did he speak any of the other names by which the Render is known. Rather he cited *croyel*, *merewives*, Sandgorgons, *skurj* and other creatures or beings of which we have no knowledge. When we pressed him to account for them, he refused disdainfully. His purpose, he averred, was to prepare the way, not to amend our shortcomings. Instead he instructed us to "Beware the halfhand". With the coming of the halfhand, the Earth would suffer its most dire peril, and if we cared aught for our home we would return to the Land's defence.'

The Manethrall snarled at her memories. 'Remembering the legends of Berek Halfhand as well as the great victory of Covenant Ringthane, we took offence that the stranger had spoken so. Because he offered no harm, we did not drive him from us. Nevertheless we invited him to depart, for he declined to honour those whose valour and worth exceeded his.

'Mocking us, he went away as he had come, leaving no sign to mark his passage.'

Then Hami sighed. 'When he had gone, we turned our way hither. Affronted by his manner, we did not wish to credit his words. Therefore we did not hasten. Yet we altered the sequence of our wandering, for he had sown disquiet among us and we wished to determine whether he had spoken sooth or no.'

Over the flames, she asked Linden, 'Are you answered, Ringthane? Will you now speak of yourself, as I have spoken of the Ramen?'

For a moment, Linden could not meet the Manethrall's gaze. The fact that an *Elohim* had approached the Ramen as well as Liand's people forced her to confront fears which she had tried to stifle.

Thomas Covenant was dead. But Jeremiah also lacked half of one hand. And as far as she knew, the *Elohim* felt only the most oblique and ambiguous concern for Lord Foul's machinations. They were Earthpower incarnate, free of Law and perhaps impervious to wild magic. In addition, they considered themselves the Würd of the Earth, the essence or purpose or fate of life; self-sufficient; beyond threat. No peril could touch them: few impinged on their notice. And fewer still stirred them from their hermetic self-contemplation.

The idea that those detached and apparently heartless beings had dispatched one of their own to forewarn the peoples of the Land made Linden want to rage and weep. Dear God, how bad was it going to get? What was Foul *doing*?

While she had known the *Elohim* Findail, he had dreaded only two things: his own Appointed doom; and the rousing of the Worm of the World's End. And during her translation to the Land, she had caught a glimpse of the Worm— Lord Foul had mocked her with a nightmare in which she awakened the Worm with wild magic, causing the destruction of the Earth.

Yet the undefined challenges of the Ramen remained. When the Manethrall said her name again, Linden looked up from her trepidation.

Awkwardly she countered, 'What was the second?'

Hami raised her eyebrows. 'Ringthane?'

'You said two events brought you here now. You told me about the first one. What was the second?'

A new tension spread through the gathering. The Manethrall's features closed: her expression became a wall. 'That event entails the first challenge. Do you choose to meet it now? Will you not rather tell us the tale of yourself, that our hearts may be eased towards you?'

No, Linden insisted in silence – not to Hami, but to herself. No, stop this. Her fears were running away with her: concern and frustration were making her crazy. She had no power to bring about the ruin of the Earth. Everything that the Despiser said or did was designed to mislead her in some way.

'I'm sorry,' she murmured, so faintly that she hardly heard her own voice.

'Of course I'll tell you my story. You've shown us nothing but kindness. I want your friendship.'

And she was certain that the Land needed the Ramen.

Hami responded with a formal bow. 'Then speak, Ringthane.' Her tone hinted at whinnying. 'The Ramen hear you.'

Standing or sitting, all of the Cords and Manethralls seemed to lean towards Linden. The mountains themselves brought their darkness nearer, and a chill breeze fell from their sides to fill the vale. In the moonless heavens, the stars glittered coldly, like the eyes of the *Elohim*; instances of disdain.

Linden made no effort to raise her voice. Hami was enough for her. The rest of the Ramen would hear her as well as they could and decide among themselves whether she spoke the truth.

'I'm like Thomas Covenant,' she said over the low crackle and hiss of the flames. 'We come from a different place. Outside this world.' Her few possessions confirmed this: her clothes, her boots. And white gold did not exist in the Land, or anywhere in the wide Earth. 'When he was summoned against the Sunbane, I came with him.

'You were brief. I'll be the same.'

Firelight filled Hami's eyes with shadows. The Manethrall seemed to watch Linden through a shroud of remembered wars and butchery, measuring Linden's words against her own knowledge of evil.

Carefully Linden described her arrival with Covenant on Kevin's Watch. She named Sunder and Hollian, whom Anele had claimed as his parents. Knowing that the ur-viles were important in some way, she told how Covenant's Dead in Andelain had given him Vain. The beginning of the Search for the One Tree; her meeting with Giants in Seareach; their encounter with the *Elohim* and with Findail the Appointed: these things she explained as concisely as possible. But she did not scant Brinn's self-sacrifice and triumph at the Isle of the One Tree. She would not make it easy for the Ramen to think ill of Stave's people. After that, however, she leaped ahead to Covenant's victory over Lord Foul, the making of the new Staff of Law and her own efforts to heal the Land.

The night around the clearing had grown impenetrable. Only the black bulk of the mountains showed against the stars. And only the campfires softened the stern faces of the Ramen.

'For me,' Linden said to the hushed gathering, 'that was only ten years ago.' A quarter of her life. 'Time is different where I come from.

'Three days ago, I was summoned again.' Shot through the heart. 'I'm not sure, but I think two other people came to the Land at the same time.' Again she made no mention of Jeremiah. She did not want to expose him to the dire pronouncements of the *Elohim.* 'If I'm right, they both serve Lord Foul. And one of them has a white gold ring.

'I don't understand Kevin's Dirt or the *caesures.* I don't know anything about *skurj* or the Durance. I've encountered *merewives,* Sandgorgons and *croyel,* but I can't imagine what they have to do with the Land. As far as I'm concerned, none of that matters as much as the other ring.

'If Lord Foul can use wild magic, the Land is already in tremendous danger, and I'm going to need all the help I can get.'

There Linden bowed her head. Praying that she had satisfied the Manethrall, she waited for Hami's response.

After a moment, Hami murmured, 'The Ramen hear you, Ringthane.' Her voice held a tone that may have been awe. 'Yet you have not spoken of your companions.'

Watching the ambivalent dance of the flames between her feet and Hami's, Linden said, 'Anele found me on Kevin's Watch. He was trying to get away from a *caesure.* When the Watch fell, wild magic saved us. Then the Masters took us prisoner. Once they knew who I was, they would have let me go, but I stayed with Anele. Liand helped us escape,' Liand and a concussive storm which the ur-viles must have sent. 'Stave found us a little while before you did.'

That was enough. If the Ramen could not recognise her honesty, no insistence of hers would convince them.

Flickering shadows concealed the Manethrall's reaction. None of the Ramen spoke or moved. They might have been willing to listen all night. In their long history, no doubt, they had met wonders aplenty, as well as bloodshed and betrayal. Yet they seemed transfixed by Linden's brief tale. Their distant ancestors had known the Seareach Giants during the ages of Damelon, Loric, and Kevin, and during the centuries of the new Lords, until the slaughter of the Unhomed. Since then, however, the Ramen may not have met anyone who had seen so many of the Earth's marvels.

'Linden Avery,' the Manethrall began. 'Ringthane.' Her tone was a knot of awe and apprehension. 'We have heard you. There remains much that we might enquire of you. Yet I do not hesitate to say that we will offer our friendship gladly – yes, both friendship and honour – if they are ours to grant.

'But you have spoken of matters which are too high for us. We are Ramen, and proud – but we are only Ramen, powerless against Fangthane as against *Elohim* or any other fell being. Our purpose is all that we are, and its ambit is too small to contain such wonders and powers. Hearing your tale, we know that we cannot measure your claim upon us, for good or ill.'

Then Hami waved her hand; and one of the Cords at the edge of the clearing hurried away into the night. Watching the young Raman go, Linden felt a new twist of apprehension.

'Linden Avery,' Hami repeated more loudly, 'Ringthane and Chosen, the time has come. You have given your consent to be challenged. This is well, for such testing is necessary to us.

'The time has come to speak of Esmer.'

At once, all of the Ramen rose to their feet. In one sense or another, they had been waiting for this moment. Hami's Cords hedged Linden within their circle. The younger Ramen seemed to form a wall around the clearing.

Esmer? Linden thought mutely. Who—?

'I have said that two events brought us timely to the Verge of Wandering, and to your aid,' the Manethrall explained with a cadence of nickering in her voice. 'This is the second. Three seasons past, we were yet far to the south, and though our way tended northwards we did not hasten, for the *Elohim* had not persuaded us to urgency. But then a new stranger came among us.

'He named himself Esmer, and he approached us courteously from afar, asking that he might be welcomed among us. To our eyes, he appeared to be a man both like and unlike any other, ruled by love and loss, as others are, and yet as puissant as a Lord in his own fashion – a figure of both power and pain. His pain we did not comprehend, however, and his power disturbed us. Therefore we were unsure of him.

'Yet he met our challenge without demur or difficulty, but rather with a seemly reverence. And when it was made plain to us that we must cede our friendship, he became a worthy member of our journey, forewarning us of pitfalls and snares, and relieving our wants, so that our sojourn has been one of safety and ease.'

Linden waited with a mounting pressure in her ears and chest, as though she were holding her breath. A figure of both power and pain—

—who did not greet new arrivals among the Ramen, or join them while they ate.

Hidden by shadows, Hami's eyes might have held eagerness or fear, empathy or suspicion.

'Because you will now be challenged in your turn,' the Manethrall continued, 'I will tell you that it was Esmer who persuaded us to hasten towards the Verge of Wandering. It was he who informed us of the Ringthane's return in peril. And it was he who summoned the ur-viles so that they might answer your need as we did, for he alone among us speaks their tongue.

'Indeed,' she added, 'because of his presence, or his summoning, we have encountered them frequently since we neared the Land.'

Then she concluded, 'It is our hope that his lore may enable us to determine our place in matters which surpass us.'

Suddenly Stave thrust himself between Hami's Cords into the circle around Linden. Resolve poured from his hard form as if he were ready for battle.

As the *Haruchai* moved, Liand called out sharply: a tight cry, unexpectedly alarmed. In the same moment, Linden felt an acrid presence touch the back of her neck. Instinctively she wheeled towards the Stonedownor.

At the edge of the clearing near him, a wedge of Demondim-spawn appeared among the Cords as if Hami had invoked them.

The black creatures barked to each other softly as they advanced. They did not sound threatening, however, and the Ramen showed only tension, not fear. None of the ur-viles held weapons.

Were they here because Hami had summoned Esmer? Or because Linden herself was in danger?

Frightened and confused, Liand pushed his way through the Ramen to join Stave beside her. Both of them seemed to think that the ur-viles posed some threat.

Linden turned back to the Manethrall. 'Hami—?'

Hami held up her hands to forestall questions. 'I know not why they have come. We did not expect them. But they have given us no cause for enmity. Since we learned of their presence among these mountains, they have offered us no harm. Rather they have aided us upon occasion, at Esmer's behest.'

Linden frowned to conceal her thoughts. If Esmer could talk to the ur-viles, he might be able to answer many of her questions.

'Ringthane,' the Manethrall hurried on, 'our challenges need not alarm you. They require naught of you, except that you abide them.

'Thus!'

Spreading her arms, she stepped back from the campfire; withdrew to the edge of the circle.

Off to her right, the crowd of Cords parted again, and a man came tensely through the firelight into the centre of the clearing.

The first sight of him made Linden's stomach churn with nausea. She was instantly certain that she was looking at the being who had driven Covenant's spirit from Anele's mind; the power who had commanded Anele to keep silent at the crest of the arête.

He resembled the *Haruchai*.

He could have been young or old: his features seemed to refuse the definition, the constriction, of time. Like Stave's people, he was flat-faced and brown-skinned, strongly built. Like them, he was not especially tall; no taller than Linden herself. And his cropped hair curled on his head. Seen from a distance, he could have been taken for Stave's brother, unscarred and untried.

However, he wore a gilded cymar formed of a strange fabric which looked like it had been woven from the froth of waves: a garment entirely unlike the raiment of the Masters – or any raiment that Linden had seen in the Land. And his eyes were the deep and running green of dangerous seas.

Now she knew why his nearness nauseated her. Her health-sense saw him as a queasy squirm of power; a knot of conflicts and capabilities like a clenched nest of worms. Poisonous. Breeding.

And yet—

If he had not been so tense, he would have seemed oddly vulnerable, even frightened. The occasion threatened him in some way. Or he was a danger to himself. In spite of her own discomfort, she felt drawn to him, as if he had appealed to her for pity; inspired her to empathy.

And yet—

Her nerves were sure of him: she perceived clearly that he was the figure of power who had twice intervened to frustrate Anele's insights, Anele's madness. He had reft her of Covenant's voice—

But he was distinctly *not* the being of fire that had possessed the old man. She could be confident of that as well. Rather he had merely blocked Covenant's spirit, impelling Anele out onto open ground. There an altogether different being had taken hold of the old man; a power that blazed with malice and hunger, as Esmer did not.

In some sense, Esmer served that other, more vicious foe – and appeared to despise himself for doing so.

'Linden,' Liand panted in astonishment or dismay, 'he is not human. Not mortal.'

Linden swallowed a rasp of sand. She wanted to ask Stave what he saw. His senses surpassed hers. And he might have knowledge which she lacked. But her throat was too dry for speech.

Stave confronted the newcomer mutely, without moving. Every line of his form had become an imminent blow.

'Esmer,' Hami announced, apparently intending to introduce him to Linden and her companions. But he stopped her with a gesture so fraught with force that it left a streak of incandescence across Linden's sight. Then he turned to Liand.

'Liand of Mithil Stonedown.' His words seemed to writhe in Linden's ears. 'You have no part in this. You will withdraw.'

Like Stave, Liand stood motionless. 'No.' His voice shook. 'I will not.'

Esmer shrugged as if with that lift of his shoulders he dismissed Liand's existence.

'Linden Avery,' he said next, 'Chosen and Sun-Sage. You have become the Wildwielder, as the *Elohim* knew that you must. Because you spurned their guidance long ago, much will now be lost which might have been preserved. You also have no part in this, and will withdraw.'

But she, too, did not comply. She could not. Instead she stood still, rooted in place by surprise and anger. He had silenced Covenant's voice; had caused Anele terrible distress. And—

And many centuries ago, the *Elohim* had expressed surprise that she did not already wield Covenant's ring. Because she did not, they had reduced Covenant's mind to blankness, striving – among other things – to persuade or compel her to claim his wedding band for herself.

How had Esmer known—?

Observing her refusal, his manner softened momentarily. 'If the Ramen heed my word, they will trust their hearts concerning you. And if they do not—' Again he shrugged; but this time the motion suggested diffidence, even timidity. 'They will be persuaded otherwise.'

Then, however, all hint of softness vanished from him. Like Liand, she might have ceased to exist. Between one instant and the next, he began to seethe with fury as he shifted his dark emerald gaze to the Master.

'*You,*' he said; and his voice gathered potency as if he could bring down the night and the stars to hear him. 'I *know* you, to my enduring cost. You are Stave, Bloodguard and Master, *Haruchai*.' With each word, his voice grew, acquired resonance, until it became the shout of great sackbuts, steerhorns, so loud that it seemed to echo off the mountainsides. 'Because of you, *I am made to be what I am*!

'Defend yourself, heartless one, lest I *destroy* you!'

At once, he launched himself at Stave like a scend, the surge of a tumbling wave.

'Esmer!' Hami cried instantly. 'No! They must not be harmed! I promised them safety!'

Together, she and several other Manethralls rushed to intervene.

Instinctively Linden reached for Covenant's ring. But she had no power. She was blocked by nausea; trapped within herself by the confusion of her senses.

The ur-viles barked savagely in unison. At the tip of their wedge, an iron rod or sceptre appeared in the loremaster's hands. The creature raised the rod high, preparing conflagration.

Esmer's response shook the encampment. Around the clearing, the ground erupted like water in spouts, geysers, hurling dirt and stubble into the air. Linden was flung backwards: the Manethralls were picked up, tossed aside. Bursts of force and soil drove the Ramen back.

But the ur-viles were not affected. Linden realised as she sprawled to the ground that Esmer spared them; or they were able to withstand him. While he made the dirt hurl and dance, they remained upright in their wedge, poised for black might which they had not unleashed.

Liand fell on his back near her. The spouts continued erratically, leaping upwards as if they had been squeezed from the guts of the Earth, first to one side, then another, back and forth at vehement intervals. But now they touched no one. Instead they kept the Ramen away; enforced a vacant place like a killing field in the middle of the clearing.

And in the midst of the geysers, Stave and Esmer fought.

Linden could not so much as whisper Stave's name. Esmer's power closed her throat.

The Master met Esmer's first attack easily: blocked a punch, then used the impact of a kick to lift him away so that he gained a little distance. 'You are a treacher, or misguided,' he informed his assailant calmly. 'The *Haruchai* also have no part in this. We do not know you.

'If you have truly been made to be who you are, and do not choose your own way' – his tone carried a sting of scorn – 'lay blame elsewhere. I know not how you have tricked or betrayed the Ramen to friendship, but I deny you. If you do not desist, I will teach you better wisdom.'

Esmer answered with a flurry of blows like a sudden squall: fists and feet so swift that Linden could not follow them. For a moment, Stave seemed to block and counter amidst the storm and the bursting geysers as if he were Esmer's equal. Strikes and gasps punctuated the air in staccato, at once sodden and sharp, flesh and bone. Then, abruptly, the *Haruchai* staggered backwards; nearly fell to his knees.

His face bled from cuts and pulped skin on his cheeks and forehead. From where she lay, Linden could feel pain grinding in his chest like splinters of bone twisting against each other.

Esmer's green eyes seethed with ferocity. 'You are mistaken, *Haruchai*!' His voice thundered across the valley. A tidal wave might have broken over the clearing: Linden seemed to hear Stave's accuser through a wall of water and chaos. 'Your folk *sired* me! I am your *descendant*, conceived by Cail among *merewives* and given birth by the Dancers of the Sea!

'Because of the *Haruchai*, there will be endless havoc!'

Tears caught the light and glowed like embers on his cheeks. In spite of his rage, he might have been sobbing.

Swift as lightning, he attacked again.

Several of the Manethralls and Cords tried to force their way into the battle. Liand joined them, ignoring his distrust of the Masters. But spouting dirt and stones repulsed them.

The *Haruchai* could be killed: Linden knew that. She had seen them slain by spears and Sandgorgons. Panting, No, no! she struggled to her feet against the overflow of Esmer's power, the shock and virulence of his geysers.

Cail's *son*?

As though he had not been bloodied, and felt no hurt, Stave sprang to meet the assault. He struck and struck, a whirlwind of blows and blocks: spinning; leaping; allowing Esmer to hit him so that he could hit back. Once he rocked Esmer's head: several times, he drove his fists and feet into Esmer's body.

Yet the punishment he received in return was worse. Linden saw his blood splash the ground; felt more of his ribs give way. A lashing elbow snapped one of his clavicles. Within herself, she scrambled frantically to find the hidden door of the ring's fire, but it eluded her. Stave's pain and Esmer's churning power and her own fear paralysed her.

And still the ur-viles did not enter the conflict. They appeared to have no interest in Stave's plight. They had come for some other purpose and ignored everything else.

Then the fight seemed to freeze for an instant, catching Stave in an attempt to fling a kick at Esmer's head. He was off-balance and slow, however, already battered almost senseless. While his kick rose, Esmer dove at him with a blow to the pelvis that wrenched his leg from its socket.

Stave fell on his face, fingers clawing at the dirt, unable to rise.

Esmer stood over the *Haruchai*. With one hand, he knotted a grip in Stave's hair, pulled Stave's head back. With the other, he punched Stave's head downwards.

Stave's head bounced once; settled to the ground like a sigh. He did not move again.

An instant later, the spouting ceased.

Fierce pressure evaporated from the air as if a squall had frayed and drifted apart. Linden stumbled at the abrupt release: her arms flailed. The ground under her boots held a residual tremor like the aftermath of a distant earthquake. Around her, the Ramen blinked dazedly, shocked by relief and the sudden end of violence. Liand stood among them with wildness in his eyes. Nothing in his life had prepared him for this.

Because of the *Haruchai*, there will be endless havoc.

Oh, Stave.

Linden felt rather than saw the ur-viles withdraw into the night; but she no longer cared what they did. Had they come to protect her? To protect Esmer from her? It made no difference now.

If they had wished Stave dead, they could easily have slain him themselves.

Shaking his head, Esmer stepped away from the beaten Master. He looked vaguely crestfallen, almost ashamed, as if he had been caught in an unjustified act of vengeance – or forbearance.

'Esmer,' Hami breathed, 'what have you done?'

He did not answer.

Stave was still alive.

Freed from her paralysis, Linden ran to his side. Ignoring Cail's son, she dropped to her knees to examine the *Haruchai*.

On the Sandwall of *Bhrathairain*, Ceer had taken a spear meant for her. With one leg shattered, he had not been able to defend her effectively, and so he had simply let himself be impaled.

Without Brinn's self-sacrifice, she and Covenant would never have been able to approach the One Tree.

Trembling with her own fury, Linden reached into Stave with her health-sense. Somehow he still lived. If he could be saved, she did not mean to let him die.

As she studied his wounds, a hush fell over the gathering. The clenched attention of the Ramen turned away from her and the Master. But she did not raise her head. In moments, she was sure that Stave needed saving.

His body was a mass of bruises and bleeding, but that damage was superficial: his native vitality would heal it. In addition to his shattered clavicle, however, and his dislocated hip, she found a collapsed sinus in one cheek, stress fractures in both femurs, a variety of badly battered internal organs and at least eight broken ribs.

One of them had splintered completely, puncturing a lung in several places. She could hear moisture rattle in his troubled breathing. The ground under him seemed to tremble with the difficulty of his respiration.

She looked up to find only Esmer gazing at her. Liand and the Ramen stared past her towards the far side of the clearing. Wonder and deference filled their faces.

Linden did not so much as glance at what they saw. The thunder in the dirt left her untouched.

'You bastard,' she spat at Esmer. 'Why didn't you just kill him? You've done everything else.'

'I have seen what you do not,' he answered ambiguously. The look in his eyes might have been gladness or remorse. 'Behold.'

With one hand, he pointed beyond her to the sound of hooves.

When she turned her head, she saw two proud horses trot into the clearing as though they had been incarnated from darkness and firelight.

She had encountered horses aplenty during her life; but she had never seen horses like these.

They were craggy and extreme, full of the essential substance of the Land, with deep chests and mighty shoulders, and a hot smoulder of intelligence in their eyes. Their coats gleamed as if they had been brushed and curried ceaselessly for generations, one a roan stallion, the other a dappled grey mare; and their long manes and tails flew like pennons.

In the centre of their foreheads, white stars blazed like heraldry, emblems of lineage and Earthpower.

As one, the Ramen bowed low to them: an action as natural and necessary as breathing to the horse-tenders of Ra. Liand gaped openly, transfixed, unable to look away.

'This is the true challenge of the Ramen,' Esmer explained gruffly. 'The Ranyhyn have accepted me.' He sounded both forlorn and proud. 'Now they have come to accept you, the *Haruchai* as well as yourself. And they are precious to me. Their approach stayed my hand. I will not gainsay them.'

The horses advanced across the clearing until they were mere strides from Linden and Stave. There they halted. She held her breath as they shook their heads and flourished their manes, gazing at her and the *Haruchai* gravely. The blowing sounds they made may have been greetings.

Then together they bent their forelegs and bowed their noses to the dirt as if in homage.

PART II

'the only form of innocence'

Chapter One:

Spent Enmity

When the Ranyhyn had departed, the Cords bore Stave into one of their open-sided shelters and laid him gently down on a bed of thick grass and bracken near the small cook fire. At Linden's command, they brought more wood and built up the fire to a sturdy blaze. Shamed that the Ramen had not kept Manethrall Hami's promises, they would have done more; but Linden sent them away when she was satisfied that Stave had been made as comfortable as possible.

She needed to be alone with his plight; and with her own.

Without some extreme intervention, he would die soon. He had begun to haemorrhage around his broken ribs and punctured lung. Even his extraordinary vitality could not ward him from death much longer.

And the Ramen had no hurtloam. Again they sent out Cords for the healing mud; but to their knowledge the nearest source lay far from the Verge of Wandering.

Because she was afraid, Linden considered simply borrowing a knife and cutting him open. But she knew better. Even with the sterile resources of a modern operating theater at her disposal, she could not have saved him surgically without transfusions; and she had none to give him. If she used a knife, she would only hasten his death from blood-loss.

And she was in no condition to work on him. She was already exhausted. The burned skin of her face throbbed in spite of the soothing effects of *amanibhavam*. And she had received too many shocks—

Yet his life was in her hands. If she did not rise above herself – and do it now – he would die.

She would have found her fears easier to bear if Stave had not regained consciousness while the Cords settled him in his bed. His eyes were glazed with agony, and he could breathe only in harsh gasps; but he recognised her beside him. Dully he watched her every movement.

Without his gaze upon her, she might have felt less ashamed of her limitations.

'Chosen,' he said at last, thinly; a blood-spattered trickle of sound between his lips. 'Do not.'

There was no room for fear in what she had to do. Because she could not be calm, she held her alarm at bay with anger.

'Shut up,' she told him. 'Save your strength. This isn't up to you.'

She also feared what he might say to sway her.

But he persisted. 'Chosen, heed me. There are tales of your healing. Do not heal me. I have failed. I am *Haruchai*. Do not shame me with my own life.'

If any tears had remained to her, Linden might have wept for him.

A few Cords lingered outside the shelter, Bhapa, Char and Pahni among them, no doubt hoping to be of assistance. She caught herself on the verge of yelling at them, ordering them furiously away, so that no one else would hear Stave beg.

Instead she instructed them to turn their backs. 'And don't let anyone else in here. I need to be alone with this.'

She did not know how else to bear her own weakness and Stave's supplication.

When the Cords had obeyed her, she confronted him as though she meant to strike him where he lay.

'Don't talk like that,' she said like an act of violence. 'Don't tell me not to heal you.' Not to at least make the attempt. 'You failed long before we came here, but you haven't used that as an excuse to give up.'

The Master swallowed blood. 'How have I failed?'

'Well, what would you call it? Anele is just a crazy old man,' whatever else he might be. 'Until I came along, the Ramen were the only friends he had, and he didn't see them very often.' *God*, she needed to be angry. 'But he's been haunting the mountains above Mithil Stonedown for *decades*.

'You're the *Haruchai*. As you keep saying. But you couldn't catch him. Wasn't that a failure?'

Stave's mien gave her no hint of his reaction. He might have felt perplexed or scornful behind his anguish. 'He was aided.'

'By ur-viles, you mean?' she countered. 'The ur-viles you didn't even know existed? That's another failure. You've made yourselves the Masters of the Land. The caretakers— But I've only been here for three days, and I've already encountered half a dozen things you didn't know.'

She had nothing to give her light except the unsteady radiance of the cook-fire; nothing to guide her except a numinous discernment which she had lacked for ten long years. And Stave would not last much longer.

'Listen to me,' she told him grimly. 'You didn't fail to capture Anele because he was aided. You failed because there aren't enough of you for the job. You're spread too thin.

'And you've isolated yourselves. Nobody can help you because you won't even let them know what the dangers are. I understand why you thought that was a good idea. At least I think I do. But you can't have it both ways. Every choice has consequences. Either you're the Masters of the Land,' alone and inviolate, beyond compromise, 'in which case there simply aren't enough of you. Or you're just the Land's friends, people like the Ramen, in which case you shouldn't even try to prevent Earthpower from being misused occasionally.'

Did he grasp what she meant? She could not tell. His dispassionate suffering seemed to defy comprehension. But that made no difference to her now. She was preaching to herself as much as to him.

'So you failed,' she assured him more gently. 'So what? It isn't your fault that Esmer beat you. You didn't lose because there's something wrong with you. You lost because he's stronger than you are.' She, too, might fail because she was not strong enough. 'It's the same problem the Bloodguard had with the Illearth Stone.

'Don't tell me not to heal you,' she repeated. 'You're wasting your breath. And you still have work to do. Somebody has to tell your people what's been going on, and I'm sure as hell not going to do it.'

Riding the thrust of that affirmation, she sent her senses into him like an appeal for understanding.

Something in her words must have reached him. Instead of clenching his will against her, Stave asked in a growing froth of blood, 'What then is your intention? If you will not forewarn the Land—?'

Her percipience slipped into him with the subtlety of a low breeze, hardly more than a sigh: a soft extension of her essence into his.

'When I figure that out, I'll let you know.' At last, the exertion of her health-sense enabled her to regain her physician's detachment. She was almost calm as she added, 'In the meantime, you can help me.' Help her to think; to concentrate unselfconsciously. 'I don't understand this grievance the Ramen have against your people. What did the *Haruchai* do that's supposed to be so terrible?

'And don't tell me they failed. I already know that.'

'As you wish.' Stave's voice was a shudder of pain.

Although she had spent ten years without this discernment, its uses returned to her readily. Because she could *see*, the pain and damage which she perceived poured into her as though they afflicted her own flesh, her own spirit. But she had learned how to accept such hurts in order to determine their sources and take action against them. The Master's agony did not daunt her.

He was silent for so long that she thought he had forgotten her question – or had lost heart. But at last he lifted his voice faintly to her.

'The Ramen resent that we ride the Ranyhyn, but that is not their grievance. The Ranyhyn choose to be ridden.'

His words and even his difficulty speaking freed Linden to focus on her task.

As her senses filtered past his superficial bruises and internal abrasions to his deepest hurts, however, she realised that she could still honour his wishes. Instead of attempting to heal him, she could simply spare him pain while he died. With her health-sense, she could intervene between his consciousness and his wounds – possess him, after a fashion – so that he felt no discomfort as he slipped away.

If she lacked the courage to do more – and if she were willing to violate his right to bear his own distress—

For her own sake as much as for his, she rejected the idea. More than ever, she needed to be able to exceed herself.

Through his pain Stave breathed words like secrets for her ears alone. 'Rather the Ramen do not forgive that the Bloodguard were accepted by the Ranyhyn, and were proved faithless. This you know. When Korik, Sill and Doar were defeated by the Illearth Stone and Ravers, they vindicated the ire of the Ramen.'

Linden heard him. On one level, she heard him acutely: his words were as sharp as etch-work. On others, however, she heeded nothing that he said. Her attention flowed in other directions, other dimensions.

There. When she had reached beyond the symptoms of his dying to their cause, she saw plainly the punctures and lacerations in his lung, the throbbing ooze of his blood. They might have been mapped in her own body. Two badly splintered ribs. Five separate perforations. Three seeping tears.

In an operating theatre she would have needed half a dozen assistants to help her cope with so much bleeding.

'Through the defeat of the Bloodguard, however,' Stave sighed, 'the fidelity of the Ramen itself is tarnished. They have never ridden the great horses, and yet their pure service has been given to beasts that in turn served willingly men who could not uphold their sworn Vow.'

With her own nerves, Linden measured the seriousness of his injuries. But it was not enough to *see*. Percipience alone would only break her heart. She required power; the ability to make a difference.

While she watched Stave haemorrhage, she groped as if blindly for wild magic, like a woman fumbling behind her to grasp the handle of a door which lay hidden or lost.

Sweat glinted in fire-lit beads on his forehead; dripped from his cheeks like the unsteady labour of his pulse. His scar underlined the pain in his eyes.

'That their service has been diminished the Ramen do not forgive, who have never broken faith.'

Somewhere among the ramified chambers of herself lay a room full of potential fire, crowded with the implications of Covenant's ring. Yet it eluded her. When she had time to think, when she went looking for that room consciously, she could not be sure of its location. Her doubting mind had too many qualms. Covenant's ring did not belong to her: she did not deserve its white flame. If she tried to become the Wildwielder, as the *Elohim* had said that she must, she might lose every aspect of herself.

Stave's voice had fallen until it was barely audible. 'Are you answered?'

'No,' she replied as softly. 'The Ramen must know why Korik and the others did what they did.' Certainly Hami's people respected their own limitations. Otherwise they would not have been content to merely serve the Ranyhyn. 'How can they *not* forgive?'

Everyone else would forgive her if she failed to save Stave; but she was not sure that she would be able to forgive herself.

'Because,' he whispered, 'they were not present.'

In the end, her choice was a simple one. She was a physician. Any one of the *Haruchai* would have given his life for her. And Lord Foul had Jeremiah.

How else could she earn her own redemption?

When she had become sure, her hand closed on the handle of the door she sought.

'How can it be said?' the broken man continued in wisps; faint puffs of life fading between his lips. 'You ask too much. Such speech does not suffice. Even in the unspoken tongue of the *Haruchai*, it transcends—'

There the difficulties of her task began in earnest.

'The Ramen cannot comprehend what transpired because only Bloodguard accompanied Lord Hyrim to the slaughter of the Giants.'

During the collapse of Kevin's Watch, she had somehow distorted the ineluctable sequences of gravity and time. But if she did such things now, she would burn Stave's life to ash.

Still he strove to answer her. 'Only Bloodguard witnessed the final murder of the Unhomed while it was yet fresh in cruelty. Only Bloodguard saw the outcome of their terrible despair.'

Even the small handful of wild magic which she had raised for Sahah's sake would be too forceful here. The Master needed delicacy from her, precision; an accuracy at once as keen as whetted steel and as gentle as trained fingers. The smallest leak of flame from its secret chamber would be enough. The merest fraction more would be too much.

If her self-command wavered for a heartbeat—

Stave was nearing the end of himself. 'Only Bloodguard,' he panted weakly, 'stood beside Lord Hyrim while Kinslaughterer endeavoured to efface every vestige of the Giants from The Grieve.'

Seeking to tune percipience and wild magic to the same feather-soft pitch, she clung to the arduous sound of Stave's voice as to a saving anchor; a point of clarity against the tug of her self-doubt.

Pierced by the touch of flame, he gasped. But he did not stop.

'The Ramen cannot know how the Bloodguard loved the Giants. They cannot grasp how the hearts of the Bloodguard were rent by what had tran-spired. Therefore they presume to scorn our fall from faith.'

The stolid demeanour of his people masked how profoundly they had been horrified. It hid the depth of their rage.

The Bloodguard had striven absolutely to succeed, and they had failed. What other conclusion could such men draw from their defeat, except that they were not worthy?

No wonder the *Haruchai* had made themselves the Masters of the Land. They sought to ensure that they would never again be found unworthy by an atrocity like the destruction of the Unhomed.

They had turned their backs on grief—

In comprehension and empathy, Linden nudged the punctures in Stave's lungs shut one by one. Then she reached into him with argence in order to bind their edges together.

'Chosen,' he murmured; his last words to her, 'hear me.

'The judgment of the *Haruchai* is not so lightly set aside. There will come a reckoning between us.'

Another man might have meant between the Masters and the Ramen; but she knew that he did not.

Wild magic was too rough for the task. Inadvertently she hurt him until he nearly screamed behind his locked teeth. Nevertheless she sealed the tissues of his lungs around each wound. Then she closed the pleural rents.

Extravagantly careful, and still unable to spare him agony, she stitched white fire along the worst of his internal lacerations until they were made whole.

Finally she bowed her head over her work. Stave had lost consciousness: he lay as still as death. But he breathed more easily now, and no new blood came to his lips.

When she believed that he would live, she let percipience and power and all the world go.

What then is your intention?

If he had asked her that question now, she might have wept.

Some time later, the sound of voices outside the shelter roused her: soft voices, thick with controlled anger and threats.

Raising her head, Linden discovered that she must have fallen asleep on her knees beside Stave's grassy bed. Her arms still rested near him. Dried bits of bracken clung to her cheek, and her folded legs had gone numb under her.

Someone – Bhapa? – was saying stubbornly, 'We care not. It is her word that she must not be disturbed.'

'You are not blind,' countered a man who may have been Esmer. 'It is plain that she has spared the *Haruchai* from death. Did you not feel the wild magic that destroys peace?

'I must speak with her while I am able.'

'As you spoke with the sleepless one?' a girl responded: a younger voice, possibly Pahni's. 'Already you have betrayed our promise of safety. Even now the Manethralls debate whether you will be permitted to remain among us.'

The man who sounded like Esmer snorted ambiguously. Contempt? Distress? Linden could not tell. 'While I am accepted by the Ranyhyn,' he retorted in scorn or alarm, 'the Ramen may not deny me, lest they break faith with the meaning of their lives.

'Stand aside, Cords. I must speak with the Wildwielder.'

Groaning, Linden brushed the bracken from her cheek; rubbed her face to restore at least a semblance of consciousness. Esmer wanted to talk to her? Fine. She had a few things to say herself.

Stave could never have stood against him: Esmer had too much power. For a moment, she relived the lurch and spout of force which had kept the Ramen from Stave's side; the numbing nausea which had eroded her defences. Esmer's unprovoked violence would delight the Despiser, if Lord Foul knew of it.

If Foul had not caused it in some way—

Just tell me what you've done.

Done? I? Naught. I have merely whispered a word of counsel here and there, and awaited events.

Angry herself now, Linden tried to rise; but her legs would not move. How long had she slept? Long enough, obviously, to deaden her nerves. With her arms, she tried to shift her weight – and gasped softly at the quick fire of returning sensation.

You need the Staff of Law.

She had not forgotten; but the advice of her dreams had taken on the weight of despair.

Abruptly hands came to her aid. With their support, she stood at last. When she could see past the pain in her legs, she found herself gazing into Char's earnest young face.

Sahah's brother, repaying a debt. As Pahni and Bhapa did by withstanding Esmer. They had watched over while she laboured for Stave's life; and while she slept.

They were still trying to obey her.

The cook-fire had died down to small flames, ruddy embers. Its dim light made Char's face look flushed. Limned in the glow of other fires around the encampment, the forms of Esmer, Bhapa, and Pahni had an infernal cast, ominous and undefined.

'You do not comprehend the difficulty,' Esmer insisted to Sahah's cousin and half-brother. 'You see what I am in part, but you do not know the cost of my nature.' His tone suggested elaborate patience, uncomfortable restraint. 'The way is open for me *now*. But the time when I may speak to the Wildwielder *for her benefit* is not long. It will soon end.

'You know that I esteem the Ramen for their service to the Ranyhyn. Do not misjudge me now. It is misguided devotion' – his tone said *folly* – 'to refuse me in this.'

Bhapa and Pahni did not stand aside. They did not so much as turn their heads to glance at Linden.

In spite of his frustration, Esmer made no attempt to force his way past them. The man who had nearly killed Stave could have knocked both Cords aside easily. Apparently, however, he had no intention of doing so.

'Let him in.' Sleep and fatigue clogged Linden's throat: she could barely make herself heard. 'I'll talk to him.'

She was not sure that anything Esmer might say would do her good. But he understood the speech of ur-viles. He possessed invaluable knowledge, if he chose to reveal it.

'The Ringthane has awakened,' Char added as if to confirm her authority. 'It is her wish to admit Esmer.'

Reluctantly Bhapa and Pahni stepped out of Esmer's way.

He had called himself the son of Cail and the Dancers of the Sea. He had demonstrated an astonishing power for which Linden had no answer. Nevertheless he entered the shelter cautiously, almost hesitantly, as if he were abashed in her presence. The low radiance of the cook-fire turned his emerald eyes the colour of shame.

Again his nearness afflicted her with a sensation of nausea, a disturbing queasiness. In some way, he seemed to undermine her perceptions, her health-sense, even her grasp on reality.

The Cords followed him, plainly concerned that Linden might need their protection.

Esmer did not meet her gaze. When he reached the head of Stave's bed, he stopped to study the *Haruchai*. With an uncomfortable frown, he murmured, 'You surpass me. Small wonder that you are named "Chosen" and "Wild-wielder". To work such healing with wild magic—'

He risked a quick glance at her face, then turned his head aside. Under his breath, he quoted:

> 'This power is a paradox,
> because Power does not exist without Law,
> and wild magic has no Law.'

In an abstracted tone, he told the Cords, 'Leave us. I will speak to the Wildwielder alone.'

'You will not,' retorted Bhapa stiffly.

Char and Pahni looked to Linden for her assent.

'It's all right,' she assured them. She had her own reasons for speaking to Esmer privately. 'You can go. He won't hurt me.'

Not now. Ranyhyn had bowed their heads to her: she had been accepted by the great horses of Ra. And Esmer had made it clear that he honoured their choices.

If the Ranyhyn had arrived sooner, Stave would not have been hurt—

Scowling their mistrust at Esmer, Pahni and Bhapa acquiesced. When Linden had seated herself beside Stave's supine form, Char also left the shelter. She did not watch where the Cords went; but she assumed that they would continue to protect her privacy.

While she slept, intentions which she could not name had begun to take shape within her. Her present straits were untenable, that was certain. They had to be altered. She could not imagine what Esmer might say to her; but she knew what she would ask him. However, her questions were mere unformed guesses, inchoate intuitive leaps; too disturbing to be shared. For the time being, at least, she did not wish to be overheard by anyone who might misunderstand her – or disapprove.

Still Esmer did not look at her directly. His arms moved awkwardly at his sides, uncertain of their purposes; restless with chagrin. Behind her, Stave bore unconscious witness to Esmer's constrained deadliness.

She did not hesitate. She was too angry. Too tired of being afraid. 'You said you wanted to talk,' she rasped. 'So talk. Tell me why I should listen to a man who nearly killed someone who couldn't possibly hurt him. Where I come from, only cowards do that.'

Esmer shrugged in discomfort. 'I am the son of Cail and *merewives*.' His tone was meek: his manner proffered no challenge. 'I descend from the blood and power and betrayal of *Elohim*, as from other theurgies. And from true service as well, the honour of *Haruchai*. The fault of my nature does not diminish your importance to me.'

Linden's guts churned suddenly. Aboard Starfare's Gem, Findail had not spoken only of Kastenessen. He had also described the doomed *Elohim*'s damaged lover. Apparently that woman had learned many forms of power from Kastenessen, but no anodyne for her bereavement. Bitter with pain, she had eventually become the mother of the *merewives*, the Dancers of the Sea, who had seduced Brinn and Cail.

For his weakness, Cail's kinsmen had judged him a failure. After the quenching of the Banefire, he had left the Land, hoping to find the *merewives* again. He had preferred the passion and imprisonment of their unending, unrelieved desire to the harshness of his people.

'That's no answer,' Linden retorted. Everything about Esmer hinted at fatal hazards: she needed to guard herself. And his present meekness only aggravated her ire. 'In any case, attacking Stave was a waste of time. What did you think you would accomplish? Even if you killed him, he's only one *Haruchai*. Someday the rest of his people will become aware of you. Then you'll have more enemies than you can count. So what was the damn point? What did you have to gain?'

Why did he wish to approach her now?

Esmer appeared to sigh, although he made no sound. 'I am made to be what I am, divided against myself and eternally at war.'

Abruptly he seated himself on the bed near Stave's head. Embers reflected greenly in his eyes as he watched the darkened movements of the Ramen within and around the neighbouring shelters.

'Do you not recall the *merewives*? Their song inspires those who hear it – those whose hearts are fierce, and can be touched – with a fathomless passion, love so needy and aspirant that the depths of the oceans cannot drown it away. Yet that song is sung in abhorrence, inspired by sorrow and the desire for death. The Dancers of the Sea loathe the love which they call forth, for they were themselves born of such vast yearning. Their nature grants them no mercy, and permits them none.

'In Cail, they found a mate to match them. I am their sum, at once more than both and less than either.'

His shoulders twitched: another shrug. 'With blows I have expended my loathing, for a little time. Until its strength is renewed, I am able to set it aside.'

Linden glared at him. 'And you had to tear into him right then? You couldn't wait until you knew whether the Ranyhyn would accept him?'

Esmer's eyes flared: the muscles at the corner of his jaw knotted. 'Did you not hear me?' he said through his teeth. 'I am made to be what I am. Every moment of my existence is conflict and pain.'

Linden shook her head. Still he had not answered her. She did not grasp how the loathing of the *merewives* required his violence against Stave. She could see, however, that she would not get a more satisfying response. He may have told her as much as he knew of his own compulsions.

Or – the thought stung her – he may have told her the exact truth. Perhaps his heritage rode and ruled him with such cruelty that he had no choice but to act on his mothers' hatred for his father.

The idea shocked her to silence. She was intimately familiar with such legacies. Her father had locked her in an attic with him so that she would be forced to watch him kill himself. And her mother—

No one, she wanted to insist, makes you what you are. You have to *choose*. She believed that. Nevertheless his mere proximity nauseated her.

In his case, she might be wrong.

Floundering to recover her intentions, her sense of purpose, she changed directions.

'You told the Cords you wanted to talk to me for my "benefit". What earthly good do you think you can do me?'

This time, he sighed aloud. 'Wildwielder, I am *Elohim* and *Haruchai*, theurgy and skill, betrayal and service. Loathing and love. I have wandered the Earth for millennia in pain, awaiting you. I have been given the knowledge of many things, and have learned more. If you ask, I will answer – while I can.'

Until his abhorrence renewed its strength.

Linden's mind reeled. Possibilities stooped through her like striking raptors. She could not hold herself upright. Involuntarily she sagged forward and braced her elbows on her knees, clutched her thoughts between her hands.

If she asked, Esmer might explain Anele's madness. He might tell her about Kastenessen, or the *skurj*, or Kevin's Dirt. He might describe how ur-viles came to be here, when Lord Foul had striven to destroy them all.

Many things—

Hell, he might even know whether she had truly heard Covenant's voice in her dreams; or in Anele's mouth.

If you ask—

Hardly aware that she spoke aloud, she whispered, 'Can you tell me where to find my son?'

Brusquely Esmer replied, 'No. The Despiser is hidden from me.'

Esmer knew that she had a son. He knew that Jeremiah had been taken from her by Lord Foul.

Nevertheless his tone gave her the impression that she had wasted a question.

God in Heaven. With an effort, she fought down an impulse to ask – no, to demand – whether she and Jeremiah would ever be able to return to their own world. She knew better. The bullet hole in her shirt confirmed that she had already lost her former life permanently. Stabbed to the heart, Covenant had not eventually awakened in the woods behind Haven Farm. Nor would she.

Instead she replied harshly, 'That's convenient. I wonder how many other crucial details just happen to be "hidden" from you.'

Then she held up her hands to forestall a response. 'All right, I'll try again. Why have you been tormenting Anele? That was you on the ridge, refusing to let him talk. And you stopped Covenant from—' A sudden clutch of grief closed her throat. She had to swallow several times before she could continue. 'He's been through so much—' She meant Anele. 'I need to know anything he can tell me, but you forced him to shut up.

'If you're going to answer questions, answer that one.'

Esmer's gaze seemed to wander the night impatiently, as if he no longer knew why he had insisted on speaking to her. His voice held a new asperity as he said, 'I have already done so. I must sate the division of my nature. The desires of the *merewives* are compulsory, as are the passions of Cail my father. That which lies hidden within the old man displeases the Dancers of the Sea.'

'Oh, hell,' muttered Linden. 'Why do they even care? They aren't exactly here, you know. And they've never had anything to do with the Land.'

As far as she knew—

Still he kept his face turned away. 'Yet the woman who made them gleaned both lore and power from Kastenessen. His fate taught her the abhorrence which defines the seductions of the *merewives*.'

Again Linden received the impression that she had wasted a question; that she should have been able to deduce his answer from the things he had said earlier. That her time was running out—

At last she found the resolve to straighten her back and raise her head so that she could look squarely at Esmer. Soon, she guessed, he would leave her to her confusion and ignorance; her useless ire. If she hoped to gain any 'benefit' from his conflicted willingness, she had to do so now.

Fearfully she asked the question on which she had half consciously decided to stake her survival – and her son's.

'All right,' she repeated roughly. 'I'll try this.

'Tell me about *caesures*, Falls. What *are* they? What do they *do*?'

Without shifting his gaze, Esmer nodded. 'They are flaws in time, caused and fed by wild magic.'

He sounded oddly gratified, as though this question, at least – or his ability to answer it – vindicated him in some way.

'Within them,' he explained, 'the Law of Time, which requires that events transpire in sequence, and that one action must lead to another, is severed. Within them, every moment which has ever passed in their ambit as they move exists at once.'

He seemed oblivious to the way in which his words intensified the air between them. Covenant had told her that white gold fed the Falls.

'Wait a minute,' she protested. Wait. 'I need to be sure I understand this. You can't mean that *I'm* doing it?'

'No,' Esmer stated as if the truth should have been obvious. 'There is other white gold in the Land, a ring in the possession of a madwoman.'

Linden groaned to herself. As she had feared from the beginning, Joan must have preceded her to the Land; summoned her. Joan was responsible for the *caesures*.

'She knows little of what she does,' Esmer continued, 'and intends less. Yet there is savagery in her, a hunger for ruin as great as that of the Raver which torments her. As her nightmares devour her, so *caesures* devour the Land, displacing objects and beings and powers, corroding the Law of Time. That the harm is not greater – that the Law of Time has not already been shattered – is due only to the form of her madness.

'There is no *willingness* in her. She is merely haunted and broken and used. She cannot choose freely to abdicate her soul. Thus is her power restrained from utter havoc.'

Oh, Joan. For a moment, Linden could not go on. Now she knew surely that she had caused the Land's peril when she had restored Joan's ring. Her fears then had been accurate; prescient. But she had set them aside because she had not understood that wild magic might reach across the boundary between realities.

Somehow Joan's wedding band, the emblem of her weaknesses and failures, had exposed her to the Despiser. The Falls were born of her despair, her self-inflicted pain.

No wonder she had grown calmer when the ring touched her skin. Inadvertently Linden had given her an outlet for her anguish.

'I did that,' Linden murmured. 'I was supposed to take care of her, but I didn't. Instead I made it possible—'

Esmer gave her one quick glance, a look full of emeralds and suffering. Sweat beaded among the shadows on his face, and his lips were pale with strain. Then he turned away once more.

Shaken, she did not immediately recognise that her nausea in his presence was growing worse; that his emanations were becoming more intense. In spite of her dismay, however, her nerves felt him clearly. He lived in endless conflict with himself; and his mothers' harsh loathing had begun to regain its force.

Trembling as if she were chilled, she forced herself to set aside her chagrin. 'Are you all right?' she asked hesitantly.

'Your time is short,' retorted Esmer. 'You waste me. If I do not depart soon, I will smother this *Haruchai* where he lies. Then the Ranyhyn will be lost to me forever.'

She swore to herself. It was too much. She had too many questions, and could not think quickly enough.

Trying to hurry, she said, 'I'm sorry. Make it easy on yourself. Just correct me if I'm wrong.

'Anele is here,' brought forward through the millennia, 'because he stumbled into a *caesure*.'

The old man had said as much. But she had not known then that the Falls were composed of severed instants. Now she guessed that within a *caesure* it might be possible to cross time; that anyone who entered a *caesure* would almost inevitably emerge somewhen else.

Esmer nodded: an angry jerk of his head.

Still guessing, Linden offered, 'So did the ur-viles.'

That would explain how they had survived Lord Foul's efforts to exterminate them.

Cail's son snorted as if she had missed the point. 'They did not "stumble". They knew what they did. They entered the Fall to flee the Despiser. Also they sought a time when they would be needed against him.'

Linden bit her lip. 'And they found it here? Now?'

'Wildwielder,' he answered, 'they have found you.' Complex ire strained his voice. 'It is their intent to serve you.'

Through her nausea, she saw implications of violence gather in him; possible lies. Cail's son would answer her honestly. Would the scion of *merewives* do the same?

'When you were imprisoned by the *Haruchai*,' he continued mordantly, 'the ur-viles sent a storm to enable your escape. When you were endangered by *kresh*, they hastened to your aid. And when I first entered your presence, they came to ensure that you would not be harmed.

'They keep watch against me. They know who I am.'

Half sneering, he muttered, 'They are puissant after their fashion. Perhaps they might withstand me. But my lore exceeds theirs. Therefore they fear me.'

Linden feared him herself.

Scrambling for some form of confirmation, reassurance, she returned to her earlier question. 'But Anele? He really is the son of Sunder and Hollian? He lost the Staff of Law because he left it in his cave?'

Esmer replied with another harsh nod.

Wrapping her arms around herself, Linden finally risked naming her unspoken intent. Hugging her heart, she asked, 'Could he find it again? If he went back to the past?'

Abruptly Esmer jumped to his feet. Linden winced, afraid that he would stride out of the shelter; leave her still too ignorant to proceed. But he did not. Instead he began to articulate his tension by pacing back and forth in front of her. His head jerked as if he were arguing with himself, debating honesty and blows. A sheen of sweat lay on his cheeks.

Still he did not look at her.

'If his madness permits,' he answered between his teeth. 'If he is able to remember. Or if he becomes sane.'

Anele had remembered often enough in the past.

Esmer would depart in moments: she felt that clearly. The bifurcation of his nature was too strong for him. He would never find peace until he had used up his mothers' loathing – or burned away his father's passion.

There was so much that she wanted to know; but she could live without it. For the time being, at least— To one question, however, she positively required an answer. Otherwise she would be helpless.

'Esmer,' she urged softly, 'hang on. Just one more.

'How do I do it?'

'Wildwielder?'

'How do I go back there? To the past? How do I find the Staff?'

She could do what Anele had done; enter one of the *caesures*. But Esmer had said that within them every moment existed simultaneously. How could she sort her way through so much time? How could she navigate every possibility of three and a half thousand years?

'For you all things are possible.' He spread his hands in a gesture too rough to be a shrug. 'You are the Wildwielder.'

Then he protested, 'But do you comprehend that we speak of *Law*? Of sequence and causality which must not be broken? If the past is altered, the Arch of Time itself is threatened. Once rent, it can never be made whole.'

'So I'll have to be careful.' She would not let him sway her. 'If the Staff is lost, then it hasn't been used. It hasn't affected anything.' And its mere existence would support the integrity of Time. 'If we can retrieve it,' she and Anele, 'after it was lost – if we can bring it back to the present without using it – the past won't be altered. Nothing that has already happened will change.'

As she spoke, Esmer stopped moving. Apparently she had surprised him. Just for a moment, his accumulating conflicts seemed to pause; and in that pause, Linden again received the impression that she had gratified him somehow, nourished some deep need.

Slowly he turned to face her. His eyes reflected green fury and supplication from the embers of the cook-fire.

'Do you regard yourself so highly?' His tone sneered at her; implored her. 'Do you deem that you are wise enough to dare the destruction of the Arch of Time?

'The Dancers of the Sea desire the end of all things. Their grief can never be assuaged.'

Then the moment passed. A feral grin twisted his lips: cunning and sorrow glinted in his gaze.

'I will say only this. Look to the Ranyhyn.'

Without another glance at her, he walked away. Five long strides took him out of the shelter. Moving among shadows and dooms, he hastened into the night.

Linden was left alone with Stave's unconsciousness and her own yearning.

Chapter Two

Dangerous Choices

Early the next morning, a group of Cords brought Sahah to the Verge of Wandering.

The injured woman was wan and weak, barely strong enough to stand; only able to walk for short distances. Her companions had conveyed her most of the way in a makeshift travois. Yet it was clear that the crisis of her wounds lay behind her.

That she had survived the rough journey on a blanket tied between wooden poles, and had arrived able to smile faintly at her friends and relatives, her people, testified eloquently to the potency of hurtloam. Her torn bowels and ripped organs were mending well, with no infection and little fever, while her other hurts improved with preternatural ease.

The wounded Cord and her companions entered the encampment accompanied by the Ramen who had gone out seeking hurtloam on Stave's behalf. The two groups had encountered each other as they returned towards the Verge of Wandering. Together they brought with them more than enough of the vital mud for Stave's needs.

Linden had been told that hurtloam would lose its virtue when it was removed from the earth; from the specific moisture and soil which had fostered it. But when she looked into the stone pot which the Cords presented to her, she saw flecks of gold aglow in the damp, sandy soil; and Earthpower called to her nerves like a tantara. Gratefully she carried the pot to Stave's bedside and stroked healing into the distended flesh of his wounds.

The eldritch celerity of the hurtloam's effects still filled her with astonishment, and she watched in wonder as Stave's injuries were transformed from mute agony to bearable pain, and then to dull, deep aching. No doubt the fact that he was *Haruchai* speeded his recovery. Nonetheless the hurtloam itself seemed miraculous to her – a gift precious beyond description or desert.

No world where such healing was possible merited the Despiser's malice.

While Stave rested, she dabbed a bit of the hurtloam onto her cheeks to ease the throbbing of her scorched features. However, its influence reached further, soothing her sore muscles and transforming her sunburned skin to a protective bronze hue; granting her the gift of the Land's vitality.

Then she might have closed her eyes for a time, released from care by simple relief. She had slept brokenly during the night, rousing herself at intervals to check on Stave's condition. As a result, she was still deeply tired. But he was conscious now, clear-eyed and determined. And the mending of his more dangerous injuries exposed the pain of a wound which hurtloam could not cure: his dislocated hip.

She had made no attempt to set it earlier. She lacked the physical strength for the task. And it had not seemed important then.

When he pronounced her name, she sighed to herself; but aloud she answered, 'Yes?'

She would not turn aside from the course she had chosen.

'Linden Avery,' he repeated, 'you have surpassed me.' Vestiges of strain still marred his tone, although he had already grown markedly stronger. 'The matter now lies beyond me. We must abide the outcome.'

She wished that she had not known what he was talking about.

She had set aside his death; spared him the natural consequences of his defeat at Esmer's hands. By the extreme logic of the *Haruchai*, she had violated his personal rectitude. What specific form the 'outcome' might take, she could not guess. But she knew that it would involve harsh judgment and repudiation.

When Brinn and Cail had been rescued from the Dancers of the Sea, they had withdrawn from Covenant's service, in the same way that the Bloodguard had turned from the Old Lords, and for the same reason: they had considered themselves unworthy. Their descendants would not deal less strictly with Stave. And the fact that he could not have prevented Linden's intervention would not spare him.

She responded with a shrug. 'Don't we always?' Certainly she had never been excused from the outcome of her own actions, for good or ill. 'Maybe this time—'

This time she intended to determine the outcome herself.

'Meanwhile,' she added after a moment, 'I should probably set your hip. The longer it stays out of joint, the more trouble you'll have with it later.'

Stave shook his head. 'Do not.' He sounded sure: as inflexible as ever. 'I will tend to it, when I have regained a little strength.'

His tone said plainly, Do not afflict me with more shame.

Inwardly Linden muttered a curse. 'All right.' She did not doubt that he would 'tend to it', no matter how much pain he caused himself. 'Orthopaedics isn't exactly my speciality anyway. Just don't expect me to watch.

'I need to talk to Manethrall Hami.' And to Liand and Anele as well. Not to mention Esmer. 'I'll come back later to see how you're doing.'

Other exigencies awaited her, which she had postponed while she cared for him. The time had come to face them.

Without waiting for a reply, she left the shelter; walked out into the growing warmth of the morning.

Around her, the encampment bustled with quiet activity. She smelled food among the scents of cook-fires and bracken; saw Cords packing bundles, tending to their shelters, cleaning or repairing their raiment. The Verge of Wandering still lay in shadow, but daylight glowed against the dark outlines of the eastward mountains and glistened on the snow-clad crests to the west. Behind the tang of wood smoke, the air held a crisp sweetness like the taste of *aliantha*.

Again and again, Linden was forced to remember that she loved the Land.

She did not belong here: she was too dirty. After the crises and urgency of the past three days, she needed a *bath*. Her hair felt like mud on her scalp. And her clothes were stiff with sweat and grime. In addition, her trudge across the vale had left a lattice-work of grass stains on the legs of her jeans.

The Ramen were able to move without disturbing the lush, tall grass. The stains which she had acquired in their company might have been the map of her limitations, or an augury of her fate.

But she could not spare the time for baths or comfort. Certainly she could not spend an hour washing her clothes. Esmer had answered a few of her questions, and her purpose was clear.

As she looked around in the piquant dawn, she found Cord Char standing nearby, gazing at her solemnly. Apparently Sahah's return had only increased her young brother's determination to attend Linden.

He met her eyes, steady as a promise. 'Are you hungry, Ringthane?' he asked respectfully. 'Will you break your fast?'

Oh, she was hungry beyond question. But other concerns compelled her. 'A little later, thanks,' she replied with wan courtesy. 'Right now, I need to talk to Manethrall Hami.'

Char turned immediately, as if she had given him an errand.

'But first,' she added quickly, 'tell me about Anele. How is he doing?'

The old man had been violated by a being of fire and abhorrence. Stave had struck him hard enough to damage his brain. Now she feared what he might suffer in the aftermath of such affronts.

Because of the way in which he had been possessed, the Ramen might no longer consider themselves his friends.

Yet she needed him badly; now more than ever. He was the son of Sunder and Hollian. And Esmer had conceded that it might be possible to find the Staff of Law—

However, Char answered without hesitation, 'It appears that he is well. He is hardy and enduring. He slept for a time. When he awakened, he accepted viands. Then he wandered away, seemingly without destination or purpose. We keep watch on him, but he' – the young Cord gave a slight shrug – 'simply wanders.

'We will retrieve him, if that is your desire.'

Uncomfortable with so much attendance, Linden shook her head. 'Not yet, thanks. The poor man doesn't seem to get much peace when I'm around.' Then she repeated, 'But I do need to talk to Manethrall Hami. Would you mind letting her know?'

She intended to take action before her courage failed.

Char acceded with a small bow. He did not seem to hurry; but he quickly disappeared among the shelters, leaving Linden to contemplate her own form of insanity.

Esmer had said, *Look to the Ranyhyn.* That may have been useful advice; but she did not know how else to follow it, except by asking Hami for help.

Restless with tension, she found it difficult to wait. Fortunately Hami soon approached between the shelters, trailing a small entourage which included two other Manethralls and Cord Bhapa.

They all bowed formally to Linden as if during the night she had somehow confirmed her status as a visiting potentate. She responded as well as she could. She lacked their fluid grace, however, and her awkwardness made her feel unsure of herself. She had done much in her life – suffered much, accomplished much – but at the moment she did not believe that she had ever done so gracefully.

Like Covenant's, all of her actions seemed stilted and effortful; expensive.

'Thanks for coming,' she replied to the query in Hami's eyes. 'I'm sure you're busy. But there are some things you might be able to help me with.' She had to put her decisions into effect. 'Can I ask you a few questions?'

The Manethrall bowed again, but less formally. 'Ringthane,' she said with a smile, 'your courtesy honours us. Yet you need feel no reluctance to speak. You have been accepted by the Ranyhyn. You are welcome among us without stint or hindrance.'

Then she gestured towards the centre of the encampment. 'Come. Let us gather together under the open sky, so that these mountains may witness our amity. You will break your fast, and we will answer your questions as we can.'

Linden nodded. Because the Ramen could not see her thoughts, their respect discomfited her. Nevertheless she hoped to make use of it. With Hami and the others, she moved towards the circle of trodden ground where Anele had burned her, and Esmer had nearly killed Stave.

Where the Ranyhyn had accepted her.

That, also, she hoped to use.

Yet she would have preferred to talk more privately; in some enclosed space. The clearing seemed rife with memories and implications. And the rising dawn was too vast to be redeemed or spared by any hazard of hers.

Hami had invoked the peaks as witnesses, as if she expected the Earth itself to acknowledge and validate what happened here.

With the confidence of long, unquestioned service, the Manethrall led Linden out into the centre of the clearing. When the Cords had set a few of their wooden blocks in a small circle, Hami sat down and gestured for her companions to join her.

Four Ramen and Linden comprised the group; but the Cords had provided seven seats. As she lowered her weariness to one of the blocks, she wondered who would occupy the two remaining places. Esmer and—?

Bhapa was the only Cord included with the three Manethralls. One of Hami's companions was the older man who had spoken the invocation for the feast. The streaks of grey in his hair resembled the scars on his arms: paler lines like galls, or the scoring of claws. The other Manethrall was a man with a narrow, avid face and a raptor's eyes. His aura gave Linden the impression that his life was not arduous enough to suit him; that he hungered for struggle and bloodshed, yearned to give battle more often than his circumstances allowed.

'Ringthane,' Hami began, 'here are Manethrall Dohn,' the older man, 'and Manethrall Mahrtiir,' the frustrated fighter. 'Cord Bhapa you know. He joins us by right of kinship with Sahah, whom you brought back from death. However,' she added with a touch of asperity, 'he has not yet gained his Maneing, and will not speak unless you wish it. Rather he will address the Cords on your behalf when our counsels are concluded.'

Bhapa met Linden's gaze gravely and inclined his head. She saw now that he had lost sight in one eye: a detail which she had somehow failed to notice the previous evening. Perhaps that explained why he had not yet become a Manethrall. At first, she suspected an injury; but when she looked more closely, she realised that he had a cataract. A simple procedure for an ophthalmologist. She might have been willing to attempt it herself, if she could have found a tool, a metaphorical scalpel, more precise than wild magic – and if she could have spared the time.

'These,' Hami was saying, nodding towards the empty seats, 'are for your companions. When they have joined us, we will begin. Until then, permit us to offer you food.'

Two—? Linden thought. Liand and—? The Ramen must have known that Stave was in no condition to sit upright on a block of wood. And Anele had left the encampment.

Cautiously she asked, 'What about Esmer?'

Manethrall Dohn looked away and Mahrtiir bared his teeth. Hami's gaze darkened as she shrugged. 'He departed into the mountains after he had spoken with you, and has not returned. Perhaps that is well. His incondign attack upon the sleepless one troubles us. He has gone beyond us. It may be that he should not remain as our companion.'

Her tone suggested that the Ramen would already have spurned Esmer if the son of the *merewives* had not been accepted, validated, by the Ranyhyn.

Mahrtiir leaned forward sharply. 'He is distressed.' The Manethrall had a voice like a rusty hinge. 'He wields a storm among the mountains, power and lightning visible across all this vale. We have witnessed his struggle, though we do not seek him out.' For a moment, Mahrtiir's gaze seemed to burn with reflected theurgy. 'It is in my heart that he strives to defy his doom.'

Linden closed her eyes, bowed her head. Instinctively, she believed Mahrtiir. *With blows I have expended my loathing*— The conflicts within Cail's son were extreme enough for storms.

She needed him as well. She had more questions for him. He understood Anele's cryptic references to Kastenessen, to *skurj*, to a broken Durance. She was sure that he could identify the fierce spirit which had possessed Anele. And he spoke the brackish tongue of the ur-viles—

His absence was not a problem which she could solve, however. When she had set aside images of his 'storm among the mountains', she raised her head and opened her eyes.

Across the clearing, she saw Liand moving towards her, accompanied by Char and another Cord, Pahni. The young woman had a waterskin tied at her waist and her hands held a bowl of food.

Unhindered by Kevin's Dirt, Linden saw at once that the Stonedownor had rested little, although he wore his fatigue lightly. The past few days had simply been too exciting to encourage sleep. And perhaps he, too, had witnessed Esmer's distress during the night. His eyes shone with an almost feverish alertness, and his strides as he approached were full of youth.

When he met Linden's gaze, however, his expression changed to one of concern and he quickened his steps. As soon as he reached the circle of seats, he announced unselfconsciously, 'Linden, you have not rested. And you are troubled. There is darkness in you.

'What is amiss? Has Esmer harmed you?'

Sighing, Linden reminded herself that he was new to health-sense and had not yet learned to interpret what he discerned.

'I'm fine, Liand.' With an effort, she smiled. 'Better than I look, at any rate. Esmer was actually' – she grimaced involuntarily – 'helpful. But I wanted to keep an eye on Stave, so I didn't get quite enough sleep.

'Please. Sit down.' She indicated one of the seats. 'We all need to talk.'

Now Liand seemed to realise that he stood among the leaders of the Ramen. Looking abashed, he bowed stiffly to the Manethralls, then dropped himself onto one of the wooden blocks.

At the same time, Pahni came to Linden's side and knelt to present the water-skin and bowl. In the bowl, Linden found *aliantha* scattered among dried fruits which she did not recognise and cut pale cubes which smelled like goat cheese.

Gratefully she accepted Pahni's offering. As the Cord withdrew, Linden placed a treasure-berry in her mouth and spent a moment savouring its sharp, tonic taste and its gift of energy. Then she raised her eyes to the Manethralls.

'I don't think Stave can join us. If you don't mind talking while I eat, you could answer some questions for me.'

Manethrall Dohn assented with a nod; and Hami replied, 'Assuredly, Ring-thane. Your plight is difficult, and we desire to aid you as we can.'

'Then tell me' – Linden spread her hands to suggest the degree of her incomprehension – 'what happened last night. I mean, with the Ranyhyn.' She had never seen such horses. 'You said they accepted me. And Stave, I assume? What does that mean?'

Feeling clumsy again, she admitted, 'I don't know anything about them.'

'Ah, the Ranyhyn.' A look of quiet joy came into Hami's face as she spoke: a look which her fellow Manethralls shared, Dohn gravely, Mahrtiir with a hint of ferocity. 'We are the Ramen, Ringthane. It is not our place to speak of them. We are their servants, and in no way their tenders, as some have named us. They are the meaning and purpose of our lives, and while one Ranyhyn remains to gallop among the glories of the world, no Raman will withdraw from their service.

'Indeed, our service itself empowers and sustains our service. We are who we are, and have remained so across the millennia, because the worth of what we serve preserves the worth of our service.'

Linden found her hands trembling slightly as she listened; and the earthenware bowl felt fragile between her fingers, as if its possibilities might break into clay and dust at any moment. The timbre of Hami's voice affected her more than the Manethrall's words. In the contentment and purity of Hami's joy, she seemed to hear the untrammelled devotion of the Ramen: a service so ancient and enduring that it humbled her.

Fearing that she might drop the bowl, she placed it in her lap. Then she folded her hands around it to conceal their unsteadiness.

'Yet you have witnessed with your own eyes,' Hami continued, 'that the Ranyhyn are Earthpowerful. They both contain and express the Land's abundance. Having beheld them, can you wonder at our service? And do you not now know all that is needful concerning the Ramen?'

Linden might have shaken her head; but the Manethrall had not paused.

'That the Ranyhyn have accepted you is beyond question. Summoned solely by your presence, they approached—' Abruptly, Hami's manner intensified. Leaning forward, she said, 'Ringthane, hear me,' urging Linden to share her sense of wonder. 'They approached and *bowed their heads*. Such homage no Raman has ever beheld, not once in all the long years of our service.'

Her gaze burned at Linden; but both Mahrtiir and Dohn watched Hami with a kind of rapture on their faces.

'To the ur-Lord Thomas Covenant, who was once the Ringthane, the Ranyhyn reared, an assembly of the great horses all rampant in his name. Neither before nor since have the Ramen witnessed such obeisance. Yet that honour contained an admixture of fear and compulsion, as the ur-Lord himself acknowledged. To you, we deem, the Ranyhyn have shown a greater homage, for they bowed their heads as though in surrender, and felt no fear.'

Then Hami sat back. For a moment, she rested her hands on the shoulders of her fellow Manethralls. Mahrtiir stared at his clenched fists between his knees; but Dohn raised a hand to squeeze Hami's fingers in consolation or support.

Liand listened as if he were transfixed: the light in his eyes was as bright as love. The Ranyhyn must have enchanted him.

When Hami spoke again, the intensity had faded from her tone.

'What does this acceptance signify? That no Raman can answer. It lies between you and Hyn, who bowed her head to you, as it lies also between the sleepless one and Hynyn.' Her manner conveyed her doubt that Hynyn had chosen wisely. 'This, however, I am able to say with certainty. Hyn and Hynyn have given their consent to be ridden.

'Such a boon is seldom granted. Once granted, however, it will not be withdrawn. While you live, the Ranyhyn will bear you wherever you wish to go. And if by some ill chance Hyn should perish while you remain alive and in need, another Ranyhyn will take her place, that their acceptance may be preserved.'

Wherever you wish to go, Linden thought in hope and alarm. *Look to the Ranyhyn.* Almost convulsively, she picked some of the dried fruit from the bowl and tossed it into her mouth, chewing to cover her apprehension. Consent to be ridden. The idea seemed fraught with vast responsibilities and perils.

Briefly she concentrated on eating while she tried to control her trembling.

When Linden did not respond, Hami enquired, 'Are you answered, Ringthane?'

With an effort, Linden faced the Manethrall. 'I need to think about it.' But her hands still shook, and she did not feel ready to pursue what Hami had said. 'I'm sure I'll want to know more. But tell me something else first, if you don't mind.'

She needed time to gather her courage.

The woman waited, expectant and willing.

Linden swallowed another treasure-berry, dropping the seed into the bowl to be scattered later. 'The Ramen here—' She gestured around the encampment. 'I hope there are more of you. Surely you have children? Old people?' Men and women unsuited to the work of Cords and Manethralls? 'You aren't all *here?*'

Dohn did not appear to hear her question. Instead he gazed away into the mountains as though he were watching for some sign of Esmer. But Mahrtiir grinned with fierce amusement; and Hami smiled.

'Indeed we are not. If we were, we would merit the concern which I hear in your words. However, the Ramen are well. After our own fashion, we flourish. But our trek among these peaks would be unnecessarily arduous for our children, as for our aged as well. And there are those Ramen – Winhomes, Curriers, Keepers – who are not apt for the rigours of Cording or Maneing. All these we have left encamped many leagues to the south, upon the foothills of the Southron Range.'

Linden did not try to hide her relief. 'I'm glad to hear it,' she said with a smile of her own. 'I've been worried.' Then her smile fell away. 'The Land is already in enough trouble. I was afraid that the Ramen were dying.'

Hami nodded her understanding. 'That loss, if no other, we have been spared.'

For a moment, she lowered her eyes. When she faced Linden again, her expression had turned sombre. 'Linden Avery, are you ready now to speak of this trouble which fills your heart?

'That the Render has returned to torment the Land is certain. If we acted of our own will, we would rather turn our backs on our ancient home than submit any Ranyhyn to Fangthane's cruelty.' Then she shrugged slightly. 'However, we are ruled by the Ranyhyn.' Her tone conveyed no taint of bitterness, although she plainly loathed any threat to the great horses. 'And it is likewise certain that you have been accepted. Nor can your wish to oppose the Render be mistaken.' In spite of its firmness, her voice held an almost subliminal tremor; a hint of dread. 'Thus we are made to understand that the Ranyhyn also will give battle, in your service.'

The three Manethralls confronted Linden squarely across their small circle as Hami asked, 'Ringthane, what is your intent?'

She may have meant, How many of the Ranyhyn are you prepared to sacrifice?

Are you ready now—? Linden would never be ready, she knew that. But Jeremiah was already in torment, and the Land's sufferings had only begun. Whether or not she would ever be ready made no difference to what was required of her.

Deliberately she finished the *aliantha* she had been given; returned the seeds to the bowl; ate another mouthful of cheese and dried fruit. While the Ramen and Liand waited, she drank from the waterskin to clear her throat. To clear her mind.

Then she said, 'Esmer knows. He understands what's happening to the Land. Most of it, anyway.' He might have given her more if she had known how to question him. 'He didn't tell me everything I need, but he gave me some hints—'

She meant to go on at once, riding words like a current so that she would not falter. But Stave stopped her.

'Hold, Chosen,' he said from the edge of the clearing. 'For the sake of the Land, I must hear what is decided.'

He spoke softly. Nonetheless strain throbbed in his voice.

Linden turned to look at him – and winced at the sight of his pain. The lacerations inside his chest had not yet healed enough to bear the effort of standing upright. Yet that hurt faded to a shadow beside the bright distress of his dislocated hip. He must have hopped to the clearing from his bed, jolting his hip abominably with every movement.

She wanted to swear at him. The damn fool should have stayed in bed.

The Manethralls also regarded Stave. Dohn softly instructed Bhapa to aid the sleepless one; but before the Cord could rise, Liand surged to his feet and hastened towards Stave. His settled distrust of the Masters had no effect on his concern.

Stave did not allow Liand to touch him. Balancing on his good leg, however, he braced one hand on the Stonedownor's shoulder for support.

So suddenly that he snatched a gasp from Linden, he clenched his free hand into a fist and punched at his dislocation.

With a sound like a muffled break, his hip snapped back into place.

Sweat stood instantly on his forehead, and he sagged against Liand. Yet he neither flinched nor cried out. Instead he lowered his foot to the ground as if he believed that now his leg would be able to bear his weight.

It did. Somehow it did. Still holding Liand's shoulder, Stave hobbled towards the ring of seats as if he were dragging Liand's consternation with him.

Involuntarily furious, Linden breathed, 'You idiot!' as Stave lowered himself onto one of the blocks. 'Next time, I'll have the Ramen tie you down. I didn't go through all that,' wild magic threatening to scale out of control, 'just so you could *cripple* yourself.'

But she perceived at once that he had not done so. He was *Haruchai*; impossibly hardy. And hurtloam had already wrought miracles of healing within him. His hip would hurt for weeks; perhaps for months. But his blow had caused no permanent harm.

'Chosen,' he replied through his pain, 'did you not say that I must warn my people? Then I must hear you now.'

Linden shrugged against her anger. 'You won't like it.'

She would show him, however, that she did not mean to be swayed.

Liand seated himself beside Stave. His concern for the Master had become a look of alarm. Bhapa frowned at Linden with his good eye. Dohn had resumed his vague study of the surrounding mountainsides; but Mahrtiir watched her like a man who had glimpsed the struggle for which his spirit hungered.

Complex uncertainties filled Hami's eyes as she murmured, 'It may be that your words will please no one among us. Yet we also must hear them. The Ranyhyn require it of us.'

Linden faced them all as well as she could. Speaking harshly to contain her fear, she said, 'Hell, even *I* don't like it, and it's *my* idea.'

Then she dropped her gaze to the ground. She could not bear to watch her companions' reactions.

'Esmer and I talked about *caesures*, Falls,' she began, clumsy again, incapable of grace. 'According to him, they're flaws in time. Rips. They tear open the barrier,' the necessary boundary, 'between the past and the present. Lord Foul wants to destroy the Arch of Time. *Caesures* are just one of the ways he's trying to accomplish that.'

One small rent at a time, over and over again, until the entire fabric tattered and fell.

'If Esmer is right, Anele really is the son of Sunder and Hollian. Three thousand and some years ago, he left the Staff of Law behind when he went to investigate a *wrongness* that turned out to be a Fall. He had no defence when the Fall snatched him out of his life.

'The ur-viles came here the same way,' Linden continued. 'Lord Foul tried to exterminate them, back in the time of the Sunbane, but a few of them escaped into a Fall.' Here she had probably encountered every remaining descendant of the Demondim. 'Esmer seems to think they came looking for a future when they would be needed.

'Apparently *caesures* first started to haunt the Land maybe a hundred years ago. They're comparatively recent. That may be why any of us are still alive. But Esmer says there are limits to what Foul can accomplish with them. The Despiser has access to a white gold ring. In theory, he already has all the power he needs. But he can't simply tear down the Arch – or even attack it directly. The ring belongs to a woman who is completely broken. Too broken to be anything more than a tool.'

And Covenant had given his life to secure the Arch. In some sense, his spirit still stood against the Lord Foul.

After a pause, she avowed grimly, 'I believe him. But we don't have to take his word for it. We already know that Time is essentially intact. We're still here. The Land is still here. Cause and effect still apply. And I doubt that even ur-viles have the power to elude Lord Foul.

'The Falls are a terrible threat, but they aren't enough. Foul needs more.'

So far Linden felt only concentration from her listeners, not denial. They all had reason to take Esmer's words seriously. And no one had suggested a better explanation for Anele's baffled predicament – or for the presence of the ur-viles.

She had harder things yet to say.

Studying the bare dirt, she said, 'The way I see it, the *caesures* are relatively small. They may span thousands of years, but they don't cover much ground. And they move slowly. That limits how much harm they can do.

'But I think there's another limitation,' a restriction in addition to Joan's insanity. 'Esmer didn't say this,' he had merely asserted that any alteration of the established past would damage the Law of Time, 'but I think the Falls only run forward. From the past to the present. Otherwise Foul could send someone into the past,' God, he could even send Joan, 'or he could go himself. He could change what's already happened. That would do more to threaten the Law of Time than the *caesures* themselves.'

Trying to reassure herself, she concluded awkwardly, 'In other words, things could be worse.'

The more she said, however, the more her intentions appalled her. Soon her companions would respond with indignation and dismay. They would certainly oppose her.

She was not Thomas Covenant: she lacked the personal extremity for such risks.

'Ringthane,' Hami responded in a neutral tone, 'this is important knowledge. It explains much. But it does not reveal how such peril may be countered. Again I must ask.

'What is your intent?'

In fear, Linden might have countered, Why do I have to make these decisions? What would you do if I weren't here? She might have demanded, Ask Esmer, not me. He knows what's going on. I don't.

But she knew better. She was Linden Avery the Chosen, named Ringthane and Wildwielder. Jeremiah was her son. There was no one else to whom she could offer her burdens.

In spite of her trepidation, she raised her eyes to gaze at each of her companions: at the Manethralls, who feared for the Ranyhyn more than for the Land; at Bhapa, who appeared to feel indebted to her, commanded by blood to repay Sahah's life; at Liand, who had already shown that he would support her whatever she did; at Stave, who might believe that she served Corruption.

Then she pronounced distinctly, 'We need the Staff of Law. I intend to go get it.'

Liand stared at her, his face wide with confusion. Stave raised his eyebrows as if she had contrived to pierce his impassivity. Frowning, Bhapa looked away. He may have been reluctant to hear what she would say next.

Dohn had covered his eyes with his hands. His posture radiated chagrin. Protests gathered on Hami's visage. But Mahrtiir looked at Linden as if he had heard the call to battle.

She held up her hands to forestall objections which her companions had not uttered. 'I know, I know. Anele lost the Staff three and a half thousand years ago. And if I'm right, I can't get there from here. *Caesures* only run forward.'

Then she knotted one fist on Covenant's ring under her shirt. 'But Lord Foul isn't the only one who has access to wild magic.' And he could not truly control Joan: her madness made her unwieldy. 'If I can find a Fall, maybe I can make it take me where I want to go.'

Linden seemed to feel the high mountainheads leaning towards her. A moment of shock held the ring. Then several of her companions protested at once.

'You will break the Law of Time! You have said so.'

'*Caesures* threaten Time. Wild magic itself threatens it.'

'It is impossible. You will fail, and be lost.'

'Anele is mad! He cannot guide you to the Staff!'

But Mahrtiir's voice rode over the others, ringing with eagerness. 'Are you adept at Time? Are such journeys common in your world? How will you find the time you seek?'

Linden closed her eyes; waited for her silence to create a space in which she could reply. She feared that Stave or Liand would cross the circle to shake her; defy her with their bare hands. But their objections, their dismay, seemed to blow past her on the dawn breeze and lose strength.

Then she heard a soft melody as Dohn began to sing:

'Grass-grown hooves, and forehead stars;
hocks and withers earth-wood bloom:
regal Ranyhyn, gallop, run—
we serve the Tail of the Sky,
Mane of the World.'

He may have been granting her permission. Or hope.

As if she had regained her heart, Linden opened her eyes. Because her companions were too many to face or answer all at once, she focused on the Manethralls; on Hami, who seemed to be her friend.

'Anele can guide me to the cave where he left the Staff,' she said with as much conviction as she could summon. 'If he gets the chance. He's already been back there any number of times. All I have to do is take him to the right year.' Any year after the loss which had broken him. 'He'll find his way.

'And I don't think I'll hurt the Law of Time. For one thing, it's not all that fragile. If it were, a hundred years of *caesures* would have shattered it already,' in spite of Covenant's poignant surrender. 'And for another—

'The Staff hasn't been used since Anele lost it. It hasn't changed anything. It hasn't done anything. That's what being lost *means*.' Surely the *Haruchai*, if no one else, would have become aware of it otherwise? 'Taking it out of the past and bringing it here won't disrupt what's already happened.'

And she had one reason to believe that her extravagant proposal might succeed. The Staff was no longer where Anele had left it. Obsessed by grief and self-recrimination, he had confirmed that fact over and over again.

Which apparently implied—

—that she had been able, or would be able, to retrieve it.

Leaving the Law of Time intact in the process.

No one contradicted her. She could not read Stave's heart through his impassivity; but the others around her were too shaken to protest further. They must have believed her; believed that she would do what she had said.

Their silence frightened her more than almost any opposition. She needed to confront and overcome their fears in order to manage her own.

Grimly she forced herself to continue.

'Of course, I'll need to locate a *caesure*.' She did not trust herself to create one: not without experiencing one first, reading it with her health-sense; learning to understand it. 'But that's not the real problem.'

Holding Hami's troubled gaze, Linden said, 'The real problem is that I'm *not* "adept at Time". I can't find my way through the confusion in a *caesure*. I need to reach the Staff at some point *after* Anele lost it,' or else she would indeed alter the past, 'and I don't know how to do that.'

She was certain that the Manethrall understood her.

'I asked Esmer. He said, "Look to the Ranyhyn".' Clenching her courage in both hands, one on Covenant's ring, the other wrapped around itself, she finished, 'I assume that means they can help me.'

Hami turned her face away as if she were flinching.

For a moment, none of the Manethralls met the demand in Linden's eyes. Instead they looked to each other. Linden had never felt in them the kind of mental communion which distinguished the *Haruchai*. Nevertheless they appeared to acknowledge each other's apprehensions mutely; to ask each other Linden's implicit question.

Then Dohn said softly, 'The Ranyhyn will choose. They must. It is not our place. This matter is beyond us.'

Mahrtiir nodded reluctantly, as if he were being asked to set aside a secret desire.

Hami's reluctance was of another kind as she faced Linden again. So hesitantly that Linden could barely hear her, the Manethrall replied, 'It may be that the Ranyhyn are able to aid you – and will elect to do so. We know nothing of *caesures* or Falls. We are bound by Time. Yet the great horses are capable of much. That is certain.

'And it is certain also' – she faltered, then went on more strongly – 'that they will answer when they are summoned. Once they have consented to be ridden, they will answer when they are summoned, though hundreds of leagues may intervene.'

Linden stared at her. 'What do you mean?'

Hami tightened her grip on herself. 'Ringthane, hear me. At this moment, there are no Ranyhyn within this vale. We are Ramen and cannot be mistaken in this. Neither Hyn nor Hynyn roams the Verge of Wandering. Yet if you were to summon her, Hyn would approach within moments.' She held up her hand to prevent questions which Linden did not know how to ask. 'If you stood in Mithil Stonedown and summoned her, she would appear at once. If you stood above ancient Revelstone itself and could not be approached except through the Westron Mountains, yet would she shortly answer your summons.

'Understand, Ringthane, that I do not speak of distance. The Ranyhyn do not transcend the difficulties of their journeys. Rather their power to answer is a power over days and seasons.'

Linden's eyes widened in wonder and apprehension. Alarm or hope swelled in her throat.

'The Ranyhyn do not spurn distance,' Hami breathed as though the knowledge dismayed her. 'They spurn time. They do not merely respond when they are summoned. Rather they hear that they *will be* summoned, and they respond. If the distance is great, and the obstacles also, the Ranyhyn will depart moons or seasons *before* they are summoned, that they may arrive when they are needed.'

On some level beyond language or explication, they had mastered time.

'Oh, God,' Linden murmured, hardly aware that she spoke aloud. 'It's possible. If they help me. I might be able to do it.'

Abruptly Stave said, 'Chosen.' The pain of his hip was palpable as he forced himself to his feet. Stiff with hurt, he moved to stand over Linden. For this one moment, at least, his characteristic dispassion had deserted him. Instead his flat features were knotted with pleading and repudiation.

'Chosen,' he said again.

She stared up at him as though she could not imagine what he would say, although she already knew every word by heart.

'You will not do this.' Complex passions yearned in his voice. 'It is abominable. Its hazards surpass endurance. The smallest error will damn the Land utterly.' With a visible effort, he swallowed some of his intensity. 'Must I remind you that the Staff supports and sustains Law by its very existence? It need not be wielded in order to affect all that is, all that transpires. If its influence upon the Land's past is removed, will not Corruption respond with delight?'

Linden bowed her head. She could not face the heat of his denial. 'Stave,' she breathed, speaking as much to her clenched hands as to him, 'I have to.'

'No,' he countered with unwonted vehemence, 'you do not. It is madness.

Have you considered that Corruption has required three millennia to regain his strength? Have you considered that he has remained so long reduced because the Staff has been potent against him? Are these matters not plain to you? Unused, the Staff has also not been misused. Therefore it hinders Corruption still. Likewise such atrocities as the Falls have been restrained and limited by the Staff's hidden suasion.

'If you will not think of such things, then consider the Masters. We are sworn to the preservation of the Land. Towards that end, we have laboured across the centuries to prevent the misuse of power which enables Corruption. You have earned my forbearance. I do not wish to oppose you. But my enmity – the enmity of the *Haruchai* – is certain if you persist. You are mighty, as we know. Yet I must prevent you. And if I cannot, even your puissance will not avail you against the combined force of the Masters.'

Every word he said was true: Linden knew that. But he had said too much, and she could no longer hear him. Crying, 'You don't understand!' she surged to her feet.

Obliquely she saw that Liand had come to Stave's side, ready to defend her if the Master attacked. However, the Manethralls remained seated, watching her with consternation in their eyes. Bhapa crouched as if he had started to rise with Liand, and had been stopped by a word from the Manethralls.

But they were all irrelevant to her now. It was Stave who confronted her, Stave who challenged her; and he could snap her neck with one sharp blow, in spite of his hurts. Even if she were capable of defending herself, she could not bear to think that he would become her enemy. Another foe among so many—

Ignoring the pain in his hip, the Master faced her. His mien resumed its familiar flat detachment. 'Then inform me, Chosen,' he replied inflexibly. The pallor of his scar seemed to reject whatever she might say. 'What is it that I do not understand?'

Desperation rose in her like fury. But it was not anger that filled her voice: it was supplication.

'Don't you remember last night? Do you even listen to yourself when you talk? I asked you why the Ramen haven't forgiven you for trying to use the Illearth Stone, and you said it's because they weren't present. They can't know what the Bloodguard suffered in Seareach because they weren't there.

'But you don't know me any better than the Ramen know you.' Transformed by pleading, she met his stare as if her own fear could no longer touch her. 'Oh, your people remember everything. But you're like the Ramen. You weren't there. You were so worried about repeating your mistake with the Illearth

Stone that you stayed behind when Covenant and I went to face Lord Foul.

'You weren't there when Covenant sacrificed himself. You weren't there when I took his ring and turned Vain and Findail into the Staff of Law, or when I erased the Sunbane, or when—' For an instant, she choked on the memory of Covenant's farewell. Then she shouted, 'And you sure as *hell* weren't there when Covenant and I were summoned in the first place!' When Jeremiah had burned away half of his right hand in the Despiser's bonfire. 'You think you have the right to pass judgment, but you don't know what's at stake for me.'

Stave appeared to consider her assertion briefly. Then he shook his head. 'You have not answered. Your words explain nothing. You make plain that you disdain the necessary choices of the *Haruchai*. You see it as a fault in us that we will never again hazard being made to serve Corruption. You also pass judgment, yet you reveal nothing.'

'We do not propose to bear white gold into the heart of a Fall. It is not our intent to dare the utter destruction of the Earth.'

'Then *listen*,' Linden begged. He had missed the point completely. Like the Ramen, he did not know how to forgive. 'I *have* to do this.

'Lord Foul has my son.'

Chapter Three:

The Will of the Ranyhyn

'Your son?'

If Stave felt any surprise or concern, his body did not show it. Linden could not read his emotions.

Nevertheless she found that she was done with pleading. 'His name,' she sighed, 'is Jeremiah.' Her efforts to persuade the Master cost her too much of her courage. 'Foul took him while we were being translated to the Land. A few days ago. I don't suppose you can imagine what he's going through, but I can.' She had been possessed by a Raver. 'You can say whatever you want. I'm not going to let anything stop me.'

The Master's stolid demeanour revealed nothing as he averred, 'You must. Your purpose is madness. The Earth will perish, and your son with it.'

Oh, hell. Mentally she threw up her hands. 'Then don't come with me. You should be able to ride in a few days.' His hip would heal sufficiently in that time. 'Take your Ranyhyn and go tell the rest of the Masters what I'm doing. They'll need time to organise your famous "enmity".'

Do anything you want. Just don't try to stop me yourself.

Stave lifted an eyebrow. Perhaps she had surprised him in spite of his restraint. However, she heard no change in his tone as he replied, 'In one thing, Chosen, you have spoken truly. I do not comprehend. Among us children are precious beyond expression. Yet no *Haruchai* would permit a greater harm in order to secure the life of any son or daughter.'

Then he stepped back. 'It will be as you say. In ages past, the *Haruchai* have doubted you – and have learned that they were mistaken. And we have not been present to share your burdens. Their cost is hidden from us. Therefore I will not strive to prevent you now. Rather I will bear word of your actions to the Masters. Together we will determine how we must respond.'

Limping, he turned away; left her to the Ramen and Liand.

Linden had gained that much, if nothing more. He had not struck her down.

Yet now her enemies numbered in the hundreds.

Liand's desire to understand her as well as the Master was tangible between them. But she felt too bereft and vulnerable to answer his unspoken questions. Deliberately she stepped past him in order to stand in front of the Manethralls.

'What about you?' she asked sadly. How could they not turn their backs on her? 'A little while ago, you assured me that I'm welcome here.' *Without stint or hindrance.* 'Do you agree with Stave? Have you changed your minds?

'I swear to you that I wouldn't do this if I could think of any other way to save my son.'

She absolutely required the Staff of Law. To that extent, at least, her dreams of Thomas Covenant had proven themselves.

And he had told her to find him. She could not imagine where else she might look, except in the past.

Hami, Dohn, and Mahrtiir shared a look. Then, together, they rose to their feet.

'Ah, Ringthane,' Hami sighed, smiling ruefully. 'Be at peace among us. You have naught to fear from the Ramen. The Ranyhyn have accepted you. Therefore we may not oppose you, though the peril which you intend for them surpasses our imagining.'

'Yet if you will accept my counsel,' Mahrtiir put in, 'you will permit me to accompany you. It will aid you to have a companion who is able to care for the Ranyhyn when you cannot. I scout as well as any Raman – and fight as well also. And I am hardy and Earth-wise. I can provide food and shelter where none appear.

'If you do not discover *aliantha*, what will you eat?' Haste quickened his words. 'If you have no shelter, where will you sleep? If you encounter no friends, who will defend you? If—'

Hami placed her hand on Mahrtiir's shoulder; and abruptly he stopped. Facing Linden with eagerness in his eyes, he repeated, 'Permit me to accompany you,' and said no more.

He troubled her. She already knew that she would miss Stave's knowledge and prowess. Mahrtiir offered her much that she could not supply for herself – and could not reasonably expect from either Liand or Anele. Yet she was reluctant to take more people into danger. And she was not entirely sure that she could trust the Manethrall. He seemed too eager to prove something—

But how could she reject any form of help? She would need more assistance than Mahrtiir could give her: that was obvious. Apart from the Ramen, however, there was no one who could aid her except Esmer and the ur-viles; and she had no idea how to ask them.

Slowly she nodded to Mahrtiir. 'If you're willing to face the risk. If your people don't need you here.'

Surely there were Cords in his care? What would happen to them? She could not lead people as young as Pahni and Char, girls and boys, *children*, into a *caesure*.

But Mahrtiir's gaze lit up as if she had set a match to tinder; and Hami and Dohn said nothing to dissuade him.

Instead the older Manethrall asked a question for the first time. 'How will you return?'

Unprepared to reveal what she had in mind, Linden blinked at him dumbly.

Dohn did not meet her stare. He had resumed watching the mountains, apparently looking for unmotivated storms and violence; for signs of Esmer.

'You will enter a Fall,' he explained quietly, 'a flaw in Time, and turn it to the past. There you will seek the Staff of Law. Very well. When you have found it' – his tone held an implicit *if* – 'what then?

'At the best, your search will require hours. It may well consume days. The Fall will move on. Perhaps it will cease to exist altogether. You will remain in the past, as unable then to regain your son as you are now.

'How will you return?'

Unwittingly he asked Linden to put her worst fear into words. Ever since she had realised the truth, during her vigil over Stave the previous night, she had avoided thinking about it; admitting it to herself. Yet the Ramen deserved an answer. Certainly Liand did.

Her pulse laboured in her temples as she said, 'If I can't use the first one, I'll have to make a new *caesure*.'

During her translation to the Land, she had seen herself rouse the Worm of the World's End with white fire. Perhaps Lord Foul had already accomplished his aim. By kidnapping Jeremiah, he may have ensured the Land's destruction. If she misjudged her power, or herself, or the stability of the Arch, she might bring Time to an end.

More because she needed some mundane activity to calm her than because she was still hungry, she resumed her seat in order to drink more water and finish the contents of her bowl. If she meant to risk the ruin of the Earth, she would at least do so on a full stomach.

Thinking sour thoughts, she ate fruit and cheese without tasting them; drank water without washing down the extremity which clogged her throat. Throughout her experience of the Land, she had only followed others: Covenant, Sunder and Hollian; the Giants. Liand had led her away from Mithil

Stonedown: the Ramen had brought her to the Verge of Wandering. Until now, she had seldom tried to impose her will on events. For Jeremiah's sake, she needed to be able to trust her own judgment, but she found that increasingly difficult to do.

Soon the Manethralls left the clearing. Perhaps they had responsibilities which they could not ignore. Or perhaps they simply recognised that she wanted to be alone. For reasons of his own, Bhapa trailed after Mahrtiir.

Liand had seated himself beside Linden, but he did not disturb her with questions. Instead he maintained a companionable silence, offering her the simple balm of his presence.

Nevertheless she could not relax with him. His naive acceptance of hazards which he could not possibly understand seemed to undermine her decisions.

She could justify taking Anele anywhere: he had nowhere else to go; and his broken mind might find mending with her. Moreover she needed him – and not only because he knew the location of the Staff. Lord Foul had spoken through him. If he became sane, he might be able to tell her where the Despiser had hidden her son.

As for the Ranyhyn, their choices were irrefragable; beyond her comprehension. And Mahrtiir clearly needed some outlet for his native intensity.

In her eyes, however, Liand belonged among his people in Mithil Stonedown. If for no other reason than because the Masters had deprived the Land of its history and lore, he seemed painfully ill-equipped to confront the dangers ahead of him.

And she was not sure that she could bear to see him killed in her cause.

When she had finished her self-imposed meal, and had spent a little while studying the high peaks for insights which their bluffs and ice disdained, she turned to the Stonedownor at last.

'What about you, Liand?' Incapable of grace, she tried to cover her stiffness by speaking softly. 'Why are you still here?

'I know we've had this conversation before. You said you want to help defend the Land. Believe me, I understand that. And you've already done a lot.' More than she could have expected from him. 'But Stave isn't wrong. What I'm planning terrifies me. So many things could go wrong—

'This might be your last chance to see your home again.'

Liand faced her soberly; but his voice held a note of affection or amusement as he replied, 'Linden, you baffle me. You are wise and valorous, yet you appear as uncomprehending as the Masters. However, your concern is well meant, and I will not take it amiss.'

He thought for a moment, then said, 'I might respond once more that the folk of Mithil Stonedown have given you no cause to doubt that they are steadfast. Or I might remark that I have beheld great wonders in your company, and would not willingly forego more. Or I might avow that the loveliness of the Land has only grown more precious to me as my senses have been opened. I have tasted with my eyes and hands and tongue the true glory of the world. To turn homeward now would be to pass from treasure-berries to dust.'

Linden wanted to protest, That's beside the point. We aren't talking about *aliantha* or dust. We're talking about slaughter or survival. But she restrained herself. She was tired of vehemence. And she had already lost Stave.

Instead she urged, 'Then stay here. With the Ramen. You don't have to waste your life in a Fall.'

The young man shook his head. 'You cannot ask it of me. For answer I will remind you of your own words.

'You said that at one time you encountered a man in need. Perhaps he sought to dissuade you from aiding him as you now seek to dissuade me. If so, you refused. Yet you acknowledged that you could not have imagined what would follow. If you had indeed grasped the nature of your peril, you doubt that you would have been able to endure it. Because of your refusal to abandon him, however, you have become the Linden Avery who now wishes to spare me a similar peril.'

Gently he placed his hand on her shoulder; permitted himself to offer her that much of an embrace. 'Do you not know that you are admirable in my sight? Can you not conceive that I have no desire to turn aside from your example? Your intent is not to destroy the Earth, but to redeem it, as you seek also to redeem your son. I will abide the outcome with you.'

Linden wept too easily. She always had. Touched by Liand's willingness, she blinked against the burn of tears in the corners of her eyes. Precisely because she hungered for hugs, however, she shrugged his hand away: his touch was not the one she craved. With her palms, she rubbed the moist salt from her cheeks. Then she did her best to match his trust.

'If that's the way you feel, I hope you'll watch my back. I'll have my hands full.' Mastering the flow of a *caesure* would demand all of her resources. 'And I'm sure you've already noticed that I'm not particularly good at taking care of myself.'

The warmth of his answering smile allowed her to hope that she had found a moment of grace after all.

Above her, daylight swelled into the dawn sky, and birds began to sprinkle the gloaming with calls and soaring. The scent of dew seemed to quicken the grass.

Sunshine glided swiftly down the westward mountainsides, pouring illumination into the Verge of Wandering. Nevertheless direct sunlight was slow to reach the depths of the vale. The eastern peaks, jagged as teeth, bit high enough into the heavens to cover her with shadows still.

Linden thought that she would wait until the light touched her before she put her feet to the path she had selected for herself. She wanted to feel the sun's consolation on her skin, let its benison warm the fear from her bones. However, her sense of urgency made her restless. Finally she could no longer sit still. She needed movement to help her manage her complex apprehensions. Rising to her feet, she asked Pahni how the Ramen took baths.

Smiling shyly, the Cord led her to one of the shelters, set out a basin of warm water for her and showed her how to wrap herself in a blanket so that she could remove her clothes and rub away grime and sweat with a soft cloth.

Linden wanted to wash her clothes as well, and her hair, but the chill in the air dissuaded her. She had no way to dry her shirt and jeans quickly, and nothing else to wear. Nevertheless she felt somewhat cleansed, slightly better prepared, when she returned to the clearing.

As Liand rose to greet her, she announced, 'Let's go. I can't keep putting this off. You should get ready.' Presumably he would want to repack his pinto's supplies. 'I'm going to ask one of the Ramen how to call Hyn.'

She felt a quick surge of tension from the Stonedownor, which he made no attempt to conceal. Yet he promised at once, 'I will be swift. I need only request viands from the Ramen and tend to Somo's burdens.'

Smiling anxiously, he hastened away.

Linden tightened her grip on herself as she looked around for someone who might answer her question.

She expected to find Bhapa, Pahni, or Char hovering somewhere nearby, but the first person she saw was Stave. He stood just outside the clearing, watching her as if he had expected her to notice him earlier.

He would know how to summon the Ranyhyn.

She did not want to talk to him, but she forced herself to cross the bare dirt towards him. When he had acknowledged her with a nod, she said severely, 'You should be in bed. You need rest. Your *hip* needs rest. If you don't stay off your feet for at least the next three days, you'll be in pain for weeks.'

Even his *Haruchai* strength could not shrug off what had happened to him.

But he ignored her admonition. 'I have not yet departed,' he replied, 'because I hoped that you would turn from your intent. However, it has become plain that you will not. I will delay no longer.'

Nodding once again, he limped out into the clearing. His damaged hip seemed to leave a groan in the air as he passed.

Involuntarily Linden followed him. 'Stave, stop. You can't ride like this. Even *you* can't. Be reasonable, for God's sake.

'Your people are too far away. They can't respond in time. It won't make any difference if they don't hear from you for a few more days.'

Stave said nothing; but he cast her a look of such disdain that she winced and fell silent. Then he put his fingers to his mouth and whistled shrilly.

For an instant, the distant birds ceased their cries, and the air itself seemed to go still, hushed with expectation.

Again Stave whistled. Suddenly Ramen crowded the rims of the clearing as if he had summoned them instead of the Ranyhyn.

A third time, his whistle pierced the sky. Now Linden felt an answering tremor under her boots; a shiver of excitement in the ground. Whinnying like the clarion call of trumpets rose above the grass-muffled rumble of hooves.

From the south and the mountains, two Ranyhyn came galloping, proud as flame in the warming day.

Linden would not have recognised them. With Stave beaten and dying in her arms the previous night, she had hardly regarded the great horses; had noticed only the stars on their foreheads and the visceral impact of their power. She assumed, however, that these were Hynyn and Hyn, come in response to Stave's call.

Both of them answered, although only Hynyn had accepted him.

In spite of their size, the beasts seemed to flow as fluidly as oil between the shelters of the Ramen. When they neared the circle of open ground, however, the smaller of the two, a mare with grave eyes and dappled flanks, slowed her pace, trotting to a halt among the gathered Ramen. Her companion, a roan stallion with a regal tail and an air of hauteur, cantered into the clearing to stand before Stave.

The Master greeted Hynyn with a deep bow. When he had raised his head again, he pronounced softly, 'Hail, Ranyhyn! Land-rider and proud-bearer.' His voice had a timbre of invocation and ritual; formal respect which his people had not uttered for thousands of years. 'Sun-flesh and sky-mane, I am glad that you have heard my call. An urgent journey lies before me. Will you bear me?'

In response, the stallion shook his mane as if in denial, although he stood ready to be mounted.

Stave appeared to hesitate. He glanced around at the assembled Ramen; but their frank adoration revealed nothing except that the Ranyhyn were revered.

Linden frowned. Had Hynyn and Hyn answered Stave's call only to refuse him? *Both* of them—?

Stave twitched one shoulder, a slight shrug. Favouring his damaged hip, he gathered himself and vaulted up onto Hynyn's back. In spite of his pain, he seemed entirely at home astride the Ranyhyn; mounted where he belonged.

Hynyn tossed his head as if to welcome his rider. The Ramen watched, transfixed and disturbed by the sight. Stave had said that the defeat of the Bloodguard had tarnished the fidelity of the Ramen. He may have been right.

Leaning forward, he murmured softly to Hynyn. Again the stallion shook his head and did not move. Stave nudged at Hynyn's sides with his heels: Hynyn flattened his ears and set his legs. To Linden's inexperienced eyes, the stallion seemed ready to buck.

Uncharacteristic uncertainty creased the Master's brows. As if to all of the Ramen, he announced, 'Hynyn will not bear me.'

From the edge of the clearing, Manethrall Dohn replied, 'You are mistaken, sleepless one. Hynyn has accepted you. However, he does not consent to your intent. He will not bear you where you wish to go.'

Stave's mien darkened. As far as Linden knew, no *Haruchai* had ever been both accepted and refused. The Master may have been shocked. And without Hynyn to bear him, he would have to return to Mithil Stonedown on foot.

How far would his stubbornness carry him with a wounded hip?

'What now, Bloodguard?' Mahrtiir asked with sardonic satisfaction. 'Will you cleave to the purposes of the Masters? Or will you honour the will of the Ranyhyn? Consult your arrogance. Surely it will not mislead you.'

Stave turned a threatening scowl towards the Manethrall. 'You are a fool,' he pronounced distinctly. 'There is no contradiction. No Ranyhyn has ever refused to serve its rider. For the sake of all the Land, the Masters must learn what this refusal portends.'

A sarcastic rejoinder flashed in Mahrtiir's eyes, but he bit it back.

Manethrall Dohn ignored both men. For a moment, he studied the daylight as it filled the vale. Then he announced, 'Ringthane, Hyn is here as well, though you did not summon her. She also will not bear you where you wish to go. Nonetheless she desires to bear you.

'Will you not mount?'

Quickly Linden looked around for Liand and Anele. She would be lost without the old man; and she had already told Liand that he could accompany her.

Will not bear you—

Anele was nowhere to be seen. After a brief search, however, she spotted Liand among the Ramen, holding Somo by the pinto's halter.

—where you wish to go.

Anxious for reasons which she could not have put into words, she turned to face Hyn.

As soon as Linden met her gaze, the mare trotted forward.

Studying the beast, Linden groaned to herself, Oh, God. I can't ride *that*. Hyn was too big: Linden's head barely reached her shoulder. And Linden was no horsewoman. If she fell from that height – and in motion—

Under the Sunbane, she had ridden the Coursers of the Clave, and they were larger than any Ranyhyn. But Cail had supported her then. With his arms around her, she could not have fallen, even by choice.

Hyn approached with a mincing step. Somehow the mare conveyed the unexpected impression that she felt shy in Linden's presence. When she drew near, however, she nudged Linden's chest, tangibly urging Linden to ride her.

Her warm breath smelled of sweet grass and freedom; of galloping wildly across illimitable vistas.

Linden looked around for help; and immediately Bhapa came towards her with wonder in his eyes. To both Linden and Hyn, he bowed deeply. Emotion thickened his voice as he said, 'Ringthane, you are reluctant to ride. For that we honour you. It is fitting to be humbled by the Ranyhyn. But in this their will must not be thwarted. The fate of the Land rides with you, and you require their aid. You will not regret that you granted their desire here.'

The Ranyhyn wanted something from her. And from Stave.

Bhapa watched her face. 'Do you fear that you may fall? There is no need. The Ranyhyn permit no harm to their riders.'

Linden shook her head. She *needed* the Ranyhyn: she was certain of that. Whether she felt ready or not, able or not, she would have to ride Hyn eventually.

She also will not bear you where you wish to go. Nonetheless she desires to bear you.

What could the great horses possibly want from her?

Linden seemed to have no choice. 'All right,' she muttered. 'I don't understand any of this. Never mind that. Help me up.'

Hyn nickered approval as Bhapa interlaced his fingers to form a stirrup. Hurrying so that she would not hesitate, Linden stepped into his hands and reached upwards.

Even then she might not have been able to mount. The distance was too great: for an instant, it seemed to symbolise or contain all of her limitations.

But Bhapa lifted her higher; and she found herself unceremoniously seated on the mare's back.

Clutching the silk of Hyn's mane in both fists, she tried to regain some sense of balance.

With elaborate consideration, Hyn turned until she faced southwards, away from the Land. At the same time, Hynyn wheeled more imperiously, bringing Stave to Linden's side. Both Ranyhyn plainly intended to return in the direction from which they had come.

'Linden!' Liand called anxiously. In haste, he tugged Somo out into the clearing, then scrambled onto the mustang's back.

Hynyn responded with a stern whinny. Hyn flicked up her hooves one at a time, showing Somo her heels.

When the Ranyhyn started into motion, Somo refused to follow.

Liand barked a command; dug his heels into the pinto's sides; hauled on the reins. His mount dropped its head and did not move. 'Linden!' he shouted again, at once angry and frightened. 'Do not—! I must accompany you.'

'Stop,' Linden muttered to Hyn, 'wait, don't go yet. I said he could come with us.'

The Ranyhyn ignored her. Together, stately as frigates, Hyn and Hynyn walked out of the clearing among the Ramen.

Linden nearly lost her seat turning to watch Liand's struggle with Somo.

Then two of the Cords intervened, obviously urging Liand to accept Somo's refusal; and Manethrall Dohn explained to Linden, 'It is the will of the Ranyhyn. They do not condone the Stonedownor's presence. Fear not, Ring-thane. You will return to find him safe among us. He will yet ride with you.'

Liand protested, an inarticulate gasp of dismay. Flinging himself from the pinto's back, he ran after Linden. The heat in his eyes and the dogged set of his shoulders proclaimed that he meant to follow her on foot as long and as far as necessary.

Almost at once, however, the Cords stopped him. He wrestled with them furiously until Manethrall Hami snapped his name.

'The will of the Ranyhyn is plain,' she told him severely. 'We will not permit you to act against it.' When at last Liand subsided, she added more kindly, 'Hyn will ward the Ringthane with her life.'

Liand may have continued to protest. Perhaps Hami reassured him further. But Linden could no longer hear them. Hyn had borne her beyond earshot.

For the moment, the ground seemed to yaw vertiginously on either side of her. She was perched too high on a mount over which she had no control; and her legs were stretched too wide. Only her grip on Hyn's mane secured her. A precarious hold: the fine hair would slip through her fingers if she relied on it.

She had made plans and promises, but she appeared to have no say at all in whether or not she ever kept her word.

She wanted to demand explanations from Stave, although she knew that he had none to give her. But his pain was vivid in the morning light, and its sharpness closed her throat. In spite of her visceral alarm, she suspected that the behaviour of the Ranyhyn disturbed him more profoundly. She was merely frightened – and frustrated by her inability to act on any of her choices. He was experiencing a violation of the ancient relationship between his people and the great horses.

More for her own sake than for his – as far as she knew, the *Haruchai* had no sense of humour – she tried to lighten the silence; distract herself from her fears. 'Well,' she said, 'here's another fine mess you've got us into.'

He did not so much as glance at her.

Linden shrugged to herself. More seriously, she asked, 'Do you have any idea where they might be taking us? Can you think of anything that might explain what they're doing?'

She hardly expected him to respond. The scale of their disagreements and conflicts might make simple conversation impossible.

Having stated his position and made his decisions, however, Stave now seemed content to comport himself as though nothing had changed. 'I have no clear answer,' he replied calmly. 'Yet there is a tale which was told by Bannor of the Bloodguard during the time of the Unbeliever. It suggests an answer.'

'Please,' Linden put in promptly. 'Tell me.'

'This tale,' he said, 'concerns the quest of High Lord Elena and ur-Lord Covenant for the Seventh Ward of Kevin's Lore. Though they knew it not, they sought the Blood of the Earth and the Power of Command.

'You have heard that when ur-Lord Covenant first summoned the Ranyhyn, a great many of them answered, each rearing in obeisance and fear, each offering to be ridden. Yet he refused them, for which the Ramen honour him above all Lords and Bloodguard. Rather than ride any Ranyhyn, he asked of them a boon.

'In Mithil Stonedown he had done cruel harm to a woman of the Land – to Lena daughter of Atiaran, she who later gave birth to High Lord Elena. Hoping, perhaps, to ease that wrong, he asked of the Ranyhyn that one of them would visit Lena each year, for she adored them.

'This service the Ranyhyn fulfilled without fail, until the Unbeliever himself released them from it.'

Gradually Linden's anxiety receded as she began to feel more secure on

Hyn's back. When they had left behind the shelters of the Ramen, the Ranyhyn increased their gait to an easy rolling canter which carried them swiftly through the deep grass. At that speed, she might have felt more alarm rather than less. But the mare was able to compensate for her uncertain balance. In spite of her initial trepidation, she found herself relaxing to the sound of Stave's voice.

She knew what he meant by 'cruel harm'. Covenant had told her of his crime against Lena. However, the rest of Stave's tale was unfamiliar to her.

'In later years,' he was saying, 'during High Lord Elena's girlhood, Lena occasionally allowed her daughter to ride in her place. The High Lord spoke of that time in Bannor's presence while she and ur-Lord Covenant floated upon the flame-burnished waters of Earthroot.

'She told of a ride which expressed the will of her mount, the Ranyhyn Myrha, rather than any wish of hers.'

Ahead of Hyn and Hynyn, the mountainsides crowded close together, leaving only a narrow gap between sharp cliffs. As the great horses stretched their canter to a run, the cut ravine seemed to sweep palpably nearer. Grass, a few shrubs, and the occasional *aliantha* blurred past Linden on both sides. To her surprise, she began to enjoy Hyn's swiftness. The adoration and service of the Ramen were not difficult to understand. Like so much of the Land outside Lord Foul's influence, the Ranyhyn were tangibly precious.

But she could not be sure that she would prove equal to what they wished of her.

'What happened?' she asked her companion.

'In the High Lord's tale,' Stave answered, 'Myrha bore her to an eldritch tarn enclosed within the Southron Range, where Ranyhyn had gathered by the hundreds. Around the vale of the tarn, the Ranyhyn galloped as though in ecstasy, only pausing at intervals to drink of the tarn's dark waters.

'When the High Lord also drank, she found herself united in spirit with the great horses, sharing their thoughts and purposes. Thus she learned that she had been brought to partake of the horserite of *Kelenbhrabanal*, Father of Horses, Stallion of the First Herd. This rite the Ranyhyn held in secret, generation after generation, so that *Kelenbhrabanal's* doom would never be forgotten.

'I know not what Hynyn and Hyn desire of us,' he added. 'It may be that they wish us also to partake of the horserite. Or they may have some purpose which lies outside the ken of the *Haruchai*.'

His tone conveyed a shrug through the muted thunder of hooves. Whatever the intentions of the Ranyhyn might be, he apparently did not mean to let them interfere with his own commitments.

Or perhaps he was not so single-minded. His people loved the great horses. And Hyn and Hynyn had imposed their will on him as well as on Linden.

And he seemed reluctant to tell her the rest—

'What was it?' she asked. '*Kelenbhrabanal*'s doom?'

What had the Ranyhyn wanted from Covenant's daughter?

'In a time before Berek Halfhand became the first High Lord,' continued the Master, 'the Ranyhyn warred against the wolves of Fangthane the Render and were slaughtered. Grieving for the decimation of the First Herd, *Kelenbhrabanal* sought to end the conflict by proposing a bargain. The Father of Horses would surrender his own throat to Fangthane. In exchange, the Render would cease his war upon the Ranyhyn.

'To this Fangthane agreed eagerly. But he did not honour his given word. When he had slain *Kelenbhrabanal*, he unleashed his wolves again upon the Plains of Ra. The slaughter of the Ranyhyn resumed. They would have perished from the Land if they had not gained the service of the Ramen to aid them in their long strife.

'This knowledge the Ranyhyn shared with High Lord Elena to warn her,' Stave concluded flatly, 'but she did not heed them.'

He seemed to believe that he had answered Linden's question. But she was not satisfied. 'What was the warning?' she insisted. 'I don't see what *Kelenbhrabanal* has to do with Elena. She wasn't looking for a way to sacrifice herself.'

Not according to the little that Linden had heard of those events.

The Master appeared to sigh. 'You know the tale. High Lord Elena sought the Seventh Ward, the Power of Command, so that she might compel Kevin Landwaster from his grave against Corruption. She believed that despair would anneal Kevin's heart, rendering him from pain to iron, making of him an indomitable tool.

'In this she was wrong, to the great cost of all the Land.

'Bannor deemed then, as do the *Haruchai* now, that the Ranyhyn had perceived a flaw in the High Lord's comprehension. By means of their horserite, they sought to alter the course of her thoughts. They wished her to grasp that despair is no more potent or salvific beyond death than it is in life.'

If Bannor and his descendants were right, the Ranyhyn had read Elena's future in her young eyes. They had seen the time ahead of her: who she would become; what she would do.

And Elena had not heeded them.

Yet they had continued to serve her. To the last, they had hoped that she would learn from their rites. Or they had forgiven in advance her human folly—

Now, like them, Stave was trying to warn Linden.

It was too bad, she thought to herself, that the Masters also were not listening.

Beyond the ravine which led them from the Verge of Wandering, Hyn and Hynyn bore their riders running across mountainsides washed with sunshine, redolent with wildflowers and springtime. Always in sunlight, they rounded one towering granite buttress after another, plunging down into the gullies and *sholas* which creased the boundaries between peaks, then clattering with undiminished speed up the far slopes. At times the ground they trod looked rocky enough to imperil mountain-goats; yet they galloped on without hesitation. For a while, Linden was sure that they would exhaust themselves. Gradually, however, she became aware that both mounts were in fact holding themselves back: that they had tremendous strength in reserve and had not yet called forth their true power.

Their restraint may have been meant as consideration for her.

Fortunately the indefeasible security of Hyn's long strides inspired an almost autonomic confidence. The mare seemed as reliable as the bones of the Earth. Lulled by trust, Linden eventually found herself drifting. The sun's warmth seeped into her bones, and the whetted atmosphere of the mountains seemed to clean the fear from her lungs. By degrees, her apprehensions faded and she fell into a doze.

Later she was startled awake by a cessation of motion. The Ranyhyn had halted in a low gully nourished by a sparkling rill. As it danced past a small clump of *aliantha*, the water chuckled to itself as if high among the mountains it had heard an amusing tale. Hyn and Hynyn had paused to let their riders eat and drink.

Stave had already dismounted. Still half asleep, Linden slipped down from Hyn's back without remembering to worry about her height from the ground. Unsteadily, she moved to the rill to quench her thirst, then joined her companion beside one of the treasure-berry bushes.

She saw at once that riding had exacerbated his wounds, his internal injuries as much as his damaged hip. His lips were pallid, his skin had taken on an ashen hue and his pains were as sharp as compound fractures.

Nonetheless he remained undaunted. He had not yet come to the end of himself. And the sapid fruit restored him as it did her. With her health-sense, she could watch the progress of renewed vitality through his body. Soon she believed that he would be able to endure more riding.

Now she noticed that the sun had reached the afternoon sky. The passing of time caused her a pang. She must have dozed longer than she realised. 'Did Bannor happen to say,' she asked Stave, 'how far away this tarn is?'

The *Haruchai* regarded her steadily. 'It is not certain that the tarn of the horserite is our destination.'

Linden nodded. 'I understand. It's just a guess. But I need something to hope for.'

'As you say.' He gazed up at the highest peaks. 'High Lord Elena spoke of riding at a gallop for a day and a night from Mithil Stonedown. Doubtless a portion of the distance was behind us in the Verge of Wandering. More than that—'

With a shrug, he turned to limp towards Hynyn.

Both Ranyhyn had cropped a little grass and drunk from the rill. Now the stallion moved unbidden to stand beside a boulder jutting from the side of the gully. Apparently Hynyn understood that his rider might no longer be able to mount without aid. Once Stave had pulled himself onto the boulder, he could reach Hynyn's back easily.

Touched by the discernment of the Ranyhyn, Linden followed his example. When she had resumed her seat, Hyn and Hynyn trotted out of the gully to continue their journey.

Thereafter the terrain became more demanding, the ground more broken and rocky, the mountainsides steeper. Bare stone loomed against the sky, grey with age and cold, mottled with lichen. Weather-stunted trees clung arduously to splits in the cliffs, and stubborn stretches of grass gave way to slopes of gravel like the detritus of glaciers. At the same time, the temperature declined as though the Ranyhyn ran towards realms of ice. Hyn and Hynyn had borne their riders far from any soil which could have sustained the rampant grass of the Verge of Wandering. Whenever the twisted thrusting of the granite blocked the sun, Linden found herself regretting that she had not thought to bring one of Liand's warm cloaks; that Liand himself was not with her.

Of necessity the Ranyhyn slowed their pace, although they still travelled swiftly.

No clouds were visible within the constricted horizons, but Linden could smell a storm on the raw breeze. Somewhere beyond the dominion of these rough peaks, rain and wind and trouble were brewing. Instinctively she feared that some bitter force gathered to repel the Ranyhyn from their purpose.

Stave betrayed no concern; but that did not comfort her.

Through Anele, Lord Foul had assured her that he had done no harm to the Land. *I have merely whispered a word of counsel here and there, and awaited events.* She suspected that he held her in too much contempt to lie. Yet he seemed to have vast powers in his service. And she did not believe for a moment that Hyn had borne her beyond his reach—

If you fear what has been 'done,' think on the Elohim *and be dismayed.*

Esmer could testify to the cruelty of such legacies.

Slowly Linden's discomfort became a remorseless ache which seemed to span her consciousness from rim to rim. She no longer noticed the evolving vistas, or watched the sun's progress down the narrow sky. At intervals an unwonted jolt roused her enough to see that her surroundings had grown as sheer as spires, as sharp as knives. Raw granite edges softened only by ice and distance cut away the daylight in swaths, making way for darkness. Then the aching in her legs and back swelled again, and her ability to regard how her world shrank slipped away.

Soon it became too small to contain her son; or Liand and Anele and the Ramen; or her memories of the man she had loved.

Time passed; and the air turned distinctly colder as the Ranyhyn dropped down the far side of a raw pass into an enclosed depth like a pit of gloom, a clenched instance of winter. Descending from remnants of sunlight into shadow, they seemed to leave behind every vestige of spring and warmth and familiarity. Under their hooves, the ground became bitter and broken, old stone warped to shards and twisted out of cognisance by eons of unrelieved ice.

Protected only by Hyn's generous heat, Linden returned shivering to herself.

Somewhere above the enveloping gloom, daylight still held the peaks, but its touch was lost in shadow, leaving only a premature dusk. In the heavens, early stars glittered coldly against the velvet dark, while ahead of the Ranyhyn midnight crouched like a waiting beast.

Until now, Hyn and Hynyn had shown themselves able and willing to care for the most basic needs of their riders; but Linden could not imagine how they might preserve her against such cold. Conditioned by Covenant's distrust of his ability to control wild magic, she had never considered calling on his ring for something as simple and necessary as warmth. If the Ranyhyn did not surprise her with some new providence, she would have no choice but to risk dangers which had dismayed him.

But then the horses sank below some unseen boundary layer like a thermocline, and the cold began to dissipate. After its first change, the air remained unpleasantly chill, reminiscent of freezing and loneliness. At least temporarily, however, it had lost its harsh edge. Soon tufts of hardy grey grass emerged among the rough stones. In the deepening shadow, the slope relaxed as grasses spread out over the ground.

Before long, Linden found herself in what appeared to be a cliff-walled glen. With only the distant disinterest of stars for illumination, she could not see its far side except as a deeper ebony amidst the gloaming; but the glen seemed to be more than broad enough to hold the horserite that Stave had described. And its grassy floor was relatively flat and smooth: it might have been beaten down by uncounted generations of hooves.

Ahead of her at the centre of the glen lay an area of complete blackness like a disk of obsidian, a rough circle impenetrable to light. It held no sheen of starlight, no reflection of any kind: she would have assumed that it was stone if Stave had not spoken of a 'tarn' – and if eldritch waters had not called out to her senses, warning her of power which had welled up from the depths of the Earth.

Hyn and Hynyn had reached their secret destination.

They trotted towards the tarn eagerly, ears pricked forward, breath snorting in their nostrils. Linden expected them to approach the waters immediately and drink; but after a few paces, Hyn abruptly shrugged her to the ground. Unprepared, she landed awkwardly and nearly fell.

Stave joined her a heartbeat later, catching himself on one leg to protect his hip.

While her knees trembled, Linden watched as the mare and the stallion together hastened to the tarn and plunged their muzzles into the unrelieved dark.

She had time to think, *Hundreds* of Ranyhyn? Where were the others? Elena had been a child, probably overwhelmed; but she could not have been so dramatically wrong about her own experience. Surely two Ranyhyn did not comprise a horserite? They were not enough—

Then Hynyn and Hyn exploded away from the waters and began to thunder around the dell as if they had plunged into frenzy.

Linden had never witnessed such galloping. She could only make out vague shapes in the caliginous air: running, the Ranyhyn appeared as little more than smears along the shrouded base of the cliffs. Yet they were loud and vivid to the enhanced dimension of her senses, fraught with Earthpower, and bright as bonfires. Drinking from the tarn seemed to have ignited their inherent vitality. They radiated an intense heat. She felt their sweat as though it were the spume of hysteria. If Stave had not described Elena's visit here, Linden would have guessed that Hyn and Hynyn had gone mad.

But they were only two—

Why were they alone? Where were the rest of the Ranyhyn?

Still shaken by cold, she breathed, 'Stave.' She needed some explanation from him. But she could find no language for what she lacked except his name. The furious race of the Ranyhyn tugged at her awareness, her ability to think, sucking her mind away with centrifugal insistence.

As if in response to her unformed question, the Master turned his back on the tarn and began to hobble towards the nearest cliff-wall.

'Wait,' she panted. She had been too long on horseback, come too far from any reality that made sense to her: she had forgotten how to claim his attention. Nevertheless she ached for his companionship. She did not know how to face even this small fragment of a horserite by herself.

'Please, Stave!' she called because he had not stopped; did not appear to have heard her past the labouring hooves of the Ranyhyn. 'I need to understand.'

He paused, balancing on one foot. 'Then drink of the tarn.' His tone had the certainty of a knell. 'Thus will you comprehend what the Ranyhyn wish you to grasp.'

Again he limped into motion.

'Wait!' she repeated. 'What do you mean? What's going on?' His air of refusal frightened her; and fear anchored her against the gyre of the Ranyhyn. 'We're *both* here. Aren't you supposed to drink, too?'

Urgently she hastened after him.

He might not have stopped, but Hyn and Hynyn flashed past in front of him, so near that he had to halt in order to avoid a collision. Then they blurred away, indistinct as hallucinations. They seemed to be submerged in the gathering darkness, barely perceptible from any position of clarity.

Stave waited for her to join him. His vague shape in the gloaming conveyed a sigh. When Linden reached him, he pronounced, 'This horserite is not for me. I was made to accompany you only so that I might provide for your safety at need.'

Now the galloping of the horses no longer frayed her attention. Instead it called to her like a demand; a form of supplication too proud for pleading.

'How do you know that?' she countered. 'Hyn and Hynyn are Ranyhyn. Do you really think they couldn't take care of me?'

'I am *Haruchai*,' he replied as if that answer sufficed. 'We have no need of horserites.'

His manner seemed to add, Or of waters which blend minds. Among themselves, his people had used a mental form of communication for millennia.

'Oh, bullshit.' Feigning anger to mask her concern, Linden put a hand on his shoulder, pulled herself or him around so that she could peer into his darkened face. 'Why not? You people are the *Masters* of the Land. You're responsible for it. And this is a warning. You said so. The Ranyhyn brought High Lord Elena here to warn her.' Hundreds of them. Not just two. 'Don't you think you need every warning you can get?'

'We do not,' Stave asserted. 'We have heeded the lesson of Kevin Landwaster. We find no value in despair.'

She could see nothing of his expression; but his aura seemed like a rejection carved in stone.

'No,' she protested as if she were sure. 'No.' Her hands insisted at his shoulders. 'Bannor heard what High Lord Elena said, but none of you heard the warning.'

Again Hyn and Hynyn pounded past, circling the valley with frenzy and fervour glaring in their eyes; the passion of beasts that could not beseech. Somewhere behind the clamour of their hooves, Linden seemed to hear the distant distress of thunder.

'Sure,' she went on, '*Kelenbhrabanal's* despair didn't save the Ranyhyn. I get that. But what did?

'It wasn't anything grand. It wasn't Lords or Bloodguard or white rings or Staffs. The Ranyhyn weren't preserved by Vows, or absolute faithfulness, or any other form of *Haruchai* mastery. *That* was the real warning.'

'Linden Avery?' Stave sounded implacable, ready for scorn.

But she had come too far, and needed him too much, to falter now. 'It was something much simpler than that. The plain, selfless devotion of ordinary men and women.' The Ramen. 'You said it yourself. The Ranyhyn were nearly destroyed until they found the Ramen to care for them.

'They wanted Elena to understand that she would be enough. She didn't need to raise Kevin from death,' or give up sleep and passion, 'or do anything else transcendent,' anything more than human. 'All she had to do was trust herself.'

In dreams, Covenant had told Linden the same thing.

Unreadable in the darkness, Stave stared at her. For a long moment while Hynyn and Hyn raced each other around the valley, he said nothing. Then, with careful precision, he asked, 'And do you not deem white gold transcendent?'

To that she had no answer except, 'Maybe it is. I'm not sure. Maybe it's nothing more than the person who wields it.' But she did not stop. 'Isn't that beside the point? If nothing else, don't you need to know why Hyn and Hynyn are alone? Don't you think it's important that there aren't more Ranyhyn here?'

She could not be sure that he had heard her, or that he cared. A moment later, however, she discovered that she had reached him, in spite of his certainty. Without a word of acquiescence or acknowledgement, he turned to hobble in the direction of the tarn.

Again thunder muttered threats in the distance. The air felt charged with power and turmoil, thick with static and expectation, as though the potent waters of the tarn were disturbed by advancing storms.

Holding her breath to contain the labour of her heart, Linden hurried to Stave's side; walked with him towards the tarn. Around them, Hyn and Hynyn constricted their circle as if they were focusing their frenzy inwards, onto their riders.

Oh, Covenant, she prayed in silence, I hope this is what you wanted. You told me to do something unexpected.

This was the result.

The force of the black waters seemed to accumulate against her at every step. She could discern it clearly enough to know that it was neither toxic nor tainted. Rather it was an expression of Earthpower purer than anything she had ever experienced before. Nonetheless its sheer strength exceeded her. She could not define its nature or guess its effects. It was too extreme for human flesh.

Yet Elena had tasted these same waters as a young girl, undefended by the lore and resources of Lordship.

Linden's eyes bled tears as she and Stave reached the rock-knuckled edge of the tarn.

Communion. Blending. The Ranyhyn wanted to share their minds with her. Their frenzy—

'Stave.' She had to drag her voice up from the bottom of her chest. 'Maybe I should go first. In case—'

She could not explain what she feared.

Energy seemed to crackle across the surface of the tarn: incipient lightning; imminent hysteria. In those unreflecting depths, no stars existed. Instead, stark blackness stretched down into the marrow of the world.

'There is naught to fear,' answered the Master. 'The Ranyhyn wish only to enlighten you. They will not make you mad.'

Although they might break her heart.

Stooping without hesitation, he lowered his face to the tarn.

His example drew her with it. In this place, with so much at stake, she could not bear to be left behind.

The touch of the water on her lips and tongue was as cold as fire. When she swallowed it, it burned within her like a blaze of absolute ice.

Then she surged upright and began to run with the Ranyhyn, run and run frantically, flinging herself like ecstasy or abjection around the dell as if she had gone out of her mind.

Chapter Four

Heedless in Rain

Linden Avery and Stave of the *Haruchai* returned to the Verge of Wandering in a scourging rain. Huddled on the necks of their Ranyhyn, they rode into the encampment of the Ramen as if driven by flails, while behind them harsh winds lashed the wracked peaks and a downpour as bitter as sleet cut into the vale from all directions, twisted to chaos by the tumbling gusts of the storm. Occasional thunder harried their heels. At intervals, shrouded streaks of lightning turned the massed thunderheads the colour of bruises and madness: a swollen, livid hue shot through with argent like unfettered wild magic.

They had been away for two days and a night.

Alerted by scouting Cords, or by some instinctive link with the great horses, a throng of Ramen accompanied by Liand hastened from their shelters to greet the Ranyhyn and their riders.

Stave was able to dismount without aid, although he wavered on his feet. Cold and cruel exposure combined with the aftereffects of his wounds had eroded even his great strength. Perhaps he would have spoken, if words would have sufficed to succour his companion – and if he could have made himself heard through the pummelling torrents.

But Linden's fingers had to be pried from their grip on Hyn's neck. She had to be dragged bodily from Hyn's back. In Liand's embrace and the support of the Ramen, she hung stiffly, unable to move: rigid with mortification and chilled to the bone; so cold and deprived and lost that she could not even shiver. She only remained clenched, and breathed in shallow, dying gasps, and wept like the rain, ceaselessly.

Hyn's steaming warmth was all that had kept her alive. Perhaps at some time earlier in the day, she had sustained herself with white fire. Stave would know, if she did not. But long hours ago the storm had whipped her capacity for power to tatters and rent it from her. If she had not lain along Hyn's neck and clung there, desolate and unyielding, her flesh would have failed her. There was malice in the gnashing rain, the fanged wind, and she could not have endured it without her mount.

Half weeping himself, and frantic, Liand carried her to the nearest shelter, the nearest cook-fire, helped by Bhapa and Pahni. Eager to be of service, Char brought armloads of wood and baskets of dried dung to stoke the flames. Hami trickled warmed water between Linden's pallid lips while the Stonedownor stroked her throat to help her swallow. With unexpected tenderness, Mahrtiir bit into two or three treasure-berries, removed the seeds, then kissed the pulp and juice into her helpless mouth.

Accepting no assistance, Stave staggered into the shelter so that he too would be warmed. And both Hyn and Hynyn shouldered their way in among the Ramen, although the sod roof was too low to let them hold up their heads and the stallion's shoulders almost brushed the lattice of the ceiling. Together they watched over Linden. Their concern steamed the rain from their coats.

Then Linden gagged; swallowed convulsively; gagged again; and some of the rigour seeped from her muscles. By slow degrees, the warmth of the water and the potency of the *aliantha* eased into her abused body, while the high heat of the fire wiped cold from the surface of her skin. Her pallid cheeks gradually acquired a hectic flush, stricken and febrile. Shivers began to surge through her, first in brief tremors like the aftershocks of a catastrophe, then in longer and more vehement waves, seizures violent enough to make her thrash in Liand's arms.

It appeared that she might rally.

After a time, the Ranyhyn withdrew as if they had been reassured. Turning away from the encampment, they disappeared into the teeth of the storm. Most of the Ramen did them homage as they departed. But Mahrtiir continued to prepare *aliantha* with his teeth; Hami offered small, steady sips of water to Linden's involuntary swallowing; and Bhapa and Pahni gently chafed her hands and feet, striving to restore her circulation.

Stave had seated himself on the opposite side of the fire. He, too, shivered heavily for a while, in spite of his toughness. But when the Ramen offered him warmed water, he drank it: he accepted a few treasure-berries, a little *rhee* and stew. Soon he stopped trembling, and his brown skin lost its rime-gnawed hue. A dullness like the glaze of exhaustion remained in his eyes, but he had sloughed away the worst effects of the storm.

Then Manethrall Hami asked him quietly, 'Will you speak now, Bloodguard? The Ringthane cannot reveal what has befallen her. Nor is she able to guide our care. The hurt of wind and rain and cold we understand, and will tend.

But a fever rises in her which we do not comprehend. It is an ague of the spirit, beyond our ken. We fear to harm her.

'Will you not tell us what has transpired?'

The *Haruchai* turned his closed features towards Hami. 'Let the Chosen speak of it,' he answered, 'if she is able.' Behind its exhaustion, his voice hinted at chagrin and old shame. 'I will not.'

Perhaps Liand would have replied with indignation or pleading. But he contained himself for Linden's sake, as did the Ramen, so that she would not be disturbed.

She seemed to sleep for a while. Her shivers receded somewhat. Then she opened her eyes briefly and stared about her with a terrible dismay, although she did not truly regain consciousness. When the moment passed, however, she began to breathe more easily. Hami cajoled more water between her lips, which she swallowed without gagging. The pulped *aliantha* which Mahrtiir placed in her mouth she swallowed as well. Little by little, she became visibly stronger.

Chills still racked her without surcease, but now their character changed. The cold gradually lifted from the marrow of her bones, the depths of her lungs, the core of her internal organs; but another fever took its place. She continued to shiver because she had fallen profoundly ill: an ailment so deep that it appeared almost metaphysical.

The Ramen would have given her hurtloam, if their small store of the eldritch mud had not been expended. They would have treated her with *amanibhavam*, if they had not feared that it would prove too potent for her – or that it was the wrong kind of febrifuge for her needs.

At last, Liand was reduced to simply murmuring her name as he held her, repeating, 'Linden. Linden,' as if by that unadorned incantation he thought he might exorcise the fever from her soul.

Still she continued to rally. When next she opened her eyes, they were bright with fever, disconsolate as stars; but a faint patina of consciousness blurred their dismay. As if deliberately, she gulped at the cup of water which Hami held to her lips. Then her tremors became coughing, and she struggled to sit up in order to clear her lungs.

Liand let her rise, although he held her shoulders so that she would not slump towards the fire or fall to the side.

'God, Stave,' she coughed weakly. Her voice sounded tortured, fatally hoarse, as if she had spent innumerable hours screaming. 'Those poor horses—

'Oh, my son.'

Tears streaked her cheeks, although she had no strength for weeping.

*

She needed time to recognise where she was. Leagues and mountains and brutal rain had intervened between her and the horserite; and at first she could recall only Stave, identify only his face across the lashing flames: the man who had accompanied her against his will.

If he had seen just a fraction of what she herself beheld—

But the horserite itself existed only in fragments. *That* she could not remember: not immediately. Not until she had reconstructed laboriously, in pain and sorrow, the links which connected her to this forgotten shelter, this lost heat; these unimagined faces, half-familiar and doomed. Shivers shattered the past, left it lying around her like splinters of broken glass.

In fever she seemed to pick them up one at a time to lacerate her aggrieved heart.

Hyn—

Very well, she remembered Hyn. The mare had kept her alive. Hyn was Earthpower defined in flesh, at once glorious and suppliant; revered and vulnerable. And Hynyn, who had borne Stave—

And the black tarn, its waters lightless as despair.

She was not ready.

Someone whom she may have recognised appeared to offer her a small bowl containing pulped treasure-berries. She ate a little of the vibrant fruit and grew stronger.

Covenant had once said, *There's only one way to hurt a man who's lost everything. Give him back something broken.*

She would have preferred to remember the storm. She had been forewarned – and did not know how to bear it.

So. Stave: Hyn and Hynyn: the bitter tarn.

And running—

—around and around the floor of the vale as if her heart would burst: as fervid as the Ranyhyn, if without their frantic speed, their fluid power. Together they pounded their shared visions into the beaten ground. She should have been able to grasp the chemical transactions taking place within her. Her health-sense should have allowed her to name the deep potency of the tarn. But her consciousness, her willing mind, had vanished at the first taste of those waters. She had become one with the Ranyhyn; no longer herself.

Only two of them. Not because the others had spurned her, or Stave, or this horserite; but because they felt too much shame. Hyn and Hynyn had been elected to bear the guilt and remorse and risk of their great kin.

Elected for sacrifice—

Beyond question, Linden preferred to remember the punishment of the storm.

Yet memories of the storm could not protect her. The blast which had broken over the mountains during the night had only hastened the fading of her transfiguration; only soaked and lashed and chilled and, finally, numbed her; only restored her mortality. And mortality was no excuse. It could not protect her from the consequences of what she had seen; or of what she meant to do.

Only death had that power.

She could not choose death. Not while the Despiser still held her son. Therefore she remembered. One by one, she retrieved whetted shards from the ground of her mind and cut—

Hyn and Hynyn, brave as martyrs. The mind-blending waters of the tarn, cruel and unutterably cold. Running.

Millennia of shame.

And Jeremiah.

Oh, my son.

'Ringthane,' said a voice which may have sounded familiar. 'Linden Avery.' Was it Manethrall Hami? Hami, who had been left behind days ago, behind vast mountains of despair? Linden could not be sure. 'You must speak. You are ill. We know not how to succour you.'

Was she ill? Oh, yes. Absolutely. But it was not an ailment of the body. Although everything within her shivered convulsively, she had spent too much time exalted by Earthpower to suffer from merely physical fevers.

She was sick with visions: the memories and prescience of the Ranyhyn.

In some sense, the great horses transcended the Law of Time. They knew when they would be needed. They knew how far they would be required to go—

Hands gripped her shoulders, attempting to steady her. A man's voice – Liand's? – murmured her name repeatedly, called her back to herself.

She feared that he would stop if she could not answer. Between tremors, she tried to say, 'The tarn.'

She thought that she spoke aloud. Certainly her strained throat felt the effort and pain of sound. But she could not hear herself. The loud rain on the roof of the shelter muffled her voice.

'The horserite.'

Around her, Cords echoed, 'Horserite,' as though in awe that she had been so privileged. Softly the woman's voice, Hami's, said, 'As we deemed. The Ranyhyn possess insight needful to her.'

They did not understand. How could they? They barely existed, rendered vague by shivering. Linden could not focus her eyes on them. Only Stave seemed fully real to her beyond the intervening flames: as irrefutable as stone.

'Just Hyn and Hynyn,' she croaked hoarsely. No other Ranyhyn. 'The others couldn't bear it. They're too ashamed.'

That shocked the Ramen. They blurred like tears. Voices protested, 'No,' and, 'No.' Someone hissed through the rain, 'It is false. She lies.'

Stave blinked at the glaze in his eyes. Sternly he retorted, 'It is sooth.' He nodded at Linden past the fire. 'Behold her. Do you discern falsehood?'

'Do not shame yourselves,' Hami told the indignation of her people. 'Do you lack sight? She has no falsehood in her.'

Fever had burned away any lies that Linden might have wished to believe.

'We are Ramen,' the Manethrall informed the Cords severely. 'We will hear the truth.'

They heeded her, but Linden did not. Her heart seemed to bleed memories for which she had no words and no courage. Running hard enough to vanquish time, she had shared the visions of the Ranyhyn: images not of *Kelenbhrabanal* and Fangthane, but of the child Elena, daughter of Lena and rape.

Another warning—

At that time, Elena was a young girl, lovely as only a child could be, and innocent in spite of her mother's instability. Lena had been deranged by violation and yearning, rendered unfit to raise a child. And both of Lena's parents, Trell and Atiaran, had been broken to some extent by the crime against their daughter. Thus Elena was effectively abandoned by her own family; left to the care of a young, unregarded man who adored Lena. For the Land's sake, he had effectively adopted Elena. His embittered tenderness, and the boon of the Ranyhyn, were all that had sustained her.

To Linden, the girl's loneliness and need were as vivid as Jeremiah's, as acute as her son's compelled maiming. The great horses had seen Elena clearly. Once each year, every year, a Ranyhyn, an old stallion, had approached Mithil Stonedown in order to relieve Lena's bereavement; and so he had witnessed again and again how the child's life was transformed for that brief time. When the mare Myrha had taken the stallion's place, she had seen her potency in Elena's heart more vividly than any man or woman who might have loved the child.

'Because of Elena,' Linden explained as clearly as she could, although she had no words. 'That's why the Ranyhyn are ashamed. The horserite doomed her.'

If Jeremiah had been granted Ranyhyn rather than hospitals and surgery after his ordeal in Lord Foul's bonfire, an excitement like Elena's might have drawn him out of himself.

Surely the Ramen remembered Elena's participation in that rite millennia ago? They had not been present. Perhaps no Raman had ever witnessed or shared a horserite. But they must have heard the tale—

'They blame themselves,' she told the eager flames, 'for what she became.'

Precisely because the Ranyhyn had recognised the nature of their power within Elena, Myrha had borne her to that long-ago conclave. They saw far ahead in time; sensed the danger which would confront Elena years later. And they had hoped to dissuade her from accepting her heritage of harm.

Now they knew that they had failed terribly.

They had shown Elena the arrogance of *Kelenbhrabanal*'s despair, thinking to teach her that failure was preferable to violation. Lena should have resisted Covenant with all her strength. Better to combat Fangthane directly and die than to believe that some grand sacrifice might alter Fangthane's nature – or the Land's fate.

But Elena had missed the lesson. She was deafened to it by the thunder of hundreds of hooves; blinded by the communion of the Ranyhyn. Covenant's gift had left her insensible. She already adored the great horses. From their rite, she had learned something akin to worship for *Kelenbhrabanal*. His sacrifice had seemed splendid to her: an act of valour so transcendental that it could not be tainted or surpassed.

The horserite had not dissuaded her from ruin. Rather it had set her more firmly on the path to destruction.

Speaking hurt Linden's mouth and throat: words bit like blades of glass, slivers of the past. Nevertheless she forced herself to say, 'They think she got the idea of commanding Kevin from *Kelenbhrabanal*.'

Perhaps she would have raised the Father of Horses himself if he had possessed the mighty lore of the Old Lords.

Now the Ranyhyn saw that they had fallen prey to an arrogance of their own. Discerning Elena's vulnerability, they had believed themselves wise enough to guide her future.

If Hyn and Hynyn had stopped there, however, Linden could have endured their self-blame; perhaps even refuted it. Her soul would not have sickened within her. The shame of the great horses, she might have said, was itself arrogant. The Ranyhyn had claimed responsibility for Elena's actions when that burden belonged properly and solely to Elena herself.

But the two horses did not stop. When they had shared their racial memories of Elena, they began their tale again from the beginning – with one appalling alteration. In their visions, they replaced Elena's visage with Linden's.

Still trying to warn her.

'Now they're afraid of me,' she moaned, 'for the same reason. They believe—'

She could not say it. It hurt too much.

Their minds united with her, Hyn and Hynyn retold the same story as if it had happened to Linden rather than Elena; as if Linden's mother and father had been Atiaran and Trell as well as Lena and Covenant. And she experienced it with them: it transpired anew. It held the same abandonment and grief, the same failed cherishing, the same loneliness – and the same exalting in-rush of love for the Ranyhyn. Mercilessly Hyn and Hynyn described Elena's introduction to the murder and betrayal of *Kelenbhrabanal* as if that crisis were indistinguishable from Linden's experience of the Land with Covenant under the Sunbane.

And still the images of the horserite did not end. The Ranyhyn had erred with Elena, perhaps, by not revealing the true extent of her peril. She had been a child, too young to apprehend the truth of their prophecies. They had feared to overwhelm her.

On behalf of all their kind, Hyn and Hynyn did not make that mistake with Linden.

Instead they found within her a still graver hurt. Galloping in frenzy, they touched the ravaged memories of *moksha* Raver's possession, the killing horror of Jehannum's malice. And with that knowledge, they caused her to experience what was being done to her son.

To damaged Jeremiah, who had no defence except blankness.

Linden could focus only on Stave. Surely he had seen the same visions, felt the same dismay? The Ranyhyn had not brought him to their horserite against his will in order to spare him. Yet he sat beyond the flames as though he were untouched, unmoved; implacable as blame.

Liand had not stopped murmuring her name. But now he crooned as if he meant to comfort her, 'Linden, no. No.

'The Ranyhyn do not fear you. They cannot.'

His support could not interrupt her trembling. She was too ill for any solace.

Belabouring the floor of the dell with her pain, she saw Jeremiah's plight as Hyn and Hynyn wished her to see it: as if he were simultaneously herself occupied by a Raver and Thomas Covenant lost in the stasis imposed by the *Elohim*. She needed him back desperately, Covenant and her son. All of their lives depended on it: the Land depended on it. And so she reached – or would reach – into him with her health-sense, seeking the place where his mind still lived.

The Ranyhyn elicited it from her, shared it with her: a field of flowers under an immaculate sun, pristine with warmth and promises. Covenant and now Jeremiah met her there, or would meet her, both children again, and unharmed; capable of a child's love, happiness, joy. Yet the visions of the horserite were unutterably cruel; for when she reached out to Covenant and Jeremiah, trying to restore them with herself, the Worm of the World's End squirmed from Covenant's mouth, and her son's dear face seemed to break open and become vile, bitter as Despite.

Hyn and Hynyn would have been kinder to simply trample Linden under their hooves.

'The Ranyhyn believe,' she said with her last strength, 'I'll do the same thing Elena did.'

Surely Stave would have admitted as much, had he chosen to speak? Yet he said nothing. His eyes held an uncharacteristic softness as he regarded her. Somehow he conveyed the impression that he, too, would have comforted her, if he had known how.

Hyn and Hynyn had given her a warning. Unlike Elena, she recognised that. And she understood that such efforts were necessary to the great horses. They needed to appease their shame. How could they see what they had seen, dread what they dreaded, and not try to guide the hope of the Land?

But she did not know where or when they wished her to step aside from her intentions. And she did not mean to recant any of her decisions.

Thomas Covenant had told her to trust herself.

She did not know that she had fallen asleep; or that her friends had stretched her out on one of the beds and covered her with blankets; or that Liand and Bhapa, Char and Pahni, had kept watch over her throughout the night. She did not know whether she dreamed, or what those insights may have cost her. When she awakened, however, *aliantha* and Earthpower had worked a transformation within her, and she was sure of herself.

Sleep and warmth and nourishment had done much to heal her; but she still could not stop shivering. Now, however, she understood what was happening to her. She shook as if she were feverish because she was sick with fear.

Her plan to enter a *caesure* and reverse its flow might damage or destroy the Arch of Time. And she had no one to guide her through history's ramified layers except a blind old man with a broken mind.

Hyn and Hynyn would aid her as they had aided Elena: she did not doubt that. They had declared their allegiance in the horserite, articulated it against the hard floor of the dell. They would bear her wherever she willed. And she had become convinced that their warnings did not pertain to her immediate choices. The dangers they foresaw lay somewhere in the distance ahead of her.

But others around her might not be so trusting; or so desperate. She had told everyone who could hear her that the Ranyhyn feared what she might do—

The visions of the horserite may have inspired Stave to renew his opposition. That was possible. On the other hand, she trusted Liand to stand by her. And Anele would certainly accompany her. Even at his most demented, he would accept any risk which might restore him to the Staff of Law.

But she did not know what to expect from the Ramen. They supported the Ranyhyn utterly, bowed to the will of the great horses in all things. However, they knew now that the Ranyhyn feared her. After millennia of service, they might decide that their responsibilities ran deeper than simple compliance.

Then there were the ur-viles. And Esmer. Both had the power to prevent her, if they elected to do so. Esmer had told her that the ur-viles wished to serve her. But he wielded forces which she could not begin to measure or counteract.

Two days ago – was it only two days? – he had spent the night among the mountains, exerting himself in ways which the Ramen had called storms.

She tried to open her eyes then, impelled by tremors; but they were caked shut. Sleep and the aftereffects of prostration blinded her. She had to lift the rough weight of her blankets in order to raise her hands to her face, rub the crust from her lids.

When she had done so, she blinked her sight clear and looked up into Liand's waiting concern.

Bhapa and Pahni stood behind him, watching her efforts to rouse herself. Nearby Char tended the fire; kept the flames hot for her sake. But the Stone-downor sat on the bed beside her, bending over her, stroking her hair. His strained visage dominated her view.

'Linden,' he said softly as she focused her eyes on him. 'It is good to see you wake. I feared that this ague would hold you until it frayed the thews of your spirit.'

Liand, she tried to say. Oh, Liand. But she could not force her throat to release words.

Tears moistened his gaze for a moment. 'If you are able, you must speak. I would urge you to rest silent, but there is an illness within you which we know not how to tend. You must name what is needed to restore you.

'Is it hurtloam? Already the Manethralls have dispatched Cords for it, but the way is long, and they will not return soon. Will treasure-berries succour you? The Ramen have gathered them in plenty. And *amanibhavam*, if that is your need. Only speak—'

She shook her head, striving to interrupt him. She wanted to tell him that she was not as sick as she appeared; or that she was sick in another way. But the residue of the horserite filled her throat with ashes, and her mouth and tongue had forgotten the shapes of language.

As Liand pleaded with her, Char left the fire and hastened from the shelter. In the distance, she heard him announce, 'The Ringthane wakes.'

Oh, God. Linden closed her eyes, covered her face with her hands. *Give me courage.*

Then Liand thrust an arm under her neck, lifted her into a half-sitting position. Carefully, almost reverently, Pahni offered a bowl of water to her lips. From the bowl came a delicate scent of *aliantha*.

Lowering her arms, Linden sipped at water mixed with the juice of treasure-berries. Succoured by that gentle touch of Earthpower, she found words.

'Liand.' Her voice was a thin croak, barely audible. 'Just hold me. You're already giving me' – she sipped more water – 'what I need. Just hold me until I'm ready to stand.'

At once, he shifted himself behind her; braced her against his chest with his arms around her. Tentatively, he protested, 'Yet this fever, Linden—'

She shook her head. 'I'll be all right.' His attention to her weakness threatened her resolve. She could not afford to acknowledge that she might fail. She was too fragile— 'You're my friend. That's enough.'

Reaching for Pahni's bowl again, she gulped down as much as she could swallow. Then she began climbing to her feet.

'No,' Liand objected. 'Linden, it is too soon. You suffered sorely in the storm – and the horserite. You must rest. Perhaps on the morrow you will be ready for these exertions.'

Still she strove to stand. He was wrong about her: she was not physically ill. And she had slept long and warmly. She had been given treasure-berries. Her bodily weakness would pass when she began to move around.

He could have held her down, but he did not. Instead he relented; helped lift her to her feet. For a moment, she had difficulty finding her balance. Then, however, her unsteadiness receded, and she was able to stand.

But she could not stop shivering.

While she tried to reassure Liand with a smile, a small group of Ramen entered the shelter: Hami, Mahrtiir and two or three Cords.

Stave accompanied them. As ever, she could not discern his emotional state.

She saw only that he had regained his strength; and that the pain in his hip had declined.

The moisture in their hair and on their faces made her aware for the first time that the rain had not stopped. But it fell more gently now, no longer lashed by the blasts of the storm. And it had become warmer, more spring-like.

The malice which had harried her after the horserite had spent its force and faded from the clouds.

Apparently Esmer had accomplished his purpose—

Or he had seen that the Ranyhyn were too enduring to be daunted, and had decided to change his tactics.

Yet the rain continued steadily, soaking the Verge of Wandering until every step outside the shelters splashed water through the thick grass. From her place between her bed and the fire, Linden could not see the sky; but the hue of the air and the texture of the rainfall conveyed the impression that it might continue for days.

Facing her, the Ramen bowed deeply, as though she had earned their admiration. Stave did not join them, however. He remained behind his companions as if he had nothing to say to her.

Hami's concern matched Liand's; but Mahrtiir's gaze caught gleams of eagerness from the firelight.

'Linden Avery,' Hami began gravely, 'Ringthane and Chosen, we are pleased to see you so much recovered. You returned from the horserite in such straits that we feared for your life.' She scrutinised Linden narrowly, then added with a touch of asperity, 'Yet you remain fevered. You must rest. Surely Liand has told you so. It is not well to expend yourself when you require sleep and healing.'

Linden felt Liand squirm. 'She is the Chosen,' he said a bit defensively. 'I have no power over her.'

Again Linden shook her head, trying to stop Hami as she had interrupted Liand a few moments ago. 'Don't worry about me.' Her voice still croaked despite the soothing effects of *aliantha*, and her throat hurt as if she had howled for hours against the scourge of the storm. 'I'm not as weak as I look.'

Before Hami could respond, she asked, 'Where's Esmer?'

The Manethrall frowned. 'Ringthane, your need is plain, but it lies beyond our lore. We know not how you may be restored. That is our first concern. What is Esmer's part in this?'

She and her companions wanted explanations which Linden did not know how to provide. Nevertheless she had to try.

'Would you get me some more *aliantha*?' she asked Liand: a husky whisper. 'And a little *amanibhavam*? That's really all I need.'

The Ramen had never shared a horserite. She did not know how to tell them that the potent waters of the tarn had preserved her from malevolence which might otherwise have slain her.

Liand hesitated for a moment: he may have looked to Hami for advice. But the Manethrall did not react, and after a moment, he referred Linden's request to Pahni and Bhapa. Clearly he meant to stay at her side; to catch her if her endurance failed.

She wanted to thank him, and the Cords as well, but that could wait. Instead she faced Hami.

'That storm,' she said as firmly as she could. 'It wasn't natural. It had malice in it.'

Still frowning, Hami nodded. 'Yet the desire for harm has passed. Only the rain remains.'

Beside the point. Linden persisted. 'Has Esmer come back?'

Hami made a sound of vexation. Apparently she distrusted Linden's insistence on Esmer. Yet she replied, 'He returned while you slept. I will summon him, if you wish it.'

Linden shook her head. 'When he came back,' she said through waves of fever, 'the malice stopped. The desire for harm.'

Mahrtiir had told her, *He wields a storm among the mountains.*

Hami's eyes widened. 'And you conceive that the malice is his? That he raised ill against you in the storm?'

The idea visibly disturbed the Cords. Mahrtiir muttered a denial through his teeth.

Too fearful to say more, Linden clutched her frangible balance and waited to Hami's response.

'Ringthane,' the Manethrall sighed, 'you judge him harshly. That you have cause to do so is beyond question. In this, however, your mistrust misleads you.

'Throughout his absence from us, we kept watch over him. Ramen witnessed closely the nature of his distress – and of his power. It was not directed against you. Of this we are certain.'

Hami's gaze urged Linden to give Esmer the benefit of the doubt. His acceptance by the Ranyhyn compelled the loyalty of the Ramen.

Abruptly Stave spoke. 'Yet that which he invoked is evil.' His tone left no room for contradiction. 'I have felt it. Even now it stalks the Verge of Wandering.

'The Ramen also have felt it,' he told Hami. 'Why otherwise do you prepare to depart?'

Depart—? For the first time, Linden met the Master's gaze. The Ramen were *leaving?*

She and Stave had returned from the horserite through a scourge of malevolence. Who had inspired the ferocity of those winds, if not Esmer?

'Chosen,' Stave informed her, 'Esmer has summoned a darkness more dire than any storm. The Ramen must flee before it.'

With a snarl of anger, Hami rounded on him. 'Have you no heart, Bloodguard? You know the severity of that which lies before her. Why then do you seek to hasten her away from rest?'

Involuntarily Linden sagged against Liand. Summoned—? Esmer, what have you done?

At once, Hami turned back to her. 'It is for your sake.' The woman's tone pleaded on Esmer's behalf. 'He seeks to aid you.'

'He has done well,' Mahrtiir put in harshly. 'She has named her purpose. He serves her as the Ramen cannot. Nor could the sleepless ones perform what he has accomplished.'

Stave's voice cut through the responses of the Manethralls. 'Assuredly rest would speed the Chosen's healing.' He sounded unexpectedly vehement. 'Where may she do so? Here? In the path of ruin? She cannot. To think otherwise is folly. If she will not flee, as the Ramen must, then she can only confront her peril. There is no rest for her.'

Hami replied with a growl of exasperation. 'Have care, Bloodguard. You demean us, and we will not suffer it.

'We intend that the Ringthane should rest until we have determined the course of this evil. Then we will bear her to safety. Already we have readied a litter so that she may continue to rest among us as we withdraw.'

Linden did not look at Hami or Stave. The hostility between them pained her. It seemed to imply that she could not trust either of them. And the Land needed all of its friends. Jeremiah needed them.

Turning away from them, she studied the Stonedownor's troubled mien. 'Liand,' she murmured, 'what did Esmer do?'

He gave her a stricken glance, then ducked his head. 'I know not. I have not left your side. No one has spoken to me. I did not know that the Ramen mean to depart.'

For a moment, everyone around her remained silent, reluctant to answer her aloud; to put her peril into words. On either side of her, Bhapa and Pahni stood motionless, stopped in the act of offering her *amanibhavam* and treasure-berries.

Then Mahrtiir said like a hawk, 'Chosen, it is your intent to enter a Fall.

Esmer has enabled you to do so. He has called Fangthane's malign creation to the Verge of Wandering.'

When Linden understood what he was saying, her heart lifted as if she had heard trumpets.

Esmer had summoned a *caesure*.

The news did nothing to ease her complex dread, relieve her emotional fever. If anything, it made her fears more immediate, brought her chosen crisis nearer. Chills and urgency shook her until she felt almost dismembered. Nevertheless Mahrtiir's announcement seemed to tap a wellspring of purpose deep within her. Days of cruel frustration fell away as if she had cut the bindings of a millstone. At last she would be able to take action; to stop following other people's decisions from emergency to emergency.

And she would not have to spend days or weeks on horseback, wandering the Land in search of a *caesure*, while Lord Foul multiplied obstacles against her. She could dare her doom *now*.

She should have been terrified. She *was* terrified. But she was also sure. The fever which threatened to paralyse her could only be annealed in fire.

At this moment, just one question remained to undermine her certainty. Her cheeks were flushed like a promise of flames as she confronted Stave past the staring Manethralls and Cords.

'Yes, it's dire,' she admitted. 'I know that.' Still she could not speak above a hoarse whisper. Nevertheless her voice was full of implied conflagration. 'But I'm going to do it. I think it's worth the risk.

'Will you come with me?'

She expected that he would refuse. He had already proclaimed his determination to ride away so that he could warn the Masters. And the horserite may have convinced him to oppose her directly. Why else had he postponed his departure? Yet last night he had gazed at her with an unwonted softness, as though he had been touched in spite of his intransigence—

He faced her flatly: she could not read him. She had never been able to see into the hearts of his people. If he decided to attack her on the spot, she would receive no warning of any kind.

Nevertheless she studied him with fever in her eyes and waited for him to declare himself.

For a few heartbeats, Stave appeared to consider his options. Then he replied, 'The wishes of the Ranyhyn have been made plain to me. If I do not accompany you, Hynyn will withdraw his acceptance.'

Stiffly the *Haruchai* shrugged. 'And the horserite has given me cause to remain at your side for a time.'

Stung by relief, Linden's eyes misted and ran. She could not clear her sight until her hands found Pahni's bowl of *aliantha*; until the taste of treasure-berries filled her mouth and throat with healing.

Already she owed the Ranyhyn a debt too great to be repaid.

While Linden ate *aliantha* lightly – very lightly – sprinkled with crushed *amanibhavam*, most of the Ramen left the shelter to continue their preparations for departure. They did not expect Esmer's *caesure* to leave any part of their encampment undamaged.

Before he went, Mahrtiir explained tersely that he had selected Bhapa and Pahni to accompany him, rather than any of his own Cords, because of their kinship with Sahah. Then he led them away to gather supplies for an extended journey into the unknown hazards of time.

Char was nowhere to be seen. Apparently he had been dispatched on an errand of some kind. Of her people, only Hami stayed with Linden. At once solicitous and alarmed, the Manethrall fretted over Linden's condition as Linden stoked her courage with treasure-berries enhanced by the dangerous roborant of *amanibhavam*.

Her shivering eased somewhat as she absorbed the sustenance of the Land, but she remained perilously frangible; close to terror.

When the Ramen had dispersed, Stave approached her. In spite of his native stoicism, he walked with a pronounced limp. Hours on horseback had inflamed his injury. Yet he proposed to ride again soon, as long and as far as she required.

At least 'for a time.' Whatever that meant.

As if Liand were not present, the Master announced, 'The Stonedownor must remain here. His mount cannot accompany the Ranyhyn. If he attempts the Fall, he will be lost.'

Liand might have retorted hotly; but Linden stopped him by touching his chest with her palm. 'Anele has the same problem,' she answered, trembling. 'But I need him. And I need Liand. We'll have to figure something out.'

The young man gave her a look of gratitude; but she kept her attention on Stave. 'The Ramen don't ride. How will they stay with us?'

Stave did not look away. 'Their bond with the Ranyhyn cannot be severed. Where the Ranyhyn lead, they will be able to follow. The Stonedownor has no such bond.'

Linden sighed. 'Then he can ride with you. I'll take Anele with me.'

The *Haruchai* raised an eyebrow. But he did not object.

When she glanced at Liand, she saw him grinning as though she had given him a gift.

Before he could speak, she muttered, 'Don't you dare thank me. I'm not doing you any favours.' Her voice shook with fear for him. 'If this doesn't kill us, we could end up in places worse than your worst nightmares. If I didn't need your help so badly, I wouldn't risk any of you.'

Except Anele, who could hardly suffer more than he already did.

Liand went on grinning; but he took her seriously enough to remain silent.

Sighing again, she told him, 'We're going to need your supplies. You'd better get them. Bring as much as you can carry.'

The Ramen might provide everything necessary; but she wanted an excuse to send the Stonedownor away. If she could, she meant to spare him the confrontation that awaited her.

'Yes, certainly,' Liand said without hesitation. At once, he hurried away as if he were eager to risk not only his life but his sanity in her name.

Within herself, Linden sagged. Devoutly she prayed that the young man would not have cause to regret his loyalty. However, a more immediate concern demanded her attention. She did not know how near the *caesure* had come. She might not have much time left.

To Stave, she said abruptly, 'Before we do this, I've got to talk to Esmer. Will you go with me?' The senses of the *Haruchai* were more discerning than hers: no doubt Stave knew exactly where to find Cail's son. 'I understand if you prefer to keep your distance. But I could use your company.'

This time, Stave raised both eyebrows. 'If you wish it.' He may have felt surprise, but his tone held no hint of alarm. 'He stands at the edge of the encampment. The way is not far.'

Gratefully she took his arm. Clinging to the tacit validation of his support, she stepped out into the ceaseless rain.

The mild, steady drizzle drenched her hair; washed the heat of fire and fever from her cheeks. It was indeed much warmer than it had been the previous day. Nevertheless it was cool enough to leech away the residual warmth of the shelter. Her chills seemed to worsen with every step as Stave took her among the busy Ramen past the open centre of the encampment.

Her fear had soaked into the marrow of her bones. She had not forgotten Covenant's words in Anele's mouth. *You need the ring. But be careful with it. It feeds the* caesures. But he had died long ago; and now she did not intend to regard his warning.

He had also said, *I can't help you unless you find me.* She did not know how to do so, except by daring the Land's past.

Esmer had prepared the way, apparently seeking to aid her. Before she went further, accepted his help, she needed to know how much she could trust him.

Limping, Stave escorted her northwards. In that direction, veiled by the rain and the teeming clouds, the Verge of Wandering narrowed gradually towards the Land. There Cail's son stood alone with his back to the last shelters, ignoring the swift preparations of the Ramen.

If he sensed Linden's approach, or Stave's, he gave no sign. Instead he concentrated through the grey drizzle as if he sought to draw the *caesure* towards him by force of will.

At her first blurred glimpse of him, Linden's guts knotted, disturbed by the nausea which had troubled her during their previous encounters. He stood like a cynosure against the shrouded background of the rain, bright with the queasy squirming of power. As soon as she saw him, she wondered how she had failed to discern him earlier. His vast capabilities, like his inbred conflicts, seemed as unmistakable as wailing.

In his presence, something within her turned numb. She was no longer sure how to question him.

Yet Stave did not hesitate, although he had more cause for apprehension. And when they were within three or four steps, Esmer turned to regard them with eyes the colour of storm-wracked seas.

Danger seethed in him. For reasons of his own, he attempted a diffident, unconvincing smile. 'You are well come, Wildwielder.' His tone was full of obscure fears. They gnawed at each other like old bones. 'The Fall is a few hundred paces distant, no more. Soon it will become manifest to your senses.'

He conveyed the impression that he thought she might take offence at his efforts on her behalf.

Deliberately Linden released Stave's arm so that he could move freely if Esmer attacked. Then she advanced to stand between Cail's son and the Master.

The Ramen were certain that Esmer had not sent malice against her after the horserite.

Fighting chills, she demanded without preamble, 'What's going on here, Esmer?' The *caesure* was too near for politeness. 'First you practically kill Stave. Then you offer to answer my questions, but you don't say much. You make it clear that you want to be my friend and my enemy at the same time. And now you're helping me?

'Do you expect me to believe that this time you aren't going to hurt anybody?'

Through the wet fabric of her shirt, she clutched Covenant's ring for courage; but the cold metal gave her no comfort. It felt inert, numb; unreachable.

'For all I know,' she finished, 'this is some crazy attempt to help Lord Foul destroy the Land.'

Esmer frowned. Abruptly his manner became acerbic, self-punishing. 'Yet you must trust me. I have served you well. And I have brought ruin upon this encampment. When the Ramen return to the Verge of Wandering, they will find wreckage rather than sanctuary. Thus is my nature satisfied. I have harmed those who have given me naught but friendship. If you do not trust me, you will render their losses valueless.'

Linden stared at him. His rapid changes disconcerted her. And she did not know what to make of his assertion. Had he consciously hurt the Ramen to aid her?

At last, she referred her doubt to the *Haruchai*. 'Stave?'

'The Fall approaches,' he stated. 'I will not trust this Esmer. I do not lightly accept his aid. Yet he has summoned a Fall like any other. It will meet your purpose, if you are able to master its evil. In this he speaks sooth.'

Harshly Linden asked Esmer, 'Is that true? Did you summon a Fall? Or did you *create* it?'

Did his power resemble wild magic?

'I have no lore to cause such rifts.' His eyes were full of advancing squalls. 'When we spoke, I discerned your purpose. Therefore I withdrew among the mountains, that my labours would occasion no other harm. In your name, Wildwielder, I have unleashed fierce theurgies, seeking first to discover the location and course of an apt *caesure*, and then to compel it hither. Thus I hope to counter the loss which the Ramen will suffer.'

Through her nausea and chills, Linden heard violence and remorse, but no falsehood. Cail's son might commit atrocities without number, but he would not lie.

For an instant or two, his struggles filled her with empathy. 'You're tearing yourself apart,' she told him more gently. 'Do you know that? You should pick a side.'

'I do so constantly.' Now his voice sounded as damp as the rain, drenched in sorrow. 'That is my doom.'

His desire to serve her was so poignant that she could feel its ache in him. Apparently Cail's legacy outweighed the fatal hunger of the *merewives*, at least for the moment. And he had already called a *caesure* for her. Perhaps in his present phase he would do more—

'All right.' Linden made a conscious attempt to catch him before his mood shifted again. 'Since you seem to be on my side at the moment, tell me about your connection to Kastenessen.'

Why had he sought to prevent Anele from speaking of the Appointed?

At once, Esmer resumed his diffidence. 'He is my grandsire. I serve him utterly. As I also serve you.'

In bafflement, she protested, 'Damn it, Esmer. You aren't making sense. Do you mean that Kastenessen and I are on the same side?'

It was possible. Kastenessen had defied the *Elohim* and his own nature for the love of a mortal woman. He and Linden might have more in common than she had imagined. If he had indeed broken free of his prison, he might be willing to take risks as extravagant as hers for the sake of his lover.

But he was *Elohim*; and the *Elohim* whom she had known had not seemed capable of any emotion that she would have recognised as love.

Esmer sighed. Quietly, humbly, he said like the water on his face, 'The *Elohim* speak of Würd as the ur-viles do of Weird. There is also the Worm of the World's End. It is my doom. I have no other answer.'

The damp soaked into Linden's bones, aggravating her fever. Chills tugged at her concentration. 'All right,' she said again. 'All right. I don't understand, but right now that doesn't matter.

'Come with me.' Guide me. 'Do some good with all that power. If you really want to help me, help me now.'

The sheer intensity of his uneasy puissance made her stomach clench whenever she studied him directly.

In response, Esmer turned his head away. 'I must not. In my presence, you will surely fail.'

She should have known what he meant. Perhaps if she had been less ill, she would have been able to think more clearly. But her fever continued to pull her away from herself. She could no longer look at Esmer. Instead she searched the grey vista of the rain in the direction of the Land as if her fate were written there, spelled out in falling droplets and cold.

'Chosen,' Stave said at her back, 'this gains nothing. He conceals his enmity in confusion, yet it remains enmity nonetheless. It is folly to heed him.'

'Then call the Ranyhyn,' she told the Master faintly. 'Let's do this.'

He complied at once, raising a shrill whistle that sounded strangely forlorn in the drizzle; devoid of resonance or echoes. Unregarded by either Linden or Esmer, he whistled again, and yet again.

When the rain had washed his call from the air, she sensed movement behind her. Ramen approached from the encampment, a throng of them. They had come to say goodbye—

Moments later, a heavy woollen cloak dropped onto her shoulders. Its hood covered her head. The sudden weight surprised her until she felt Liand beside her.

'Linden,' he said severely, 'this is madness. You are ill, yet you stand unprotected in the rain. Already your ailment worsens. Are you a child, that you must be warded at every step?'

Before she could reply, Stave commanded, 'Attend, Chosen.'

With an effort, Linden withdrew her gaze from the shrouded north, turned her head – and found herself confronted by ur-viles. Somehow they had concealed themselves from her senses; or she was shivering too hard to notice them.

Esmer's manner had shifted again. Scornfully he pronounced, 'They watch against me, as I have said. You did not discern them. Their lore enables them to veil their presence.'

They must have been nearby for some time. Esmer had been aware of them – and had not considered them worthy of comment.

Trembling more violently, Linden leaned on Liand. Now beyond the ur-viles she could see the approaching Ramen, Hami and Mahrtiir first among them. As the Manethralls and Cords came near, the ur-viles moved to form a wedge; concentrate their power.

Its tip pointed, not at Cail's son, but at Linden.

The leading Ramen quickened their strides. Soon Hami and Mahrtiir stood in front of Linden, with Pahni and Bhapa at their shoulders. Deliberately they interposed themselves between Linden and the Demondim-spawn.

Behind them, Char guided Anele forward. The young Cord looked vaguely crestfallen, as if his pride had suffered a blow. He may have considered himself old enough, experienced enough, to accompany Linden and Mahrtiir in Sahah's name. If so, he had been refused.

Anele shuffled towards Linden as though he had no say in his own movements. He appeared bedraggled and bewildered, his tattered raiment drenched, as if he had spent days wandering aimlessly about the vale. In spite of his blindness, however, he conveyed the impression that he was aware of her.

The thought that he might have been possessed in her absence disturbed her. With the last of her lucidity, she turned to Char. 'Is he all right?' she asked. 'Did anything happen to him while I was away?'

The Cord bowed uncomfortably, as if he feared that he had committed some affront. 'He has been as he is, Ringthane. Since your departure, he has betrayed little cognisance of us, though he permitted us to tend his needs. He appeared to await your return.'

Again Char bowed. When Linden said nothing, he backed away from her until she lost sight of him among the gathered Ramen.

At the focus of the wedge, the largest of the ur-viles, the loremaster, abruptly began to bark: an insistent guttural gush of sound fretted with peril. Anele cocked his head in a listening attitude, but did not react in any other way. Esmer gazed up into the rain as if he did not deign to hear the loremaster. Yet when the flow of barking stopped, he responded in kind, still letting raindrops splash into his eyes.

The loremaster answered, and Esmer replied: they seemed to argue with each other. The sound of their voices scraped along Linden's nerves, accentuating her chills until her skin itched and her ears ached.

Mahrtiir held his garrote in both hands, ready for use. Anticipation glinted in his eyes. But he did not speak. Like the rest of the Ramen, he deferred to Hami where Linden was concerned.

Hami ignored the ur-viles and Esmer. 'Ringthane,' she said, 'we have come to bid you farewell. You must depart soon, as must the Ramen. Ere then, however—'

The woman hesitated, then said intently, 'Linden Avery, I will not challenge your choices. The Land's needs rest heavily upon you – and more so upon you than any other, though all are affected. Both your worth and your risk surpass my estimation.

'Yet it must be said – if the saying of it will not offend you – that your purpose appears unwise. You are ill, and worsening. If you hope to master a Fall, will you not require health and strength?

'You have said that the Ranyhyn fear you. Is this not the cause? That your resolve imperils the Land?'

Linden heard Hami's words, but she could not attend to them. The clashing speech of the ur-viles confused her. If she listened to their harsh language much longer, she would start to howl.

Unaware of her own motions, she raised her hands to cover her ears. 'Tell them to stop,' she urged the Manethrall. 'I can't stand this.'

'You do well to suffer it,' Esmer retorted immediately. 'I serve you still, though you disdain my efforts.'

The loremaster fell silent, clamping shut the thin slit of its mouth until the muscles of its jaw bulged with urgency.

Linden sagged against Liand as if a bubble of distress had burst, releasing her to fever.

'Explain,' Stave demanded of Esmer in her stead.

Cail's son faced the *Haruchai* with green threats seething in his eyes. 'The

ur-viles distrusted her purpose as it appeared to them. They demanded explanation. I have informed them that she will dare the past, seeking the Staff of
Law with only a madman's memory to guide her. Now they have determined
to aid her.

'They will accompany her. With their lore, they will pierce the madman's
confusion, sharing that which they descry with the Ranyhyn. Thus she may
hope to be guided accurately.'

None of this made sense to Linden: she was too far gone in tremors. Instead of
listening, trying to understand, she lifted her face to the rain, as Esmer had done.

Through the spatter on her face, she found that she could hear the distant
mutter of hooves. While Stave confronted Esmer, and the Ramen waited in
suspense, she wondered vaguely how Hyn and Hynyn alone made so much
noise on the sodden grass.

'And this you name service,' Stave countered. 'Do you also call it sooth?'
Esmer could have killed him where he stood, but he did not falter. 'Speak truly,
scion of *Elohim*. I have heard the contention in your words, and theirs. What
have you urged of them that they refuse to countenance?'

Another swift change overtook Esmer. He seemed to shrink before Stave,
almost cringing. 'The ur-viles mean to accompany her, yet they insist that she
will fail. Her purpose will serve their former master, whom they have betrayed.
I have averred that she is the Wildwielder and must endure the outcome of
her choices, but they do not relent.'

More firmly, he added, 'Also they do not trust me. That is our dispute.'

Then he turned to Linden; and the pressure of his regard – the sense of
troubled seas mounting towards storms – pulled her attention away from the
advancing rumble. Involuntarily she looked into the depths of his eyes as if
she were capable of comprehending him.

The scale of his distress made her want to vomit.

Diffident again, he said like raindrops, 'Wildwielder, they will oppose you if
you do not permit them to heal you.'

'"Heal"—?' Liand asked. 'Are they able to do so? Does their lore encompass
her affliction?'

To Linden, Esmer's words were indistinguishable from the sound of hooves.
It seemed impossible that Hyn and Hynyn could be so loud. But Jeremiah was
the Despiser's prisoner. As soon as the Ranyhyn arrived, she meant to ride
straight down the throat of the Fall, and to hell with anyone or anything that
stood in her way.

Esmer did not reply. Instead he stepped aside, barking dismissively to the ur-
viles.

As if in answer, the wedge nudged its way forward, gently urging the Ramen aside until the loremaster stood directly in front of Linden.

The black creature was little more than an arm's length from her. The wide nostrils in the centre of its eyeless face gaped for her scent wetly.

Liand quickly shifted to Linden's side; held her with his left arm so that his right was free to defend her. At the same time, Mahrtiir gave his fighting cord a snap and stepped closer. Bhapa and Pahni poised themselves to spring.

Stave now stood at Linden's shoulder opposite Liand, although she had not seen him move.

Somewhere behind them, Esmer laughed like a crash of surf.

'Ringthane,' Manethrall Hami said urgently. 'The Ramen know no ill of these ur-viles. Their service to the Render is many centuries past, and has not been renewed. Yet in your name we will oppose them, if that is your wish. Only speak so that we may know your desire.

'If you are too ill to answer,' she warned Linden, 'then I must believe that you require their healing.'

Something was expected of her: Linden knew that. It plucked at her wordlessly. Liand and Stave, the Ramen, Esmer, the ur-viles: they all wanted something. Anele asked her for nothing because he could not. Nevertheless his madness made its own demands. Only the Ranyhyn were simply content to aid her. They had given her their warning in the horserite. Now they would keep their promises.

Unaware of what she did, she watched the encampment for Hyn and Hynyn. When they appeared, her heart lifted as it had when Mahrtiir had informed her of Esmer's *caesure*. The stars on their foreheads shone in spite of the gloom and moisture. No mere rainfall could dampen their glory.

And they were not alone. Other Ranyhyn, three, four, five of them, followed Hyn and Hynyn galloping between the shelters towards Linden and her companions.

Seven Ranyhyn. Stave and herself. Anele and Liand. Mahrtiir, Bhapa, and Pahni. Of their own accord, the great horses offered all the help for which Linden could have asked.

No Raman had ever ridden a Ranyhyn; but she did not wish Mahrtiir and his Cords to refuse. The time had come to redefine old commitments.

Fever and sudden joy surged through her. As her heart rose, she raised her arms and her voice as well; shouted in celebration as well as welcome, 'Yes!'

She did not see the loremaster produce a knife with a curved and burning blade as if the creature had created the weapon within its black flesh. Nor did she hear the ur-viles growling together as though in invocation. Power swelled through the wedge as the loremaster sliced open its palm, then cupped its fingers to catch the viscid welling of its ebony blood; but she took no notice of it.

She did not realise that the ur-viles had interpreted her cry as permission until the loremaster snatched at her arm, pulling her hand towards it.

In the brief shock before she remembered fear, Linden saw the blade glow like molten metal over her palm: ruddy and lambent; potent as ichor. Then, while she tried to snatch back her hand, the loremaster drew a line of red pain across the base of her thumb. At once, the creature upended its palm over hers; clasped its fingers around hers so their cuts and their blood met and mingled.

Liand struck at the ur-vile's wrist, but could not break its grip: the loremaster held the power of the whole wedge. At the same time, Mahrtiir flung his garrote around the loremaster's neck. Instantly a flash of vitriol and flame incinerated the cord.

Alone among Linden's immediate companions, Stave made no attempt to defend her. He may have believed that the ur-viles could prevent her from entering the *caesure*.

Her call of welcome to the Ranyhyn became a wail—

—which died in her throat as strength like a charge of coursers pounded from her hand up her arm into the centre of her heart. Between one throb of her pulse and the next, she was exalted; translated from pain and fever and terror into a realm of illimitable possibilities; suffused with cascading health and vitality and *life* as though she had become Earthpower.

In that instant, she seemed suddenly equal to her fate.

The surge of transcendence vanished almost at once. Yet its brevity was essential. If it had endured too long, she might have torn herself apart in sheer ecstasy. Instead the rush of power left her shaken, simultaneously drained and galvanised, and shivering as if she were still feverish. But she was not ill now. Oh, she was *not*. Instead she felt reborn, made new, positively redeemed: as fresh with potential as a sunrise.

She could not speak. Waves of renewal rolled through her, tumbling her into a confusion of tears and gratitude and yearning. Somewhere beyond her, Liand pleaded for her attention, although his health-sense must have told him that she was well. In the background, Stave and the Ramen welcomed the Ranyhyn, while Esmer exchanged imprecations or promises with the ur-viles. But she did not return to herself until she felt a hand plucking at her cloak and blinked her eyes clear to find Anele in front of her.

Thomas Covenant's love shone from him, as it had once before. Standing ankle-deep in the sodden grass, he said to her in Covenant's familiar voice –

but softly, softly, so that only she would hear him – 'Go now, beloved. While you can. Just be wary of me. Remember that I'm dead.'

Beware the halfhand.

She stared at the old man, too surprised – and too entirely transformed – to react. Some part of her tried to cry out, but her heart had no words—

Then the light of possession disappeared from Anele's mien, snatched away by the sudden interruption of the loremaster. Before Linden could protest, the ur-vile reached out with its molten blade and flicked a small gouge in the thin flesh of Anele's forearm. Snuffling damply, the creature put its mouth to the wound and sucked.

With their lore, they will pierce the madman's confusion—

Anele suffered the loremaster's actions without protest or struggle: he seemed unaware of them. Covenant's brief presence must have reassured him. Mere days ago he had yelled in distress, *Creatures make Anele* remember!

Had the ur-viles themselves searched for the Staff of Law? For what purpose?

Until the loremaster finished with the old man and stepped back, Linden did not notice that the Ranyhyn had grown restive.

They had arrived together as she had imagined them entering the dell for Elena's horserite; but now they separated, stamping their hooves and tossing their manes among the Ramen. Hyn came purposefully towards Linden: Hynyn approached Stave. The others ranged themselves before Anele and Liand, Mahrtiir and his Cords.

The three Ramen stared, stricken dumb, as star-browed horses urged them to mount.

As one, the throng drew back. Voices rose through the rain: whispers of astonishment; low cries of expostulation. Hami's eyes went wide and white as if her ready pride had become chagrin.

Responding to their people as well as to the Ranyhyn, Mahrtiir, Pahni and Bhapa immediately prostrated themselves like supplicants in the sodden grass. They may have feared that what happened now would undermine the foundations of everything the Ramen had ever done; that the meaning of their lives might crack and fall.

No Raman had ever ridden a Ranyhyn – but nor had any Raman refused the will of the great horses.

Through the confusion of voices, the Ranyhyn made blowing noises that sounded like affectionate jeers as they lowered their heads to nudge at the three prone Ramen.

Linden watched Mahrtiir, Bhapa, and Pahni in suspense, afraid that none of them would move; that the *caesure* would overtake her before the Ramen could redefine themselves. But then the Manethrall shook himself as if he were gathering his courage and climbed unsteadily to his feet. His voice shook like Linden's as he announced, 'The will of Ranyhyn is plain. We cannot serve the Ringthane – or the Land – if we do not ride.'

The horses replied with a resounding whinny of approval.

'No Raman has ever done so,' objected Hami thinly.

'No Ranyhyn,' Mahrtiir answered, gaining strength, 'has ever offered to bear a Raman.'

Still Bhapa and Pahni remained prostrate. Like their people, they were caught in a contradiction that they could not resolve. Softly in the background, Esmer exchanged a harsh commentary with the ur-viles.

'Then let it be so,' said a new voice; and Linden saw that Manethrall Dohn had moved to the forefront of the crowd. His years and his scars gave him an air of authority. He did not speak loudly, but his words seemed to carry through the rain into the future. 'Too long have the Ranyhyn and their Ramen been exiled from the Plains of Ra. Once in this place we determined that we would never again allow Fangthane to ravage the Ranyhyn. We have held to that promise. Yet now my heart misgives me. I fear that we have entered the last days of the Land. If we do not accept this opportunity to strike against the Render, we will be forever homeless.'

For a moment longer, no one moved. Than Mahrtiir reached down abruptly, grabbed Pahni and Bhapa by the backs of their jerkins, and tugged them erect. 'Up, Cords,' he growled with hectic eagerness. 'Are we craven, that we fear to give our lives a new meaning?'

Under her breath, Linden muttered, 'Thank God.' *Go now, beloved. While you can.* She did not know how much longer she could contain the pressure building within her.

As if Mahrtiir had broken a trance, all of the Ramen seemed to slough off their wonder and dismay. They looked around them; studied the sky; peered anxiously into the north. Singly and in groups, they turned back towards the encampment. Soon only Hami remained with Linden and her companions.

'Ringthane, we must depart,' said the Manethrall. Now that a decision had been reached, she seemed resigned to its implications. 'We cannot withstand this Fall.'

Linden turned towards the woman. 'Then go, Hami. Take care of yourselves. Protect the Ranyhyn. I'm grateful for everything you've done.

'I'll come back if I can,' she told the concern in Hami's eyes. 'If I can't, look for me in the Land. You'll always be needed.'

Hami's gaze clouded; and her throat worked as if she wished to say more. Instead, however, she bowed deeply, mutely, in the fashion of her people. After that, she wheeled and trotted away after the other Ramen.

Before he left, Char spoke privately to Mahrtiir. Linden winced, thinking that Mahrtiir might rebuff the young Cord in some hurtful way. But then she saw Char offer his garrote to the Manethrall – and noticed as well that Mahrtiir's hands had been scorched in his attempt to throttle the loremaster.

Mahrtiir accepted Char's cord with taut grace. Although his fingers hurt, he rumpled Char's hair: a quick gesture of affection. Then the Cord ran after the rest of the Ramen, and Mahrtiir turned to Bhapa and Pahni, and to the champing Ranyhyn.

Satisfied and urgent, Linden faced Liand at last.

'Linden,' he began like a man in shock, 'I—'

She stopped him gently. 'Liand, thank you. For everything.' She felt almost frantic to be on her way. Nevertheless she took the time to add, 'I'm lucky I met you. If you decide you want to go with the Ramen, I'll still consider myself lucky.'

Her words seemed to pluck away his apprehensions. 'Are you mad?' he replied with a sudden grin. 'Can you believe that I will let pass an occasion to cross time upon the back of a Ranyhyn? I have been too long a mere Stone-downor. Here I will become more than I was.' He laughed. 'I mean to teach Stave and the Masters the error of their mastery.'

Linden nodded. What else could she do? She had already tried to dissuade him too often.

Hurrying now, she strode towards Hyn, calling over her shoulder, 'Mahrtiir, it's time! We need to *go*.'

Her senses had caught their first taste of the *caesure*. If it did not slacken its advance or drift aside, it would soon be visible to ordinary sight.

Mahrtiir came promptly to help her mount while Bhapa and Pahni guided Anele to the smallest of the Ranyhyn, a muscular pinto with flaring eyes and shaggy hocks which they called Hrama. Linden worried that Anele might be afraid to ride; but some visceral interaction between Hrama's vitality and his own Earthpower seemed to calm him, and he did not protest as the Cords boosted him onto Hrama's back.

By the time Hyn had turned towards the north, Stave and Mahrtiir were mounted as well. The Manethrall looked exultant, elevated beyond himself, and crowded with anticipation. Stolidly Stave brought Hynyn to Hyn's side as Bhapa helped Liand vault onto a palomino stallion named Rhohm. Mahrtiir joined Linden opposite the *Haruchai*. Then Pahni and Bhapa sprang onto their own Ranyhyn, following behind Liand and Anele to ensure that no one fell back or was lost.

At the same time, the ur-viles changed their formation. Running on all fours, they scattered around the riders to form a black ring with their loremaster in the lead. As they did so, they chanted together like a chorus of dogs.

Once in position, the loremaster exchanged its ruddy blade for a pointed iron rod like a sceptre or javelin; and from the metal, dark force flowed around the riders, enclosing them with vitriol.

Esmer had disappeared. Linden scanned the rain quickly, but felt no hint of him. Apparently he had simply folded his power around himself and winked away.

She remained where she was, staring into the gloom. After the brief respite of Esmer's absence, her stomach felt a renewed nausea as the swirling *wrongness* of the *caesure* approached. Peering through the raindrops, she began to discern the visible outlines of the Fall.

The *caesure* she had seen from Kevin's Watch had resembled the aura of a migraine: a sickening phosphene dance which seemed to cast every individual mote of reality into chaos. Without her health-sense, she might have believed that the swirl took place among the neurons of her brain rather than within the fabric of existence. But this Fall looked worse; stronger. Multiplied, perhaps, by the pressure of Esmer's summons, it formed a howl of distortion and madness against the grey backdrop of the rain.

The sight reminded her of damnation. *Abandon hope—*

Although she was soaked, the *caesure*'s ill covered her skin with formication, as if fire ants crawled through her clothes.

'Chosen?' Stave asked, questioning her hesitation – or her resolve.

'Oh, hell.' Frightened now on a scale that surpassed prolonged frustration and metaphysical chills, Linden reached into the front of her shirt; drew out Covenant's ring. Closing the cold circle in her fist, she muttered, 'Let's do it.'

If Joan were indeed the cause of the *caesures*, then entering one might resemble being plunged into her madness. But Linden had already survived Joan's torment once—

Joan was stronger now. In the Land, white gold inherited its true power; and her despair fed on itself, swelling ceaselessly. But Linden had grown as well. She was strengthened by the support of her friends as by the healing of the ur-viles. She also held a white ring. And when gunfire had first stripped her of her former life, she had not known that the Despiser would claim her son.

The loremaster heard her and understood. It began to pace forward through the water-heavy grass, holding high its sceptre. Grimly Linden touched Hyn's flanks with her heels. The Ranyhyn quivered under her, but did not falter.

Then all of the riders were in motion, trotting ahead within the ur-viles' protective theurgy.

The chanting of the creatures rose. Gradually the Ranyhyn quickened their pace to match the rhythm of the invocation.

Rain splashed past Linden's hood into her eyes. Now the *caesure* resembled a vast swarm of hornets. Its power shocked her senses: it seemed to swallow the north in its frenzy. She no longer wondered why Kevin's Watch had fallen. The wonder was that any aspect of the living world could endure the *caesure*'s evil.

Anele had done so. His inborn Earthpower had preserved him then. It would again. But the rest of the company would have to rely on the Demondim-spawn – and on Linden's uncertain ability to use wild magic.

With Stave and Mahrtiir beside her, she gripped Covenant's ring and followed the ur-viles at a canter into the turmoil of the Fall. At the last instant, she may have shouted Jeremiah's name. If so, she did not hear herself. The firestorm assault of the *caesure* had already stricken her deaf and dumb and blind.

Chapter Five:

Against Time

In an instant, formication became the world. It filled Linden's senses as though biting ants had burrowed into her flesh, chewing their way deeper and deeper towards the essential fibres – the thews of will and purpose, experience and memory – which bound her identity into a coherent whole. She felt that she was being torn from herself strand by strand; ripped to agony.

She would not have believed that she could endure such pain and remain conscious of it. Surely the human mind could call upon blankness or insanity to defend it? How else had Jeremiah kept himself alive; able to be loved? How else had Anele borne the cost of his bereavements?

Nevertheless she had no means to protect herself. No aspect of her being remained intact to ward her against the meticulous excruciation of the *caesure*. She had entered a demesne of flux, inchoate and chaotic; altogether devoid of Time's necessary sequences. Life could not exist outside the stricture of chronology. She remained alive only because she occupied no consecutive moments during which she could have ceased to be.

Instead of dying, she was caught in an eternity of incineration as though she had been struck by a bolt of lightning which would never end.

And yet—

Formication, devouring, was only one of the *caesure's* avatars. It had others. Her entire being had become a timeless shriek. Simultaneously, however, she stood alone in a realm of utter white and cold.

It had no features and no dimensions in any direction. It was simply gelid white multiplied to infinity, faceless as snow, demeaning as ice: vast and desolate, entirely uninhabitable: a heatless interstice between the possible moments of existence. The cold was an infinite fire. It would have peeled the skin from her bones if this moment could have modulated forward in time. But here there was no time, no movement, no possible modulation.

Only her solitary presence in that place defined it.

There her loneliness was complete. It seemed less bearable than pain. She could have wailed forever and gone unheard.

Nevertheless some form of movement was permitted to her. She could turn her head. Take steps as though she stood on solid ground. Gasp as freezing bit into her lungs. She could feel the cold stab like a *krill* through the bullet-hole in her shirt. Surely that implied a state of being in which one thing led to another? A condition in which her pain might be heeded?

But she saw only bitter white, and her steps took her nowhere, and her gasping puffed no vapour into the isolation.

And yet—

Formication tore her apart and white emptiness bereft her simultaneously. And simultaneously again, in still another avatar of the *caesure*'s evil, she found herself gazing out at a wasteland of shattered stone and rubble. She heard the lorn hiss of the wind punctuated by the rhythmic fall and retreat of surf; and although she did not look, she knew that behind her the seas crashed perpetually against a broken cliff.

The raw damaged rocks before her appeared to be chunks of time, discrete instances of the substance which should have made existence possible; woven the world whole. They were badly battered, torn from their natural union with each other by violence or lunacy. Yet they were intact in themselves; and each of them still implied its place in the former cliff.

Once they had formed a buttress against the sea, an assertion of structure and endurance in the teeth of the surging waves. Although they had been shattered, they retained their essential identity, their obdurate granite selves.

And among them moved sad gleaming creatures like misshapen children.

As the creatures squirmed over and among the stones, they emitted a sick emerald radiance; light the hue of acid and gangrene. They might have been the fouled progeny of the Illearth Stone, if that condensed bane had not been destroyed by wild magic millennia before her own time in the Land.

Nonetheless she recognised them. They were *skest*, and their touch was death: they were formed of a rank corrosive which devoured flesh. At one time, they had served the lurker of the Sarangrave, herding prey to the lurker's hungry tentacles. Without aid, she and Covenant and their Quest for the One Tree would not have survived their passage through Lifeswallower, the Great Swamp.

Now the acid-children appeared to serve her, occasionally placing tasteless food and brackish water in her mouth, offering their bitter warmth to her wind-chilled skin, and mewling for pity which she did not deign to provide.

At other times, they dissolved from sight, perhaps melting between the rocks in order to replenish her viands, or to restore their own lambent green lives. When they reappeared, they resumed their diligence.

Sharp formication: lost white and cold: a wasted vista of torn stone and *skest*. All simultaneous, overlapping around her and within her as though they occupied the same space at the same time. If the *caesure* took other forms as well, they lay beyond the reach of her senses.

Tearing ants and fiery cold slowed her perceptions. Gradually, however, she became aware that in the wasteland among the *skest* she was someone else: that she inhabited a flesh not her own; gazed about her through eyes which did not answer to her will; made choices over which she had no control. Although she wailed and grieved, she altered nothing, affected nothing. None of her pain or her yearning escaped the mind where she was imprisoned.

She should have died, consumed by fire ants and cold. She should have been driven mad by the loss of her friends and her purpose; of her son. She had brought them all to ruin and deserved no less. Yet she could not escape.

Instead she felt a hand which was not hers clench and rise abruptly towards her head. Through the eyes of her prison, she saw the body's right fist strike against its temple. Nerves that did not belong to her felt blood weep from an aggravated sore, dripping like tears down an abused cheek. Dissociated whimpers leaked from a mouth that had lost most of its teeth. When the throat swallowed, she tasted the seepage of bleeding gums.

At the same time, a flash of argent fire burst from the ring hanging against a sternum on its chain. Silver anguish blazed and coruscated among the stones, the rent instances, until one of them had been torn to confusion and dust.

Then, simultaneous with her other agonies, Linden understood that she was trapped in Joan's mind; that the woman who tortured this wasteland of rubble with the sea at her back, the woman whom the *skest* served, was Covenant's ex-wife. Charred by the Despiser's lightning, Joan had indeed found her way to the Land, as Linden had feared.

And here Joan herself had been found by *turiya* Herem.

Linden knew the Raver's touch intimately: she could not fail to recognise it. During her own translation to the Land, she had met *turiya* in Joan's mind. She had been afflicted with visions of pain and destruction which she still did not know how to bear. But there were no visions now. Even they required sequences and causality which did not exist within the *caesure*. Instead she felt only the Raver's insatiable abhorrence of life.

Goaded by *turiya* Herem's malice, Joan continued to strike herself, measuring out her despair against her temple. And with each blow, her power lashed out to create Falls, shattering coherent fragments of time until every moment with that fragment was torn apart.

Wild magic could have unmade the entire landscape in one towering gout of power; broken the Arch of Time instantly. Trapped in Joan's mind, however, Linden understood that she was incapable of such an act. Coercion and insanity fettered her pain: she could utter no cry louder or more sustained than this piecemeal devastation.

Gauged by the scale of Joan's blasts, the wasteland around her was immense. The Earth might endure and suffer for centuries before the damage became irrecoverable.

To Linden, that seemed still worse than formication and emptiness. Had she remained alive in any coherent sense, able to make choices and act, she might have striven to counteract Joan's suffering; to hold back the harm of Joan's self-loathing. But that possibility also Linden had lost.

Her plight surpassed endurance, yet she could not escape it. When the *skest* had fed her, Joan savaged another of the littered moments – and freezing white loneliness filled Linden's senses, featureless and forever unrelieved – and myriad upon myriad gnawing pincers bit her flesh to shreds – and she could not escape it.

Then she might have attempted deliberately to abandon consciousness and knowledge, hoping to find relief. More than once in the past, however, she had felt the same desire; the same impulse to abdicate herself. Watching her father's suicide. Tortured in every nerve by the ravages of the Sunbane. Imprisoned in Revelstone. Possessed by a Raver while Covenant surrendered to Lord Foul. In some sense, she had sacrificed volition when she had entered Covenant's mind in order to free him from the imposed stasis of the *Elohim*.

Now she could not forget what her desire for absence had cost her in the past. Or what it would cost Jeremiah here.

Nor could she forget that her companions suffered as well; that Anele and Liand, Stave, the Ramen and the Ranyhyn, even the ur-viles, had entered this demesne of horror at her behest.

And she remembered that no time had passed.

She was trapped in all moments and none simultaneously. She might spend eternity searching for an escape, and still nothing would have been lost. Nothing would be lost until the bounds of her identity frayed and failed; until she truly and entirely abandoned hope.

Until then, she could still think.

Both Anele and the ur-viles had once survived this same experience. She intended to do the same.

But they had merely entered a *caesure*, or been taken by it. And when the chaos had flung them forth again, by accident of Earthpower or design of lore, they had emerged thousands of years later. She needed more: not merely to survive and emerge, but to defy the inherent attributes of the Fall. Within itself, it was all moments and none, impossible confusion. Externally, however, it was a specific rock on the littoral of Joan's madness; a discrete force which moved from place to place through time. Despite its internal insanity, it was like a river: it ran in only one direction.

Linden needed to do more than simply endure until the *caesure* cast her onto its banks. She needed to swim against the current, drawing her companions with her.

She needed wild magic.

Thinking was a form of movement. And the avatar of freezing whiteness was the only one which allowed her the illusion of movement. Therefore she selected a direction at random – all directions were the same in that place – and began to walk. Then she began to run—

—seeking the door within herself which opened on white fire.

The cold attacked her lungs with relentless ferocity: she should have collapsed in bloody coughing. Yet she did not. No time had passed. She did not need air. Therefore the rending in her chest never changed. She could continue to run, no matter how vast her pain.

In that way, she clung to herself through formication and loss and blazing madness.

But she had lost the door. It lay hidden somewhere within her. Twice before, she had found her way there consciously, and it had opened to her hand. Now, however, the path which might have led towards it had been transformed to chaos. She was in too much pain to rediscover the route inwards.

In this excruciating tumult, only Joan had power.

Nevertheless Linden kept running. She believed now that if she stopped she would never become herself again.

Nothing changed. Nothing could change in a realm devoid of cause and sequence. Fire ants and utter loneliness ruled here. Yet Joan continued to feed occasionally, drink occasionally, and strike out; and Linden still ran, fleeing her own despair.

Then the lash of argent from Joan's ring caused a jagged chunk of granite to detonate in incandescence, momentarily dimming the emerald glow of the *skest* – and Linden stumbled to an unsteady halt in front of Anele.

He gazed straight at her as if he were aware of her presence, although he could not see her. They did not exist for each other here, and he was blind.

Yet his eyes were a milky gleam of Earthpower and intention.

She had not seen him appear: he was simply there, as he both had and had not been all along. Without his inherited strength, he would have remained beyond the reach of her perceptions. Yet here he was more real than she was. Unlike hers, his breath plumed in the frigid air.

In a gust of steam, he said as if he were invoking her, 'Please.'

Then he was gone.

He had never been there. He was a figment of her desperation, a reification of her loss.

Nevertheless he had saved her.

Please? Please *what*?

She knew the answer.

The richness of the Land was written in grass-stains on the fabric of her pants: a map like a metaphor for her own heart, both revealing and disguising the location of vitality and treasure. If she could not find the way to wild magic, she could make other use of such guidance.

She was a physician, a giver of care. Her response to pleading and need reached as deep as any pain. And Joan's violence, against herself as against time, was a form of supplication. In the only language which remained to her, Joan cried out her long madness, her self-loathing, and her hunger for release.

Linden's years in Berenford Memorial had taught her that the form in which damaged people repulsed aid expressed with terrible eloquence the nature of their wounds. In her own crippled way, Joan needed Linden's intervention as badly as Jeremiah did.

Linden could not contain her voiceless wailing; had no control over her agony. The cold white emptiness burned as fiercely as scoria, and she had no hands with which she might have reached out to Joan. But she was not helpless.

Despair and isolation and gnawing searched her to the root of her soul. She could do the same. If she had no power herself, she would use Joan's.

Riding the force of her own anguish and empathy, Linden tuned her heart to the pitch of Joan's madness.

It was possible: she knew that now. As if accidentally – as if accidents were possible for a soul in such pain – Joan had raised Anele like an echo inside Linden, a knell of death and life. With his appearance and his pleading to guide her, Linden could choose to participate in each new exertion of Joan's ring.

And she knew how to do so. Once before, briefly, she had been trapped in Joan's mind. She had met Joan's ghouls and spectres; Joan's tormentor. She could find her way because Lord Foul – perhaps unaware that he was aiding her – had allowed her to hear the true name of Joan's pain.

Knowing that name, Linden added Joan's agony to her own, and became stronger.

She had no means to impose her will on Joan; could do nothing to stop the remorseless blows which Joan struck against herself. Joan still lived in the Land, still inhabited time: Linden did not. But Linden had no desire for that form of power. Instead of trying to stay Joan's hand, she used her presence in Joan's mind, her comprehension of Joan's despair, to tap into the force of Joan's blasts.

With Joan's wedding ring, Linden summoned her companions.

She could find them. If they had not been severed from themselves by anguish, shredded by the cruelty of the *caesure*'s avatars, she could hope to touch them. They were mounted upon Ranyhyn, as she was. And they were warded in some fashion by ur-viles, whose lore encompassed enormous transgressions of Law.

If she still endured, surely they did also?

Through Esmer, the ur-viles had promised to aid her. The loremaster had mingled its strength with hers. It had sucked memories from Anele's wounded forearm. And Esmer had suggested that the creatures could communicate with the Ranyhyn.

Thus she may hope to be guided—

With wild magic which she siphoned from Joan's violence, Linden turned against the current of the *caesure* and called the ur-viles to join her.

They had made Anele remember—

At first, her borrowed and oblique argence accomplished nothing. In spite of its purity, it did not repulse the fire ants, or soften the cold, or ease Joan's desolation. Linden remained in her prison, tormented by ruin.

But then Joan made a whimpering sound which brought the *skest* scurrying to her side; and Linden rode the bitter whiteness on Hyn's back. The mare trotted through the cold confidently, as though she had always been there and knew exactly where she was going; as though she had waited only for Linden to rouse herself from some unexplained stupor.

The Ranyhyn's breath sent thick gusts of steam curling past her shoulders to Linden's face, filling Linden's nose with the scent of cropped grass; reinforcing the bond between them. Thus tangibly Hyn seemed to recreate the lovable world which should have existed instead of the Fall's chaos.

Oh, yes.

Lord Foul preached despair. But Linden Avery the Chosen was not helpless.

Again she called out to the Demondim-spawn.

Joan's whimpers became moaning; nascent sobs. The *skest* fretted around her, sensing distress which their compelled attentions could not relieve. But now her silver blasts were shot through with blackness and vitriol like streaks of poison in mortifying flesh.

Beside Linden, Anele sat on Hrama's back with an air of disdain, as though the *caesure*'s afflictions were trivial.

Opposite him, Liand huddled over Rhohm's neck like a man whose back had been broken. Linden feared to meet his eyes. She could not bear to see how badly he had been hurt.

Still dark acid insinuated itself throughout Joan's violence. The frigid waste-land appeared to break apart like floes of ice, calving smaller chunks of lone-liness; and through the cracks and breaches shone streams of midnight.

The gnawing insects of the *caesure*'s swirl became hornets again; vibrating augers loud for the taste of Linden's frailty. Stave held himself stolidly erect, impassive as stone. Under him, Hynyn stamped his massive hooves and tossed his head, imperiously demanding release, while the hornets attacked the encroaching obsidian and burst into flames.

Mahrtiir's gasping sounded like a splash of blood. Pain crippled his Cords.

Now Joan sobbed aloud, beating at her forehead repeatedly to invoke blasts and breakage. *Turiya* Herem multiplied her torment. Her *skest* blundered over the rocks, aimlessly dissolving and reforming themselves. For one brief moment in the tangible Land, her power had become darkness, and she could not expend her pain.

Ur-viles surrounded all of the riders. Their barking chant was palpable in Linden's ears, a solid thing rife with power, at once frantic and resolute, tattered and untorn. Fed by their lore, vitriol swelled in the *caesure*, defying the white void and the hornets; enforcing the distinction between chaos and identity.

Then Anele clenched his fist, shedding a thin drop of blood from the gouged flesh of his forearm. As one, the ur-viles seemed to redouble their vehemence.

Together the Ranyhyn lifted their heads. To the beat of the harsh chant, they began surging into the teeth of formication and cold; plunging against the current of severed time.

For a while which might have been an instant or an eon, Linden feared that the Demondim-spawn would falter. That the Ranyhyn would lose their way. That Joan's unanswerable madness would regain its efficacy. That the hornets howling into and through her flesh would devour the last of her sanity.

Then the migraine aura of the Fall parted on either side of her and she and her companions ran onto solid earth under a bright sky as though they had been spat out from the belly of Hell's own leviathan.

Chapter Six:

The Staff of Law

Convulsed with relief, Linden slumped from Hyn's back, stumbled to her hands and knees, then sprawled face-down on the stiff grass as though she sought to embrace the earth. At that moment, the ordinary solidity of the ground seemed infinitely precious; as healing as hurtloam.

She heard retching nearby. Without looking, she knew that Liand and both Cords had also collapsed from their mounts. She sensed them distinctly, in spite of the aftershocks, the residual excruciation, of the *caesure*. Sick with distress, Liand and one of the Cords – Bhapa – spewed bile and anguish onto the hardy grass.

The grass was tough because it needed to be. The soil in which it grew was thinly layered over old shale. It received comparatively little rain, and that moisture was soon leeched away. Nevertheless its sharp-edged blades grew thickly enough to soften the ground. When Linden breathed, she did not inhale dust, but rather the clenched dampness of roots and the prolonged heat of late summer.

She had been so cold— Now the warmth of the day was bliss, soothing her abraded senses.

Mahrtiir was in no better condition than the other Ramen, but he did not vomit. Instead he lowered himself carefully from the back of his mount and walked away from his companions, tottering as breakably as an old man. His stiffness told Linden that he was ashamed of his weakness and wanted to distance himself while he recovered.

Stave also dismounted, although he displayed none of the battered nausea which afflicted Liand and the Ramen. Rather he seemed essentially whole; proof against pain and distortion. Only his involuntary limp showed that he could be hurt.

'Chosen,' he said near Linden's head, 'are you able to move? We have survived the Fall. That feat deserves acknowledgement.' His tone admitted that he had not expected so much from her. 'I know not when we are, but where is plain. Arise and gaze about you.'

She did not lift her head: the sun's comfort held her. Ignoring the Master, she continued to cast her percipience around her, verifying in the most tangible way possible that she was still alive – and intact.

Only Anele remained mounted, apparently studying his surroundings blindly. She could not tell whether he recognised what he saw.

As for the great horses, they gave no sign that they had just endured an extraordinary ordeal. Hrama seemed content to stand still, providing a safe seat for Anele. The other Ranyhyn had scattered slightly, giving each other room to crop the dry grass. Occasionally one or another of them tasted the air as if searching for the scent of water.

In the background of Linden's awareness, the ur-viles barked quietly among themselves. They may have been discussing the situation, or debating what should be done now. Like Stave, they did not appear to have suffered in the Fall, although their weariness was obvious.

But the Fall was gone, leaving no evidence of its passage.

Linden and her companions had been marooned.

'Chosen?' Stave asked more insistently. 'It is not well to delay. If we have indeed entered the past of the Land, then we must be wary that we do not alter it in some way, endangering the Arch of Time. We are neither seers nor oracles. Our actions may have consequences which we cannot foresee.'

Still she did not rise to answer him. As she tested her circumstances, she caught a hint – the merest whiff – of *wrongness*.

It did not arise from the air, which held only the rising heat of a summer morning. The Ranyhyn certainly had no *wrong* in them. Nor did her companions, in spite of their lingering hurts. And the ur-viles, like Stave, exceeded her evaluation.

The suggestion of *wrongness*, of imposed and unnatural harm, seemed to arise from the earth under her.

And it was familiar—

Abruptly she surged up onto her hands and knees; pressed her fingers through the grass to touch the dirt. 'Here,' she told Stave softly, almost whispering. 'Put your hands here. Tell me what you feel.'

A slight frown knotted the Master's brows as he knelt in front of her and eased his fingers into the grass.

'Linden?' croaked Liand. Hunching over his stomach as if it were full of broken glass, he crawled weakly towards her. 'What is amiss?'

But she was concentrating too hard to speak; and Stave did not reply.

Uncertainly Liand worked his hands into the grass as well, trying to feel what they felt.

Yes, Linden thought as she probed the ground. Familiar. And *wrong*. Its touch evoked a kind of visceral memory; a recall too deeply buried for consciousness and too disturbing to be forgotten.

It breathed along her nerves, suggesting echoes of rain and pestilence; of fearsome deserts and terrible fecundity.

Then Liand gasped sharply and snatched back his hands. 'Heaven and Earth!' he panted. 'That is *evil*. A great wrong has been done here.' Wrapping his arms around his stomach, he struggled to contain his nausea.

Stave met Linden's gaze and nodded in confirmation.

At last, she lifted her hands from the grass. 'Not just here,' she said harshly. 'Everywhere in the Land.' Everywhere west of Landsdrop and Mount Thunder. 'That's the Sunbane.'

Her senses had found traces of Lord Foul's assault upon Law, persistent and vile.

'Indeed,' Stave agreed without inflection. 'The *Haruchai* have not forgotten it. Yet already in this time it is long past.'

She knew that he was right. Any more recent atrocity would have left its effect closer to the surface. Nevertheless her dire recollections of the Sunbane hit her hard. At its height, it had transformed every living and lovely aspect of the Land into a victim of torture; an instance of unforgivable hurt.

'But it's fresh enough to feel,' she muttered. Then she swallowed her past. More quietly, she asked, 'How long ago do you think it was?'

Everything depended upon that. If the ur-viles had misread Anele's memories – or if the Ranyhyn had erred—

Stave considered the question. 'I cannot speak with certainty. Ten score years, perhaps more. Not more than fifteen.' Then he shrugged. 'So I estimate.'

Between two and three hundred years? Surely that was long enough—? Surely Linden and her companions had not arrived before Anele lost the Staff?

She trusted Stave's perceptions; but still her nerves needed reassurance. Even this distant reminder of the Sunbane afflicted her with dread. Raising her head, she flicked a quick glance towards the sun.

It arced across a blue sky already flattened, deprived by depth, by heat and haze. Around it, high clouds made noncommittal shapes against the azure. But it showed no sign of the disturbing corona which had defined the effects of the Banefire.

Nor did the sky betray any indication of Kevin's Dirt. Here, at least, her health-sense would not be taken from her.

Her stomach still squirmed on the brink of rebellion, but at last she felt strong enough to ignore it. Gathering her courage, she rose to her feet to look around her.

Anele drew her gaze. He sat loosely on Hrama's back, head bowed and arms dangling, as if he had fallen asleep. In that posture, the angle of the light across his shoulders caught at the raindrops which remained on his cloak, transforming them into a net of pearls; a web woven of reflections and prophecy.

And behind him mountains piled into the heavens, holding up their granite heads in defiance or refusal. The foothills of the range were no more than a league distant.

Percipience and the position of the sun told her that she was facing south. Therefore these mountains were part of the Southron Range. Off to her left, a spur of peaks jutted past her northwards: to her right, the cliffs and peaks retreated into the southwest. However, she recognised none of the vistas.

She had entered a region of time and place where she had never been before.

Stave would tell her what he knew, if she asked him; but she did not. Instead she set the question aside temporarily. Other concerns compelled her attention.

Clenching her teeth against the aftereffects of the Fall, she turned to her companions.

Stave and Anele were essentially well, but the Ramen and Liand were another matter. Of them all, only the Manethrall had been able to stand; and he could no longer do so. Now he sat with his back to his companions a short distance away, hugging himself and rocking back and forth like a battered child.

Pahni sprawled where she had first fallen, too shocked to move. Bhapa had crawled a few paces from his vomit: he lay curled into a ball around the memory of his pain. And Liand was in little better condition. His momentary contact with the Sunbane's residue had cost him the last of his endurance. He had collapsed supine with his hands over his face, panting softly.

The fact that Linden could remain upright testified to the dark lore and blood of the ur-viles. Their power had protected her from the worst of the *caesure*.

Remembering that the loremaster had cut her, she glanced down at her hand and saw that the small wound had already closed. No, more than that: it had sealed completely, leaving behind nothing more than a faint scar to mark what the ur-viles had done for her.

At one time, they had been the bitter enemies of the Land. Now their desire to serve her was beyond question.

Unfortunately her companions had not received the same eldritch gift.

Apart from Stave and Anele, they were in no condition to go on. They needed rest, perhaps hours of it. And *aliantha*, if she could find any – and if they could force themselves to swallow it.

Hurtloam would restore them, of course. Or the Staff of Law. In this time and place, she might as well have asked for Covenant's resurrection.

But the ur-viles might be able to provide *vitrim*. If they had not exhausted themselves—

Even after all that they had done for her, she felt strangely reluctant to approach them; timid in the face of their bestial forms and their black past. Nevertheless she walked cautiously towards the loremaster.

The creatures stopped their low barking as she approached. They turned their faces towards her, sniffing wetly. Their ears twitched. The thin slits of their mouths looked as cruel as cuts.

A few paces from the loremaster, she halted. Staring at the creature's forehead to avoid the sight of its wide nostrils, she said uncomfortably, 'I hate doing this. It feels disrespectful. I can ask you for help, and you can't even tell me how to thank you. You certainly can't ask *me* for anything. And you've already done so much—'

Then she admitted, 'But Stave is right. Everything we do here is dangerous. And the longer we stay, the more dangerous it becomes. We should get started, but we can't. Liand and the Ramen are too sick to ride.'

In response, the loremaster made a gesture that she could not interpret. Her health-sense told her nothing except that the creature was alien to her; beyond explication.

Then, however, the loremaster wove its hands as though in invocation; muttered a few guttural sounds which seemed to hang in the air, telic and oddly resonant. Almost at once, an iron bowl as black as obsidian took form in its palms, apparently transubstantiated from within the creature's flesh.

The bowl held a fluid that gave off the musty aroma of *vitrim*.

Because she was touched and did not know how else to express her gratitude, Linden sank to her knees in order to accept the bowl from the loremaster's hands.

The ur-viles spoke in unison, barking a response which told her nothing. The raw sound could have been a curse or a paean – or a warning.

Again they had given her what she needed. Their dark liquid sang to her senses of concentrated restoration. Struggling unsteadily to her feet, she carried the bowl to the nearest of her companions, the Manethrall, and offered it to his lips.

Mahrtiir did not hesitate. His need was great; and his discernment was as keen as Linden's. Accepting the *vitrim*, he sipped it carefully.

Its effect was swift. Between one heartbeat and the next, new strength burgeoned in him. The pain was swept from his muscles, and his nausea faded. He seemed to rise up within himself, although he remained seated, hardly able to credit his own recovery.

In a voice still husky with strain, he urged Linden, 'Aid the Cords. And the Stonedownor.'

He did not need to add, And yourself.

She ached for some of the roborant. The Fall's effects clung to her still, aggravating old memories of the Sunbane and loss. But her companions took precedence.

From Mahrtiir, she went to kneel beside Pahni.

The young woman could not raise her head. The bile in her guts threatened to overflow at any moment; and her muscles hung slack along her bones, stretched past exhaustion. But Stave joined Linden then, supporting Pahni so that Sahah's cousin could take a mouthful of *vitrim*.

When Pahni had tasted the dusky fluid, Linden and Stave turned to assist Bhapa.

By then Liand had seen what was happening. Still cradling his aggrieved stomach, he crept to the older Cord's side. He had his own memories of *vitrim*.

Soon both he and Bhapa were on their feet, with Pahni beside them. They did not stand easily, but Linden saw that their recovery would not take long. Doubtless they would be ready to ride before she was.

Finally she allowed herself to drink from the bowl.

As before, the heavy liquid had a neglected flavour, as if it had been left too long in a lightless room, exposed to dust and stagnation. Yet she swallowed it gladly; and in moments, the *caesure*'s brutality lost its hold on her, dropping from her shoulders like a shed cloak. The *vitrim* seemed to expand the boundaries of her mortality. When she returned the bowl to the loremaster, her steps no longer wavered and her bow of thanks was as deep as an obeisance.

Then at last she turned to Stave; to the only member of her company who may have wished her to fail. She could no longer postpone the larger concerns of her situation.

She had too many fears. She might still be days away from Anele's lost cave. The Staff of Law may have been found and moved – and used – since Anele's departure. She may not have arrived at the right time to retrieve it. And any significant alteration of the past might violate the integrity of time.

She believed that the Law of Time was sturdy enough to withstand an occasional shock. How else had it endured the affront of Joan's attacks? And she believed as well that the mere existence of the Staff would have a sustaining influence on all Law. Surely she could search for it without inflicting any irreparable harm?

Still she wanted some form of reassurance.

Covenant had told her, *You need the Staff of Law*. But he had also said, *Just be wary of me. Remember that I'm dead.*

And somewhere millennia from now an *Elohim* wandered the Earth, warning people to *Beware the halfhand.*

'All right,' she said to the Master. 'I'm ready now. You said you know where we are?'

He nodded. 'Indeed. We stand among the South Plains. The Southron Range rises before us. The mountains to the east form the western bound of the Mithil Valley. Many leagues to the west lies Doom's Retreat. And there' – he pointed across the foothills towards the curving line of scarps and slopes where the spur met the southwestward sweep of the Range – 'we will be able to ascend towards the region where I judge that the old man once made his home.'

Clearly *caesures* traversed distance as well as time: Linden had seen them move. Indeed, she was fortunate that the Fall had not carried her further from her goal during the intervening centuries.

Studying the mountains, she asked, 'How far do you think we have to go?'

Stave glanced at the sun. 'We will be among the heights before midday. There, however, the way may become too difficult for riding. Beyond that—' He shrugged.

Linden understood him: he did not know the location of Anele's cave. But surely it would be somewhere accessible? While Ramen and ur-viles battled *kresh* in the rift, Anele had said that his dwelling was *not so distant from Mithil Stonedown that I could not hasten to the Land's aid at need, but far enough to attain the freedom from astonishment which my spirit craved.*

'Good enough,' she murmured half to herself. 'We'll ride as far as we can. Then we'll figure out what to do next.'

As she turned towards Hyn, she slipped off her cloak. Warmed by the summer sun and *vitrim*, she no longer needed the heavy wool. At once, Liand accepted it from her. When he had removed his own as well, he went to Hrama and tugged the cloak from Anele's back. Then he packed the three garments away among his supplies.

At the same time, Mahrtiir approached Linden with Bhapa and Pahni. The usual fierceness of his mien was complicated by chagrin, and when he spoke his voice held a note of defensive belligerence.

'Ringthane,' he rasped, 'we are shamed by our weakness. It ill becomes us.' Sharply he promised, 'We will not again be overcome.'

Both Bhapa and Pahni nodded, but without his combative assurance. Already the prospect of their next encounter with a *caesure* seemed to cast shadows in their eyes.

'We know our peril now,' the Manethrall continued, 'and are forewarned. When next we dare a Fall, we will provide for our own endurance.'

He did not say how he proposed to protect himself and his Cords.

'Don't be so hard on yourself,' Linden sighed. 'I'm not worried about you.' In fact, the thought of entering another Fall made her entire being flinch. And she had no more patience for people who judged themselves by inhumane standards. She did too much of that herself. 'We aren't Ranyhyn. We don't have their gift for time.'

Mahrtiir accepted her reply with a bow, but his manner remained defiant.

Linden glanced around; found the ur-viles ready and the Ranyhyn waiting. It was time to go.

With Liand's help, she gained Hyn's back. Stave and the Stonedownor placed themselves on either side of her. After they had prostrated themselves before the Ranyhyn once more, the Ramen brought up the rear of the small company, herding Anele ahead of them. This time, however, the ur-viles did not girdle the riders. Instead they formed a loose wedge off to one side, dropping to all fours for speed.

As Linden touched Hyn's flanks with her heels, all of the Ranyhyn sprang into a gallop southwards, pounding the thin grass as fast as the Demondim-spawn could run.

Stave had gauged the distance accurately. More swiftly than Linden had anticipated, the riders left the plains behind and surged up the first slopes of the foothills. And here the terrain had been softened by long ages of wind and rain, heat and cold. The Ranyhyn would be able to sustain their pace for a while yet. If the ur-viles did not falter, the company might be high among the mountains by noon.

Nevertheless a sense of trepidation grew in Linden as the company ascended the hillsides. If she ever hoped to return to her proper present, she would have to rend time with her own hands. She dreaded that prospect.

After a while, however, Anele distracted her. As the heat of the plains gave way to the sharper, thinner exhalation of the peaks, she noticed a shift in his emanations. His earlier passivity was gone. Instead he radiated urgency, and he rode leaning forward with a look of frenzy in his milky eyes.

But he had not suddenly become sane: that was obvious. Rather his madness had resolved into focus. Perhaps he recognised his surroundings. He was being driven now by the same obsession which had impelled him to return to his former home over and over across the decades, searching uselessly for his lost inheritance.

At the same time, another change demanded her attention. Although the ur-viles continued to scramble doggedly upwards, they were growing restive. Occasionally at first, then more and more often, one or another of them paused to taste the air, falling behind the other creatures, and barking insistently before they resumed their haste. As a result, the whole wedge lost ground.

Did they scent danger? Foes? Linden had no way of knowing. But the possibilities, the potential hazards, left her dry-mouthed and winded, as though the air were becoming too thin to breathe.

Surely it was impossible that Lord Foul might oppose her here? If her senses had not misled her, and Stave's perceptions were accurate, the Despiser's defeat at Covenant's hands had taken place less than three hundred years ago. And Foul had been *thoroughly* defeated. The beaten being that remained unextinguished in this time could hardly threaten her.

Yet the ur-viles were troubled, for no apparent reason. And Lord Foul was not Linden's only enemy. *Elohim* wandered the Earth at will. For all she knew, they could traverse time as well, or manipulate *caesures*. And the strange dictates of their Würd were incomprehensible to her.

If Kastenessen had indeed broken free of his Appointed prison; if his bonds were the Durance of which Anele had spoken—

In addition, the Earth might hold other banes as fearsome as the Illearth Stone. Somewhere *kresh* lived and multiplied. More than once, Anele had referred to *skurj*. And Linden feared that Roger Covenant had accompanied his mother to the Land. Because he had power over Joan, he might be able to manipulate her use of wild magic.

Anele's headlong urgency might lead the company into an ambush—

Finally Linden called over the pounding din of hooves, 'Stave! The ur-viles. Something is wrong!'

The Master nodded without a glance at the straggling wedge. 'They have lore which even the Old Lords could not equal.' Then he added, 'I discern no peril.'

Linden looked over her shoulder at Mahrtiir. Glowering, the Manethrall shrugged: he had no answer.

A moment later, the creatures began to slacken their pace. They had apparently reached an agreement. As the Ranyhyn crossed a low hollow between the hillsides with cliffs soaring ahead of them, the Demondim-spawn halted altogether. At once, they gathered around their loremaster, bickering like a pack of wild dogs.

Damn it. Linden tried to slow Hyn; and in an instant, all of the Ranyhyn responded together, turning in a curve as they reduced their strides.

When he understood what was happening, Anele wailed, 'No!' But Hrama ignored his protest, stamping to a standstill with the other Ranyhyn.

In a fury, the old man flung himself from Hrama's back. As soon as he gained his feet, he began to run.

Above him, a narrow ravine marked by a dry streambed separated the cliffs. Shallow at first, it grew deeper as it cut into the hills; and after a few hundred paces, it disappeared around a bulge in its eastern wall. With surprising speed, Anele headed for the ravine, sure of his destination and determined to reach it. Earthpower and intensity made him preternaturally fleet.

Swearing again under her breath, Linden wheeled towards Mahrtiir. 'You'd better go after him,' she panted. 'Don't try to stop him. Just don't lose him. We'll catch up with you when we find out what's bothering the ur-viles.'

The Manethrall nodded his acquiescence. Calling Pahni and Bhapa with him, he sent his Ranyhyn cantering after Anele.

Of his own accord, Hrama joined them. Like the Ramen, the shaggy pinto appeared to respect Linden's wishes.

Temporarily relieved for the old man, she turned her attention to the Demondim-spawn. 'What's going on?' she asked rhetorically. 'Are we in danger? What do they expect us to do?'

But Liand knew no more than she did, and Stave did not respond. The air held no threats. It smelled only of summer and wildflowers, warmed granite and shale, and the slow, distant trickling of melted ice. The breeze carried nothing that might have warned her.

Impelled by uncertainty, she asked the loremaster, 'What should we do? Do you need us here? Can I help you? You understand me, but I don't know what you want.'

But the creatures ignored her while they continued their harsh debate. Some of them had produced short black daggers with blades like forged magma, seething redly. Others made abrupt, intricate gestures as if they were weaving expostulations. Even the loremaster paid no heed to Linden's appeal.

For a moment, she glared at them with frustration beating like anger in her temples and nameless fears aching in her chest. Then she muttered a curse and turned Hyn away.

'Come on,' she told Liand and Stave. 'If they want us here, they can figure out some way to stop us. Otherwise we're going with Anele.'

At once, Hynyn and Rhohm joined Hyn; and in unison the three Ranyhyn stretched their strides to pursue their companions.

The others had already passed out of sight behind the bulge in the ravine. When Linden, Stave, and Liand reached that point, however, and followed the ascending curve of the streambed beyond it, they spotted Bhapa some distance ahead of them, waiting near a break in the east wall. As they approached, the Cord led them up into the break and darkness.

Its sheer sides, rugged and uncompromising, rose above them. Even at noon, the sun's light did not reach the floor of the break. But the surface had been softened by millennia of weather and run-off. It posed no threat to the footing of the Ranyhyn. They managed the slope at a trot.

Silt and moss swallowed the sounds of their passage. They followed the crooked path unheralded and unforewarned.

Overhead, an arch of granite spanned the walls like a flying buttress. Beyond it, the last twist of the break revealed sunshine splashed across a slow hillside covered with mountain grasses and wildflowers. When Linden and her companions emerged, they found their mounts wading through rich swaths of eglantine, cornflowers, blue columbine and paintbrush as stark as blood.

There they joined Pahni. She greeted them with a bow, but did not speak. Instead she pointed beyond her towards a wide, low basin surrounded on the east, south and west by grey cliffs and grass-dappled mountainsides.

When she followed Pahni's gesture, Linden spotted Anele halfway across the bottom of the basin, with Mahrtiir mounted beside him and Hrama trailing nearby.

The old man no longer moved so swiftly. Even at this distance, his weariness was plain. Yet he stumbled onwards, half falling from stride to stride, his urgency undiminished.

He may have been unaware of Mahrtiir's presence, and Hrama's.

Mahrtiir could have stopped him, perhaps even placed him on Hrama's back. But the Manethrall seemed content to let Anele labour along on foot, presumably so that he would not run too far ahead of Linden and her companions.

The old man was heading towards the southeastern edge of the basin, where a high pile of boulders sprawled against the base of the mountain. Long ago, monolithic slabs and menhirs must have fallen from the cliffs and broken there. Watching him, she guessed that his former home lay hidden among those massive, ragged stones.

He has no friend—

If so, he had chosen a lovely spot for his escape from astonishment. The bluff grandeur of the surrounding peaks contrasted dramatically with the profuse fertility of the basin. And it had plenty of water. Several streams tumbled down from the heights, catching the sunlight in a cascade of sparkles, and gathered to form a lively creek which babbled and ran towards the south and east. Anele could have grown food here easily. And in the heavy winters, he could have warmed himself with wood fires and Earthpower.

To Linden's eyes, the whole basin seemed to show the benignant influence of the Staff of Law. Even unused, the Staff's very existence sustained and promoted the natural Law, the essential structures and vitality, of the Land. She herself had formed it for that purpose. In Andelain, she had finally learned to love the Land, and with all her heart she had yearned to preserve and defend its beauty.

The vista ahead of her had the look of a place which had been adored.

Nevertheless an inarticulate foreboding troubled her. The high clouds cast vague shadows across the wildflowers, transforming them from vividness to uncertainty and back again; shedding mute premonitions across the basin. And in the distance, Anele appeared to flounder, hindered by recollections of failure and loss. Suddenly she felt reluctant to follow him. Instead of sending Hyn down into the basin, she remained where she was.

Beside her, Liand leaned forward as if he were eager to discover the future. Both Pahni and Bhapa studied her with puzzlement in their eyes, confused by her hesitation. But she turned from them to Stave, half consciously seeking to postpone the moment when she would learn whether she herself would fail or succeed; whether she had endangered the Arch of Time for nothing.

'So tell me,' she began awkwardly. 'Why did you change your mind?'

She meant, What am I going to do if the Staff isn't there? But she could not ask that question: it searched her too deeply. She would not have trusted anyone except Covenant to hear her without reproach or dismay.

Stave met her gaze, raising an eyebrow in enquiry.

Linden wanted to look away, but she did not. 'You were planning to leave. You wanted to warn the Masters. God knows you have plenty to tell them. But then you changed your mind.' After the horserite. 'I can't help wondering why.'

Stave held her troubled stare. 'Chosen,' he replied, 'I have elected to accompany you. I will defend you with my life. But I will not account for my choices. I await the proper time and place.

'When it is meet to do so, I will speak of what is in my heart.'

He had promised her a reckoning—

In this time, her need for the Staff was absolute. She could not return to her proper present without entering another Fall. In order to do so, she would first have to create it with wild magic. But whenever she attempted to wield Covenant's ring, its power might scale out of control. In that eventuality, that likely danger, only Law could preserve the Arch.

By entering Esmer's *caesure*, she had created a situation in which any failure or misstep would bring about Lord Foul's victory.

'One matter, however,' Stave added after a moment, 'I will explain, for I deem that you are unaware of it.

'We partook of the horserite together, you and I, but we did not share the same vision. That which the Ranyhyn revealed to you, they did not impart to me. Nor did they grant to you that which they wished me to see and understand.'

Linden stared at him. She had assumed that they had participated in the same memories, the same prophecies; that he had seen the same dangers. And she had felt that he had finally become her friend, in spite or because of those dangers.

But she was wrong. The Ranyhyn had given him other insights, other knowledge. He had accompanied her for reasons which he kept from her.

As if he knew what disturbed her, he continued, 'They made plain to me that I must not be parted from you. Therefore I will remain your companion until I have discovered or devised an opportunity to consult the will of my people.'

Because she was afraid, she wanted to say something sarcastic; but she refrained. She recognised that he had given her as much reassurance as he could. For the present, at least, she could rely on him.

With that she had to be content.

While she gnawed on her doubts, Liand touched her arm; asked for her attention. 'Linden,' he said tentatively, 'Anele and the Manethrall proceed while we delay. Will they not gain the location of this Staff before us? And if they do, is it wise for Anele to hold the Staff? You have explained that any use of such power in this time is perilous.'

Linden sighed to herself. He was right. Hell, even Stave was right. This was not the time or the place—

Nodding to the Stonedownor, she touched Hyn's sides with her heels; and immediately the mare started down into the basin at a swift canter.

Stave and Liand joined her. Hynyn and Rhohm stretched their legs with Hyn's, matching the mare's strides; and the Cords followed a heartbeat behind them. Gathering speed as they went, Linden and her companions followed Anele and Mahrtiir.

Among the wildflowers, butterflies scattered before the swift passage of the Ranyhyn and occasional bees hummed away in alarm; but she had no attention to spare for them. Liand's words had crystallised her fears into shapes as sharp as knives.

Ahead of her, Anele's stamina was flagging, and Mahrtiir did nothing to hasten him. But they had gained ground while Linden spoke with Stave. Already they were nearing the rocks. Before she could overtake the old man, he found his path among the boulders and stumbled out of sight.

At the edge of the piled monoliths, Mahrtiir dismounted, leaving the horses behind in order to accompany Anele.

Moments seemed to stretch out ahead of Linden, longer than the strides of the Ranyhyn. Despite the breeze of their passage, the air between the mountains felt viscid and still; cloying. Yet the great horses were wonderfully swift. If she had not hesitated earlier, she might have caught up with Anele before he reached his goal.

Then finally the riders thudded to a halt beside Hrama and Mahrtiir's mount. In a rush, Linden slipped from Hyn's back; stumbled running towards the rocks.

There, however, she faltered: she could not find Anele's path. Every gap and cranny between the boulders looked the same to her, truncated and depthless, leading nowhere. But Stave sprang ahead of her. His sight was keener than hers and he must have identified the place where Anele had entered the pile.

Past a leaning slab of granite which appeared to rest squarely against still larger stones, he found a gap like a crevice just wide enough to admit him. Without hesitation, he moved into it.

'Follow the Bloodguard, Ringthane,' Bhapa offered encouragingly. 'The Manethrall has marked the path.'

Linden saw no indications among the boulders; but she believed the Cord implicitly – and did not doubt Stave's instincts. Hurrying, she began to make her way between the stones.

His passage through the *caesure* had not restored Anele's mind. If he found the Staff, he might be made whole; or he might lose himself completely.

Deep behind the slab, another gap appeared, a crooked aisle between monoliths propped against each other. Only shafts and streaks of sunlight penetrated the pile, leaving much of the way shrouded in gloom. Beyond Stave's dark shoulders, however, Linden saw flickering hints of light, dancing flames. And when she reached the end of the aisle, she found herself in the mouth of a cave like an entombed tunnel. The rockfall had concealed the entrance without burying it.

Mahrtiir met her there, holding a torch that burned hotly, dried almost to tinder by age. The rough wood must have hurt his scorched palms, but he ignored the pain.

Linden ran a few steps to catch at Stave's arm, hold him back. Then she panted to Mahrtiir, 'Anele—?'

'He goes ahead,' answered the Manethrall. 'This was once a dwelling, though many years have passed since it served that purpose. When I discovered torchwood, I returned to assist you. He will not be lost. The signs of his passing' – Mahrtiir indicated the disturbed dirt of the floor – 'will guide us.'

Still gripping Stave's arm, Linden pushed the Raman ahead of her. As they strode down the throat of the cave, she asked, 'How big is this place?'

'I know not, Ringthane,' Mahrtiir replied. 'Mayhap it extends for leagues. But the place of habitation is near.' He hesitated briefly, then added, 'If the old man once dwelt here, he abandoned it long ago. However, others have also entered.'

Linden's heart thudded. 'Others—?'

'Time and dust have obscured the marks of their feet,' Mahrtiir told her. The light of his torch cast grotesque shadows across his features. 'I cannot determine their kind or number. Nor am I able to declare when they entered and departed. I am certain only that they have preceded us by years or decades.'

Oh, God. Suddenly the darkness ahead of her seemed crowded with catastrophes. Memories of the ordeal of the Fall mocked her as she started forward again.

Then the gullet of the cave opened into a larger space like a chamber in the rock. By the unsteady torchlight, Linden saw the signs of habitation: they seemed to flicker in and out of existence as the flames gusted and leaned.

A neat pile that might once have been bedding lay against one wall. Even in the cave's dry atmosphere, however, much of the fabric of the blankets and the stuffing of the mattress had rotted away. The rest had been gnawed apart by vermin.

Opposite it stood a trestle table and three-legged stool, both precariously balanced on legs as brittle as twigs. Another, smaller table held clay urns and amphorae for storage, most of which were still intact, although one amphora had slumped to mud, dissolved from within by its contents, and an urn had cracked open, spilling husks of grain like dust across the table.

Near the bed, Linden saw the remains of a large wicker basket which may once have held clothing, but which now contained only nests for mice. A scattering of faggots obviously intended as torches lay on the floor. From them, Pahni and Bhapa took sticks and lit them at Mahrtiir's torch, adding their light to his.

As they did so, threatening shadows writhed and gibbered across the ceiling.

Lastly Linden noticed a tidy stone hearth designed as much for warmth as for cooking. At one time, its fires had spread soot up the wall behind it; but now most of the black had flaked away, leaving behind bare packed dirt and stone.

Nothing else remained to indicate that Anele, son of Sunder and Hollian, and inheritor of the Staff of Law, had ever lived here.

He was not in the chamber, but Linden knew where he had gone. There was only one other egress, a small opening like a portal in the wall near the hearth. And from it came small sounds which she had heard too often and knew too well: the bereft, inarticulate whimpering of the old man's desolation.

The opening gave access to another cave, an unassuming space, hardly more than a niche or closet in the heart of the mountain. There Anele sprawled on the floor. Too broken even to weep, he slowly raised and then dropped his head over and over again, beating his forehead bloody against the stone. With each lift of his head, he moaned softly. But when he let it fall, the only sound was the sodden thump of his damp flesh hitting the floor.

Linden felt no surprise at all to see that the Staff of Law was gone. Yet she believed that it had once been there; and for a moment she felt herself transported out of tangible reality into a demesne of pure and irreducible woe.

Chapter Seven:

Aid and Betrayal

Linden did not know how to contain her dismay.

Somewhere hundreds of leagues and thousands of years away from her, her son was being tortured. Mere hours ago, she had subjected all of her companions to the exquisite agonies of a *caesure*. And the Staff of Law was gone.

She desired nothing except to save Jeremiah and defend the Land; but she had gained only an empty cave and despair.

On some level, she had believed, trusted, *assumed* that she would find the Staff here. Millennia from now, when Anele searched his abandoned home, the Staff would be gone. Hardly conscious of what she was doing, she had chosen to think that the Staff would be gone because she herself had taken it; that Anele's searching would fail because her venture into the past had succeeded.

She had blinded herself to other possibilities—

In her imagination, she heard Lord Foul laughing like the destruction of stones. When he had led her to hurtloam, he had set her on the path to this place. Without that healing, she would not have been able to elude the Masters long enough to hear Anele's tale. She would not have known who the old man was, or how he had lost the Staff; would never have imagined violating Time in this way.

With Covenant's ring, she was a danger to the Despiser; but he had effectively neutralised her by enabling her to do what she had done.

Anele still lay on the floor, stigmatising the packed dirt and rock with his spilled blood. Liand stared at him in shock, as though the depth of the old man's loss exceeded comprehension. Chagrin trapped the Ramen within the light of their torches, so that their features appeared to waver and blur as the flames gusted. And Stave scowled at the absence of the Staff as if his anger at Linden's folly had overcome his dispassion.

She did not know how to bear it. It was intolerable. Therefore she refused to accept it.

Her companions deserved a better outcome.

'All right,' she said. 'This is bad.' Her voice shook like the torchlight; like flames consuming wood which had dried for decades. 'But it could be worse. We aren't beaten yet.'

The Cords gaped at her. Even Mahrtiir, the eager fighter, stared as though she had begun to froth at the mouth. Liand could find no words or air adequate to his shock.

Because she trusted the Stonedownor, Linden held up her hand as if to refuse his unspoken appeal. 'Don't say it. Don't say anything at all.' Then she swept her arm to include all of her companions. 'None of you.' They could have broken her heart. 'Don't interrupt me. I need to think.'

But Anele continued pounding his head on the floor. In desperation, Linden snapped, 'Anele, God *damn* it—!' Then she whipped a look towards Liand. 'For pity's sake, *stop* him. He shouldn't punish himself like this.'

The young man heard her: he could still recognise pain and feel compassion. Shaking off his consternation, he hastened to Anele's side. With Pahni's help, he turned the old man over. Then he wrapped his strong arms around Anele's grief, cradling it against his chest.

At once, Linden turned on Stave.

'You,' she said like an accusation, although she blamed no one but herself. 'The Masters. The *Haruchai*. You remember everything.' She had reason to wonder what he might have withheld. 'So tell me this.

'What's been going on here since Anele disappeared with the Staff? I mean in this time. This region, this part of the South Plains. Have there been any battles? Any signs of power? Strange fertility, unnatural wastes? Unexplained enemies? Dangerous occurrences of any kind?'

Stave tried to respond, but she rushed on. 'What about the people who live here? What are their lives like? How have they recovered from the Sunbane? What—?'

'Chosen,' the Master interrupted sternly. 'Your question is plain. Permit me to reply.'

With an effort, Linden restrained herself. Chewing on her lower lip, she waited for his answer.

'It is sooth,' he said more quietly, 'that we remember much. Yet there are matters which you must understand.

'First, the *Haruchai* did not lightly undertake to become the Masters of the Land. Until the Staff of Law was lost, the Land had no need of such care. Even then, centuries passed before the decision was made, for we are not hasty in these things. And as new Masters we did not extend our bourn to encompass all the upper Land until centuries more had passed.

'Between the time of your own knowledge and the time in which we now stand, few *Haruchai* sojourned so far into the South Plains. To Mithil Stonedown my people rode, that they might honour Sunder and Hollian. And later, when the loss of the Staff had become certain, they aided in searching for it. But they conceived that if the Staff had been removed towards Doom's Retreat, they would have caught some glimpse of its presence or its use. Therefore they believed that its fate lay among the heights of the Southron Range, where no quest would discover it.'

Stave seemed to consider how much he should reveal. Then he said, 'But there is a second reason why the *Haruchai* made no thorough search in this region. Since the time of the Old Lords, the South Plains to the west of the Mithil River and the south of the Black have been little inhabited. The soil is ill-nourished and knows scant rain. The folk of the Land have found no welcome there.'

Mahrtiir nodded. Apparently the long tales of the Ramen confirmed the Master's assertion.

'In the time of Berek Heartthew,' Stave went on, 'before he became the first of the Old Lords, much of his vast war against Corruption and the servants of evil was waged in the South Plains. The violence of that war blighted the earth, leaving too much harm to encourage human life.'

The *Haruchai* held Linden's urgent stare. 'Because there are no dwellings in this region, it has no need of Masters. We know the South Plains because our duty to the Land requires it. But we seldom journey here.'

'So you don't know,' Linden retorted. 'Anything could have happened here – anything at all – and you wouldn't know about it. The Staff could have been destroyed, or used for centuries, and you wouldn't have any idea.'

'No, Chosen.' An undercurrent of reproach disturbed Stave's flat tone. 'Have you quested so long and arduously in the company of *Haruchai* and not learned that we are sensitive to power? Such forces as you imagine could not fail to draw our notice. Kevin's Dirt does not blind us, and the reach of our senses is great.

'Also I have said that we seldom journey here. I did not say never. Across the centuries, our care has been bounded only by the bounds of the Land. Small theurgies, perhaps, we would not discern. But that is not your fear.

'Your concern is groundless. Of that I am certain.'

Linden should have been grateful for his reassurance; but her emotions burned too hotly. Nevertheless she believed him. Their straits could indeed be worse.

Biting her lip again, she shifted her attention to Mahrtiir.

'You said others have been here. Human or not.' Friendly or not. 'Can you tell me anything else about them?'

In spite of his fierceness, the Manethrall looked suddenly timid; or the torchlight cast shadows like fears across his visage. He swallowed roughly. 'I cannot. As you have seen, this habitation is well protected. Wind and rain do not enter. Yet dust settles ceaselessly here. Too much has been obscured.'

'But you can still track them?' Linden demanded. 'Can't you?'

Her tone drew a wince from Bhapa.

Mahrtiir squared his shoulders. 'We cannot, Ringthane. I am a Manethrall of the Ramen. The Cords with me are skilled. In such things we are adept beyond any other people we have known.

'But we have been preceded by years or decades, as I have said. Many seasons have combined to efface any outward path. And the lowland beyond this cave is both open and fertile, rich with grass. I cannot follow those that preceded us because it cannot be done.'

His answer rebuffed Linden's hopes; but now she did not hesitate. She could not. If she faltered for an instant, the enormity of what she had done would overtake her. Then she might collapse like Anele, beating out her despair against the stone.

'In that case,' she muttered, hardly aware that she spoke aloud, 'we'll have to trust the ur-viles.'

Creatures make Anele remember!

Outside the encampment of the Ramen, the ur-viles had drawn the old man's blood in order to reach his memories. But they had previously done something similar to him. They may have done it several times. Surely they had learned enough of his past to know where and how – and when – he had lost the Staff? They must have sought it themselves, for their own reasons. Why else had they continued to probe his madness? Why else had they aided Linden—?

They had not followed Anele to his cave now because they had known that the Staff was gone. Instead they meant to search for it in some other way.

They had served Linden valiantly, but she did not know why. Perhaps they desired the Staff for themselves. She – and Covenant's ring – might be nothing more than a means to an end. They could not have reached this time, their own past, without her.

She might already be too late.

Immediately she began to run, rushing ahead of the torchlight into the dark.

An instant of surprise held her companions. Then Liand called urgently after her, 'Linden! Wait!'

She did not slacken her pace. She trusted him. He would bring Anele as swiftly as he could. If he needed help, the Ramen would not forsake him.

Harried by images of disaster, she crossed Anele's abandoned home and raced into the throat of the cave.

Stave seemed to overtake her easily, in spite of his damaged hip. Mahrtiir followed close behind them, lighting their way with his unsteady torch.

The ur-viles were too far away—

Ahead of her, precise streaks of sunshine fell among the piled boulders. She no longer needed torchlight. The Manethrall discarded his brand as he ran.

The aisle beyond the mouth of the cave was too narrow to allow either Stave or Mahrtiir past her; but as soon as the passage widened, the Master vaulted over the rocks to block her path. She collided headlong with his hard form.

'Chosen,' he insisted severely, 'this is madness. The Staff is lost. Haste and wildness will not recover it.'

Linden thrust against him, trying uselessly to force him aside. 'Damn it,' she protested, 'why do you think the ur-viles *stopped*? You saw them. They *smelled* something.

'We have to catch up with them before they find the Staff.'

She should have stayed with them. But how could she have known that Anele's desperation would mislead her?

Stave's visage showed no reaction; but he turned to run ahead of her, leading her between the tall stones. With Mahrtiir behind them, they burst free of the rocks and dashed for their waiting Ranyhyn.

When they reached the ravine above the hollow where they had left the ur-viles, Linden began to believe that she was not too late. She could feel power throbbing in the air: the walls of the ravine channelled emanations of darkness and force upwards. Then she knew that the creatures were at work nearby. They had not yet moved away.

To her senses, their theurgy felt like questing.

Still responding to her urgency, the Ranyhyn galloped through the ravine and down the hillside. As they neared the knotted wedge of the Demondim-spawn, however, they slowed to a canter, then a walk. With Hynyn and Mahrtiir's mount beside her, Hyn came to a halt half a dozen strides from the spot where the ur-viles laboured. There Linden stared, transfixed, at what the creatures were doing. She had never seen power used in this fashion before.

Its obsidian force stung her health-sense so that her vision blurred and her nose ran. A flush like remorse spread across her skin, and her mouth was filled with the taste of copper and yearning.

A low rise swelled in the bottom of the hollow. At the crown of the rise, the ur-viles had gouged or dug a narrow ditch like a gutter in a circle eight or ten paces wide. Now the loremaster, with the other creatures packed tightly behind it, held its iron jerrid or sceptre with the point planted in the ditch; and as the ur-viles chanted together, black power as fluid as oil and as rank as offal streamed from the iron into the gutter.

The liquid seemed to suck away the day's brightness. Within the ditch, the circle was crowded with shadows that writhed and wailed, although they made no sound.

Linden rubbed the damp from her eyes, trying to see more clearly. The loremaster's iron bled force slowly, yet the ditch was already full. The ur-viles must have begun their invocation soon after she and her companions had departed for Anele's cave.

Within the circle, the twisting shadows refused to take definite forms. They remained indistinct: shapeless and tormented; allusive as a masque. Yet their very vagueness conveyed a sense of intention; of desire and searching.

'Stave?' she murmured softly.

What the hell are they doing?

But the Master did not answer.

Still the shadows roiled and yearned. But now by increments they appeared to direct their attention away from the wedge and the mountains, across the foothills into the west. Their squirming forms seemed to beckon in that direction.

As they did so, the ditch began to overflow. Viscid black fluid poured like a serpent from the gutter, slithering through the soil and grass as if in obedience to the commands of the trapped shadows.

Slowly at first, then with more celerity, the snake of power glided across the hollow and went questing down the hillside. In moments, it was long enough to have drawn all of the liquid from the ditch. However, the ur-viles contrived to replenish the fluid as rapidly as it flowed away. Their ditch remained full, holding the shadows in place against the direct contradiction of the sun.

The black serpent called to Linden's percipience, urging her to follow where it led.

After a time, a small group of ur-viles – perhaps a third of the creatures – broke from the wedge and trotted away beside the serpent's squirming length.

They did not run, but they moved quickly enough to outpace their liquid power.

Each of them carried an iron dagger with a crimson blade as bright as burning blood.

With an effort, Linden wrenched herself out of her transfixion. If the lore of the ur-viles could locate the Staff of Law in this fashion, she did not mean to be left behind. Murmuring, 'Come on,' to Mahrtiir and Stave, she urged Hyn into motion. 'We should see where this is going.' Obediently the mare began to canter around the hollow after the creatures.

The line of darkness did not appear to flow swiftly. And its progress had slowed. Perhaps its power was attenuated by its distance from the circle and the shadows. Or it may have been diminished by the fact that fewer creatures now fed it. Yet it had already dropped into a fold of ground between foothills and begun to squirm up the far slope, searching the rocks and tufts of grass as if it were unsure of its way.

There the trailing ur-viles caught up with it. At once, they placed themselves near the serpent's head, four in a row on each side, and dropped to their knees facing each other. Raucous as crows, their harsh voices rose as each of them plunged its dagger into the snake's fluid body.

Fresh power thrummed in the air: the serpent writhed as though it had been goaded. Then it began to move ahead with more speed and certainty.

The ur-viles remained where they were to sustain the fluid.

Its course ran almost due west. In this region, however, the mountains gradually withdrew into the south, drawing their foothills with them. As a result, the serpent's path angled slowly towards the plains, leading Linden and her companions deeper and deeper into the piled heat of summer.

The moisture in her eyes became sweat as she rode. Helpless to do anything else, she wiped them on the sleeve of her shirt, and concentrated on the tortuous progress of the search.

The serpentine blackness soon began to falter again as its elongation weakened it. Shortly, however, eight more ur-viles came trotting across the slopes, dispatched by the loremaster and the dwindling wedge to extend the reach of their power. These creatures also knelt behind the serpent's head in order to stab their glowing daggers into its liquid flesh.

Once again, the dark fluid flowed ahead with renewed strength.

Softly, fearing to disturb the ur-viles' concentration, Linden asked Stave, 'How much longer can they keep this up?'

She did not expect an answer; but her constrained urgency demanded an outlet. As far ahead as she could see, the foothills continued to unfold in sequence, as rumpled as a dropped blanket, and devoid of any features – caves or copses, ravines, fallen stones – which might have concealed the Staff.

The Master shrugged. 'They are Demondim-spawn. Who can measure the extent of their lore? The *Haruchai* have seen them perform far greater feats, in Corruption's service.'

Linden could not think of any reason why the Staff might not have been taken tens or even hundreds of leagues from the place where Anele had lost it.

In the heat of her concentration, she had forgotten the rest of her companions. Fortunately Stave had not. Turning to the Manethrall, he asked Mahrtiir to ride back towards the hollow in case Liand, Anele, and the Cords needed help or guidance.

The Manethrall visibly disliked accepting a suggestion from Stave. However, he apparently recognised that the request was reasonable. Inclining his head more to Linden than to the *Haruchai*, he turned his Ranyhyn and cantered away.

She hardly saw him go. She had no attention to spare for pragmatic concerns. She had risked too much by coming here and could think of nothing except the search before her.

Again the flowing liquid began to lose its way. Before it failed altogether, however, the last of the ur-viles arrived to sustain it, leaving only the loremaster behind to command the shadows.

Until then, Linden's attention had been fixed on the serpent's progress: she had given no thought to the price which the ur-viles paid for their exertions. They were too alien to be understood in human terms. But now she saw that the Demondim-spawn were trembling with weariness. Their peculiar nature did not protect them from strain and limitation: the necessary, ineluctable and crippling strictures of time.

Earlier she had feared that they sought the Staff for reasons which might conflict with hers. Now she began to worry that they might exhaust themselves before they found it.

Overhead, the sun slipped towards mid-afternoon. Linden was dimly conscious of thirst and hunger, and of her own deep fatigue. She had known no real rest since the hour when she had first met Roger Covenant. Nevertheless the efforts and lore of the ur-viles held her. Her need for the Staff of Law outweighed every other consideration.

Ahead of her, the lore-serpent slid past an outcropping of rock in a narrow gully and seemed to become confused, no longer able to taste its prey in the thin soil. At the same time, Mahrtiir returned, accompanied by the rest of Linden's companions as well as by a group of ur-viles.

Tersely the Manethrall explained that when Liand, Anele, and the Cords had emerged from the ravine, the loremaster had led them westwards, abandoning its solitary efforts to replenish the ditch and compel the shadows. Instead of simply advancing to the serpent's head, however, the loremaster had stopped to replace the rearmost ur-viles. Driving its power into the black flow, the largest of the creatures had freed the others to extend the reach of their lore.

They staggered with fatigue as they loped forward. Nonetheless they plunged unsteadily to their knees beside their fading search. Their blades seemed to gutter in their hands, lapsing to iron and then resuming a molten glow spasmodically. Yet they bent as one to their task, chanting in raw voices.

If Bhapa and Pahni felt any weariness, they did not show it. Instead they evinced the unassuming stoicism of Cords in the presence of their Manethrall. But Anele sprawled on Hrama's neck as though he had given up hope. And Liand made no attempt to conceal his worry and wonder. Nothing in his life had prepared him to comprehend an exertion of power like the lore-serpent.

When he had drawn Rhohm to Linden's side, the Stonedownor said, 'The Manethrall deems that the ur-viles quest for the Staff.' He spoke in a whisper, plainly hoping that the creatures would not hear him. 'Yet your apprehension is clear. Do you not desire their aid? Do you mistrust them, Linden?'

'I'm not sure.' She hardly knew what she felt. 'Everything they've done for us so far has been good. But I don't know why they're doing it.

'I've heard that they're driven by some kind of racial purpose.' Their Weird. 'For thousands of years, they served Lord Foul. Then they turned against him.' They had created Vain so that a new Staff of Law could be made. 'I don't know what changed.'

Nor did she know the limits of their lore. Were they capable of prescience; of reading Time? Was it possible that they had enabled her to fashion the Staff so that later – now – they would have an opportunity to claim it for themselves?

If they shared the loathing of the Viles and the Demondim for their own forms, they might believe that they needed the Staff in order to transform themselves.

Liand nodded. He had learned enough about the ur-viles from Stave to understand her uncertainty. Softly he said, 'I confess that I have envied your knowledge of the Land and power. But now I find that I do not envy the burdens imposed by your knowledge.'

Smiling ruefully, he left her to study the progress of the lore-serpent in silence.

Linden could see signs that it would soon fail altogether. It was stretched too thin: its power dwindled as if the black fluid were being denatured by the summer heat. The ur-viles knelt behind its head in relays, leaving its tail so that their vitriol could continue its search. But each time they did so, weariness sapped more of their strength; and no new power fed the snake.

The sun seemed to cook Linden's heart as she watched, bringing her closer and closer to Anele's despair.

Then the black fluid neared the bottom of a narrow crease between hills, and there it stopped altogether. She could see no obstacle in its path – and no feature to distinguish this particular crease from others she had passed. The sand and stone of its bottom suggested a watercourse, fed during the spring by rain and melting snow, but now entirely dry. However, a scattering of low brush grew along the scant ravine's sides: more shrubs and grass than Linden had noticed on the surrounding hills. Perhaps a little water still seeped through the sand, helping the deep roots of the brush cling to life.

For no apparent reason, the liquid line of the ur-viles' questing ended in a flat plane as though it had encountered an invisible wall.

Behind Linden, the creatures slumped away from the serpent, withdrawing their blades from its body, allowing its power to wither and fade. In moments, the dark fluid began to evaporate. Its macerated strength curled into the air in midnight plumes and wisps like remnants of shadows.

As the serpent died, she urged Hyn forward. She wanted to study the spot where it had ended. Had the ur-viles simply failed? Or had their searching met a barrier of some kind, an expression of lore which ordinary sight could not detect?

The Demondim-spawn barked at her hoarsely: they may have been trying to warn her. But their cries were too weak and weary to hold her back.

Stave came after her at once. Liand and Mahrtiir did the same. But their Ranyhyn were a stride behind Hyn as Linden neared the line where the dying liquid had been cut off.

Abruptly the mare shied; stopped. Tossing her head, she snorted in disapproval.

'Have care, Chosen,' advised the Master. 'There is power here.'

Still Linden could discern nothing. 'What kind of power?'

Stave gazed across the hills. 'It resembles a Word of Warning such as the Lords wrought to forbid the approach of their foes.'

Harshly Mahrtiir put in, 'It lacks such force.' He appeared to relish contradicting the *Haruchai*.

Stave nodded. 'Indeed. It conceals. It does not threaten.'

Linden gaped at the blank air as though she had gone blind. Why could she not perceive—?

She glanced around for Liand to ask him what he could see; and as she did so the edge of her vision caught a faint shimmering in the bottom of the dry streambed, an elusive distortion like a hint of mirage. Instinctively she looked directly at the sand and brush again; and again her senses detected nothing. Yet when she glanced aside, the watercourse seemed to waver slightly.

Guided by uncertainty, as she had been ever since she had first met Thomas Covenant, Linden gradually refined her percipience until, like Stave and Mahrtiir, she could feel the character of the shimmering.

They were right: there was power in the air. If Hyn had carried her into the bottom of the crease, she would have been stung by forces strong enough to stun her. Yet any harm that she might have suffered would have been a necessary side-effect of the power, not its intent. It had been placed here for another purpose.

To conceal something, as Stave had suggested? Or to forewarn its wielders? Or both?

In any case, its evanescent presence implied—

'Linden—?' Liand began; but he was too bewildered to complete his question.

—that the lore of the ur-viles had not failed. Some potent being or beings lurked nearby.

And it or they did not wish to be found. Or taken by surprise.

'All right,' she murmured under her breath. 'All right.'

She could still hope.

Then she asked more loudly, 'Now what?'

At her side, Stave shrugged. 'I know little of such lore. The *Haruchai* do not require it. If you will not turn aside, we must continue to rely upon the guidance of the ur-viles.'

Unless Linden called up white fire and simply tore the shimmering aside—

She no longer trusted that she would be able to do so. Her failure to find her own power in the *caesure* had nearly doomed her and everyone with her.

Thinking that she should return to the ur-viles, see if they were in any condition to take action, she touched Hyn's neck; and the Ranyhyn turned to trot back towards the creatures.

Already most of their fluid had wisped away into the sunlight; and another group of ur-viles had joined those nearby, sprawling exhausted beside their fellows. More limped over the crest of the hill, their black skin streaked with dust and expenditure. They, too, sagged to the ground with the other ur-viles, too worn out to go further. Now only the loremaster remained absent. When it reached her, Linden's company would be complete.

Pitying their prostration, she slipped from Hyn's back, walked a few steps to stand among the creatures, then slowly lowered herself to her knees so that she would not appear to be looking down on them.

Her companions also dismounted, leaving only Anele astride his Ranyhyn. He ignored them as he had ignored everything since he had been taken from his cave. His battered forehead he veiled in Hrama's mane.

For a moment, Linden hesitated, unsure of herself. But the pressure of her plight did not release her. Wiping the sweat from her forehead, she addressed the creatures softly, pleading with them yet again.

'I don't know what to do. I keep saying that. This is beyond me. I know you're exhausted. You've already done more than I have any right to ask. But I need even more.'

The thought of confronting the mirage with Covenant's ring made her stomach clench.

'Is there anything we can do for you? Do you eat *aliantha*?' She had seen none, but she did not doubt that the Ramen – or the Ranyhyn – would be able to find treasure-berries. 'Do you need water?' Liand and the Ramen carried several waterskins. 'Can you make more *vitrim*?'

The ur-viles regarded her with their wide nostrils and did not respond.

All right, she insisted, trying to reassure herself. She could not tell whether the situation required action or not. Nonetheless *she* did. A form of madness crouched in the background of her mind, awaiting its opportunity to spring. She had to do something—

Somehow she needed to find her way back to wild magic.

Surging to her feet, she turned roughly away and strode past her companions down the hillside towards the dry streambed.

So that she would not blunder into the shimmering, she watched for it askance, approaching it cautiously. Whoever or whatever had placed the barrier there might have no desire to do harm. It or they might recognise the presence of white gold. Hell, they might even recognise *her*. The ur-viles had certainly done so.

She had to take the chance.

Liand followed a step or two behind her, murmuring her name as though he did not know how else to aid her. And Stave walked at her shoulder. At a word from the Manethrall, Bhapa and Pahni unslung their waterskins and went to offer water to the Demondim-spawn. Mahrtiir himself followed Linden, Liand and Stave down the slope.

This time, the ur-viles uttered no warnings. All of her companions seemed to understand what she meant to do.

A few paces from the watercourse, Linden stopped. She no longer needed to sense the mirage obliquely: she could feel its implications like a faint tingle on the skin of her face. When she had chosen a steady place to stand, a stretch of bare dirt where the thin soil did not shift under her feet, she lifted Covenant's ring from under her shirt and wrapped her fingers around it. Then she closed her eyes and went looking within herself for fire; for the hidden door which opened on wild magic.

She should have been able to find it. She was certainly desperate enough. And twice now she had summoned argence by conscious choice. But the knowledge that she had failed in the *caesure* hampered her concentration. The possibility that she might fail once more – that she might never again have access to the power she needed – blocked her from clarity. She could not rediscover the door.

A low breeze skirled around her, carrying heat to her skin, drawing sweat from her temples and ribs. The pressure of the sun made her feel weak, denatured like the lore-serpent. Instead of white fire, she found a sensation of nausea twisting in her guts as if she were dehydrated or ill.

Abruptly all of the ur-viles began to bark. Their raucous shouts held a note of alarm. Startled, Linden looked back up the slope towards the creatures.

The loremaster had rejoined them. As weary as its fellows, it could barely support itself on all fours. The stain of dust on its eyeless face gave it a stricken aspect, as if it had caught a scent which appalled it.

The heads of the ur-viles were turned, not towards Linden and the streambed, but in the direction of the open plains.

Liand gasped softly; and Stave said with sudden harshness, 'Attend, Chosen.'

Wheeling to face northwards, Linden muttered involuntarily, 'Oh, hell. What's *he* doing here?'

Less than a stone's cast below her, Esmer came striding up the hillside. He moved smoothly, easily, ascending the slope with unspoken puissance. His gilded cymar flowed like water on the breeze, alternately caressing and concealing his limbs. The strange fabric seemed to shift in hue with each step, modulating from the bright blue-and-gold of sun-burnished waves to the ominous shade of storm-frothed seas.

The plain shock of his appearance here, millennia before his proper time, made Linden feel like retching.

He was headed towards a point midway between her and the ur-viles. As he drew near, however, he paused as if to consider both groups. Then he advanced on the Demondim-spawn with a spume of hauteur in his eyes.

Some of them struggled to rise. Others cowered on the ground, nearly grovelling. Only the loremaster managed to haul itself erect. With its sceptre in its hands, it confronted Esmer's approach unsteadily; but the iron looked cold, inert. To Linden's eyes, the creature seemed too weak withstand a blow – or even a rough word. Esmer's vast power would sweep the loremaster from the face of the hills.

And still she could not find the door— She had lost her access to wild magic entirely.

When he reached the ur-viles, Esmer stopped, clenching his fists on his hips. 'This is abject,' he sneered. 'Has the mighty lore of the Demondim become so frail? And do you dare to set yourselves against me? You do well to grovel, lest my betrayals destroy you utterly.'

The loremaster responded with a bark of defiance. But Linden felt no force from the creature; no strength at all.

As if he had decided to begin a slaughter, Esmer stooped suddenly to slap a prone ur-vile with the palm of his hand.

Linden felt her heart labouring in her chest. Esmer's palm struck between the creature's shoulder-blades. She expected a gout of blood; expected to see the ur-vile's spine shattered. But instead a small iron bowl appeared in Esmer's hand. He seemed to have snatched it out of the ur-vile's flesh.

From the bowl, she sensed the unmistakable must and potency of *vitrim*.

Pacing imperiously among the creatures, Esmer carried the bowl to the loremaster and thrust it at the big ur-vile. 'Drink,' he commanded. '*Drink*, and may the Seven Hells consume your bones. This weakness is intolerable.

'You are needed.'

Then he turned his back on the creatures to stride like an act of violence towards Linden and her companions.

She breathed in hard gasps, trying to quell her nausea. Esmer's conflicted emanations left her half stunned: she could hardly think. What was he *doing* here? How had he come?

And why was he so angry?

Fearlessly Stave stepped forward to stand in front of Linden. After an instant's hesitation, Liand joined him. Muttering Ramen curses, Mahrtiir placed himself shoulder-to-shoulder with Stave and Liand. And Pahni and Bhapa followed Esmer down the slope. The set of their faces said that they were ready to sacrifice themselves, if they were needed.

The Ranyhyn had accepted Esmer. He had been the friend of the Ramen—

'Stand aside!' he barked at Linden's guardians. For a moment, he sounded like an ur-vile, guttural and enraged; and distant lightnings glared in his eyes. 'This delay is fatal. The defenders of the Staff are unsure of you. And they are blinded to white gold. Already they prepare to abandon their covert. They will flee if they are not given battle.

'Then will you be betrayed in earnest, and nothing will undo the harm that I have wrought.'

He could easily have gone around Linden and her companions; but he seemed to need a kind of permission from them.

Or from her.

'Go ahead,' she breathed, although she hardly heard herself. Her head reeled. The defenders of the Staff—? She wanted to challenge him; demand an explanation. The Staff was *here*? But surprise and confusion seemed to compel her acquiescence.

Some part of him wanted to help her.

He had already betrayed—?

When she spoke, Stave, Liand, and Mahrtiir stepped out of Esmer's way. He swept past them scornfully, ignoring Linden as if she had fulfilled her role and no longer had any significance.

Together, she and her companions turned to watch him approach the dry streambed.

He did not pause as he neared the shimmering. Instead he plunged into the crease between the hills like the onset of a gale.

And like a gale, he tore reality asunder.

A tremendous concussion shook the ground. For an instant, dirt and grass and rocks sprang into the air like waterspouts, force-driven geysers. Unable to keep her feet, Linden pitched headlong down the slope; landed with dust in her eyes and mouth. Liand fell beside her: even Mahrtiir staggered to his knees. Only Stave contrived to remain upright.

The blast passed quickly, leaving in its wake a rain of broken stones, rent grass, clods of soil. Blinking desperately to clear her sight, Linden saw Esmer standing undisturbed in the bottom of the watercourse, facing up the ravine. The fall of debris came nowhere near him.

She coughed convulsively at the dust in her lungs; but she made no sound. Liand appeared to call her name, yet his voice did not reach her. The concussion had taken her hearing.

And—

Oh, God.

The sand on which Esmer stood was no longer the bottom of a small ravine. The crease between the hills was gone; ripped out of existence. In its place stood a wider streambed, higher and more rugged walls. As the slopes rose on either side, the walls piled upwards, forming a deep cut in the bedrock of the hills – an incision filled with shadows and implied peril.

At the end of the cut, fifty or a hundred paces up the ravine, gaped the broad mouth of a cave. It seemed as full of darkness as a sepulchre.

Esmer, Linden tried to say. God in Heaven. Esmer! But she heard nothing.

Then Stave came to her side. His hands clasped her shoulders, lifted her to her feet as if she were weightless. His lips moved, conveying nothing.

Liand scrambled upright a moment later. He shook his head, raised his hands to his ears. Fear flashed in his eyes as he realised that he had been deafened. In a rush, he flung his arms around Linden and held her close as if to assure himself that she was whole.

Their deafness would pass: she knew that already. The concussion had only shocked her auditory nerves. If her eardrums had ruptured, she would have felt more pain. In a moment, Liand would discern the same for himself.

Struggling against his embrace, she turned to see what Esmer was doing.

At the same time, the ur-viles launched themselves down the slope, galvanised by alarm or *vitrim*. Their jaws worked: they appeared to bark frenetically. In spite of their weariness, they held their blades glowing in their fists. As they hastened towards the new ravine, they contrived to form a ragged wedge.

At the point of the wedge, the loremaster staggered weakly, hardly able to keep its balance. Nevertheless its sceptre seemed to ache with power, and dark vitriol glistened on the surface of the iron.

Esmer gave them a jeering glance, then returned his attention to the cave at the end of the ravine.

Made visible only by its own intensity, by the discrepancy between its force and the calm of summer, a shockwave lashed through the air from the mouth of the cave. Channelled and focused by the rough stone of the walls, it struck at Esmer like a scourge; fell on him with such vehemence that Linden almost saw the flesh stripped from his bones. She expected him to fall backwards in a clutter of disarticulated limbs.

At the last instant, however, he erupted like a burst of sunfire, blinding and incandescent.

Then Linden was blind as well as deaf, lost in a glare that blotted out vision. Heat licked through her clothes as though the air had become flame.

Yet somehow she broke free of Liand's grasp and began to run, sightless and desperate, in the direction of the ravine. This had to stop. The Staff was in that cave. Its defenders were not her enemies.

When she could see again, she squinted through a chaos of splotches and power-echoes and found Esmer standing unharmed a few strides ahead of her, wrapped in disdain as if it were armour; as if the force unleashed against him were no more than a petty affront.

Covenant's ring bounced against her chest as she landed heavily in the sand of the watercourse. No! she cried silently at Esmer. Stop this! Get out of here! They aren't our *enemies*!

But she did not pause to see whether he heard her; heeded her. Thrusting him aside, she staggered frantically up the ravine.

No! she cried again, appealing now to the beings hidden in the cave. Please! We don't want to fight you. We won't fight you!

Confused by phosphenes, little suns and nebulae, she could not see her footing clearly. Sand shifted under her boots and rocks tripped her, making her stumble. Still she ran.

In the darkness ahead of her, another shockwave gathered, powerful enough to be palpable through the residual burning of her skin. If it struck her, she would suffer the rent flesh and scattered bones which she had imagined for Esmer. Yet she did not stop.

Before she reached the mouth of the cave, however, and the shockwave ripped through her, she heard a howl in spite of her deafness, a cry of warning in Esmer's voice. So suddenly that she could not avoid colliding with him, he appeared between her and the poised assault.

He faced into the cave, obviously shouting something which once again she did not hear. With one hand, he pointed urgently at the ring swinging on its chain outside her shirt. With the other, he directed a wall of force back down the ravine, a barrier which prevented Linden's companions and the ur-viles from following her.

Beyond his forbidding, Liand and Bhapa appeared to call for her; and Pahni clung to them both as if she had lost her voice. But Stave and Mahrtiir had already flung themselves up the hillsides beside the ravine, seeking to bypass Esmer's barrier. In the streambed, the ur-viles concentrated their wedge, preparing an acid counter-stroke.

Linden turned her back on them to continue struggling towards the cave.

Esmer caught her arm to restrain her – and at once released her as a small form emerged from the darkness within the cave.

Of her own volition, she halted.

The figure before her was a Waynhim.

She recognised it instantly, although ten years had passed since its kind had saved her life and Covenant's in the Northron Climbs. But she had never expected to see one of them again. She had believed that all of the Waynhim, every community or *rhysh*, had gathered long ago to oppose the depredations of the *arghuleh*. There most of them had perished, overpowered by the unexpected might of the ice-beasts.

Had enough of the creatures survived to form one last *rhysh*?

If so, they were absolutely not her enemies. Throughout their long existence, they had served the Land with all the cunning of their strange lore.

But they had always been the deadly foes of the ur-viles—

Like the rest of its kind, the Waynhim was smaller than any of the ur-viles: standing erect, its head reached no higher than the centre of her chest. And its skin was an ambiguous grey, a colour which would have looked pale in direct sunlight, but which appeared darker, tinged with illness or sorrow, in the shadows that filled the ravine. Yet the creature could only be a making of the Demondim. Its pointed ears perched high on its bald skull; its entire body was hairless; and instead of eyes, two wide damp nostrils gaped above its lipless mouth.

It stood just outside the cave. Its mouth moved as though it were speaking; but if Linden had been able to hear she would not have understood what the Waynhim said.

The ur-viles must have known that the Waynhim were here as soon as they had detected the scent of the Staff. Without Esmer's intervention, they and the Waynhim would have already attacked each other.

He replied to the creature: a buzz of implied noise in the bones of Linden's skull. Again he indicated Covenant's ring. This time when the Waynhim spoke, she heard a low spatter of sound like the phosphenes which lingered in her vision, complicating the shadows.

The rasp of Esmer's voice returned; but she did not realise that he had addressed her until he gripped her shoulders and turned her to face him. Like the Waynhim's, his mouth moved incomprehensibly.

With gestures, she tried to tell him that she could not hear.

Esmer scowled in vexation and his green eyes seethed. He said something over his shoulder to the Waynhim, then spoke as if he were issuing commands to Linden's companions. But he did not wait for a response. Instead he raised his hands to her ears and tapped them lightly with his fingertips.

The ur-viles held their formation, waiting.

For a moment, Esmer's touch tingled on Linden's eardrums. Then she was struck by a blare of sound as loud and compulsory as the calling of sirens.

Suddenly she could hear the strident apprehension of Liand's breathing, the harsh chanting of the ur-viles. Pahni's whispers seemed to roar up the ravine.

In spite of their surefootedness, Stave's and Mahrtiir's movements along the rims of the walls sounded like the grinding of boulders.

When Esmer asked, 'Now do you hear?' he might as well have yelled in her face.

She flinched. 'Too loud.' Her own voice bellowed at her. She clamped her hands over her ears. 'It's too loud.'

Esmer looked stricken; inexplicably ashamed of himself. Then he covered his chagrin with a feigned sneer. 'It will pass.'

Before she could reply, he turned to bark something at the Waynhim.

Clamorous as an avalanche, Stave and Mahrtiir landed in the sand of the ravine. Confused by the exaggeration of her hearing, Linden feared that they would hurl themselves at Esmer; or at the Waynhim. But they ignored Cail's son, and her. Instead of attacking, they bowed deeply to the grey creature.

Their actions left Linden momentarily weak with relief.

Esmer seemed vexed, but he did not regard the *Haruchai* and the Manethrall. When the Waynhim had answered him, he faced Linden again.

'Wildwielder,' he said darkly, 'I have introduced you and your companions. As much as I am able, I have explained your purpose here. This is their reply.

'Your name they acknowledge. They know the ur-Lord Thomas Covenant's companion against the Sunbane. By their lore, they have learned of her role in fashioning the Staff of Law. And assuredly they understand the importance of white gold. For the sake of the great good that she accomplished at Thomas Covenant's side, in the name of the wild magic that destroys peace, and because I have spoken on your behalf, they concede that you are indeed Linden Avery the Chosen, as you appear to be. Therefore they will make you welcome.'

Gradually the volume of Esmer's voice receded to a more bearable level. Lowering her hands, Linden found that she could hear him now without discomfort. Stave's and Mahrtiir's feet no longer sounded like thunder as they crossed the sand towards her.

'They concede as well,' Esmer continued, 'that you have passed through a rupture in the Law of Time. Their lore speaks of this peril. And I am able to compel their belief. They cannot deny my knowledge of such powers.'

His tone darkened to bitterness as he said, 'The *Haruchai* also they recognise, and the Ramen. They, too, will be welcomed, as well as the Stonedownor, for the same reason.'

Esmer paused while a look of savagery mounted in his gaze. 'But never,' he concluded, 'will they permit the presence of ur-viles in their covert. And they will not give the Staff of Law into your hands.'

Stave nodded as though he had expected this and approved. But Mahrtiir glared a warning at the Waynhim, and his sore fingers hinted at his garrote.

Instinctively Linden dismissed the refusal of the Waynhim. It was too much: she could not afford to believe that she would fail now. Her head still reeled with the aftereffects of the Waynhim's defences, and Esmer's. She had no choice but to act as though she could not be thwarted.

They were Waynhim, and they had the Staff: that was all that mattered. She had nowhere else to turn. If they did not trust her, she would simply have to persuade them.

Quietly, almost calmly, she asked Esmer, 'Why not? They know I made it. Don't they think it belongs to me?'

His ferocity faded at once. Now he appeared to squirm.

'They fear you,' he admitted. 'Your presence in this time is a profound violation of the very Law which the Staff supports. How can they believe that your purpose is benign, when you have chosen to pursue that purpose by such hazardous means?'

'Also,' he added in a smaller voice, 'they fear me. They perceive the peril of my nature. That I act on your behalf tells against you.'

Linden shook her head. The reasoning of the Waynhim did not surprise her. They were not her enemies.

Esmer, on the other hand—

'They have a point,' she said more sharply. 'What in hell are you *doing* here, Esmer?' Then she stopped herself. 'No, don't answer that yet. First tell me how you *got* here.'

Earlier, he had refused to enter the *caesure* with her. *In my presence, you will surely fail.* What had he meant, if not that his nature would not permit passage through a Fall?

'You are acquainted with *Elohim*,' he answered, still squirming. 'You know that they stand apart from all Law. I have not inherited their untrammelled separateness, but I have been granted a measure of their freedom.' He shrugged uncomfortably. 'Time seldom hinders me.'

'Then why didn't you just come get the Staff for me? You keep saying you want to help. Why did we have to go through all that pain?'

Esmer looked away. 'The *Elohim* respect the Law of Time. It preserves the Earth. They have no wish to rouse the Worm of the World's End. To that extent, I am bound by their Würd.'

Linden swore to herself. As usual, his response was too conflicted and ambiguous to help her. Instead of pursuing the subject, she changed directions.

'You said the Waynhim were blind to my ring. Why is that?'

Esmer's mien reflected a rolling wave of emotions: anxiety, defensiveness, shame. 'It is an effect of my nearness.'

She heard hints in his words, suggestions of insight, but their meaning eluded her. There were conclusions which she should have been able to draw— Too many truths had already slipped through her fingers, leaving her less and less prepared for each succeeding crisis. But she could not think beyond the exigencies of her immediate situation.

Esmer had mentioned *betrayal*. As if treachery were essential to his identity. And he had avowed that his presence would ensure her failure.

'So if you hadn't showed up here and broken down their defences,' she said grimly, 'we wouldn't be in this mess. The Waynhim would have sensed the ur-viles, sure, but they would have felt my ring at the same time.

'And the ur-viles wouldn't have attacked them.' She would not have permitted that. 'As far as I can see, the Waynhim are refusing me now because you came all this way to threaten them.'

Stave nodded again.

'So explain it to me, Esmer,' she insisted. 'What in hell *are* you doing here?'

'Wildwielder,' he retorted, 'you understand nothing.' His words were scornful, but his tone and his manner ached with regret, apology; self-recrimination. 'I feared what might transpire if the ur-viles accosted the Waynhim.

'The breaking of their wards is nothing. If you chose, you might have torn the barrier asunder. Or the ur-viles, given time, could have accomplished as much in your name. But such efforts would have been prolonged, allowing the Waynhim to withdraw. Nor would your actions have relieved their mistrust.

'My intervention has not harmed them. It was necessary only to prevent them from flight, so that you might be granted an opportunity to beseech them.

'Also the enmity among these Demondim-spawn is deep and ancient. That the ur-viles have seen their Würd in a new way does not comfort the Waynhim. In my absence, how would you mediate between them? And how would you counter their doubt of you? You do not know their speech. You cannot answer their concerns if you do not comprehend them.

'You must not spurn my aid.' Yearning ached in his gaze. 'How otherwise may I be redeemed?'

But Linden had no tolerance left for his self-justifications. 'That's not my problem,' she told him trenchantly. 'You like to talk about betrayals. I don't think I can afford your help.'

Turning her back on his puissance, she took a few steps towards the Waynhim.

'You know me,' she told the waiting creature. 'I don't care what Esmer says about me – or about you either. He's making this all sound complicated when it's actually simple.

'I'm the woman who made the Staff. Covenant sacrificed himself to protect the Arch of Time, and I used his ring to transform Vain and Findail so that I could stop the Sunbane.

'I came here through a *caesure*. That's true. And *caesures* are evil. That's true, too. But it doesn't change who I am.' She believed that. 'I just didn't have any other way to get here.'

She could not read the creature's reactions. It might have regarded her with empathy or terror and she would not have known the difference. Yet somehow the Waynhim conveyed the impression that it was not well; that some old sorrow or wound sapped its vitality, leaving it more frail than it should have been. Grief over the near-extermination of its kind? Some other loss or burden? Linden could not tell. Like the ur-viles, the Waynhim baffled her health-sense.

Nevertheless its condition moved her. When she went on, she spoke more gently.

'If I'm going to fight Lord Foul, I need the Staff. I'm no "Wildwielder". That was Covenant, and he's dead. And white gold can't stop *caesures*. You know that better than I do. Only Law can undo that kind of rupture.

'But that's not all.' She glanced back at Cail's son, then told the Waynhim urgently, 'Esmer may not have mentioned that Lord Foul has my son, my Jeremiah. Maybe I can rescue him with wild magic, maybe I can't. But I can't do it without risking the Arch, and that's too dangerous. I need the Staff. Otherwise I might do enough harm to end the Earth.'

Even Jeremiah would be destroyed.

'And the Staff belongs to me,' she asserted. 'Not just because I made it, but because I'm a healer. That's what I do.' She chose her words with care. 'I'm the right person to use it.'

You're the only one who can do this.

The creature responded with a spate of harsh barking, bitter as a denial. When the Waynhim finished, Esmer said as if he had lost interest, 'They were unaware that you have a son. They sorrow on his behalf. But all else that you have said they knew, and they are not swayed. Your presence is a violation of Law. Good cannot be accomplished by evil means.'

At any other time, that argument would have stopped Linden. She recognised its validity. But she could not heed it now. She had already taken risks which she could not undo. She could only hope to justify them with her actions.

'Wait here,' she told the Waynhim abruptly. 'I'll show you why you should give me the Staff.'

The creature inclined its head: a motion which could have meant anything, but which she chose to interpret as consent.

At once, she swung away to stride down the ravine towards her companions.

Deliberately she ignored Esmer. Accompanied by Stave and Mahrtiir, she hastened along the streambed, rushing to find her way through her ramified dilemmas before her instincts faltered or failed.

Although Esmer had withdrawn his barrier, the rest of her company still stood in mid-afternoon sunlight at the end of the ravine. The ur-viles remained undecipherable to her; but Liand's charged confusion and the alarm of the Cords reached her across the intervening sand and stone.

They were as human as she was; their needs as great. Any explanation might have eased their hearts. But she could not pause for them. Holding up her hand to silence their questions, she spoke first to the ur-viles.

'You can't go any further,' she said brusquely. 'You know that. The Waynhim won't have it. And I suspect you don't want to.' Unless they craved the Staff for themselves. But if they did, they were too weak to act on their desire. 'You've already done your part. You'll have to wait here.'

Then she turned to Liand and the Cords. 'Bhapa, Pahni, I want you to take care of the Ranyhyn. Keep them nearby. I don't know when we're going to need them again, but it might be sudden.

'As for you—' She faced Liand's open concern squarely. 'Get Anele for me. Bring him into the ravine. If he can't convince the Waynhim—'

She left the thought unfinished: if the old man could not move the Waynhim, they had no hearts; and she was powerless.

Liand's gaze still pleaded with her, but he did not protest. When Pahni and Bhapa bowed in acquiescence, he smiled crookedly and did the same.

Touched by his generosity, Linden might have taken a moment to thank him; but her fears did not let her go.

As if she had released them, the ur-viles surrendered to their weariness again. Abandoning their wedge, they sank down to rest in the bottom of the watercourse. At the same time, the Cords and Liand started up the hillside towards the Ranyhyn and Anele.

With Mahrtiir and Stave beside her still, Linden returned to Esmer and the lone Waynhim, walking among the shadows as if she meant to challenge the dark.

Esmer and the creature were talking quietly, but they broke off their exchange as she approached. She could not be sure, but she thought that she saw tears in Esmer's indefinite gaze.

Too tense to remain silent, she asked, 'Now what?'

Esmer lifted his shoulders: a shrug, perhaps, or a clench of self-restraint. 'The Waynhim are valiant,' he answered in a low voice, 'and too many of them will perish if you do not contrive their salvation. They know their plight, yet they do not flinch from it. I grieve for them, as I do for myself.'

Oh, great, Linden thought to herself. Just what I need. More riddles.

Aloud, she muttered, 'So this is what your help is like. You summoned a *caesure* for me, and the Ramen were driven out of their homes. Now you're here to "mediate" for me, and something terrible is going to happen to the Waynhim.'

He nodded stiffly.

A new concern occurred to her. 'What about all the help you gave the Ramen before they came to the Verge of Wandering? How are you going to betray them for that?'

Esmer withheld his damp gaze. 'I have already done so. I have brought them near to the Land when you had need of them. No more terrible doom has been required of me.'

Linden wanted to snarl at him; but she kept her ire to herself. While she remained in this time, she could do nothing for the Ramen.

'Then,' Stave remarked to Esmer, 'the Chosen and all the Land would be better served without your aid.'

Remembering Esmer's earlier violence, Linden braced herself to jump between him and the *Haruchai*. But Cail's son did not answer Stave's accusation.

'Ringthane,' Mahrtiir offered slowly, 'I cannot account for him.' The Manethrall sounded troubled. 'He has been a friend to the Ramen as to the Ranyhyn, giving us no cause for mistrust. Of one thing I am certain, however. No urging of his has caused us to act against the will of the Ranyhyn. For that reason, we regret nothing that we have done, though we have indeed returned to the Verge of Wandering in a time of peril.'

Before Linden could respond, she heard movement behind her. Glancing over her shoulder, she saw Liand enter the streambed with Anele. The Stonedownor supported Anele with his arm around the old man's waist. Anele appeared to have lost all volition and strength: he accompanied Liand only because the young man half-carried him along.

Nonetheless Linden was sure of him. He was an argument which would persuade the Waynhim to aid her. If they were deaf to him, they would hear no other appeal.

'Thank you,' she murmured as Liand and the old man drew near. Then she said, 'Let him go. Let's see what he does.'

Liand complied with a nod. When he had released Anele, he stepped back.

Shadows made pools of darkness in the sockets of Anele's blind eyes. He appeared entirely lost; too far gone in dismay to be aware of his surroundings or situation. In some preterite way, however, he may have understood what was needed of him. Or perhaps his inborn Earthpower reacted to the lore of the Waynhim. As soon as Liand removed his support, the old man took a few tottering steps towards the creature and dropped to his knees.

Clasping his hands before his face as if he were praying, he bowed his face to the sand. Then he spread out his arms and prostrated himself like an act of supplication.

The Waynhim considered him carefully. It came to stand over him; sniffed all around him as though tasting the tale of his life in his aggrieved scent. And as it did so, the creature increasingly gave the impression that it had been wounded; galled by sorrow or suffering.

If Linden could have seen its cause, the creature's care and pain would have explained the Waynhim to her. One more hint, a final glimpse or insight, might enable her to comprehend their dilemma.

Trying to elicit that hint, she told the Waynhim softly, 'This is Anele, son of Sunder and Hollian. They were chosen to hold the Staff of Law when I passed from the Land and Covenant was lost. He inherited it from them. You found it in the cave where he lived while he studied the Land, trying to determine the form of service that was right for him.'

She did not add, He only made one mistake. Look at what it cost him. The creature could discern the truth for itself.

When the Waynhim had finished its examination, it barked a few guttural syllables into the gloom and retreated to stand once more near the mouth of the cave. There it stayed, apparently forbidding Linden to enter; refusing her—

After a moment, Mahrtiir demanded tensely, 'Esmer, what was said? Has the Waynhim given its answer?'

Esmer hid his surging gaze in the crook of his arm and did not reply.

Stave waited with his arms folded across his chest. His flat features betrayed no reaction.

Linden kept her attention fixed on the creature and the cave.

As the sun declined past mid-afternoon, the shadows thickened, obscuring the face of the Waynhim, filling the mouth of the cave with potential night. Within herself, Linden fretted; but outwardly she remained calm. The Waynhim could argue that the end did not justify the means, but they could not deny that Anele was the rightful wielder of the Staff – or that he was in no condition to bear that responsibility. Nor could they believe that the Staff was not desperately needed. Anele's plight demonstrated the Land's more eloquently than any words.

And the delay was not prolonged. Soon the darkness within the cave appeared to condense, concentrating gradually into the form of a second Waynhim.

This creature moved with an arduous limp, as if every movement tormented its sore and swollen joints. As it emerged from the cave, Linden saw that its flesh was afflicted with oozing galls and eruptions like the stigmata of a plague. From half of its face the skin had peeled away, leaving raw tissues which throbbed and bled with each beat of its heart. Boils and blisters distorted its mouth as if it had swallowed acid, and a rank green fluid dripped like pus from both of its nostrils.

Its pain cried out to her, as articulate as weeping, although the Waynhim made no sound.

It came forward a few steps, then stopped, wavering on its feet as if it had reached the end of its strength.

'Heaven and Earth!' Liand breathed. 'What has befallen it? Is this an ailment? Has some cruel force wrought such harm?'

'Esmer?' demanded Mahrtiir harshly.

Linden understood now: the poor creature's suffering gave her the hint she needed. How else might the Waynhim have responded to Anele's plight, except by revealing their own?

Nevertheless the truth appalled her. And she had no power. Some force or confusion had sealed shut the door to wild magic within her.

Like Anele, still prostrate in the sand beside her, she sank to her knees before the damaged creature and bowed her head.

Gruffly Esmer responded, 'The Demondim-spawn are not creatures of Law. They were not born as natural creatures, nor do they wither and perish as the Law of Life requires. Rather they were conceived by lore, created to redeem the loathing of the Demondim for their own forms.'

Ah, God. Linden feared that this crisis would be too much for her; that the dilemma of the Waynhim exceeded her scant strength. But these creatures were not her enemies. And they had shown her what they required in order to trust her.

'Those offspring,' Esmer continued, 'which the Demondim deemed worthy, they nurtured. Those which failed their intent, they cast aside. Yet the ur-viles and the Waynhim differ primarily in their interpretations of the Weird or Wyrd or Word which gives them purpose. In their physical substance, they are alike, and the Law which gives form to mortal life has no place in them.'

On her knees with her eyes closed and her chest full of yearning, Linden considered her straits. She could not use Covenant's ring. But the Waynhim held the Staff of Law; her Staff. How distant was it? How deeply had the Waynhim sequestered it?

Could her health-sense extend so far?

The damaged creature had taken some time to reach the ravine. But its pain was terrible and all its steps were slow. It could not have come a long way.

With her eyes closed, she listened to Esmer's voice. It moved her like a lament.

'For that reason,' he explained, 'the Staff of Law is inimical to them. Though the Waynhim serve the Land, and have always done so, their service stands outside the bounds of Law. Their lore is in itself a violation of Law. The fact of their service does not alter their nature.

'Therefore the mere proximity of the Staff harms them. If its influences are not guided and controlled by a condign hand, its power must destroy them. Unprotected, no Waynhim or ur-vile can long endure its presence and remain whole.'

And therefore the Waynhim understood Linden's dilemma; the dilemma of every white gold wielder. The damaged creature in front of her demonstrated that they could be persuaded.

Comforted by the knowledge, she sank into Esmer's words and the Waynhim's pain; and as she did so, her percipience expanded outwards, following the hard guidance of the ravine's stone walls into the cave.

She did not consciously search for the Staff. The wrong kind of concentration would block her senses. Instead she simply drifted. And she found herself thinking, not of the Staff itself, or of how she had made it, or of its cost, but rather of Andelain and beauty.

If she had not visited that bastion of loveliness with Thomas Covenant, she would not have loved the Land as he did. Until that time, she had known only the Sunbane; and so the ineffable glory of Earthpower had been hidden from her.

'Sensing that the Staff had been abandoned,' Esmer said as if from an impossible distance, 'these Waynhim sought it out, that they might preserve it from the Despiser's servants.'

Linden could almost hear the Forestal of Andelain's song. It had been retained in the depths of her memories, melodic as trees, poignant as flowers: an eldritch music which had spangled and enumerated with glory every blade of grass, every petal, every leaf, every woodland creature.

'Yet the nearness of the Staff harms all Demondim-spawn.' Esmer's voice had become a threnody in the dim ravine. 'Over the years, it would unmake these Waynhim entirely. Therefore they selected from among their number one to bear the burden – one to transport the Staff from its former resting place and here to become its final guardian. Thus the Waynhim hoped to satisfy their Weird without bringing ruin upon this *rhysh*, for it is the last in all the Land.

'The outcome of their choosing stands before us.'

Perpetually wounded in the name of service.

Like the Waynhim, the Forestal's song was full of sorrow, carried on an undercurrent of woe. And like the Waynhim, it did not flinch from its own resolve.

> *Oh, Andelain! Forgive! For I am doomed to fail this war.*
>   *I cannot bear to see you die – and live,*
> *Foredoomed to bitterness and all the grey Despiser's lore.*
>   *But while I can I heed the call*
>   *Of green and tree; and for their worth*
> *I hold the glaive of Law against the Earth.*

Linden's memories of Andelain and music bore her along until she found what she sought: the precise aura and potency of the Staff of Law.

'And yet,' Mahrtiir put in, 'they would refuse the Staff to the Ringthane, she who above all others has the greatest need—'

He stopped, unable to express his bafflement and chagrin.

'Manethrall,' answered Esmer, 'they must satisfy their Weird. I have named their reasons. They do not count the cost to themselves.'

They did not; but Linden counted it for them. She had spent her life responding to such needs.

Her nerves recognised the Staff with gladness. The Land had gifted her with health-sense, and she could not mistake the Staff's particular emanations. It was the incarnation of *rightness*, the tangible bulwark of the strictures, sequences, necessities – the commandments – which made life and beauty possible. While it remained intact, Lord Foul could never entirely extinguish hope.

And she was its maker. Inspired by her love for Covenant and the Land, for all of her friends, she had expended herself in white fire to create an instrument against the Sunbane. She did not need to be in contact with it in order to wield its benison. She needed only to feel its strength and know that it was hers.

Guided and controlled, Esmer had said. By a condign hand.

Kneeling still, with her eyes closed and her head bowed, Linden Avery the Chosen reached out to claim the only power which had ever truly belonged to her.

Somewhere in the distance, Liand whispered, 'Heaven and Earth! Look to her. She is exalted—'

Together, as if they had momentarily set aside their antagonism, Esmer and Stave replied, 'She has discovered the Staff.'

'What will she do?' Liand asked in wonder.

Stave did not reply; but Esmer murmured softly, 'Behold.'

Filling her hands with the vast possibilities of Law, Linden turned her thoughts to the damaged Waynhim standing unsteadily before her.

Her eyes remained closed. She did not need to gaze upon the creature to know its suffering. Its wounds – the inadvertent and unavoidable corrosion of its substance – were plain to her in every detail. Her own flesh felt them.

The Staff of Law had inflicted these hurts. With the Staff, she could heal them.

Thus she answered the denial of the Waynhim. They were the last remnant of their kind, and deserved no less than to be made whole.

When her task was complete, the sun had fallen further down the sky, and the slow approach of evening left the ravine deep in shadows. Nevertheless her heart felt like daybreak, bright and full of promise.

Chapter Eight:
'Contrive their salvation'

When Linden rose at last to her feet, nearly staggering with weariness, the healed Waynhim and its companion made raw-edged sounds which Esmer translated as welcome. Courteously Stave and Mahrtiir returned grave thanks. Leaving Bhapa and Pahni with the Ranyhyn and the ur-viles to fend for themselves, Linden and her small company followed the Waynhim into the cave.

She leaned heavily against Liand, needing his support. And Mahrtiir held Anele upright: the old man seemed too lost to fend for himself. Stave walked alone, while Esmer trailed behind as if he had been dispossessed.

Formal as a procession, they proceeded along the dark stone throat until they reached a turning where the passage opened into a wide chamber lit like a meeting-hall. There the rest of the *rhysh* waited to offer welcome also, bowing after their fashion and chittering among themselves like delighted birds.

Healing the creature that warded the Staff, Linden had apparently healed them all. Even the Waynhim which had first met her in the ravine had lost its grieving air, and none of the others showed any signs of harm.

She had in some sense validated the meaning of their lives.

After the summer heat on the South Plains, the atmosphere of the cave felt blessedly cool, soothing to her raw nerves. The Waynhim guided their guests to ledges like seats in the wall of the cave; and when she sat down the worn stone seemed to embrace her in spite of its unyielding surfaces. This sensation, she knew, was an effect created by the Waynhim. They wished her to understand that she had arrived in a place of peace.

The light in the cave had a warm luminescence tinged with emerald and flickers of rust. It arose from a number of stone pots spaced like braziers around the wide floor; and flames danced and twisted at their rims. Yet Linden could see that the fires were fed, not by oil or wood, but by lore. Instead of smoke, they cast a scent of cloves and coriander into the air.

Liand sat near her, although now she did not need his care. The Waynhim had brought her closer to the Staff of Law: she could feel its nearness effortlessly. Its stern beneficence filled her with an unfamiliar contentment.

Stave remained standing as if to do the Demondim-spawn honour. And Esmer wandered aimlessly around the chamber, looking vaguely rueful, troubled by sorrows which he did not explain. But Mahrtiir also sat on one of the ledges, studying the Waynhim as though he meant to memorise every detail so that he would be able to tell his people a tale worthy of his fierce ambitions.

Seated as well, Anele rested against the stone, mumbling into his thin beard. But some essential change had taken place in him. When Linden looked at him, she saw that his old rue and shame had lost some of their vehemence. He had been ground down by too many years and too much regret; and yet, in spite of his mumbling, he appeared almost sane. His proximity to the Staff seemed to soothe him, easing his long bereavement.

The Waynhim offered an iron cup of *vitrim* to each of their guests, although Esmer waved his aside with apparent disdain. Then they gathered together in the centre of the chamber, forming themselves into a loose wedge with the Staff's guardian at its tip. Again the healed creature bowed to Linden, barking words which she could not understand. When she also had bowed, it walked slowly out of the chamber into one of several side-tunnels which interrupted the walls of the cave. Hushed and expectant, everyone waited while the creature disappeared on its errand.

Soon it returned, bearing the Staff of Law in its hands.

Linden's heart lifted again at the sight. The Staff's unique nature spoke to her senses. It was taller than the Waynhim – nearly as tall as she was herself – and formed of a pale wood which gleamed in the lore-light; wood so pale that it might have been carved from the heart of a tree. Its length was smooth, as if it had been polished lovingly for centuries. But its ends were bound with iron bands, the heels of the original Staff of Law which Berek Halfhand had formed from a limb of the One Tree.

Vain and Findail had given their lives to it, rigid structure and fluid vitality. But their qualities had been transformed by wild magic and the passion of Linden's torn spirit. And their union had been shaped, guided, by the deep knowledge with which Berek had forged his iron. Thus the lore of the ur-viles and the Earthpower of the *Elohim* had become the pure instrument of Law.

Eagerly Linden rose to meet the Staff. When the creature placed it in her grasp, she felt a rush of warmth from the wood. Its possibilities flowed into her like heat. At the same time, she was filled with memories of Andelain: of hillsides as lush as lawns bedizened with wildflowers and *aliantha*; of the proud out-stretched health of Gilden trees with their wreaths of golden leaves thick about them; of small streams, and groves of oak, and swaths of briar-rose, all vibrant with Earthpower.

She felt that she was remembering the Land as it had once existed in the mind of its Creator, before Lord Foul was imprisoned within the Arch of Time; before Foul had corrupted the Land with hidden banes like the Illearth Stone, and had gained the service of fell beings like the Ravers. And she tasted as well the Creator's grief. Having created the Arch, the structure of beginning and end which allowed life to exist, the Creator could not alter events within that structure without violating it. Therefore Lord Foul's imprisonment itself gave him the freedom to destroy what the Creator had made.

Such treasures as the Staff of Law had been brought into being so that the inhabitants of the Land would have the means to oppose Lord Foul themselves; to fight for the intended beauty of the world.

For a moment, at least, while she held the Staff for the first time in many years, Linden felt equal to her enormous task. Unlike Covenant's ring, the Staff suited her. She understood its uses instinctively; trusted herself with it. Its natural *rightness* seemed to send healing into every cell and impulse of her being.

She did not realise that she was weeping until she thought to thank the Waynhim and discovered that she could see nothing clearly. Tears blurred her gaze, turning the light to streaks of consolation and confusing the definition of the figures around her.

When she blinked the tears from her eyes, however, she found that the Staff's guardian no longer stood before her. The creature had stepped back, making way for Anele.

The old man faced her with his hands poised near the Staff as though he meant to wrest it from her grasp.

Liand and Mahrtiir hovered behind him, waiting to see what he would do; ready to intervene. But they were visibly reluctant to disturb him.

Anele's hands trembled as he studied the Staff, and his blind gaze seemed to ache with yearning. How many decades had passed since he had last stood in the presence of his birthright? How much recrimination and self-loathing had he suffered before he had fallen into madness?

The touch of the Staff might heal him as well.

Yet he did not close his hands on the immaculate wood; did not so much as brush it with his fingertips. Instead he stood motionless while Linden grieved for him and the entire chamber seemed to hold its breath. Then, trembling, he lowered his arms.

In a small voice, he murmured unsteadily, 'I am unworthy of such astonishment. The day has not yet come when I may be whole.' His throat closed on a sob. When he had swallowed it, he whispered, 'Until that time, I must remain as I am.

'Do not mourn for me.' The effort of renunciation left him desolate. 'Know that I am content to behold the Staff in your care.'

Then he turned away and hid his face in his hands.

Liand's eyes were damp as he watched the old man. Mahrtiir scowled fiercely, too proud for sadness; but his manner was gentle as he guided Anele back to his seat and offered *vitrim* to his lips.

For a while, Linden could not stop her tears. The day has not yet come— She believed him: there was no falsehood in him. But the thought that he needed to remain as he was hurt her more than she could express. With the Staff, she possessed the power to impose any healing that he might require. Yet he refused her. He was not ready – or his circumstances were not.

'Linden,' asked Liand softly, 'will you heed his desire for forbearance? Your weariness is extreme, but surely it does not outweigh his suffering?'

Hugging the Staff of Law to her chest, Linden cast her health-sense deeply into the old man, as she had once before in the Verge of Wandering: again she sought the means to succour him. But he had changed in more ways than one. The same yearning or compulsion which had brought him close to sanity had also galvanised his native puissance. She would have to force her way past powerful defences in order to reach him.

That violence might do him harm that she could not repair.

She wiped her eyes on her sleeve. 'Look at him,' she told Liand. 'He's choosing to be this way.' His madness, like his blindness, was necessary to him still. 'If I try to heal him, he'll fight me. And maybe he's right. He certainly *has* the right.'

And she had neither the wisdom nor the arrogance to make his decisions for him.

After a moment, Liand answered sadly, 'I see what you see, though it baffles me. Perhaps he must determine the time and place of his healing.' Then the Stonedownor asked in a tone of pleading, 'What does he desire, if not the Staff which he lost?'

'You heard him,' Linden sighed. 'He needs to believe in himself. He still thinks he's unworthy.'

Grieving, she returned to her seat on the stone ledge. Anele had assured her that he was content. And she, too, needed healing. Her tasks were far from complete. She still had to return to her proper time, and could not do so without entering a *caesure*. But her first experience had nearly destroyed her. Until she became stronger, she would not be able to endure a second.

And Esmer had warned her of betrayals— *The Waynhim are valiant*, he had said, *and too many of them will perish if you do not contrive their salvation*. He had brought with him or elicited some peril when he had appeared in this time. Now she and her companions as well as the Ranyhyn were in danger.

Fervidly she clung to the smooth wood of the Staff for comfort. When she had settled herself on the ledge, she drank a few swallows of the musty *vitrim* and let its potency carry the Staff's warmth like chrism into the depths of her weariness.

She had rested there for only a short time, however, when Stave and Esmer approached her together. Animosity bristled between them, yet they were momentarily united in their resolve to question her.

Holding the Staff across her lap, she looked into the shifting green of Esmer's gaze and the steady brown of Stave's and waited wearily for them to speak.

'What will you do,' Esmer demanded abruptly, 'now that you have obtained your desire? It appears that you are indeed the Chosen, for the Demondim-spawn have chosen you. Perhaps they are not alone in their selection. Will you now cease to be the Wildwielder, setting aside white gold that you may dedicate yourself to the service of Law? If you do so, how will you return to your proper time? And if you do not, how will you bear the burden of such powers?

'Either alone will transcend your strength, as they would that of any mortal. Together they will wreak only madness, for wild magic defies all Law. That is its power and its peril.

'You must declare yourself, so that I' – he caught himself – 'that all those here may find their own paths.'

He did not need to ask, If you set aside the ring, who will take it up? That question was implicit in every line of his face.

He may have wished to possess Covenant's ring himself.

While Esmer spoke, Stave stepped aside as if to dissociate himself from his antagonist's demand. But when Esmer was finished, the Master said, 'I also ask this. We must not remain in this time. The hazard is too great. And you must not wield both wild magic and Law, lest you be torn asunder.

'Therefore I ask it. What is your intent?'

Linden considered both men through a blur of fatigue. Stave remained suspicious of her, she was sure of that. Yet she trusted him. Esmer, on the other hand—

Deliberately she turned to Mahrtiir and Liand.

'This depends on you,' she told the Manethrall carefully, 'at least to some extent. I already know what Liand will say. And Anele needs to stay near the Staff. But I haven't asked you.

'Do you want to go back to your people? It should be possible.' Once she had created a Fall, the Ranyhyn would be able to find their way. 'But if we do that, I can't stay with you. I have too many—'

'Ringthane,' Mahrtiir put in before she could explain, 'this is needless.' The light from the stone pots glinted in his eyes. 'I will accompany you wherever your purpose leads. I seek a tale which will remain in the memories of the Ramen when my life has ended. Such renown I will never earn among them. They are' – his mouth twisted – 'too cautious to be remembered.'

Then he shrugged. 'In this I will not command the Cords. However, they feel a debt which they wish to repay.' He grinned at a thought which he kept to himself. 'And you have found favour in their sight. They will not be parted from you.'

'All right.' Linden did not try to argue with him, although he and the Cords might well perish in her company. She needed as much rest as she could get. And some buried part of her had already made her decision. Raising her eyes to Esmer and Stave again, she repeated, 'All right.

'I'm going to Andelain. I know I've got too much power. And I don't know where to look for my son.' Long ago, the spirits of Covenant's friends had guided and comforted him there. Perhaps she, too, would find her loved Dead. 'I'm hoping that someone there can tell me what to do.'

Esmer made a sound like a hiss of vexation and turned away; but Stave continued to face her with his usual flat stoicism. Whatever her answer meant to him remained shrouded. When her silence made it clear that she had no more to say, however, his manner seemed to intensify.

'Very well,' he replied. 'You wish to enter Andelain. Perhaps you will do so. Yet you have not named a more immediate intention. What will you do *now*?

'As I have said, we must not remain in this time. And the peril grows with every moment of delay. Esmer has threatened a betrayal which it would be unwise to confront. And the hazard that our actions may violate Time accumulates against us. It is folly to indulge in rest when the need for departure becomes ever more urgent.'

Linden groaned to herself. She had hoped to postpone arduous questions for a while; until the benignant warmth of the Staff could knit together her frayed resources. Yet Stave deserved an answer. All of her companions did, the Waynhim has much as the Ramen and Liand.

Searching for a way to convey what she felt, she turned to the Stonedownor as to a touchstone of honesty. 'Liand?'

At once, he stopped tending Anele to look at her. 'Yes?'

'What was it like for you? In the *caesure*? What happened to you while we were there?'

His eyes widened, then seemed to grow dark, benighted by memory. 'Linden—' He ducked his head to hide his discomfort. Yet he concealed nothing. 'To speak of it is difficult. The pain— I had not conceived it possible to experience such pain.

'And to endure it—' His voice sank until it was barely audible. 'That I could not have done, had the ur-viles left me unprotected. But I felt their blackness about me through the pain, warding away the worst of the Fall.'

Then he raised his head again. 'There is a disturbance in their lore which sickened me,' he told Linden's concerned gaze. 'Yet it was a little thing in the greater evil of the Fall. I would not have survived to speak of it if the ur-viles had not preserved me.'

Linden thanked him quietly, and released him.

'That's bad enough,' she said to Stave. 'The rest of us aren't *Haruchai*. And we don't have Anele's Earthpower. We're' – she shuddered – 'vulnerable.

'But it's not the only problem. I don't know if you realise that I failed. In the *caesure*. I almost let us all—' Her own memories nearly choked her. 'I couldn't use Covenant's ring. I was in too much pain.

'We're only here because the ur-viles saved us. The ur-viles and the Ranyhyn.' And because she had found a way to make use of Joan's madness – which she would not have been able to do if the creatures had not given her their strength. 'Since I healed you, I've been cut off from wild magic.'

A moment of restless movement passed among the Waynhim; but Linden ignored it. 'I'm aware of the danger. I need rest' – badly – 'but that wouldn't stop me if I knew how to get us out of here. I wouldn't let the fact that I'm terrified of all that pain stop me. But somehow I'm going to have to relearn how to use Covenant's ring, and I'm not sure I can do that.'

The Staff of Law would restore her, if she gave it time. It would ward her against the Fall's torment. But it would not give her access to argence. That she had to rediscover within herself; and she did not know how she had lost the way.

Stave stood before her, impassive and unswayed. 'The pain will be less severe,' he pronounced. 'You will not be required to oppose the current of the Fall.' He paused to glance around the cave. When he faced Linden again, he said, 'And you will not be blocked from wild magic. That hindrance is caused by Esmer's presence, as he has said, and he is gone.'

Startled, Linden looked quickly for Cail's son. But Stave was right. Esmer had simply faded away; evaporated like water.

She tried to ask, 'Why—?' but she could not complete the question.

Moments ago, the Waynhim had seemed restive. They must have been reacting to Esmer's disappearance.

'Your intention to enter Andelain displeased him,' replied the Master. 'Therefore he has departed.'

Displeased—?

While Linden stared at Esmer's absence, she scrambled to understand Stave's revelation.

Esmer had refused to enter the *caesure* with her. *In my presence, you will surely fail.* And he had said that the Waynhim were blinded to the proximity of white gold. *It is an effect of my nearness.*

Damn it, she should have known—

But he could not have caused her failure in the Fall. That was the result of her own weakness, not of his interference.

'Chosen.' Stave's concentration gave his tone a cutting edge. 'We must depart now, while Esmer is absent and his betrayal has not yet come upon us.'

Abruptly Liand jumped to his feet. 'You mislead us, Master,' he put in. 'The decisions which Linden must make are not as plain as you wish them to appear.'

Before Stave could retort, Liand rushed on. 'If I comprehend aright, our presence here endangers the Arch of Time. And we are in peril of Esmer's betrayal. But there is another peril which you do not name.' He seemed suddenly furious at everything that the Masters had done in the name of their unyielding convictions. 'If we hasten to depart, the harm which Esmer has wrought will fall upon the Waynhim alone. Without our aid, it may be that they will be destroyed.

'You are a Master of the Land. Do you deem the Waynhim unworthy of our concern?'

The young man's anger – and his loyalty – raised an echo of determination in Linden. With an effort, she set aside her confusion and self-doubt. Tightening her grip on the Staff, she concentrated instead on the hope that Stave had given her; and on the passion of Liand's support.

Stave's mien hinted at scorn as he answered the young man. 'Esmer's harm is directed against the Chosen. If she is no longer present in this time, the peril to the Waynhim will dissipate. He gains naught by their destruction.'

'Nothing,' Linden countered, defending Liand in her turn, 'except a violation of the Land's history.'

Stave studied her as though she had surprised him.

'You said yourself,' she continued, 'that there haven't been any significant battles or powers in the South Plains. If the danger doesn't dissipate, and the Waynhim defend themselves, that might change.

'But even if they let themselves be exterminated—' *They know their plight, yet they do not flinch from it.* 'We don't know what Esmer might have unleashed. Whatever it is, it could be powerful enough to change history no matter what the Waynhim do.'

Liand's eyes shone as if Linden had vindicated him.

Stave gave a slight shake of his head. 'If he were capable of such things, he would have done so ere now. The Arch of Time would already have fallen.'

Yet time remained intact: she knew that. Stave's words still reached her in sequence. One thing still led to another—

'No,' she said like a sigh. 'It doesn't work that way for him. He's too conflicted. We're his friends, or his enemies. He hates you and approves of me. Or maybe it's the other way around. As far as I can tell, the only simple thing about him is his respect for the Ranyhyn.' Nothing else had compelled him to refrain from killing Stave. 'He doesn't want them hurt.'

Mahrtiir nodded in confirmation.

Closing her eyes, Linden rubbed at the frown knotted between her brows. 'Maybe he is powerful enough to bring down the Arch. I don't know. But he can't do it. He needs a balance of some kind. He can't do anything really destructive if he doesn't help us at the same time. He can't help us without betraying us.

'He had to at least warn us. He needs that. And if he didn't, we wouldn't have a chance to save the Ranyhyn.'

The Master regarded her closely. 'You cannot be certain of this.'

'No,' she admitted. When had she ever been certain of anything except her loves? 'But neither can you. And until we *are* sure, I'm not leaving. The Waynhim have already suffered enough. I won't leave them until I know they aren't going to be wiped out.'

Esmer had threatened even the ur-viles with destruction.

For a long moment, Stave appeared to consider her words. Then he lifted his shoulders in a small shrug. 'Very well,' he said. 'You will do as you wish, and I will serve you as well as I am able. In this time, it is useless to oppose you. But understand that nothing has been resolved between us.'

As he turned away, Linden bowed her head over the Staff. She was content with his response. He was *Haruchai*, inflexible by nature as well as conviction. Yet he had already conceded more than she could have expected from him.

*

She might have closed her eyes then and slept; let *vitrim* and the Staff work within her undisturbed. But Liand was too restless to leave her alone. And she had been postponing his questions for hours. Sighing to herself, she gave up on sleep in order to relieve some of his imposed ignorance.

While she told him tales of her time with Thomas Covenant, one rambling anecdote after another in no particular order, the Waynhim began to busy themselves around the cave. At first, she wondered what they were doing; but then she saw that they were preparing a meal. Apparently they did not live on *vitrim* alone – or did not expect their guests to do so.

From a side tunnel, they produced a stone pot shaped like a cauldron. One of their flaming urns they placed near the centre of the chamber; and when they had muttered over it for a few moments, intensifying its heat with chants and gestures, they balanced the larger pot on top of it. Then they began sorting ingredients which Linden could not identify into the cooking pot.

As they worked, she continued to talk; and gradually her oblique narrative began to take on another purpose. Instead of answering questions which Liand did not know how to ask, she mined her memories: words were the picks and shovels with which she delved for courage and insight. And the names of her lost friends were an incantation. By their magic, she created a place for herself in the Land, a role – and imagined herself able to fulfil it.

'I thought that the Sunbane and the Ravers were as bad as things could get. For a long time, I didn't think I would ever see anything worse than the shedding of the *Haruchai*.' Through the Clave, Lord Foul had attempted genocide against Stave's ancestors, draining their blood to feed the Banefire. 'But when Caer-Caveral was gone, and the Sunbane broke into Andelain for the first time—'

The people and places and needs that she remembered explained her to herself.

'Lord Foul was responsible for all of it,' she said quietly. 'He isn't called the Despiser and Corruption for nothing. He's contempt and despair. Every time any being or power tramples on life, he's there. Laughing—'

Only the agony of an entire world could appease his own innominate anguish.

'I'm sure there are times when I act like I've lost my mind. I probably confuse the hell out of you. But you already know what's happening for me. Whenever I do something that looks insane, just remember that Lord Foul has my son.'

When she stopped at last, she found all of the attention in the chamber focused on her. The Waynhim had paused in their preparations to regard her as they would an oracle. Mahrtiir's concentration was as precise as a hawk's. Even Stave's posture conveyed an unexpected impression of respect.

Liand had been listening with wonder on his face. As she looked at him, however, he drew an unsteady breath and shook off his entrancement.

'Now I am able to grasp why Anele is troubled when he speaks of "astonishment". I know not how to name what you have become to me. I feel that I have gained the experience of years in these past days, and every fact or detail which once seemed commonplace has taken on a new significance.

'To my eyes, you do not appear "insane". Rather, you surpass my capacity for expression. When you speak of that which you have done, and of those whom you have known, you appear to inhabit a realm of antiquity and grandeur. I would say that at your side I seem paltry to myself, yet that belies what is in my heart, for it is not I who am diminished, but rather you who are exalted.'

He glanced around the cave as if he sought confirmation, but only Mahrtiir nodded an acknowledgement. Stave and the Waynhim simply studied Linden and listened as if the fates of worlds were being decided; and Anele sprawled on his ledge, sleeping soundly.

Linden did not know how to respond. If he believed that she occupied 'a realm of antiquity and grandeur', how could he understand that she was terrified and confused, or that she depended on his uncomplicated support?

After a moment, she said, 'It isn't like that. I'm more ordinary than you think.' Covenant fit Liand's description. She did not. 'I just can't afford to let it get in my way.'

Holding the young man's gaze, she added, 'Do you think that I *belong* in this position? That I was *born* to wield tremendous powers and make decisions that could affect the world? No. I do it because I don't know how else to fight for what I love.' Or for herself. 'If Lord Foul hadn't kidnapped Jeremiah, I wouldn't even *be* here.'

As she spoke, her weariness seemed to slip from her shoulders, shrugged aside by the importance of what she was trying to say.

'That makes you braver than I am,' she told Liand. 'Don't you know that? You didn't have to leave Mithil Stonedown. You didn't have to help me. Hell, as far as you knew, there wasn't even anything at stake. But you did it anyway.

'You did it because you didn't believe in your own life. The Masters made it too small for you, and you jumped at your first chance to make it bigger.'

Let Stave take offence if he would. She had not kept secret her reaction to what his people had done.

'If there's anyone here,' she pronounced like an article of faith, 'who deserves to "inhabit a realm of antiquity and grandeur," it's you. And Mahrtiir.' She met the Manethrall's gaze briefly. 'Bhapa. Pahni. You're less selfish than I am. You haven't lost a helpless kid who needs you. Instead you decided to risk your entire lives for the simple reason that you consider it worth doing.'

In response, Liand regarded her as though she had lifted him out of himself. All of the Waynhim appeared to study her closely, and Mahrtiir's eagerness for battle shone in his eyes.

But Stave stood near the centre of the chamber with his arms folded across his chest and his emotions hidden. His native reticence defied her discernment. But the scar under his eye caught the light of the urns and gleamed redly.

Eventually the Waynhim resumed their preparations; and Linden watched them, haunted by Esmer's dark promises. *Too many of them will perish if you do not contrive their salvation.* He might conceivably have been referring to the harm that the creatures suffered from the Staff; but she did not believe so. He had spoken too often of betrayal.

When she realised that she was fretting, she asked the Manethrall if Pahni and Bhapa should be warned of the danger. He assured her, however, that the Cords had been trained as hunters and scouts; sentinels for the great horses. No doubt the ur-viles were wary as well: they had their own reasons to distrust Esmer. And the senses of the Ranyhyn were preternaturally acute. They would be able to detect any threat before it fell upon the Waynhim.

With as much patience as she could muster, Linden waited for the creatures to ready their meal.

Fortunately they did so without further delay. Using wooden ladles, they filled stone bowls with a steaming broth that looked like sludge and smelled like stagnant pond-water. These they offered to their guests before partaking themselves.

In spite of its superficial reek, the steam curling from the bowls spoke to Linden's senses of much-needed sustenance. The aura of the broth was redolent with nourishment; and she was surprised to find that she was hungry. Her first sip threatened to gag her, but the second went down more easily and the third she swallowed almost eagerly.

Meeting her glance, Liand gave her a rueful smile. Politely he consumed some of his broth. Then he set down his bowl with an air of relief and turned to assist Mahrtiir with Anele.

Together Liand and the Manethrall roused the old man and encouraged him to sup.

While she ate, Linden studied the stone of the cave, trying to read its old, slow, imponderable sentience, as Anele sometimes did. With the Staff in her lap, she thought for a moment that she could detect hints of knowledge in the clenched rock. But her human mind slid past them too rapidly to be sure of their presence.

Because her attention was elsewhere, she did not notice Pahni's approach until the Cord appeared at the mouth of the outward tunnel.

The young woman – Linden still thought of her as a girl – ventured hesitantly into the cave. She may have feared to interrupt some important conclave or invocation. Her face was set, however, and she did not allow timidity or self-consciousness to hold her back. Avoiding the Waynhim, she advanced towards Linden and Mahrtiir.

All of the creatures stopped what they were doing and turned to consider her with their moist nostrils.

Liand flashed a broad smile at the Cord. But the pleasure fell from him when he recognised the quality of her determination.

Instinctively Linden rose to her feet. She held the Staff upright beside her, its heel planted on the floor, as if she meant to call forth its power.

Mahrtiir stood also; and Stave joined them. Liand mopped unceremoniously at a spill of broth in Anele's beard, then surged erect as well.

Hurrying now, the young woman offered them a quick Ramen bow.

The Manethrall replied with a brusque nod. 'Speak, Cord. We have awaited some word of what transpires in the night.'

In the night—? Linden was surprised to realise that so much time had passed. Darkness would limit even the unquantified perceptions of the Ranyhyn.

'Manethrall.' Pahni bowed again reflexively. Her voice held a tremor of anxiety as she said, 'Shortly before sunset, Esmer came among us. He attempted to draw the Ranyhyn away.' She frowned to mask a distinctly Ramen disdain. 'I had not thought him so foolish. He should have known that they would not abandon their riders.'

'He is troubled,' Mahrtiir replied. His tone made it clear that he did not consider being troubled an adequate excuse.

Pahni nodded. 'Yet we were concerned, Bhapa and I, for he spoke slightingly to us, foretelling death. Then he departed, though we could not name where or how he had gone.

'Because of his words, we widened our guard over the Ranyhyn. Still we found no sign of peril.

'Shortly after moonrise, however, came Naharahn – the proud mare who has shown me such honour—'

Abruptly the Cord fell silent, flustered by her awe and gratitude.

Mahrtiir did not rush her.

When Pahni had taken a deep breath to steady herself, she was able to continue. 'Naharahn made it known to me that something discomfited her. What it was I could not determine by scent or sight or sound. But Whrany, who bears Bhapa, felt likewise disturbed. And their unrest spread swiftly among the other Ranyhyn.'

To herself, Linden groaned. She was not ready to attempt another *caesure*. But she did not interrupt the Cord.

'Sure of them,' Pahni finished, 'Bhapa has descended towards the plains, seeking the cause of their concern. Before he departed, however, we agreed that you must be forewarned.'

As she said this, Pahni looked through her lashes at the Manethrall as if she half expected him to reprimand her for leaving her assigned duties.

He did not. Instead he said, 'You have done rightly. Return now to the Ranyhyn.' In spite of his apparent calm, his voice held a rising eagerness. 'We will follow when we have offered our respect to the Waynhim.'

With another nod, he dismissed the Cord.

Bowing once more, Pahni turned and hastened, fleet as a colt, out of the cave.

Liand watched her go as if he wanted to run after her; but he made no move to leave Linden's side.

'It comes,' Stave said impassively. Outside the cave, Esmer's dark hints were approaching fruition.

Mahrtiir nodded, eager as a blade. He looked like a man who could hear the call of battle.

Linden leaned heavily on the Staff. She was weary yet, deeply in need of rest; entirely unprepared. Yet this was the moment for which she had been waiting. Now the nature of Esmer's betrayal would declare itself, and she would know what she had to do to save the Waynhim and her companions.

The Staff was a powerful tool, fraught with dangerous possibilities; but it could not help her return to her proper time. Somehow she would have to find her way back to wild magic.

'Linden?' asked Liand. 'Does your knowledge of the Land suggest a name for this disturbance?' He glanced at Stave. 'Is this another dark wonder which the Masters have concealed from us?'

'I don't know.' Abruptly she pulled herself upright. She had needs more profound than rest. At this moment, they began with the Waynhim, although they extended far beyond her ability to measure them. 'Stave will tell us as much as he can. When the time comes.'

Esmer had asked, *How will you bear the burden of such powers? Either alone will transcend your strength. Together they will wreak only madness—*

Apparently he had always intended to 'help' her face his betrayal by removing the barrier that his presence imposed on her access to Covenant's ring.

'Mahrtiir is right,' she added. 'It's time to go.'

At once, she turned towards the waiting creatures.

The Waynhim knew what threatened them: she was certain of that. Like the ur-viles, they understood Esmer's intentions better than she did. Yet they had made no obvious move to prepare a defence. And she suspected that they would not, unless she led the way. Surrendering the Staff, they had to some extent made her responsible for the outcome of their lives.

'I wish you could tell me what's coming,' she said gravely. 'I can't even imagine how much danger I've put you in.' She had brought Cail's son to them. 'But it doesn't change my debt to you. I don't know what would have happened to the Staff without you – or what would happen to the Land – but I think we would all be doomed.

'One thing I'm sure of. You did the right thing. You've been faithful to your Weird.'

With all the dignity she could muster, she bowed, holding the Staff before her in acknowledgement. Then, so that she would not falter, she turned to Stave and said, 'We've waited long enough. Let's find out how bad this is.'

The *Haruchai* also bowed to the Waynhim, as did Mahrtiir and Liand. Then the Stonedownor urged Anele to his feet; Mahrtiir hastened into the lead; and Stave accompanied Linden across the cave towards the egress.

As she and her companions passed, the creatures formed a wedge and followed more slowly, chittering encouragement or farewells to each other.

The angle of the tunnel beyond the cave soon blocked out the light. With the last reflected glow of the urns behind her, Linden could see nothing ahead. At her back, the bare feet of the Waynhim made a faint susurrus on the stone. The sound seemed to pursue her, sibilant and apprehensive, echoing softly about her ears like supplication.

Too many of them will perish—

Trepidation confused her steps; but Stave guided her with a light touch on her arm, ensuring that she did not stumble. The warm certainty of the Staff also sustained her. And soon the darkness receded on either side as the tunnel opened into the ravine and the night sky spread a swath of starlight overhead. Sand yielding under her boots, she walked along the bottom of the ravine towards the open night of the foothills.

There Mahrtiir awaited her with Pahni. When Linden and Stave reached him, the Manethrall announced in a contained whisper, 'Cord Bhapa has not yet returned. The Ranyhyn remain on the hillside above us. They are restive, for the peril draws near. But they will not flee it.' His tone suggested pride in the great horses.

'If you will heed my word,' he added, 'we will mount so that they may respond swiftly to your desires.'

Bhapa had only one good eye. His night vision would be hampered—

'What about the ur-viles?' Linden asked, whispering as the Manethrall did.

'An unwary foe,' he replied, 'might deem that they have abandoned us, but they have not. Rather they have secreted themselves among the shadows below us.' Between Linden's company and the advancing danger. 'Doubtless they will attempt surprise on our behalf.' He considered the hillside briefly, then said, 'It may be, also, that they seek to distance themselves from the Waynhim. If so, they are wise. The Demondim-spawn will not readily trust each other, or fight in each other's defence.'

Linden peered down the slopes, looked for some hint of the creatures. But she found none. Their lore and their blackness concealed them from her senses.

Yet she could see better than she had expected. Above the jagged line of mountains distant in the east, a sallow moon a few days from its full had risen, shedding its wan light, bilious and unresolved, over the rumpled foothills and sprawling plains. In that uncertain illumination, the undulations of the lowland seemed to seethe gradually towards the horizon, ponderous and fluid as seas, and the shallow vales and clefts which defined the hills were crowded with darkness. The vague shapes of the Ranyhyn, off to her right and uphill from her, were as ill-defined as shadows.

'Ringthane,' insisted Mahrtiir. 'Will you mount?'

She shook her head. 'Not yet. First I want you to talk to them.' She meant the ur-viles. 'You or Pahni. They'll understand.

'Tell them to come when they hear me shouting.' If she succeeded at tearing open a Fall – and if she could devise no other response to the peril— 'I don't care how they feel about the Waynhim. I won't be able to save anyone who isn't near me.'

Nodding sharply, the Manethrall turned away and strode into the night. For a moment, he slipped down the crease of the dry watercourse. Then he seemed to fade from sight as if, like the ur-viles, he had cloaked himself in darkness.

Beyond question the Ramen understood stealth.

'Stave,' Linden breathed to the Master, 'tell the Waynhim. I need to know they'll come to me when I call.'

He did not ask why she did not speak to the creatures herself. Nevertheless she told him, 'I have to think.'

Noiselessly the *Haruchai* withdrew into the ravine; and Liand came to take his place at her side, bringing Anele with him.

The old man stood as though he were alone, wrapped in madness. Holding his head up, he studied the dark with senses other than vision; alert to the nuances of the night. As if to himself, he murmured, 'It is wrong. Wrong and terrible. Beings of nightmare walk the hills. They must not be permitted.'

At that moment, he appeared as sane as Linden had ever seen him.

She had to *think*.

Summon a Fall: that was the obvious solution. Recover her grasp on wild magic and rip open time. Commit her companions, all of them, ur-viles and Waynhim as well, to the known horrors of a *caesure* so that they would not fall prey to Esmer's betrayal. But she had pointed out the flaw in that reasoning to Stave. Something fatal had been unleashed on the South Plains; and it would not simply disappear, unmake itself, if she escaped. Deprived of its intended victims, it might seek to vent its destructiveness elsewhere.

It might turn towards Mithil Stonedown. Liand's ancestors would have no defence. And such an attack would violate the known history of the Land. It would weaken the essential integrity of time.

Therefore Linden could not flee. First she had to meet the danger. She had brought it here: it was her responsibility.

And still she could see nothing. Even her health-sense gave her no hints. The Ranyhyn scented peril on the air, or felt it through the earth. The Waynhim and the ur-viles knew their danger. In some fashion, Anele tasted the approach of nightmares. Yet Linden herself remained effectively blind.

She held her breath for Bhapa's return, hoping that the Cord would tell her what she needed to know. But when the imprecise night condensed at last into the form of a man, it was Mahrtiir rather than Bhapa who whispered her name.

'I have done as you required. Now I urge you to heed me. We must mount. The swiftness of the Ranyhyn will ward us more surely than any garrote or fist.'

'The Manethrall counsels well,' Stave observed. Linden had not seen him return: like Mahrtiir, he appeared to join her from among the secrets of the dark. 'It is said that there is no glory to compare with riding a Ranyhyn in battle.'

Now Linden did not delay. The Ranyhyn were under her protection as much as the Waynhim and the ur-viles. As much as Liand and Anele and the Ramen—

With Mahrtiir in the lead, she and her companions climbed the hillside towards the great horses. Pahni took charge of Anele so that Liand could stay with Linden. And behind them came the Waynhim in formation, chanting rhythmically the rituals of their lore.

However, the creatures did not ascend the slope. Instead they positioned themselves below the Ranyhyn, with the tip of their wedge pointing downwards and somewhat to the east. There they awaited the attack.

A warm breeze drifted into Linden's face. The air had cooled little since sunset, and baked shale, loose dirt, and sparse grass held the heat. The minor exertion of climbing towards the Ranyhyn drew sweat from her temples, made her shirt cling to her back.

Two or three of the horses whinnied softly in greeting. Others tossed their manes or stamped their hooves as if they were eager to run. Linden could not see clearly enough to tell them apart; but Hyn came to her and nuzzled her shoulder, urging her to mount.

With the Staff in her hands, Linden relied on Stave to boost her onto the mare's back. As he did so, the strained muscles in her legs protested. And she felt Hyn's disquiet at once. It spoke to her nerves, flesh to flesh: a visceral quiver like a harbinger of panic. The great horses were not easily frightened, but Hyn was afraid now, champing for movement.

When Linden touched the mare's flank with the Staff, however, Hyn calmed herself and her quivering subsided.

Around them, the other riders went to their Ranyhyn. Pahni needed Liand's help to seat Anele on Hrama: the old man had not relaxed his concentration northwards and made no effort to assist them. But the Master mounted Hynyn unaided, and Mahrtiir appeared to glide up onto his horse's back. When Pahni had given Liand a subtle lift, she sprang lightly onto Naharahn. In moments, Whrany alone remained unridden.

Still Bhapa had not returned.

A silence spread around them, punctuated only by the restless movements of the horses and the low, focused barking of the Waynhim. No night birds called: no insects chirred or whined. The darkness seemed to be holding its breath, and the moon's yellow light illumined little, as though it winced away from what it might witness. Linden felt an old malice gather among the slopes below her as if it welled up from within the ground. She did not know how to reply to it.

'Chosen,' Stave pronounced suddenly, 'be warned. It is dire. We did not know that this evil still endured. The old tellers have said that the ur-Lord destroyed it utterly.'

As he spoke, Linden felt pressure rise against her percipience. At the limit of its reach, her health-sense decried malevolence swelling into the night.

A moment later, she saw a distant flash of emerald like a flaring instance of sickness, an ignition of pure desecration. It was swallowed almost immediately by a black concussion which shook the night, a thunderclap of vitriol flung by one or several of the ur-viles. Before the vicious green vanished, however, she recognised it. It had been etched into her memory by horror.

'God!' she panted. 'Oh, God. It can't be.'

Beyond mistake that flash of rank emerald was the power of the Illearth Stone.

Which should have been impossible. Stave was right: with wild magic, Covenant had extirpated that ancient bane from the Land. And he had won his expensive victory thousands of years before Linden had first been translated to the Land.

Yet she knew from cruel experience that at least one small corrupt flake of the original Stone had survived Covenant's victory. In the years before that final contest, Lord Foul had given fragments of the Illearth Stone to each of his Giant-Ravers so that they could command his armies. One such fragment had been wielded against the defenders of the Land somewhat to the south and west of Andelain; and during the conflict, a shard had broken off from that piece of the Stone: had broken off and been lost.

The air seemed to grow warmer. It felt like a touch of steam. Nevertheless a chill slid along Linden's spine as if her sweat had turned to ice.

Lost, the green flake had remained so for centuries, leaking slow ruin into the hills, until it was discovered by a village of Woodhelvennin. By then, the Clave had come to rule the Land, and the lore of the Lords, which might have warned or protected the Woodhelven, had been corrupted. So the village was itself corrupted, generation after generation, until at last the evil shard was used against Linden, Sunder and Hollian while Covenant rambled in Andelain alone.

Later Covenant had destroyed that virulent flake as he had once shattered the Illearth Stone itself. But Linden remembered it still. She had felt its evil at a time when she did not know how to bear such knowledge.

Now, staring appalled at the lurid emerald after-flash on her retinas, she wondered: if one little piece of that terrible bane had survived, why not more than one? The Giant-Ravers had fought a number of battles against the Land's defenders. They had channelled immense forces through their fragments of the Stone. Other pieces could have broken off and been lost.

She could imagine no other explanation. Somehow an enemy of the Land had found such a piece. Or Esmer had—

It was possible. *Time seldom hinders me.* His access to the past made almost any act of treachery conceivable.

The thought that she would have to confront the old bane which had nearly undone both the Council of Lords and Thomas Covenant shrilled along her nerves, making her guts squirm with dread.

Another quick flare of green stained the night. Detonations of acid volleyed around it. The breeze falling from the mountainsides carried intimations of slaughter out into the moonlight.

Among the Ranyhyn, shadows seemed to melt and solidify. Then Bhapa stood at Mahrtiir's knee, gazing urgently up at the Manethrall. Even in the dark, his left arm and shoulder blazed with damage: Linden's dismayed nerves discerned a wound like a deep burn. Lingering emerald flickered among fine droplets of black fluid in the hurt. He had been caught at the fringe of a blast; lashed with power.

'Manethrall—' His throat clenched in pain. Forcing himself, he gasped softly, 'I know not what they are. But they are many. And they hold—'

He could not find words for what he had beheld.

'We have seen it,' Mahrtiir replied through his teeth. 'Mount at once. I cannot now tend to your wound.'

The Cord nodded. For a moment, he appeared to crouch, huddling over his injury; and his hurt burned at Linden as if she, too, had been splashed with acid. Then he flung himself onto Whrany's back.

'Describe them, Cord.' Stave spoke quietly, but his tone cut through the restiveness of the horses. 'What is their appearance? What did you discern of them?'

Green malignance slashed the night, momentarily limning the exposed shape of the foothills. It looked more savage now, and reached further: its wielders were advancing up the slope, or the ur-viles opposing it had been decimated. Frantic barking rose against the breeze. Scattered blooms and geysers of obsidian tattered the flash of emerald, but could not tear it apart.

Linden clung to the warm wood of the Staff and the broad strength of Hyn's back, and tried to believe that she was capable of combating a piece of the Illearth Stone.

Without wild magic—

'They are bitter,' Bhapa answered in a congested voice, 'and ancient beyond estimation. So I have felt. They appear to rise from the ground as if they have been freed from graves. Some have the size and semblance of trees, though they walk like men. Others resemble Cavewights and similar creatures. Still others wear monstrous shapes— I have never beheld the like, or heard them named.'

Through his teeth, he groaned, 'They are too many. Far too many. The ur-viles cannot hold them.'

Linden's heart quailed to hear him. Freed from graves— Oh, God. She seemed to hear Stave's response before he spoke. *Animate dead—*

'It should not be so,' said the Master. 'Yet it is. In this the recall of the *Haruchai* is sure.'

Earlier, days ago, he had spoken of *the lore and bitterness of the Viles made manifest in slain flesh, corpses with the puissance of Lords.*

Again emerald beat in the air like the throbbing of a diseased heart. It had come a long way up the hillside. A spatter of blackness answered it, and fell still.

The Ranyhyn stamped and whickered anxiously.

'We have shared it mind to mind across the millennia,' Stave continued, 'undiminished and unconfused.'

The vitriol which the ur-viles wield for destruction pulsed in their hearts.

'At first I was reluctant to name what I perceive. It offends Time and all Law. Yet now I am certain.'

Abruptly he stopped.

Clad in cerements and rot, their touch was fire.

Sitting Rhohm at Linden's side, Liand was a dark ache in the moonlight, an outpouring of innominate alarm. Behind them, Pahni leaned from her mount to succour Bhapa as best she could, while Anele muttered execrations into his beard.

'Speak the name, Bloodguard,' Mahrtiir put in harshly. 'Your knowledge is needed.'

Bursts of green evil echoed through the night, accumulating like summer lightning. Linden thought she heard the sound of running; desperate haste. Small swirls of blackness coalesced along the slope below her, still some distance from the Waynhim.

The ur-viles had been routed.

As did the Viles, they persisted outside or beyond life and death. As do the ur-viles, they had forms which could be touched and harmed.

'They are Demondim,' Stave answered. If he felt either fear or uncertainty, he did not show it. 'Esmer has brought them to this time.'

Apparently Cail's son had betrayed Linden and her companions with a vengeance.

If the legends of the Demondim were accurate, and their lore as vast and insidious as Stave had reported, the creatures might be able to destroy the Staff of Law. Given a little time, they could easily exterminate the last of the ur-viles and Waynhim. Even wild magic might not surpass their powers.

'Ringthane,' Mahrtiir asked avidly, 'will we not give battle? The ur-viles cannot hold. In moments they will be swept aside, and the Waynhim with them. We must ride to their defence.'

'No!' Linden protested. 'We can't. Not here. Don't you remember what Stave said? There haven't been any battles,' any extravagant exertions of power, 'in this part of the Land.' Not since she had unmade the Sunbane. 'If we fight now,' or if she did, 'we'll violate history. We'll damage the Arch of Time.'

The mere presence of the Demondim and a flake of the Illearth Stone might suffice to undermine the foundations of reality.

Yet the plight of the ur-viles cried out to her. Their desperate barking had become ragged, frenetic: they were being overwhelmed. And the Waynhim would be next. Already the grey creatures stood at the verge of the Stone's reach. With each mounting flash of emerald, each multiplied burst of virulence, their doom advanced on them. She could hear them chanting, and knew that they were too weak, too few—

Shapes that she could not define crowded up the slope, dark forms like a storm-lashed wave breaking impossibly upwards. They seemed to devour the moonlight so that they were illumined only by green evil. But now other forces were visible as well, quick eruptions of a killing opalescence which appeared to flash from indistinct hands.

'Then what must we do?' snarled Mahrtiir. 'It is intolerable that all who aid us must be slain while we stand aside.'

'Protect me,' she answered, acrid with self-restraint. The Waynhim had preserved the Staff for her. The ur-viles had exhausted themselves to help her find it. She wanted to rush to their defence, regardless of the consequences. But she had recognised her true peril. 'I need time—'

It is an effect of my nearness.

You will not be blocked from wild magic.

She needed time to rediscover the truth about herself.

At last, the Waynhim released the results of their steady invocation. From their wedge, a shockwave poured down the hillside; a blast which dwarfed the one that had warded their cave. Perceptible only because it was so potent, it crashed against the rising tsunami of the attackers.

A staggering emerald jolt answered the collision. Murderous nacre blazed soundlessly from the hands of the Demondim. Instantly an electric discharge as cruel as fangs and as lurid as the lightning lit the night; and for that brief moment Linden saw the Demondim clearly.

Eyeless like the creatures they had spawned, they resembled their creations in no other way except darkness. Bhapa was right. They looked like huge trees ripped somehow intact from centuries of mould and rot; like Cavewights corroded by time to skeletons and ferocity; like *kresh* and other rapt beasts resurrected to repay their deaths. Among them marched human corpses, men and women who knew only the animating lust of their possessors. And there were other figures as well, monsters in the shape of nightmares. The Demondim appeared to number in the hundreds, all surging upwards against the assault of the Waynhim – and all so long abandoned to the hungry embrace of worms that they had forgotten whatever they had once known of their mortality.

Linden could not tell which among them held their fragment of the Illearth Stone. Perhaps several did in concert. She saw only that while the Stone blazed its evil seemed to rave from many of the Demondim at once, casting back the darkness; tainting the moonlight with the hues of atrocity.

She no longer believed that her foes held a mere flake of the ancient bane. To her horrified senses, its power seemed as absolute as that of the original Illearth Stone.

When the Waynhim fell, the onslaught would reach Linden and her companions. She had only a little time left. A scattering of moments: a few dozen heartbeats.

Too few to save the world—

The Ranyhyn were growing frantic. Whrany skittered and flinched, apparently feeling Bhapa's pain, yearning to protect his rider. Pahni walked her mount in tight circles to calm the mare; and Mahrtiir leaned along his stallion's neck, murmuring fierce promises to the horse's ears. But Stave sat motionless, with Hynyn as stolid as a statue under him. And Hrama bore Anele steadily in spite of the old man's angry muttering.

Linden gripped the Staff until her hands were slick with sweat, thinking that she would have no choice except to call forth its power – and praying fervently that an exertion of Law by its very nature would sustain rather than weaken the Arch; that the insult to the integrity of Time would not prove irreparable.

Another tremendous concussion shook the night, emerald shot through with opalescence and ruin, dropping the Waynhim to their knees. Faint bursts of vitriol still attacked the dire force of the bane, but they were few and widely separated. Only a handful of the ur-viles remained alive—

Esmer had foretold death for the Waynhim. He had not mentioned the ur-viles. They had discerned treachery in him from the first, and had set themselves to guard against him. He may have been glad to think that they would all perish.

Yet he could do nothing without contradicting his own intentions. For every betrayal, his conflicted nature required him to offer help. That was why he had left.

So that Linden could use Covenant's ring.

Stave had assured her that she would be able to do so.

Abruptly she shook off her hesitation. 'Here,' she said to Liand. Prompted by an instinct which she could not have explained, she tossed the Staff to him, trusting him to catch it. 'Keep it safe for me. I'll need it later.'

It would only distract her now – and might hinder her in other ways as well. Its essential nature contradicted wild magic.

Liand fumbled for it in surprise, secured his grasp on it; hugged it to his chest. But she did not see his nod of acceptance, or the promise in his eyes. She had already dropped away from him in her mind, bowing her head and covering her face with her hands as if to isolate herself from him and all her companions.

Esmer was gone. And she held Covenant's ring by right and need. She had inherited it from him in Kiril Threndor; had confirmed her claim upon it by wielding its illimitable fire to shape the new Staff of Law. It had healed a bullet's passage through her vulnerable flesh. It had preserved her from the collapse of Kevin's Watch. If she needed it now, it would not be denied to her.

It could not.

Scrambling along the twisted pathways of herself, the lost route to the hidden door, she found the truth. Stave was right. The door had not vanished. It had merely been masked by Esmer's aura. In his absence, she seemed to rediscover it with ease. She was already desperate: she had forgotten agony and formication and utter bereavement. And at times the ring's argence had answered her urgent impulses more naturally, more readily, than her deliberate choices.

Between one heartbeat and the next, white fire bloomed from the hard circle under her shirt as though it had arisen straight out of her heart.

If she had opened her eyes, she would have seen the faces of her companions turning towards her, defined by wonder and white fire. If she had reached out with her percipience, she would have felt a shock of recognition and eagerness galvanise the Ranyhyn. Her nerves might have tasted the more distant awe of the Waynhim and the grim determination of the remaining ur-viles. She could have found comfort in the sudden apprehension which momentarily halted the Demondim.

But she had no attention to spare for the external details of her situation. As soon as she found the door and felt the silver fire of Covenant's ring spring forth like exaltation, she squeezed her eyes more tightly shut, bowed more deeply into herself and pulled her concentration down to a point as fine as the tip of a dirk.

With that delicate instrument, she probed the necessary structure of time.

At once, she felt the *wrongness* of what she did. She was attempting a violation as cruel as possession or rape. On a level too deep for words or understanding, she seemed to feel the woven fabric of existence shudder in dismay. If she made even the smallest mistake, all of reality would be torn apart; and the rending shriek of ruin would be the last sound that the world ever heard.

Nevertheless she did not falter now. She was Linden Avery the Chosen, and she meant to prove herself against the Land's doom.

Lord Foul had taught her to know her own evil. She could still fear what might happen; but she no longer feared herself.

She needed to focus her power and her senses so keenly that she would be able to detect the ligatures which connected one instant to the next; the bonds of sequence which caused one heartbeat, one thought, one event to follow another. If she could identify the ceaseless, evanescent, and ineluctable fact of transition which defined time, she would be able to insert her fire there and sever—

—detaching one moment from the next. Opening a *caesure*, as Joan did whenever her madness impelled her to strike herself.

Yet she knew that it would not be enough to simply replicate Joan's actions; to slow and refine her perceptions to the pitch which empowered Joan. If she did, she would have no control over what ensued. Her task was more complex. While she emulated Joan's insanity, she had to remember that what she did was evil. She had to remember its consequences.

Therefore she cast herself deliberately back into the instant when she had first entered the Fall; when formication had become the world, leaving her capable of nothing except featureless gelid whiteness and Joan's torment. That excruciation she recreated in her mind as she focused her argence closer and closer to the gap between the instants. With every piercing breath, she relived agony.

That pain helped her cling to herself. It reminded her that she was not Joan; that she was prepared to accept the cost of her own actions.

She had caused this crisis by the extravagance of her choices. Uncounted ur-viles had been slain, and most of the Waynhim would follow. Her friends would die. The Staff of Law might be destroyed. She herself might fall in spite of her powers, abandoning Jeremiah and the Land to Lord Foul's malice. And all because she had risked leaving her proper time.

Set beside the potential cost of failure, the anguish and evil of creating a *caesure* were prices that she was willing to pay.

Somewhere beyond her attention, emerald flared and raved, adumbrating malice into the betrayed night. The Waynhim were driven back. The waves of their theurgy, shock after shock like combers in a high wind, were barely adequate to defend them: they could not stand their ground. The explosions of vitriol from the ur-viles had become pitifully brief and slight; too small to hamper the Demondim. The bitter gleaming of the attackers swept resistance aside.

Watching the doomed contest, Mahrtiir and his mount could no longer restrain themselves. Howling defiance, the Manethrall launched his Ranyhyn like thunder down the hillside. At once, Pahni and Naharahn pounded after him, chased unsteadily by Bhapa on Whrany. Pahni added her girlish shout to Mahrtiir's stentorian roar; but Bhapa was silent.

Only Whrany's fleet skill enabled the injured Cord to keep his seat. Unable to use his garrote and fatally weak, he could not fight. Nevertheless he raced after his Manethrall and Pahni, trusting the hooves of his mount to strike for him.

Liand might have followed the Ramen into battle, but his responsibility for the Staff held him back. Stave did not move from Linden's side. And Anele remained where he was, consumed by his useless imprecations.

If the onslaught came near Linden, she would be defended only by an untried Stonedownor, a madman and one lone *Haruchai*.

With some part of her mind, she must have been aware of her companions and the Demondim; must have felt the proximity of the Illearth Stone and slaughter. Her sense of urgency increased moment by moment, and white fire from Covenant's ring spired higher into the dark, shedding a stark luminescence across the bare hillsides and the thronging battleground.

Nevertheless her peril only fed her concentration, sending her deeper into her task.

It was hard. God, it was hard! Intending to violate time, she violated as well every instinct for healing and health which had shaped her life. *Caesures* were evil: they attacked the fundamental structures which made existence possible. And she had committed herself to wholeness rather than ruin.

Still she did not hold back. She knew the depth of the Despiser's malice.

She felt the lust and hatred of the Demondim and the destructiveness of the Illearth Stone. She understood what would happen if she allowed such hungers to feed unopposed and her whole being rose up in repudiation.

And Liand held the Staff of Law in her name: the only instrument of power in all the Land which might be able to halt or contain the vast wrong of a Fall. If he did not fail her, she could hope to impose limits on the harm she meant to cause.

Guilt is power. Only the damned can be saved.

When she was ready, she cast a silent appeal to Hyn and all of the Ranyhyn. Without them, she would be unable to reach her necessary goal.

Then she released a slash of silver flame which sundered the night.

Through the riven dark, chaos tumbled forth. A tremendous migraine swirl of distortion appeared in the night, destructive as a tornado and maddening as a swarm of wasps. It seethed with force as though every link and interstice of material reality had been torn apart.

Remembered agony squalled in Linden's nerves as she saw that she had succeeded.

The *caesure* boiled no more than a stone's throw to her right. It seemed to drift towards her with a kind of hideous nonchalance, sure of its might and in no hurry to devour.

Stave barked a warning and Liand called her name; but she hardly heard them. With a gesture of wild magic, a sweep of fire, she redirected the Fall, sent it sprawling like an avalanche in slow motion down towards the heart of the battle. At the same time, she scourged it with flame so that it swelled over the ground, growing wider until it was vast enough to consume the entire horde of the Demondim. Then she urged Hyn into motion after it.

As the mare stretched into a gallop, Linden shouted in a voice of argence, '*Come now!*' praying that the Waynhim and the ur-viles would be able to hear her through the tumult.

At the same time, she prayed that Mahrtiir and his Cords still lived, and could respond.

Stave and Liand rode at her sides. Silver fire lit the stern concentration on the Master's visage: he looked like a man who believed that he could determine the outcome of Linden's gamble by sheer force of will. Liand clung grimly to the Staff, holding it ready. His fear of the Fall glared in his eyes, but he did not try to restrain his mount.

Behind them ran Hrama, bearing Anele whether or not the old man wished to follow.

Linden glimpsed Waynhim racing towards her on all fours. Among them, a few ur-viles appeared, splashed with blood as black as night. As Hyn pounded among the massed forces of the Demondim, more Ranyhyn joined her, two or three. But in the light of Covenant's ring, Linden caught only a brief flash of them. She could not be sure that more than one of them still carried a rider.

Then she plunged into the *caesure* as though it were a lake of nightmares.

In an instant, utter anguish seemed to swallow her whole. And as the roiling torment closed over her head, she began to drown—

At that moment, she had no reason to believe she had not brought death to all that she held dear.

Chapter Nine:

Pursuit

The unspeakable pain of the Fall was the same: the disorientation: the sensory insanity. She was trapped as she had been once before in the simultaneous shattering of too many realities. Every moment which would ever come and go in the *caesure*'s path was torn apart and flung at her like a bleeding gobbet; and every scrap of time's shredded flesh as it struck her became a burrowing insect, a wasp or chigger driven mad by dissociation and avid to lay its ruinous eggs within her. At the same time, all perceptible meaning and structure were wiped away, leaving behind only white emptiness and illimitable cold.

Drowning in all the world's distress at once, Linden could easily have perished, suffocated by icy formication and loss. She could just as easily have been driven mad. But even madness and death required causality, sequence, interconnection; and the Fall had severed every link which would have made such consequences possible.

Yet this experience was essentially unlike her first such immersion. She did not need to compel the current of distortion backward, into the past. Nor was she required to trust that the ur-viles would impose her will upon it. Instead she could let the terrible forces of the *caesure* carry her forward according to their own peculiar logic. The Earthpowerful instincts of the Ranyhyn would provide for her redemption.

In addition, she was spared another encounter with Joan Covenant's demented grief. Somewhere Joan still stood among her attending *skest*, reaching out with wild magic and self-loathing to name her endless pains. But she had not created this Fall, and did not occupy it. Her madness played no part in its ravening.

And Linden had one other advantage as well. Covenant's ring still shone like a beacon through the fabric of her shirt, lighting her way to survival. Wild magic was in some sense as disruptive as the *caesure*, untrammelled by restriction. For that reason, it had the power to violate the strictures of time.

For the same reason, however, white gold formed the keystone of the Arch of Time. Its unfettered passion anchored the paradox which made finite existence possible within the infinite universe.

Similarly, the hot blaze of Linden's heart anchored her within herself, enabling her to continue to be who she was when every mote and particle of her specific being had been torn asunder.

Duration could not exist within the Fall. Nothing was possible there except devouring pain and infinite cold and devastation. Therefore no tangible interval passed before Hyn galloped free of agony, bearing Linden out into a flood of sunlight and dazzled blindness.

They had arrived on a slowly rising slope which jolted the mare's hooves like packed dirt.

Because she had been anchored, and wild magic shone from her yet, Linden was not overwhelmed by her passage through time and torment. She could still think, and feel, and choose. Although the intense glare of the sun filled her vision, effacing sight, her other senses reached out acutely. With the nerves of her skin, she felt Stave riding strongly on one side of her, impervious to the harm of the *caesure*. On the other side, Liand held his seat on Rhohm, clinging grimly to the Staff of Law. Protected by its warm clarity, he also was not as sick as he would otherwise have been.

Close on their heels followed Anele, as unmistakably himself as his inborn Earthpower could make him – and as unquestionably insane as the Fall at his back.

Behind Hrama ran three more Ranyhyn, all of them injured, but still essentially whole. For a moment, Linden could not tell if they bore riders. The rampant seething of the Fall and the sudden brightness of the sun blocked her perceptions. Then she discerned Mahrtiir clutching his appalled stomach at Anele's back; Pahni vomiting helplessly past Naharahn's withers; Bhapa stretched nearly unconscious along Whrany's neck. Blood throbbed from Bhapa's arm and shoulder, streaking his mount's torn flanks.

Beside the last Ranyhyn raced more than a dozen Waynhim and perhaps half that many ur-viles, all that remained of the bereft creatures which had committed their lives to Linden and the Staff.

And behind them came the Demondim in a teeming horde, ecstatic with power and ravenous for victims.

She had accomplished this much, if no more: she had brought her assailants with her out of the past; had defused their power to disrupt the integrity of time.

Now she would have to fight them. Hyn would be able to outrun the

Demondim, but Linden's company could not flee indefinitely. The ur-viles and the Waynhim were badly hurt; close to exhaustion. And the Ramen were too ill to defend themselves. Pahni and Bhapa might not be able to sit their mounts much longer. Even Mahrtiir's aura felt fragile. The Manethrall could hardly contain the heaving of his stomach.

Linden had to make a stand.

She intended to turn and strike as soon as she could see.

As soon as she knew where she was. And *when*.

If the Ranyhyn had misjudged their passage through the *caesure* – or if some effect of the Fall had cast them out prematurely – she might still be in danger of altering the Land's history.

The midday brilliance of the sun still blinded her, however. While Hyn bore her racing over the hard ground, she blinked her eyes frantically, trying to clear the dazzle from her sight, and strove to extend her senses further around her.

In spite of the sun's brightness, the air was cool on her sweating cheeks: it smelled of spring. And ahead of her the ground rose gradually, uninterrupted by swelling hills or narrow ravines or streambeds. She was no longer among the foothills of the Southron Range in late summer. Somehow Hyn's urgent run must have carried her out into the South Plains.

Or the Ranyhyn were able to navigate distance as well as time within a Fall. Linden and her companions may have crossed many leagues while they traversed the years.

But whatever the Ranyhyn had done, the Demondim had matched it. They could not have prevented Linden's Fall from engulfing them; yet they had emerged still on the heels of their prey. And their passage did not daunt them, or diminish their hunger for slaughter. Stave had said that their lore was profound and oblique, reaching depths which had surpassed the Old Lords. Their understanding of *caesures* could easily be greater than Linden's.

And they were unexpectedly swift. They rushed forward as if they were boiling over the ground. For all her speed, Hyn pulled away from the harrying creatures slowly. Perhaps she could not run faster. Or perhaps she held back so that she would not outdistance the rest of Linden's companions.

Behind them, the Fall still moiled viciously. Linden had made it large, dangerously large, so that it would swallow all of the horde. Now its swirling forces seemed to blot out the world in that direction; and it flowed after the Demondim as though they sucked it in their wake.

Nevertheless Linden and those with her gained distance by increments, creating a small interval of safety between their desperation and the powers which pursued them.

How much time had passed? A score of heartbeats? Two score? In another moment, Linden told herself, when the gap was a bit wider, she would turn to counterattack.

With Covenant's ring, she might be able to slow the Demondim so that her companions could escape; but she feared to take the risk. Wild magic might inadvertently draw the Fall towards her too swiftly to be avoided, or feed its destructiveness in some way which she could not foresee.

As her vision began to clear, she deliberately silenced the argence shining through the fabric of her shirt. Then, without a word, as if she expected Liand to read her mind, she reached out for the Staff.

He did not fail her. Almost immediately, she felt the smooth wooden shaft slap into her palm.

Its touch sent a thrill of vitality through her, wiping away the last effects of the *caesure*; retrieving her from the harm which she had imposed on time. In some fundamental way, wild magic did not suit her: it was too extravagant and unpredictable for her. She was a physician by choice, trained to precision and care; and the teeming ramifications of Covenant's ring threatened at every moment to expand beyond her control.

In contrast, the Staff of Law was a healer's implement, as careful as any scalpel or suture. When she held it, she grew stronger: at once calmer and more capable, firmly poised between passion and restraint.

Elevated by the essential certainty of Law, she spoke a silent word to Hyn, nudged the mare with her heels. Without hesitation, Hyn peeled away from her course, carrying Linden in a steady curve out of the path of the other Ranyhyn and the Demondim-spawn and back towards the onrushing horde.

Stave and Liand accompanied her as if they – or their mounts – had known exactly what she would do. But Hrama bore Anele onwards with the Ramen thundering behind them while the ur-viles and Waynhim scrambled to keep pace.

Moment by moment, blinking tears and brightness from her eyes, Linden regained her sight.

With her companions, she galloped down a slow, wide slope which stretched ahead of her until it vanished under the feet of the Demondim and was covered by the towering storm of the *caesure*. The sun and its shadows suggested that she was riding eastward.

As the Ramen raced past her in the opposite direction, she sensed that Mahrtiir had begun to rally. Hours or days or centuries ago, he had promised that he and his Cords would not again be crippled by the effects of a Fall. Now from a small pouch at his waist he fumbled out a leaf of dried *amanibhavam*. Crumbling it in his hand, he held it under his nose; inhaled a little of the sharp powder.

The potent grass stung him like a flick of lightning. A seizure took him, and he thrashed violently on his mount's back. But the spasm passed in an instant. When it ended, it left him restored and eager, galvanised for combat.

Guiding his stallion to Naharahn's side, he thrust his hand at Pahni's nose until she breathed in a taste of the *amanibhavam*. She, too, thrashed for a moment, then recovered visibly.

But Mahrtiir offered none of the leaf to Bhapa. The injured Cord lay unconscious along Whrany's neck, and might have been unseated by the healing grass. Instead the Manethrall left Bhapa to his mount's care and led Pahni after Linden towards the charging Demondim.

As soon as the last of the Waynhim and ur-viles had passed her, Linden called Hyn to a halt, and looked out over the army of her attackers.

At her side, Liand stopped and stared in dismay. But Stave gazed at the Demondim like a man who had long ago forgotten how to be afraid.

Seen by daylight on the wide plain instead of by moonlight rising among the hills, the horde seemed less vast; no longer as measureless as night and slaughter. Nevertheless the sun did not diminish the creatures. Rather, its glare seemed to accentuate their stature and potency.

Linden could not discern them precisely. They wavered in and out of definition as if they passed in front of a rippled glass. At one moment, they appeared as tangible as flesh and pain: at the next, they were translucent, nearly invisible. Whenever she tried to focus on a specific creature, it blurred away and then emerged several paces closer to her. And as the Demondim advanced, their forms steamed and frothed like acid.

Paled by sunlight, the flaring of power from their hands was barely visible to ordinary sight; but it howled at Linden's percipience. And it left behind stains of midnight which persisted in the air as if the inherent vitriol of the Demondim had burned holes in the substance of reality. Until the onrushing *caesure* swallowed those stains, they looked vicious enough to tear down trees and blast boulders.

Still the individual powers of the monstrous creatures were evanescent compared to the raving evil of the Illearth Stone. Among them the Demondim bore an outpouring of emerald so avid and malefic that it seemed to daunt the sun. From the vantage of higher ground and Hyn's back, Linden could see now that the dire green did not arise from any one place or creature among the horde. The Demondim carried no discrete fragment of the original Stone.

Rather they appeared to bring its essence with them as if they could draw on it from some distant source.

'What will you do, Chosen?' demanded Stave. 'Is it your purpose to give combat? That is madness. We must flee.'

The sound of his voice distracted her from the horde; and as soon as she understood what he had said, she remembered that he was right. She could not afford to unleash her power until she knew where she was, and when.

The Demondim rushed savagely towards her with the *caesure* looming behind them. She had only moments left—

'I have to stop this,' she panted. 'It's too big—' She had made it too big. 'For God's sake, tell me where we are!'

Had they reached the time in which they belonged?

'Linden,' Liand breathed in sudden astonishment. 'Heaven and Earth, Linden!'

She did not so much as glance at him. Gripping the Staff, she waited for Stave's answer.

'I am not yet certain,' he replied flatly. 'The season is condign. And Kevin's Dirt impends above us. It appears that our proper time is nigh.'

Kevin's Dirt, she thought. Oh, shit! She had not noticed it overhead because she could not force her gaze away from the Demondim. But she believed the Master. Soon her health-sense would begin to fray and fail.

She had to act *now*, before the horde advanced further; before the truncation of her senses began to hamper her.

Could she risk wielding the Staff of Law?

She did not know. Yet the Staff itself might protect her from an irreparable mistake. And she had no time left for doubt. The Demondim were almost upon her. Behind them, the *caesure* which she had created surged forward. It was her responsibility.

Good cannot be accomplished by evil means.

'Linden!' Liand called again, insisting on her attention. 'Have you beheld—?'

She did not give him a chance to finish. Slipping abruptly from Hyn's back, she took three stiff strides towards the leading edge of the horde, then halted to plant one heel of the Staff in the hard dirt.

The Stonedownor shouted after her: a cry rife with alarm. She ignored him. Stave and Mahrtiir sprang from their mounts, poised themselves for battle. She ignored them as well.

From the vibrant wood of the Staff, she brought forth a burst of incandescence as bright as sunlight and as defiant as an oriflamme. While it blazed, she yelled at the Demondim, '*Stop right there!* This is as far as you go!'

Her unexpected challenge threw the creatures into confusion. She did not know whether they could understand her, and did not care. They were lorewise enough to recognise the Staff of Law. And they had already felt the presence of Covenant's ring. At once, the first Demondim scrambled to a halt, blocking the way for the dire shapes behind them. Nacre power spat and frothed, pale as air and ruinous as magma, shedding blackness like glimpses into the heart of the Lost Deep. Indistinct forms steamed darkly, while among them rapt emerald seethed for release.

They could not know that she was bluffing—

Or perhaps they could. They might perceive that she was too human and frail to control both of her powers simultaneously. They needed only a few heartbeats to resolve their uncertainty and resume their ravening onrush.

Nevertheless they had given Linden enough time. As the horde paused, she leaped past it in her mind to confront the Fall.

She had caused this rent in the fabric of sequence and causality herself. And she had been swept up in its chaos only a short while ago. She knew it intimately.

With percipience to guide her, she raised the Staff, directed it over the heads of the Demondim, and unleashed its warm puissance into the swarming core of the *caesure.*

From the iron-shod end of the wood, flame the rich yellow hue of sunflowers and ripe corn lashed out, a streaming ceaseless flail of fire. The Fall was huge: she had made it so. And it had fed on millennia of severed instants. But the Staff of Law could draw on the fathomless reservoir of Earthpower which defined the Land. Indeed, its possibilities were limited only by the capacities of its wielder. And Linden had already proved herself equal to the Sunbane. The evil before her now was enormous and consuming. Yet it was a small thing in comparison.

Challenged by the direct vitality of the Staff, the Fall failed rapidly. For an instant, it mounted upwards, screaming into the heavens. Then it collapsed in on itself with a noise like a thunderclap, sucking down its own viciousness until it winked away like a snuffed candle.

More swiftly than Linden would have believed possible, the *caesure* was gone, leaving her with warm wood quiescent in her hands. Stave and Mahrtiir stood ready at her sides; and all around her was the sweet scent of meadows in sunlight, swales of grass and wildflowers adorned with dew, and trees budding into leaf.

No longer aware of herself, Linden sank to her knees. Exerting the Staff, she had expended her own substance. Her determination was gone, and the very ground beneath her no longer felt necessary or immediate.

Apparently howling, although they made no sound, the Demondim flung themselves towards her. In the distance, Liand shouted her name as if he had never stopped calling for her.

Then suddenly Stave took hold of her. Lifting her into the air, he threw her onto Hyn's back. At the same time, Mahrtiir sprang astride his mount; and immediately their two Ranyhyn surged into a gallop, fleeing the horde. Behind them, Stave followed on Hynyn.

Uncertain of her balance, and clinging fervently to the Staff of Law, Linden returned to herself.

There Liand and Pahni joined her. Pounding the hard ground close together, the five horses stretched their strength to out-distance the Demondim.

At first, Linden barely noticed them. For a while, she hardly knew where she was. She felt harried by exigencies which she no longer recognised or understood. By degrees, however, their urgency reclaimed her. Still reeling internally, she glanced around to check on her companions.

Both Stave and Liand were unhurt: they had not encountered the Demondim. But Mahrtiir's legs had been burned, his hands held bleeding sores and one cheek wore a swath of blisters. The opalescent blasts of the creatures had nearly slain him. Perhaps he had attempted to garrote one of them. Its acid would have eaten away his fighting cord; chewed into his hands.

Pahni's pain was obvious; but for a moment, Linden could not determine where the Cord had been injured. Then she noticed that Pahni rode leaning to one side, protecting the blood which had soaked her tunic along her ribs.

Reflexively Linden studied Mahrtiir's and Pahni's wounds until she was sure that they were not mortal. Given time, the Ramen would heal. With the Staff, Linden herself could heal them. If the Ranyhyn outran the horde far enough – and if she recovered her ability to concentrate—

The great horses had also been scored with corrosion. Blood oozed from galls and welts in their sides. But the Ranyhyn had avoided hurts severe enough to hamper their strides.

Reassured, Linden allowed herself to relax a little. As Hyn strained for speed under her, she grew gradually stronger.

Then Liand gestured ahead. Shouting over the labour of hooves, he repeated, 'Linden! Have you beheld it?'

She had not. Since emerging from the *caesure*, she had not glanced in that direction.

When at last she lifted her gaze towards the west, she saw Revelstone looming there like the prow of a mighty ship.

God in Heaven— Revelstone: Lord's Keep. A few hundred paces directly in front of her – and some three hundred leagues from the place where she and her companions had entered the Fall.

For a moment, the sight left her stunned; too stupefied to think. Revelstone? Impossible! Even Hyn's tremendous strength could not have carried her so far in less than ten days—

Then panic clutched her heart, and she urged Hyn to a halt, forcing Stave to wheel back towards her; face her. Ignoring the tumult and hunger of the Demondim, she demanded, 'Revelstone, Stave? How in hell did we get *here?*'

Once the habitation of the Lords, the vast stone castle had later become the fortress from which the Clave had ruled the Land. Ten years ago she had entered Lord's Keep twice: first as a prisoner of the Riders; then as their foe. For her, the intricately carved castle was flagrant with memories of anguish and bloodshed.

How had the Ranyhyn brought her so far astray?

Liand had told her that Revelstone was important to the Masters.

Stave gazed past her to gauge the pace of the horde. Then he met her shaken stare. Deliberately patient, he replied, 'I have said that I would bear tidings to the Masters. When we entered the Fall, you asked no clear destination of the Ranyhyn. Therefore they heeded me. Answering my will, they have borne us hither.'

'God *damn* it—!' Linden began, then bit down her indignation. What had she expected of Stave? That he would forsake his responsibilities and beliefs merely because she disagreed with him? The *Haruchai* were not so easily swayed. And he may have served her well. One destination was as good as another when she did not know where to look for her son. In addition, Revelstone might provide a temporary refuge, if she could convince the Masters to aid her – if enough of Stave's people lived here – and if the Keep's walls could withstand the Demondim—

Nevertheless Anele would suffer for what Stave had done.

Clenching her hands on the Staff until her knuckles ached, she called Hyn into motion again.

As the mare sped forward once more, Linden stared hard at Revelstone; and her brief hope fell away. She could not imagine how plain granite might rebuff the Demondim. Perhaps the creatures would be unable to pass through solid obstacles; but they had access to the Illearth Stone—

In ancient times, the Keep's walls had been defended by Lords and lore.

Now there were no Lords, or any men and women like them. Yet she and her company raced towards Revelstone simply because Stave had willed it so.

She could not believe that she would find safety there. But where else could she go? The Demondim had not slowed their pace, and she doubted that she would ever be strong enough to withstand them all.

And Revelstone should have been a sanctuary. It had been formed by Giants during the time of High Lord Damelon, many long centuries before Thomas Covenant had first entered the Land; delved by stone-lore and stone-love into the foundations of a wedge-shaped promontory jutting beyond a spur of the Westron Mountains. From the sealed watchtower which guarded its entrance to the elaborately graven ramparts and balconies, embrasures and coigns which defined its walls, it stood just as she remembered it: proudly, like a work of art, articulating the long-lived adoration and homage of the lost Giants.

Looking at the Keep now, however, another realisation struck Linden like a blow to the heart; another flash of anger and fear—

Her son had tried to warn her.

That also should have been impossible. In his condition, it must have been. Yet Jeremiah, who knew nothing of this place, and had never responded to her love – ah, Jeremiah had used Lego to build an image of Revelstone in her living room only a few hours before Roger Covenant had kidnapped him.

Never having seen them before, he had devised motley models of both Revelstone and Mount Thunder; messages in red and blue and yellow bricks. Using the only language available to him, he had tried to prepare her for his plight – and hers. But she had failed to understand him.

In spite of her chagrin, however, she now knew where to find to him.

But first she needed to reenter Revelstone. That message had become clear to her as well. Why else had Jeremiah included it in his construct?

Yet the fact that Stave had brought her here implied that Lord's Keep was more than simply important to the Masters. It was the seat of their Mastery. Here they made their decisions and kept their prisoners. They would not let Anele go. And they might oppose any use of the Staff, or of Covenant's ring. Indeed, they might believe that their commitments required them to wrest Linden's powers from her.

Ahead of her, Hrama and Whrany waited with their riders. Bhapa remained unconscious and feverish, sickened by the burst of vitriol which had torn open his arm and shoulder. And Whrany's injuries appeared to be festering, as if the nacre of the Demondim still gnawed at them. But Anele gazed blindly about him with a look of confusion, apparently wondering where he was, or how he had come here.

The Ranyhyn panted with exertion, blowing froth from their nostrils. Linden could tell at a glance, however, that they were far from the end of their strength. Not so the ur-viles and Waynhim. Utterly spent and gasping hoarsely, they sprawled in the dirt beside the horses, unable even to hold up their heads. If their makers came upon them now, they would be helpless to defend themselves.

At a thought from Linden, Hyn halted there. Stave and Liand remained mounted on either side of her; but Mahrtiir slipped to the ground at once and hastened to attend to Bhapa.

Now he gave the Cord a scent of his crumbled *amanibhavam*. The dried grass-blade did not rouse him, in spite of its potency. Nevertheless it appeared to stabilise his condition, reinforcing his body's natural defences. He coughed a few times and squirmed unquietly, then began to breathe with more ease. By degrees, his fever receded somewhat.

While the Manethrall cared for Bhapa, Pahni also dismounted. Although she looked like she might collapse herself, weakened by the wound in her side, she went quickly to each of the injured Ranyhyn in turn, offering them *amanibhavam*.

Liand watched Linden with his eyes full of apprehension. He seemed more aware of the gnashing Demondim than anyone around him. And, like her, he distrusted the Masters.

Struggling to contain her fears, Linden confronted Stave. 'All right,' she panted urgently. 'You brought us here. Now what? How many Masters *are* there?' She meant in Revelstone. 'And what do you think they can do?' They had no power except their native strength and skill. 'We need help, Stave. How can your people fight those things?'

He had promised her a reckoning. How high a price was he willing to pay for his convictions?

She was the only one here who could oppose the horde – and she was already exhausted.

Stave regarded her steadily. Instead of speaking, he extended his hand towards the high bulk of Lord's Keep against its background of mountains; and at that moment the interlocking stone gates in the base of the watchtower swung open. From the tunnel under the tower, riders cantered outwards as if he had summoned them forth.

Four abreast, they emerged row after row, first a dozen of them, then a score; two score; more— and still they appeared: more men on horseback than Linden had ever seen at one time. When the last of them had left the darkness under the watchtower, they must have numbered eighty or a hundred.

And they were *Haruchai*, all of them: fell-handed warriors mounted on hardy mustangs and heavy destriers, dray-horses and racers. They bore no weapons and no pennons; wore no armour; carried no shields; wielded no lore or instruments of power. Nevertheless they rode out from Revelstone to challenge the horde of the Demondim as if no foe could stand against them.

'We will not fail,' Stave replied to Linden. 'While one of us remains alive, you will be warded.'

As soon as the full force of the riders had left the Keep, they quickened their pace, accelerating from an easy canter to a headlong charge. Apparently they meant to reach Linden and her company before the Demondim could overtake them.

'Revelstone?' Anele asked in bewilderment. 'Is it Revelstone?' But Linden had no time to comfort him.

Briefly Stave cocked his head as if he were listening. Then he informed Linden, 'The Ranyhyn have served us well. This day is the second since our departure from the Verge of Wandering.'

His people could communicate so, mind to mind.

But the assurance that she had regained her proper time gave her little relief. The horde would soon draw near enough to strike at her small company. And the Masters might prove as fatal in their own way as the Demondim.

Quickly she urged Stave, 'Tell them about the ur-viles.' She did not doubt that his people would defend the Waynhim; but the *Haruchai* and the ur-viles had been foes for millennia. 'I don't care whether you approve of anything I've done. This isn't about me. The ur-viles have earned your protection.'

Stave nodded his agreement.

Again Anele asked the air plaintively, 'Revelstone?'

Linden could feel the Demondim massing at her back: Kevin's Dirt had not yet dimmed her percipience. And when she turned to look at them, she saw that they were too close. The Masters would barely reach her before the horde did. If their charge did not immediately throw back the onslaught, she and her friends would find themselves in the midst of the battle.

When she had gathered her reserves, she called up a soothing current of strength from the Staff and sent it flowing towards the Waynhim and the ur-viles.

They were not creatures of Law. And her senses could not read them. Still she knew that she would not harm them. She trusted herself here. She had already healed the Staff's guardian among the Waynhim.

They would die if they remained helpless, unable to fight or run.

The Waynhim stirred almost at once, rousing to lift their heads and sniff at the fraught air. Then the ur-viles did the same. Some of them slapped at their skin as if to beat off insects. Others flung themselves from side to side, or scrabbled at the dirt. Yet they grew stronger.

As soon as they began to regain their feet, Linden called back her power.

Behind her, the horde slowed its pace. New forces gathered and swirled among the monsters. Apparently the Demondim were preparing to meet the charge of the Masters.

'Come on,' she muttered to her companions. 'Let's go.' She had been in danger for too long. 'We need some distance.'

With a touch of her hand, she asked Hyn to bear her away.

The *Haruchai* thundered closer. The hooves of their mounts raised banners of dust from the bare ground.

Twisting on Hrama's back, Anele appeared to look straight at Linden, in spite of his blindness. 'Anele is betrayed,' he announced bitterly. 'You have given him to *them*.'

While she gazed at him in sorrow, he slipped suddenly to the ground, ducked past Rhohm, and dashed away—

'Anele!' she shouted: too late. She had already missed the instant when she might have deflected him.

—directly towards the massed forces of the Demondim.

As his bare feet touched the dirt, his entire aura changed. His baffled bitterness vanished, replaced by savage fire like a yowl of repudiation. Running towards the horde, he seemed to set the air aflame, igniting it with outrage. His feet left smoking burns on the ground, and his whole form glowed like iron in the forge, too hot to be touched or endured.

Any other mortal being would have been flash-burned to ash and cinders. Only his inherited Earthpower enabled him to withstand the abrupt magma which had taken possession of him.

Linden shouted his name. This had happened to the old man once before. In the communal centre of the Ramen encampment, he had become a con-flagration in human form. Raging at her, he had nearly scorched the eyes from her skull.

That same spirit had claimed Anele again.

In a clattering rush, the first wave of the Masters swept around Linden and her company towards the Demondim; and Anele flung himself against the monsters as if he meant to challenge their vast evil with the lava of his own pain.

He had taken even Stave by surprise; yet Stave reacted before Linden could do more than flinch and cry out. At his silent command, Hynyn reared and turned, springing away to join the tumultuous charge of the *Haruchai*.

The Master may have intended to strike Anele down, as he had among the Ramen.

Leaping for their mounts, Mahrtiir and Pahni positioned themselves to defend Linden. The ur-viles and Waynhim rallied together; staggered chanting into loose formations on either side of her. Liand yelled at her, but she could not hear him through the din of hooves. *Haruchai* pounded past her, row after row of them. Then they seemed to disappear in their own dust.

Desperately she groped for power – and found none. She could not concentrate: the implications of Anele's transformation seemed to beat about her head, confusing her attention. When she tried to wield both Covenant's ring and the Staff of Law, neither answered her.

In the Verge of Wandering, Anele had been possessed by flame and fury when he had moved from the rich grass around the shelters onto the bare ground of the clearing. And here he had been similarly changed when he had dropped from Hrama's back; when his feet had found the dirt–

Oh my God— *Anele!*

Linden felt more than heard the clash of flesh and bone and force as the *Haruchai* crashed into the front lines of the Demondim. Too many riders and too much dust blocked her view. Her senses had other dimensions, however. She could still witness the battle.

In spite of their numbers, each of the Masters seemed as distinct as stone: they slammed into the horde like a fall of boulders, heavy and irrefusable. But the monstrous creatures were rife with power. Nacre corrosion beat in their veins, poured from their hands. Any one of them singly had the might to shatter walls, tear down houses. And they had seen the *Haruchai* coming: they were ready.

As the riders struck, concerted emerald as vehement and fatal as the Despiser's own ichor erupted in response, coruscating through the hues of gems and verdure to the blinding incandescence of sunfire.

In an instant, the conflict became chaos.

Without transition, the screaming of horses filled the air. Blood and shredded flesh articulated the dust. The first rows of the Masters went down like mown wheat, scythed from their mounts by the vicious strength of the Vile-spawn and the incarnate puissance of the Illearth Stone.

The slaughter among the horses was hideous, but in the initial assault few of the Masters were slain. Prodigiously swift and skilled, they dove from their falling mounts between gouts of ruin unleashed by the hands and limbs and beaks of the Demondim; ducked under staggering concussions of green force;

attacked their foes and spun away. Yet each quick evasion and abrupt blow carried them further into the horde, deeper among the massed creatures; closer to the centre of the Stone's power. And the Demondim were too many, the Stone too potent.

Monsters fell around the *Haruchai*; but none of the leading warriors survived.

Yet among the tumult Anele remained palpable, vivid to Linden's discernment: a figure compacted of scoria and rage. He strode some distance into the battle, then paused there as if he were contemplating carnage. But he struck at none of the creatures. None of them struck at him. Instead he appeared to gather them about him in swirling eddies which veered closer and then were flung away by the forces of the fight.

Her fear for him snatched Linden out of her confusion. Banishing Covenant's ring from her mind, she raised the Staff high; and from its end shone forth a beacon of flame as yellow as sunshine and as compelling as trumpets.

Holding the wooden shaft before her like a standard, she nudged Hyn into motion.

The mare tossed her head and nickered anxiously, but did not flinch or falter. At a slow canter, she bore Linden towards the battle.

Towards Anele.

Immediately Liand, Mahrtiir and Pahni placed themselves protectively around her, bringing Hrama with them, while the ur-viles and Waynhim adjusted their formations to guard her back.

Ahead of her, the shape of the fighting shifted. Reacting to the outcome of their first attack, the Masters changed their tactics. Instead of hurtling into the fray, they fanned out on either side of the horde and leaped down from their mounts. There they slapped their horses away so that no more of the vulnerable beasts would be burned or eviscerated. Then they fought the onslaught along its edges rather than forging inwards. By so doing, they gave themselves space in which to dodge and duck and strike back and dance away.

At once, they became more effective, altering the proportions of the conflict. More of the *Haruchai* were able to keep their feet and take advantage of their lightning reflexes: more of the monsters dropped.

Still the Demondim were too many. Too few were stricken down. And they had not yet made concerted use of the Illearth Stone. Effectively focused, that bane could sweep away every living being between the horde and Revelstone.

Then Linden saw in horror that the extravagant efforts of the Masters did not diminish the horde. Instead the trees and Cavewights and men and monsters which fell, apparently slain, seemed to melt out of existence, disappearing into the ground; and from the dirt emerged new shapes to replace them. Now creatures in the form of ur-viles stood among the combatants; monsters that resembled Giants; savage yellow beasts like *kresh*.

The Demondim arose from the graves of the fallen, Stave had said, *and their touch was fire*. They could resurrect themselves in every form which had ever been slain before the gates of Revelstone.

It was only a matter of time before all of the *Haruchai* were killed.

Abruptly Anele vanished from her perceptions. He had stood alone amidst the clamour, a cynosure of red heat and fury surrounded by the fading and solidifying forms of the Demondim, the splashing of opalescent corrosion, the daunting concussions of the Stone. Then, without warning, she could no longer discern him. Blankness answered her questing health-sense. As far as she could tell, he was utterly gone, erased from the face of the plain.

Holding a shout of Staff-fire before her, Linden urged Hyn faster. With her companions braced about her, she carried her power into the battle.

The Masters parted from her path. They may have assumed that she meant to measure herself against the Illearth Stone. But she had no such intention. She was too weary and mortal to contend with the Stone's virulence directly. Not while its source remained hidden from her; unapproachable; immune to assault. Her only thought was to find Anele.

Like the *Haruchai*, the Demondim withdrew to allow her passage. Or she may have driven them back with the Staff's lucid flame. She no longer knew what she did. She knew only that she did not mean to turn aside.

Then from within the chaos Hynyn burst into her path, sides heaving, coat soaked and glossy with blood. And on his back sat Stave as if they had endured a furnace together. Acid had charred the Master's tunic to tatters, scored galls across his ribs and down his arms. And it had eaten away the left side of his face. The bones of his cheek showed through the streaming wound, and his eye was lost in burns. Nonetheless he somehow contrived to support Anele's limp form in front of him.

The old man still lived. His heart beat: air leaked in and out of his lungs. The Earthpower which had preserved him through so many other ordeals had sustained him again.

Linden might have shouted his name, but he would not have heard her. The heat which had carried him into the fray was gone, leaving him unconscious.

Frantic now, and stretched past her limits, she whirled the fire of the Staff around her, forcing more of the Demondim to pull back. As she did so, she yelled to her friends and Stave – to the Waynhim and ur-viles – to all of the embattled *Haruchai* – 'Run! We've got to get out of here!'

The clangour of blows and powers swallowed her cry; yet the Ranyhyn understood her instantly. As one, they turned, half sitting on their haunches in order to launch themselves back the way they had come. With Hynyn among them, they stretched for Revelstone at a pounding gallop.

But now Linden hardly noticed what they did. Between one heartbeat and the next, the battle had dropped away from her. All of her attention was fixed on Anele. She clung to him with her senses as if that might keep him alive.

The Waynhim and ur-viles had been behind her, guarding her back. Now in an instant the Ranyhyn rushed past them, leaving them exposed to the assault of their makers.

Linden did not see that the Masters must have heard her, or had made their own decision to withdraw. As she and her companions broke free of the horde, however, the *Haruchai* abruptly jumped back from their opponents and began to run. Some of them whistled for their mounts. And some of those calls were answered. But most of the warriors simply ran. A few followed after the Ranyhyn as if to shield their flight. A large majority, however, headed for the ur-viles and Waynhim.

In their own way, the Waynhim had served the Land as diligently as any of the Lords. And Linden had told the Masters through Stave that the ur-viles deserved protection.

Encircling the creatures, the *Haruchai* took up positions to fight a rearguard action back towards the entrance to Lord's Keep.

But Linden was unaware of them. She had closed herself to all distractions; and so she did not see that the horde had slowed its pace, allowing its foes to retreat ahead of it. Apparently the Demondim did not desire to overwhelm their last descendants and the surviving warriors, but preferred rather to herd their opponents towards the illusory haven of Revelstone. They let the opportunity for carnage escape them.

While Hyn's hooves beat the hard ground, Linden counted Anele's heartbeats until she began to believe that they were not failing; that his peculiar strength had preserved him somehow. Then, gradually, she expanded her awareness to include Stave's wounds and Hynyn's laboured gait.

They would live because she did not mean to let them die. She had already lost too many people who had trusted her, and had come no nearer to rescuing her son. Nevertheless she was relieved to discern that they were in no immediate danger.

Hynyn had lost too much blood: the stallion was in acute pain. Yet his hurts were not as severe as Stave's. The Master's pulse had a ragged, thready beat, hampered by agony, and his burns fumed hotly, exacerbated by the lingering vitriol of the Demondim. An ordinary man would already have died—

But even Stave's preternatural toughness might fail him if his injuries were not treated soon. His left eye was already lost, and his other wounds were worse. She was not certain that even the theurgy of the Staff would be enough to save him; and the convictions of the Masters would probably require them to spurn hurtloam.

Linden's choices had become too expensive. The prices that other people paid in her name, because she had done what she did, seemed too high to be borne.

She was aware of nothing except the hurts of her companions as the Ranyhyn flashed from sunlight into the shadows of the tunnel under Revelstone's watch-tower. For a long moment, their hooves raised a tumult of trod stone and echoes, so that they seemed to gallop through the residue of the battle which they had left behind. Then they burst back into the sun's warmth in the walled courtyard which separated the watchtower from the main bulk of the Keep, and there the Ranyhyn scrambled to a halt, stopping urgently on stiffened legs.

Before them were the massive inner gates of Revelstone.

The gates stood open as if in welcome. But no lamps or torches lit the hall beyond them, and the wide jaws of Lord's Keep offered only darkness.

Chapter Ten:

Troubled Sanctuary

As she entered Revelstone for the third time in her life, Linden Avery yearned for illumination.

In a sense, she knew the high forehall well. She had struggled and survived here against the Clave and the na-Mhoram's *Grim*. But it was dark now, and she could see nothing to assure her that she knew where she was.

Apparently the Masters did not need light. Their sight was acute. And their senses were not truncated by Kevin's Dirt.

She lacked their abilities. Already she could feel her percipience fading, eroded by the tainted pall which overhung the Land. Soon she would be able to discern only the surfaces around her, none of the depths. She would be blind to all that was not lit and plain.

But she was not blind yet. The Staff of Law in her hands sustained her when she felt too weary to hold up her head.

When she and those with her had entered into the prow-shaped promontory of Revelstone – her companions and their mounts, the ragged and gasping Demondim-spawn and the Masters who had survived the horde, along with most of their horses – the heavy gates were closed, both those at the base of the watchtower and those within the courtyard. The Demondim had advanced too slowly to kill more of the Land's retreating defenders; and now the monsters were sealed out of Revelstone. Scores of people, creatures and mounts crowded the forehall, awaiting decisions.

With the gates shut, Linden could no longer taste the approach of the Illearth Stone; but she trembled to think what would happen when that immeasurable evil was unleashed against the wrought stone of Lord's Keep.

The choices of the Masters had left Revelstone virtually defenceless. They had denied the Land its heritage of lore and Earthpower. And Stave's kinsmen had just demonstrated that mere skill and strength could not stand against the powers of the Demondim.

Linden did not dismount. She was reluctant to leave the security of Hyn's back. Like the Staff, Hyn's fortitude and loyalty enabled her to exceed herself. In spite of her exhaustion, she called up fire from the Staff and held it flaming over her head. If she could not accomplish anything else, she meant to at least *see*—

As the warm buttery light reached for the walls of the cavernous hall, she studied the condition of her companions. Only Stave and Bhapa needed care immediately. Mahrtiir and Pahni had suffered less dangerous hurts. Indeed, they had already slipped down from their Ranyhyn to tend Whrany and Hynyn with *amanibhavam* and tenderness, stifling their wonder at the legendary Keep as well as their ancient animosity towards the *Haruchai*. And neither Liand nor the Demondim-spawn had been exposed to acid and emerald since passing through the Fall. As for Anele, the old man had emerged scatheless from the horde. He remained unconscious – perhaps Stave had struck him again – but he breathed more easily now, relaxing into natural sleep.

A significant number of the Masters had been wounded, but none as grievously as Stave. Apparently every warrior with serious injuries had fallen to the Demondim. The rest had been able to evade the worst attacks of the monsters.

Gazing around the entry hall, Linden estimated that a score or two of the *Haruchai* had spent their lives to purchase escape for her and her companions.

So much bloodshed— Too much. She had surpassed the limits of what she could accept.

A Master whom she did not know approached her through the restless throng, the wavering shadows, and asked for her attention. He knew her name. No doubt they all did. Stave had already spoken of her.

She could not imagine what else he might have told his kinsmen.

This Master carried himself with a commanding certainty. He may have been a leader among his people. The silver in his hair lent him dignity: the scars on his face and arms testified to his prowess. He wore no insignia or emblems, no marks of status, but the other *Haruchai* deferred to him subtly, honouring him more by posture and stance than by any overt signs of respect.

Nevertheless Linden ignored him. She had been pushed beyond herself, and other needs were more important to her.

While she could still rely on her health-sense to inform her actions, she sent tendrils of force curling from the comfortable wood in her hands; extended Law and healing to both Stave and Bhapa at once.

Stave's eye was a scalded mess. She could not repair it: she could only clean it and stop the bleeding. Therefore she closed her heart to it. Fortunately his other injuries were similar to Bhapa's: far more severe, but alike in kind. She could apply the same balm of Earthpower to both men. However, she did not neglect Stave's sore hip. And she cleared the cataract from Bhapa's eye. He might have avoided the worst of his hurts if he had been able to see more clearly; if she had thought to treat his vision when she had first gained the Staff.

Finally she stretched out her care to the worst hurts of the Ranyhyn. She did not know how else to thank them for all that they had done in her name.

While she worked, a hush filled the hall. Pahni, Liand and Mahrtiir regarded her gravely. The older Master held his peace. None of the other *Haruchai* made a sound. The Ranyhyn and even the lesser horses ceased their restive stamping, their snorted whimpers. Huddling together, the Waynhim tended to each other in silence, while the ur-viles licked their wounds.

When she was done, a wave of exhaustion broke over her and she nearly faded from consciousness. She had been under too much strain for far too long. The Staff's strength lapsed in her tired hands, restoring the darkness of the forehall, leaving her isolated in her personal night.

Then Mahrtiir said softly, 'My thanks, Ringthane,' and she roused herself with a jerk. Perhaps she would be able to rest later: she could not do so now. She had other responsibilities which she did not mean to ignore.

'You are Linden Avery the Chosen,' announced a nearby voice, 'and you hold both white gold and the Staff of Law. Stave has spoken of you. I am Handir, by right of years and attainment the Voice of the Masters. In their name, I bid you welcome.'

His tone suggested his scars and his years, in spite of its lack of inflection.

'Good for you,' Linden muttered gracelessly. The forehall was as dark as a tomb. It seemed crowded with fears and suffering; demands which she did not know how to meet. 'If we're so welcome and all, how about giving us some light?'

Stave had saved her by bringing her here. Without the aid of the Masters, she would not have been able to keep her companions, or herself, alive. But he had also betrayed her. His people would imprison Anele. And they might well do the same to her.

Jeremiah had tried to warn her—

The horses nickered and snorted, clattering their distress against the stone floor with their hooves; but no one answered Linden's query until Mahrtiir rasped, 'It is the Ringthane who asks it, sleepless ones. She has ridden Hyn of the Ranyhyn across fifteen score leagues and uncounted centuries to this fell place. Will you disdain even her?'

As if in response to the Manethrall's indignation, a torch sputtered and took flame at the far end of the forehall, away from the gates. It revealed a Master carrying an armload of brands. Without haste, he began distributing torches among his people.

Vaguely Linden wondered how many *Haruchai* had not ridden out to meet the Demondim. How many losses could they sustain and still hold fast to their convictions?

Were there enough Masters to defend the Keep?

As small fires spread from brand to brand, a flickering light slowly filled the hall. It cast ambiguous shadows among the people and horses until they resembled Demondim, fading in and out of definition.

Liand remained mounted behind Handir, two other Masters and Mahrtiir's stallion. As soon as she met the Stonedownor's worried gaze, he said, 'My sight fails, Linden. Soon I will be reduced to what I was in Mithil Stonedown.' The thought clearly grieved him, but he set it aside. 'Yet I see naught to trouble me. But my heart misgives me still. I do not trust these Masters, though they have snatched us back from death.'

For his sake, she sighed, 'We're safe enough,' although her voice shook, 'at least for now. They may be Masters, but they're still *Haruchai*. They'll take care of us as well as they can.'

And they would do so as long as they could, with Demondim massed beyond the gates, and the power of the Illearth Stone rampant against them.

Handir waited until she was finished. Then he informed Liand, 'I have bid you welcome. In the Chosen's name, I have welcomed you all. Has this no meaning among Stonedownors?'

Facing Linden again, he asserted, 'We have become the Masters of the Land because we are *Haruchai*. While Revelstone stands, you are guests among us and need fear no harm.'

'Does that include the ur-viles?' she asked promptly. 'And the Waynhim? None of us would have survived without them. Even Stave—'

Her throat closed. Too many *Haruchai* lay dead beyond the Keep's gates. The Demondim may have already assumed their corpses—

'We know nothing of their needs,' the Voice of the Masters said inflexibly. 'They will be released to the plateau of Glimmermere, where they may care for themselves as they are able.'

At his words, one of her fears fell away. She had once visited the eldritch lake of Glimmermere: she had seen the unassailable purity of its waters. And she had heard long ago that the plateau above and behind the promontory of Lord's Keep was guarded by sheer cliffs for many leagues. In Glimmermere's vicinity, the Waynhim and ur-viles would be beyond the immediate reach of the Demondim; safe as long as the Masters could hold back the horde.

A moment of yearning for the cleanliness of the tarn undermined Linden's attention, and she missed what Handir said next. Something about the Ranyhyn—? Because he appeared to expect a response, she murmured distantly, 'Thank you. I'm sorry I haven't been more gracious. We've been through a lot.'

And her difficulties were far from ended. Entering into Revelstone had merely transformed them.

Before Handir could reply, Mahrtiir snapped, 'The Ringthane may accept your wishes, Bloodguard. The Ramen do not. The Ranyhyn will *not* submit to your care. Rather you will release them also to the upland plateau, where they will be tended by the Ramen, and where they may remain or depart, as they choose. To propose otherwise is arrogance.

'And your welcome is without substance. You avow that you will provide for our safety "while Revelstone stands". That is scant comfort, sleepless one. You cannot cast down the Demondim and are utterly surpassed by the Illearth Stone. Yet you make no preparation for defence.'

Shadows shifted ominously across the Manethrall's visage. 'You name yourself "the Voice of the Masters". Heed *my* voice, Bloodguard. The gates of Revelstone are mighty, but they will not long remain unbreached. Ere the sun sets, the Demondim will enter this hall, and then it will be revealed that your welcome is as empty as your arrogance. If the Ringthane does not preserve you, the Masters will perish from the Land.'

The gates, Linden thought unexpectedly. Something about the gates—

Handir continued to regard her for a moment as though he wondered whether Mahrtiir spoke for her. Then he turned impassively to the Raman.

'You are mistaken, Manethrall, in many things.' If the Master felt either impatience or scorn, his tone concealed it. 'We have offered to care for the Ranyhyn because we seek to do them honour. They have been too long absent from the Land, and we have craved their return. But we intend no disregard towards the Ramen. Nor will we gainsay your word. The Ranyhyn will be released, as you have instructed, and you will tend to them.'

Handir paused, apparently offering Mahrtiir an opportunity to respond. But the Manethrall said nothing, and his fierce glare seemed to defy the Masters. With a shrug, Handir continued his reply.

'Preparations against the Demondim have begun, though you do not witness our efforts. As you have observed, we cannot equal the might of the Demondim. Therefore the watchtower is being filled with wood and oil, and made ready for fire. Any approach to the gates of Revelstone will fall in flames.'

And rise again, Linden thought darkly, until you run out of fuel. If the gates hold at all.

They troubled her for some reason. There was a question that she wanted to ask, but it eluded her. She was too tired to remember—

'Other preparations also have begun,' the Voice of the Masters promised. 'You may partake in them, and in the defence of the Keep, if that is your desire.'

Still Mahrtiir glared at the Master on Linden's behalf, and said nothing.

Again Handir shrugged. The *Haruchai* with him did not react to Mahrtiir's belligerence.

'In one matter, however,' explained Handir, 'you have spoken sooth. No defence will ward us from the evil of the Illearth Stone. Yet at present the Demondim do not wield it against us. Nor do they approach the gates. For reasons which we do not comprehend, they appear content to remain at some distance, ensuring that we cannot flee, but threatening us in no other form.

'We have heard your voice, Manethrall. Hear mine. Until we have determined how we must respond to the Chosen, we have no better course than to make our guests welcome as best we may.'

Abruptly Linden jerked up her head. Responsive to her mood, Hyn took a step or two forward, moving between Mahrtiir and the Voice of the Masters.

'The gates,' Linden said. 'Now I remember. Where in hell did you get *gates?*'

When she had entered here three and a half thousand years ago, there were no gates below the watchtower. They had been destroyed long before. And the Sandgorgon Nom had shattered the Keep's inner defences at Covenant's behest. Yet now both sets of gates were closed: great interlocking stone doors which sealed the Keep as effectively as blank walls.

Stave had said that Giants still visited the Land—

Handir paused as if he were consulting with his people. Then he asked, 'Do you require to speak of this now, Chosen? You are weary. Your questions will be answered when you have rested.'

'I don't know how to trust you,' Linden countered thinly. 'Stave knows why. Tell me about the damn gates.'

Handir met her gaze with the ambiguous light of the torches in his eyes. 'They were gifted to Revelstone by the Giants of the Search. More I will not say now. We will speak of all that lies between us when you are better able to do so.

'Here is Galt.' With a nod, he indicated a Master standing behind his shoulder. 'He will guide you to chambers where you may sleep. We will gather on the morrow to speak of your plight, and of Revelstone's. There your questions will be answered.'

Linden nodded. 'All right. That's fair enough, I guess. God knows I'm exhausted,' so tired that she could barely keep her thoughts in order. 'So are my friends.

'There's just one more thing.'

One more absolute responsibility. Then she would let herself sleep. With an effort, she pushed down the rising force of her weariness and looked around for Anele.

She spotted him across the hall from her just as two Masters reached up to lift him down from Hrama's back.

He was still asleep. Otherwise he would not have suffered their touch without protest. But he roused as soon as they took hold of him and immediately began to struggle, thrashing against them as if the touch of their hard hands burned him.

Reacting to Anele's distress, Hrama whinnied sharply. The other Ranyhyn tossed their heads and stamped their hooves anxiously. But they did not move against the *Haruchai*.

However, Hyn answered Linden's swift alarm by shouldering her way between the warriors and their horses towards the old man. Alert now, and frantic, Linden shouted over the crowd, 'Just a minute! Anele stays with *me*!'

In her hands, she held up the Staff like a threat.

At once, half a dozen Masters came together across her path, forming a barricade against her. Hyn shoved at them with her chest, then stepped back, awaiting Linden's will.

'God *damn* it,' Linden protested, 'aren't you listening?' She could have swept them apart in an instant; but she would not. No matter what happened, they were not her enemies. 'I said he stays with me! I promised him my protection.'

'Protect!' the old man panted as he twisted against the grasp of his captors. 'Linden Avery! Protect Anele!'

Impassively Handir joined the barrier of Masters. The torches cast indecipherable shadows across his face. Galt stood at Hyn's head as if his mere presence might restrain the mare.

Mahrtiir moved quickly to Linden's side, with Pahni and Liand close behind him. Like Linden, the Stonedownor had not yet dismounted. Apprehension and resolve clenched his face.

'The old man is ours,' announced Handir. Stave had said the same when he had first captured Anele, after the collapse of Kevin's Watch. 'We do not permit freedom to such beings.'

'Oh, for God's sake!' Linden snapped back. 'Not this again. Hasn't Stave talked to you? Don't you people ever *learn*?'

Gasping and unable to break free, Anele abruptly ceased his struggles. His blind gaze reproached Linden.

She did not doubt that Hyn and Rhohm could have thrust past the Masters. No *Haruchai* would lift his hand against the Ranyhyn. But that forbearance might not extend to her and Liand – or to the Ramen – in spite of Handir's welcome.

'Sure,' she went on, 'he's full of Earthpower. So are the Ranyhyn. He can do things other people can't. So can they. That doesn't make them a *threat*. His power isn't something he *uses*. It's something he *is*.

'Hasn't Stave told you that Anele loves the Land as much as you do? That the only thing he wants is to be of use?' Anele's helpless stare tore at her heart. 'He can't forgive himself for losing the Staff until he does something to make restitution.' And his madness made that impossible. 'That's why being a prisoner hurts him so much. He can't do anything to help the Land when you've got him locked away.'

Handir may have shrugged. 'Yet the Earthpower within him cannot be set aside. Therefore his deeds will serve Corruption, whatever his intentions may be. And therefore we will not release him.'

Furiously Linden turned to scan the hall for Stave. She had healed him. More than once— He could vouch for Anele.

She found him moving slowly towards her. His wounds had left him painfully weak. Nevertheless he spurned his frailty, holding up his head as though he defied anyone to challenge him.

'Stave,' she urged at once, 'tell them. You heard Anele's story. You know what he's been through. You've seen what he can do. *Tell* them.'

As if in response, Stave walked arduously past her to join the barricade between her and the old man.

When he had positioned himself among his kinsmen, he faced her. 'Chosen,' he said in a wan voice, 'you also do not appear to learn. Again you have shamed me with your healing. And I have permitted you to lift the burden of my failures from me. Do you now imagine that my people will heed whatever I might say?

'Anele will not be harmed. That is the given word of the *Haruchai*. There is no need to fear for him.'

But I *promised* him! Linden wanted to cry out. Yet she knew that she could not sway the Master. She could not sway any of them.

She felt like tearing her hair in frustration. 'I can stop you,' she told Handir through her teeth. 'You know I can.'

The Voice of the Masters shook his head. His gaze did not waver. 'You hold great powers. Yet if we determine that we must wrest them from you, do you truly doubt that we will prevail?'

Her worst fear—

Perhaps he could see into her heart. He may have known that she would not strike out at him.

'Linden.' Carefully Liand leaned from Rhohm's back to rest his hand like an appeal on her arm. 'They have offered us rest and sustenance, which we sorely need. Many of them were slain to procure our escape. And they have vowed that they will not harm Anele. Would it not be well to grant them their will until the morrow, when we may speak of him again?'

If we're still alive, Linden thought bitterly. If the Demondim haven't torn this whole place apart.

Mahrtiir made a spitting sound, but did not protest.

Helpless in the hands of the Masters, Anele's gasping sounded like sobs.

Linden did not glance at Liand. Instead she glared into Handir's flat visage.

'He's terrified of you. With good reason, as it turns out. If you hurt just one hair on his poor old head—' Abruptly she thrust her face closer to the Master. Whispering, she warned him, 'If you do that, I'll know whose side you're really on.'

Before Handir could respond, she turned Hyn and rode away to the far end of the forehall, seeking to lose herself in shadows because she could no longer bear the reproach in Anele's eyes.

A while later, still fuming, she entered the chambers which had been prepared for her and closed the door on Galt; nearly slammed it in his face. He was the only Master present, and her distress required an outlet.

She had seen the Ranyhyn led away, accompanied by the Ramen and followed by the Demondim-spawn. She had watched Anele taken from the forehall as gently as his frail resistance permitted. And she had nodded a temporary farewell to Liand when one of the Masters had urged him from her side. Now she was alone with her anger and her fear.

Anele had survived worse affronts than imprisonment by the Masters. Physically he would be well. But his despair might grow too great for his broken mind to contain.

In addition, most of the ur-viles and Waynhim had been killed for her sake. A frightening number of the *Haruchai* had been slain. Revelstone was besieged: it would soon fall. In spite of all her efforts, she had earned no support from Stave. She had risked the Arch of Time in order to retrieve the Staff; but she still had done nothing to rescue her son.

She was alone because she needed to be. She did not know how else to bear her sense of futility.

She had no idea where in the great Keep her rooms were located. Her scant familiarity with Revelstone was useless when few of the passages and stairways were lit. In fact, few of them seemed to be frequented at all. More than once, her boots had raised dust from the stone. Occasionally Galt had led her through pockets of stale air. And they had encountered no one along the way. The Masters believed that they served the Land; but Lord's Keep was nearly empty.

Yet her quarters showed signs of care. The rooms were clean and fresh, with oil lamps glowing on small tables and stands and a faint scent of soap in the air. Rough-woven rugs softened the smooth granite floors, while similar hangings eased the starkness of the walls. And when she closed the door and latched it, the old stone seemed to seal her away from the rest of the Keep, warding her from Masters and peril.

Here she was safe, at least temporarily, and could rest.

There were three rooms, a compact suite. The outer door had admitted her to a chamber with a few stone chairs, a low table for food and a fireplace with a supply of wood. Beyond it lay a bedroom, empty except for a narrow bed, a large rug and a shuttered window. And beyond that she found a bathroom with a basin, a rudimentary commode, a small tub, an urn filled with fine sand for scrubbing and a system of simple valves which opened to release streams of water. A stand in the corner held a pile of flaxen towels neatly folded.

When she thought of bathing, she began to tremble.

Reaction setting in, she told herself. For days she had been under more strain than she knew how to handle: now she had been given rooms that felt *safe*, even though they were threatened by siege and betrayal. Here she could finally wash off days of grime and frenzy. With the Staff beside her, she might even be able to sleep.

Shivering in the cool air, she returned to the main room where she built a fire in the hearth, lighting it with one of the lamps and feeding it with slivers of wood until it burned strongly. Then she went back to the bathroom.

Setting aside the Staff cost her an effort. Instinctively she clung to its severe cleanliness. But she *needed* a bath. When she had propped the wood against the wall, she ran water into the tub and stripped off her clothes.

In the bath, the cold of the water stung her skin. It must have arisen from a mountain spring and been drawn by gravity into pipes and conduits within Revelstone's walls, where it was kept cold by the surrounding rock. But she fought the chill. Fumbling sand onto her arms and legs, her torso, her head, she rubbed them until she felt raw. Then she pulled her clothes into the water and did the same to them.

For all of her scrubbing, however, she could not remove the grass stains from her pants. They had become part of the fabric, indelible, and cryptic as runes.

And soon the chattering of her teeth drove her from the tub. Wrapping one of the rough towels around her, she hastened towards the warmth of the fire. There gradually the crackling heat soaked into her, easing the clench of her muscles and the deep pang of the cold; and she began to relax.

When she was warm, she returned to the bathroom, wrung out her clothes and brought them to the fire, hanging them over the backs of chairs near the hearth to dry.

Now she wished that she had a comb. Her hair would be a mess when it dried. But she ran her fingers through it by the comfortable flames, untangling it as best she could. That would have to suffice. She had no energy left for vanity.

Then she began to feel hungry. Knowing the *Haruchai*, she felt sure that one of them – Galt, presumably – stood outside her door, guarding her; or guarding against her. If she opened the door, she could ask him for something to eat.

She did not. Instead she continued to sit by the fire, staring into the indecipherable dance of the flames while she forced herself to think about her circumstances.

And about Anele.

She told herself that she should prepare for the morrow; for the confrontation she had been promised. Always assuming, of course, that the Demondim could be held back so long. More than that, however, she needed to devise some stratagem which would allow her to bypass the horde and head for Mount Thunder.

She had not forgotten her desire to visit Andelain. If any guidance remained in the Land, she would find it there. But every day that slipped away from her only multiplied Jeremiah's suffering. Now that she knew where to look for him, she intended to postpone other considerations.

But she could not concentrate: her weary thoughts seemed to bleed away from her. Rather than making plans, she found herself remembering the hazard and bloodshed which had purchased her escape from the Demondim.

Slain *Haruchai* and slaughtered horses haunted her. Blasts of opalescent acid devoured raw chunks of pain and death, while blurred forms shifted in and out of definition. Fanged flails of emerald scourged flesh to tatters, and yet represented only a small portion of the Illearth Stone's potential evil.

Despite the peril, however, Anele had dropped from Hrama's back to become an avatar of fire and rage. When his feet had touched the bare dirt, the bitterness of some other being had taken possession of him. He had been transformed—

—just as he had been in the open centre of the Verge of Wandering.

Linden struggled to grasp the implications.

In at least one phase of his madness, apparently, the old man's vulnerability was defined or controlled by the nature of the ground on which he stood. For the few days that she had known him in her proper time, she had only seen his feet touch bare dirt twice; and both times he had immediately begun to rave with heat and flame. But in the Land's past he had evinced nothing similar. Instead every aspect of his madness with which she was familiar had been modified beyond recognition. There, in the presence of the Staff, he had come close to ordinary sanity.

Perhaps his passage through the first *caesure* had taken him out of reach—

And the same was true, she realised suddenly, whenever Anele was on horseback. More than once, she had observed that he seemed less troubled when he rode. During their escape from Mithil Stonedown, Lord Foul's grasp on his spirit had disappeared when he had been lifted onto Somo's back. And after that it had not recurred until—

No, it had not recurred at all; not fully. From Somo's back, Anele had climbed onto the rocks around the Mithil's Plunge. Behind the Plunge, he had been wracked by an entirely different form of pain. And after that, during their ascent towards the cleft where they had later been attacked by the *kresh* – during that difficult trudge—

Damn it, she could not remember. But she seemed to recall that he had vacillated between varying manifestations of his insanity, shedding glimpses of Despite and woe. And where they walked had been primarily a kind of scrub-grass, hardy and thin, interspersed with patches of bare dirt and sections of fallen stone.

He had been standing on grass of that same kind when Lord Foul had guided her to hurtloam. And earlier, when the Despiser had first spoken to her through Anele: the same grass.

Dear God, was it *possible*?

He has no friend but stone.

Did the surface on which he stood determine the phase of his madness? Or did that surface control which of several beings or spirits could locate and possess him?

Thomas Covenant had spoken to her through Anele twice, on the lush grass of the Verge of Wandering: grass so rich and high that she had been unable to walk through it without floundering; the same grass which had stained her pants with a script which she did not know how to interpret.

In the rubble of Kevin's Watch, and again among the shattered rocks which had filled the cleft, as well as on the piled granite of the ridge above the Verge of Wandering, he had professed to read what was written within the stones. He had seemed almost lucid— On more polished stone, he had appeared more broken and fearful; but still he had seemed able to understand what was said to him – and to offer an occasional coherent response. And—

Linden groaned at the memory.

On a plane of exposed gutrock between the walls of the rift, he had briefly become sane enough to reveal his past.

If she were right – if her memories had not misled her – it was God's truth that he had *no friend but stone*. Every other surface under his feet in this time exposed him to possession and torment.

As she had understood it until now, Anele's madness had seemed adequately cruel: bitter and undeserved. But this new vision of his plight was far worse. He had become the pawn of powers which would have savaged any less Earthpowerful flesh than his.

She might have stopped then to grieve for him; but implications continued to tumble through her. If she were right, Lord Foul could not know where she was or what she did when Anele was not accessible to him. That probably accounted for the attack of the *kresh*. The Despiser must have expected her to flee Mithil Stonedown northwards, into the South Plains – away from the Ramen and the Ranyhyn and hope. And Anele had been hidden from him on Somo's back. When the old man had reentered Lord Foul's reach beyond the Mithil's Plunge, the Despiser must have been taken by surprise. Realising his error, he must have sent the *kresh* in an attempt to prevent Linden from reaching the mountains.

In addition, Anele's particular vulnerability might explain why the Demondim had slowed their attack. By her reasoning, it was no accident that the horde had not assailed him when he was filled with fire and rage. The dire creatures had recognised an ally. In their midst, Anele's possessor had spoken to them – and they had heeded him.

For some reason, they wanted Linden and her companions enclosed in Revelstone.

Deep within herself, she trembled at the possibilities. Evils other than the Despiser also used Anele to keep track of her; oppose her; guard against her. *I have merely whispered a word of counsel here and there*— And Covenant had warned her to beware of him.

Almost involuntarily, she imagined ways in which she might benefit from her new understanding. If it proved true— She could take Anele to the upland plateau, to the rich grass around Glimmermere, and ask him for Covenant's guidance. Or she could—

The mere consideration of such ideas shamed her. Anele was a broken old man, and he had already experienced too many forms of violation. He did not deserve to be used, even by someone who cared for him.

But the Despiser had taken her son. And Anele's madness was defended by Earthpower. Unconsciously he had shaped his birthright into a bulwark for his insanity. She could not succour him without committing an act of violence against the choices which he had made for himself.

And his plight did not outweigh Jeremiah's. It could not; not with her. The old man had friends: Liand and the Ramen; Linden herself; even the ur-viles to some extent. He had episodes of sanity which enabled him to articulate his dilemma. And his heritage of Earthpower protected his underlying identity from the ravages of his possessors. Jeremiah had none of those things.

He had only Linden. If she did not redeem him from Lord Foul, there would be no limit to his agonies.

Therefore—

She hid her face in her hands.

—she had no choice. If she could find no alternative, no other way to reach her son, she would have to make use of Anele. To manipulate his madness so that it served her needs.

The prospect dismayed her; but she did not shrink from it. She had already risked the Arch of Time in the same cause.

Good cannot be accomplished by evil means.

She understood that. But such convictions, like the beliefs of the Masters, were too expensive. She could not afford them.

She might have remained where she was for some time, warming her weariness by the fire and considering possibilities which shamed her. Before she could remember that she was hungry, however, or that she needed sleep, she heard a muted knock at her door.

Sighing, she uncovered her face and rose to her feet.

Her clothes were still too damp to wear. After a moment's hesitation, she wrapped a couple of towels tightly around her, then retrieved the Staff and carried it with her as she went to unlatch the door.

The door was stone, and massive as a cenotaph, yet it swung easily on its hinges. It must have been counterbalanced in some way, perhaps by weights within the walls. Lord's Keep had been wrought by Giants, and they were wizards of stone-work.

In the corridor outside her chambers stood Liand, Galt and a woman whom she had never seen before. The woman held a wicker tray laden with dried fruit, dark bread, cheese and a steaming bowl of soup.

Liand smiled uncertainly. 'Linden.' He seemed reluctant to enter; unsure of his welcome. 'This is the Mahdoubt.' He indicated the woman. 'I glean that she is *the* Mahdoubt, though I do not presume to know what the title may signify. When she brought food to my rooms, I enquired of you, and she replied that she had not yet served you. Wishing to ascertain that you were well, I craved her leave to accompany her.'

'Yes. Assuredly.' The woman plainly did not doubt her own welcome. Bustling past Linden, she swept into the room: a short dowdy figure apparently well past middle age, with a crow's nest of hair askew on her head, plump flesh hanging from her arms and features which might have been sculpted by an unruly child during a tantrum. About her she wore a robe of astonishing ugliness, a motley patchwork of scraps and swaths seemingly selected for their unsuitability to each other and stitched together at random.

'The Mahdoubt, indeed,' she pronounced as she bent to place her tray on the low table. 'Assuredly. Who else?' She may have been speaking to herself. 'Meagre fare for two. Does the Mahdoubt comprehend this? She does. But this flirtatious young man' – she indicated Liand – 'has mazed her with blandishments, and so she did not return to the kitchens for a second tray.

'A long trudge, that,' she remarked to the air. 'Long and weary. And the Mahdoubt can no longer recall her first youth, though she has been shamelessly charmed.'

For a moment, she studied her tray. Then she bent again and adjusted its position until it occupied the exact centre of the table. When she straightened her back, her manner suggested satisfaction.

'Pssht. It is no matter,' she informed the room. 'One tray may feed as many as two, if it be kindly shared.'

In an effort to make herself stop staring, Linden turned to Galt. ' "The Mahdoubt"?' she asked unsteadily.

The Master replied with a *Haruchai* shrug, at once subtle and expressive. 'She is a servant of Revelstone. The name is her own. More than that we do not know.'

A servant— Linden scowled reflexively. Well, of course, she thought. If the Land had Masters, it naturally required servants as well. Men and women who had been born here for uncounted generations had been reduced to waiting on the *Haruchai*.

What fun.

Riding a wave of renewed irritation, she beckoned Liand into the room and started to close the door on Galt. But then she caught herself. Facing the Master past the edge of the door, she demanded, 'Wait a minute. I know you're here to guard me, but I assume you're also going to at least pretend that I'm a guest. So tell me something.'

Galt lifted an eyebrow. 'Chosen?'

'The gates.' She held him with her glare. 'I'm tired of waiting for answers. Where did you get them?'

He cocked his head, apparently consulting his kinsmen. Then he shrugged again. 'Very well. As you have heard, the gates were wrought by the Giants of the Search. It transpired thus.

'When the First of the Search and Pitchwife, her mate, had borne the Staff of Law to Sunder and Hollian, they returned to The Grieve. There they awaited some word of what had befallen Starfare's Gem and the other Giants of the Search.' Covenant, Linden, and their companions had left the Giantship far to the north in the Sunbirth Sea, half crippled among floes of ice. 'But when at last the *dromond* gained *Coercri*, the Giants did not then return to their homeland. Rather the First led them to Revelstone, that they might behold the handiwork of their lost kindred, the Unhomed.'

At first while Galt spoke, Linden simply listened, glad to hear what had become of her long-dead friends. When she was satisfied that he would indeed answer her question, however, she began to study the Master himself. Distracted by other concerns, she had paid no attention to him in the forehall. And she had seen little of him except his back during their ill-lit trek to her rooms. Now she looked at him as if they had never met before.

He appeared to be less than Stave's age. The characteristic flat cheeks and brown skin of the *Haruchai* resisted the definition of years. But Galt's lack of scars made him seem untried; therefore young.

'You are aware,' he continued, 'that the Giants are a deliberate folk, hasty in neither speech nor deed. Though they had been long absent from their Home, they remained in the Land for several years. At first their efforts were dedicated to the restoration of Starfare's Gem, which had been sorely damaged. Later, however, their hearts turned towards Revelstone, for Lord's Keep also had known harm.

'They admired greatly the craft of the Unhomed, who had lived and perished in Seareach. In addition, they wished to honour the valour of all those who had striven against the Sunbane. And they desired to express their gratitude for the *caamora* which the ur-Lord Thomas Covenant granted to the dead of The Grieve. Therefore they determined to offer what they named a "small" restoration to Revelstone.

'They professed that many of the hurts which the Keep had suffered lay beyond their skill. However, the fashioning of gates did not surpass them. Here the Giants of the Search laboured long and mightily so that Revelstone might once again withstand its foes.'

Linden lowered her eyes to mask her own gratitude. Instinctively she did not want the Master to see what his explanation meant to her.

She was about to ask him if her friends had ever found their way Home; but when she looked down, she noticed his right hand.

It might have belonged to Thomas Covenant. The last two fingers had been cut away, leaving a ragged scar in their place. Its smooth pallor suggested that the mutilation had been performed long ago, perhaps in Galt's youth – or his childhood.

At the sight, she flinched, stung by a sudden host of memories. With his maimed right hand, Covenant had drawn her towards sunlight and love aboard Starfare's Gem. He had worn his wedding ring on the last finger of that hand. And she herself had cut away two of Jeremiah's fingers in order to save the rest.

Beware the halfhand. Covenant and Jeremiah.

Now she had found another among the Masters.

'Linden?' Liand asked anxiously. She could not conceal her reactions from him. He had begun to know her too well; or his proximity to the Staff preserved the vestiges of his health-sense.

But she ignored his concern. The inferences which she had drawn about Anele seemed to carry her further. Now she saw implications, portents, too complex for her to articulate. Hugging the Staff to her chest, she asked brusquely, 'Tell me about your hand.'

The Master did not deign to glance down at his missing fingers. 'I am honoured to be among the Humbled.'

She swallowed curses and waited for him to go on.

'When the *Haruchai* determined to take upon themselves the burdens of Mastery,' Galt said flatly, 'they recognised their peril. It is the peril of Korik, Sill and Doar.

'Their tale is surely known to you. Ruled by the Illearth Stone, they were made to serve Corruption. First they were maimed to resemble the Halfhand, ur-Lord Thomas Covenant the Unbeliever. Then they were sent to bear battle and despair against the Council of Lords. Thus was the Vow of the Bloodguard tarnished, and their service brought to an end.'

Linden knew the story: she had heard it from Stave only a few days ago. Still it filled her with dread.

Without haste or emphasis, Galt stated, 'The fault of Korik and Sill and Doar lay in this, that they allowed their ire at the destruction of the Unhomed to sway them. They believed that the outrage in their hearts would raise them to the stature of terrible banes and deathless malice. From their example, the *Haruchai* learned the peril of such passions. When we determined to become the Masters of the Land, we determined also that we would commit no similar fault.

'Therefore in each generation three among us are selected to be the Humbled, so that the Masters will not neglect their resolve, or set it aside. Our hands are severed to resemble Korik's and Sill's and Doar's. Among our people, we embody the error which destroyed the service of the Bloodguard. While the Humbled live, the Masters will not forget their peril.'

Linden stared at him in dismay. The judgments of the *Haruchai* continued to appall her. *Again you have shamed me with your healing.* Stave believed that he deserved the consequences of his failure to defeat insurmountable odds. And Galt considered his mutilation an honour—

Her voice nearly failed as she asked, 'How did they pick you?'

'Chosen,' he replied, 'I challenged others of my people, and was not defeated.'

Linden winced. 'You *wanted* this? You wanted to be *maimed?*'

He regarded her gravely. 'There is no higher place among us. Only the Voice of the Masters commands greater deference, and even he will accede when the Humbled speak as one.'

Commands greater deference— Abruptly new suggestions swept through her; hints of insight like a glimpse into the secret hearts of the Masters. Hardly aware of what she did, she closed the door on Galt. Then she leaned her forehead against the cool stone. He had given her what she needed.

Now she knew how she would argue for Anele's release. The *Haruchai* had founded their Mastery of the Land on a profound misapprehension.

Perhaps she would be able to postpone making use of the old man's madness a little longer.

When the rush of inferences had passed, she turned back to Liand and the Mahdoubt. The older woman was looking at her, apparently studying her; and for the first time Linden could see the mismatched colour of her eyes. Her left was the rich blue of violets, but her right held a startling orange which gave the impression that it was about to burst from her head.

In spite of her strangeness, however, the Mahdoubt emanated a comfortable kindness that appealed to Linden. With the last of her dwindling percipience, she saw both solid health and untroubled beneficence in the woman. In response, she felt unexpectedly protective of the Mahdoubt. At the same time, she yearned to be protected by her.

Before either the older woman or Liand could speak, Linden asked, 'You're a servant? Why do you do it? Let the Masters wait on themselves. Why should it be your job to make their lives easier?'

Liand nodded his agreement.

But the question did not ruffle the Mahdoubt. Indeed, she appeared to occupy a space beyond the reach of disturbance. 'Pssht, lady,' she replied. 'Fine sentiments, assuredly. The Mahdoubt sees that your heart is great. Upon occasion, however, it misleads you.

'There is no dishonour in service. The Mahdoubt labours here, assuredly, and her tasks are weary. Yet by her efforts she is fed and clad and warmed. At night she sleeps beyond harm in a kindly bed, with no rough words.

'Lady, the Mahdoubt has lived too many years to find pleasure in the tending of sheep and cattle. The endless labours of crops and farming exceed her old bones. She and others – pssht, lady, there are many others – are grateful to end their days in the service of Revelstone. How otherwise should they provide for themselves?'

The older woman's orange eye appeared to flare briefly. 'Is there some miscomprehension here?' she asked herself. 'Assuredly.

'Lady, the Mahdoubt does not "wait" upon the Masters. They are who they are, and require no care. Her labours serve the great Keep and all those within it who lack the sufficiency of Masters.'

Comforted by the Mahdoubt's answer, Linden found herself smiling at last. 'I'm sorry.' She could hardly remember the last time she had smiled at all. 'I shouldn't jump to conclusions like that. I'm just frustrated by all this *Haruchai* purity and absolutism. After a while, I can't help assuming the worst.'

Again Liand nodded.

'Assuredly, lady,' muttered the Mahdoubt. 'Assuredly. Think no more on it. Is the Mahdoubt affronted? She is not. Indeed, the days when aught vexed her are long past.'

In the same tone, she added, 'Does the wonder of my gown please you?' She indicated her jarring robe. 'Are you gladdened to behold it? Yes, assuredly, it must be so. How should it be otherwise? Every scrap and patch was given to the Mahdoubt in gratitude and woven together in love.'

Linden smiled again. 'It's extraordinary.' She did not know what else to say.

Certainly she had no wish to deny the older woman's pride in her garment.

Liand cleared his throat. 'That it is woven in love cannot be mistaken,' he remarked politely. 'If I may say so without offence, however, the gratitude is less plain to me. Will you not speak of it, that I may see your gown more clearly?'

The Mahdoubt faced him with her plump fists braced on her hips. 'Foolish boy, you must not tease the Mahdoubt so.' Her tone suggested tart amusement. 'Matters of apparel are the province of women, beyond your blandishment. The lady grasps the presence of gratitude. And if she does not' – her blue eye flicked a quick glance at Linden – 'yet she will. Oh, assuredly. It is as certain as the rising and setting of the sun.'

Before he could respond, she turned for the door. 'You must have food. And then you must sleep. Assuredly. Your need for both is great.

'The Mahdoubt will return with a second tray.'

At once, she bustled out of the room as if her movements were as irresistible as tides.

As the door closed, Liand met Linden's gaze with a perplexed smile. 'That,' he said in bafflement, 'is an unforeseen woman. I suspect that I should be wary of her, yet I feel only fondness. She has comforted me, Linden.' He sighed. 'I do not understand it.'

Linden frowned. 'Makes you want to curse Kevin's Dirt, doesn't it.' Because her percipience had dwindled, she had felt unable to see deeply into the Mahdoubt.

A grin quirked Liand's mouth. 'Assuredly.' But then his humour fell away. 'It is as you say. The loss of my senses is bitter to me. Until we sojourned among the mountains, and all the Land was reborn in my sight, I did not comprehend evil. It has become plain to me now.' Sadness darkened his eyes as he spoke. 'Beyond question the Falls are a great evil. Yet I deem them a little wrong beside the deprivation imposed by Kevin's Dirt. It has blinded the people of my home, and perhaps all the folk of the Land, to the meaning of their lives.'

The lament in his words touched Linden. 'Maybe there's something I can do about that,' she said grimly. 'This is the Staff of Law, for God's sake.' She held its reassuring clarity close to her heart. 'Once I've slept for a while,' and had some food, 'I intend to find out just how powerful Kevin's Dirt is.'

Liand replied with a dark grin of anticipation. In the brief time that she had known him, he had become a man who wanted to fight; to strike blows in the Land's defence, although he had no power, and could not hope to stand against Lord Foul.

The change in him affected her like the Mahdoubt's strange aura. She had relied on his protection from the first. And in turn she ached to protect him. But she did not know how.

She and Liand shared the contents of the Mahdoubt's tray in silence. His desire for talk was palpable; yet tact or empathy kept him quiet. Wordlessly he seemed to recognise that Linden needed to be left in peace.

She valued his consideration. For the most part, however, her thoughts had shifted, leaving him in the background. Galt had evoked memories which she was too weary to suppress. With the last of her waning strength she clung to images of Jeremiah, and tried to think clearly.

Years before she had met him, Thomas Covenant had once refused the Land for the sake of a snake-bitten girl. Linden understood his decision. She would do the same for Jeremiah, if she could find no other way to save him. But in his place the Masters would not have made the same choice. For them, the Land's peril would outweigh the suffering of one lost child.

She knew, however, that she was not being fair to them. Her situation, and theirs, differed from Covenant's in one important respect. He had refused the Land's distant plight for the sake of a child in immediate peril. For Linden and the Masters, the immediate peril was the Land's: the distant plight, Jeremiah's.

Good cannot be accomplished by evil means.

She could not use Covenant's example to explain or excuse her decisions.

At last Liand rose to his feet and announced that he would leave: he must have been able to see that she was about to fall asleep in her chair. She thanked him wanly and let him go.

Trapped in her thoughts, she had not realised how badly she wanted sleep.

But possible horrors followed her into the bedroom. When she had unwrapped the towels and stretched herself out among the rough blankets, she feared that she would not be able to relax. Then she feared that she would, and that ghouls would ride her dreams, tormenting her with sorrow.

Rising to use the bathroom a short time later, however, she found that the daylight filtering through the shutters over her window had become darkness, and the fire in her hearth had died to embers. Somehow night had fallen without her notice.

And in her front room a tray mounded with food had replaced the one which she and Liand had emptied. The Mahdoubt must have slipped into her quarters while she slept.

Linden had forgotten to latch the door when Liand left.

Nevertheless this evidence of the older woman's care released knots of tension in her. The Mahdoubt's kindliness seemed to dismiss nightmares and doom.

Hardly aware of what she did, Linden set the latch, tossed more wood into the fireplace and extinguished all but one of the lamps. Then she toppled like a felled tree back into bed and slept again.

Chapter Eleven:

The Masters of the Land

Later she heard Covenant calling her name. 'Linden,' he said, and again, 'Linden,' insistently, warning her of imminent danger. She knew that she ought to heed him, rouse herself; make choices which her companions could not gainsay or refuse. But instead she endeavoured not to hear him, thinking that if she could make herself deaf he would go away. Perhaps he would cease to exist, and then all of her woes would end at last.

Nevertheless he continued to insist. For reasons which she could not explain, he shone a flashlight into her eyes. He commanded an illumination which pierced her, made her squirm.

A muted thudding accompanied it, a sound like the distant drumbeat which heralded the collapse of worlds.

But when she tried to blink away the dazzle and coercion, she found herself squinting into a fine slit of sunlight which struck her face between the slats of the shutter above her bed. The voice intruding on her dreams was Liand's, not Covenant's: less strict than Covenant's; and anxious for her. At intervals, he knocked on her door, attempting to urge her awake.

With a groan, Linden hauled herself out of bed.

How long had she slept? She had no idea. She felt sodden with sleep, waterlogged with dreams: she had soaked up too much rest to reach wakefulness easily.

'Coming,' she muttered, although she knew that her muffled voice would not be heard through the heavy door. 'Damn it, I'm coming. Let me get some clothes on.'

Even in the worst emergencies, her former life had not required her to leave home without clothes.

By the time she had pulled on her jeans, however, and buttoned her shirt, the familiar urgency of sudden awakenings had caught up with her. God, what could have happened? Had the Demondim broken into Revelstone?

Why had they taken so long? They had the Illearth Stone—

Still barefoot, she padded to the door and opened it on Liand's concern and Galt's impassivity.

'What?' Her voice was rough with alarm. 'What is it?'

Then she stopped, silenced by the abrupt realisation that her health-sense was now entirely gone. She could not discern the extent or nature of Liand's concern. The polished stone of the Keep was closed to her, lifeless as a sepulchre.

Although she had expected the loss, it hurt her nonetheless.

'Linden,' the Stonedownor murmured as if he were embarrassed. 'I crave your pardon. I was loathe to awaken you, but the Master would have done so if I did not. The Voice of the Masters has summoned you. The time has come to speak of Anele's imprisonment' – he dropped his gaze uncomfortably – 'and of other matters.'

She waved a hand to dismiss his apology. 'Don't worry about it.' She could not afford to grieve over the effects of Kevin's Dirt. 'I should have been awake hours ago.'

How had she slept so long? She would not have believed that her fears and frustrations would allow her to rest so deeply.

Turning to the Humbled, she asked, 'What are the Demondim doing? Are we under attack?'

Without her health-sense, she would not have known it if the Vile-spawn had torn down the watchtower and shattered the gates.

Galt regarded her without expression. 'It is strange, Chosen,' he admitted as though the information did not interest him. 'Yesterday they arrayed them-selves as they would in preparation for a siege. During the night, however, they withdrew. There is now no sign of them within sight of Lord's Keep. Scouts have been sent to determine if they have truly abandoned their intent against us. Those Masters have not yet returned.'

Linden stared at him. 'They're gone? Is that even possible?' The horde had seemed so single-minded in its hunger for bloodshed. 'Kevin's Dirt doesn't affect you. Do you mean to tell me that you can't even *sense* the Illearth Stone?'

What had Anele's possessor said to the Demondim? What did that fiery being want? And why were its desires heeded by the Demondim?

Galt faced her steadily. 'It is as I have said. There is now no sign of them. Our scouts have not yet returned.'

Well, damn, Linden thought dumbly. She might be able to leave Revelstone after all. As soon as she had persuaded the Masters to release Anele, she could gather her companions and head for Mount Thunder, following the hints which Jeremiah had constructed for her.

As soon as she had persuaded—

Only then did she notice that Galt had not bowed to her: not once since they had first been introduced. Apparently he or his people esteemed her less than Stave did.

Galt may have wished her to understand that the Masters had no intention of letting Anele go.

Well, damn, she thought again, this time angrily. Let them try it. If they think—

Nevertheless the prospect of contending for Anele's soul calmed her. A physician's detachment came to her aid, a separation of emotion which she had learned from years of training. Precisely because a struggle awaited her, she comported herself as though she were unafraid.

Quietly she asked the Humbled, 'Is Handir waiting? Can we take the time to eat something? I haven't had breakfast yet.'

Let them try to keep Anele from her.

'There is no need for haste,' replied Galt. His tone seemed to imply that the Masters could wait indefinitely for a woman as weak as she was.

Linden turned back into the room. 'In that case,' she suggested to Liand, 'why don't you cut up some of that bread and cheese' – she nodded at the Mahdoubt's tray – 'while I get my boots on? We'll take it with us.'

Her attitude appeared to confuse Liand, but he promptly stifled his reaction, obeying without hesitation. He may have realised that there were large issues at stake for her, issues which transcended Anele's release and the departure of the Demondim.

You hold great powers. Yet if we determine that we must wrest them from you, do you truly doubt that we will prevail?

Without the Staff of Law and Covenant's ring, she would be helpless to defend the Land, or rescue her son.

Carefully, preparing herself, Linden donned her socks and then her boots while Liand sliced bread and cheese into convenient pieces. Then, still calm, she returned to her bedroom to retrieve the Staff.

She had promised the Stonedownor that she would attempt to restore their percipience. Without it, she feared that she would be powerless to sway the Masters.

But when she took the warm shaft in her hands, she found that she did not know how to call upon its strength.

A surge of panic threatened her detachment. She *needed* the Staff; perhaps more than she needed wild magic. She had pinned all of her hopes on Law and Earthpower. They were the organic antitheses of *caesures* and Kevin's Dirt and Despite. And she had fashioned this Staff with her own hands and heart. It *belonged* to her more profoundly than Covenant's ring. Yet she could discover no power in it. It was merely wood: lovely to the touch, and flawless, but nothing more.

Panic would not serve her, however. Instead of trying to force some response from the Staff, she required herself to step back emotionally and think.

When she did so, she realised that she had never before been able to raise any kind of power without health-sense to guide her. Not during the collapse of Kevin's Watch: not when she had summoned the ur-viles to aid Sahah: not in the Verge of Wandering on Stave's behalf. On each occasion, she had been above the blinding shroud of Kevin's Dirt. In the Rift, she had failed to find wild magic. But during her time with Thomas Covenant, she had never lacked percipience. In the past, Kevin's Dirt had not existed. And when she had used the Staff the previous day, her senses had still retained most of their discernment.

She had always been able to feel the Staff's potential like a geyser waiting to be released. Without that sight, she was trapped. She needed the Staff to restore her health-sense, and needed percipience to use the Staff.

Trust yourself. You're the only one who can do this. But she could not.

Again panic threatened her. She did not hear Liand enter the bedroom; did not notice him until he placed his hands on her shoulders.

'Linden,' he whispered, trying not to be overheard, 'what is amiss? Has Kevin's Dirt deprived the Staff of potency?'

Urgently she stared into his eyes; and the sight of his unaffected worry steadied her. She could not afford to lose her way now. Too many people had staked their lives on her.

She had to *think*.

Liand's question gave her a place to start. 'No,' she began weakly. 'It can't. This is the Staff of *Law*. Kevin's Dirt can't change what it *is*. That's not the problem.' As she spoke, however, her voice grew stronger. She drew courage from the gentleness of his touch on her shoulders. 'I am. I can't figure out how to use it. I need my health-sense.'

The Stonedownor knew virtually nothing about power. For that very reason, he might be able to aid her. He was not hampered by her preconceptions.

If he had trusted her less implicitly, he might have hesitated. But he seemed to believe beyond question that her dilemma was a problem which she could resolve rather than an inadequacy which she would be unable to overcome.

Still whispering, he said firmly, 'Yet you also have not changed. Kevin's Dirt is merely a veil. It cannot alter you.'

Linden nodded. Her reliance on him was as implicit as his trust. And of course he was right. Otherwise the effects of the shroud would have been permanent.

He smiled to encourage her. 'Is the wood not warm?'

Warmth, yes. She could feel that. She shifted her hands to confirm it, and was sure. The shaft radiated a palpable heat, delicate and reassuring.

Again she nodded.

'If the wood retains its warmth,' he asked softly, 'can you not also touch the source of that warmth?'

She did not know. She had not made the attempt.

Prompted by his clear assumption that she would not fail, she closed her eyes and focused all of her attention on the sensation of the Staff in her grasp.

The surface of the wood was so smooth that it felt almost slick; as immaculate as a clear sky, and yet as full of life and possibilities as the Andelainian Hills. Its energy was unmistakable. And the more she concentrated on it, the deeper that vitality seemed to run. It was a geyser indeed, a tangible wellspring. There was no measurable limit to the amount of Earthpower which might pour forth if the Staff were opened.

All she needed—

—was the warmth itself. Kevin's Dirt might close her senses, but it could not seal the Staff. By its very nature, the wood's strength would heal her if she simply immersed herself in its heat.

Wrapping her arms around the Staff, she hugged it to her heart; and as she did so, her senses began to bloom.

In moments, she could feel the shaft glowing like hope in her embrace. With her eyes still shut, she could discern Liand's simple belief in her. The nerves of her skin tasted the life in his veins; enjoyed the confident beating of his heart. And behind him—

Ah, behind him stood the living gutrock of the promontory, the vital and ageless granite into which the Unhomed had engraved their intricate, enduring and passionate love of stone. If she had been content to do so, she could have spent days or years entranced by the slow pulse of Revelstone's rock. Eventually she would have been able to sense and share every life that inhabited the vast Keep, every love, every fear, every desire. Given time, she might learn to hear the words which the stone spoke to itself, as Anele did.

But the thought of the old man brought her back to herself. She had too much to do. Now she would be able to do it.

Tears of relief ran down her cheeks as she reached out to Liand with the Staff's beneficence and freed his senses from Kevin's Dirt. She did not need to look at him to recognise his sudden bliss.

'This is temporary,' she told him in a husky voice. 'I'll probably have to renew it every day.' Or every few hours. 'But now I know how.'

'My thanks,' he breathed when she was finally able to open her eyes and face him. 'There are no words— Only know that you have my' – he swallowed roughly – 'entire gratitude.'

'Then we're even.' Without transition, Linden found that she was eager to confront the Masters. She felt fundamentally restored, in full possession of her powers, as if she had reclaimed a birthright. Armed with the Staff of Law and Covenant's ring, as with Liand's trust, she was ready for any challenge. 'I could not have done this without you.'

Grinning, he replied, 'And still your estimate of yourself falls too low.' Then he indicated the room where Galt waited. 'I am inclined to try the patience of these Masters as far as I may. Yet Anele's plight remains. And I do not doubt that the Ramen grow restive.' After a brief hesitation, he added, 'Also I fear that Pahni's blindness torments her. She lacks Bhapa's years, and the Manethrall's, and has not learned to harden her heart.'

'You're right.' Linden wiped away her tears; secured her grip on the Staff. 'We should go.'

He gave her a humorous bow, which she returned. She was smiling as they left her bedroom to rejoin the Humbled.

If Galt had ever experienced impatience, he did not show it. Linden was sure that he knew what had just happened. With his *Haruchai* senses, he had probably heard every word, felt every change. Nevertheless he remained stolid; impenetrable. Her restoration gave him no discernible qualms. He merely acknowledged her with a nod and turned towards the door.

When Liand had taken a double handful of bread and cheese and tucked the food into the front of his jerkin, he and Linden followed the Master out into the corridors of Revelstone.

She was vaguely surprised to find them lit at wide intervals by oil lamps and torches. Since the previous day, someone – the Mahdoubt, perhaps, or another servant of Revelstone – had heeded her desire for light. She could see her way along the disused passages, down the echoing stairways, across the uninhabited halls.

If anything, the sparse illumination made the great Keep seem more abandoned than it had earlier. Now she could not imagine hosts of people thriving beyond the reach of her senses. Instead the long stone corridors and high chambers ached with emptiness. Lord's Keep had been made by Giants to be occupied by men and women who loved it; and now those inhabitants were gone.

Doubtless the Masters respected Revelstone. They may even have admired it. But they could not take the place of people who served Earthpower and stone. The huge gutrock warren needed more than light: it needed use and warmth.

By complex stages, Galt led Linden and Liand inwards and downwards, deeper into the old heart of the Keep; and as they descended, both the air and the stone grew colder. The shadows beyond the lamps and torches intensified until they became as dark as coverts. Beyond the flat retort of her boot heels, the softer clap of Liand's sandals and the nearly inaudible susurrus of Galt's steps, Linden seemed to hear the muffled breaths and whispers of lurking enmity. With her health-sense, she could feel the tremendous weight of Revelstone's rock leaning over her as if to watch what she would do.

'Where are we going?' she asked Galt abruptly. The deserted Keep oppressed her in spite of her new confidence. She wanted to hear something other than ramified echoes and emptiness.

'It is near,' replied the Humbled. 'We will speak together in the Close, where in ancient times the Council of Lords gathered to debate the Land's need and to determine their response.'

Linden sighed. No doubt the Close held meaning for the *Haruchai*, but she had never seen it. Too much of the Land's long history was hidden from her, or lost. Its undefined significance seemed to bear down on her like Revelstone's impending mass.

'Anele will be there?'

'Chosen,' Galt answered, 'all of your companions await you, saving only the Demondim-spawn. Already they have dispersed among the upland hills. We do not know if they will return.'

Gone, she thought. The obscure dictates of their Weird – or of their Weirds, if the ur-viles and Waynhim did not agree – had commanded them elsewhere. She had no idea what their departure meant; but at least she could believe that they were safe.

Liand offered her a few pieces of bread and cheese. She accepted them and began to eat while she followed Galt's strict back.

Then ahead of them she saw an arched entryway which looked like it might once have held doors. If so, however, they were long gone; neglected until they had fallen away. Now the opening gaped like a scream petrified in granite, an outcry so old that only the stone could remember it.

But a brighter illumination shone from the entryway. When Galt led his charges through the entrance, Linden found herself in a huge chamber lit by many lamps: the Close. It was a round cavity, both high and deep, which appeared to have been formed with conflicting purposes. Above her, almost beyond the reach of the light, the groined ceiling was intricately crafted, shaped with reverence, as if to honour everything that was done and said within the chamber. But below the entryway the floor slumped to form a crude pit. At first, the surface sank down in stages which may once have been tiers. Further down, however, the stone resembled poured magma. She could almost believe that a once-fine audience hall had been subjected to a terrible heat; fire so hot that the floor melted and ran, cooling at last into contorted patterns like memorials of pain at the bottom of the pit.

In the wall opposite her, Linden saw a pair of gaps which may once have been smaller doors. But they had suffered the same damage which had marred the lower half of the Close, and did not appear to be usable.

Among the wracked shapes at the bottom of the Close waited Handir, Stave and perhaps a score of other Masters. Among them, Linden saw Anele as well as Manethrall Mahrtiir and his two Cords. The old man stood at the back of the gathering, guarded or restrained by two of the Masters. Linden knew at a glance that he had not been harmed; but his physical wellbeing failed to reassure her.

As soon as she entered the hall, the Ramen ascended the rumpled stone towards her. All three of them were pale with loss and oppression. Bhapa concentrated on protecting his newly healed arm and shoulder as he moved; but Pahni mustered a thin smile for Linden and Liand. Mahrtiir betrayed more discomfort, however. He had difficulty holding up his head, and his fierce features looked uncharacteristically daunted. He climbed the stone with a slight hitch in his strides, a subtle flinch.

The Manethrall stopped a step below Linden, Liand and Galt, with his Cords behind him in deference. Avoiding Linden's eyes, he bowed in the Ramen fashion, then asked uncertainly, 'Ringthane, are you well? Have you been treated courteously?'

He may have expected her to say that she had not.

Because his distress was vivid to her, Linden held up the Staff of Law like an emblem of authority and bowed formally. 'I'm glad you're here, Manethrall. Liand and I are fine.' The Stonedownor nodded in confirmation, grinning at Pahni. 'Mostly the Masters ignored us. But a woman called the Mahdoubt took good care of us.

'How about you? Are you all right?'

Mahrtiir made a transparent effort to gather his resolve. 'We are not. At our word, the Ranyhyn were released to the grasses of the upland plateau and to the eldritch waters of Glimmermere. We accompanied them, preferring service and the open sky to the veiled disdain of these Bloodguard. The Ranyhyn remain there, although we have answered the summons of the sleepless ones in your name. So much is well.'

Linden nodded, waiting for him to go on.

'But, Ringthane—' He faltered; had to force himself to lift his head so that she could see the shame in his eyes. 'I fear that I will fail you here. This dire place bears down upon me. The Ramen are born to open skies. Such enclosure darkens our hearts. Yet there is a deeper pain which hampers me.'

He stepped closer, lowered his voice. 'Ringthane, we are blinded. We were aware of the nature of Kevin's Dirt, but we had not experienced it in our own flesh. We—' He scowled in dismay. 'I had not known that its bereavement would be so extreme. I am more than half crippled, unfit for your service.'

Still holding up the Staff, Linden shook her head. 'Manethrall, you're wrong. You and Bhapa and Pahni are who you've always been,' as worthy as loyalty and valour could make them. 'With your permission, I'll show you what I mean.'

He stared at her, perplexed and uncertain. He could not see her health, or the potency of the Staff. Yet he assented without hesitation.

Law and Earthpower came easily now. They were natural to her: as long as she held the Staff, they could not be taken away. If she had not felt diminished by Kevin's Dirt earlier, she would not have panicked. With the warm wood in her hands, she had only to desire the cleansing of the Ramen's senses and her desire was accomplished.

The joy that lit their faces when they could *see* again was wonderful to behold. And it was especially acute in Bhapa. Until this moment, apparently, he had not fully appreciated the fact that his ordinary sight had been restored. For years, his vision had been impaired: now he could see in every sense of the word.

As one, the Ramen prostrated themselves at Linden's feet as though she were as majestic as the Ranyhyn.

Embarrassed, she lowered the Staff, muttering, 'Oh, get up. Please. I don't want to be treated this way.' Again she explained, 'It's temporary. Kevin's Dirt is still there. But I can renew it as often as we need. And eventually we'll figure out how to get rid of the cause.'

Obediently the Ramen rose to their feet. Now a palpable current of pleasure flowed between Pahni and Liand; and Bhapa gazed at Linden with gratitude in his clear eyes. But Mahrtiir turned away to glare fiercely down at the waiting Masters.

'Sleepless ones,' he called out in a voice that rang with scorn, 'your purpose here has no meaning. Doubtless you will require the Ringthane to defend her actions and intentions. Stave has promised a reckoning, has he not? And you will attempt to account for your mistreatment of sad Anele, who harms no one. But your words and your choices are empty.

'The Ranyhyn have accepted the Ringthane. More, they have honoured her, bowing their heads when they have never bowed to any living being. And in her name they have likewise accepted all of her companions, not excluding Anele. Indeed, at their will they have been ridden by Ramen, a thing which no Raman has ever done before.

'Sleepless ones, Bloodguard, you who have ridden so many Ranyhyn to their deaths, there is no more to be said. No more! All of your doubts and arrogance have been answered. If you will not serve the Ringthane, then you must set aside your Mastery, for you have declared your infidelity to the Land!'

From the floor of the Close, the Masters regarded Mahrtiir in silence. Linden could not read their reactions. Nevertheless their flat stoicism conveyed the impression that they did not consider Mahrtiir's indignation worthy of a response.

Their lack of affect vexed Linden. It was no wonder, she thought grimly, that the *Haruchai* spoke to each other mind to mind. They were too enclosed, too deeply immured within themselves, for any other form of communication.

Snarling, Mahrtiir turned back to Linden. 'Ringthane, do you choose to submit to this false council?'

'Submit?' Her tone resembled his. 'No. But I'll hear what they have to say, and I'll answer it. I need them, Manethrall. The Land needs them. I can't turn my back on that.'

He held her gaze, apparently searching for some flaw in her determination. Then he nodded once, brusquely. 'Very well. The Ramen will stand beside you, whatever befalls.

'But heed my warning. These *Masters*' – he spat the word – 'will not treat honestly with you.'

Summoning her professional detachment, she replied, 'I'll take that chance.'

The *Haruchai* would not deign to lie; not under any compulsion. Not unless they had first lied to themselves.

When she started down into the Close, Liand and Mahrtiir walked at her sides and the Cords arrayed themselves behind her. Followed by Galt, and deliberate as a cortège, they descended the hurt stone. At the bottom of the pit, however, she paused to see how the gathered Masters would greet her arrival.

For a moment, Stave regarded her with his remaining eye as if he wished to measure her against his shame. Then he bowed as he had often done before, impassive in his respect. But Handir merely inclined his head. He might have done more to acknowledge one of the servants of Revelstone.

The rest of the Masters only gazed at her and waited.

Now Linden was near enough to see that both of Anele's guards had lost the last two fingers of their right hands. Like Galt, they were the Humbled.

She swallowed a curse; refused to allow herself that show of emotion. As Mahrtiir had just demonstrated, the Masters would not be swayed by outrage.

If they could be swayed at all.

Standing passively between the Humbled, Anele did not react to Linden's presence. He may have been lost in the labyrinth of his dismay; unaware of her.

'Chosen,' Handir began when she looked towards him again, 'you have been made welcome in Revelstone. Yet the Manethrall your companion conceives that he has cause to denounce us. Do you also fault our purpose here? If so, speak plainly, and you will be plainly answered.'

Mahrtiir stiffened at Linden's side, but did not retort. He had committed himself to her service, and remained silent.

Linden faced the Voice of the Masters squarely. 'You know why I'm here. Anele is under my protection. I want you to let him go. And I hope I can convince you to help me. The Land needs you. What you've done so far isn't enough anymore – if it ever was.

'As for your welcome, the Mahdoubt took good care of me. And she did the same for Liand.' The Stonedownor nodded. 'We have no complaints.'

Handir held her gaze. 'Then I bid you a further welcome to the Close of Revelstone, where in ages long past the Council of Lords gathered to consider the perils of their times. We have selected this to be our meeting-place because it has been harmed by despair and Earthpower.

'When the first Staff of Law had been destroyed, the former Bloodguard Bannor sojourned to Revelstone to discover what had befallen the Lords. From his tales of that time, the *Haruchai* learned that here Trell Atiaran-mate performed a Ritual of Desecration which nearly brought about the ruin of Lord's Keep. The outcome of his mad grief is written in this wounded stone.

'Here you may behold clearly the reasons which have led us to assume the Mastery of the Land. You stand upon the consequences of mortal power and passion. Here you may see explained the purposes of the Masters, if your eyes are open and your heart is not inured to pain.

'It is here,' Handir concluded inflexibly, 'that you will be accused. Here you will make answer as you are able. And here the judgment of the Masters will rendered.'

'"Accused"?' Liand objected in surprise. 'Do you jest?'

'It is as I have said, Ringthane,' snarled Mahrtiir. 'The sleepless ones have grown too haughty to be endured. Do they welcome us? Then let us depart, that they may no longer be constrained. We have no need of their judgment.'

But Linden gestured both of them to silence. Behind her chosen detachment, she seethed with indignation; yet she exposed none of it. She had expected something like this. Stave had promised her a reckoning. And in some sense she was ready for it.

'All right,' she told Handir quietly. 'Accuse away. I'm eager to hear what you think I should have done differently.' Then she let a flick of anger into her voice. 'But make no mistake about it. I am going to answer you. And when I'm done, you will by God answer *me*.'

She had earned that right.

The Voice of the Masters studied her for a moment. Then he pronounced, 'Let it be so.'

At his word, most of his people left the bottom of the pit to position themselves like sentinels or judges around the lower slopes. Only Handir, Stave and the Humbled, with Anele among them, remained facing Linden.

Firmly she turned her back on the Masters and stepped aside to sit on a bulge of stone at the edge of the bottom. Placing the Staff across her knees, she beckoned for her companions to join her.

Reluctantly Mahrtiir and Liand sat on either side of her, while the Cords placed themselves behind her. 'Linden,' Liand whispered at once, 'I mislike this. The Masters do not relent. Permitting them to accuse you, you grant them a credence which they do not merit.'

'The Stonedownor speaks truly,' Mahrtiir put in more loudly. 'You are beyond these Bloodguard. Your heed does them too much honour.'

'And there is no fault in what you have done,' added Liand. 'Why then should they be suffered to speak against you?'

Linden did not glance at either of them. Nor did she meet Handir's gaze. Instead she focused her attention on Stave.

'Trust me,' she answered softly. 'This has to be done.' Anele's plight required it – as did Jeremiah's. 'They may call themselves Masters, but they're still *Haruchai*,' men so moved by the grandeur of the Old Lords that they had surrendered love and sleep and death to their Vow of service. 'They can be persuaded.'

Somehow High Lord Kevin had persuaded them—

The Manethrall glared about him, but did not protest further. After a squirming moment, Liand subsided as well.

Linden went on watching Stave and waited for the accusations to begin. Handir was the Voice of the Masters; yet she did not expect him to recite her crimes. Every question that mattered lay between her and Stave. He had travelled with her, aided her; had been badly injured in her name. And she had shamed him— She was intuitively sure that he would be her accuser.

'In courtesy,' Handir announced, 'we will speak as do the folk of the Land, though it is not natural to us. The Chosen should hear all that is said of her.'

With a grave nod, Stave stepped into the centre of the contorted floor. Ignoring Linden's gaze, he addressed the Close as though his entire race were in attendance.

'She is Linden Avery the Chosen,' he said stolidly, 'the companion of ur-Lord Thomas Covenant the Unbeliever during the time of the Sunbane. So much is certain. I have ascertained it beyond doubt. She accompanied the Unbeliever on his quest for the One Tree. She shared his return to Revelstone, putting an end to the evils of the Clave and the Banefire. At his side in Kiril Threndor, she formed the new Staff of Law – the Staff which was then lost, and has now been regained.

'From him she received the white gold ring which is at once the Land's greatest boon and its most fatal bane.'

At least, Linden thought as she listened to him, he plays fair. He was willing to acknowledge who she was and what she had done, if Handir and the Humbled were not.

'When I had learned that she is indeed the Chosen,' Stave continued without pausing, 'I sought to do her honour by explaining the convictions and purposes of the Masters. I described the harm which attends inevitably upon any use of Earthpower. And I offered the support and aid of the Masters in any condign quest which might oppose Corruption.

'She has responded with unfailing defiance. At every turn, she has acted against my counsel. At every turn, she has striven to deny Anele from us, though his madness only accentuates the peril of his Earthpower.'

Feigning calm, Linden helped herself to some of Liand's bread and cheese; ate as if her own heart and Jeremiah's life were not at stake. Yet inwardly she squirmed with frustration and yearning and she could barely swallow.

'I grant,' Stave declared, 'that her defiance has yielded unforeseen boons. Because she fled from me, we now know that the Ranyhyn and their Ramen yet live. That is a benison which all who serve the Land must acknowledge.

'And the Staff of Law has been reclaimed. That is of inestimable worth. In itself, it is not a use of power. Yet it is a bastion of Law, and its nature sustains the life of the Land. Unused, its presence among us may hamper the proliferation of Falls, or diminish the pall of Kevin's Dirt.'

The Master was still trying to be fair.

But then he resumed his accusations. 'By the same defiance, however, she has admitted new perils. I have spoken of Esmer, who professes to be the son of Cail and the Dancers of the Sea, and whose dark puissance concerns and dismays even the ur-viles, despite their ancient loathing for the Land. And there are the Demondim, of which I will say more.

'However, the greatest accusation is this. She has a son who has been captured by Corruption. Her desire to redeem him is both proper and seemly. Yet her actions in his name have threatened the destruction of the Arch of Time.'

Mahrtiir muttered imprecations under his breath. Softly Liand asked Linden, 'Why do you suffer this? What manner of men advocate the sacrifice of threatened children?'

Placing her hand on the young man's arm, she gripped him hard to quiet him. She already knew what Stave would say.

The Master ignored her companions. 'For the sake of her son,' he proclaimed, 'she entered a Fall of Esmer's summoning, daring the past to seek for the Staff of Law. There she forged an alliance between the Waynhim and the ur-viles, which have ever opposed each other. And when we were beset by the Demondim, as well as by the power of the Illearth Stone, she herself caused the Fall which has delivered both them and us to Revelstone. Doing so, she has inflicted yet another dire bane upon the Land.

'I am *Haruchai* and fear nothing. Yet I fear to enquire what else she may attempt in her son's name.'

Mahrtiir breathed an obscenity, but did not interrupt.

'Now she has entered Revelstone holding both white gold and the Staff of Law.' At last, Stave turned to gaze at Linden. His face held no expression, but shadows which she could not interpret haunted his single eye like ghosts. 'I do not doubt that she is a woman of honour, and that all of her purposes are benign. Indeed, she has spoken eloquently of her love for the Land. Nevertheless she is mortal, and her powers surpass the strictures of mortal flesh and desire. If ever she knows a moment of despair – which is surely Corruption's intent – she will wreak such ruin as the Earth has never known.'

Then he looked away. 'Thus she reenacts the error which destroyed the fidelity of the Bloodguard. As did Korik, Sill and Doar, she commands powers which exceed her. Yet none will question that those Bloodguard were men of honour.

'The first principle of our Mastery,' he told his people, 'is that the uses of such power must ultimately serve Corruption. Is it not therefore certain that Linden Avery the Chosen will in the end become a servant of the Despiser?

'She will perhaps reply that she is warded from doom by the purity of her purpose. Her desire, she may assert, is merely to redeem her son rather than to defeat Corruption. Yet her own deeds gainsay her. Twice she has imposed healing upon me against my desires. Thus she has demonstrated that she cares nothing for the honour of those who do not share her purpose.

'Beyond question she has already begun to tread the path of Corruption's service.'

There he stopped, leaving Linden daunted in spite of herself. His recitation eroded her detachment; her certainty. In his own way, he had told the truth about her. If she accepted his assumptions, she could not contest his conclusion. It was as ineluctable as loss.

Good cannot be accomplished by evil means.

After Esmer had almost beaten Stave to death, she believed that the *Haruchai* had given her permission to treat him. But she could not say the same for her actions the previous day. In the forehall, she had reached out with the Staff reflexively; had responded to Stave's wounds simply because he was hurt.

Again you have shamed me— There she had violated her own convictions as well as his. If power could corrupt, then it had already begun to corrupt her.

Now she clutched Mahrtiir's forearm as well, holding both men to keep them from speaking – and to assure herself that she was not alone. She could not answer Stave's charges directly. She had already sacrificed her right to do so. And the Masters would not yield to simple contradiction. She had to go further.

She had to show them that their fundamental assumptions were false. That good could come of deeds and risks and even purposes which appeared evil.

'Are you done?' she asked grimly. 'Is it my turn yet?'

She was angry at herself; but she knew that anger would not serve her. She could not undo her mistakes. And her ire was merely a defence against pain and fear. Deliberately she put such things aside. Surgeries were full of bleeding which could not be staunched, wounds which resisted repair, deaths which defied refusal. Anger and grief only prevented the surgeon from accomplishing as much as possible.

When Handir replied with a severe nod, she said more gently, 'I'm not going to contradict anything Stave told you. It's the truth. Instead I'll give you a better answer. In fact, I'll give you three.

'But just so you'll know—' she added to Stave, 'I'm sorry I didn't ask your permission yesterday. You're right. I should have done that.'

And accepted his answer.

Her accuser faced her regret without a word. He had already gone too far to be turned aside.

Sighing, she released her grasp on her friends, wrapped her hands around the Staff and rose to her feet. As Stave withdrew from the centre of the floor, she took a few steps over the twisted stone, then stopped to plant the heel of the Staff between her feet and hold up her head.

Briefly she considered revealing the advice which she had received from Covenant in her dreams. No doubt Stave had already told his kinsmen what Anele had said when he had spoken for her dead love. And Covenant's name might carry weight with the Masters. But she did not know what to make of his messages – if in fact they were messages at all, and not the byproducts of her dreaming dreads.

Whatever happened, she needed to withstand the Masters on her own terms.

Still facing Stave as if he were the only one of his people who mattered, she said quietly, 'We're wasting time here. The Demondim will be back,' she was sure of that. 'We should be deciding what to do, not blaming each other.

'But you're the Masters of the Land. You've done me the courtesy of explaining what you think I've done wrong,' when they could have simply left her to the horde, or taken Covenant's ring and the Staff from her. 'You deserve the same from me.'

Only then did she shift her attention to Handir. Obliquely her words were still addressed to Stave. But she had already contradicted and defied him enough. He might hear her more clearly now if she spoke to the Voice of the Masters.

'Tell me something,' she asked abruptly. 'How do they do it?'

Handir lifted an eyebrow. 'Chosen?'

'The Demondim. How do they use the Illearth Stone? You can sense them.' And the discernment of the *Haruchai* exceeded hers. 'Explain it to me.

'At first I thought they must have found some lost fragment of the original Stone. But now I don't think so. They have too much power – and too many of them have it at once. And we all know that the Illearth Stone was destroyed.

'So how do they do it?'

The older *Haruchai* paused for a moment, apparently considering his response. He may have thought that the capabilities of the Demondim were irrelevant to Stave's accusations. Still he decided to answer.

'The Demondim wield a Fall. Among them they both command and sustain it, causing it to serve them. This Fall spans time to a distant age when the Illearth Stone remained intact. Similarly it extends deep among the roots of Gravin Threndor, to the place where the Stone lay hidden until Drool Rockworm discovered it. Therefore the might which the Demondim employ is great. It arises unhindered from its source.'

Linden frowned. He might be right— Like the Lost Deep, where the Demondim had bred their descendants, the Illearth Stone had once been buried far beneath Mount Thunder. The Vile-spawn could conceivably have known the Stone's location centuries or millennia before Drool Rockworm uncovered it.

But she needed confirmation. 'Are you sure? If they can do that, why don't they just shatter Time and be done with it? Instead they're toying with us. Why do they even bother?'

'If Corruption were able to destroy the Arch,' replied Handir, 'he would have done so ere now. Some Law or power constrains him, and his servants with him.

'Observe that the Fall violates the Law of Time, but that the use of the Illearth Stone which the Fall enables does not. The Demondim do not alter the past. In some fashion, the Law of Time intervenes to preserve itself.

'This we do not comprehend. We know only that the Falls are perilous and terrible. We cannot say why their evil does not suffice to undo the Arch. The Lords spoke of restrictions inherent to the nature of power. They named "the necessity of freedom", among others. However, such lore is beyond our ken. It is only plain to us that the Demondim act as they do because their power extends no further.'

'All right.' Linden nodded, accepting the idea. 'For some reason, they have limits.' Obviously *something* prevented Lord Foul from using Joan's ring directly. 'That might help us. But it's not enough. Here's the important question.

'Can you beat them? All of you together?' Every living *Haruchai*? 'Can you prevent them from turning this whole place into a pile of rubble?'

Handir faced her as if nothing she might say could disturb him. 'We cannot.'

Trying to pierce his impassivity, Linden made a show of surprise. 'And you don't think you need me? You don't think you need power? You admit you can't save Revelstone, much less the Land, but you don't want help?'

From the edge of the floor, Liand nodded vigorous approval. Mahrtiir watched her with encouragement gleaming in his eyes.

But the Voice of the Masters was not swayed. 'Kevin Landwaster heeded such concerns,' he countered. 'We do not. Our worth and our purposes are measured by the forces arrayed against us, but we are not judged by victory or defeat, life or death. Rather we value ourselves according to our honour and steadfastness. That the Demondim are able to wield the might of the Illearth Stone does not require us to abandon who we are.

'Knowing this, we do not choose to emulate the Landwaster's despair.'

Linden stifled a groan. In Handir's response, she recognised the passion of the *Haruchai* for absolute judgments. Even Cail, who had served the Search for the One Tree with an almost limitless valour and fidelity: even he had not questioned the final denunciation of the *Haruchai*. His fault was not that he had succumbed to the *merewives*, but that he had lived on after his seduction. She did not doubt that the Masters would rather die as a race than retract their chosen form of service.

But she was not prepared to simply strive and fail and die. Not while her son needed her. Not while the Land was in such peril.

And she knew that Handir had not told her the whole truth. He had said nothing of his people's fear that they would be taken by the passion which had overcome Cail as well as Korik, Sill and Doar. Liand was right about the Masters. They feared to grieve.

Tightening her grasp on the Staff, she frowned at Handir. 'I think I understand,' she said slowly. 'You're mortal. You can't afford to judge yourselves by standards that transcend your limitations. That was Korik's mistake. It may even have been Kevin's.'

There her detachment faltered. Anger began to throb in her voice as she continued.

'But that doesn't explain why you don't want help. It doesn't explain your so-called Mastery of the Land.

'It's one thing to give your best and then accept what happens. You do that. You've always done it. But this time you've gone further. *This* time you think you have the right to prevent other people from doing the same. Isn't that true? As far as I can tell, you didn't become Masters because you want to save the Land. You did it because you want to stop anyone else from saving it.

'Am I wrong?' she demanded. 'Then say so. Tell me why.'

The Voice of the Masters remained relaxed in front of her; apparently untouched. But his nostrils flared slightly with each breath, and a small muscle clenched and released at the corner of his jaw.

Linden thought that she heard indignation in his tone as he retorted, 'That is unjust. We prevent nothing except the use of power.'

'No, you don't,' she insisted. 'You've gone much further than that. Stave accused me of healing him without giving him a choice. You've prevented anyone from having the choice to use power. In effect, you've decided *in advance* that there hasn't ever been and won't ever be anyone in the Land wise enough to use Earthpower well. You've prejudged every person and every decision and every action since the day you became Masters. And that just doesn't make sense.

'Look at it this way,' she said, hurrying so that she would not be interrupted, 'you know what's going to happen when the Demondim come back. You'll fight them with everything you've got, and you'll be slaughtered. But you *don't* know what would happen if you trusted me to help you. Or if you helped me find my son.'

Then Linden shook her head. 'But that's not a good example. I'm not ignorant. And so far you haven't done anything to get in my way. Here's a better one.

'You can't possibly know what the result would be if Liand had the training and resources to be a Graveler.' She did not glance at the Stonedownor, although she felt his surprise. 'Sunder did. You know that. And you also know that Covenant would not have lived long enough to save your people from the Clave if Sunder hadn't helped him. So how can you believe that Liand doesn't have the right to know as much as Sunder did?'

Abruptly she stopped, nearly panting with the force of her assertion.

Handir raised an eyebrow; but he did not pause to consult with the other Masters. 'Linden Avery,' he replied flatly, 'we act as we do because the alternative is plainly impossible. We cannot intervene in decisions and actions after their effects have become known. The opportunity to prevent them has passed. And we are too few. All the *Haruchai* who have ever lived would not suffice to ward from evil every person who might seek to make use of Earthpower.

'Yet we have determined that we cannot stand aside. The evil is too great. And Brinn has become the Guardian of the One Tree. Are we less than he? Must we do less than serve as the guardians of the Land? No. You cannot ask it of us. But if we will serve, how otherwise may our task be accomplished? We must prevent the use of Earthpower. No other way is possible for us.'

Linden did not hesitate. She could not. And in her chambers she had prepared herself for this moment. Handir had given her the opening she needed.

Breathing hard, she glared at him. 'Then look at it *this* way,' she continued, carried on a rising wave of anger. 'There stand the Humbled.' With the back of her hand, she slapped a gesture towards the Masters holding Anele. 'Galt and—'

Momentarily she stumbled. She did not know their names.

'The Humbled,' Handir informed her, 'are Galt, Clyme and Branl.'

'Fine,' she returned. 'The Humbled. They're supposed to be living reminders that you can't *master* evils like the Illearth Stone and Ravers and Corruption. Which sounds good, I have to admit. But how did they *get* the job? How did you *choose* them?'

Again she did not grant their Voice a chance to interrupt her. 'Christ, Handir, they *fought* for the privilege.' Her words were flames. They leaped and burned as she uttered them. 'They think it's an *honour* to be maimed like that. They beat the shit out of each other for the *status* of reminding you that you need *humility*.'

Responding to her passion, the Staff began to burn in her grasp. Its fire reached higher with every utterance. If she did not restrain it, the rush of power would light the unharmed ceiling of the Close.

She would be able to see what the love of the Giants had crafted there.

For a moment, she let her fire rise. Then, deliberately, she swallowed her ire until the Staff was quenched. The force of her emotions served only to remind her that she was not helpless. It would not increase her credibility.

Quietly now, she said, 'I think you've missed the point of what happened on the Isle of the One Tree. I don't know how Cail told the story, but I was there. I saw it.

'Brinn didn't win that fight. He lost. In fact, he surrendered,' just as Covenant had surrendered to Lord Foul in Kiril Threndor. 'He let the Guardian kill him. And he became the new Guardian by taking the old one with him when he died.

'I'm sorry, Handir,' she finished as calmly as she could. 'If you and the Humbled and the rest of the Masters are trying to follow Brinn's example, you're going about it the wrong way. You haven't just denied everyone else the right to make their own choices. You've missed the point.'

Handir held up his hand. In spite of his apparent relaxation, however, his gesture had the certainty of a blow. With one small motion, he dominated the Close as if the rectitude and indignation of all his people were invested in him. Even the light seemed to concentrate on him, focused by his underlying authority.

The Cords and Liand stared at him in chagrin. Mahrtiir swore under his breath.

'It is enough,' the Voice of the Masters pronounced like a knell. 'We have heard you. Now you will desist. Because you are the Chosen, we have suffered the challenge of your words. But you fault us to no purpose.

'Perhaps you have described us justly. Perhaps not. It alters nothing. Your recriminations do not pertain to the hazard of your actions in the Land. The truth remains that you have dared the destruction of all the Earth for the sake of your son. And now you do not assure us that the danger is past. Rather you seek to disguise your actions by diminishing ours.

'Yet this answer I will grant to you.' The muscles at the corners of the jaw knotted and released to the beat of his words. 'It is true that we have placed ourselves foremost in the Land's defence. For this we might claim to merit respect rather than accusation. But if we fall, the Land will remain, and all who wish to strive against Corruption may do so in any fashion which seems good to them.'

'No, Handir,' Linden retorted at once. 'Now you're just being dishonest.' She had come too far to hold back. 'You've done everything you can to erase that possibility. You've kept the people of the Land from knowing anything about Earthpower, or their own history, or the evils they'll have to face. I tell you, it's wrong. You've made too many decisions for other people, and you never had the right.

'But I'm not done,' she added immediately. 'I've given you two answers.' Inadequacy. Arrogance. 'I've pointed out that you aren't in a position to judge me. If you refuse to listen, that's your problem, not mine.

'I've got one more answer for you.'

Ignorance.

She was desperate now; on the verge of a risk as great in its own way as daring to enter a *caesure*. *Good cannot be accomplished by evil means*. But the Masters had denied every other argument. And she had believed almost from the first that she would not be able to rescue her son without Anele's help.

As if she knew that she would not be refused, she looked at the son of Sunder and Hollian among the Humbled and said softly, 'Anele, come here.'

The old man had given no sign that he had heard or understood what was being said around him. He seemed unaware of anything except the fact that the Masters had claimed him. Without Linden's protection, he had no defence.

Yet when she spoke his name, he jerked up his head and his moonstone eyes caught a flare of fire from the lamps. Threshing his arms as if to break free of the Humbled, although they made no effort to restrain him, he crossed the tormented stone and flung himself down in front of her. His thin arms embraced her knees and the Staff in supplication.

'Protect,' he panted. 'Oh, protect Anele. They are heartless. They will devour his soul. They devour all things, leaving only pain.'

Liand started forward to attend to the old man; but Linden waved him back.

She needed Anele where he was. His contact with the Staff might calm him so that he could heed her.

To Handir, she said, 'You don't really care about keeping him prisoner. You just want to control him so he can't do any harm. You've explained that. I think I understand it. But you haven't thought it through.'

Her heart ached in her chest as she considered what she meant to do. She had found no gap in the Masters' defences. Her intentions might taint Anele irredeemably in their eyes. They might go to any extreme to keep him. But she had no recourse that she could see – or accept. Apart from Anele, she had no arguments left except power. And she would not fight the *Haruchai*. The Land needed them. Too many of them had already spent their lives for her sake.

The old man was her last hope. Therefore she chose to place him in danger.

With one hand, she clenched her courage to the smooth shaft of the Staff. The other she lowered so that it rested on Anele's dismayed head, hoping that the touch of her palm would reassure him.

Doing so, she also reassured herself.

Although the Masters had conceded nothing, she met Handir's flat gaze and began.

'Stave must have told you that Anele reads stone. He's like an Unfettered One. He's taught himself to hear slowly enough to understand what the rocks are saying.

'Sure, that means he can tell people about the Land's history.' If he stood on the right kind of stone. 'You don't want that. But it also means he can tell us what the Earth is saying about its own pain.

'He's already identified threats we wouldn't know about otherwise. *Skurj*. A broken Durance. Kastenessen. That alone makes him too useful to be locked away.

'But he has more to offer. A lot more. If he's free.'

Urgently she wished that she could interpret Handir's expression. But she had no idea whether he heard her with sympathy or scorn. She had to trust that the Masters saw her more clearly than she did them; that what was in her heart would show through the inadequacy of her ability of express it.

'If I'm right,' she said carefully, 'the – I'm not sure what to call it – the "content" of his madness is controlled by the surface under his feet. When he stands on broken stones, he hears them. When he's on native gutrock, he becomes sane. But when the stone has been worked in some way' – by Giants in Revelstone, or by Liand's people in Mithil Stonedown – 'then he's like this. He seems to understand what's happening, but he can't always respond appropriately.

'But there's more. Stave wasn't with us all the time. He didn't see everything that happened.'

Impulsively she glanced at Stave. She had withheld some of her experience with Anele's madness from him; had distrusted him to that extent. Her concern that he might take umbrage impelled her to turn away from Handir for a moment.

The look on his face gave her nothing. The puckering of his new scars seemed to imply that he would not forgive her.

It was possible that he did not understand the concept. Perhaps none of the *Haruchai* did.

Aching, she faced the older Master again.

'When Anele,' oh, Anele, 'stands on something other than stone – bare dirt, or different kinds of grass – he can be possessed. Sometimes Lord Foul reaches into him and takes over. The Despiser can see through his eyes, talk through his mouth.

'And there are other beings—' She would not mention Covenant: not here, out of desperation. 'You've seen one of them, when you were fighting the Demondim. I don't know who it was, but it wasn't Anele. When his feet touched bare dirt, someone else claimed him.'

A spirit or power whose hatred was magma.

'You probably think that's a good reason to keep him locked up.' Linden shook her head to dismiss Handir's objections. 'An even better reason than preventing him from saying too much about the Land's history. But you're wrong.

'Don't you see?' In spite of her shame, she spoke as though she had no qualms about sacrificing the old man to her own needs. 'If we understand who can possess him, and when, we'll have a tremendous advantage. By hearing what our enemies say, even when they're trying to mislead us, we might be able to figure out who they are and what they're doing.

'But there's more. Think about how we could mislead *them*. My God, if we were clever enough, we could make them believe anything we wanted.'

Abruptly Liand put in, 'Linden, this troubles me.' His aura had become an ache of worry. 'Would not Anele suffer in such use?'

Manethrall Mahrtiir nodded sharply. Bhapa and Pahni watched Linden with uncertainty on their faces.

It seemed that none of her companions had expected her to sound so callous.

Vexed by the interruption, and privately sickened by her own actions, Linden sighed, 'Oh, hell, we're all suffering. Do you actually think it would be any worse than what he's going through right now? And he wants to be of use.

You heard him.' In the cave of the Waynhim. 'He doesn't think he's earned the right to be healed.'

Then she faced Handir again. 'I don't see how you can call yourselves the Masters of the Land and still believe that he should be kept prisoner.'

Briefly Handir gazed around at the other Masters. He seemed to be communing with them in spite of his promise that their deliberations would be conducted aloud. Before Linden could object, however, he turned back to her.

'We are not persuaded,' he announced. 'You must demonstrate his worth.'

She flinched, although Handir's demand did not surprise her. She had expected it; feared it. Indeed, she had proposed something similar herself. Now, however, her heart rebelled at the idea of asking Anele to perform like a trained animal. She still wanted to postpone the moment when she would be forced to misuse him.

And she could not be certain of his response.

But she had created a situation in which she had no choice but to surrender or forge ahead. When she had risked damaging the Arch of Time to seek for the Staff, she had in some sense misused everyone with her. And the Masters had made it plain that she could not answer them alone, any more than she could rescue Jeremiah or defeat Lord Foul by herself. She had to ask for help, and pray that she would get it.

With a silent groan, she stooped to the old man and urged him to stand.

He seemed reluctant to release her knees. Or perhaps it was the Staff to which he clung, consoling himself with its apt warmth. After a moment, however, he loosened his grasp and rose.

When he had gained his feet, she put her arm around him and hugged him close. 'Anele,' she murmured gently, 'I need you. I said I would protect you, and I want to keep my promise. But I can't do this without you.'

'We're standing on stone,' surrounded by stone. 'It's your friend.' His only friend. 'It's always been your friend.

'I need you to tell us what it says.'

He was no longer the Anele who had averred that he was content to see the Staff of Law in her hands. That avatar of his dilemma had been left many centuries in the past. In *this* time – Linden's proper time, if not his own – he had been hounded to destitution by loneliness and loss as much as by the Masters. Linden could not be sure that he understood her. She had no reason to assume that he would comply.

By small shifts and stages, however, as if he had to remember separately how to move each muscle, he withdrew from her clasp. Reluctantly he trailed his fingertips along the Staff. Then he let it go.

'It is sooth.' His voice was a low croak which seemed to hurt his throat. 'Anele has no friend but stone. It does not comfort him. It is not kindly. It is strict, and full of hurt. But it only speaks. It does not judge. It does not demand. It does not punish.'

The old man shook his head sadly. 'For him there is no other solace.'

Hampered by the burden of too much time, he took a few steps towards the centre of the floor. His head began to flinch from side to side. Apparently trying to stop it, he covered his face with his hands. Still his head jerked back and forth as if he feared what he might see in spite of his blindness.

A moan slipped between his lips and fell away, leaving the Close hushed and expectant; waiting.

Linden held her breath. Hardly aware of herself, she retreated to sit once more between Liand and Mahrtiir. Her attention was fixed on Anele. At that moment, nothing else mattered.

Barely audible through his hands, Anele breathed, 'Ah, stone. Bone of the world. Forlorn and unregarded. It weeps eternally, yet none heed its sorrow. None hear its endless plaint.

'This stone has known love which the Land has forgotten, the adoration of Giants and Lords. It has suffered rage. It has been afflicted with Desecration.

'In grief and understanding, it speaks to me of fathers.'

Unselfconsciously Linden rested the Staff between her knees and reached out to her companions. But now simply gripping Liand's forearm, and Mahrtiir's, did not suffice. She needed to entwine her fingers with theirs and grip them until her knuckles ached.

That tight human clench, the Stonedownor on one side and the Manethrall on the other, seemed to make it possible for her to bear Anele's words.

Muffled by his hands, his voice was a thin thread of sound in the huge chamber, as inadequate as the lamps to fill the Close, and as necessary.

'First,' he murmured, 'always first, it speaks of the father who wrought this harm. He was Trell Atiaran-mate, Gravelingas of Mithil Stonedown. The stone remembers him compassionately, for he was of the *rhadhamaerl*, beloved of all the Earth's rock, and the plight of his daughter, his only child, had surpassed his heart's capacity for healing. Rent by her violation and pain, he here betrayed his love and his lore and himself, and when his hand was stayed the weight of his despair bore him down. What remains is the spilth and contortion of his anguish.'

Anele's head jerked, and jerked again. 'That sorrow would exceed any less enduring flesh. But this stone has more.'

His voice seemed to limp between his hands, wincing to the rhythm of words which only he could interpret.

'It speaks of the *Elohim* Kastenessen in his Durance, father to the malice of the *merewives*. His daughters are the Dancers of the Sea and they swim the fathomless deeps in hunger and cruelty, insatiable for retribution, while their own scion is torment. Yet they know glee as well as hunger, for their father has broken his imprisonment, and at his behest the *skurj* which he once unwillingly restrained have unleashed their cunning and frenzy against the Land.

'And in the same breath, it speaks of the *Haruchai* Cail, who succumbed to the *merewives* and fathered their scion. He also is remembered with compassion, for only death has spared him from desolation at his son's torment. Indeed, there is keening here on his behalf, keening and great sadness. He had been repudiated by his kindred, and his heart could not distinguish between its own yearning and the desire of the *merewives*. Yet that desire was not love but malice.'

Slowly Anele sank to his knees, borne down by knowledge. He kept his hands pressed over his eyes, and his head beat from side to side as if his ears were full of threnodies. His voice had become a long-breathed gasping, scarcely strong enough to sustain the sentences which the stone required of him.

'And it speaks as well of Thomas Covenant, of the white gold wielder, whose daughter rent the law of death, and whose son is abroad in the Land, seeking such havoc that the bones of mountains tremble to contemplate it. For the wielder also this stone grieves, knowing him betrayed.

'It speaks of Sunder son of Nassic, Graveler of Mithil Stonedown, who abandoned all that he had known for the sake of the wielder and the Land. Him the stone names because the son whom he brought back from death in Andelain lost the Staff of Law. In spite of this father's valour and love, his legacy is sorrow.

'Also it names the Despiser, who is the father of woe. Yet of him the stone says little. His darkness is beyond its ken.'

Then the old man moaned again, a sound like distant winds complaining past jagged granite teeth. He began to pant heavily as if he were suffocating on words.

'And last, at the furthest extent of hearing, it speaks of Berek the Lord-Fatherer. It has not known him, for Revelstone had not been fashioned in that age, and he did not enter here. Yet he and his line prized and honoured deep rock passionately, and until the Landwaster's Desecration all the Land's stone knew the savour of joy.'

Abruptly he dropped his hands to the floor, crouching over them as if he could no longer support the weight of what he heard.

'More,' he panted, 'Anele cannot read. A seer might spend his life in study and not hear all that this stone would tell.'

Yet he was not done. While Linden and her companions still watched him and waited, he flung up his head and turned to face her, unerring in spite of his blindness.

'You,' he gasped between ragged gulps of air. 'You who promised. Anele begs— Oh, he begs of you.

'Tell him that he has not failed your need.'

Before she knew that she had moved, Linden knelt at his side, her friends and the Staff and all of the Masters forgotten. Wrapping her arms around him, she hugged him to her heart. 'Oh, Anele.' Tears which she could not refuse streamed down her cheeks. 'Anele.' His old body trembled in her embrace. 'Of *course* you haven't failed me. Dear God, no. You've done more than I could have asked. You always have.

'You poor man.' Releasing one hand, she brushed straggling hair out of his face. Then tenderly she kissed his forehead. 'Sometimes you astonish me.'

He had told her, *I am unworthy of such astonishment*. But he was wrong.

If he understood her – if he remembered any of his own past – he did not show it. Gradually, however, his respiration eased and the tension receded from his muscles. By degrees, he grew quiet in her arms.

Liand had joined her while she concentrated on the old man. When Anele was still at last, the Stonedownor helped her raise him to his feet. Carefully they supported him to the edge of the floor and seated him between Pahni and Bhapa.

Only then did Linden retrieve the Staff and return her attention to the Masters; to Handir and Stave, who had not spoken since she had asked for Anele's help.

Shamed by what the old man had endured at her bidding, she no longer made any distinction between the two *Haruchai*.

'I hope you're satisfied,' she said thinly. 'I've had enough of this. Don't trust us, or do. Just make up your minds. I'm done trying to convince you.'

She seemed to see nothing in Handir's mien except denial. Yet it was not the Voice of the Masters who replied to her.

It was Stave.

Although he stood at Handir's side as if the two of them were united against her, he gave her a deliberate bow. 'You are Linden Avery the Chosen,' he began without inflection, 'and we have heard you. You have said much, to your cost, and to that of your companions, and to our own. Now I will speak again.

'I have named your perilous deeds. And I have said that I fear what you may do in your son's name. I do fear it. For such reasons the Masters withhold their trust. Yet one other matter remains unaddressed.'

Linden's hopes seemed to gutter until she heard Stave say, 'My people did not participate in the horserite which you and I have shared. I have not yet spoken of the will of the Ranyhyn.'

What—?

Suddenly she sat up straighter. Her eyes burned as she met his flat gaze. Tightening her grip on the Staff, she waited for Stave to go on.

He had told his people everything else—

'You have observed,' he remarked almost casually, 'that my stance towards you was altered by the horserite. You enquired of the cause. I declined to answer. I replied only that I awaited the proper time and place to speak. Both now are upon me.'

Still he spoke to Linden as though his words were meant for her alone. She could only stare at him in mute surprise as he continued.

'When the Ranyhyn Hynyn and Hyn had borne us to the vale and the eldritch tarn of their ancient gathering place, I avowed that I would not take part in their mind-blending rituals.'

She remembered his refusal vividly. *I am* Haruchai. *We have no need of horserites.*

'You sought there to humble me,' he said, 'as you have done here as well. Yet your words persuaded me when I did not wish to be swayed.

'You spoke of the time which followed *Kelenbhrabanal's* failure to redeem the Ranyhyn from Fangthane's depredations. And you reminded me that the great horses were restored to the Land, not by Lords or Bloodguard, or by any great power.'

Facing Linden, but clearly speaking for the benefit of the other Masters, Stave explained the point which she had made.

'Rather their return to the Plains of Ra was made possible by the Ramen. You spoke of "the plain, selfless devotion of ordinary men and women". And you averred that the Ranyhyn endeavoured to make this known as a warning, so that such men as we are would not conceive that we must redeem the Land through any form of Mastery. To do so, you suggested, would be to repeat the folly of High Lord Elena, and perhaps of Kevin Landwaster and *Kelenbhrabanal* as well.'

Stave paused as if to consult his memories; to assure himself that he had described her argument fairly. Then he lifted his shoulders in a slight shrug and went on.

'Also you observed that both the form and the substance of the horserite offered a warning which I must not ignore. Therefore I consented to the will of the Ranyhyn. With you I partook of their dark waters, and was transformed.'

Linden nodded, although he had not asked for her confirmation. Intent on him, she listened, unable to turn away.

At last, he lifted his face to the few Masters among the broad empty spaces of the Close. 'The perils which the Ranyhyn have foreseen for the Chosen are strait and arduous. They fear her as I do. They fear that the burdens of this age may be too great for her to bear.

'To me the great horses offered no such caution.

'Masters, kinsmen—' Again Stave paused for thought; and again he shrugged. Without raising his voice, he announced distinctly, 'When I had drunk of the mind-blending waters, I learned that the Ranyhyn laughed at me.'

Linden stared, unable to conceal her amazement. At her side, Liand's aura showed that he, too, had expected to hear something very different. But Mahrtiir gave a snort of vindication, which his Cords echoed more discreetly.

Yet the Masters around the Close listened as if they felt nothing: no surprise or indignation; no uncertainty. The features of Handir and the Humbled were as unreactive as engravings.

Stolidly Stave explained, 'Their laughter did not resemble Corruption's, scornful and demeaning. The Giants laugh so, and it gives no hurt. Rather it was kindly and—' He hesitated for a moment, murmuring, 'Such speech is awkward.' But then he pronounced clearly, 'Their laughter was both kindly and affectionate. The Ranyhyn conceived no ill of me. They merely wished to express that they found amusement in my belief that our service is sufficient to the Land's need.

'Our Mastery amuses them. In their sight, we are too small to comprehend or gauge all of the paths which may lead to triumph or Desecration. Though they are beings of Earthpower and mystery, they do not claim for themselves either the discernment or the courage to determine the Land's defence.'

For a few heartbeats, Stave fell silent. He may have felt that his people needed time to absorb what he had said. Then he resumed.

'At the same time, laughing, they desired me to grasp that they have declared themselves utterly to the service of the Chosen. They will bear her wheresoever she wills, until the end of days. Her paths may enter Falls and the hazardous depths of time. Each and all of her choices may conduce to ruin. Yet will they bear her gladly. Indeed, they deem themselves fortunate to serve her.

'It is sooth,' he pronounced as if he were passing sentence, 'that she may damn the Land. Yet the Ranyhyn believe that she will not. In their eyes, the Land's life and hope require them to believe that she will not.'

Around him, tension gathered. It seemed to well up from the twists and flaws of the floor, drift down from the obscured ceiling, until it became so thick that the light of the lamps flickered and dimmed.

Stave's kinsmen were taking umbrage.

Now his tone appeared to quicken, although his words maintained their uninflected tread.

'Masters, you will decide as you must, according to your beliefs. Doubtless it is difficult for the people who gave birth to the Guardian of the One Tree to consider themselves small. But the Manethrall has spoken aptly, though he knew it not.

'I have shared the horserite of the Ranyhyn, and have learned that we are not greater than they. Nor are we greater than the Ramen, who are content with service, and who do not attempt to alter that which lies beyond them.'

Mahrtiir muttered gruff approval. Surprise and wonder shone from the faces of his Cords.

Stave's voice took on a palpable sharpness. 'Nor are we greater than this Stonedownor, the least of the Chosen's companions, for he seeks only to join his cause with hers, and to partake in beauties and powers which we have withheld from him.'

As he spoke, the assembled Masters watched him with darkness in their eyes, despite the many lamps; and the muscles at the corners of Handir's jaw knotted and released with the heaviness of a death-watch. Slowly the Humbled closed their hands into fists.

But Liand seemed not to notice the tightening among the *Haruchai*. Instead he simply stared at Stave, astonished to hear a Master say such things. And Linden, who felt the rise of tension, ignored it to listen and hold her breath, waiting for Stave's conclusion.

Finally he turned again so that he stood facing the Voice of the Masters across the distorted stone. The lamplight emphasised the unwonted intensity in his gaze as he announced, 'Because I have heard the laughter of the great horses, I will cast my lot with the Chosen. I cannot do less than the Ranyhyn. Whatever may befall her, I will endeavour to prove that I am equal to my fears.'

Linden hugged the Staff of Law to her chest with both arms, blinking furiously to hold back her tears. She wept too easily and did not mean to do so now.

At last— she breathed to herself. God, at last!

Stave of the *Haruchai* had brought her to Revelstone for this: so that he could declare himself in front of his people.

He had finally become her friend.

Chapter Twelve:

Find Me

She could not imagine what the Masters would do now. But their accumulated judgment had a tangible force which seemed to bear down upon her from the sides of the Close, as heavy as Revelstone's unillumined rock.

It felt like animosity.

She spared a glance and a quick nod for Liand's open relief and Mahrtiir's begrudged approval. Then she rose to her feet, holding the Staff before her like a talisman. At once, Liand and the Manethrall came to stand beside her.

Escorted by her friends, she approached Stave and bowed deeply, hoping that he would recognise the scale of her gratitude. However, the bow which he returned to her resembled a farewell more than an acknowledgement. His manner conveyed the impression that for her sake he had turned his back on more things than she could understand.

She wanted to ask him how the Masters would respond to his profession of faith; but her throat was full of other words which demanded utterance.

Meeting his single gaze, she said with her whole heart, 'Thank you. I owe you more than I can ever repay.

'You've already done so much for me. You've been true—' Her voice broke momentarily. 'I can't even begin to describe how glad I am—'

In this place, she could not go further. Handir had not yet pronounced judgment upon her.

Dispassionately, as if he had no interest in her gratitude, Stave replied, 'You are Linden Avery the Chosen. The Ranyhyn have taught me that I cannot refuse your service.'

'Still,' she countered, smiling sadly. 'I hope that someday you'll be sure you did the right thing.'

Because she was determined not to weep, she bowed again, as deeply as before. Then she turned towards the Voice of the Masters.

There she froze. The merciless clarity in his eyes chilled her: it seemed to settle like frost on her bones. She had to swallow a mouthful of dread before she could speak.

Awkwardly she asked, 'So what's it going to be? Are we on the same side?' His gaze covered her with rime. She had to cling to the Staff's warmth to keep her voice from shaking. 'Will you let me have Anele? Will you give me your help?'

'How will the sleepless ones refuse?' put in Mahrtiir. His tone held a sting of asperity. 'Stave has confirmed the will of the Ranyhyn. Naught else signifies.'

But Handir did not choose to heed the Manethrall. Instead he replied, 'Stand aside, Linden Avery. Another matter requires precedence. I will reply when it has been addressed.'

Commanded by his certainty, she stepped back, drawing Mahrtiir and Liand with her.

For a moment, Handir appeared to commune with all of the Masters mutely, mind to mind. When he was satisfied with their response, he nodded sternly; and the three Humbled moved closer.

Instinctively Linden lifted the Staff higher, thinking that the Humbled meant to reclaim Anele. But they did not. When they reached Handir's side, Galt moved forward to confront Stave.

They faced each other in silence, as poised as predators, and as relaxed. They might have been living statues, motionless except for the subtle flex of their respiration; sculptures positioned to form a tableau of arcane and ambiguous intent. Then without warning Galt lashed a kick at Stave's chest.

Stave made no move to defend himself. Only a hard flat exhalation indicated that he was prepared for the blow. He stood like stone to receive it.

The kick drove him backwards a step; two. Linden could see its impact jolt through him, forceful as a sledgehammer. But then he regained his poise. Only a brief accentuation of his breathing betrayed that he had been struck.

'Heaven and Earth!' Liand cried. Whipping his garrote from his hair, Mahrtiir launched himself at Galt's back with the suddenness of a panther. At the same time, Bhapa and Pahni leaped to their feet and rushed forward.

'No!' Linden gasped after the Manethrall, '*stop!*'

An arm's length from Galt, Mahrtiir halted; wheeled to face her.

She seemed to feel the power of Galt's kick in her own chest. She could hardly choke out words.

'This is between them.' She understood Galt's attack. Long ago she had watched the *Haruchai* pass judgment on Cail. She had feared that their violence would kill him. 'Stave has to do this. You know how he feels about help.'

Unwitting flames licked along the surface of the Staff. Grimly she quenched them.

Mahrtiir hesitated. His desire for battle burned like the fires which lit the Close. But he heard Linden – and respected her judgment. Growling, 'Sleepless ones,' as though the words were an obscenity, he returned to her side. With a brusque wave of his hand, he motioned the Cords back to their seats.

'Linden,' protested Liand under his breath, 'they are Masters. They may be able to slay him.'

Through her teeth, she repeated, 'This is between them.' She could not forget how Esmer had torn into Stave, delivering millennia of rage despite the *Haruchai*'s best efforts to defend himself. 'He's already been shamed enough.'

Galt did not renew his attack. Instead he withdrew; and Clyme came forward to take his place.

Again the two Masters faced each other in stillness. They may have been sparring mentally, probing each other's minds for openings or weakness. When Clyme exploded into motion, he did not kick or punch. Rather he leaped high into the air, driving down at Stave's shoulder with his elbow and all of his weight.

The Master was trying to cripple Stave—

Once again, Stave made no effort to defend himself. This time, however, he shifted slightly at the last instant so that Clyme's elbow struck muscle rather than bone. The blow almost drove him to his knees; but it broke nothing.

Like Galt, Clyme withdrew, and the last of the Humbled advanced to challenge Stave.

Apparently Branl had decided to try for surprise by attacking immediately. Before Stave could set aside the pain in his shoulder, Branl hooked a vicious punch to the left side of his face: the blind side. Branl's knuckles dug deep into the puckered flesh of Stave's scar, pounding against the damaged tissue and bone beneath it.

Stave's head rocked as if he had been clubbed: he barely kept his balance. But he did not repay the blow. The flat stare of his right eye suggested an acceptance more profound than resignation.

Branl may or may not have been satisfied. Linden could not tell. Sympathetic hurts ached in her chest, her shoulder, her cheek. But the Humbled moved aside without hesitation.

Slowly the Voice of the Masters stepped in front of Stave.

Linden's restraint broke. 'Oh, come on!' she snapped, although she knew that Stave did not desire her intervention, and would not approve. 'How much longer are you going to do this? There's just *one* of him, for God's sake! How much of your self-righteousness do you think he can stand?'

Neither Handir nor Stave answered her. But the Voice of the Masters may have been tired of her objections. Instead of probing mentally, he addressed Stave aloud.

'You have set yourself against the will of the Masters, when that will has not yet been decided. Indeed, you have endeavoured to impose your will upon us, shaming us with your words and your example. But the Masters are not shamed. We will not be shamed.

'We will consider your words and your example when we are ready to determine our path. But we will no longer heed you. Henceforth you are severed from the Masters, as from all of the *Haruchai*. When the rite of our disapproval has been completed, no hand will be raised against you. If you speak as I do now, you will be answered. But you are excluded from the true speech of the *Haruchai*, and if you call out you will not be heard. Nor will you be permitted to return to your home among the mountains. There will be no place for you. You have declared your allegiance. Now you must abide its outcome.

'This is my word. I will not alter it.'

So suddenly that Linden hardly saw him move, Handir attacked.

Like the Humbled, he struck only once. Unlike them, however, he used just the palm of his hand. And his blow seemed easy and fluid, hardly more than a light thrust. Yet Stave burst backwards as though he had been kicked by a Ranyhyn. He tumbled through the air; slammed helplessly to the rough stone. For a heartbeat or two, he lay motionless.

Before Linden could start towards him, however, he raised his head. When he had braced his hands on the floor, he climbed slowly to his feet. Bright blood pulsed from the corner of his mouth as he resumed his stance. She could not imagine where he found the strength to remain standing.

The Voice of the Masters held Stave's gaze for a long moment. Then he turned to Linden. 'Be content,' he told her stolidly. 'The rite has been completed.'

Blood splashed the front of Stave's tunic, staining the ochre fabric with darkness. He did not deign to wipe it away.

'You're wrong,' Linden panted. 'It's not over.' She needed all of her resolve to withhold fire from the Staff. 'It'll never be over. Someday you're going to understand that you've made a terrible mistake.'

Handir replied with a slight shrug. When she fell silent, still panting, he said in the same tone, 'There is much here which the Masters must consider.

We will not choose our response in haste. Nevertheless our debate must now be curtailed.

'Certain of our scouts seek to return. They run before the host of the Demondim, calling to forewarn us as they ride. And they are not alone. They have retrieved two' – he paused and glanced away as if consulting the air, then met Linden's gaze again – 'two strangers from the path of the Vile-spawn.' Complex intentions seemed to undermine the flatness of his gaze. 'They hasten towards us, pursued by the Demondim.

'We are summoned to greet the approach of our scouts, and of the strangers with them, as well as to answer an imminent siege.'

Linden scowled bitterly; but before she could pose a question, Handir announced, 'This much I may grant, however. The madman Anele we release to you. Let it be upon your head if harm should befall the Land through any deed or inaction of his.

'All else which lies between us must remain unresolved until events permit consideration and decision.'

Expressionless and impenetrable, the Voice of the Masters strode past Linden towards the uneven slope leading up to the entrance of the Close. As one, the Humbled and the other *Haruchai* followed after him, leaving only Stave behind to guide Linden and her companions.

She would have sworn at his back if she could have thought of a curse harsh enough to breach his dispassion.

As soon as Handir and the other Masters had passed, she hurried towards Stave. 'Are you all right?' His bleeding filled her with shame. She felt an almost unbearable yearning to cleanse it from him; to heal him. 'Do you want my help?'

He shook his head. 'Hurts of the flesh have no significance. The severance from my people is a deeper wound, beyond your succour.' His eye held her stricken gaze without flinching. 'In their place, I would have done as they have.'

'But, Stave—' She tried to protest, but her dismay surpassed her.

Swallowing blood, he continued, 'We must witness the approach of the Demondim and these strangers.' A lift of his undamaged shoulder seemed to indicate the silence in his mind. His voice held an added stiffness like a hint of denied bereavement. 'If we do not, we will be ignorant of what transpires.'

Still Linden wanted to weep for him; rail at the Masters; demand their acquiescence with fire. But there had been something in Handir's tone when he had mentioned strangers— Although she could not read him, she had felt a change in his demeanour; a slippage behind his impassivity.

He had recognised the newcomers—

She remained motionless for a moment while her mind wheeled, grasping at possibilities which she could not define. Then she sighed. 'You're right. Let's go.'

In spite of his injuries, the *Haruchai* turned at once to lead the way.

When she looked towards her friends, Liand nodded in spite of his chagrin. Glowering, Mahrtiir beckoned for his Cords to join him; and together Pahni and Bhapa brought Anele, encouraging him gently.

As she began the ascent to the entryway, Linden's sense of loss grew. She felt that she was treading across Trell's pain; that her boot heels wounded the twisted stone. When she reached the entrance, her mouth had gone dry; and the air beyond the chamber smelled of smoke and ashes, as if something more essential than lamp oil and torches were being consumed.

Now she wished that she had asked Liand to bring water as well as bread and cheese from her quarters. She had gained Stave's support and freed Anele. The Staff in her hands reassured her. But the price— Revelstone was threatened by Demondim and the Illearth Stone because she had dared the past. The ur-viles and Waynhim had been decimated in her name, and many *Haruchai* had died. Her defiance had alienated the Masters. And because he had declared himself, Stave had suffered a hurt far more profound than the beating he had received from Esmer. She wanted water to wash down the taste of what she had accomplished.

Nevertheless she trudged onwards, following her guide into the unmapped complications of Revelstone.

At first, she and her companions walked the unfamiliar passages in silence. This part of the Keep had not been prepared for guests: there were no lamps, and the torches were far apart, leaving only a faint tang of smoke in the air. But Stave knew the way and did not hesitate.

However, Liand emitted a growing disquiet, and his need to speak soon became palpable. Clearing his throat, he began awkwardly, 'Stave—' Then he admitted, 'I know not how to address you. I have considered you a Master, but now that title seems' – he faltered briefly – 'false.'

'I am Stave,' the *Haruchai* replied. 'I need no other name.'

'Very well.' Liand tried again. 'Stave. I wish to say—' For a moment longer, he struggled. Then he took on the dignity which Linden had first seen in him during their flight from Mithil Stonedown. In a firmer voice, he announced, 'I regret that I have thought ill of you. Yes, and spoken ill as well. Your courage shames me.'

Stave may have shrugged. 'We are all shamed, you no more than I' – he glanced at Linden – 'and neither of us more than the Chosen, who should not have been subjected to the disapproval of the Masters.'

He waited until he had led his companions through the intersection of several corridors. Then he assured the Stonedownor, 'Yet you need have no fear of me. I have claimed a place at the side of the Chosen, and will not withdraw from it.'

'I do not doubt you,' Mahrtiir put in gruffly. 'You have won my esteem as well, Stave of the *Haruchai*. The Ramen will never again err by demeaning you.'

Stave nodded, but made no other reply.

I have claimed— Again Linden fought back tears. She feared that she would never be done with weeping. She had only been in the Land for a few days, and already she needed so much forgiveness—

Even Anele had refused to let her heal him.

They walked on; and Linden's thirst increased; and the passages of Revelstone seemed to have no end. Eventually, however, they reached a broad stair which appeared to curve up indefinitely into the dark rock of the Keep. And at the foot of the stair they found a stout figure waiting for them.

The nearest torch was some distance away. In spite of the gloom, however, Linden soon recognised the Mahdoubt. The comfortable complacency of the older woman's aura was unmistakable.

Still shadows seemed to trail about the Mahdoubt like wisps of fog. But then she faced Linden with her startling eyes; and at once every scrap and tatter of obscurity dissipated, evaporated by her oblique warmth. Now she became more vivid to Linden's health-sense than any of her companions; more distinct than the stone of the halls. The Mahdoubt's presence shone in the dimness, lambent with abundance and implications. She appeared to command a personal dimension which was at once more ordinary and more numinous than any other place in the Keep.

Apparently Mahrtiir had not encountered the Mahdoubt before. He started forward to place himself between Linden and the older woman. But Liand caught his arm and explained quickly, 'She is the Mahdoubt. She serves Revelstone. And she has cared for us kindly.'

Mahrtiir peered through the dimness. 'She serves?' He sounded surprised. 'Yet she is—' He hesitated. 'There is that about her which—' Then he shook his head. 'Perhaps I am mistaken.' To the Mahdoubt, he added, 'I crave your pardon. My concerns have misled me.'

Stave said nothing. However, he bowed to the older woman as he had to Linden, acknowledging her worth in spite of his injuries.

The Mahdoubt ignored all of the men. 'The lady is thirsty,' she huffed as if to reprove some fault in Revelstone's hospitality – or in Linden. 'She neglects her own needs. Is the Mahdoubt pleased? She is not. Oh, assuredly. Yet it is her burden and her gift to supply care where it is found lacking.'

From within her miswoven robe she produced a flagon of water which she thrust unceremoniously at Linden.

As Linden accepted it, the Mahdoubt continued, 'The lady must not delay. Peril awaits her. Peril and pain, most assuredly. Yet the Mahdoubt will hinder her a moment. A little moment.'

The woman stepped closer. 'Heed her, lady,' she urged, whispering. 'The Masters know not what they do.' She appeared to believe that Stave and the others could not hear her. 'Nor does the lady.' She sighed lugubriously. 'Nor does the Mahdoubt, alas.'

Then she breathed with an air of intensity, 'This, however, she knows assuredly. Be cautious of love. It misleads. There is a glamour upon it which binds the heart to destruction.'

Linden stared at her. 'What do you mean? I don't understand.'

The Mahdoubt did not answer. Instead she turned and walked away. As she moved, she appeared to wrap herself in shadows so that she slipped from sight almost at once.

Be cautious of *love*?

'Strange—' Mahrtiir murmured, gazing after the woman. 'For a moment – a moment only – I seemed to see another in her place. Yet the seeming was brief. It mystifies me.'

'Stave—?' Linden asked without knowing how to put her question into words.

'She is the Mahdoubt,' he replied stolidly. 'She serves Revelstone. Naught else is certain of her.'

With one hand, he gestured towards the stair, urging his companions to ascend.

Linden eyed the heights. She was too tired for this – and understood too little. But the Mahdoubt had given her water, and when she drank deeply she began to feel somewhat stronger. Handing the flagon to Liand, she said with a sigh, 'All right. I'm ready. This can't go on forever.'

With her companions, she followed Stave up the stairs.

They seemed to ascend for a long time; but when the *Haruchai* at last guided his small company into a side passage, the way became easier. And soon Linden saw more light ahead: not the flickering of torches, or the yellow glow of lamps, but the bright illumination of day.

Stave had brought them to a balcony in the prow of the Keep, a walled projection overlooking the courtyard above the inner gates. From a gap in the ramparts, a narrow bridge of wooden slats hung suspended between the Keep and the watchtower, supported by ropes as thick as hawsers. More ropes served as railings and handholds on either side of the span.

Stave strode out onto the slats without hesitation. After a moment, Linden followed, balancing herself with the Staff and trusting the ropes to keep her safe.

When she and her companions had crossed the span, Stave led them past tall piles of firewood and clay tubs of oil – the Keep's first defence against the Demondim – to another walled projection like a coign several levels above the open gates of the tower. From this vantage, they could see a wide arc of Revelstone's environs: north towards a region of newly planted fields, south and west among the hills that buttressed the Keep's jutting plateau, and east down the long gradual slope of the bare plain where the previous day Linden and her company had emerged from her *caesure*, pursued by monsters.

Glancing down, she saw Handir and the Humbled on a similar coign one level below her. Their attention was fixed to the east. As soon as she looked in that direction, she saw what held their eyes.

Some distance away, perhaps half a league, the horde of the Demondim was plainly visible, advancing in an undifferentiated tumult. Even from so far away, the Vile-spawn seemed potent enough to overwhelm the Keep. Their malice howled at Linden's senses, and a clangour of opalescence stung the skin of her cheeks. At intervals, rank emerald flashed into the skies, staining her vision with images of violence; and concussions followed after them, hard blows which kicked up spouts and ripples of dust all around the horde. Despite the distance, faint tremors reached the watchtower. The stone seemed to shiver in reply, spreading visceral dread along her nerves.

Briefly the effects of the Illearth Stone consumed Linden's attention. But then Stave pointed out over the plain; and she saw a small cluster of riders racing ahead of the onslaught.

Four Masters mounted on horses galloped for their lives. She could not guess how long or how far they had fled: the frenzy of the horses suggested that they had been ridden hard. But they had opened a gap between themselves and the Demondim. If they did not fall or falter, they would reach the watchtower ahead of their pursuers; in time for Revelstone's defenders to close the gates.

Peering fearfully across the distance, Linden counted four horses, four Masters. But two of the mounts bore other riders as well: the beasts were badly overburdened. Although their terror goaded them, they were falling behind their companions. And they looked like they were about to founder. At erratic intervals, they stumbled under the weight of their riders.

When she saw them clearly, Linden's heart seemed to fail her, and she sank to her knees. The Staff clattered, forgotten, to the stone beside her.

The Masters had not rescued *strangers*. She knew both of them intimately.

One was Jeremiah; her son, beyond question. As the Master's mount pounded the dirt, the boy waved his arms, urging the horse to run faster, and shouted encouragement to the other riders.

Even from so far away, Linden could see that his eyes were afire with excitement.

The other *stranger* was unmistakably Thomas Covenant.

Here ends
The Runes of the Earth
Book One of
'The Last Chronicles of Thomas Covenant'.
The story continues in Book Two
Fatal Revenant.

COMBINED GLOSSARY

THE CHRONICLES OF
THOMAS COVENANT THE UNBELIEVER
Lord Foul's Bane, The Illearth War and *The Power that Preserves*

THE SECOND CHRONICLES
OF THOMAS COVENANT
The Wounded Land, The One Tree and *White Gold Wielder*

THE LAST CHRONICLES
OF THOMAS COVENANT
The Runes of the Earth

Acence: a Stonedownor, sister of Atiaran

Ahamkara: Hoerkin, 'the Door'

Ahanna: painter, daughter of Hanna

Aimil: daughter of Anest, wife of Sunder

a-Jeroth of the Seven Hells: Lord of wickedness; Clave-name for Lord Foul
  the Despiser

ak-Haru: a supreme *Haruchai* honorific

Akkasri na-Mhoram-cro: a member of the Clave

aliantha: treasure-berries

Alif, the Lady: a woman Favoured of the *gaddhi*

amanibhavam: horse-healing grass, poisonous to humans

Amatin: a Lord, daughter of Matin

Amith: a woman of Crystal Stonedown

Amok: mysterious guide to ancient Lore

Amorine: First Haft, later Hiltmark

Anchormaster: second-in-command abroad a Giantship

Andelain, the Hills of Andelain, the Andelainian Hills: a region of the Land
  which embodies health and beauty

Andelainscion: a region in the Center Plains

Anele: deranged old man; son of Sunder and Hollian

Anest: a woman of Mithil Stonedown, sister of Kalina

Annoy: a Courser

anundivian yajña: 'lost' Ramen craft of bone-sculpting

Appointed, the: an *Elohim* chosen to bear a particular burden; Findail

Arch of Time, the: symbol of the existence and structure of time; conditions
  which make the existence of time possible

arghule/arghuleh: ferocious ice-beasts

Asuraka: Staff-Elder of the Loresraat

Atiaran Trell-mate: a Stonedownor, daughter of Tiaran; mother of Lena

Aumbrie of the Clave, the: storeroom for former Lore

Auspice, the: throne of the *gaddhi*

aussat Befylam: child-form of the *jheherrin*

Bahgoon the Unbearable: character in a Giantish tale

Banas Nimoram: The Celebration of Spring

Bandsoil Bounds: region north of Soulsease River

Banefire, the: fire by which the Clave affects the Sunbane

Bann: a Bloodguard, assigned to Lord Trevor

Bannor: a Bloodguard, assigned to Covenant

Baradakas: a Hirebrand of Soaring Woodhelven

Bareisle: an island off the coast of *Elemesnedene*

Benj, the Lady: a woman Favored by the *gaddhi*

Berek Halfhand: Heartthew, Lord-Fatherer, first of the Old Lords

Bern: *Haruchai* lost to the Clave

Bhapa: a Cord of the Ramen; Sahah's half-brother; companion of Linden Avery

Bhrathair: a people met by the wandering Giants; residents of *Bhrathairealm* on the verge of the Great Desert

Bhrathairain: the city of the *Bhrathair*

Bhrathairain Harbour: the port of the *Bhrathair*

Bhrathairealm: the land of the *Bhrathair*

Birinair: a Hirebrand, Hearthrall of Lord's Keep

Bloodguard, the: *Haruchai*, a people living in the Westron Mountains; the defenders of the Lords

bone-sculpting: ancient Ramen craft, marrowmeld

Borillar: a Hirebrand and Hearthrall of Lord's Keep

Bornin: a *Haruchai*; a Master of the Land

Brabha: a Ranyhyn, Korik's mount

Brannil: man of Stonemight Woodhelven

Branl: a *Haruchai*; a Master of the Land; one of the Humbled

Brinn: a leader of the *Haruchai*; protector of Covenant; later Guardian of the One Tree

Brow Gnarlfist: a Giant; father of the First of the Search

caamora: Giantish ordeal of grief by fire

Cable Seadreamer: a Giant; brother of Honninscrave; member of the Search; possessed of the Earth-Sight

Caer-Caveral: Forestal of Andelain; formerly Hile Troy

Caerroil Wildwood: Forestal of Garroting Deep

caesure: a Fall; a rent in the fabric of time

Cail: one of the *Haruchai*; protector of Linden

Caitiffin: a captain of the armed forces of *Bhrathairealm*

Callindrill Faer-mate: a Lord

Callowwail, the River: stream arising from *Elemesnedene*

Cavewights: evil creatures existing under Mount Thunder

Ceer: one of the *Haruchai*

Celebration of Spring, the: the Dance of the Wraiths of Andelain on the dark of the moon in the middle of spring

Centerpith Barrens: a region in the Center Plains
Cerrin: a Bloodguard, assigned to Lord Shetra
Chant: one of the *Elohim*
Char: a Cord of the Ramen; Sahah's brother
Chatelaine, the: courtiers of the *gaddhi*
Chosen, the: title given to Linden Avery
Circle of Elders: Stonedown leaders
clachan, **the**: demesne of the *Elohim*
Clang: a Courser
Clangor: a Courser
Clash: a Courser
Clave, the: group which wields the Sunbane and rules the Land
clingor: adhesive leather
Close, the: the Council-chamber of Lord's Keep
Clyme: a *Haruchai*; a Master of the Land; one of the Humbled
Coercri: The Grieve; former home of the Giants in Seareach
Colossus of the Fall, the: ancient stone figure guarding the Upper Land
Consecear Redoin: a region north of the Soulsease River
Cord: Ramen second rank
Cording: Ramen ceremony of becoming a Cord
Corimini: Eldest of the Loresraat
Corruption: Bloodguard/*Haruchai* name for Lord Foul
Council of Lords, the: protectors of the Land
Courser: a beast made by the Clave using the Sunbane
Creator, the: maker of the Earth
Croft: Graveler of Crystal Stonedown
Crowl: a Bloodguard
croyel, **the**: mysterious creatures which grant power through bargains, living off their hosts
Crystal Stonedown: home of Hollian
Currier: a Ramen rank

Damelon Giantfriend: son of Berek Halfhand, second High Lord of the Old Lords
Dance of the Wraiths, the: Celebration of Spring
Dancers of the Sea, the: *merewives*; suspected to be the offspring of the *Elohim* Kastenessen and his mortal lover
Daphine: one of the *Elohim*
Dawngreeter: highest sail on the foremast of a Giantship

Dead, the: spectres of those who have died

Defiles Course, the: river in the Lower Land

Demondim, the: creatures created by Viles; creators of ur-viles and Waynhim

Demondim-spawn: another name for ur-viles and Waynhim; Vain

Desolation, the: era of ruin in the Land, after the Ritual of Desecration

Despiser, the: Lord Foul

Despite: evil; name given to the Despiser's nature and effects

dharmakshetra: 'to brave the enemy', a Waynhim

dhraga: a Waynhim

dhubha: a Waynhim

dhurng: a Waynhim

diamondraught: Giantish liquour

Din: a Courser

Doar: a Bloodguard

Dohn: a Manethrall of the Ramen

Dolewind, the: wind blowing to the Soulbiter

drhami: a Waynhim

Drinishok: Sword-Elder of the Loresraat

Drinny: a Ranyhyn, Lord Mhoram's mount, foal of Hynaril

dromond: a Giantship

Drool Rockworm: a Cavewight; leader of the Cavewights, finder of the Illearth Stone

dukkha: 'victim', Waynhim name

Dura Fairflank: a mustang, Covenant's mount

Durance: a cryptic barrier, apparently broken

durhisitar: a Waynhim

During Stonedown: village destroyed by the *Grim*; home of Hamako

Duroc: one of the Seven Words

Durris: a *Haruchai*

EarthBlood: concentrated fluid Earthpower; only known to exist under *Melenkurion* Skyweir; source of the Power of Command

Earthfriend: title first given to Berek Halfhand

Earthpower: natural power of all life; the source of all power in the Land

Earthroot: lake under *Melenkurion* Skyweir

Earth-Sight: Giantish power to perceive distant dangers and needs

eftmound: gathering-place for the *Elohim*

eh-Brand: one who can use wood to read the Sunbane

Elemesnedene: home of the *Elohim*

Elena: daughter of Lena and Covenant; later High Lord
Elohim, the: a mystic people encountered by the wandering Giants
Elohimfest: a gathering of the *Elohim*
Emacrimma's Maw: a region in the Center Plains
Enemy: Lord Foul's term of reference for the Creator
Eoman: a unit of the Warward of Lord's Keep, twenty warriors and a Warhaft
Eoward: twenty Eoman plus a Haft
Esmer: tormented son of Cail and the Dancers of the Sea

fael Befylam: serpent-form of the *jheherrin*
Faer: mare of Lord Callindrill
Fall: *Haruchai* name for a *caesure*
Fangs: the Teeth of the Render; Ramen name for the Demondim
Fangthane the Render: Ramen name for Lord Foul
Far Woodhelven: a village of the Land
Father of Horses, the: *Kelenbhrabanal*; legendary sire of the Ranyhyn
Favoured, the: courtesans of the *gaddhi*
Findail: one of the *Elohim*; the Appointed
Fields of Richloam: a region in the Center Plains
Fire-Lions: living fire-flow of Mount Thunder
fire-stones: graveling
First Betrayer: Clave-name for Berek Halfhand
First Circinate: first level of the Sandhold
First Haft: third-in-command of the Warward
First Mark: Bloodguard commander
First of the Search, the: leader of the Giants who follow the Earth-Sight
First Ward of Kevin's Lore: primary cache of knowledge left by High Lord Kevin
Fleshharrower: a Giant-Raver, Jehannum, *moksha*
Foamkite: *tyrscull* belonging to Honninscrave and Seadreamer
Fole: a *Haruchai*
Foodfendhall: eating-hall and galley aboard a Giantship
Forbidding: a wall of power
Forestal: a protector of the remnants of the One Forest
Fostil: a man of Mithil Stonedown; father of Liand
Foul's Creche: the Despiser's home; Ridjeck Thome
Furl Falls: waterfall at Revelstone
Furl's Fire: warning fire at Revelstone

gaddhi, the: sovereign of *Bhrathairealm*

Gallows Howe: a place of execution in Garroting Deep

Galt: a *Haruchai*; a Master of the Land; one of the Humbled

Garroting Deep: a forest of the Land

Garth: Warmark of the Warward of Lord's Keep

Gay: a Winhome of the Ramen

ghohritsar: a Waynhim

ghramin: a Waynhim

Giantclave: Giantish conference

Giantfriend: title given first to Damelon, later to Thomas Covenant

Giants: the Unhomed, ancient friends of the Lords; a seafaring people of the Earth

Giantship: a stone sailing vessel made by Giants; *dromond*

Giantway: path made by Giants

Giant Woods: a forest of the Land

Gibbon: the na-Mhoram; leader of the Clave

Gilden: a maple-like tree with golden leaves

Gildenlode: a power-wood formed from the Gilden trees

Glimmermere: a lake on the plateau above Revelstone

Gorak Krembal: Hotash Slay, a defence around Foul's Creche

Gossamer Glowlimn: a Giant; the First of the Search

Grace: a Cord of the Ramen

Graveler: one who uses stone to wield the Sunbane

graveling: fire-stones, made to glow and emit heat by stone-lore

Gravelingas: a master of the stone-lore

Gravin Threndor: Mount Thunder

Great Desert, the: a region of the Earth; home of the *Bhrathair* and the Sandgorgons

Great Swamp, the: Lifeswallower; a region of the Land

Grey Desert, the: a region south of the Land

Grey River, the: a river of the Land

Grey Slayer: plains name for Lord Foul

Greywightswath: a region north of the Soulsease River

Greshas Slant: a region in the Center Plains

griffin: lion-like beast with wings

Grim, the: (also the na-Mhoram's *Grim*) a destructive storm sent as an attack by the Clave

Grimmand Honninscrave: a Giant; Master of Starfare's Gem; brother of Seadreamer

Grimmerdhore: a forest of the Land

Guard, the: *hustin*; soldiers serving the *gaddhi*

Guardian of the One Tree, the: mystic figure warding the approach to the One Tree; *ak-Haru Kenaustin Ardenol*

Haft: commander of an Eoward

Halfhand: title given to Thomas Covenant and to Berek

Hall of Gifts, the: large chamber in Revelstone devoted to the artworks of the Land

Hamako: sole survivor of the destruction of During Stonedown

Hami: a Ramen Manethrall

Handir: a *Haruchai* leader; the Voice of the Masters

Harbour Captain: chief official of the port of *Bhrathairealm*

Harn: one of the *Haruchai*; protector of Hollian

Haruchai: a warrior people from the Westron Mountains

Healer: a physician

Hearthrall of Lord's Keep: a steward responsible for light, warmth and hospitality

Heart of Thunder: cave of power in Mount Thunder; Kiril Threndor

Hearthcoal: a Giant; cook of Starfare's Gem; wife of Seasauce

Heartthew: a title given to Berek Halfhand

heartwood chamber: meeting-place of a Woodhelven, within a tree

Heer: leader of a Woodhelven

Heft Galewrath: a Giant; Storesmaster of Starfare's Gem

Herem: a Raver, Kinslaughterer, *turiya*

Hergrom: one of the *Haruchai*

High Lord: leader of the Council of Lords

High Lord's Furl: banner of the High Lord

High Wood: *lomillialor*, offspring of the One Tree

Hile Troy: a man formerly from Covenant's world; Warmark of High Lord Elena's Warward

Hiltmark: second-in-command of the Warward

Hirebrand: a master of wood-lore

Hoerkin: a Warhaft

Hollian: daughter of Amith; eh-Brand of Crystal Stonedown

Home: original homeland of the Giants

Horizonscan: lookout atop the midmast of a Giantship

Horse, the: human soldiery of the *gaddhi*

horserite: a gathering of Ranyhyn in which they drink mind-blending waters in order to share visions, prophecies and purpose

Hotash Slay: flow of lava protecting Foul's Creche; Gorak Krembal

Hower: a Bloodguard, assigned to Lord Loerya

Hrama: a Ranyhyn stallion; mount of Anele

Humbled, the: three *Haruchai* maimed to resemble Thomas Covenant; a reminder to the Masters of their limitations

Hurn: a Cord of the Ramen

hurtloam: a healing mud

Huryn: a Ranyhyn, Terrel's mount

husta/hustin: partly human soldiers bred by Kasreyn to be the *gaddhi*'s Guard

Hyn: a Ranyhyn mare; mount of Linden Avery

Hynaril: a Ranyhyn, mount of Tamarantha and then Mhoram

Hynyn: a Ranyhyn stallion; mount of Stave

Hyrim: a Lord, son of Hoole

Illearth Stone, the: powerful bane long buried under Mount Thunder

Illender: title given to Thomas Covenant

Imoiran Tomal-mate: a Stonedownor

Infelice: reigning leader of the *Elohim*

Irin: a warrior of the Third Eoman of the Warward

Isle of the One Tree, the: location of the One Tree

Jain: a Manethrall of the Ramen

Jass: a *Haruchai*; a Master of the Land

Jehannum: a Raver, Fleshharrower, *moksha*

jheherrin: soft ones, misshapen by-products of Foul's making

Jous: a man of Mithil Stonedown; son of Prassan; father of Nassic; inheritor of an Unfettered One's mission to remember the Halfhand

Kalina: wife of Nassic; mother of Sunder; woman of Mithil Stonedown

Kam: a Manethrall of the Ramen

Kasreyn of the Gyre: a thaumaturge; the *gaddhi*'s Kemper (advisor) in *Bhrathairealm*

Kastenessen: one of the *Elohim*; former Appointed

Kelenbhrabanal: Father of Horses in Ranyhyn legends

Keep of the na-Mhoram, the: Revelstone

Keeper: a Ramen rank; one of those unsuited to the rigours of being a Cord or a Manethrall

Kemper, the: chief advisor of the *gaddhi*; Kasreyn

Kemper's Pitch: highest level of the Sandhold

Kenaustin Ardenol: a figure of *Haruchai* legend; paragon and measure of all *Haruchai* virtues

Kevin Landwaster: son of Loric Vilesilencer; last High Lord of the Old Lords

Kevin's Dirt: smog-like pall covering the Upper Land; invisible from below, it blocks health-sense

Kevin's Lore: knowledge of power left hidden by Kevin in the Seven Wards

Kevin's Watch: mountain lookout near Mithil Stonedown

Khabaal: one of the Seven Words

Kinslaughterer: a Giant-Raver, Herem, *turiya*

Kiril Threndor: chamber of power deep under Mount Thunder; Heart of Thunder

Koral: a Bloodguard, assigned to Lord Amatin

Korik: a Bloodguard

kresh: savage giant yellow wolves

krill, **the**: knife of power forged by High Lord Loric, awakened to power by Thomas Covenant

Kurash Plenethor: region of the Land formally named Stricken Stone, now called Trothgard

Kurash Qwellinir: the Shattered Hills; region of the Lower Land protecting Foul's Creche

Lake Pelluce: a lake in Andelainscion

Lal: a Cord of the Ramen

Landsdrop: great cliff separating the Upper and Lower Lands

Land, the: generally, area found on the map; a focal region of the Earth where Earthpower is uniquely accessible

Landsverge Stonedown: a village of the Land

Landwaster: title given to High Lord Kevin

Law, the: the natural order

Law of Death, the: the natural order which separates the living from the dead

Law of Life, the: the natural order which separates the dead from the living

Lena: a Stonedownor, daughter of Atiaran; mother of Elena

Lifeswallower: the Giant Swamp

lianar: wood of power used by an eh-Brand

Liand: a man of Mithil Stonedown; son of Fostil; companion of Linden Avery

lillianrill: wood-lore; masters of wood-lore

Lithe: a Manethrall of the Ramen

Llaura: a Heer of Soaring Woodhelven
Loerya Trevor-mate: a Lord
lomillialor: High Wood; a wood of power
Lord: one who has mastered both the Sword and the Staff aspects of Kevin's Lore
Lord-Fatherer: title given to Berek Halfhand
Lord Foul: the Enemy of the Land; the Despiser
'Lord Mhoram's Victory': a painting by Ahanna
Lord of Wickedness: a-Jeroth
Lord's-fire: staff-fire used by the Lords
Lord's Keep: Revelstone
Lords, the: primary protectors of the Land
loremaster: a leader of ur-viles
Loresraat: Trothgard school at Revelwood where Kevin's Lore is studied
Lorewarden: a teacher in the Loresraat
loreworks: Demondim power-laboratory
Loric Vilesilencer: a High Lord; son of Damelon Giantfriend
lor-liarill: Gildenlode
Lost, the: Giantish name for the Unhomed
Lost Deep, the: loreworks; breeding pit/laboratory under Mount Thunder where Demondim, Waynhim and ur-viles were created
Lower Land, the: region of the Land east of Landsdrop
lucubrium: laboratory of a thaumaturge
lurker of the Sarangrave, the: monster inhabiting the Great Swamp

Mahdoubt, the: a strange old woman; a servant of Revelstone
Mahrtiir: a Ramen Manethrall; companion of Linden Avery
maidan: open land around *Elemesnedene*
Maker, the: *jheherrin* name for Lord Foul
Maker-place: *jheherrin* name for Foul's Creche
Malliner: Woodhelvennin Heer, son of Veinnin
Mane: Ramen reference to a Ranyhyn
Maneing: Ramen ceremony of becoming a Manethrall
Manethrall: highest Ramen rank
Manhome: main dwelling place of the Ramen in the Plains of Ra
Marid: a man of Mithil Stonedown; Sunbane victim
Marny: a Ranyhyn, Tuvor's mount
marrowmeld: bone-sculpting; *anundivian yajña*
master-rukh: iron triangle at Revelstone which feeds and reads other *rukhs*

Master, the: Clave-name for Lord Foul

Masters of the Land, the: *Haruchai* who have claimed responsibility for protecting the Land from Corruption

Mehryl: a Ranyhyn, Hile Troy's mount

Melenkurion abatha: phrase of invocation or power; two of the Seven Words

Melenkurion **Skyweir:** a cleft peak in the Westron Mountains

Memla na-Mhoram-in: a Rider of the Clave

merewives: the Dancers of the Sea

metheglin: a drink; mead

Mhoram: a Lord, later High Lord; son of Variol

Mill: one of the Seven Words

Minas: one of the Seven Words

mirkfruit: papaya-like fruit with narcoleptic pulp

Mistweave: a Giant

Mithil River: a river of the Land

Mithil Stonedown: a village in the South Plains

Mithil's Plunge, the: waterfall at the head of the Mithil valley

moksha: a Raver, Jehannum, Fleshharrower

Morin: First Mark of the Bloodguard; commander in original *Haruchai* army

Morinmoss: a forest of the Land

Morninglight: one of the *Elohim*

Morril: a Bloodguard, assigned to Lord Callindrill

Mount Thunder: a peak at the centre of Landsdrop

Murrin Odona-mate: a Stonedownor

Myrha: a Ranyhyn, Elena's mount

Naharahn: a Ranyhyn mare; mount of Pahni

na-Mhoram, the: leader of the Clave

na-Mhoram-cro: lowest rank of the Clave

na-Mhoram-in: highest rank of the Clave below the na-Mhoram

na-Mhoram-wist: middle rank of the Clave

Nassic: father of Sunder; son of Jous, inheritor of an Unfettered One's mission to remember the Halfhand

Nelbrin: son of Sunder; 'heart's child'

Nicor, the: great sea-monster; said to be offspring of the Worm of the World's End

Nom: a Sandgorgon

North Plains, the: a region of the Land

Northron Climbs, the: a region of the Land

Oath of Peace, the: oath by the people of the Land against needless violence
Odona Murrin-mate: a Stonedownor
Offin: a former na-Mhoram
Old Lords: Lords prior to the Ritual of Desecration
Omournil: Woodhelvennin Heer, daughter of Mournil
One Forest, the: ancient forest covering most of the Land
One Tree, the: mystic tree from which the Staff of Law was made
orcrest: a stone of power; Sunstone; used by a Graveler
Osondrea: a Lord, later High Lord; daughter of Sondrea

Padrias: Woodhelvennin Heer, son of Mill
Pahni: a Cord of the Ramen; cousin of Sahah; companion of Linden Avery
Peak of the Fire-Lions: Mount Thunder; Gravin Threndor
Pietten: Woodhelvennin child damaged by Lord Foul's minions; son of Soranal
pitchbrew: a beverage combining *diamondraught* and *vitrim*, conceived by
  Pitchwife
Pitchwife: a Giant; member of the Search; husband of the First of the Search
Porib: a Bloodguard
Power of Command, the: Seventh Ward of Kevin's Lore
Pren: a Bloodguard
Prothall: High Lord, son of Dwillian
Prover of Life: title given to Thomas Covenant
Puhl: a Cord of the Ramen
Pure One, the: redemptive figure of *jheherrin* legend

Quaan: Warhaft of the Third Eoman of the Warward; later Hiltmark, then
  Warmark
Quest for the Staff of Law: quest to recover the Staff of Law from Drool
  Rockworm
Questsimoon, the: the Roveheartswind; a steady, favourable wine, perhaps
  seasonal
Quirrel: a Stonedownor, companion of Triock

Ramen: people who serve the Ranyhyn
Rant Absolain: the *gaddhi*
Ranyhyn: the great horses of the Plains of Ra
Ravers: Lord Foul's three ancient servants
Raw, the: fjord into the demesne of the *Elohim*
Rawedge Rim, the: mountains around *Elemesnedene*

Reader: a member of the Clave who tends and uses the *master-rukh*
Rede, the: knowledge of history and survival promulgated by the Clave
Revelstone: Lord's Keep; mountain city formed by Giants
Revelwood: seat of the Loresraat; tree city grown by Lords
rhadhamaerl: stone-lore; masters of stone-lore
rhee: a thick mush; a Ramen food
Rhohm: a Ranyhyn stallion; mount of Liand
rhysh: a community of Waynhim; 'stead'
rhyshyshim: a gathering of *rhysh*; a place in which such gathering occurs
Riddenstretch: a region north of the Soulsease River
Rider: a member of the Clave
Ridjeck Thome: Foul's Creche
rillinlure: healing wood dust
Ringthane: Ramen name for Thomas Covenant
ring-wielder: *Elohim* term of reference for Covenant
Rire Grist: a Caitiffin of the *gaddhi*'s Horse
Rites of Unfettering: the ceremony of becoming Unfettered
Ritual of Desecration: act of despair by which High Lord Kevin destroyed
  the Old Lords and ruined most of the Land
Riversward: a region north of the Soulsease River
Rockbrother, Rocksister: terms of affection between men and Giants
rocklight: light emitted by glowing stone
roge Befylam: Cavewight-form of the *jheherrin*
Roveheartswind, the: the *Questsimoon*
Rue: a Manethrall, formerly named Gay
Ruel: a Bloodguard, assigned to Hile Troy
rukh: iron talisman by which a Rider wields the power of the Sunbane
Runnik: a Bloodguard
Rustah: a Cord of the Ramen

sacred enclosure: Vespers-hall at Revelstone
Sahah: a Cord of the Ramen
Saltheart Foamfollower: a Giant, friend of Covenant
Saltroamrest: bunk hold for the crew in a Giantship
Salttooth: jutting rock in the harbour of Giants' Home
samadhi: a Raver, Sheol, Satansfist
Sandgorgons: monsters of the Great Desert of *Bhrathairealm*
Sandgorgons Doom: imprisoning storm created by Kasreyn to trap the
  Sandgorgons

Sandhold, the: the *gaddhi*'s castle in *Bhrathairealm*

Sandwall, the: the great wall defending *Bhrathairain*

Santonin na-Mhoram-in: a Rider of the Clave

Sarangrave Flat: a region of the Lower Land; the Great Swamp

Satansfist: a Giant-Raver, Sheol, *samadhi*

Satansheart: Giantish name for Lord Foul

Search, the: quest of the Giants for the wound in the Earth; later the quest for the Isle of the One Tree

Seareach: region of the Land occupied by the Unhomed

Seasauce: a Giant; cook of Starfare's Gem; husband of Hearthcoal

Seatheme: dead wife of Sevinhand

Second Circinate: second level of the Sandhold

Second Ward: second unit of Kevin's hidden knowledge

setrock: a type of stone used with pitch to repair stone

Seven Hells, the: a-Jeroth's demesne: desert, rain, pestilence, fertility, war, savagery and darkness

Seven Wards, the: collection of knowledge hidden by High Lord Kevin

Seven Words, the: words of power from Kevin's Lore

Sevinhand: Anchormaster of Starfare's Gem; a Giant

Shattered Hills: a region of the Land near Foul's Creche

Sheol: a Raver, Satansfist, *samadhi*

Shetra Verement-mate: a Lord

Shipsheartthew: the wheel of a Giantship

shola: a small wooded glen where a stream runs between unwooded hills

Shull: a Bloodguard

Sill: a Bloodguard, assigned to Lord Hyrim

Sivit na-Mhoram-wist: a Rider of the Clave

skest: acid-creatures serving the lurker of the Sarangrave

skurj: ominous, unexplained beings

Slen Terass-mate: a Stonedownor

soft-ones: the *jheherrin*

Somo: horse taken by Liand from Mithil Stonedown

soothreader: a seer

soothtell: ritual of revelation practiced by the Clave

Soranal: a Woodhelvennin Heer, son of Thiller

Soulbiter, the: a dangerous ocean of Giantish legend

Soulbiter's Teeth: reefs in the Soulbiter

Soulcrusher: Giantish name for Lord Foul

Sparlimb Keelsetter: a Giant, father of triplets

Spikes, the: guard-towers at the mouth of *Bhrathairain* Harbour

Spray Forthsurge: a Giant; mother of the First of the Search

springwine: a mild, refreshing liquour

Staff, the: a branch of the study of Kevin's Lore

Staff of Law, the: a tool of Earthpower; the first Staff was formed by Berek from the One Tree and later destroyed by Thomas Covenant; the second was formed by Linden Avery by merging Vain and Findail with wild magic

Stallion of the First Herd, the: *Kelenbhrabanal*

Starfare's Gem: Giantship used by the Search

Starkin: one of the *Elohim*

Stave: a *Haruchai*; a Master of the Land; companion of Linden Avery

Stell: one of the *Haruchai*; protector of Sunder

Stonedown: a stone-village

Stonedownor: one who lives in a stone-village

Stonemight, the: a fragment of the Illearth Stone

Stonemight Woodhelven: a village in the South Plains

Storesmaster: third-in-command aboard a Giantship

Stricken Stone: region of the Land; now called Trothgard

Sunbane, the: a power arising from the corruption of nature by Lord Foul

Sunbirth Sea: ocean east of the Land

Sunder: son of Nassic; Graveler of Mithil Stonedown

Sun-Sage: one who can affect the Sunbane

Sunstone: *orcrest*

sur-jheherrin: descendants of the *jheherrin*; inhabitants of Sarangrave Flat

suru-pa-maerl: an art using stone

Swarte: a Rider

Swordmain/Swordmainnir: a Giant trained as a warrior

Sword, the: a branch of the study of Kevin's Lore

Sword-Elder: chief Lorewarden of the Sword at the Loresraat

Tamarantha Variol-mate: a Lord, daughter of Enesta

Teeth of the Render, the: Fangs; Ramen name for the Demondim

Terass Slen-mate: a Stonedownor, daughter of Annoria

Terrel: a Bloodguard, assigned to Lord Mhoram; a commander of the original *Haruchai* army

test of silence: test of integrity used by the people of the Land

test of truth, the: test of veracity by *lomillialor* or *orcrest*

The Grieve: *Coercri*; home of the Giants in Seareach

Thelma Twofist: character in a Giantish tale

The Majesty: throne room of the *gaddhi*; fourth level of the Sandhold

Thew: a Cord of the Ramen

Third Ward: third unit of Kevin's hidden knowledge

Thomin: a Bloodguard, assigned to Lord Verement

Three Corners of Truth, the: basic formulation of beliefs promulgated by the Clave

Tier of Riches, the: showroom of the *gaddhi*'s wealth; third level of the Sandhold

thronehall, the: the Despiser's seat in Foul's Creche

Tohrm: a Gravelingas; Hearthrall of Lord's Keep

Tomal: a Stonedownor craftmaster

Toril: *Haruchai* lost to the Clave

Treacher's Gorge: ravine opening into Mount Thunder

treasure-berries: *aliantha*, nourishing fruit found throughout the Land in all seasons

Trell Atiaran-mate: Gravelingas of Mithil Stonedown, father of Lena

Trevor Loerya-mate: a Lord

Triock: a Stonedownor, son of Thuler; loved Lena

Trothgard: a region of the Land, formerly Stricken Stone

Tull: a Bloodguard

turiya: a Raver, Herem, Kinslaughterer

Tuvor: First Mark of the Bloodguard; a commander of the original *Haruchai* army

tyrscull: a Giantish training vessel for apprentice sailors

Unbeliever, the: title claimed by Thomas Covenant

Unfettered, the: lore-students freed from conventional responsibilities to seek individual knowledge and service

Unfettered One, the: founder of a line of men waiting to greet Thomas Covenant's return to the Land

Unhomed, the: the Giants living in Seareach

upland: plateau above Revelstone

Upper Land: region of land west of Landsdrop

ur-Lord: title given to Thomas Covenant

ur-viles: Demondim-spawn, evil creatures

ussusimiel: nourishing melon grown by the people of the Land

Vailant: former High Lord before Prothall

Vain: Demondim-spawn; bred by ur-viles for a secret purpose

Vale: a Bloodguard

Valley of Two Rivers, the: site of Revelwood in Trothgard

Variol Tamarantha-mate: a Lord, later High Lord, son of Pentil; father of Mhoram

Verement Shetra-mate: a Lord

Verge of Wandering, the: valley in the Southron Mountains southeast of Mithil Stonedown; gathering-place of the Ramen

Vespers: self-consecration rituals of the Lords

viancome: meeting place at Revelwood

Victuallin Tayne: a region in the Center Plains

Viles, the: monstrous beings which created the Demondim

vitrim: nourishing fluid created by the Waynhim

Voice of the Masters, the: a *Haruchai* leader; spokesman for the Masters as a group

voure: a plant-sap which wards off insects

Vow, the: *Haruchai* oath of service which formed the Bloodguard

vraith: a Waynhim

Ward: a unit of Kevin's lore

Warhaft: commander of an Eoman

Warlore: Sword knowledge in Kevin's Lore

Warmark: commander of the Warward

Warrenbridge: entrance to the catacombs under Mount Thunder

Warward, the: army of Lord's Keep

Wavedancer: Giantship commanded by Brow Gnarlfist

Wavenhair Haleall: a Giant, wife of Sparlimb Keelsetter, mother of triplets

Waymeet: resting place for travellers maintained by Waynhim

Waynhim: tenders of the Waymeets; rejected Demondim-spawn, opponents and relatives of ur-viles

Weird of the Waynhim, the: Waynhim concept of doom, destiny or duty

Whane: a Cord of the Ramen

white gold: a metal of power not found in the Land

white gold wielder: title given to Thomas Covenant

White River, the: a river of the Land

Whrany: a Ranyhyn stallion; mount of Bhapa

Wildwielder: white gold wielder; Esmer's name for Linden Avery

Wightburrow, the: cairn under which Drool Rockworm is buried

Wightwarrens: home of the Cavewights under mount Thunder; catacombs

wild magic: the power of white gold; considered the keystone of the Arch of time

Windscour: region in the Center Plains

Windshorn Stonedown: a village in the South Plains

Winhome: Ramen lowest rank

Woodenwold: region of trees surrounding the *maidan* of *Elemesnedene*

Woodhelven: wood-village

Woodhelvennin: inhabitants of wood-village

Word of Warning: a powerful, destructive forbidding

Worm of the World's End, the: creature believed by the *Elohim* to have formed the foundation of the Earth

Wraiths of Andelain, the: creatures of living light that perform the Dance at the Celebration of Spring

Würd of the Earth, the: term used by the *Elohim* to describe their own nature, destiny or purpose; could be read as Word, Worm or Weird

Yeurquin: a Stonedownor, companion of Triock

Yolenid: daughter of Loerya

Stephen Donaldson spent thirteen years in India, where his father was a medical missionary and orthopaedic surgeon; the idea for Thomas Covenant grew out of his father's work with lepers. The first trilogy, *Lord Foul's Bane*, *The Illearth War* and *The Power That Preserves*, won Donaldson the British Fantasy and John W. Campbell Awards. The second Covenant trilogy, *The Wounded Land*, *The One Tree*, and *White Gold Wielder*, won Donaldson the Balrog and Saturn Awards. Donaldson is also the author of the collection *Daughter of Regals and Other Tales*, which won the Balrog Award, the Gap SF novels, the World Fantasy Award-winning collection *Reave the Just and Other Tales* and, as Reed Stephens, a series of mystery novels. He has also won, amongst others, two Science Fiction Book Club Awards, the French Julia Verlanger Award, and the President's Award from The International Association for the Fantastic in the Arts. Donaldson got his BA in English Literature from the College of Wooster in Ohio, who went on to give him the Distinguished Alumni Award and, in 1993, a D. Litt. (Honorary). He also earned an MA in English literature from Kent State University. He lives with his family in New Mexico, where he is at work on the second novel of 'The Last Chronicles of Thomas Covenant'.